THE YEAR'S BEST SCIENCE FICTION

Sixth Annual Collection

THE
YEAR'S BEST
SCIENCE FICTION
Sixth Annual Collection

Edited by
Gardner Dozois

ST. MARTIN'S PRESS

New York

TO MY IN-LAWS
Norton and Sylvia Casper
Anne Berger
Judith Kohn

ISBN 0-312-03009-6 (paperback)

ISBN 0-312-03008-8 (hardcover)

First Edition
10 9 8 7 6 5 4 3 2 1

ACKNOWLEDGMENTS

The editor would like to thank the following people for their help and support: first and foremost, Susan Casper, for doing much of the thankless scut-work involved in producing this anthology; Virginia Kidd, Ellen Datlow, Sheila Williams, Tina Lee, Michael Swanwick, Pat Cadigan, Arnie Fenner, Janet and Ricky Kagan, Shawna McCarthy, Lou Aronica, Edward Ferman, Anne Jordan, Beth Meacham, Claire Eddy, Susan Allison, Ginjer Buchanan, Pat LoBrutto, Patrick Delahunt, Patrick L. Price, Charles C. Ryan, John Betancourt, Tim Sullivan, Bob Walters, Tess Kissinger, Kristine Kathryn Rusch, Michael G. Adkisson, Diane Mapes, Nicholas Robinson, David S. Garnett, Mike Resnick, David G. Hartwell, Melinda M. Snodgrass, Lucius Shepard, David Pringle, Mark Van Name, and special thanks to my own editors, Gordon Van Gelder and Stuart Moore.

Thanks are also due to Charles N. Brown, whose magazine *Locus* (Locus Publications, Inc., P.O. Box 13305, Oakland, California 94661, $28.00 for a one-year subscription, twelve issues) was used as a reference source throughout the Summation, and to Andrew Porter, whose magazine *Science Fiction Chronicle* (Algol Press, P.O. Box 2730, Brooklyn, N.Y. 10202–0056, $27.00 for one year, twelve issues) was also used as a reference source throughout.

CONTENTS

INTRODUCTION

Summation: 1988

This was a year of contradictory signals and ambiguous omens for science fiction. On one hand, it was yet another record year, commercially, for the field. The familiar litany of Big Name SF writers—Stephen King, Arthur C. Clarke, Piers Anthony, Isaac Asimov, Stephen R. Donaldson, and so forth—dominated nationwide bestseller lists again. Some 177 different publishers produced SF or fantasy in 1988, according to the newsmagazine *Locus*, turning out a record total of 1,936 books (1,186 of them new titles!), up 16 percent from last year. New book lines continued to appear, including a line of Tor Doubles (short novels published back-to-back, in the style of the old Ace Doubles line); a line of softcover reprints of the Isaac Asimov Presents hardcover novels from Worldwide Books; a line packaged by Byron Preiss Productions for Lynx Books, to be called Omeiga Books, edited by Dave Harris; and a new line of up to a dozen titles per year, coming up later in 1989 from Bantam Spectra.

On the other hand, an uneasy awareness that a recession of *some* size—whether major or minor—is almost inevitably on the way seems to have spread over the American publishing industry, and many insiders seem to be emotionally battening down the hatches and waiting to ride out the coming storm, if they can. This uneasiness may be responsible for the buying slowdowns that are rumored to have affected several major publishers. There were plenty of ill omens to be found, if you looked for them. Postal rate increases, for instance, drove up mail-order book prices and magazine subscription rates throughout the field last year. Pageant Books—the mass-market line produced by Crown Books in partnership with the giant bookstore chain Waldenbooks—died, as did several genre magazines. Tor announced cuts of 25 percent of its mass-market lists, and St. Martin's Press announced that it will drop its entire mass-market SF program. Waldenbooks announced that it will reduce the number of titles it buys, and increase the nonbook display space in its stores at the expense of book space. Sharecropping, the practice of hiring lesser-known authors to create new novels set ''in the world of'' some famous SF novel (for instance, a novel set in the world of Robert Silverberg's

Lord Valentine's Castle) continues to increase; the newest twist on sharecropping is "franchising," hiring a well-known SF writer to write a sequel to some work by another well-known SF writer, or even to expand some shorter work of a well-known writer out to novel size. For instance, Gregory Benford has been asked to write a sequel to Arthur C. Clarke's short novel *Against the Fall of Night*, and Robert Silverberg has been hired to expand three short pieces by Isaac Asimov —"Nightfall," "The Martian Way," "The Ugly Little Boy"—into full-length novels. "Sharecropper" and "Franchise" novels join a flood of similar items in recent years—Star Trek novels, choose-your-own-adventure books, shared-world anthologies, TV and movie novelizations, "Robotech" books, "Dungeons and Dragons" scenarios and books based on other games, "Thieves' World" novels, and so on—that are filling an ever-increasing number of slots in publisher's schedules and eating up rack display space in bookstores, making it more and more difficult for unknown young writers to place individual novels of merit. Taken to an extreme, which is just where many publishers (who would love to be able to publish only surefire "brand name" bestsellers) would like to take it, this could mean that it would become extremely difficult for a young writer to get into print at all, unless he hires out to write books in some more famous writer's universe . . . which could spell the creative death of the field.

Quite probably—I hope—this scenario is far too bleak. There are still publishing houses concentrating on producing individual novels of merit, new writers are still finding it possible to get into print without resorting to sharecropping . . . and there are some tentative early indications that the public may not be responding to sharecropper books anywhere near as enthusiastically as publishers had hoped that they would. As for recession and retrenchment—the "bust" phase of the periodic boom-and-bust cycle that has repeated ever since there *was* such a thing as SF as a distinct publishing category—undoubtedly it will come. But as it has been pointed out before, every boom-and-bust cycle has left the habitual SF-reading audience *larger than it was before the boom began*. Some of the gains are always held. Retrenchment may come, but even so, the "retrenched" genre will probably still be larger than the genre *as a whole* was prior to the start of the most recent boom. It's hard to realistically predict any "bust" cycle, for example, that would reduce SF to pre-1974 levels of readership or advances or sales, unless most of the publishing industry collapses with it. History also shows us that even in the midst of the blackest recessions, some writers will survive . . . and may even prosper. And finally, we should remember that a cycle implies that things will eventually turn *up* again as well. At the beginning of the '80s, for instance, the British SF publishing world was a dreary ruin—and now SF publishing in Britain is booming, so much so that British publishers are now frequently able to pay considerably *more* for the British rights to American books than the American publishers were able to pay in the first place!

So keep your fingers crossed. We'll just have to wait and see what happens.

*   *   *

It was a year of changes in the SF magazine market, with old magazines dying, and new magazines struggling to establish themselves. Just as I was preparing a clean copy of this summation, I received the worst news of the year in the magazine market: that *The Twilight Zone Magazine* had died. This is saddening news—the magazine had improved greatly in quality under the creative editorship of Tappan King during the last couple of years, and I had real hopes for its survival. The death of *TZ*, coupled with the demise last year of the digest-sized horror magazine *Night Cry*, leaves a real hole in the market for horror fiction at shorter lengths— in fact, there are no longer *any* professional horror magazines left on the market, so that a horror writer with a short story to sell has no recourse but to sell it to one of the slew of horror semiprozines, or to the occasional original horror an- thology. With horror booming in the novel market, it's hard to believe that this vacuum will remain unfilled—the question is, who will fill it? My own money would be on the new semiprozine *Weird Tales*, simply because it is edited by canny magazine veteran George Scithers, but other possible candidates include *American Fantasy* and *Midnight Graffiti*, two slick, large-format semiprozines, and *Fear*, a new slick British semiprozine. It'll be interesting to see which, if any, of these magazines manage to take over this particular ecological niche. At *Amazing*, editor Patrick L. Price resigned as a full-time TSR employee, but will continue to edit the magazine "on a free-lance basis"; at year's end there were some rumors that Price had left the magazine entirely, but we were unable to confirm or deny those by presstime. *Amazing*'s overall circulation remains dan- gerously low, and many insiders have speculated that it may be next major mag- azine to die—which would be a shame, since the quality of the magazine has increased dramatically under Patrick Price, and *Amazing* is now publishing better stuff than it has in years. Elsewhere, the British magazine *Interzone* and *Aboriginal SF* both went bi-monthly, and both raised their circulations above the 10,000- copy per issue mark, which, according to the Hugo eligibility rules, raises them into the professional magazine category. *Interzone* is partially supported by a British Arts Council grant, but *Aboriginal SF* has already defied the experts by surviving as long as it has—founding a new magazine (particularly a large-format slick magazine, which costs far more to produce than a digest-sized magazine) is an extremely chancy enterprise, and the field is littered with the bleaching bones of magazines that failed after a few issues or died stillborn, most of them killed by undercapitalization. *Aboriginal SF* is making many of the right moves—an aggressive advertising policy, direct mail solicitation, getting chain distribution to major bookstores like Dalton's and Waldenbooks—but they are also danger- ously undercapitalized, and have yet to get through their first major cash-flow crunch; a similar crunch helped to kill off Charles C. Ryan's last SF magazine *Galileo*, in the '70s. So we'll see. I wish both of them luck—the field can use all the short-fiction markets it can get.

As most of you probably know, I, Gardner Dozois, am also editor of *Isaac Asimov's Science Fiction Magazine*. And that, as I've mentioned before, does pose a problem for me in compiling this summation, particularly the magazine-by-magazine review that follows. As *IAsfm* editor, I could be said to have a vested interest in the magazine's success, so that anything negative I said about another SF magazine (particularly another digest-sized magazine, my direct competition), could be perceived as an attempt to make my own magazine look good by tearing down the competition. Aware of this constraint, I've decided that nobody can complain if I only say *positive* things about the competition . . . and so, once again, I've limited myself to a listing of some of the worthwhile authors published by each.

Omni published first-rate fiction this year by George Alec Effinger, Bruce McAllister, Howard Waldrop, Bruce Sterling, Robert Silverberg, Tom Maddox, Sharon N. Farber, and others. *Omni*'s fiction editor is Ellen Datlow.

The Magazine of Fantasy and Science Fiction featured excellent fiction by Brian Stableford, Harry Turtledove, Pat Cadigan, Lucius Shepard, Mike Resnick, Bruce Sterling, and others. *F & SF*'s long-time editor is Edward Ferman.

Isaac Asimov's Science Fiction Magazine featured critically acclaimed work by Walter Jon Williams, James Patrick Kelly, Lucius Shepard, Pat Cadigan, Judith Moffett, John Kessel, Connie Willis, Kim Stanley Robinson, Robert Silverberg, Nancy Kress, Howard Waldrop, Neal Barrett, Jr., and others. *IAsfm*'s editor is Gardner Dozois.

Analog featured good work by Michael Flynn, Charles Sheffield, James White, Steven Gould, Elizabeth Moon, W. T. Quick, Stephen Kraus, Ben Bova, and others. *Analog*'s long-time editor is Stanley Schmidt.

Amazing featured good work by James Lawson, Kristine Kathryn Rusch, David E. Cortesi, John Barnes, Phillip C. Jennings, Susan Palwick, and others. *Amazing*'s editor is Patrick L. Price.

The Twilight Zone Magazine featured good work by Susan Casper, Jane Yolen, Chet Williamson, B. W. Clough, Stanley Schmidt, James Killus, Elizabeth Mitchell, Robert Frazier, and others. *TZ*'s editor was Tappan King.

Interzone featured good work by Brian Stableford, Kim Newman, Paul J. McAuley, Phillip Mann, David Langford, Christopher Burns, and others. *Interzone*'s editors are Simon Ounsley and David Pringle.

Aboriginal Science Fiction featured interesting work by Jamil Nasir, Howard V. Hendrix, Kristine Kathryn Rusch, Elaine Radford, Phillip C. Jennings, and others. The editor of *Aboriginal Science Fiction* is Charles C. Ryan.

Short SF continued to appear in many magazines outside genre boundaries. *Playboy* in particular continues to run a good deal of SF, under fiction editor Alice K. Turner.

(Subscription addresses follow for those magazines hardest to find on the newsstands: *The Magazine of Fantasy and Science Fiction*, Mercury Press, Inc., Box

56, Cornwall, CT, 06753, annual subscription—twelve issues—$21.00 in U.S.; *Amazing*, TSR, Inc., P.O. Box 72089, Chicago, IL, 60678, annual subscription $9.00 for six issues; *Isaac Asimov's Science Fiction Magazine*, Davis Publications, Inc., P.O. Box 1933, Marion, OH 43305, $25.97 for thirteen issues; *Interzone*, 124 Osborne Road, Brighton, BN1 6LU, England, $26.00 for an airmail one-year—six issues—subscription; *Aboriginal Science Fiction*, P.O. Box 2449, Woburn, MA 01888–0849, $14.00 for six issues, $22.00 for twelve.)

Among the fiction semiprozines, with *Interzone* and *Aboriginal SF* having escaped up into the professional category, the most prominent survivor is probably *Weird Tales*, edited by George H. Scithers. *Weird Tales* is a thoroughly professional magazine, lacking only in circulation to qualify it for the professional category; maybe it'll make it next year, if it survives. There was no issue of *Whispers* this year, although it has been your most reliable value among the horror semiprozines for many years. There is also a slew of new horror semiprozines, too many to list here, although the most visible of them were probably *Midnight Graffiti, American Fantasy, The Horror Show*, and *Grue. New Pathways*, edited by Michael G. Adkisson, seems to still be healthy; it's a quirky, intriguing, and frequently deliberately outrageous magazine, well worth a look. The promising new fiction semiprozine *Argos*, edited by Diane Mapes, died this year, unfortunately, another victim of undercapitalization. The British *Fantasy Tales* died as a semiprozine, but was reborn as a hardcover anthology series. As ever, *Locus* and *SF Chronicle* remain your best bet among the semiprozines if you are looking for news and/or overview of the genre. *Thrust* is the longest-running of those semiprozines that concentrate primarily on literary criticism. Two other more recent criticalzines, Steve Brown and Dan Steffan's *Science Fiction Eye* and Orson Scott Card's *Short Form*, are interesting, but both magazines had trouble sticking to their announced publishing schedules this year—*Short Form* was particularly unreliable, and some people have wondered if the next issue ever is going to appear at all. A new contender in this category is *The New York Review Of Science Fiction*, an interesting and pleasantly eccentric journal that, so far at least, has been fairly good at keeping to schedule.

(Subscription addresses: *Locus*, Locus Publications, Inc., P.O.Box 13305, Oakland, CA 94661, $28.00 for a one-year subscription, twelve issues; *Science Fiction Chronicle*, Algol Press, P.O. Box 2730, Brooklyn, N.Y. 10202–0056, $27.00 for one year, twelve issues; *Thrust*, Thrust Publications, 8217 Langport Terrace, Gaithersburg, MD 20877, $8.00 for four issues; *Science Fiction Eye*, Box 43244, Washington, DC 20010–9244, $10.00 for one year; *Short Form*, 546 Lindley Road, Greensboro, NC 27410; *Weird Tales*, Terminus Publishing Company, Box 13418, Philadelphia, PA 19101–3418, $18.00 for six issues; *New Pathways, MGA* Services, P.O. Box 863994, Plano, TX 75086–3994, $10.00 for one year—four issues—subscription, $18.00 for a two-year subscription; *Whispers*, 70 Highland Ave., Binghamton, NY 13905, two double issues $13.95;

Fantasy Tales, Stephen Jones, 130 Parkview, Wembley, Middlesex, HA9 6JU, England, Great Britain, $11.00 for three issues; *The Horror Show*, Phantasm Press, 1488 Misty Springs Lane, Oak Run, CA 96069, $14.00 per year; *Grue Magazine*, Hells Kitchen Productions, Box 370, Times Square Sta., New York, NY 10108, $11.00 for three issues; *American Fantasy*, P.O. Box 41714, Chicago, IL 60641, $16.00 a year; *The New York Review Of Science Fiction*, Dragon Press, P.O. Box 78, Pleasantville, NY, 10570, $24.00 per year; *Midnight Graffiti*, 13101 Sudan Rd., Poway, CA 92604, one year for $24.00.)

Overall, 1988 was a weaker year than 1987 in the original anthology market, with nothing as strong as last year's *In the Fields of Fire*, although some good material did appear. The two strongest original SF anthologies of the year were probably: *Full Spectrum* (Bantam Spectra), edited by Lou Aronica and Shawna McCarthy, and *Terry's Universe* (Tor), edited by Beth Meacham. *Full Spectrum* is the very promising start of a proposed annual anthology series; the level of fiction is remarkably consistant here—almost all the stories are quite good, there are very few dogs . . . but, on the other hand, with one possible exception, none of them strike me as really *major* stories, either. *Terry's Universe*, a one-shot memorial anthology honoring the late Terry Carr, strikes me as almost the exact opposite—it contains three of the very best stories of the year (works by Robinson, Swanwick, and Silverberg), but many of the *rest* of the stories are mediocre, and a few are flat failures. *Full Spectrum* has the potential to develop into a major anthology series, although the departure of Shawna McCarthy from Bantam's editorial staff has raised some questions among industry insiders about the series' ultimate survival. There will definitely be at least a *Full Spectrum II*, however; it's already in the works for next year.

Also promised for next year is a new edition of the long-running *Universe* anthology series, now being edited by Robert Silverberg and Karen Haber, and I'm looking forward to that. There were also rumors at year's end that Orson Scott Card would be editing a new annual anthology series in 1989. *Synergy* (Harcourt Brace Jovanovich), George Zebrowski's new anthology series published two volumes, Two and Three, this year—*Synergy* is an interesting and ambitious series, and I wish it well, but at $8.95 for a normal mass-market sized paperback, and a rather slender one at that (by comparison, *Full Spectrum* costs $4.95 and contains 483 pages, as opposed to *Synergy 3*'s 221 pages), I fear that they may be pricing this series out of existence; only time will tell. Another ambitious new series started this year, *Pulphouse* (Pulphouse Publishing), edited by Kristine Kathryn Rusch, a small-press ''hardback magazine''—really a quarterly hardcover anthology, available primarily by subscription. Each issue of *Pulphouse* is supposed to have a specific theme. Of the two volumes available so far, *Pulphouse One*, the Horror issue, is rather good, with interesting work by Edward Bryant, Don Webb, Nina Hoffman, Harlan Ellison, and others; *Pulphouse Two*, the Speculative Fiction issue, is awful, full of obvious trunk stories masquerading as "experimental" work. Coming up are their Science Fiction and Fantasy issues (then I suppose they start cycling again), and I'm curiously looking forward to see what they're like; this is a series worth keeping an eye on. (Subscription address: Pulphouse Publishing, Box 1227, Eugene OR 97440; $17.95 per single issue, $30 for a half-year subscription [two issues] or $56 for a full-year subscription [four issues]); *Other Edens II* (Unwin), edited by Christopher Evans and Robert Holdstock, is a continuation of a new British anthology series that started last year; it's not quite as impressive as the first *Other Edens*, but it does contain interesting work by Scott Bradfield, Garry Kilworth, Josephine Saxton, and others. The *New Destinies* series (Baen), edited by James Baen, put out two solid volumes this year, with a particularly good Vernor Vinge story in Vol VI. *L. Ron Hubbard Presents Writers of the Future Vol. IV* (Bridge), edited by Algis Budrys, presents the usual array of novice work; some of the writers included here may well become well-known in the future, as the jacket copy suggests, but it won't be for any work to be found in this particular anthology. There was a one-shot small-press anthology of stories by SF writers who live in New Mexico, *A Very Large Array* (University of New Mexico Press), edited by Melinda M. Snodgrass; a dubious premise, but an enjoyable book.

It's encouraging to see that suddenly there are a number of original SF anthology series jostling to establish themselves—only a few years back, they seemed well on their way to extinction.

Far from being an Endangered Species, that literary curiosity, the shared-world anthology, is proliferating—several new series were added this year, and there are now fifteen or more of them, according to *Locus*. Shared-world anthologies are perhaps the least pernicious form of sharecropping—stories from them usually strike me as too dependent on the background framework to function well as individual units, but there are many exceptions; I've published a few shared-world stories in *IAsfm*, after all, and even reprinted some in this anthology, so it would be hypocritical of me to be too sternly censorious about the existence of such anthologies. Nevertheless, I am growing somewhat tired of them, and there are signs (including industry rumors about poor sales for at least two of the major series) that the buying public may be becoming tired of them as well. If this is true, then this year's expansion, rather than a sign of health, may be an indication of an oncoming glut that will eventually produce a drastic winnowing in this market. We'll see. In the meantime, there were two volumes in the *Wild Cards* (Bantam Spectra) series, edited by George R. R. Martin (this is probably the major SF shared-world series, but there are some signs that it is running out of steam; certainly the later volumes seem weaker than the initial two were); a volume in the *Liavek* (Ace) series, edited by Will Shetterly and Emma Bull; several *Heroes In Hell* (Baen) volumes by various hands, mostly edited by Janet Morris; a volume in the *Merovingen Nights* (DAW) series, edited by C. J. Cherryh; one in the

Tales of the Witch World (Tor) series, edited by Andre Norton; and doubtless others that I've overlooked. *Arabesques: More Tales of the Arabian Nights* (Avon), edited by Susan Shwartz, was a rather pleasant start to a new shared-world series, featuring enjoyable work by Gene Wolfe, Tanith Lee, Jane Yolen, M. J. Engh, and others. Much the same could be said of another series start-off, *Invitation to Camelot* (Ace), which features enjoyable work by Tanith Lee, John M. Ford, Jane Yolen and others. The other new series are all military themed, some of them depicting, with often undisguised admiration, the exploits of mercenary soldiers: *The Fleet* (Ace), edited by David Drake and Bill Fawcett; *The Man-Kzin Wars* (Baen), edited by Larry Niven; and *War World* (Baen), edited by Jerry Pournelle.

As usual, there was a lot of activity in the original horror anthology market. Sadly, Charles L. Grant's *Shadows*, the long-running anthology series that was your best bet in the horror field most years, seems to have died; it will be missed. There was also no *Whispers* anthology this year, so the market was mostly left to younger hands. Your best value this year was probably *Tropical Chills* (Avon), edited by Tim Sullivan, a varied and entertaining anthology containing good work by Pat Cadigan, Charles Sheffield, Gene Wolfe, and others. *Prime Evil* (NAL), edited by Douglas E. Winter, was being hyped as a major collection, a new *Dark Forces* (in other words, another contender for the title of "the *Dangerous Visions* of horror"), but although it contained good work by Peter Straub, M. John Harrison, and others, on the whole it fell short of that goal. On the other hand, *Night Visions 5* (Dark Harvest), also edited by Douglas E. Winter, may well be the best volume yet in this series, featuring good work by Stephen King, Dan Simmons, and George R. R. Martin. *Silver Scream* (Tor), edited by David J. Schow, was widely hailed as the definitive splatterpunk anthology, and blows wide open the widening schism in the horror field between the "quiet" school of horror writing and the gleefully gore-splattered Grand Guignol "splatterpunk" school, a conflict that is producing bitter rhetoric and fiery public attacks worthy of the New Wave wars of the '60s in science-fiction. There is some good material in *Silver Scream*, but the constant parade of deliberate gross-out scenes gets annoying after a while . . . and many of the stories aren't particularly *scary*, either, a trait some of them share with "splatter" films. A distinction can also be made, and perhaps should be, between gross-out gore and old-fashioned *meanness*—the casual, off-hand murders depicted here in Joe Lansdale's "Night They Missed the Horror Show," for instance, have far more real impact than the thirteen pages of gross-to-the-max (and rather silly) slaughter and mutilation that mar the ending of Mark Arnold's otherwise interesting "Pilgrims to the Cathedral." So the splatterpunks score high here for vigor and ambition . . . but their work would often be more effective if they learned to add some restraint and creative control to the mixture. *Pulphouse, Issue One* was discussed above. *Women of Darkness* (Tor), edited by Kathryn Ptacek, was disappointing. Noted without comment is *Ripper!* (Tor), edited by Gardner Dozois and Susan Casper, a mixed original (mostly) and reprint anthology of stories about Jack-the-you-know-what.

There were no clearly dominant novels in 1988, the way there have been in other years, nothing clearly destined to sweep the awards, but it was a decent year for novels overall, even so. Once again, I must admit that I was unable to read all the new novels released this year, or even the majority of them. *Locus* estimates that there were 317 new SF novels, 264 new fantasy novels, and 182 new horror novels (up sharply from last year's count of 92!) published in 1988 —for a staggering total of 763 new novels released. Clearly the novel field has expanded far beyond the ability of any one reviewer to keep up with it—even a reviewer who *doesn't* have as much other reading at shorter lengths to do as I have. So therefore, as usual, I am going to limit myself here to commenting that of the novels I did read this year, I was the most impressed by: *Mona Lisa Overdrive*, William Gibson (Bantam Spectra); *Islands in the Net*, Bruce Sterling (Arbor House); *The Gold Coast*, Kim Stanley Robinson (Tor); *The Last Coin*, James P. Blaylock (Ace); *Deserted Cities of the Heart*, Lewis Shiner (Bantam Spectra); *Wetware*, Rudy Rucker (Avon); *Unicorn Mountain*, Michael Bishop (Morrow); *Hellspark*, Janet Kagan (Tor); *Eternity*, Greg Bear (Warner); and *Neon Lotus*, Marc Laidlaw (Bantam Spectra).

Other novels that have gotten a lot of attention this year include: *Red Prophet*, Orson Scott Card (Tor); *Prelude to Foundation*, Isaac Asimov (Doubleday Foundation); *There Are Doors*, Gene Wolfe (Tor); *Adulthood Rites*, Octavia E. Butler (Warner); *Fire on the Mountain*, Terry Bisson (Morrow); *House of Shards*, Walter Jon Williams (Tor); *Marco Polo and the Sleeping Beauty*, Avram Davidson & Grania Davis (Baen); *Koko*, Peter Straub (E. P. Dutton); *Falling Free*, Lois McMaster Bujold (Baen); *Memory Wire*, Robert Charles Wilson (Bantam Spectra); *Dreams of Flesh and Sand*, W. T. Quick (NAL); *Starfire*, Paul Preuss (Tor); *Venus of Shadows*, Pamela Sargent (Doubleday Foundation); *Crazy Time*, Kate Wilhelm (St. Martin's); *Ivory*, Mike Resnick (Tor); *The Story of the Stone*, Barry Hughart (Doubleday Foundation); *The Reindeer People*, Megan Lindholm (Ace); *Sister Light, Sister Dark*, Jane Yolen (Tor); *Metrophage*, Richard Kadrey (Ace); *Tower to the Sky*, Phillip C. Jennings (Baen); *Who's Afraid of Beowulf?*, Tom Holt (St. Martin's); *Chronosequence*, Hilbert Schenck (Tor); *Neverness*, David Zindell (Donald I. Fine); *The Armageddon Blues*, Daniel Keys Moran (Bantam Spectra); *Inner Eclipse*, Richard Paul Russo (Tor); *A Splendid Chaos*, John Shirley (Franklin Watts); *Wheel of the Winds*, M. J. Engh (Tor); *At Winter's End*, Robert Silverberg (Warner); *The Wooden Spaceships*, Bob Shaw (Baen); *Cyteen*, C. J. Cherryh (Warner); *Wyvern*, A. A. Attanasio (Ticknor & Fields); *Narabedla Ltd.*, Frederik Pohl (Del Rey); *Destiny's End*, Tim Sullivan (Avon); *Desolation Road*, Ian McDonald (Bantam Spectra); *Krono*, Charles L. Harness (Franklin Watts); *Sleeping in Flame*, Jonathan Carroll (Legend); *Four Hundred Billion Stars*, Paul

J. McAuley (Del Rey); *The Heavenly Horse from the Outermost West*, Mary Stanton (Baen); *Walkabout Woman*, Michaela Roessner (Bantam Spectra); *Journey to Fusang*, William Sanders (Questar); *Through a Brazen Mirror*, Delia Sherman (Ace); *Waiting for the Galactic Bus*, Parke Godwin (Doubleday Foundation); *Consider Phlebas*, Iain M. Banks (St. Martin's); *The Dark Door*, Kate Wilhelm (St. Martin's); *The Last Deathship Off Antares*, Walter Jon Williams (Questar) and *The Drive In*, Joe R. Lansdale (Bantam Spectra).

(I should set off mention here of books I bought and edited myself for the Isaac Asimov Presents line for Congdon & Weed/Worldwide Library, so that you can make the proper allowances for bias: *Antibodies*, David J. Skal; *A Different Flesh*, Harry Turtledove; and *Sin of Origin*, John Barnes.)

There were still a lot of good first novels published this year, although none of them had as much of an impact on the field as first novels by Gibson and Robinson had a few years back. Still, it is encouraging to see so many worthwhile first novels continuing to make it into print; that they can, and are, is one of the bright spots of the last few years. Novels by Kadrey, Moran, McDonald, Quick, Stanton, and Zindell seemed to get the most attention this year among this group. It's a good bet that many of these first novelists will be turning up in print again and again in coming years; some of them may even be among the Big Names of the '90s.

Nineteen eighty-eight was not as strong a year for short-story collections as 1986 or 1987, but some worthwhile collections did appear, including several valuable retrospectives. Among the most interesting of the year's collections were: *Crown of Stars*, James Tiptree Jr. (Tor); *Angry Candy*, Harlan Ellison (Houghton Mifflin); *The Knight and Knave of Swords*, Fritz Leiber (Morrow); *Green Magic*, Jack Vance (Tor); *The Hidden Side of the Moon*, Joanna Russ (St. Martin's); *Other Americas*, Norman Spinrad (Bantam Spectra); *The Day the Martians Came*, Frederik Pohl (St. Martin's); and *Threats . . . And Other Promises*, Vernor Vinge (Baen). My own personal favorite this year, though, was *John the Balladeer*, Manly Wade Wellman (Baen), a landmark fantasy collection that brings back into print Wellman's best short work, long unavailable. There were five retrospective collections this year that should be in the libraries of any serious student of the field: *The Best of John Brunner*, (Baen); *A Rendezvous in Averoigne*, Clark Ashton Smith (Arkham); the massive, three-volume *The Selected Stories of Robert Bloch*, (Underwood-Miller); *Charles Beaumont: Selected Stories* (Dark Harvest); and *Memories of the Space Age*, J. G. Ballard (Arkham). Also worthwhile were: *The Bug Life Chronicles*, Phillip C. Jennings (Baen), a first collection from a madly inventive new writer; *The Blood Kiss*, Dennis Etchison (Scream/Press); *A Thread of Silver Madness*, Jessica Amanda Salmonson (Ace); *Empire Dreams*, Ian McDonald (Bantam Spectra); *The Heat Death of the Universe*, Pamela Zoline (McPherson & Co.); *Azazel*, Isaac Asimov (Doubleday Foundation); *Merlin Dreams*, Peter

Dickinson (Delacorte); and *The Wine-Dark Sea*, Robert Aickman (Morrow).

Two offbeat but interesting small-press collections are: *The Early Lafferty*, R. A. Lafferty (United Mythologies Press, P.O. Box 390, Station 'A', Weston, Ontario, Canada, M9N–3N1; $3.50 plus 50 cents postage) and *Uncle Ovid's Exercise Book*, Don Webb (Illinois State Univ. Fiction Collective, $8.95—available by mail from Mark Zeising Books, P.O. Box 806, Willimantic, CT 06226).

As you can see, small-press publishers—Arkham House, Dark Harvest, Underwood-Miller, Scream/Press—continue to play an important role in bringing short-story collections to the reading public. Even major new writers like Lucius Shepard and Bruce Sterling, who almost certainly would have had trade collections a decade ago, are turning to small-press publishers to get their first short-story collections into print. On the other hand, there *were* more collections from the regular trade publishers this year than last year, which is a good sign. St. Martin's, Baen, Morrow, and Bantam Spectra all published more than one collection this year, and are to be commended for it, but I'd still like to see them publish still *more* collections in years to come. For too many years there have been too few collections published—I'd like to see the trade publishers play catchup in this area, for a change.

The reprint anthology market also seemed a bit weaker this year. As usual, your best bets in the reprint market were the various "Best of the Year" anthologies. This year there were again three covering science fiction, including this one (we lost one series—the later Terry Carr's—but a new series was started in England, edited by David S. Garnett), one covering fantasy, one covering horror, one covering *both* fantasy and horror, and the annual Nebula Award anthology —it's hard to go wrong with any of these. As for nonseries anthologies, the best value was probably *Masterpieces of Fantasy and Enchantment* (Nelson Doubleday and St. Martin's), edited by David G. Hartwell, a solid and worthwhile volume, if not quite as spectacular as last year's *The Dark Descent*. Other worthwhile SF anthologies were: *Interzone: The 3rd Anthology* (Simon & Schuster Ltd.), edited by John Clute, David Pringle, & Simon Ounsley; *Isaac Asimov Presents the Great SF Stories 18: 1956* (DAW), edited by Isaac Asimov and Martin H. Greenberg; and *The Mammoth Book of Classic Science Fiction: Short Novels of the 1930s* (Robinson/Carroll & Graf), edited by Isaac Asimov, Charles Waugh, and Martin H. Greenberg. Noted without comment are *The Best of Isaac Asimov's Science Fiction Magazine* (Ace), edited by Gardner Dozois and *Dogtales!* (Ace), edited by Jack Dann and Gardner Dozois. There were two light fantasy reprint anthologies: *Unknown* (Baen), edited by Stanley Schmidt, and *Werewolves* (Harper & Row), edited by Jane Yolen and Martin H. Greenberg. And several interesting reprint horror anthologies: *The Best of Shadows* (Doubleday Foundation), edited by Charles L. Grant; *The Best Horror Stories from the Magazine of Fantasy and Science Fiction* (St. Martin's), edited by Edward L. Ferman and Anne Jordan;

Fine Frights: Stories That Scared Me (Tor), edited by Ramsey Campbell; *Haunted New England* (Yankee), edited by Charles G. Waugh, Martin H. Greenberg, and Frank McSherry, Jr.; *Haunting Women* (Avon), edited by Alan Ryan; and *Yankee Witches* (Lance Tapley), edited by Frank McSherry, Jr., Martin H. Greenberg, and Charles Waugh.

The rest of the reprint anthology market this year was *heavily* flooded with military themed anthologies, to an even greater extent than the shared-world anthology market was: *Space-Fighters* (Ace), edited by Joe Haldeman, Martin H. Greenberg, and Charles G. Waugh; *Space Wars* (Tor), edited by Poul Anderson, Martin H. Greenberg, and Charles G. Waugh; *There Will Be War, Vol. VII* (Tor), edited by J. E. Pournelle; *Nuclear War* (Ace), edited by Gregory Benford and Martin H. Greenberg; *Men Hunting Things* (Baen), edited by David Drake; *Things Hunting Men* (Baen), edited by David Drake; and *Robert Adam's Book of Soldiers* (NAL), edited by Robert Adams, Pamela Crippen Adams, and Martin H. Greenberg. The overall best of this lot was probably Benford's and Greenberg's *Nuclear War*, and many of the others also contained good stories, but the sheer *number* of these books is somewhat unnerving, particularly when you combine their total with the military themed shared-world anthologies like *War World* and *The Fleet*. Apparently war is one of the most popular themes in SF these days, and the *prospect* of it is greeted with great enthusiasm and gusto by most of these writers (only *Nuclear War* could be said to contain any real cautionary note). I suppose that only custard-headed liberals will be dismayed by all this martial ardor . . . but it does make one wonder, somewhat uneasily, what the future has in store for us—and hope that SF's famed predictive capacity is not working all that well these days.

Two of the silliest ideas for anthologies in recent years were to be found in: *Hunger for Horror* (DAW), edited by Robert Adams, Pamela Adams Crippen, and Martin H. Greenberg (Killer Food), and *14 Vicious Valentines* (Avon), edited by Rosalind M. Greenberg, Martin H. Greenberg, and Charles G. Waugh (self-explanatory).

There were no real outstanding items in the SF-oriented nonfiction SF reference book field in 1988, although it was another solid year, with some interesting stuff seeing print. The book that should have been 1988's standout reference work, but which instead became one of the year's most controversial books, was *The New Encyclopedia of Science Fiction* (Viking), edited by James Gunn. Clearly much earnest effort went into the compilation of this book, and some of the individual essays and entries are excellent, but my overall general reaction to the book is one of mild disappointment, a reaction that seems to have been pretty generally shared. A few reasons for disappointment: many of the entries are sketchy and too many of them are not significantly updated over the information available in 1979's *Science Fiction Encyclopedia* edited by Peter Nicholls; many authors who by rights really ought to be covered here are omitted; and much too much space is devoted to plot summaries of bad B science fiction and monster movies—this last is particularly annoying, since the space devoted to *The Beast from 20,000 Fathoms* or *The Deadly Mantis* could more profitably have been devoted to some of the authors who should have been discussed here. Gunn's *New Encyclopedia* still has value as a reference work, but it's not the book it might have been, and it does not adequately replace Nicholls's *Encyclopedia*—we will have to continue to hope for an updating of the Nicholls's *Encyclopedia* sometime in the future. More solid references are: *Science Fiction, Fantasy And Horror: 1987* (Locus), edited by Charles N. Brown and William G. Contento; *Jules Verne Rediscovered: Didacticism and the Scientific Novel* (Greenwood), Arthur B. Evans; *Fantasy: The 100 Best Books* (Xanadu), James Cawthorn and Michael Moorcock; and *Horror: 100 Best Books* (Xanadu), Stephen Jones and Kim Newman. Another controversial book this year was *Bare-Faced Messiah: The True Story of L. Ron Hubbard* (Holt), by Russell Miller; it makes fascinating reading. Also controversial were two autobiographies, *The Motion of Light in Water* (Morrow), by Samuel R. Delany, and *Bio Of An Ogre* (Ace), by Piers Anthony—two books that couldn't be more different. There was also yet *another* book about the late Philip K. Dick: *Philip K. Dick* (Twayne), by Douglas A. Mackey; it's a shame that he couldn't have received some of this attention while he was still alive. John Clute is a controversial *critic*, speaking of controversy, and certainly he has never hesitated to speak his mind, but, as the reviews collected in *Strokes: Essays and Reviews 1966–1986* (Serconia Press) show, he is also often brilliant and incisive—if sometimes acerbic. More essays, varying in quality and interest, are to be found in *Women of Vision: Essays by Women Writing Science Fiction* (St. Martin's), edited by Denise Du Pont. And if you are a *Silverlock* fan, you'll definitely want *A Silverlock Companion* (Niekas Publications), edited by Fred Lerner; if you're not, however, or haven't read it, then don't bother, because you'll find it incomprehensible. There were two good art books this year: *First Maitz: Selected Works by Don Maitz* (Ursus Imprints), by Don Maitz and *Imagination: The Art and Technique of David A. Cherry* (Donning), by David A. Cherry, as well as a rare reference book about SF art: *A Biographical Dictionary of Science Fiction and Fantasy Artists* (Greenwood), by Robert Weinberg.

My favorite nonfiction book of the year, though, is also the hardest to categorize: *The New Dinosaurs* (Salem House) by Dougal Dixon, a brilliant—and often slyly witty—biological extrapolation of what the world's fauna might look like today if dinosaurs had *not* become extinct, magnificently rendered. Art book? Speculative biology? Whatever it is, it's well worth buying.

Nineteen eighty-eight was apparently a good year for SF and fantasy films, as far as box-office receipts were concerned, anyway, but except for *Who Framed Roger Rabbit*, an extremely enjoyable technological movie, I didn't really *like* any of them very much. Being lukewarm about *Willow* was okay—nobody else seemed to be able to work up much enthusiasm about it anyway—but then I didn't like *Beetlejuice* either, which was everyone else's favorite movie, and I began to wonder if my taste had drifted too far away from that of the average moviegoer to make this review section germane—especially as I now find it physically difficult to force myself into any more slasher/satanist/exploding-head movies. With television it's even worse—*Star Trek: The Next Generation* strikes me as a lackluster second-rate retread of a series I never liked that much in the *first* place. I have lost interest in *Beauty and the Beast*, with all the best will in the world, and the idea of *Freddy's Nightmares*, a weekly TV series based on the *Nightmare on Elm Street* slasher movies, is one that I find repugnant, something that would have been a satirical bit of business in a Pohl/Kornbluth novel a few years back. Grumble. Bah Humbug.

So I've asked Tim Sullivan, someone who really *likes* exploding-head movies—and a noted authority on SF/Horror films, having contributed many of the film reviews for the recent *Penguin Encyclopedia of Horror and the Supernatural*—to give us *his* list of the year's ten best SF/Fantasy films instead, hoping they'll be more useful. Tim's list of the year's top ten films is: 1. *Who Framed Roger Rabbit*; 2. *The Trouble with Dick*; 3. *Dead Ringers*; 4. *Monkeyshines*; 5. *Brain Damage* (about "a singing and dancing brain parasite named Elmer," according to Tim); 6. *The Milagro Beanfield War*; 7. *Lair of the White Worm*; 8. *Wings of Desire*; 9. *DA*; 10. *They Live*.

Actually, now that Tim reminds me of it, I liked *The Milagro Beanfield War*, too. So there. *Two* movies I liked in 1988! Call *me* an unhip old fart, will you . . .

The 46th World Science Fiction convention, Nolacon II, was held in New Orleans, Louisiana, September 1–5, 1988, and drew an estimated attendance of 5,343. The 1988 Hugo Awards, presented at Nolacon II, were: Best Novel, *The Uplift War*, by David Brin; Best Novella, "Eye for Eye," by Orson Scott Card; Best Novelette, "Buffalo Gals, Won't You Come Out Tonight," by Ursula K. Le Guin; Best Short Story, "Why I Left Harry's All-Night Hamburgers," by Lawrence Watt-Evans; Best NonFiction, *Michael Whelan's Works of Wonder*, by Michael Whelan; Best Other Forms, *Watchmen*, by Alan Moore and Dave Gibbons; Best Professional Editor, Gardner Dozois; Best Professional Artist, Michael Whelan; Best Dramatic Presentation, *The Princess Bride*; Best Semiprozine, *Locus*; Best Fanzine, *The Texas SF Inquirer*; Best Fan Writer, Mike Glyer; Best Fan Artist, Brad Foster, plus the John W. Campbell Award for Best New Writer to Judith Moffett.

The 1987 Nebula Awards, presented at a banquet at the Hollywood Roosevelt Hotel, on May 21, 1988, were Best Novel, *The Falling Woman*, by Pat Murphy; Best Novella, "The Blind Geometer," by Kim Stanley Robinson; Best Novelette, "Rachel in Love," by Pat Murphy; Best Short Story, "Forever Yours, Anna," by Kate Wilhelm; plus the Grand Master Award to Alfred Bester.

The World Fantasy Awards, presented at the Fourteenth Annual World Fantasy

Convention in London, England, over Halloween weekend, were: Best Novel, *Replay*, by Ken Grimwood; Best Novella, "Buffalo Gals, Won't You Come Out Tonight," by Ursula K. Le Guin; Best Short Story, "Friend's Best Man," by Jonathan Carroll; Best Collection, *The Jaguar Hunter*, by Lucius Shepard; Best Anthology (tie) *The Architecture of Fear*, edited by Kathryn Cramer and Peter D. Pautz, and *The Dark Descent*, edited by David G. Hartwell. Best Artist, J. K. Potter; Special Award (Professional), David G. Hartwell; Special Award (Non-professional), (tie) David B. Silva, and Robert and Nancy Garcia; plus a Life Achievement Award to Everett F. Bleiler.

The 1988 Bram Stoker Awards, presented at a banquet at the Warwick Hotel in New York City on June 5, 1988 by The Horror Writers of America, were: Best Novel (tie) *Misery*, by Stephen King and *Swan Song*, by Robert McCammon; Best First Novel, *The Manse*, by Lisa Cantrell; Best Collection, *The Essential Ellison*, by Harlan Ellison; Best Nonfiction, *Mary Shelley* by Muriel Spark; Best Novelette, (tie) "The Pear-Shaped Man," by George R. R. Martin and "The Boy Who Came Back from the Dead," Alan Rodgers; Best Short Story, "The Deep End," by Robert McCammon; plus Life Achievement Awards to Fritz Leiber, Frank Belknap Long, and Clifford D. Simak.

The 1987 John W. Campbell Memorial Award-winner was *Lincoln's Dreams*, by Connie Willis.

The 1987 Theodore Sturgeon Award was won by "Rachel in Love," by Pat Murphy.

The 1988 Philip K. Dick Memorial Award-winner was *Strange Toys*, by Patricia Geary.

The Arthur C. Clarke award was won by *The Sea and the Summer*, by George Turner.

Death hit the SF field hard yet again in 1988, taking several of the giants of the industry. The dead include: **Robert A. Heinlein,** 80, one of the most famous SF authors of all time and arguably the most *influential* SF writer since H. G. Wells, multiple award-winner, author of such books as the cult classic *Stranger in a Strange Land*, the controversial *Starship Troopers, The Moon is a Harsh Mistress*, and a long sequence of so-called "juvenile" novels like *Red Planet* and *Starman Jones* that were an introduction to SF for generations of readers; **Clifford D. Simak,** 83, another Golden Age giant, winner of the Hugo, Nebula, and International Fantasy Award, probably best known for the novels *Way Station, Time and Again*, and the classic novel/collection *City*, one of the cornerstone works of the field; **C.L. Moore,** 76, another prominent writer of the '30s and '40s, who, alone or in collaboration with her husband, the late Henry Kuttner, produced a distinguished body of work, including the classic stories "Vintage Season," "No Woman Born," "The Twonky," and "Mimsy Were the Boro-groves"; veteran author **Ross Rocklynne,** 75, author of "Time Wants a Skeleton,'' and ''Jackdaw,'' as well as dozens of other stories for the pulp magazines of the '30s and '40s; **Randall Garrett,** 60, prolific author best known for his ''Lord Darcy'' series, such as *Too Many Magicians* and *Murder and Magic*, in which he adroitly blended the mystery and fantasy fields; **John Myers Myers,** 82, primarily known as the author of the fantasy novel *Silverlock*, which has become a cult classic since its first publication in 1949; **Lin Carter,** 57, writer and editor, often credited, as editor of the Ballantine Adult Fantasy line in the late '60s and early '70s, with helping to revive public interest in high fantasy and sword and sorcery; **Michael Shaara,** 58, SF writer of the '50s who also won a Pulitzer Prize for his Civil War novel, *The Killer Angels*; veteran writer, **E. Hoffmann Price,** author of *Strange Gateways* and *Far Lands, Other Days*; **Neil R. Jones,** 79, author of the long-running ''Professor Jameson'' series, as well as many other novels and stories; **Linda Haldeman,** 52, fantasy writer, author of *Esbae: A Winter's Tale*; **Alice M. Lightner,** 83, author of *The Day of the Drones*; **Louis L'Amour,** 80, perhaps the premier Western writer of all time, rivaled only by Zane Grey; **John Ball,** 77, author of the mystery novel *In the Heat of the Night*, as well as some SF; **Donald E. Keyhoe,** 91, author of *The Flying Saucers Are Real* and other flying saucer books; **Lurton Blassingame,** 84, well-known literary agent; **Charles Addams,** 76, well-known cartoonist with a macabre bent; **Hank Jankus,** 59, SF interior illustrator and cover artist for most of the SF magazines; **John D. Clark,** long-time fan and friend of L. Sprague De Camp, Fletcher Pratt, and other SF notables; **Oswald Train,** 72, long-time fan and small press publisher, long involved in Philadelphia fannish circles; **Eva McKenna,** 67, long-time fan and widow of SF writer Richard McKenna; **Leonard N. Isaacs,** 49, professor at Michigan State University, one of the founders of the Clarion Workshop; **Roy Squires,** 68, book dealer, specialty printer, long-time fan; **James Friend,** 55, academician interested in SF scholarship: **James French,** 55, SF fan and convention staffer; **John Carradine,** 82, veteran actor and film star who appeared in dozens of SF/Horror movies, including *The Bride of Frankenstein* and *The Invisible Man*; and **Billy Curtis,** 79, actor, one of the original munchkins in the *Wizard of Oz*, among many other roles.

WALTER JON WILLIAMS

Surfacing

Walter Jon Williams was born in Minnesota and now lives in Albuquerque, New Mexico. Regarded as one of the hottest new talents in science fiction, Williams has sold stories to *Isaac Asimov's Science Fiction Magazine, Omni, Far Frontiers, Wild Cards*, and *The Magazine of Fantasy and Science Fiction*. His novels include *Ambassador of Progress, Knight Moves, Hardwired, The Crown Jewels*, and *Voice of the Whirlwind*. His most recent novels are *House of Shards* and *Angel Station* (out soon). His story "Side Effects" was in our Third Annual Collection; his story "Video Star" was in our Fourth Annual Collection; and "Dinosaurs" was in our Fifth Annual Collection.

Here he takes us sailing on mysterious alien seas on distant alien worlds, in search of elusive and dangerous prey.

SURFACING

Walter Jon Williams

There was an alien on the surface of the planet. A Kyklops had teleported into Overlook Station, and then flown down on the shuttle. Since, unlike humans, it could teleport without apparatus, presumably it took the shuttle for the ride. The Kyklops wore a human body, controlled through an *n*-dimensional interface, and took its pleasures in the human fashion.

The Kyklops expressed an interest in Anthony's work, but Anthony avoided it: he stayed at sea and listened to aliens of another kind.

Anthony wasn't interested in meeting aliens who knew more than he did.

The boat drifted in a cold current and listened to the cries of the sea. A tall grey swell was rolling in from the southwest, crossing with a wind-driven easterly chop. The boat tossed, caught in the confusion of wave patterns.

It was a sloppy ocean, somehow unsatisfactory. Marking a sloppy day.

Anthony felt a thing twist in his mind. Something that, in its own time, would lead to anger.

The boat had been out here, both in the warm current and then in the cold, for three days. Each more unsatisfactory than the last.

The growing swell was being driven toward land by a storm that was breaking up fifty miles out to sea: the remnants of the storm itself would arrive by midnight and make things even more unpleasant. Spray feathered across the tops of the waves. The day was growing cold.

Spindrift pattered across Anthony's shoulders. He ignored it, concentrated instead on the long, grating harmonic moan picked up by the microphones his boat dangled into the chill current. The moan ended on a series of clicks and trailed off. Anthony tapped his computer deck. A resolution appeared on the screen. Anthony shaded his eyes from the pale sun and looked at it.

Anthony gazed stonily at the translation tree. ''I am rising toward and thinking hungrily about the slippery-tasting coordinates'' actually made the most objective sense, but the righthand branch of the tree was the most literal and most

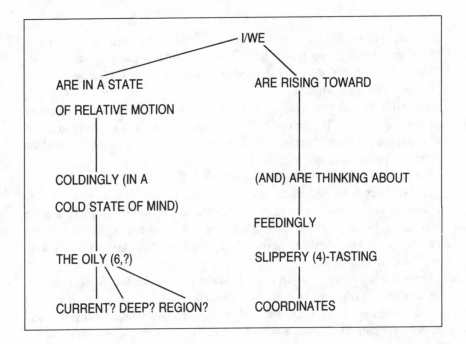

of what Anthony suspected was context had been lost. "I and the oily current are in a state of motion toward one another" was perhaps more literal, but "We (the oily deep and I) are in a cold state of mind" was perhaps equally valid.

The boat gave a corkscrew lurch, dropped down the face of a swell, came to an abrupt halt at the end of its drogue. Water slapped against the stern. A mounting screw, come loose from a bracket on the bridge, fell and danced brightly across the deck.

The screw and the deck are in a state of relative motion, Anthony thought. The screw and the deck are in a motion state of mind.

Wrong, he thought, there is no Other in the Dwellers' speech.

We, I and the screw and the deck, are feeling cold.

We, I and the Dweller below, are in a state of mutual incomprehension.

A bad day, Anthony thought.

Inchoate anger burned deep inside him.

Anthony saved the translation and got up from his seat. He went to the bridge and told the boat to retrieve the drogue and head for Cabo Santa Pola at flank speed. He then went below and found a bottle of bourbon that had three good swallows left.

The trailing microphones continued to record the sonorous moans from below, the sound now mingled with the thrash of the boat's screws.

The screw danced on the deck as the engines built up speed.

Its state of mind was not recorded.

*   *   *

The video news, displayed above the bar, showed the Kyklops making his tour of the planet. The Kyklops' human body, male, was tall and blue-eyed and elegant. He made witty conversation and showed off his naked chest as if he were proud of it. His name was Telamon.

His real body, Anthony knew, was a tenuous uncorporeal mass somewhere in n-dimensional space. The human body had been grown for it to wear, to move like a puppet. The nth dimension was interesting only to a mathematician: its inhabitants preferred wearing flesh.

Anthony asked the bartender to turn off the vid.

The yacht club bar was called the Leviathan, and Anthony hated the name. His creatures were too important, too much themselves, to be awarded a name that stank of human myth, of human resonance that had nothing to do with the creatures themselves. Anthony never called them Leviathans himself. They were Deep Dwellers.

There was a picture of a presumed Leviathan above the bar. Sometimes bits of matter were washed up on shore, thin tenuous membranes, long tentacles, bits of phosphorescence, all encrusted with the local equivalent of barnacles and infested with parasites. It was assumed the stuff had broken loose from the larger Dweller, or were bits of one that had died. The artist had done his best and painted something that looked like a whale covered with tentacles and seaweed.

The place had fake-nautical decor, nets, harpoons, flashing rods, and knick-nacks made from driftwood, and the bar was regularly infected by tourists: that made it even worse. But the regular bartender and the divemaster and the steward were real sailors, and that made the yacht club bearable, gave him some company. His mail was delivered here as well.

Tonight the bartender was a substitute named Christopher: he was married to the owner's daughter and got his job that way. He was a fleshy, sullen man and no company.

We, thought Anthony, the world and I, are drinking alone. Anger burned in him, anger at the quality of the day and the opacity of the Dwellers and the storm that beat brainlessly at the windows.

"*Got* the bastard!" A man was pounding the bar. "Drinks on me." He was talking loudly, and he wore gold rings on his fingers. Raindrops sparkled in his hair. He wore a flashing harness, just in case anyone missed why he was here. Hatred settled in Anthony like poison in his belly.

"Got a thirty-foot flasher," the man said. He pounded the bar again. "Me and Nick got it hung up outside. Four hours. A four-hour fight!"

"Why have a fight with something you can't eat?" Anthony said.

The man looked at him. He looked maybe twenty, but Anthony could tell he was old, centuries old maybe. Old and vain and stupid, stupid as a boy. "It's a game fish," the man said.

Anthony looked into the fisherman's eyes and saw a reflection of his own contempt. "You wanna fight," he said, "you wanna have a *game*, fight something *smart*. Not a dumb animal that you can outsmart, that once you catch it will only rot and stink."

That was the start.

Once it began, it didn't take long. The man's rings cut Anthony's face, and Anthony was smaller and lighter, but the man telegraphed every move and kept leading with his right. When it was over, Anthony left him on the floor and stepped out into the downpour, stood alone in the hammering rain and let the water wash the blood from his face. The whiskey and the rage were a flame that licked his nerves and made them sing.

He began walking down the street. Heading for another bar.

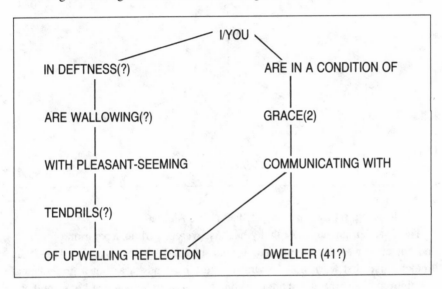

GRACE(2) meant grace in the sense of physical grace, dexterity, harmony of motion, as opposed to spiritual grace, which was GRACE(1). The Dweller that Anthony was listening to was engaged in a dialogue with another, possibly the same known to the computer as 41, who might be named "Upwelling Reflection," but Deep Dweller naming systems seemed inconsistent, depending largely on a context that was as yet opaque, and "upwelling reflection" might have to do with something else entirely.

Anthony suspected the Dweller had just said hello.

Salt water smarted on the cuts on Anthony's face. His swollen knuckles pained him as he tapped the keys of his computer deck. He never suffered from hangover, and his mind seemed filled with an exemplary clarity; he worked rapidly, with burning efficiency. His body felt energized.

He was out of the cold Kirst Current today, in a warm, calm subtropical sea on the other side of the Las Madres archipelago. The difference of forty nautical miles was astonishing.

The sun warmed his back. Sweat prickled on his scalp. The sea sparkled under a violet sky.

The other Dweller answered.

Through his bare feet, Anthony could feel the subsonic overtones vibrating through the boat. Something in the cabin rattled. The microphones recorded the sounds, raised the subsonics to an audible level, played it back. The computer made its attempt.

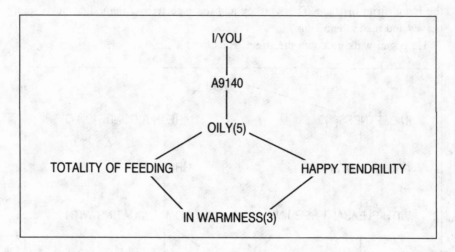

A9140 was a phrase that, as yet, had no translation.

The Dweller language, Anthony had discovered, had no separation of subject and object; it was a trait in common with the Earth cetaceans whose languages Anthony had first learned. "I swim toward the island" was not a grammatical possibility: "I and the island are in a condition of swimming toward one another" was the nearest possible approximation.

The Dwellers lived in darkness, and, like Earth's cetaceans, in a liquid medium. Perhaps they were psychologically unable to separate themselves from their environment, from their fluid surroundings. Never approaching the surface—it was presumed they could not survive in a non-pressurized environment—they had no idea of the upper limit of their world.

They were surrounded by a liquid three-dimensional wholeness, not an air-earth-sky environment from which they could consider themselves separate.

A high-pitched whooping came over the speakers, and Anthony smiled as he listened. The singer was one of the humpbacks that he had imported to this planet, a male called The One with Two Notches on His Starboard Fluke.

Two Notches was one of the brighter whales, and also the most playful. Anthony ordered his computer to translate the humpback speech.

ANTHONY, I AND A PLACE OF BAD SMELLS HAVE FOUND ONE ANOTHER, BUT THIS HAS NOT DETERRED OUR HUNGER.

The computer played back the message as it displayed the translation, and Anthony could understand more context from the sound of the original speech: that Two Notches was floating in a cold layer beneath the bad smell, and that the bad smell was methane or something like it—humans couldn't smell methane, but whales could. The over-literal translation was an aid only, to remind Anthony of idioms he might have forgotten.

Anthony's name in humpback was actually He Who Has Brought Us to the Sea of Rich Strangeness, but the computer translated it simply. Anthony tapped his reply.

What is it that stinks, Two Notches?

SOME KIND OF HORRID JELLYFISH. WERE THEY-AND-I FEEDING, THEY-AND-I WOULD SPIT ONE ANOTHER OUT. I/THEY WILL GIVE THEM/ME A NAME: THEY/ME ARE THE JELLYFISH THAT SMELL LIKE INDIGESTION.

That is a good name, Two Notches.

I AND A SMALL BOAT DISCOVERED EACH OTHER EARLIER TODAY. WE ITCHED, SO WE SCRATCHED OUR BACK ON THE BOAT. THE HUMANS AND I WERE STARTLED. WE HAD A GOOD LAUGH TOGETHER IN SPITE OF OUR HUNGER.

Meaning that Two Notches had risen under the boat, scratched his back on it, and terrified the passengers witless. Anthony remembered the first time this had happened to him back on Earth, a vast female humpback rising up without warning, one long scalloped fin breaking the water to port, the rest of the whale to starboard, thrashing in cetacean delight as it rubbed itself against a boat half its length. Anthony had clung to the gunwale, horrified by what the whale could do to his boat, but still exhilarated, delighted at the sight of the creature and its glorious joy.

Still, Two Notches ought not to play too many pranks on the tourists.

We should be careful, Two Notches. Not all humans possess our sense of humor, especially if they are hungry.

WE WERE BORED, ANTHONY. MATING IS OVER, FEEDING HAS NOT BEGUN. ALSO, IT WAS NICK'S BOAT THAT GOT SCRATCHED. IN OUR OPINION NICK AND I ENJOYED OURSELVES, EVEN THOUGH WE WERE HUNGRY.

Hunger and food seemed to be the humpback subtheme of the day. Humpback songs, like the human, were made up of text and chorus, the chorus repeating itself, with variations, through the message.

I and Nick will ask each other and find out, as we feed.

Anthony tried to participate in the chorus/response about food, but he found himself continually frustrated at his clumsy phrasing. Fortunately the whales were tolerant of his efforts.

HAVE WE LEARNED ANYTHING ABOUT THE ONES THAT SWIM DEEP AND DO NOT BREATHE AND FEED ON OBSCURE THINGS?

Not yet, Two Notches. Something has interrupted us in our hungry quest.

A CONDITION OF MISFORTUNE EXISTS, LIKE UNTO HUNGER. WE MUST LEARN TO BE QUICKER.

We will try, Two Notches. After we eat.

WE WOULD LIKE TO SPEAK TO THE DEEP DWELLERS NOW, AND FEED WITH THEM, BUT WE MUST BREATHE.

We will speak to ourselves another time, after feeding.

WE ARE IN A CONDITION OF HUNGER, ANTHONY. WE MUST EAT SOON.

We will remember our hunger and make plans.

The mating and calving season for the humpbacks was over. Most of the whales were already heading north to their summer feeding grounds, where they would do little but eat for six months. Two Notches and one of the other males had remained in the vicinity of Las Madres as a favor to Anthony, who used them to assist in locating the Deep Dwellers, but soon—in a matter of days—the pair would have to head north. They hadn't eaten anything for nearly half a year; Anthony didn't want to starve them.

But when the whales left, Anthony would be alone—again—with the Deep Dwellers. He didn't want to think about that.

The system's second sun winked across the waves, rising now. It was a white dwarf and emitted dangerous amounts of X-rays. The boat's falkner generator, triggered by the computer, snapped on a field that surrounded the boat and guarded it from energetic radiation. Anthony felt the warmth on his shoulders decrease. He turned his attention back to the Deep Dwellers.

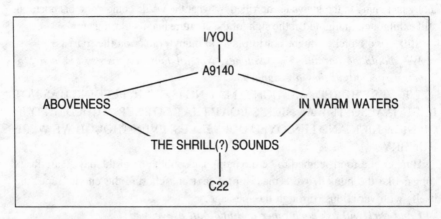

A blaze of delight rose in Anthony. The Dwellers, he realized, had overheard his conversation with Two Notches, and were commenting on it. Furthermore, he knew, A9140 probably was a verb form having to do with hearing—the Dwellers had a lot of them. "I/You hear the shrill sounds from above" might do as a working translation, and although he had no idea how to translate C22, he suspected it was a comment on the sounds. In a fever, Anthony began to work. As he bent over his keys he heard, through water and bone, the sound of Two Notches singing.

The Milky Way was a dim watercolor wash overhead. An odd twilight hung over Las Madres, a near-darkness that marked the hours when only the dwarf star was in the sky, providing little visible light but still pouring out X-rays. Cabo Santa Pola lay in a bright glowing crescent across the boat's path. Music drifted from a waterfront tavern, providing a counterpoint to the Deep Dweller speech that still rang in Anthony's head. A familiar figure waited on the dock, standing beneath the yellow lamp that marked Anthony's slip. Anthony waved and throttled the boat back.

A good day. Even after the yellow sun had set, Anthony still felt in a sunny mood. A9140 had been codified as "listen(14)," meaning listen solely in the sense of listening to a sound that originated from far outside the Dwellers' normal sphere—from outside their entire universe, in fact, which spoke volumes for the way the Dwellers saw themselves in relation to their world. They knew something else was up there, and their speech could make careful distinction between the world they knew and could perceive directly and the one they didn't. C22 was a descriptive term involving patterning: the Dwellers realized that the cetacean speech they'd been hearing wasn't simply random. Which spoke rather well for their cognition.

Anthony turned the boat and backed into the slip. Nick Kanellopoulos, whom the humpbacks called The One Who Chases Bad-Tasting Fish, took the sternline that Anthony threw him and tied it expertly to a cleat. Anthony shut off the engines, took a bowline, and hopped to the dock. He bent over the cleat and made his knot.

"You've gotta stop beating up my customers, Anthony," Nick said.

Anthony said nothing.

"You even send your damn whales to harass me."

Anthony jumped back into the boat and stepped into the cabin for a small canvas bag that held his gear and the data cubes containing the Dweller's conversation. When he stepped back out of the cabin, he saw Nick standing on one foot, the other poised to step into the boat. Anthony gave Nick a look and Nick pulled his foot back. Anthony smiled. He didn't like people on his boat.

"Dinner?" he asked.

Nick gazed at him. A muscle moved in the man's cheek. He was dapper, olive-skinned, about a century old, the second-youngest human on the planet. He looked in his late teens. He wore a personal falkner generator on his belt that protected him from the dwarf's X-rays.

"Dinner. Fine." His brown eyes were concerned. "You look like hell, Anthony."

Anthony rubbed the stubble on his cheeks. "I feel on top of the world," he said.

"Half the time you don't even talk to me. I don't know why I'm eating supper with you."

"Let me clean up. Then we can go to the Mary Villa."

Nick shook his head. "Okay," he said. "But you're buying. You cost me a customer last night."

Anthony slapped him on the shoulder. "Least I can do, I guess."

A good day.

Near midnight. Winds beat at the island's old volcanic cone, pushed down the crowns of trees. A shuttle, black against the darkness of the sky, rose in absolute silence from the port on the other side of the island, heading toward the bright fixed star that was Overlook Station. The alien, Telamon, was aboard, or so the newscasts reported.

Deep Dwellers still sang in Anthony's head. Mail in hand, he let himself in through the marina gate and walked toward his slip. The smell of the sea rose around him. He stretched, yawned. Belched up a bit of the tequila he'd been drinking with Nick. He intended to get an early start and head back to sea before dawn.

Anthony paused beneath a light and opened the large envelope, pulled out page proofs that had been mailed, at a high cost, from the offices of the *Xenobiology Review* on Kemps. Discontent scratched at his nerves. He frowned as he glanced through the pages. He'd written the article over a year before, at the end of the first spring he'd spent here, and just glancing through it he now found the article over-tentative, over-formal, and, worse, almost pleading in its attempt to justify his decision to move himself and the whales here. The palpable defensiveness made him want to squirm.

Disgust filled him. His fingers clutched at the pages, then tore the proofs across. His body spun full circle as he scaled the proofs out to the sea. The wind scattered thick chunks of paper across the dark waters of the marina.

He stalked toward his boat. Bile rose in his throat. He wished he had a bottle of tequila with him. He almost went back for one before he realized the liquor stores were closed.

"Anthony Maldalena?"

She was a little gawky, and her skin was pale. Dark hair in a single long braid, deep eyes, a bit of an overbite. She was waiting for him at the end of his slip, under the light. She had a bag over one shoulder.

Anthony stopped. Dull anger flickered in his belly. He didn't want anyone taking notice of the bruises and cuts on his face. He turned his head away as he stepped into his boat, dropped his bag on a seat.

"Mr. Maldalena. My name is Philana Telander. I came here to see you."

"How'd you get in?"

She gestured to the boat two slips down, a tall FPS-powered yacht shaped like a flat oval with a tall flybridge jutting from its center so that the pilot could see over wavetops. It would fly from place to place, but she could put it down in the water if she wanted. No doubt she'd bought a temporary membership at the yacht club.

"Nice boat," said Anthony. It would have cost her a fair bit to have it gated here. He opened the hatch to his forward cabin, tossed his bag onto the long couch inside.

"I meant," she said, "I came to this *planet* to see you."

Anthony didn't say anything, just straightened from his stoop by the hatch and looked at her. She shifted from one foot to another. Her skin was yellow in the light of the lamp. She reached into her bag and fumbled with something.

Anthony waited.

The clicks and sobs of whales sounded from the recorder in her hand.

"I wanted to show you what I've been able to do with your work. I have some articles coming up in *Cetology Journal* but they won't be out for a while."

"You've done very well," said Anthony. Tequila swirled in his head. He was having a hard time concentrating on a subject as difficult as whale speech.

Philana had specialized in communication with female humpbacks. It was harder to talk with the females: although they were curious and playful, they weren't vocal like the bulls; their language was deeper, briefer, more personal. They made no songs. It was almost as if, solely in the realm of speech, the cows were autistic. Their psychology was different and complicated, and Anthony had had little success in establishing any lasting communication. The cows, he had realized, were speaking a second tongue: the humpbacks were essentially bilingual, and Anthony had only learned one of their languages.

Philana had succeeded where Anthony had found only frustration. She had built from his work, established a structure and basis for communication. She still wasn't as easy in her speech with the cows as Anthony was with a bull like Two Notches, but she was far closer than Anthony had ever been.

Steam rose from the coffee cup in Philana's hand as she poured from Anthony's vacuum flask. She and Anthony sat on the cushioned benches in the stern of Anthony's boat. Tequila still buzzed in Anthony's head. Conflicting urges warred in him. He didn't want anyone else here, on his boat, this close to his work; but Philana's discoveries were too interesting to shut her out entirely. He swallowed more coffee.

"Listen to this," Philana said. "It's fascinating. A cow teaching her calf about life." She touched the recorder, and muttering filled the air. Anthony had difficulty understanding: the cow's idiom was complex, and bore none of the poetic repetition that made the males' language easier to follow. Finally he shook his head.

"Go ahead and turn it off," he said. "I'm picking up only one phrase in five. I can't follow it."

Philana seemed startled. "Oh. I'm sorry. I thought—"

Anthony twisted uncomfortably in his seat. "I don't know every goddamn thing about whales," he said.

The recorder fell silent. Wind rattled the canvas awning over the flybridge. Savage discontent settled into Anthony's mind. Suddenly he needed to get rid of this woman, get her off his boat and head to sea right now, away from all the things on land that could trip him up.

He thought of his father upside-down in the smokehouse. Not moving, arms dangling.

He should apologize, he realized. We are, he thought, in a condition of permanent apology.

"I'm sorry," he said. "I'm just . . . not used to dealing with people."

"Sometimes I wonder," she said. "I'm only twenty-one, and . . ."

"Yes?" Blurted suddenly, the tequila talking. Anthony felt disgust at his own awkwardness.

Philana looked at the planks. "Yes. Truly. I'm twenty-one, and sometimes people get impatient with me for reasons I don't understand."

Anthony's voice was quiet. "I'm twenty-six."

Philana was surprised. "But. I thought." She thought for a long moment. "It seems I've been reading your papers for . . ."

"I was first published at twenty," he said. "The finback article."

Philana shook her head. "I'd never have guessed. Particularly after what I saw in your new XR paper."

Anthony's reaction was instant. "You saw that?" Another spasm of disgust touched him. Tequila burned in his veins. His stomach turned over. For some reason his arms were trembling.

"A friend on Kemps sent me an advance copy. I thought it was brilliant. The way you were able to codify your conceptions about a race of which you could really know nothing, and have it all pan out when you began to understand them. That's an incredible achievement."

"It's a piece of crap." Anthony wanted more tequila badly. His body was shaking. He tossed the remains of his coffee over his shoulder into the sea. "I've learned so much since. I've given up even trying to publish it. The delays are too long. Even if I put it on the nets, I'd still have to take the time to write it, and I'd rather spend my time working."

"I'd like to see it."

He turned away from her. "I don't show my work till it's finished."

"I . . . didn't mean to intrude."

Apology. He could feel a knife twisting in his belly. He spoke quickly. "I'm sorry, Miss Telander. It's late, and I'm not used to company. I'm not entirely well." He stood, took her arm. Ignoring her surprise, he almost pulled her to her feet. "Maybe tomorrow. We'll talk again."

She blinked up at him. "Yes. I'd like that."

"Good night." He rushed her off the boat and stepped below to the head. He didn't want her to hear what was going to happen next. Acid rose in his throat. He clutched his middle and bent over the small toilet and let the spasms take him. The convulsions wracked him long after he was dry. After it was over he stood shakily, staggered to the sink, washed his face. His sinus burned and brought tears to his eyes. He threw himself on the couch.

In the morning, before dawn, he cast off and motored out into the quiet sea.

The other male, The One Who Sings of Others, found a pair of Dwellers engaged in a long conversation and hovered above them. His transponder led Anthony to the place, fifty miles south into the bottomless tropical ocean. The Dwellers' conversation was dense. Anthony understood perhaps one word-phrase in ten. Sings of Others interrupted from time to time to tell Anthony how hungry he was.

The recordings would require days of work before Anthony could even begin to make sense of them. He wanted to stay on the site, but the Dwellers fell silent, neither Anthony nor Sings of Others could find another conversation, and Anthony was near out of supplies. He'd been working so intently he'd never got around to buying food.

The white dwarf had set by the time Anthony motored into harbor. Dweller mutterings did a chaotic dance in his mind. He felt a twist of annoyance at the sight of Philana Telander jumping from her big air yacht to the pier. She had obviously been waiting for him.

He threw her the bowline and she made fast. As he stepped onto the dock and fastened the sternline, he noticed sunburn reddening her cheeks. She'd spent the day on the ocean.

"Sorry I left so early," he said. "One of the humpbacks found some Dwellers, and their conversation sounded interesting."

She looked from Anthony to his boat and back. "That's all right," she said. "I shouldn't have talked to you last night. Not when you were ill."

Anger flickered in his mind. She'd heard him being sick, then.

"Too much to drink," he said. He jumped back into the boat and got his gear.

"Have you eaten?" she asked. "Somebody told me about a place called the Villa Mary."

He threw his bag over one shoulder. Dinner would be his penance. "I'll show you," he said.

"Mary was a woman who died," Anthony said. "One of the original Knight's Move people. She chose to die, refused the treatments. She didn't believe in living forever." He looked up at the arched ceiling, the moldings on walls and ceiling, the initials ML worked into the decoration. "Brian McGivern built this place in her memory," Anthony said. "He's built a lot of places like this, on different worlds."

Philana was looking at her plate. She nudged a ichthyoid exomembrane with her fork. "I know," she said. "I've been in a few of them."

Anthony reached for his glass, took a drink, then stopped himself from taking a second swallow. He realized that he'd drunk most of a bottle of wine. He didn't want a repetition of last night.

With an effort he put the glass down.

"She's someone I think about, sometimes," Philana said. "About the choice she made."

"Yes?" Anthony shook his head. "Not me. I don't want to spend a hundred years dying. If I ever decide to die, I'll do it quick."

"That's what people say. But they never do it. They just get older and older. Stranger and stranger." She raised her hands, made a gesture that took in the room, the decorations, the entire white building on its cliff overlooking the sea. "Get old enough, you start doing things like building Villa Marys all over the galaxy. McGivern's an oldest-generation immortal, you know. Maybe the wealthiest human anywhere, and he spends his time immortalizing someone who didn't want immortality of any kind."

Anthony laughed. "Sounds like you're thinking of becoming a Diehard."

She looked at him steadily. "Yes."

Anthony's laughter froze abruptly. A cool shock passed through him. He had never spoken to a Diehard before: the only ones he'd met were people who mumbled at him on streetcorners and passed out incoherent religious tracts.

Philana looked at her plate. "I'm sorry," she said.

"Why sorry?"

"I shouldn't have brought it up."

Anthony reached for his wine glass, stopped himself, put his hand down. "I'm curious."

She gave a little, apologetic laugh. "I may not go through with it."

"Why even think about it?"

Philana thought a long time before answering. "I've seen how the whales accept death. So graceful about it, so matter-of-fact—and they don't even have the myth of an afterlife to comfort them. If they get sick, they just beach themselves; and their friends try to keep them company. And when I try to give myself a reason for living beyond my natural span, I can't think of any. All I can think of is the whales.''

Anthony saw the smokehouse in his mind, his father with his arms hanging, the fingers touching the dusty floor. "Death isn't nice."

Philana gave him a skeletal grin and took a quick drink of wine. "With any luck," she said, "death isn't anything at all."

Wind chilled the night, pouring upon the town through a slot in the island's volcanic cone. Anthony watched a streamlined head as it moved in the dark windwashed water of the marina. The head belonged to a cold-blooded amphibian that lived in the warm surf of the Las Madres; the creature was known misleadingly as a Las Madres seal. They had little fear of humanity and were curious about the new arrivals. Anthony stamped a foot on the slip. Planks boomed. The seal's head disappeared with a soft splash. Ripples spread in starlight, and Anthony smiled.

Philana had stepped into her yacht for a sweater. She returned, cast a glance at the water, saw nothing.

"Can I listen to the Dwellers?" she asked. "I'd like to hear them."

Despite his resentment at her imposition, Anthony appreciated her being careful with the term: she hadn't called them Leviathans once. He thought about her request, could think of no reason to refuse save his own stubborn reluctance. The Dweller sounds were just background noise, meaningless to her. He stepped onto his boat, took a cube from his pocket, put it in the trapdoor, pressed the PLAY button. Dweller murmurings filled the cockpit. Philana stepped from the dock to the boat. She shivered in the wind. Her eyes were pools of dark wonder.

"So different."

"Are you surprised?"

"I suppose not."

"This isn't really what they sound like. What you're hearing is a computer-generated metaphor for the real thing. Much of their communication is subsonic, and the computer raises the sound to levels we can hear, and also speeds it up. Sometimes the Dwellers take three or four minutes to speak what seems to be a simple sentence."

"We would never have noticed them except for an accident," Philana said. "That's how alien they are."

"Yes."

Humanity wouldn't know of the Dwellers' existence at all if it weren't for the subsonics confusing some automated sonar buoys, followed by an idiot computer assuming the sounds were deliberate interference and initiating an ET scan. Any human would have looked at the data, concluded it was some kind of seismic interference, and programmed the buoys to ignore it.

"They've noticed *us*," Anthony said. "The other day I heard them discussing a conversation I had with one of the humpbacks."

Philana straightened. Excitement was plain in her voice. "They can conceptualize something alien to them."

"Yes."

Her response was instant, stepping on the last sibilant of his answer. "And theorize about our existence."

Anthony smiled at her eagerness. "I . . . don't think they've got around to that yet."

"But they are intelligent."

"Yes."

"Maybe more intelligent than the whales. From what you say, they seem quicker to conceptualize."

"Intelligent in certain ways, perhaps. There's still very little I understand about them."

"Can you teach me to talk to them?"

The wind blew chill between them. "I don't," he said, "talk to them."

She seemed not to notice his change of mood, stepped closer. "You haven't tried that yet? That would seem to be reasonable, considering they've already noticed us."

He could feel his hackles rising, mental defenses sliding into place. "I'm not proficient enough," he said.

"If you could attract their attention, they could teach you." Reasonably.

"No. Not yet." Rage exploded in Anthony's mind. He wanted her off his boat, away from his work, his existence. He wanted to be alone again with his creatures, solitary witness to the lonely and wonderful interplay of alien minds.

"I never told you," Philana said, "why I'm here."

"No. You didn't."

"I want to do some work with the humpback cows."

"Why?"

Her eyes widened slightly. She had detected the hostility in his tone. "I want to chart any linguistic changes that may occur as a result of their move to another environment."

Through clouds of blinding resentment Anthony considered her plan. He couldn't stop her, he knew: anyone could talk to the whales if they knew how to do it. It might keep her away from the Dwellers. "Fine," he said. "Do it."

Her look was challenging. "I don't need your permission."

"I know that."

"You don't own them."

"I know that, too."

There was a splash far out in the marina. The Las Madres seal chasing a fish. Philana was still staring at him. He looked back.

"Why are you afraid of my getting close to the Dwellers?" she asked.

"You've been here two days. You don't know them. You're making all manner of assumptions about what they're like, and all you've read is one obsolete article."

"You're the expert. But if my assumptions are wrong, you're free to tell me."

"Humans interacted with whales for centuries before they learned to speak with them, and even now the speech is limited and often confused. I've only been here two and a half years."

"Perhaps," she said, "you could use some help. Write those papers of yours. Publish the data."

He turned away. "I'm doing fine," he said.

"Glad to hear it." She took a long breath. "What did I *do*, Anthony? Tell me."

"Nothing," he said. Anthony watched the marina waters, saw the amphibian surface, its head pulled back to help slide a fish down its gullet. Philana was just standing there. We, thought Anthony, are in a condition of non-resolution.

"I work alone," he said. "I immerse myself in their speech, in their environment, for months at a time. Talking to a human breaks my concentration. I don't know *how* to talk to a person right now. After the Dwellers, you seem perfectly . . ."

"Alien?" she said. Anthony didn't answer. The amphibian slid through the water, its head leaving a short, silver wake.

The boat rocked as Philana stepped from it to the dock. "Maybe we can talk later," she said. "Exchange data or something."

"Yes," Anthony said. "We'll do that." His eyes were still on the seal.

Later, before he went to bed, he told the computer to play Dweller speech all night long.

Lying in his bunk the next morning, Anthony heard Philana cast off her yacht. He felt a compulsion to talk to her, apologize again, but in the end he stayed in his rack, tried to concentrate on Dweller sounds. I/We remain in a condition of solitude, he thought, the Dweller phrases coming easily to his mind. There was a brief shadow cast on the port beside him as the big flying boat rose into the sky, then nothing but sunlight and the slap of water on the pier supports. Anthony climbed out of his sleeping bag and went into town, provisioned the boat for a week. He had been too close to land for too long: a trip into the sea, surrounded by nothing but whales and Dweller speech, should cure him of his unease.

Two Notches had switched on his transponder: Anthony followed the beacon north, the boat rising easily over deep blue rollers. Desiring sun, Anthony climbed to the flybridge and lowered the canvas cover. Fifty miles north of Cabo Santa Pola there was a clear dividing line in the water, a line as clear as a meridian on a chart, beyond which the sea was a deeper, purer blue. The line marked the boundary of the cold Kirst current that had journeyed, wreathed in mist from contact with the warmer air, a full three thousand nautical miles from the region of the South Pole. Anthony crossed the line and rolled down his sleeves as the temperature of the air fell.

He heard the first whale speech through his microphones as he entered the cold current: the sound hadn't carried across the turbulent frontier of warm water and cold. The whales were unclear, distant and mixed with the sound of the screws, but he could tell from the rhythm that he was overhearing a dialogue. Apparently Sings of Others had joined Two Notches north of Las Madres. It was a long journey to make overnight, but not impossible.

The cooler air was invigorating. The boat plowed a straight, efficient wake through the deep blue sea. Anthony's spirits rose. This was where he belonged, away from the clutter and complication of humanity. Doing what he did best.

He heard something odd in the rhythm of the whalespeech; he frowned and listened more closely. One of the whales was Two Notches: Anthony recognized his speech patterns easily after all this time; but the other wasn't Sings of Others. There was a clumsiness in its pattern of chorus and response.

The other was a human. Annoyance hummed in Anthony's nerves. Back on Earth, tourists or eager amateur explorers sometimes bought cheap translation programs and tried to talk to the whales, but this was no tourist program: it was too eloquent, too knowing. Philana, of course. She'd followed the transponder signal and was busy gathering data about the humpback females. Anthony cut his engines and let the boat drift slowly to put its bow into the wind; he deployed the microphones from their wells in the hull and listened. The song was bouncing off a colder layer below, and it echoed confusingly.

DEEP SWIMMER AND HER CALF, CALLED THE ONE THAT NUDGES, ARE POSSESSED OF ONE ANOTHER. I AND THAT ONE AM THE FATHER. WE HUNGER FOR ONE ANOTHER'S PRESENCE.

Apparently hunger was once again the subtheme of the day. The context told Anthony that Two Notches was swimming in cool water beneath a boat. Anthony turned the volume up:

WE HUNGER TO HEAR OF DEEP SWIMMER AND OUR CALF.

That was the human response: limited in its phrasing and context, direct and to the point.

I AND DEEP SWIMMER ARE SHY. WE WILL NOT PLAY WITH HUMANS. INSTEAD WE WILL PRETEND WE ARE HUNGRY AND VANISH INTO DEEP WATERS.

The boat lurched as a swell caught it at an awkward angle. Water splashed over the bow. Anthony deployed the drogue and dropped from the flybridge to the cockpit. He tapped a message into the computer and relayed it.

I and Two Notches are pleased to greet ourselves. I and Two Notches hope we are not too hungry.

The whale's reply was shaded with delight. HUNGRILY I AND ANTHONY GREET OURSELVES. WE AND ANTHONY'S FRIEND, AIR HUMAN, HAVE BEEN IN A CONDITION OF CONVERSATION.

Air Human, from the flying yacht. Two Notches went on.

WE HAD FOUND OURSELVES SOME DEEP DWELLERS, BUT SOME MOMENTS AGO WE AND THEY MOVED BENEATH A COLD LAYER AND OUR CONVERSATION IS LOST. I STARVE FOR ITS RETURN.

The words echoed off the cold layer that stood like a wall between Anthony and the Dwellers. The humpback inflections were steeped in annoyance.

Our hunger is unabated, Anthony typed. *But we will wait for the non-breathers' return.*

WE CANNOT WAIT LONG. TONIGHT WE AND THE NORTH MUST BEGIN THE JOURNEY TO OUR FEEDING TIME.

The voice of Air Human rumbled through the water. It sounded like a distant, throbbing engine. OUR FINEST GREETINGS, ANTHONY. I AND TWO NOTCHES WILL TRAVEL NORTH TOGETHER. THEN WE AND THE OTHERS WILL FEED.

Annoyance slammed into Anthony. Philana had abducted his whale. Clenching his teeth, he typed a civil reply:

Please give our kindest greetings to our hungry brothers and sisters in the north.

By the time he transmitted his speech his anger had faded. Two Notches' departure was inevitable in the next few days, and he'd known that. Still, a residue of jealousy burned in him. Philana would have the whale's company on its journey north: he would be stuck here by Las Madres without the keen whale ears that helped him find the Dwellers.

Two Notches' reply came simultaneously with a programmed reply from Philana. Lyrics about greetings, hunger, feeding, calves, and joy whined through the water, bounced from the cold layer. Anthony looked at the hash his computer made of the translation and laughed. He decided he might as well enjoy Two Notches' company while it lasted.

That was a strange message to hear from our friend, Two Mouths, he typed. "Notch" and "mouth" were almost the same phrase: Anthony had just made a pun.

Whale amusement bubbled through the water. TWO MOUTHS AND I BELONG TO THE MOST UNUSUAL FAMILY BETWEEN SURFACE AND COLD WATER. WE-ALL AND AIR BREATHE EACH OTHER, BUT SOME OF US HAVE THE BAD FORTUNE TO LIVE IN IT.

The sun warmed Anthony's shoulders in spite of the cool air. He decided to leave off the pursuit of the Dwellers and spend the day with his humpback.

He kicked off his shoes, then stepped down to his cooler and made himself a sandwich.

*   *   *

The Dwellers never came out from beneath the cold layer. Anthony spent the afternoon listening to Two Notches tell stories about his family. Now that the issue of hunger was resolved by the whale's decision to migrate, the cold layer beneath them became the new topic of conversation, and Two Notches amused himself by harmonizing with his own echo. Sings of Others arrived in late afternoon and announced he had already begun his journey: he and Two Notches decided to travel in company.

NORTHWARD HOMING! COLD WATERING! REUNION JOYOUS! The phrases dopplered closer to Anthony's boat, and then Two Notches broke the water thirty feet off the port beam, salt water pouring like Niagara from his black jaw, his scalloped fins spread like wings eager to take the air . . . Anthony's breath went out of him in surprise. He turned in his chair and leaned away from the sight, half in fear and half in awe . . . Even though he was used to the whales, the sight never failed to stun him, thrill him, freeze him in his tracks.

Two Notches toppled over backwards, one clear brown eye fixed on Anthony. Anthony raised an arm and waved, and he thought he saw amusement in Two Notches' glance, perhaps the beginning of an answering wave in the gesture of a fin. A living creature the size of a bus, the whale struck the water not with a smack, but with a roar, a sustained outpour of thunder. Anthony braced himself for what was coming. Salt water flung itself over the gunwale, struck him like a blow. The cold was shocking: his heart lurched. The boat was flung high on the wave, dropped down its face with a jarring thud. Two Notches' flukes tossed high and Anthony could see the mottled pattern, grey and white, on the underside, distinctive as a fingerprint . . . and then the flukes were gone, leaving behind a rolling boat and a boiling sea.

Anthony wiped the ocean from his face, then from his computer. The boat's auto-baling mechanism began to throb. Two Notches surfaced a hundred yards off, spouted a round cloud of steam, submerged again. The whale's amusement stung the water. Anthony's surprise turned to joy, and he echoed the sound of laughter.

I'm going to run my boat up your backside, Anthony promised; he splashed to the controls in his bare feet, withdrew the drogue and threw his engines into gear. Props thrashed the sea into foam. Anthony drew the microphones up into their wells, heard them thud along the hull as the boat gained way. Humpbacks usually took breath in a series of three: Anthony aimed ahead for Two Notches' second rising. Two Notches rose just ahead, spouted, and dove before Anthony could catch him. A cold wind cut through Anthony's wet shirt, raised bumps on his flesh. The boat increased speed, tossing its head on the face of a wave, and Anthony raced ahead, aiming for where Two Notches would rise for the third time.

The whale knew where the boat was and was able to avoid him easily; there was no danger in the game. Anthony won the race: Two Notches surfaced just aft of the boat, and Anthony grinned as he gunned his propellers and wrenched the rudder from side to side while the boat spewed foam into the whale's face. Two Notches gave a grunt of disappointment and sounded, tossing his flukes high. Unless he chose to rise early, Two Notches would be down for five minutes or more. Anthony raced the boat in circles, waiting. Two Notches' taunts rose in the cool water. The wind was cutting Anthony to the quick. He reached into the cabin for a sweater, pulled it on, ran up to the flybridge just in time to see Two Notches leap again half a mile away, the vast dark body silhouetted for a moment against the setting sun before it fell again into the welcoming sea.

GOODBYE, GOODBYE. I AND ANTHONY SEND FRAGRANT FARE-WELLS TO ONE ANOTHER.

White foam surrounded the slick, still place where Two Notches had fallen into the water. Suddenly the flybridge was very cold. Anthony's heart sank. He cut speed and put the wheel amidships. The boat slowed reluctantly, as if it, too, had been enjoying the game. Anthony dropped down the ladder to his computer.

Through the spattered windscreen, Anthony could see Two Notches leaping again, his long wings beating air, his silhouette refracted through seawater and rainbows. Anthony tried to share the whale's exuberance, his joy, but the thought of another long summer alone on his boat, beating his head against the enigma of the Dwellers, turned his mind to ice.

He ordered an infinite repeat of Two Notches' last phrase and stepped below to change into dry clothes. The cold layer echoed his farewells. He bent almost double and began pulling the sweater over his head.

Suddenly he straightened. An idea was chattering at him. He yanked the sweater back down over his trunk, rushed to his computer, tapped another message.

Our farewells need not be said just yet. You and I can follow one another for a few days before I must return. Perhaps you and the non-breathers can find one another for conversation.

ANTHONY IS IN A CONDITION OF MIGRATION. WELCOME, WEL-COME. Two Notches' reply was jubilant.

For a few days, Anthony qualified. Before too long he would have to return to port for supplies. Annoyed at himself, he realized he could as easily have victualed for weeks.

Another voice called through the water, sounded faintly through the speakers. *Air Human and Anthony are in a state of tastiest welcome.*

In the middle of Anthony's reply, his fingers paused at the keys. Surprise rose quietly to the surface of his mind.

After the long day of talking in humpback speech, he had forgotten that Air Human was not a humpback. That she was, in fact, another human being sitting on a boat just over the horizon.

Anthony continued his message. His fingers were clumsy now, and he had to go back twice to correct mistakes. He wondered why it was harder to talk to Philana, now that he remembered she wasn't an alien.

He asked Two Notches to turn on his transponder, and, all through the deep shadow twilight when the white dwarf was in the sky, the boat followed the whale at a half-mile's distance. The current was cooperative, but in a few days a new set of northwest trade winds would push the current off on a curve toward the equator and the whales would lose its assistance.

Anthony didn't see Philana's boat that first day: just before dawn, Sings of Others heard a distant Dweller conversation to starboard. Anthony told his boat to strike off in that direction and spent most of the day listening. When the Dwellers fell silent, he headed for the whales' transponders again. There was a lively conversation in progress between Air Human and the whales, but Anthony's mind was still on Dwellers. He put on headphones and worked far into the night.

The next morning was filled with chill mist. Anthony awoke to the whooping cries of the humpbacks. He looked at his computer to see if it had recorded any announcement of Dwellers, and there was none. The whales' interrogation by Air Human continued. Anthony's toes curled on the cold, damp planks as he stepped on deck and saw Philana's yacht two hundred yards to port, floating three feet over the tallest swells. Cables trailed from the stern, pulling hydrophones and speakers on a subaquatic sled. Anthony grinned at the sight of the elaborate storebought rig. He suspected that he got better acoustics with his homebuilt equipment, the translation softwear he'd programmed himself, and his hopelessly old-fashioned boat that couldn't even rise out of the water, but that he'd equipped with the latest-generation silent propellers.

He turned on his speakers. Sure enough, he got more audio interference from Philana's sled than he received from his entire boat.

While making coffee and an omelette of mossmoon eggs Anthony listened to the whales gurgle about their grandparents. He put on a down jacket and stepped onto the boat's stern and ate breakfast, watching the humpbacks as they occasionally broke surface, puffed out clouds of spray, sounded again with a careless, vast toss of their flukes. Their bodies were smooth and black: the barnacles that pebbled their skin on Earth had been removed before they gated to their new home.

Their song could be heard clearly even without the amplifiers. That was one change the contact with humans had brought: the males were a lot more vocal than once they had been, as if they were responding to human encouragement to talk—or perhaps they now had more worth talking about. Their speech was also more terse than before, less overtly poetic; the humans' directness and compactness of speech, caused mainly by their lack of fluency, had influenced the whales to a degree.

The whales were adapting to communication with humans more easily than the humans were adapting to them. It was important to chart that change, be able to say how the whales had evolved, accommodated. They were on an entire new planet now, explorers, and the change was going to come fast. The whales were good at remembering, but artificial intelligences were better. Anthony was suddenly glad that Philana was here, doing her work.

As if on cue she appeared on deck, one hand pressed to her head, holding an earphone: she was listening intently to whalesong. She was bundled up against the chill, and gave a brief wave as she noticed him. Anthony waved back. She paused, beating time with one hand to the rhythm of whalespeech, then waved again and stepped back to her work.

Anthony finished breakfast and cleaned the dishes. He decided to say good morning to the whales, then work on some of the Dweller speech he'd recorded the day before. He turned on his computer, sat down at the console, typed his greetings. He waited for a pause in the conversation, then transmitted. The answer came back sounding like a distant buzzsaw.

WE AND ANTHONY WISH ONE ANOTHER A PASSAGE FILLED WITH SPLENDID ODORS. WE AND AIR HUMAN HAVE BEEN SCENTING ONE ANOTHER'S FAMILIES THIS MORNING.

We wish each other the joy of converse, Anthony typed.

WE HAVE BEEN WONDERING, Two Notches said, IF WE CAN SCENT WHETHER WE AND ANTHONY AND AIR HUMAN ARE IN A CONDITION OF RUT.

Anthony gave a laugh. Humpbacks enjoyed trying to figure out human relationships: they were promiscuous themselves, and intrigued by ways different from their own.

Anthony wondered, sitting in his cockpit, if Philana was looking at him.

Air Human and I smell of aloneness, unpairness, he typed, and he transmitted the message at the same time that Philana entered the even more direct, WE ARE NOT.

THE STATE IS NOT RUT, APARTNESS IS THE SMELL, Two Notches agreed readily—it was all one to him—and the lyrics echoed each other for a long moment, *aloneness, not, unpairness, not. Not.* Anthony felt a chill.

I and the Dwellers' speech are going to try to scent one another's natures, he typed hastily, and turned off the speakers. He opened his case and took out one of the cubes he'd recorded the day before.

Work went slowly.

By noon the mist had burned off the water. His head buzzing with Dweller sounds, Anthony stepped below for a sandwich. The message light was blinking on his telephone. He turned to it, pressed the play button.

"May I speak with you briefly?" Philana's voice. "I'd like to get some data, at your convenience." Her tone shifted to one of amusement. "The condition," she added, "is not that of rut."

Anthony grinned. Philana had been considerate enough not to interrupt him, just to leave the message for whenever he wanted it. He picked up the telephone, connected directory assistance in Cabo Santa Pola, and asked it to route a call to the phone on Philana's yacht. She answered.

"Message received," he said. "Would you join me for lunch?"

"In an hour or so," she said. Her voice was abstracted. "I'm in the middle of something."

"When you're ready. Bye." He rang off, decided to make a fish chowder instead of sandwiches, and drank a beer while preparing it. He began to feel buoyant, cheerful. Siren wailing sounded through the water.

Philana's yacht maneuvered over to his boat just as Anthony finished his second beer. Philana stood on the gunwale, wearing a pale sweater with brown zigzags on it. Her braid was undone, and her brown hair fell around her shoulders. She jumped easily from her gunwale to the flybridge, then came down the ladder. The yacht moved away as soon as it felt her weight leave. She smiled uncertainly as she stepped to the deck.

"I'm sorry to have to bother you," she said.

He offered a grin. "That's okay. I'm between projects right now."

She looked toward the cabin. "Lunch smells good." Perhaps, he thought, food equaled apology.

"Fish chowder. Would you like a beer? Coffee?"

"Beer. Thanks."

They stepped below and Anthony served lunch on the small foldout table. He opened another beer and put it by her place.

"Delicious. I never really learned to cook."

"Cooking was something I learned young."

Her eyes were curious. "Where was that?"

"Lees." Shortly. He put a spoonful of chowder in his mouth so that his terseness would be more understandable.

"I never heard the name."

"It's a planet." Mumbling through chowder. "Pretty obscure." He didn't want to talk about it.

"I'm from Earth."

He looked at her. "Really? Originally? Not just a habitat in the Sol system?"

"Yes. Truly. One of the few. The one and only Earth."

"Is that what got you interested in whales?"

"I've *always* been interested in whales. As far back as I can remember. Long before I ever saw one."

"It was the same with me. I grew up near an ocean, built a boat when I was a boy and went exploring. I've never felt more at home than when I'm on the ocean.''

''Some people live on the sea all the time.''

''In floating habitats. That's just moving a city out onto the ocean. The worst of both worlds, if you ask me.''

He realized the beer was making him expansive, that he was declaiming and waving his free hand. He pulled his hand in.

''I'm sorry,'' he said, ''about the last time we talked.''

She looked away. ''My fault,'' she said. ''I shouldn't have—''

''You didn't do anything wrong.'' He realized he had almost shouted that, and could feel himself flushing. He lowered his voice. ''Once I got out here I realized . . .'' This was really hopeless. He plunged on. ''I'm not used to dealing with people. There were just a few people on Lees and they were all . . . eccentric. And everyone I've met since I left seems at least five hundred years old. Their attitudes are so . . .'' He shrugged.

''Alien.'' She was grinning.

''Yes.''

''I feel the same way. Everyone's so much older, so much more . . . sophisticated, I suppose.'' She thought about it for a moment. ''I *guess* it's sophistication.''

''They like to think so.''

''I can feel their pity sometimes.'' She toyed with her spoon, looked down at her bowl.

''And condescension.'' Bitterness striped Anthony's tongue. ''The attitude of, oh, we went through that once, poor darling, but now we know better.''

''Yes.'' Tiredly. ''I know what you mean. Like we're not really people yet.''

''At least my father wasn't like that. He was crazy, but he let me be a person. He—''

His tongue stumbled. He was not drunk enough to tell this story, and he didn't think he wanted to anyway.

''Go ahead,'' said Philana. She was collecting data, Anthony remembered, on families.

He pushed back from the table, went to the fridge for another beer. ''Maybe later,'' he said. ''It's a long story.''

Philana's look was steady. ''You're not the only one who knows about crazy fathers.''

Then you tell me about yours, he wanted to say. Anthony opened the beer, took a deep swallow. The liquid rose again, acid in his throat, and he forced it down. Memories rose with the fire in Anthony's throat, burning him. His father's fine madness whirled in his mind like leaves in a hurricane. We are, he thought, in a condition of mutual trust and permanent antagonism. Something therefore must be done.

"All right." He put the beer on the top of the fridge and returned to his seat. He spoke rapidly, just letting the story come. His throat burned. "My father started life with money. He became a psychologist and then a fundamentalist Catholic lay preacher, kind of an unlicensed messiah. He ended up a psychotic. Dad concluded that civilization was too stupid and corrupt to survive, and he decided to start over. He initiated an unauthorized planetary scan through a transporter gate, found a world that he liked, and moved his family there. There were just four of us at the time, dad and my mother, my little brother, and me. My mother was—is—she's not really her own person. There's a vacancy there. If you're around psychotics a lot, and you don't have a strong sense of self, you can get submerged in their delusions. My mother didn't have a chance of standing up to a full-blooded lunatic like my dad, and I doubt she tried. She just let him run things.

"I was six when we moved to Lees, and my brother was two. We were—" Anthony waved an arm in the general direction of the invisible Milky Way overhead. "—we were half the galaxy away. Clean on the other side of the hub. We didn't take a gate with us, or even instructions and equipment for building one. My father cut us off entirely from everything he hated."

Anthony looked at Philana's shocked face and laughed. "It wasn't so bad. We had everything but a way off the planet. Cube readers, building supplies, preserved food, tools, medical gear, wind and solar generators—Dad thought falkner generators were the cause of the rot, so he didn't bring any with him. My mother pretty much stayed pregnant for the next decade, but luckily the planet was benign. We settled down in a protected bay where there was a lot of food, both on land and in the water. We had a smokehouse to preserve the meat. My father and mother educated me pretty well. I grew up an aquatic animal. Built a sailboat, learned how to navigate. By the time I was fifteen I had charted two thousand miles of coast. I spent more than half my time at sea, the last few years. Trying to get away from my dad, mostly. He kept getting stranger. He promised me in marriage to my oldest sister after my eighteenth birthday." Memory swelled in Anthony like a tide, calm green water rising over the flat, soon to whiten and boil.

"There were some whale-sized fish on Lees, but they weren't intelligent. I'd seen recordings of whales, heard the sounds they made. On my long trips I'd imagine I was seeing whales, imagine myself talking to them."

"How did you get away?"

Anthony barked a laugh. "My dad wasn't the only one who could initiate a planetary scan. Seven or eight years after we landed some resort developers found our planet and put up a hotel about two hundred miles to the south of our settlement." Anthony shook his head. "Hell of a coincidence. The odds against it must have been incredible. My father frothed at the mouth when we started seeing their flyers and boats. My father decided our little settlement was too exposed and we moved farther inland to a place where we could hide better. Everything was camouflaged. He'd hold drills in which we were all supposed to grab necessary supplies and run off into the forest.''

''They never found you?''

''If they saw us, they thought we were people on holiday.''

''Did you approach them?''

Anthony shook his head. ''No. I don't really know why.''

''Well. Your father.''

''I didn't care much about his opinions by that point. It was so *obvious* he was cracked. I think, by then, I had all I wanted just living on my boat. I didn't see any reason to change it.'' He thought for a moment. ''If he actually tried to marry me off to my sister, maybe I would have run for it.''

''But they found you anyway.''

''No. Something else happened. The water supply for the new settlement was unreliable, so we decided to build a viaduct from a spring nearby. We had to get our hollow-log pipe over a little chasm, and my father got careless and had an accident. The viaduct fell on him. Really smashed him up, caused all sorts of internal injuries. It was very obvious that if he didn't get help, he'd die. My mother and I took my boat and sailed for the resort.''

The words dried up. This was where things got ugly. Anthony decided he really couldn't trust Philana with it, and that he wanted his beer after all. He got up and took the bottle and drank.

''Did your father live?''

''No.'' He'd keep this as brief as he could. ''When my mother and I got back, we found that he'd died two days before. My brothers and sisters gutted him and hung him upside-down in the smokehouse.'' He stared dully into Philana's horrified face. ''It's what they did to any large animal. My mother and I were the only ones who remembered what to do with a dead person, and we weren't there.''

''My God. Anthony.'' Her hands clasped below her face.

''And then—'' He waved his hands, taking in everything, the boat's comforts, Overlook, life over the horizon. ''Civilization. I was the only one of the children who could remember anything but Lees. I got off the planet and got into marine biology. That's been my life ever since. I was amazed to discover that I and the family were rich—my dad didn't tell me he'd left tons of investments behind. The rest of the family's still on Lees, still living in the old settlement. It's all they know.'' He shrugged. ''They're rich, too, of course, which helps. So they're all right.''

He leaned back on the fridge and took another long drink. The ocean swell tilted the boat and rolled the liquid down his throat. Whale harmonics made the bottle cap dance on the smooth alloy surface of the refrigerator.

Philana stood. Her words seemed small after the long silence. ''Can I have some coffee? I'll make it.''

"I'll do it."

They both went for the coffee and banged heads. Reeling back, the expression on Philana's face was wide-eyed, startled, faunlike, as if he'd caught her at something she should be ashamed of. Anthony tried to laugh out an apology, but just then the white dwarf came up above the horizon and the quality of light changed as the screens went up, and with the light her look somehow changed. Anthony gazed at her for a moment and fire began to lap at his nerves. In his head the whales seemed to urge him to make his move.

He put his beer down and grabbed her with an intensity that was made ferocious largely by Anthony's fear that this was entirely the wrong thing, that he was committing an outrage that would compel her shortly to clout him over the head with the coffee pot and drop him in his tracks. Whalesong rang frantic chimes in his head. She gave a strangled cry as he tried to kiss her and thereby confirmed his own worst suspicions about this behavior.

Philana tried to push him away. He let go of her and stepped back, standing stupidly with his hands at his sides. A raging pain in his chest prevented him from saying a word. Philana surprised him by stepping forward and putting her hands on his shoulders.

"Easy," she said. "It's all right, just take it easy."

Anthony kissed her once more, and was somehow able to restrain himself from grabbing her again out of sheer panic and desperation. By and by, as the kiss continued, his anxiety level decreased. I/You, he thought, are rising in warmness, in happy tendrils.

He and Philana began to take their clothes off. He realized this was the first time he had made love to anyone under two hundred years of age.

Dweller sounds murmured in Anthony's mind. He descended into Philana as if she were a midnight ocean, something that on first contact with his flesh shocked him into wakefulness, then relaxed around him, became a taste of brine, a sting in the eyes, a fluid vagueness. Her hair brushed against his skin like seagrass. She surrounded him, buoyed him up. Her cries came up to him as over a great distance, like the faraway moans of a lonely whale in love. He wanted to call out in answer. Eventually he did.

Grace(1), he thought hopefully. Grace(1).

Anthony had an attack of giddiness after Philana returned to her flying yacht and her work. His mad father gibbered in his memory, mocked him and offered dire warnings. He washed the dishes and cleaned the rattling bottlecap off the fridge, then he listened to recordings of Dwellers and eventually the panic went away. He had not, it seemed, lost anything.

He went to the double bed in the forepeak, which was piled high with boxes of food, a spool of cable, a couple spare microphones, and a pair of rusting Danforth anchors. He stowed the food in the hold, put the electronics in the compartment under the mattress, jammed the Danforths farther into the peak on top of the anchor chain where they belonged. He wiped the grime and rust off the mattress and realized he had neither sheets nor a second pillow. He would need to purchase supplies on the next trip to town.

The peak didn't smell good. He opened the forehatch and tried to air the place out. Slowly he became aware that the whales were trying to talk to him. ODD SCENTINGS, they said, THINGS THAT STAND IN WATER. Anthony knew what they meant. He went up on the flybridge and scanned the horizon. He saw nothing.

The taste is distant, he wrote. *But we must be careful in our movement.* After that he scanned the horizon every half hour.

He cooked supper during the white dwarf's odd half-twilight and resisted the urge to drink both the bottles of bourbon that were waiting in their rack. Philana dropped onto the flybridge with a small rucksack. She kissed him hastily, as if to get it over with.

"I'm scared," she said.

"So am I."

"I don't know why."

He kissed her again. "I do," he said. She laid her cheek against his woolen shoulder. Blind with terror, Anthony held onto her, unable to see the future.

After midnight Anthony stood unclothed on the flybridge as he scanned the horizon one more time. Seeing nothing, he nevertheless reduced speed to three knots and rejoined Philana in the forepeak. She was already asleep with his open sleeping bag thrown over her like a blanket. He raised a corner of the sleeping bag and slipped beneath it. Philana turned away from him and pillowed her cheek on her fist. Whale music echoed from a cold layer beneath. He slept.

Movement elsewhere in the boat woke him. Anthony found himself alone in the peak, frigid air drifting over him from the forward hatch. He stepped into the cabin and saw Philana's bare legs ascending the companion to the flybridge. He followed. He shivered in the cold wind.

Philana stood before the controls, looking at them with a peculiar intensity, as though she were trying to figure out which switch to throw. Her hands flexed as if to take the wheel. There was gooseflesh on her shoulders and the wind tore her hair around her face like a fluttering curtain. She looked at him. Her eyes were hard, her voice disdainful.

"Are we lovers?" she asked. "Is that what's going on here?" His skin prickled at her tone.

Her stiff-spined stance challenged him. He was afraid to touch her.

"The condition is that of rut," he said, and tried to laugh.

Her posture, one leg cocked out front, reminded him of a haughty water bird. She looked at the controls again, then looked aft, lifting up on her toes to gaze at the horizon. Her nostrils flared, tasted the wind. Clouds scudded across the sky. She looked at him again. The white dwarf gleamed off her pebble eyes.

"Very well," she said, as if this was news. "Acceptable." She took his hand and led him below. Anthony's hackles rose. On her way to the forepeak Philana saw one of the bottles of bourbon in its rack and reached for it. She raised the bottle to her lips and drank from the neck. Whiskey coursed down her throat. She lowered the bottle and wiped her mouth with the back of her hand. She looked at him as if he were something worthy of dissection.

"Let's make love," she said.

Anthony was afraid not to. He went with her to the forepeak. Her skin was cold. Lying next to him on the mattress she touched his chest as if she were unused to the feel of male bodies. "What's your name?" she asked. He told her. "Acceptable," she said again, and with a sudden taut grin raked his chest with her nails. He knocked her hands away. She laughed and came after him with the bottle. He parried the blow in time and they wrestled for possession, bourbon splashing everywhere. Anthony was surprised at her strength. She fastened teeth in his arm. He hit her in the face with a closed fist. She gave the bottle up and laughed in a cold metallic way and put her arms around him. Anthony threw the bottle through the door into the cabin. It thudded somewhere but didn't break. Philana drew him on top of her, her laugh brittle, her legs opening around him.

Her dead eyes were like stones.

In the morning Anthony found the bottle lying in the main cabin. Red clawmarks covered his body, and the reek of liquor caught at the back of his throat. The scend of the ocean had distributed the bourbon puddle evenly over the teak deck. There was still about a third of the whiskey left in the bottle. Anthony rescued it and swabbed the deck. His mind was full of cotton wool, cushioning any bruises. He was working hard at not feeling anything at all.

He put on clothes and began to work. After a while Philana unsteadily groped her way from the forepeak, the sleeping bag draped around her shoulders. There was a stunned look on her face and a livid bruise on one cheek. Anthony could feel his body tautening, ready to repel assault.

"Was I odd last night?" she asked.

He looked at her. Her face crumbled. "Oh no." She passed a hand over her eyes and turned away, leaning on the side of the hatchway. "You shouldn't let me drink," she said.

"You hadn't made that fact clear."

"I don't remember any of it," she said. "I'm sick." She pressed her stomach with her hands and bent over. Anthony narrowly watched her pale buttocks as she groped her way to the head. The door shut behind her.

Anthony decided to make coffee. As the scent of the coffee began to fill the boat, he heard the sounds of her weeping. The long keening sounds, desperate throat-tearing noises, sounded like a pinioned whale writhing helplessly on the gaff.

A vast flock of birds wheeled on the cold horizon, marking a colony of drift creatures. Anthony informed the whales of the creatures' presence, but the humpbacks already knew and were staying well clear. The drift colony was what they had been smelling for hours.

While Anthony talked with the whales, Philana left the head and drew on her clothes. Her movements were tentative. She approached him with a cup of coffee in her hand. Her eyes and nostrils were rimmed with red.

"I'm sorry," she said. "Sometimes that happens."

He looked at his computer console. "Jesus, Philana."

"It's something wrong with me. I can't control it." She raised a hand to her bruised cheek. The hand came away wet.

"There's medication for that sort of thing," Anthony said. He remembered she had a mad father, or thought she did.

"Not for this. It's something different."

"I don't know what to do."

"I need your help."

Anthony recalled his father's body twisting on the end of its rope, fingertips trailing in the dust. Words came reluctantly to his throat.

"I'll give what help I can." The words were hollow: any real resolution had long since gone. He had no clear notion to whom he was giving this message, the Philana of the previous night or this Philana or his father or himself.

Philana hugged him, kissed his cheek. She was excited.

"Shall we go see the drifters?" she asked. "We can take my boat."

Anthony envisioned himself and Philana tumbling through space. He had jumped off a precipice, just now. The two children of mad fathers were spinning in the updraft, waiting for the impact.

He said yes. He ordered his boat to circle while she summoned her yacht. She held his hand while they waited for the flying yacht to drift toward them. Philana kept laughing, touching him, stropping her cheek on his shoulder like a cat. They jumped from the flybridge to her yacht and rose smoothly into the sky. Bright sun warmed Anthony's shoulders. He took off his sweater and felt warning pain from the marks of her nails.

The drifters were colony creatures that looked like miniature mountains twenty feet or so high, complete with a white snowcap of guano. They were highly organized but unintelligent, their underwater parts sifting the ocean for nutrients or reaching out to capture prey—the longest of their gossamer stinging tentacles was up to two miles in length, and though they couldn't kill or capture a humpback, they were hard for the whale to detect and could cause a lot of stinging wounds before the whale noticed them and made its escape. Perhaps they were unintelligent, distant relatives of the Deep Dwellers, whose tenuous character they resembled. Many different species of sea birds lived in permanent colonies atop the floating islands, thousands of them, and the drifters processed their guano and other waste. Above the water, the drifters' bodies were shaped like a convex lens set on edge, an aerodynamic shape, and they could clumsily tack into the wind if they needed to. For the most part, however, they drifted on the currents, a giant circular circumnavigation of the ocean that could take centuries.

Screaming sea birds rose in clouds as Philana's yacht moved silently toward their homes. Philana cocked her head back, laughed into the open sky, and flew closer. Birds hurtled around them in an overwhelming roar of wings. Whistlelike cries issued from peg-toothed beaks. Anthony watched in awe at the profusion of colors, the chromatic brilliance of the evolved featherlike scales.

The flying boat passed slowly through the drifter colony. Birds roared and whistled, some of them landing on the boat in apparent hopes of taking up lodging. Feathers drifted down; birdshit spattered the windscreen. Philana ran below for a camera and used up several data cubes taking pictures. A trickle of optimism began to ease into Anthony at the sight of Philana in the bright morning sun, a broad smile gracing her face as she worked the camera and took picture after picture. He put an arm around Philana's waist and kissed her ear. She smiled and took his hand in her own. In the bright daylight the personality she'd acquired the previous night seemed to gather unto itself the tenebrous, unreal quality of a nightmare. The current Philana seemed far more tangible.

Philana returned to the controls; the yacht banked and increased speed. Birds issued startled cries as they got out of the way. Wind tugged at Philana's hair. Anthony decided not to let Philana near his liquor again.

After breakfast, Anthony found both whales had set their transponders. He had to detour around the drifters—their insubstantial, featherlike tentacles could foul his state-of-the-art silent props—but when he neared the whales and slowed, he could hear the deep murmurings of Dwellers rising from beneath the cold current. There were half a dozen of them engaged in conversation, and Anthony worked the day and far into the night, transcribing, making hesitant attempts at translation. The Dweller speech was more opaque than usual, depending on a context that was unstated and elusive. Comprehension eluded Anthony; but he had the feeling that the key was within his reach.

Philana waited for the Dwellers to end their converse before she brought her yacht near him. She had heated some prepared dinners and carried them to the flybridge in an insulated pouch. Her grin was broad. She put her pouch down and embraced him. Abstracted Dweller subsonics rolled away from Anthony's mind. He was surprised at how glad he was to see her.

With dinner they drank coffee. Philana chattered bravely throughout the meal. While Anthony cleaned the dishes, she embraced him from behind. A memory of the other Philana flickered in his mind, disdainful, contemptuous, cold. Her father was crazy, he remembered again.

He buried the memory deliberately and turned to her. He kissed her and thought, I/We deny the Other. The Other, he decided, would cease to exist by a common act of will.

It seemed to work. At night his dreams filled with Dwellers crying in joy, his father warning darkly, the touch of Philana's flesh, breath, hands. He awoke hungry to get to work.

The next two days a furious blaze of concentration burned in Anthony's mind. Things fell into place. He found a word that, in its context, could mean nothing but light, as opposed to fluorescence—he was excited to find out the Dwellers knew about the sun. He also found new words for darkness, for emotions that seemed to have no human equivalents, but which he seemed nevertheless to comprehend. One afternoon a squall dumped a gallon of cold water down his collar and he looked up in surprise: he hadn't been aware of its slow approach. He moved his computer deck to the cabin and kept working. When not at the controls he moved dazedly over the boat, drinking coffee, eating what was at hand without tasting it. Philana was amused and tolerant; she buried herself in her own work.

On preparing breakfast the morning of the third day, Anthony realized he was running out of food. He was farther from the archipelago than he'd planned on going, and he had about two days' supply left; he'd have to return at flank speed, buy provisions, and then run out again. A sudden hot fury gripped him. He clenched his fists. He could have provisioned for two or three months—why hadn't he done it when he had the chance?

Philana tolerantly sipped her coffee. "Tonight I'll fly you into Cabo Santa Pola. We can buy a ton of provisions, have dinner at Villa Mary, and be back by midnight."

Anthony's anger floundered uselessly, looking for a target, then gave up. "Fine," he said.

She looked at him. "Are you ever going to talk to them? You must have built your speakers to handle it."

Now the anger had finally found a home. "Not yet," he said.

In late afternoon, Anthony set out his drogue and a homing transponder, then boarded Philana's yacht. He watched while she hauled up her aquasled and programmed the navigation computer. The world dimmed as the falkner field increased in strength. The transition to full speed was almost instantaneous. Waves blurred silently past, providing the only sensation of motion—the field cut out both wind and inertia. The green-walled volcanic islands of the Las Madres archipelago rolled over the horizon in minutes. Traffic over Cabo Santa Pola complicated the approach somewhat; it was all of six minutes before Philana could set the machine down in her slip.

A bright, hot sun brightened the white-and-turquoise waterfront. From a cold Kirst current to the tropics in less than half an hour.

Anthony felt vaguely resentful at this blinding efficiency. He could have easily equipped his own boat with flight capability, but he hadn't cared about speed when he'd set out, only the opportunity to be alone on the ocean with his whales and the Dwellers. Now the very tempo of his existence had changed. He was moving at unaccustomed velocity, and the destination was still unclear.

After giving him her spare key, Philana went to do laundry—when one lived on small boats, laundry was done whenever the opportunity arose. Anthony bought supplies. He filled the yacht's forecabin with crates of food, then changed clothes and walked to the Villa Mary.

Anthony got a table for two and ordered a drink. The first drink went quickly and he ordered a second. Philana didn't appear. Anthony didn't like the way the waiter was looking at him. He heard his father's mocking laugh as he munched the last bread stick. He waited for three hours before he paid and left.

There was no sign of Philana at the laundry or on the yacht. He left a note on the computer expressing what he considered a contained disappointment, then headed into town. A brilliant sign that featured aquatic motifs called him to a cool, dark bar filled with bright green aquaria. Native fish gaped at him blindly while he drank something tall and cool. He decided he didn't like the way the fish looked at him and left.

He found Philana in his third bar of the evening. She was with two men, one of whom Anthony knew slightly as a charter boat skipper whom he didn't much like. He had his hand on her knee; the other man's arm was around her. Empty drinks and forsaken hors d'oeuvres lay on a table in front of them.

Anthony realized, as he approached, that his own arrival could only make things worse. Her eyes turned to him as he approached; her neck arched in a peculiar, balletic way that he had seen only once before. He recognized the quick, carnivorous smile, and a wash of fear turned his skin cold. The stranger whispered into her ear.

"What's your name again?" she asked.

Anthony wondered what to do with his hands. "We were supposed to meet."

Her eyes glittered as her head cocked, considering him. Perhaps what frightened him most of all was the fact there was no hostility in her look, nothing but calculation. There was a cigaret in her hand; he hadn't seen her smoke before.

"Do we have business?"

Anthony thought about this. He had jumped into space with this woman, and now he suspected he'd just hit the ground. "I guess not," he said, and turned.

"Que pasó, hombre?"

"Nada."

Pablo, the Leviathan's regular bartender, was one of the planet's original Latino inhabitants, a group rapidly being submerged by newcomers. Pablo took Anthony's order for a double bourbon and also brought him his mail, which consisted of an inquiry from *Xenobiology Review* wondering what had become of their galley proofs. Anthony crumpled the note and left it in an ashtray.

A party of drunken fishermen staggered in, still in their flashing harnesses. Triumphant whoops assaulted Anthony's ears. His fingers tightened on his glass.

"Careful, Anthony," said Pablo. He poured another double bourbon. "On the house," he said.

One of the fishermen stepped to the bar, put a heavy hand on Anthony's shoulder. "Drinks on me," he said. "Caught a twelve-meter flasher today." Anthony threw the bourbon in his face.

He got in a few good licks, but in the end the pack of fishermen beat him severely and threw him through the front window. Lying breathless on broken glass, Anthony brooded on the injustice of his position and decided to rectify matters. He lurched back into the bar and knocked down the first person he saw.

Small consolation. This time they went after him with the flashing poles that were hanging on the walls, beating him senseless and once more heaving him out the window. When Anthony recovered consciousness he staggered to his feet, intending to have another go, but the pole butts had hit him in the face too many times and his eyes were swollen shut. He staggered down the street, ran face-first into a building, and sat down.

"You finished there, cowboy?" It was Nick's voice.

Anthony spat blood. "Hi, Nick," he said. "Bring them here one at a time, will you? I can't lose one-on-one."

"Jesus, Anthony. You're such an asshole."

Anthony found himself in an inexplicably cheerful mood. "You're lucky you're a sailor. Only a sailor can call me an asshole."

"Can you stand? Let's get to the marina before the cops show up."

"My boat's hundreds of miles away. I'll have to swim."

"I'll take you to my place, then."

With Nick's assistance Anthony managed to stand. He was still too drunk to feel pain, and ambled through the streets in a contented mood. "How did you happen to be at the Leviathan, Nick?"

There was weariness in Nick's voice. "They always call me, Anthony, when you fuck up."

Drunken melancholy poured into Anthony like a sudden cold squall of rain. "I'm sorry," he said.

Nick's answer was almost cheerful. "You'll be sorrier in the morning."

Anthony reflected that this was very likely true.

Nick gave him some pills that, by morning, reduced the swelling. When Anthony awoke he was able to see. Agony flared in his body as he staggered out of bed. It was still twilight. Anthony pulled on his bloody clothes and wrote an incoherent note of thanks on Nick's computer.

Fishing boats were floating out of harbor into the bright dawn. Probably Nick's was among them. The volcano above the town was a contrast in black stone and green vegetation. Pain beat at Anthony's bones like a rain of fists.

Philana's boat was still in its slip. Apprehension tautened Anthony's nerves as he put a tentative foot on the gunwale. The hatch to the cabin was still locked. Philana wasn't aboard. Anthony opened the hatch and went into the cabin just to be sure. It was empty.

He programmed the computer to pursue the transponder signal on Anthony's boat, then as the yacht rose into the sky and arrowed over the ocean, Anthony went into Philana's cabin and fell asleep on a pillow that smelled of her hair.

He awoke around noon to find the yacht patiently circling his boat. He dropped the yacht into the water, tied the two craft together, and spent half the afternoon transferring his supplies to his own boat. He programmed the yacht to return to Las Madres and orbit the volcanic spire until it was summoned by its owner or the police.

I and the sea greet one another, he tapped into his console, and as the call wailed out from his boat he hauled in the drogue and set off after the humpbacks. Apartness is the smell, he thought, aloneness is the condition. Spray shot aboard and spattered Anthony, and salt pain flickered from the cuts on his face. He climbed to the flybridge and hoped for healing from the sun and the glittering sea.

The whales left the cold current and suddenly the world was filled with tropic sunshine and bright water. Anthony made light conversation with the humpbacks and spent the rest of his time working on Dweller speech. Despite hours of concentrated endeavor he made little progress. The sensation was akin to that of smashing his head against a stone wall over and over, an act that was, on consideration, not unlike the rest of his life.

After his third day at sea his boat's computer began signaling him that he was receiving messages. He ignored this and concentrated on work.

Two days later he was cruising north with a whale on either beam when a shadow moved across his boat. Anthony looked up from his console and saw without surprise that Philana's yacht was eclipsing the sun. Philana, dark glasses over her deep eyes and a floppy hat over her hair, was peering down from the starboard bow.

"We have to talk," she said.

JOYOUSLY WE GREET AIR HUMAN, whooped Sings of Others.

I AND AIR HUMAN ARE PLEASED TO DETECT ONE ANOTHER'S PRESENCE, called Two Notches.

Anthony went to the controls and throttled up. Microphones slammed at the bottom of his boat. Two Notches poked one large brown eye above the waves to see what was happening, then cheerfully set off in pursuit.

ANTHONY AND AIR HUMAN ARE IN A STATE OF EXCITEMENT, he chattered. I/WE ARE PLEASED TO JOIN OUR RACE.

The flying yacht hung off Anthony's stern. Philana shouted through cupped hands. "Talk to me, Anthony!"

Anthony remained silent and twisted the wheel into a fast left turn. His wake foamed over Two Notches' face and the humpback burbled a protest. The air yacht seemed to have little trouble following the turn. Anthony was beginning to have the sense of that stone wall coming up again, but he tried a few more maneuvers just in case one of them worked. Nothing succeeded. Finally he cut the throttle and let the boat slow on the long blue swells.

The trade winds had taken Philana's hat and carried it away. She ignored it and looked down at him. Her face was pale and beneath the dark glasses she looked drawn and ill.

"I'm not human, Anthony," she said. "I'm a Kyklops. That's what's really wrong with me."

Anthony looked at her. Anger danced in his veins. "You really are full of surprises."

"I'm Telamon's other body," she said. "Sometimes he inhabits me."

Whalesong rolled up from the sea. WE AND AIR HUMAN SEND ONE ANOTHER CHEERFUL SALUTATIONS AND EXPRESSIONS OF GOOD WILL.

"Talk to the whales first," said Anthony.

"Telamon's a scientist," Philana said. "He's impatient, that's his problem."

The boat heaved on an ocean swell. The trade wind moaned through the flybridge. "He's got a few more problems than that," Anthony said.

"He wanted me for a purpose but sometimes he forgets." A tremor of pain crossed Philana's face. She was deeply hung over. Her voice was ragged: Telamon had been smoking like a chimney and Philana wasn't used to it.

"He wanted to do an experiment on human psychology. He wanted to arrange a method of recording a person's memories, then transferring them to his own . . . sphere. He got my parents to agree to having the appropriate devices implanted, but the only apparatus that existed for the connection of human and Kyklops was the one the Kyklopes use to manipulate the human bodies that they wear when they want to enjoy the pleasures of the flesh. And Telamon is . . ." She waved a dismissive arm. "He's a decadent, the way a lot of the Kyklopes turn once they discover how much fun it is to be a human and that their real self doesn't get hurt no matter what they do to their clone bodies. Telamon likes his pleasures, and he likes to interfere. Sometimes, when he dumped my memory into the nth dimension and had a look at it, he couldn't resist the temptation to take over my body and rectify what he considered my errors. And occasionally, when he's in the middle of one of his binges, and his other body gives out on him, he takes me over and starts a party wherever I am.''

''Some scientist,'' Anthony said.

''The Kyklopes are used to experimenting on pieces of themselves,'' Philana said. ''Their own beings are tenuous and rather . . . detachable. Their ethics aren't against it. And he doesn't do it very often. He must be bored wherever he is— he's taken me over twice in a week.'' She raised her fist to her face and began to cough, a real smoker's hack. Anthony fidgeted and wondered whether to offer her a glass of water. Philana bent double and the coughs turned to cries of pain. A tear pattered on the teak.

A knot twisted in Anthony's throat. He left his chair and held Philana in his arms. ''I've never told anyone,'' she said.

Anthony realized to his transient alarm that once again he'd jumped off a cliff without looking. He had no more idea of where he would land than last time.

Philana, Anthony was given to understand, was Greek for ''lover of humanity.'' The Kyklopes, after being saddled with a mythological name by the first humans who had contacted them, had gone in for classical allusion in a big way. Telamon, Anthony learned, meant (among other things) ''the supporter.'' After learning this, Anthony referred to the alien as Jockstrap.

''We should do something about him,'' Anthony said. It was late—the white dwarf had just set—but neither of them had any desire to sleep. He and Philana were standing on the flybridge. The falkner shield was off and above their heads the uninhibited stars seemed almost within reach of their questing fingertips. Overlook Station, fixed almost overhead, was bright as a burning brand.

Philana shook her head. ''He's got access to my memory. Any plans we make, he can know in an instant.'' She thought for a moment. ''If he bothers to look. He doesn't always.''

''I'll make the plans without telling you what they are.''

''It will take forever. I've thought about it. You're talking court case. He can sue me for breach of contract.''

''It's your parents who signed the contract, not you. You're an adult now.''

She turned away. Anthony looked at her for a long moment, a cold foreboding hand around his throat. ''I hope,'' he said, ''you're going to tell me that you signed that contract while Jockstrap was riding you.''

Philana shook her head silently. Anthony looked up into the Milky Way and imagined the stone wall falling from the void, aimed right between his eyes, spinning slightly as it grew ever larger in his vision. Smashing him again.

''All we have to do is get the thing out of your head,'' Anthony said. ''After that, let him sue you. You'll be free, whatever happens.'' His tone reflected a resolve that was absent entirely from his heart.

''He'll sue you, too, if you have any part of this.'' She turned to face him again. Her face pale and taut in the starlight. "All my money comes from him —how else do you think I could afford the yacht? I owe everything to him."

Bitterness sped through Anthony's veins. He could feel his voice turning harsh. "Do you want to get rid of him or not? Yes or no."

"He's not entirely evil."

"Yes or no, Philana."

"It'll take years before he's done with you. And he could kill you. Just transport you to deep space somewhere and let you drift. Or he could simply teleport me away from you."

The bright stars poured down rage. Anthony knew himself seconds away from violence. There were two people on this boat and one of them was about to get hurt. *"Yes or no!"* he shouted.

Philana's face contorted. She put her hands over her ears. Hair fell across her face. "Don't shout," she said.

Anthony turned and smashed his forehead against the control panel of the flybridge. Philana gave a cry of surprise and fear. Anthony drove himself against the panel again. Philana's fingers clutched at his shoulders. Anthony could feel blood running from his scalp. The pain drained his anger, brought a cold, brilliant clarity to his mind. He smashed himself a third time. Philana cried out. He turned to her. He felt a savage, exemplary satisfaction. If one were going to drive oneself against stone walls, one should at least take a choice of the walls available.

"Ask me," Anthony panted, "if I care what happens to me."

Philana's face was a mask of terror. She said his name.

"I need to know where you stand," said Anthony. Blood drooled from his scalp, and he suppressed the unwelcome thought that he had just made himself look ridiculous.

Her look of fear broadened.

"Am I going to jump off this cliff by myself, or what?" Anthony demanded.

"I want to get rid of him," she said.

Anthony wished her voice had contained more determination, even if it were patently false. He spat salt and went in search of his first aid kit. We are in a condition of slow movement through deep currents, he thought.

In the morning he got the keys to Philana's yacht and changed the passwords on the falkner controls and navigation comp. He threw all his liquor overboard. He figured that if Jockstrap appeared and discovered that he couldn't leave the middle of the ocean, and he couldn't have a party where he was, he'd get bored and wouldn't hang around for long.

From Philana's cabin he called an attorney who informed him that the case was complex but not impossible, and furthermore that it would take a small fortune to resolve. Anthony told him to get to work on it. In the meantime he told the lawyer to start calling neurosurgeons. Unfortunately there were few neurosurgeons capable of implanting, let alone removing, the rider device. The operation wasn't performed that often.

Days passed. A discouraging list of neurosurgeons either turned him down flat or wanted the legal situation clarified first. Anthony told the lawyer to start calling *rich* neurosurgeons who might be able to ride out a lawsuit.

Philana transferred most of her data to Anthony's computer and worked with the whales from the smaller boat. Anthony used her yacht and aquasled and cursed the bad sound quality. At least the yacht's flight capability allowed him to find the Dwellers faster.

As far as the Dwellers went, he had run all at once into a dozen blind alleys. Progress seemed measured in microns.

"What's B1971?" Philana asked once, looking over his shoulder as he typed in data.

"A taste. Perhaps a taste associated with a particular temperature striation. Perhaps an emotion." He shrugged. "Maybe just a metaphor."

"You could ask them."

His soul hardened. "Not yet." Which ended the conversation.

Anthony wasn't sure whether or not he wanted to touch her. He and Jockstrap were at war and Philana seemed not to have entirely made up her mind which side she was on. Anthony slept with Philana on the double mattress in the peak, but they avoided sex. He didn't know whether he was helping her out of love or something else, and while he figured things out, desire was on hold, waiting.

Anthony's time with Philana was occupied mainly by his attempt to teach her to cook. Anything else waited for the situation to grow less opaque. Anthony figured Jockstrap would clarify matters fairly soon.

Anthony's heart lurched as looked up from lunch to see the taut, challenging grin on Philana's face. Anthony realized he'd been foolish to expect Telamon to show up only at night, as he always had before.

Anthony drew his lips into an answering grin. He was ready, no matter what the hour.

"Do I know you?" Anthony mocked. "Do we have business?"

Philana's appraisal was cold. "I've been called Jockstrap before," Telamon said.

"With good reason, I'm sure."

Telamon lurched to his feet and walked aft. He seemed not to have his sea legs yet. Anthony followed, his nerves dancing. Telamon looked out at the sea and curled Philana's lip as if to say that the water held nothing of interest.

"I want to talk about Philana," Telamon said. "You're keeping her prisoner here."

"She can leave me anytime she wants. Which is more than she can say about you."

"I want the codes to the yacht."

Anthony stepped up to Telamon, held Philana's cold gaze. "You're hurting her," he said.

Telamon stared at him with eyes like obsidian chips. He pushed Philana's long hair out of his face with an unaccustomed gesture. "I'm not the only one, Maldalena. I've got access to her mind, remember."

"Then look in her mind and see what she thinks of you."

A contemptuous smile played about Philana's lips. "I know very well what she thinks of me, and it's probably not what she's told you. Philana is a very sad and complex person, and she is not always truthful."

"She's what you made her."

"Precisely my next point." He waved his arm stiffly, unnaturally. The gesture brought him off-balance, and Philana's body swayed for a moment as Telamon adjusted to the tossing of the boat. "I gave her money, education, knowledge of the world. I have corrected her errors, taught her much. She is, in many ways, my creation. Her feelings toward me are ambiguous, as any child's feelings would be toward her father."

"Daddy Jockstrap." Anthony laughed. "Do we have business, Daddy? Or are you going to take your daughter's body to a party first?"

Anthony jumped backwards, arms flailing, as Philana disappeared, her place taken by a young man with curly dark hair and bright blue eyes. The stranger was dressed in a white cotton shirt unbuttoned to the navel and a pair of navy blue swimming trunks. He had seen the man before on vid, showing off his chest hairs. The grin stayed the same from one body to the next.

"She's gone, Maldalena. I teleported her to someplace safe." He laughed. "I'll buy her a new boat. Do what you like with the old one."

Anthony's heart hammered. He had forgotten the Kyklopes could do that, just teleport without the apparatus required by humans. And teleport other things as well.

He wondered how many centuries old the Kyklops' body was. He knew the mind's age was measured in eons.

"This doesn't end it," Anthony said.

Telamon's tone was mild. "Perhaps I'll find a nice planet for you somewhere, Maldalena. Let you play Robinson Crusoe, just as you did when you were young."

"That will only get you in trouble. Too many people know about this situation by now. And it won't be much fun holding Philana wherever you've got her."

Telamon stepped toward the stern, sat on the taffrail. His movements were fluid, far more confident than they had been when he was wearing the other, unaccustomed body. For a moment Anthony considered kicking Telamon into the drink, then decided against it. The possible repercussions had a cosmic dimension that Anthony preferred not to contemplate.

"I don't dislike you, Maldalena," the alien said. "I truly don't. You're an alcoholic, violent lout, but at least you have proven intelligence, perhaps a kind of genius.''

"Call the kettle black again. I liked that part.''

Two Notches' smooth body rose a cable's length to starboard. He exhaled with an audible hiss, mist drifting over his back. Telamon gave the whale a disinterested look, then turned back to Anthony.

"Being the nearest thing to a parent on the planet,'' he said. "I must say that I disapprove of you as a partner for Philana. However—'' He gave a shrug. "Parents must know when to compromise in these matters.'' He looked up at Anthony with his blue eyes. "I propose we share her, Anthony. Formalize the arrangement we already seem to possess. I'll only occupy a little of her time, and for all the rest, the two of you can live out your lives with whatever sad domestic bliss you can summon. Till she gets tired of you, anyway.''

Two Notches rolled under the waves. A cetacean murmur echoed off the boat's bottom. Anthony's mind flailed for an answer. He felt sweat prickling his scalp. He shook his head in feigned disbelief.

"Listen to yourself, Telamon. Is this supposed to be a scientist talking? A researcher?''

"You don't want to share?'' The young man's face curled in disdain. "You want everything for yourself—the whole planet, I suppose, like your father.''

"Don't be ridiculous.''

"I know what Philana knows about you, and I've done some checking on my own. You brought the humpbacks here because you needed them. Away from *their* home, *their* kind. You *asked* them, I'm sure; but there's no way they could make an informed decision about this planet, about what they were doing. You needed them for your Dweller study, so you took them.''

As if on cue, Two Notches rose from the water to take a breath. Telamon favored the whale with his taut smile. Anthony floundered for an answer while the alien spoke on.

"You've got data galore on the Dwellers, but do you publish? Do you share it with anybody, even with Philana? You hoard it all for yourself, all your specialized knowledge. You don't even talk to the Dwellers!'' Telamon gave a scornful laugh. "You don't even want the *Dwellers* to know what Anthony knows!''

Anger poured through Anthony's veins like a scalding fire. He clenched his fists, considered launching himself at Telamon. Something held him back.

The alien stood, walked to Anthony, looked him up and down. "We're not so different,'' he said. "We both want what's ours. But *I'm* willing to share. Philana can be our common pool of data, if you like. Think about it.''

Anthony swung, and in that instant Philana was back, horror in her eyes. Anthony's fist, aimed for the taller Telamon's chin, clipped Philana's temple and she fell back, flailing. Anthony caught her.

"It just happened, didn't it?" Her voice was woeful.

"You don't remember?"

Philana's face crumpled. She swayed and touched her temple. "I never do. The times when he's running me are just blank spots."

Anthony seated her on the port bench. He was feeling queasy at having hit her. She put her face in her hands. "I hate when that happens in front of people I know," she said.

"He's using you to hide behind. He was here in person, the son of a bitch." He took her hands in his own and kissed her. Purest desire flamed through him. He wanted to commit an act of defiance, make a statement of the nature of things. He put his arms around her and kissed her nape. She smelled faintly of pine, and there were needles in her hair. Telamon had put her on Earth, then, in a forest somewhere.

She strained against his tight embrace. "I don't know if this is a good idea," she said.

"I want to send a message to Telamon," Anthony said.

They made love under the sun, lying on the deck in Anthony's cockpit. Clear as a bell, Anthony heard Dweller sounds rumbling up the boat. Somewhere in the boat a metal mounting bracket rang to the subsonics. Philana clutched at him. There was desperation in her look, a search for affirmation, despair at finding none. The teak punished Anthony's palms. He wondered if Telamon had ever possessed her thus, took over her mind so that he could fuck her in his own body, commit incest with himself. He found the idea exciting.

His orgasm poured out, stunning him with its intensity. He kissed the moist juncture of Philana's neck and shoulder, and rose on his hands to stare down into Telamon's brittle grin and cold, knowing eyes.

"Message received, Anthony." Philana's throat convulsed in laughter. "You're taking possession. Showing everyone who's boss."

Horror galvanized Anthony. He jumped to his feet and backed away, heart pounding. He took a deep breath and mastered himself, strove for words of denial and could not find them. "You're sad, Telamon," he said.

Telamon threw Philana's arms over her head, parted her legs. "Let's do it again, Anthony." Taunting. "You're so masterful."

Anthony turned away. "Piss off, Telamon, you sick fuck." Bile rose in his throat.

"What happened?" Anthony knew Philana was back. He turned and saw her face crumple. "We were making love!" she wailed.

"A cheap trick. He's getting desperate." He squatted by her and tried to take her in his arms. She turned away from him.

"Let me alone for a while," she said. Bright tears filled her eyes.

Misplaced adrenaline ran charges through Anthony's body—no one to fight, no place to run. He picked up his clothes and went below to the main cabin. He drew on his clothing and sat on one of the berths, hands helpless on the seat beside him. He wanted to get blind drunk.

Half an hour later Philana entered the cabin. She'd braided her hair, drawn it back so tight from her temples it must have been painful. Her movements were slow, as if suddenly she'd lost her sea legs. She sat down at the little kitchen table, pushed away her half-eaten lunch.

"We can't win," she said.

"There's got to be some way," Anthony said tonelessly. He was clean out of ideas.

Philana looked at Anthony from reddened eyes. "We can give him what he wants," she said.

"No."

Her voice turned to a shout. "It's not *you* he does this to! It's not you who winks out of existence in the middle of doing laundry or making love, and wakes up somewhere else." Her knuckles were white as they gripped the table edge. "I don't know how long I can take this."

"All your life," said Anthony, "if you give him what he wants."

"At least then he wouldn't use it as a *weapon!*" Her voice was a shout. She turned away.

Anthony looked at her, wondered if he should go to her. He decided not to. He was out of comfort for the present.

"You see," Philana said, her head still turned away, "why I don't want to live forever."

"Don't let him beat you."

"It's not that. I'm afraid . . ." Her voice trembled. "I'm afraid that if I got old I'd *become* him. The Kyklopes are the oldest living things ever discovered. And a lot of the oldest immortals are a lot like them. Getting crazier, getting . . ." She shook her head. "Getting less human all the time."

Anthony saw a body swaying in the smokehouse. Philana's body, her fingernails trailing in the dust. Pain throbbed in his chest. He stood up, swayed as he was caught by a slow wave of vertigo. Somewhere his father was laughing, telling him he should have stayed on Lees for a life of pastoral incest.

"I want to think," he said. He stepped past her on the way to his computer. He didn't reach out to touch her as he passed. She didn't reach for him, either.

He put on the headphones and listened to the Dwellers. Their speech rolled up from the deep. Anthony sat unable to comprehend, his mind frozen. He was helpless as Philana. Whose was the next move? he wondered. His? Philana's?

Whoever made the next move, Anthony knew, the game was Telamon's.

At dinnertime Philana made a pair of sandwiches for Anthony, then returned to the cabin and ate nothing herself. Anthony ate one sandwich without tasting it, gave the second to the fish. The Dweller speech had faded out. He left his computer and stepped into the cabin. Philana was stretched out on one of the side berths, her eyes closed. One arm was thrown over her forehead.

Her body, Anthony decided, was too tense for this to be sleep. He sat on the berth opposite.

"He said you haven't told the truth," Anthony said.

Anthony could see Philana's eyes moving under translucent lids as she evaluated this statement, scanning for meaning. "About what," she said.

"About your relationship to him."

Her lips drew back, revealing teeth. Perhaps it was a smile.

"I've known him all my life. I gave you the condensed version."

"Is there more I should know?"

There was another pause. "He saved my life."

"Good for him."

"I got involved with this man. Three or four hundred years old, one of my professors in school. He was going through a crisis—he was a mess, really. I thought I could do him some good. Telamon disagreed, said the relationship was sick." Philana licked her lips. "He was right," she said.

Anthony didn't know if he really wanted to hear about this.

"The guy started making demands. Wanted to get married, leave Earth, start over again."

"What did you want?"

Philana shrugged. "I don't know. I hadn't made up my mind. But Telamon went into my head and confronted the guy and told him to get lost. Then he just took me out of there. My body was half the galaxy away, all alone on an undeveloped world. There were supplies, but no gates out."

Anthony gnawed his lip. This was how Telamon operated.

"Telamon kept me there for a couple weeks till I calmed down. He took me back to Earth. The professor had taken up with someone else, another one of his students. He married her, and six weeks later she walked out on him. He killed her, then killed himself."

Philana sighed, drew her hand over her forehead. She opened her eyes and sat up, swinging her legs off the berth. "So," she said. "That's one Telamon story. I've got more."

"When did this happen?"

"I'd just turned eighteen." She shook her head. "That's when I signed the contract that keeps him in my head. I decided that I couldn't trust my judgment about people. And Telamon's judgment of people is, well, quite good."

Resentment flamed in Anthony at this notion. Telamon had made his judgment of Anthony clear, and Anthony didn't want it to become a subject for debate. "You're older now," he said. "He can't have a veto on your life forever."

Philana drew up her legs and circled her knees with her arms. "You're violent, Anthony."

Anthony looked at her for a long moment of cold anger. "I hit you by accident. I was aiming at *him*, damn it."

Philana's jaw worked as she returned his stare. "How long before you aim at *me*?"

"I wouldn't."

"That's what my old professor said."

Anthony turned away, fury running through him like chill fire. Philana looked at him levelly for a moment, then dropped her forehead to her knees. She sighed. "I don't know, Anthony. I don't know anymore. If I ever did."

Anthony stared fixedly at the distant white dwarf, just arrived above the horizon and visible through the hatch. We are, he thought, in a condition of permanent bafflement. "What do you want, Philana?" he asked.

Her head came up, looked at him. "I want not to be a tennis ball in your game with Telamon, Anthony. I want to know I'm not just the prize given the winner."

"I wanted you before I ever met Telamon, Philana."

"Telamon changed a few things." Her voice was cold. "Before you met him, you didn't use my body to send messages to people."

Anthony's fists clenched. He forced them to relax.

Philana's voice was bitter. "Seems to me, Anthony, that's one of Telamon's habits you're all too eager to adopt."

Anthony's chest ached. He didn't seem able to breathe in enough air. He took a long breath and hoped his tension would ease. It didn't. "I'm sorry," he said. "It's not . . . a normal situation."

"For you, maybe."

Silence hung in the room, broken only by the whale clicks and mutters rising through the boat. Anthony shook his head. "What do we do, then?" he asked. "Surrender?"

"If we have to." She looked at him. "I'm willing to fight Telamon, but not to the point where one of us is destroyed." She leaned toward him, her expression intent. "And if Telamon wins, could you live with it?" she asked. "With surrender? If we had to give him what he wanted?"

"I don't know."

"I *have* to live with it. You don't. That's the difference."

"That's *one* difference." He took a breath, then rose from his place. "I have to think," he said.

He climbed into the cockpit. Red sunset was splattered like blood across the windscreen. He tried to breathe the sea air, clear the heaviness he felt in his chest, but it didn't work. Anthony went up onto the flybridge and stared forward. His eyes burned as the sun went down in flames.

*   *   *

The white dwarf was high overhead when Anthony came down. Philana was lying in the forepeak, covered with a sheet, her eyes staring sightlessly out the open hatch. Anthony took his clothes off and crawled in beside her.

"I'll surrender," he said. "If I have to, I'll surrender." She turned to him and put her arms around him. Hopeless desire burned in his belly.

He made love to Philana, his nerves numb to the possibility that Telamon might reappear. Her hungry mouth drank in his pain. He didn't know whether this was affirmation or not, whether this meant anything other than the fact there was nothing left to do at this point than stagger blindly into one another's embrace.

A Dweller soloed from below, the clearest Anthony had ever heard one. WE CALL TO OURSELVES, the Dweller said, WE SPEAK OF THINGS AS THEY ARE. Anthony rose from bed and set his computer to record. Sings of Others, rising alongside to breathe, called a hello. Anthony tapped his keys, hit TRANS-MIT.

Air Human and I are in a condition of rut, he said.

WE CONGRATULATE ANTHONY AND AIR HUMAN ON OUR CON-DITION OF RUT, Sings of Others responded. The whooping whale cries layered atop the thundering Dweller noises. WE WISH OURSELVES MANY HAPPY COPULATIONS.

HAPPY COPULATIONS, HAPPY COPULATIONS, echoed Two Notches.

A pointless optimism began to resonate in Anthony's mind. He sat before the computer and listened to the sounds of the Deep Dwellers as they rumbled up his spine.

Philana appeared at the hatch. She was buttoning her shirt. "You told the whales about us?" she said.

"Why not?"

She grinned faintly. "I guess there's no reason not to."

Two Notches wailed a question. ARE ANTHONY AND AIR HUMAN COP-ULATING NOW?

Not at present, Anthony replied.

WE HOPE YOU WILL COPULATE OFTEN.

Philana, translating the speech on her own, laughed. "Tell them we hope so, too," she said.

And then she stiffened. Anthony's nerves poured fire. Philana turned to him and regarded him with Telamon's eyes.

"I thought you'd see reason," Telamon said. "*I'll surrender*. I like that."

Anthony looked at the possessed woman and groped for a vehicle for his message. Words seemed inadequate, he decided, but would have to do. "You haven't won yet," he said.

Philana's head cocked to one side as Telamon viewed him. "Has it occurred to you," Telamon said, "that if she's free of me, she won't need you at all?"

"You forget something. I'll be rid of *you* as well."

"You can be rid of me any time."

Anthony stared at Telamon for a moment, then suddenly he laughed. He had just realized how to send his message. Telamon looked at him curiously. Anthony turned to his computer deck and flipped to the Dweller translation file.

I/we, he typed, *live in the warm brightness above. I am new to this world, and send good wishes to the Dwellers below.*

Anthony pressed TRANSMIT. Rolling thunder boomed from the boat's speakers. The grammar was probably awful, Anthony knew, but he was fairly certain of the words, and he thought the meaning would be clear.

Telamon frowned, stepped to gaze over Anthony's shoulder.

Calls came from below. A translation tree appeared on the screen.

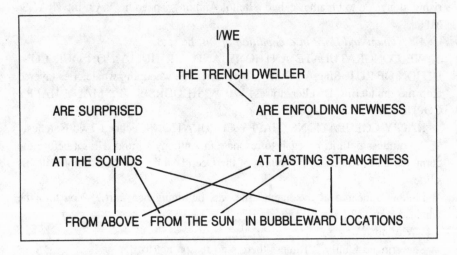

"Trench Dweller" was probably one of the Dwellers' names. "Bubbleward" was a phrase for "up," since bubbles rose to the surface. Anthony tapped the keys.

We are from far away, recently arrived. We are small and foreign to the world. We wish to brush the Dwellers with our thoughts. We regret our lack of clarity in diction.

"I wonder if you've thought this through," Telamon said.

Anthony hit TRANSMIT. Speakers boomed. The subsonics were like a punch in the gut.

"Go jump off a cliff," Anthony said.

"You're making a mistake," said Telamon.

The Dweller's answer was surprisingly direct.

Anthony's heart crashed in astonishment. Could the Dwellers stand the lack

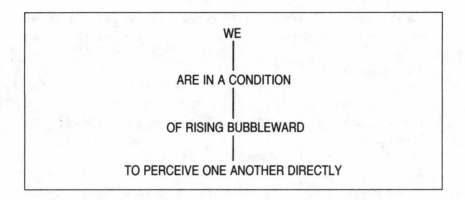

WE
|
ARE IN A CONDITION
|
OF RISING BUBBLEWARD
|
TO PERCEIVE ONE ANOTHER DIRECTLY

of pressure on the surface? *I/We*, he typed, *Trench Dweller, proceed with consideration for safety. I/We recollect that we are small and weak.* He pressed TRANSMIT and flipped to the whalespeech file.

Deep Dweller rising to surface, he typed. *Run fast northward.*

The whales answered with cries of alarm. Flukes pounded the water. Anthony ran to the cabin and cranked the wheel hard to starboard. He increased speed to separate himself from the humpbacks. Behind him, Telamon stumbled in his unfamiliar body as the boat took the waves at a different angle.

Anthony returned to his computer console. *I/We are in a state of motion*, he reported. *Is living in the home of the light occasion for a condition of damage to us/Trench Dweller?*

"You're mad," said Telamon, and then Philana staggered. "He's done it *again*," she said in a stunned voice. She stepped to the starboard bench and sat down. "What's happening?" she asked.

"I'm talking to the Dwellers. One of them is rising to say hello."

"Now?"

He gave her a skeletal grin. "It's what you wanted, yes?" She stared at him.

I'm going over cliffs, he thought. One after another.

That, Anthony concluded, is the condition of existence.

Subsonics rattled crockery in the kitchen.

Anthony typed, *I/We happily await greeting ourselves* and pressed TRANSMIT, then REPEAT. He would give the Dweller a sound to home in on.

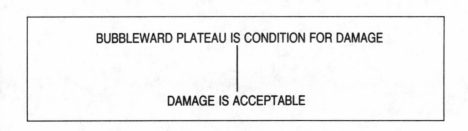

BUBBLEWARD PLATEAU IS CONDITION FOR DAMAGE
|
DAMAGE IS ACCEPTABLE

"I don't understand," Philana said. He moved to join her on the bench, put his arm around her. She shrugged him off. "Tell me," she said. He took her hand.

"We're going to win."

"How?"

"I don't know yet."

She was too shaken to argue. "It's going to be a long fight," she said.

"I don't care."

Philana took a breath. "I'm scared."

"So am I," said Anthony.

The boat beat itself against the waves. The flying yacht followed, a silent shadow.

Anthony and Philana waited in silence until the Dweller rose, a green-grey mass that looked as if a grassy reef had just calved. Foam roared from its back as it broke water, half an ocean running down its sides. Anthony's boat danced in the sudden white tide, and then the ocean stilled. Bits of the Dweller were all around, spread over the water for leagues—tentacles, filters, membranes. The Dweller's very mass had calmed the sea. The Dweller was so big, Anthony saw, it constituted an entire ecosystem. Sea creatures lived among its folds and tendrils: some had died as they rose, their swim bladders exploding in the release of pressure; others leaped and spun and shrank from the brightness above.

Sunlight shone from the Dweller's form, and the creature pulsed with life.

Terrified, elated, Philana and Anthony rose to say hello.

JAMES PATRICK KELLY

Home Front

Not all battles are fought on the battleground; some are won considerably closer to home . . .

One of the hottest new writers in science fiction, James Patrick Kelly was born in Mineola, New York, and now lives in Durham, New Hampshire. Kelly made his first sale in 1975, and has since become a frequent contributor to *The Magazine of Fantasy and Science Fiction* and *Isaac Asimov's Science Fiction Magazine*; his stories have also appeared in *Universe, Galaxy, Amazing, Analog, The Twilight Zone Magazine*, and elsewhere. His first solo novel *Planet of Whispers* came out in 1984, followed by *Freedom Beach*, written in collaboration with John Kessel. His most recent novel is *Look Into the Sun*. His story "Friend," also in collaboration with Kessel, was in our First Annual Collection; his story "Solstice" was in our Third Annual Collection; his story "The Prisoner of Chillon" was in our Fourth Annual Collection; his story "Glass Cloud" was in our Fifth Annual Collection.

HOME FRONT

James Patrick Kelly

"Hey, Genius. What are you studying?"

Will hunched his shoulders and pretended not to hear. He had another four pages to review before he could test. If he passed, then he wouldn't have to log onto eighth grade again until Wednesday. He needed a day off.

"What are you, deaf?" Gogolak nudged Will's arm. "Talk to me, Genius."

"Don't call me that."

"Come on, Gogo," said the fat kid, whose name Will had forgotten. He was older: maybe in tenth, more likely a dropout. Old enough to have pimples. "Let's eat."

"Just a minute," said Gogolak. "Seems like every time I come in here, this needle is sitting in this booth with his face stuck to a schoolcomm. It's ruining my appetite. What is it, math? Español?"

"History." Will thought about leaving, going home, but that would only postpone the hassle. Besides, his mom was probably still there. "The Civil War."

"You're still on that? Jeez, you're slow. I finished that weeks ago." Gogolak winked at his friend. "George Washington freed the slaves so they'd close school on his birthday."

The big kid licked his lips and eyed the menu above the vending wall at the rear of the Burger King.

"Lincoln," said Will. "Try logging on sometime, you might learn something."

"What do you mean? I'm logged on right now." Gogolak pulled the comm out of his backpack and thrust it at Will. "Just like you." The indicator was red.

"It doesn't count unless someone looks at it."

"Then you look at it, you're so smart." He tossed the comm onto the table and it slid across, scattering a pile of Will's hardcopy. "Come on Looper. Get out your plastic."

Will watched Looper push his ration card into the french-fry machine. He and Gogolak were a mismatched pair. Looper was as tall as Will, at least a hundred and ninety centimeters; Looper, however, ran to fat, and Will looked like a sapling.

Looper was wearing official Johnny America camouflage and ripped jeans. He didn't seem to be carrying a schoolcomm, which meant he probably was warbait. Gogolak was the smallest boy and the fastest mouth in Will's class. He dressed in skintight style; everyone knew that girls thought he was cute. Gogolak didn't have to worry about draft sweeps; he was under age and looked it, and his dad worked for the Selective Service.

Will realized that they would probably be back to bother him. He hit save so that Gogolak couldn't spoil his afternoon's work. When they returned to Will's booth, Looper put his large fries down on the table and immediately slid across the bench to the terminal on the wall. He stuck his fat finger into the coin return. Will already knew it was empty. Then Looper pressed select, and the tiny screen above the terminal lit up.

"Hey," he said to Will, "you still got time here."

"So?" But Will was surprised; he hadn't thought to try the selector. "I was logged on." He nodded at his comm.

"What did I tell you, Loop?" Gogolak stuffed Looper's fries into his mouth. "Kid's a genius."

Looper flipped channels past cartoons, plug shows, catalogs, freebies, music vids, and finally settled on the war. Johnny America was on patrol.

"Gervais buy it yet?" said Gogolak.

"Nah." Looper acted like a real fan. "He's not going to either; he's getting short. Besides, he's wicked smart."

The patrol trotted across a defoliated clearing toward a line of trees. With the sun gleaming off their helmets, they looked to Will like football players running a screen, except that Johnny was carrying a minimissile instead of a ball. Without warning, Johnny dropped to one knee and brought the launcher to his shoulder. His two rangefinders fanned out smartly and trained their lasers on the far side of the clearing. There was a flash; the jungle exploded.

"Foom!" Looper provided the sound effects. "Yah, you're barbecue, Pedro!" As a sapodilla tree toppled into the clearing, the time on the terminal ran out.

"Too bad," Gogolak poured salt on the table and smeared a fry in it. "I wanted to see the meat."

"Hey, you scum! That's my dinner." Looper snatched the fries pouch from Gogolak. "You hardly left me any."

He shrugged. "Didn't want them to get cold."

"Stand-ins." A girl in baggy blue disposables stood at the door and surveyed the booths. "Any stand-ins here?" she called.

It was oldie Warner's granddaughter, Denise, who had been evacuated from Texas and was now staying with him. She was in tenth and absolutely beautiful. Her accent alone could melt snow. Will had stood in for her before. Looper waved his hand hungrily until she spotted them.

"Martin's just got the monthly ration of toilet paper," she said. "They're limiting sales to three per customer. Looks like about a half-hour line. My grandpa will come by at four-thirty.''

"How much?" said Looper.

"We want nine rolls." She took a five out of her purse. "A quarter for each of you."

Will was torn. He could always use a quarter and he wanted to help her. He wanted her to ask his name. But he didn't want to stand in line for half an hour with these stupid jacks.

Gogolak was staring at her breasts. "Do I know you?"

"I may be new in town, sonny—" she put the five on the table "—but you don't want to rip me off."

"Four-thirty." Gogolak let Looper take charge of the money. Will didn't object.

Martin's was just next door to the Burger King. The line wasn't bad, less than two aisles long when they got on. There were lots of kids from school standing in, none of them close enough to talk to.

"Maybe she got tired of using leaves," said Gogolak.

Looper chuckled. "Who is she?"

"Seth Warner's granddaughter," said Will.

"Bet she's hot." Gogolak leered.

"Warner's a jack," said Looper. "Pig-faced oldie still drives a car."

Most of the shelves in aisle 2 were bare. There was a big display of government surplus powdered milk, the kind they loaded up with all those proteins and vitamins and tasted like chalk. It had been there for a week and only three boxes were gone. Then more empty space, and then a stack of buckets with no labels. Someone had scrawled "Korn Oil" on them: black marker on bare metal. At the end of the aisle was the freezer section, which was mostly jammed with packages of fries. Farther down were microwave dinners for the rich people. They wound past the fries and up aisle 3, at the end of which Will could see Mr. Rodenets, the stock boy, dispensing loose rolls of toilet paper from a big cardboard box.

"How hard you think it is to get chosen Johnny America?" Looper said. "I mean really."

"What do you mean, really?" said Gogolak. "You think J.A. is real?"

"People die. They couldn't fake that kind of stuff." Looper's face got red. "You watch enough, you got to believe."

"Maybe," Gogolak said. "But I bet you have to know someone."

Will knew it wasn't true. Gogolak just liked to pop other people's dreams. "Mr. Dunnell swears they pick the team at random," he said.

"Right," Gogolak said. "Whenever somebody gets dead."

"Who's Dunnell?" said Looper.

"Socialization teacher." Will wasn't going to let Gogolak run down Johnny

America's team, no matter who his father was. "Most of them make it. I'll bet seventy percent at least."

"You think that many?" Looper nodded eagerly. "What I heard is they get discharged with a full boat. Whatever they want, for the rest of their lives."

"Yeah, and Santa is their best friend," Gogolak said. "You sound like recruiters."

"It's not like I'd have to be J.A. himself. I just want to get on his team, you know? Like maybe in body armor." Looper swept his arm down the aisle with robotic precision, exterminating bacon bits.

"If only you didn't have to join the army," said Will.

Silence.

"You know," said Looper, "they haven't swept the Seacoast since last July."

A longer silence. Will figured out why Looper was hanging around Gogolak, why he had not complained more about the fries. He was hoping for a tip about the draft. Up ahead, Mr. Rodenets opened the last carton.

"I mean, you guys are still in school." Looper was whining now. "They catch me, and I'm southern front for sure. At least if I volunteer, I get to pick where I fight. And I get my chance to be Johnny."

"So enlist already." Gogolak was daring him. "The war won't last forever. We've got Pedro on the run."

"Maybe I will. Maybe I'm just waiting for an opening on the J.A. team."

"You ever see a fat Johnny with pimples?" said Gogolak. "You're too ugly to be a vid. Isn't that right, Mr. Rodenets?"

Mr. Rodenets fixed his good eye on Gogolak. "Sure, kid." He was something of a local character—Durham, New Hampshire's only living veteran of the southern front. "Whatever you say." He handed Gogolak three rolls of toilet paper.

Will's mom was watching cartoons when Will got home. She watched a lot of cartoons, mostly the stupid ones from when she was a girl. She liked the Smurfs and the Flintstones and Roadrunner. There was an inhaler on the couch beside her.

"Mom, what are you doing?" Will couldn't believe she was still home. "Mom, it's quarter to five! You promised."

She stuck out her tongue and blew him a raspberry.

Will picked up the inhaler and took a whiff. Empty. "You're already late."

She held up five fingers. "Not 'til five." Her eyes were bright.

Will wanted to hit her. Instead he held out his hands to help her up. "Come on."

She pouted. "My shows."

He grabbed her hands and pulled her off the couch. She stood, tottered, and fell into his arms. He took her weight easily; she weighed less than he did. She didn't eat much.

"You've got to hurry," he said.

She leaned on him as they struggled down the hall to the bathroom; Will imagined he looked like Johnny America carrying a wounded buddy to the medics. Luckily, there was no one in the shower. He turned it on, undressed her, and helped her in.

"Will! It's cold, Will." She fumbled at the curtain and tried to come out.

He forced her back into the water. "Good," he muttered. His sleeves got wet.

"Why are you so mean to me, Will? I'm your mother."

He gave her five minutes. It was all that he could afford. Then he toweled her off and dressed her. He combed her hair out as best he could; there was no time to dry it. The water had washed all her brightness away, and now she looked dim and disappointed. More like herself.

By the time they got to Mr. Dunnell's house, she was ten minutes late. At night, Mr. Dunnell ran a freelance word-processing business out of his kitchen. Will knocked; Mr. Dunnell opened the back door, frowning. Will wished he'd had more time to get his mom ready. Strands of wet stringy hair stuck to the side of her face. He knew Mr. Dunnell had given his mom the job only because of him.

"Evening, Marie," Mr. Dunnell said. His printer was screeching like a cat.

"What so good about it?" She was always rude to him. Will knew it was hard for her, but she wouldn't even give Mr. Dunnell a chance. She went straight to the old Apple that Mr. Dunnell had rewired into a dumb terminal and started typing.

Mr. Dunnell came out onto the back steps. "Christ, Will. She's only been working for me three weeks and she's already missed twice and been late I don't know how many times. Doesn't she want this job?"

Will couldn't answer. He didn't say that she wanted her old job at the school back, that she wanted his father back, that all she really wanted was the shiny world she had been born into. He said nothing.

"This can't go on, Will. Do you understand?"

Will nodded.

"I'm sorry about last night."

Will shrugged and bit into a frozen fry. He was not sure what she meant. Was she sorry about being late for work or about coming home singing at three-twenty-four in the morning and turning on all the lights? He slicked a pan with oil and set it on the hot plate. He couldn't turn the burner to high without blowing a fuse but his mom didn't mind mushy fries. Will did; he usually ate right out of the bag when he was at home. He'd been saving quarters for a french fryer for her birthday. If he unplugged the hot plate, there'd be room for it on top of the dresser.

He was through with her dumb questions. He didn't want to talk to her anymore. He opened the door.

"I said I was sorry."

He slammed it behind him.

It wasn't so much that it was Gogolak's dad this time. Will wasn't going to judge his mom; it was a free country. He wanted to live life, too—except that he wasn't going to make the same mistakes that she had. She was right in a way: it was none of his business who she made it with or what she sniffed. He just wanted her to be responsible about the things that mattered. He didn't think it was fair that he was the only grown-up in his family.

Because he had earned a day off from school, Will decided to skip socialization, too. It was a beautiful day and volleyball was a dumb game anyway, even if there were girls in shorts playing it. Instead he slipped into the socialization center, got his dad's old basketball out of his locker, and went down to the court behind the abandoned high school. It helped to shoot when he was angry. Besides, if he could work up any kind of jumper, he might make the ninth basketball team. He was already the tallest kid in eighth, but his hands were too small, and he kept bouncing the ball off his left foot. He was practicing reverse lay-ups when Looper came out of the thicket that had once been the baseball field.

"Hey, Will." He was flushed and breathing hard, as if he had been running. "How you doing?"

Will was surprised that Looper knew his name. "I'm alive."

Looper stood under the basket, waiting for a rebound. Will put up a shot that clanged off the rim.

"Hear about Johnny America?" Looper took the ball out to the foul line. "Old Gervais got his foot blown off. Stepped on a mine." He shot: swish. "Some one-on-one?"

They played two games and Looper won them both. He was the most graceful fat kid Will had ever seen. After the first game, Looper walked Will through some of his best post-up moves. He was a good teacher. By the end of the second game, sweat had darkened Looper's T-shirt. Will said he wouldn't mind taking a break. They collapsed in the shade.

"So they're recruiting for a new Johnny?" Will tried in vain to palm his basketball. "You ready to take your chance?"

"Who, me?" Looper wiped his forehead with the back of his hand. "I don't know."

"You keep bringing it up."

"Someday I've got to do something."

"Johnny Looper." Will made an imaginary headline with his hands.

"Yeah, right. How about you—ever think of joining? You could, you're tall enough. You could join up today. As long as you swear that you're fifteen, they'll take you. They'll take anyone. Remember Johnny Stanczyk? He was supposed to have been thirteen."

"I heard he was fourteen."

"Well, he looked thirteen." Looper let a caterpillar crawl up his finger. "You know what I'd like about the war?" he said. "The combat drugs. They make you into some kind of superhero, you know?"

"Superheroes don't blow up."

Looper fired the caterpillar at him.

Will's conscience bothered him for saying that; he was starting to sound like Gogolak. "Still, it is our country. Someone has to fight for it, right?" Will shrugged. "How come you dropped out, anyway?"

"Bored." Looper shrugged. "I might go back, though. Or I might go to the war. I don't know." He swiped the basketball from Will. "I don't see you carrying a comm today."

"Needed to think." Will stood and gestured for his ball.

"Hey, you hear about the lottery?" Looper fired a pass.

Will shook his head.

"They were going to announce it over the school channels this morning; Gogo tipped me yesterday. Town's going to hire twenty kids this summer. Fix stuff, mow grass, pick up trash, you know. Buck an hour—good money. You got to go register at the post office this afternoon, then next month they pick the lucky ones."

"Kind of early to think about the summer." Will frowned. "Bet you that jack Gogolak gets a job."

Looper glanced at him. "He's not that bad."

"A jack. You think he worries about sweeps?" Will didn't know why he was so angry at Looper. He was beginning to like Looper. "He's probably rich enough to buy out of the draft if he wants. He gets everything his way."

"Not everything." Looper laughed. "He's short."

Will had to laugh too. "You want to check this lottery out?"

"Sure." Looper heaved himself up. "Show you something on the way over."

There was blood on the sidewalk. A crowd of about a dozen had gathered by the abandoned condos on Coe Drive to watch the EMTs load Seth Warner into the ambulance which was parked right behind his Peugeot. Will looked for Denise but didn't see her. A cop was recording statements.

"I got here just after Jeff Roeder." Mrs. O'Malley preened as she spoke into the camera; it had been a long time since anyone paid attention to her. "He was lying on the sidewalk there, all bashed up. The car door was open and his disk was playing. Jeff stayed with him. I ran for help."

The driver shut the rear doors of the ambulance. Somebody in the crowd called out, "How is he?"

The driver grunted. "Wants his lawyer." Everyone laughed.

"Must've been a fight," Jeff Roeder said. "We found this next to him." He handed the cop a bloody dental plate.

"Did anyone else here see anything?" The cop raised her voice.

"I would've liked to've seen it," whispered the woman in front of Will. "He's one oldie who had it coming." People around her laughed uneasily. "Shit. They all do."

Even the cop heard that. She panned the crowd and then slammed the Peugeot's door.

Looper grinned at Will. "Let's go." They headed for Madbury Road.

"He wanted me to get in the car with him," Looper said as they approached the post office. "He offered me a buck. Didn't say anything else, just waved it at me."

Will wished he were somewhere else.

"A stinking buck," said Looper. "The pervert."

"But if he didn't say what he wanted . . . maybe it was for a stand-in someplace."

"Yeah, sure." Looper snorted. "Wake up and look around you." He waved at downtown Durham. "The oldies screwed us. They wiped their asses on the world. And they're still at it."

"You're in deep trouble, Looper." No question Looper had done a dumb thing, yet Will knew exactly how the kid felt.

"Nah. What are they going to do? Pull me in and say 'You're fighting on the wrong front, Johnny. Better enlist for your own good.' No problem. Maybe I'm ready to enlist now, anyway." Looper nodded; he looked satisfied with himself. "It was the disk, you know. He was playing it real loud and tapping his fingers on the wheel like he was having a great time." He spat into the road. "Boomer music. I hate the damn Beatles, so I hit him. He was real easy to hit."

There was already a ten-minute line at the post office and the doors hadn't even opened yet. Mostly it was kids from school who were standing in, a few dropouts like Looper and one grown-up, weird Miss Fisher. Almost all of the kids with comms were logged on, except that no one paid much attention to the screens. They were too busy chatting with the people around them. Will had never mastered the art of talking and studying at the same time.

They got on line right behind Sharon Riolli and Megan Brown. Sharon was in Will's class, and had asked him to a dance once when they were in seventh. Over the summer he had grown thirteen centimeters. Since then she'd made a point of ignoring him; he looked older than he was. Old enough to fight.

"When are they going to open up?" said Looper.

"Supposed to be one-thirty," said Megan. "Hi, Will. We missed you at socialization."

"Hi, Megan. Hi, Sharon."

Sharon developed a sudden interest in fractions.

"Have you seen Denise Warner?" said Will.

"The new kid?" Megan snickered. "Why? You want to ask her out or something?"

"Her grandpa got into an accident up on Coe Drive."

"Hurt?"

"He'll live." Looper kept shifting from foot to foot as if the sidewalk was too hot for him.

"Too bad." Sharon didn't look up.

"Hey, Genius. Loop." Gogolak cut in front of the little kid behind Looper, some stiff from sixth who probably wasn't old enough for summer work anyway. "Hear about Gervais?"

"What happened?" said Sharon. Will noticed that she paid attention to Gogolak.

"Got his foot turned into burger. They're looking for a new Johnny."

"Oh, war stuff." Megan sniffed. "That's all you guys ever talk about."

"I think a girl should get a chance," said Sharon.

"Yeah, sure," said Looper. "Just try toting a launcher through the jungle in the heat."

"I could run body armor." She gave Looper a pointed stare. "Something that takes brains."

The line behind them stretched. It was almost one-thirty when Mr. Gogolak came running out of the side door of the post office. The Selective Service office was on the second floor. He raced down the line and grabbed his kid.

"What are you doing here? Go home." He grabbed Gogolak's wrist and turned him around.

"Let go of me!" Gogolak struggled. It had to be embarrassing to be hauled out of a job line like some stupid elementary school kid.

His dad bent over and whispered something. Gogolak's eyes got big. A flutter went down the line; everyone was quiet, watching. Mr. Gogolak was wearing his Selective Service uniform. He pulled his kid into the street.

Mr. Gogolak had gone to the western front with Will's dad. Mr. Gogolak had come back. And last night he had been screwing Will's mom. Will wished she were here to see this. They were supposed to be old friends, maybe he owed her a favor after last night. But the only one Mr. Gogolak whispered to was *his* kid. It wasn't hard to figure out what he had said.

Gogolak gazed at Looper and Will in horror. "It's a scam!" he shouted. "Recruiters!"

His old man slapped him hard and Gogolak went to his knees. But he kept shouting even as his father hit him again. "Draft scam!" They said a top recruiter could talk a prospect into anything.

Will could not bear to watch Mr. Gogolak beat his kid. Will's anger finally boiled over; he hurled his father's basketball and it caromed off Mr. Gogolak's shoulder. The man turned, more surprised than angry. Will was one hundred and ninety centimeters tall and even if he was built like a stick, he was bigger than this little grown-up. Lucky Mr. Gogolak, the hero of the western front, looked shocked when Will punched him. It wasn't a very smart thing to do but Will was sick of being smart. Being smart was too hard.

"My mom says hi." Will lashed out again and missed this time. Mr. Gogolak dragged his crybaby kid away from the post office. Will pumped his fist in triumph.

"Run! Run!" The line broke. Some dumb kid screamed, "It's a sweep!" but Will knew it wasn't. Selective Service had run this scam before: summer job, fall enlistment. Still, kids scattered in all directions.

But not everyone. Weird Miss Fisher just walked to the door to the post office like she was in line for ketchup. Bobby Mangann and Eric Orr and Danny Jarek linked arms and marched up behind her; their country needed them. Will didn't have anywhere to run to.

"Nice work." Looper slapped him on the back and grinned. "Going in?"

Will was excited; he had lost control and it had felt *great*. "Guess maybe I have to now." It made sense, actually. What was the point in studying history if you didn't believe in America? "After you, Johnny."

BRIAN STABLEFORD

The Man Who Loved the Vampire Lady

One of the most respected as well as one of the most prolific British SF writers, Brian Stableford is the author of more than thirty books, including *Cradle of the Sun, The Blind Worm, Days of Glory, In The Kingdom of the Beasts, Day of Wrath, The Halcyon Drift, The Paradox of the Sets*, and *The Realms of Tartarus*. His nonfiction books include *The Sociology of Science Fiction* and, with David Langford, *The Third Millennium: A History of the World A.D. 2000–3000*. His most recent book is the acclaimed new novel *The Empire of Fear*. A biologist and sociologist by training, Stableford lives in Reading, England.

In the chilling story that follows, he suggests that sometimes *what* you know may be just as dangerous as who . . .

THE MAN WHO LOVED
THE VAMPIRE LADY

Brian Stableford

A man who loves a vampire lady may not die young, but cannot live forever.
—Walachian proverb

It was the thirteenth of June in the Year of Our Lord 1623. Grand Normandy was in the grip of an early spell of warm weather, and the streets of London bathed in sunlight. There were crowds everywhere, and the port was busy with ships, three having docked that very day. One of the ships, the *Freemartin*, was from the Moorish enclave and had produce from the heart of Africa, including ivory and the skins of exotic animals. There were rumors, too, of secret and more precious goods: jewels and magical charms; but such rumors always attended the docking of any vessel from remote parts of the world. Beggars and street urchins had flocked to the dockland, responsive as ever to such whisperings, and were plaguing every sailor in the streets, as anxious for gossip as for copper coins. It seemed that the only faces not animated by excitement were those worn by the severed heads that dressed the spikes atop the Southwark Gate. The Tower of London, though, stood quite aloof from the hubbub, its tall and forbidding turrets so remote from the streets that they belonged to a different world.

Edmund Cordery, mechanician to the court of the Archduke Girard, tilted the small concave mirror on the brass device that rested on his workbench, catching the rays of the afternoon sun and deflecting the light through the system of lenses.

He turned away and directed his son, Noell, to take his place. "Tell me if all is well," he said tiredly. "I can hardly focus my eyes, let alone the instrument."

Noell closed his left eye and put his other to the microscope. He turned the wheel that adjusted the height of the stage. "It's perfect," he said. "What is it?"

"The wing of a moth." Edmund scanned the polished tabletop, checking that the other slides were in readiness for the demonstration. The prospect of Lady Carmilla's visit filled him with a complex anxiety that he resented in himself. Even in the old days, she had not come to his laboratory often but to see her here—on his own territory, as it were—would be bound to awaken memories that were untouched by the glimpses that he caught of her in the public parts of the Tower and on ceremonial occasions.

"The water slide isn't ready," Noell pointed out.

Edmund shook his head. "I'll make a fresh one when the time comes," he said. "Living things are fragile, and the world that is in a water drop is all too easily destroyed."

He looked farther along the bench-top, and moved a crucible, placing it out of sight behind a row of jars. It was impossible—and unnecessary—to make the place tidy, but he felt it important to conserve some sense of order and control. To discourage himself from fidgeting, he went to the window and looked out at the sparkling Thames and the strange gray sheen on the slate roofs of the houses beyond. From this high vantage point, the people were tiny; he was higher even than the cross on the steeple of the church beside the Leathermarket. Edmund was not a devout man, but such was the agitation within him, yearning for expression in action, that the sight of the cross on the church made him cross himself, murmuring the ritual devotion. As soon as he had done it, he cursed himself for childishness.

I am forty-four years old, he thought, *and a mechanician. I am no longer the boy who was favored with the love of the lady, and there is no need for this stupid trepidation.*

He was being deliberately unfair to himself in this private scolding. It was not simply the fact that he had once been Carmilla's lover that made him anxious. There was the microscope, and the ship from the Moorish country. He hoped that he would be able to judge by the lady's reaction how much cause there really was for fear.

The door opened then, and the lady entered. She half turned to indicate by a flutter of her hand that her attendant need not come in with her, and he withdrew, closing the door behind him. She was alone, with no friend or favorite in tow. She came across the room carefully, lifting the hem of her skirt a little, though the floor was not dusty. Her gaze flicked from side to side, to take note of the shelves, the beakers, the furnace, and the numerous tools of the mechanician's craft. To a commoner, it would have seemed a threatening environment, redolent with unholiness, but her attitude was cool and controlled. She arrived to stand before the brass instrument that Edmund had recently completed, but did not look long at it before raising her eyes to look fully into Edmund's face.

"You look well, Master Cordery," she said calmly. "But you are pale. You should not shut yourself in your rooms now that summer is come to Normandy."

Edmund bowed slightly, but met her gaze. She had not changed in the slightest degree, of course, since the days when he had been intimate with her. She was six hundred years old—hardly younger than the archduke—and the years were impotent as far as her appearance was concerned. Her complexion was much darker than his, her eyes a deep liquid brown, and her hair jet black. He had not stood so close to her for several years, and he could not help the tide of memories rising in his mind. For her, it would be different: his hair was gray now, his skin creased; he must seem an altogether different person. As he met her gaze, though, it seemed to him that she, too, was remembering, and not without fondness.

"My lady," he said, his voice quite steady, "may I present my son and apprentice, Noell."

Noell bowed more deeply than his father, blushing with embarrassment.

The Lady Carmilla favored the youth with a smile. "He has the look of you, Master Cordery," she said—a casual compliment. She returned her attention then to the instrument.

"The designer was correct?" she asked.

"Yes, indeed," he replied. "The device is most ingenious. I would dearly like to meet the man who thought of it. A fine discovery—though it taxed the talents of my lens grinder severely. I think we might make a better one, with much care and skill; this is but a poor example, as one must expect from a first attempt."

The Lady Carmilla seated herself at the bench, and Edmund showed her how to apply her eye to the instrument, and how to adjust the focusing wheel and the mirror. She expressed surprise at the appearance of the magnified moth's wing, and Edmund took her through the series of prepared slides, which included other parts of insects' bodies, and sections through the stems and seeds of plants.

"I need a sharper knife and a steadier hand, my lady," he told her. "The device exposes the clumsiness of my cutting."

"Oh no, Master Cordery," she assured him politely. "These are quite pretty enough. But we were told that more interesting things might be seen. Living things too small for ordinary sight."

Edmund bowed in apology and explained about the preparation of water slides. He made a new one, using a pipette to take a drop from a jar full of dirty river water. Patiently, he helped the lady search the slide for the tiny creatures that human eyes were not equipped to perceive. He showed her one that flowed as if it were semiliquid itself, and tinier ones that moved by means of cilia. She was quite captivated, and watched for some time, moving the slide very gently with her painted fingernails.

Eventually she asked: "Have you looked at other fluids?"

"What kind of fluids?" he asked, though the question was quite clear to him and disturbed him.

She was not prepared to mince words with him. "Blood, Master Cordery," she said very softly. Her past acquaintance with him had taught her respect for his intelligence, and he half regretted it.

"Blood clots very quickly," he told her. "I could not produce a satisfactory slide. It would take unusual skill."

"I'm sure that it would," she replied.

"Noell has made drawings of many of the things we *have* looked at," said Edmund. "Would you like to see them?"

She accepted the change of subject, and indicated that she would. She moved to Noell's station and began sorting through the drawings, occasionally looking up at the boy to compliment him on his work. Edmund stood by, remembering how sensitive he once had been to her moods and desires, trying hard to work out now exactly what she was thinking. Something in one of her contemplative glances at Noell sent an icy pang of dread into Edmund's gut, and he found his more important fears momentarily displaced by what might have been anxiety for his son, or simply jealousy. He cursed himself again for his weakness.

"May I take these to show the archduke?" asked the Lady Carmilla, addressing the question to Noell rather than to his father. The boy nodded, still too embarrassed to construct a proper reply. She took a selection of the drawings and rolled them into a scroll. She stood and faced Edmund again.

"We are most interested in this apparatus," she informed him. "We must consider carefully whether to provide you with new assistants, to encourage development of the appropriate skills. In the meantime, you may return to your ordinary work. I will send someone for the instrument, so that the archduke can inspect it at his leisure. Your son draws very well, and must be encouraged. You and he may visit me in my chambers on Monday next; we will dine at seven o'clock, and you may tell me about all your recent work."

Edmund bowed to signal his acquiescence—it was, of course, a command rather than an invitation. He moved before her to the door in order to hold it open for her. The two exchanged another brief glance as she went past him.

When she had gone, it was as though something taut unwound inside him, leaving him relaxed and emptied. He felt strangely cool and distant as he considered the possibility—stronger now—that his life was in peril.

When the twilight had faded, Edmund lit a single candle on the bench and sat staring into the flame while he drank dark wine from a flask. He did not look up when Noell came into the room, but when the boy brought another stool close to his and sat down upon it, he offered the flask. Noell took it, but sipped rather gingerly.

"I'm old enough to drink now?" he commented dryly.

"You're old enough," Edmund assured him. "But beware of excess, and never drink alone. Conventional fatherly advice, I believe."

Noell reached across the bench so that he could stroke the barrel of the microscope with slender fingers.

"What are you afraid of?" he asked.

Edmund sighed. "You're old enough for that, too, I suppose?"

"I think you ought to tell me."

Edmund looked at the brass instrument and said: "It were better to keep things like this dark secret. Some human mechanician, I daresay, eager to please the vampire lords and ladies, showed off his cleverness as proud as a peacock. Thoughtless. Inevitable, though, now that all this play with lenses has become fashionable.''

''You'll be glad of eyeglasses when your sight begins to fail,'' Noell told him. ''In any case, I can't see the danger in this new toy.''

Edmund smiled. ''New toys,'' he mused. ''Clocks to tell the time, mills to grind the corn, lenses to aid human sight. Produced by human craftsmen for the delight of their masters. I think we've finally succeeded in proving to the vampires just how very clever we are—and how much more there is to know than we know already.''

''You think the vampires are beginning to fear us?''

Edmund gulped wine from the flask and passed it again to his son. ''Their rule is founded in fear and superstition,'' he said quietly. ''They're long-lived, suffer only mild attacks of diseases that are fatal to us, and have marvelous powers of regeneration. But they're not immortal, and they're vastly outnumbered by humans. Terror keeps them safe, but terror is based in ignorance, and behind their haughtiness and arrogance, there's a gnawing fear of what might happen if humans ever lost their supernatural reverence for vampirekind. It's very difficult for them to die, but they don't fear death any the less for that.''

''There've been rebellions against vampire rule. They've always failed.''

Edmund nodded to concede the point. ''There are three million people in Grand Normandy,'' he said, ''and less than five thousand vampires. There are only forty thousand vampires in the entire imperium of Gaul, and about the same number in the imperium of Byzantium—no telling how many there may be in the khanate of Walachia and Cathay, but not so very many more. In Africa the vampires must be outnumbered three or four thousand to one. If people no longer saw them as demons and demi-gods, as unconquerable forces of evil, their empire would be fragile. The centuries through which they live give them wisdom, but longevity seems to be inimical to creative thought—they learn, but they don't *invent*. Humans remain the true masters of art and science, which are forces of change. They've tried to control that—to turn it to their advantage—but it remains a thorn in their side.''

''But they do have power,'' insisted Noell. ''They *are* vampires.''

Edmund shrugged. ''Their longevity is real—their powers of regeneration, too. But is it really their magic that makes them so? I don't know for sure what merit there is in their incantations and rituals, and I don't think even *they* know—they cling to their rites because they dare not abandon them, but where the power that makes humans into vampires really comes from, no one knows. From the devil? I think not. I don't believe in the devil—I think it's something in the blood. I think vampirism may be a kind of disease—but a disease that makes men stronger instead of weaker, insulates them against death instead of killing them. If that *is* the case—do you see now why the Lady Carmilla asked whether I had looked at blood beneath the microscope?''

Noell stared at the instrument for twenty seconds or so, mulling over the idea. Then he laughed.

"If we could *all* become vampires,'' he said lightly, "we'd have to suck one another's blood.''

Edmund couldn't bring himself to look for such ironies. For him, the possibilities inherent in discovering the secrets of vampire nature were much more immediate, and utterly bleak.

"It's not true that they *need* to suck the blood of humans,'' he told the boy. "It's not nourishment. It gives them . . . a kind of pleasure that we can't understand. And it's part of the mystique that makes them so terrible . . . and hence so powerful.'' He stopped, feeling embarrassed. He did not know how much Noell knew about his sources of information. He and his wife never talked about the days of his affair with the Lady Carmilla, but there was no way to keep gossip and rumor from reaching the boy's ears.

Noell took the flask again, and this time took a deeper draft from it. "I've heard,'' he said distantly, "that humans find pleasure, too . . . in their blood being drunk.''

"No,'' replied Edmund calmly. "That's untrue. Unless one counts the small pleasure of sacrifice. The pleasure that a human man takes from a vampire lady is the same pleasure that he takes from a human lover. It might be different for the girls who entertain vampire men, but I suspect it's just the excitement of hoping that they may become vampires themselves.''

Noell hesitated, and would probably have dropped the subject, but Edmund realized suddenly that he did not want the subject dropped. The boy had a right to know, and perhaps might one day *need* to know.

"That's not entirely true,'' Edmund corrected himself. "When the Lady Carmilla used to taste my blood, it did give me pleasure, in a way. It pleased me because it pleased *her*. There is an excitement in loving a vampire lady, which makes it different from loving an ordinary woman . . . even though the chance that a vampire lady's lover may himself become a vampire is so remote as to be inconsiderable.''

Noell blushed, not knowing how to react to this acceptance into his father's confidence. Finally he decided that it was best to pretend a purely academic interest.

"Why are there so many more vampire women than men?'' he asked.

"No one knows for sure,'' Edmund said. "No humans, at any rate. I can tell you what I believe, from hearsay and from reasoning, but you must understand that it is a dangerous thing to think about, let alone to speak about.''

Noell nodded.

"The vampires keep their history secret,'' said Edmund, "and they try to control the writing of human history, but the following facts are probably true. Vampirism came to western Europe in the fifth century, with the vampire-led horde of Attila. Attila must have known well enough how to make more vampires—he converted both Aëtius, who became ruler of the imperium of Gaul, and Theodosius II, the emperor of the east who was later murdered. Of all the vampires that now exist, the vast majority must be converts. I have heard reports of vampire children born to vampire ladies, but it must be an extremely rare occurrence. Vampire men seem to be much less virile than human men—it is said that they couple very rarely. Nevertheless, they frequently take human consorts, and these consorts often become vampires. Vampires usually claim that this is a gift, bestowed deliberately by magic, but I am not so sure they can control the process. I think the semen of vampire men carries some kind of seed that communicates vampirism much as the semen of humans makes women pregnant—and just as haphazardly. That's why the male lovers of vampire ladies don't become vampires.''

Noell considered this, and then asked: "Then where do vampire lords come from?''

"They're converted by other male vampires,'' Edmund said. "Just as Attila converted Aëtius and Theodosius.'' He did not elaborate, but waited to see whether Noell understood the implication. An expression of disgust crossed the boy's face and Edmund did not know whether to be glad or sorry that his son could follow the argument through.

"Because it doesn't always happen,'' Edmund went on, "it's easy for the vampires to pretend that they have some special magic. But some women never become pregnant, though they lie with their husbands for years. It is said, though, that a human may also become a vampire by drinking vampire's blood—if he knows the appropriate magic spell. That's a rumor the vampires don't like, and they exact terrible penalties if anyone is caught trying the experiment. The ladies of our own court, of course, are for the most part onetime lovers of the archduke or his cousins. It would be indelicate to speculate about the conversion of the archduke, though he is certainly acquainted with Aëtius.''

Noell reached out a hand, palm downward, and made a few passes above the candle flame, making it flicker from side to side. He stared at the microscope.

"*Have* you looked at blood?'' he asked.

"I have,'' replied Edmund. "And semen. Human blood, of course—and human semen.''

"And?''

Edmund shook his head. "They're certainly not homogeneous fluids,'' he said, "but the instrument isn't good enough for really detailed inspection. There are small corpuscles—the ones in semen have long, writhing tails—but there's more . . . much more . . . to be seen, if I had the chance. By tomorrow this instrument will be gone—I don't think I'll be given the chance to build another.''

"You're surely not in danger! You're an important man—and your loyalty has never been in question. People think of you as being almost a vampire yourself. A black magician. The kitchen girls are afraid of me because I'm your son—they cross themselves when they see me."

Edmund laughed, a little bitterly. "I've no doubt they suspect me of intercourse with demons, and avoid my gaze for fear of the spell of the evil eye. But none of that matters to the vampires. To them, I'm only a human, and for all that they value my skills, they'd kill me without a thought if they suspected that I might have dangerous knowledge."

Noell was clearly alarmed by this. "Wouldn't. . . ." He stopped, but saw Edmund waiting for him to ask, and carried on after only a brief pause. "The Lady Carmilla . . . wouldn't she . . . ?"

"Protect me?" Edmund shook his head. "Not even if I were her favorite still. Vampire loyalty is to vampires."

"She was human once."

"It counts for nothing. She's been a vampire for nearly six hundred years, but it wouldn't be any different if she were no older than I."

"But . . . she did love you?"

"In her way," said Edmund sadly. "In her way." He stood up then, no longer feeling the urgent desire to help his son to understand. There were things the boy could find out only for himself and might never have to. He took up the candle tray and shielded the flame with his hand as he walked to the door. Noell followed him, leaving the empty flask behind.

Edmund left the citadel by the so-called Traitor's Gate, and crossed the Thames by the Tower Bridge. The houses on the bridge were in darkness now, but there was still a trickle of traffic; even at two in the morning, the business of the great city did not come to a standstill. The night had clouded over, and a light drizzle had begun to fall. Some of the oil lamps that were supposed to keep the thoroughfare lit at all times had gone out, and there was not a lamplighter in sight. Edmund did not mind the shadows, though.

He was aware before he reached the south bank that two men were dogging his footsteps, and he dawdled in order to give them the impression that he would be easy to track. Once he entered the network of streets surrounding the Leathermarket, though, he gave them the slip. He knew the maze of filthy streets well enough—he had lived here as a child. It was while he was apprenticed to a local clockmaker that he had learned the cleverness with tools that had eventually brought him to the notice of his predecessor, and had sent him on the road to fortune and celebrity. He had a brother and a sister still living and working in the district, though he saw them very rarely. Neither one of them was proud to have a reputed magician for a brother, and they had not forgiven him his association with the Lady Carmilla.

He picked his way carefully through the garbage in the dark alleys, unperturbed by the sound of scavenging rats. He kept his hands on the pommel of the dagger that was clasped to his belt, but he had no need to draw it. Because the stars were hidden, the night was pitch-dark, and few of the windows were lit from within by candlelight, but he was able to keep track of his progress by reaching out to touch familiar walls every now and again.

He came eventually to a tiny door set three steps down from a side street, and rapped upon it quickly, three times and then twice. There was a long pause before he felt the door yield beneath his fingers, and he stepped inside hurriedly. Until he relaxed when the door clicked shut again, he did not realize how tense he had been.

He waited for a candle to be lit.

The light, when it came, illuminated a thin face, crabbed and wrinkled, the eyes very pale and the wispy white hair gathered imperfectly behind a linen bonnet.

"The lord be with you," he whispered.

"And with you, Edmund Cordery," she croaked.

He frowned at the use of his name—it was a deliberate breach of etiquette, a feeble and meaningless gesture of independence. She did not like him, though he had never been less than kind to her. She did not fear him as so many others did, but she considered him tainted. They had been bound together in the business of the Fraternity for nearly twenty years, but she would never completely trust him.

She lead him into an inner room, and left him there to take care of his business.

A stranger stepped from the shadows. He was short, stout, and bald, perhaps sixty years old. He made the special sign of the cross, and Edmund responded.

"I'm Cordery," he said.

"Were you followed?" The older man's tone was deferential and fearful.

"Not here. They followed me from the Tower, but it was easy to shake them loose."

"That's bad."

"Perhaps—but it has to do with another matter, not with our business. There's no danger to you. Do you have what I asked for?"

The stout man nodded uncertainly. "My masters are unhappy," he said. "I have been asked to tell you that they do not want you to take risks. You are too valuable to place yourself in peril."

"I am in peril already. Events are overtaking us. In any case, it is neither your concern nor that of your . . . masters. It is for me to decide."

The stout man shook his head, but it was a gesture of resignation rather than a denial. He pulled something from beneath the chair where he had waited in the shadows. It was a large box, clad in leather. A row of small holes was set in the longer side, and there was a sound of scratching from within that testified to the presence of living creatures.

"You did exactly as I instructed?" asked Edmund.

The small man nodded, then put his hand on the mechanician's arm, fearfully. "Don't open it, sir, I beg you. Not here."

"There's nothing to fear," Edmund assured him.

"You haven't been in Africa, sir, as I have. Believe me, *everyone* is afraid—and not merely humans. They say that vampires are dying, too."

"Yes, I know," said Edmund distractedly. He shook off the older man's restraining hand and undid the straps that sealed the box. He lifted the lid, but not far—just enough to let the light in, and to let him see what was inside.

The box contained two big gray rats. They cowered from the light.

Edmund shut the lid again and fastened the straps.

"It's not my place, sir," said the little man hesitantly, "but I'm not sure that you really understand what you have there. I've seen the cities of West Africa—I've been in Corunna, too, and Marseilles. They remember other plagues in those cities, and all the horror stories are emerging again to haunt them. Sir, if any such thing ever came to London. . . ."

Edmund tested the weight of the box to see whether he could carry it comfortably. "It's not your concern," he said. "Forget everything that has happened. I will communicate with your masters. It is in my hands now."

"Forgive me," said the other, "but I must say this: there is naught to be gained from destroying vampires, if we destroy ourselves, too. It would be a pity to wipe out half of Europe in the cause of attacking our oppressors."

Edmund stared at the stout man coldly. "You talk too much," he said. "Indeed, you talk a *deal* too much."

"I beg your pardon, sire."

Edmund hesitated for a moment, wondering whether to reassure the messenger that his anxiety was understandable, but he had learned long ago that where the business of the Fraternity was concerned, it was best to say as little as possible. There was no way of knowing when this man would speak again of this affair, or to whom, or with what consequence.

The mechanician took up the box, making sure that he could carry it comfortably. The rats stirred inside, scrabbling with their small clawed feet. With his free hand, Edmund made the sign of the cross again.

"God go with you," said the messenger, with urgent sincerity.

"And with thy spirit," replied Edmund colorlessly.

Then he left, without pausing to exchange a ritual farewell with the crone. He had no difficulty in smuggling his burden back into the Tower, by means of a gate where the guard was long practiced in the art of turning a blind eye.

When Monday came, Edmund and Noell made their way to the Lady Carmilla's chambers. Noell had never been in such an apartment before, and it was a source of wonder to him. Edmund watched the boy's reactions to the carpets, the wall hangings, the mirrors and ornaments, and could not help but recall the first time *he* had entered these chambers. Nothing had changed here, and the rooms were full of provocations to stir and sharpen his faded memories.

Younger vampires tended to change their surroundings often, addicted to novelty, as if they feared the prospect of being changeless themselves. The Lady Carmilla had long since passed beyond this phase of her career. She had grown used to changelessness, had transcended the kind of attitude to the world that permitted boredom and ennui. She had adapted herself to a new aesthetic of existence, whereby her personal space became an extension of her own eternal sameness, and innovation was confined to tightly controlled areas of her life—including the irregular shifting of her erotic affections from one lover to another.

The sumptuousness of the lady's table was a further source of astonishment to Noell. Silver plates and forks he had imagined, and crystal goblets, and carved decanters of wine. But the lavishness of provision for just three diners—the casual waste—was something that obviously set him aback. He had always known that he was himself a member of a privileged elite, and that by the standards of the greater world, Master Cordery and his family ate well; the revelation that there was a further order of magnitude to distinguish the private world of the real aristocracy clearly made its impact upon him.

Edmund had been very careful in preparing his dress, fetching from his closet finery that he had not put on for many years. On official occasions he was always concerned to play the part of mechanician, and dressed in order to sustain that appearance. He never appeared as a courtier, always as a functionary. Now, though, he was reverting to a kind of performance that Noell had never seen him play, and though the boy had no idea of the subtleties of his father's performance, he clearly understood something of what was going on; he had complained acidly about the dull and plain way in which his father had made *him* dress.

Edmund ate and drank sparingly, and was pleased to note that Noell did likewise, obeying his father's instructions despite the obvious temptations of the lavish provision. For a while the lady was content to exchange routine courtesies, but she came quickly enough—by her standards—to the real business of the evening.

"My cousin Girard," she told Edmund, "Is quite enraptured by your clever device. He finds it most interesting."

"Then I am pleased to make him a gift of it," Edmund replied. "And I would be pleased to make another, as a gift for Your Ladyship."

"That is not our desire," she said coolly. "In fact, we have other matters in mind. The archduke and his seneschal have discussed certain tasks that you might profitably carry out. Instructions will be communicated to you in due time, I have no doubt."

"Thank you, my lady," said Edmund.

"The ladies of the court were pleased with the drawings that I showed to them," said the Lady Carmilla, turning to look at Noell. "They marveled at the thought that a cupful of Thames water might contain thousands of tiny living creatures. Do you think that our bodies, too, might be the habitation of countless invisible insects?''

Noell opened his mouth to reply, because the question was addressed to him, but Edmund interrupted smoothly.

"There are creatures that may live upon our bodies," he said, "and worms that may live within. We are told that the macrocosm reproduces in essence the microcosm of human beings; perhaps there is a small microcosm within us, where our natures are reproduced again, incalculably small. I have read. . . .''

"I have read, Master Cordery," she cut in, "that the illnesses that afflict humankind might be carried from person to person by means of these tiny creatures.''

"The idea that diseases were communicated from one person to another by tiny seeds was produced in antiquity," Edmund replied, "but I do not know how such seeds might be recognized, and I think it very unlikely that the creatures we have seen in river water could possibly be of that character.''

"It is a disquieting thought," she insisted, "that our bodies might be inhabited by creatures of which we can know nothing, and that every breath we take might be carrying into us seeds of all kinds of change, too small to be seen or tasted. It makes me feel uneasy.''

"But there is no need," Edmund protested. "Seeds of corruptibility take root in human flesh, but yours is inviolate.''

"You know that is not so, Master Cordery," she said levelly. "You have seen me ill yourself.''

"That was a pox that killed many humans, my lady—yet it gave to you no more than a mild fever.''

"We have reports from the imperium of Byzantium, and from the Moorish enclave, too, that there is plague in Africa, and that it has now reached the southern regions of the imperium of Gaul. It is said that this plague makes little distinction between human and vampire.''

"Rumors, my lady," said Edmund soothingly. "You know how news becomes blacker as it travels.''

The Lady Carmilla turned again to Noell, and this time addressed him by name so that there could be no opportunity for Edmund to usurp the privilege of answering her. "Are you afraid of me, Noell?" she asked.

The boy was startled, and stumbled slightly over his reply, which was in the negative.

"You must not lie to me," she told him. "You *are* afraid of me, because I am a vampire. Master Cordery is a skeptic, and must have told you that vampires have less magic than is commonly credited to us, but he must also have told you that I can do you harm if I will. Would you like to be a vampire yourself, Noell?''

Noell was still confused by the correction, and hesitated over his reply, but he eventually said: "Yes, I would."

"Of course you would," she purred. "All humans would be vampires if they could, no matter how they might pretend when they bend the knee in church. And men *can* become vampires; immortality is within our gift. Because of this, we have always enjoyed the loyalty and devotion of the greater number of our human subjects. We have always rewarded that devotion in some measure. Few have joined our ranks, but the many have enjoyed centuries of order and stability. The vampires rescued Europe from a Dark Age, and as long as vampires rule, barbarism will always be held in check. Our rule has not always been kind, because we cannot tolerate defiance, but the alternative would have been far worse. Even so, there are men who would destroy us—did you know that?"

Noell did not know how to reply to this, so he simply stared, waiting for her to continue. She seemed a little impatient with his gracelessness, and Edmund deliberately let the awkward pause go on. He saw a certain advantage in allowing Noell to make a poor impression.

"There is an organization of rebels," the Lady Carmilla went on. "A secret society, ambitious to discover the secret way by which vampires are made. They put about the idea that they would make all men immortal, but this is a lie, and foolish. The members of this brotherhood seek power for themselves."

The vampire lady paused to direct the clearing of one set of dishes and the bringing of another. She asked for a new wine, too. Her gaze wandered back and forth between the gauche youth and his self-assured father.

"The loyalty of your family is, of course, beyond question," she eventually continued. "No one understands the workings of society like a mechanician, who knows well enough how forces must be balanced and how the different parts of a machine must interlock and support one another. Master Cordery knows well how the cleverness of rulers resembles the cleverness of clockmakers, do you not?"

"Indeed, I do, my lady," replied Edmund.

"There might be a way," she said, in a strangely distant tone, "that a good mechanician might earn a conversion to vampirism."

Edmund was wise enough not to interpret this as an offer or a promise. He accepted a measure of the new wine and said: "My lady, there are matters that it would be as well for us to discuss in private. May I send my son to his room?"

The Lady Carmilla's eyes narrowed just a little, but there was hardly any expression in her finely etched features. Edmund held his breath, knowing that he had forced a decision upon her that she had not intended to make so soon.

"The poor boy has not quite finished his meal," she said.

"I think he has had enough, my lady," Edmund countered. Noell did not disagree, and, after a brief hesitation, the lady bowed to signal her permission.

Edmund asked Noell to leave, and, when he was gone, the Lady Carmilla rose from her seat and went from the dining room into an inner chamber. Edmund followed her.

"You were presumptuous, Master Cordery," she told him.

"I was carried away, my lady. There are too many memories here."

"The boy is mine," she said, "if I so choose. You do know that, do you not?"

Edmund bowed.

"I did not ask you here tonight to make you witness the seduction of your son. Nor do you think that I did. This matter that you would discuss with me— does it concern science or treason?"

"Science, my lady. As you have said yourself, my loyalty is not in question."

Carmilla laid herself upon a sofa and indicated that Edmund should take a chair nearby. This was the antechamber to her bedroom, and the air was sweet with the odor of cosmetics.

"Speak," she bade him.

"I believe that the archduke is afraid of what my little device might reveal," he said. "He fears that it will expose to the eye such seeds as carry vampirism from one person to another, just as it might expose the seeds that carry disease. I think that the man who devised the instrument may have been put to death already, but I think you know well enough that a discovery once made is likely to be made again and again. You are uncertain as to what course of action would best serve your ends, because you cannot tell whence the greater threat to your rule might come. There is the Fraternity, which is dedicated to your destruction; there is plague in Africa, from which even vampires may die; and there is the new sight, which renders visible what previously lurked unseen. Do you want my advice, Lady Carmilla?"

"Do you *have* any advice, Edmund?"

"Yes. Do not try to control by terror and persecution the things that are happening. Let your rule be unkind *now*, as it has been before, and it will open the way to destruction. Should you concede power gently, you might live for centuries yet, but if you strike out . . . your enemies will strike back."

The vampire lady leaned back her head, looking at the ceiling. She contrived a small laugh.

"I cannot take advice such as that to the archduke," she told him flatly.

"I thought not, my lady," Edmund replied very calmly.

"You humans have your own immortality," she complained. "Your faith promises it, and you all affirm it. Your faith tells you that you must not covet the immortality that is ours, and we do no more than agree with you when we guard it so jealously. You should look to your Christ for fortune, not to us. I think you know well enough that we could not convert the world if we wanted to. Our magic is such that it can be used only sparingly. Are you distressed because it has never been offered to you? Are you bitter? Are you becoming our enemy because you cannot become our kin?''

"You have nothing to fear from me, my lady," he lied. Then he added, not quite sure whether it was a lie or not: "I loved you faithfully. I still do."

She sat up straight then, and reached out a hand as though to stroke his cheek, though he was too far away for her to reach.

"That is what I told the archduke," she said, "when he suggested to me that you might be a traitor. I promised him that I could test your loyalty more keenly in my chambers than his officers in theirs. I do not think you could delude me. Edmund. Do you?"

"No, my lady," he replied.

"By morning," she told him gently, "I will know whether or not you are a traitor."

"That you will," he assured her. "That you will, my lady."

He woke before her, his mouth dry and his forehead burning. He was not sweating—indeed, he was possessed by a feeling of desiccation, as though the moisture were being squeezed out of his organs. His head was aching, and the light of the morning sun that streamed through the unshuttered window hurt his eyes.

He pulled himself up to a half-sitting position, pushing the coverlet back from his bare chest.

So soon! he thought. He had not expected to be consumed so quickly, but he was surprised to find that his reaction was one of relief rather than fear or regret. He had difficulty collecting his thoughts, and was perversely glad to accept that he did not need to.

He looked down at the cuts that she had made on his breast with her little silver knife; they were raw and red, and made a strange contrast with the faded scars whose crisscross pattern still engraved the story of unforgotten passions. He touched the new wounds gently with his fingers, and winced at the fiery pain.

She woke up then, and saw him inspecting the marks.

"Have you missed the knife?" she asked sleepily. "Were you hungry for its touch?"

There was no need to lie now, and there was a delicious sense of freedom in that knowledge. There was a joy in being able to face her, at last, quite naked in his thoughts as well as his flesh.

"Yes, my lady," he said with a slight croak in his voice. "I had missed the knife. Its touch . . . rekindled flames in my soul."

She had closed her eyes again, to allow herself to wake slowly. She laughed. "It is pleasant, sometimes, to return to forsaken pastures. You can have no notion how a particular *taste* may stir memories. I am glad to have seen you again, in this way. I had grown quite used to you as the gray mechanician. But now. . . ."

He laughed, as lightly as she, but the laugh turned to a cough, and something in the sound alerted her to the fact that all was not as it should be. She opened her eyes and raised her head, turning toward him.

"Why, Edmund," she said, "you're as pale as death!"

She reached out to touch his cheek, and snatched her hand away again as she found it unexpectedly hot and dry. A blush of confusion spread across her own features. He took her hand and held it, looking steadily into her eyes.

"Edmund," she said softly. "What have you done?"

"I can't be sure," he said, "and I will not live to find out, but I have tried to kill you, my lady."

He was pleased by the way her mouth gaped in astonishment. He watched disbelief and anxiety mingle in her expression, as though fighting for control. She did not call out for help.

"This is nonsense," she whispered.

"Perhaps," he admitted. "Perhaps it was also nonsense that we talked last evening. Nonsense about treason. Why did you ask me to make the microscope, my lady, when you knew that making me a party to such a secret was as good as signing my death warrant?"

"Oh Edmund," she said with a sigh. "You could not think that it was my own idea? I tried to protect you, Edmund, from Girard's fears and suspicions. It was because I was your protector that I was made to bear the message. What have you done, Edmund?"

He began to reply, but the words turned into a fit of coughing.

She sat upright, wrenching her hand away from his enfeebled grip, and looked down at him as he sank back upon the pillow.

"For the love of God!" she exclaimed, as fearfully as any true believer. "It is the plague—the plague out of Africa!"

He tried to confirm her suspicion, but could do so only with a nod of his head as he fought for breath.

"But they held the *Freemartin* by the Essex coast for a full fortnight's quarantine," she protested. "There was no trace of plague aboard."

"The disease kills men," said Edmund in a shallow whisper. "But animals can carry it, in their blood, without dying."

"You cannot know this!"

Edmund managed a small laugh. "My lady," he said, "I am a member of that Fraternity that interests itself in everything that might kill a vampire. The information came to me in good time for me to arrange delivery of the rats— though when I asked for them, I had not in mind the means of using them that I eventually employed. More recent events. . . . ." Again he was forced to stop, unable to draw sufficient breath even to sustain the thin whisper.

The Lady Carmilla put her hand to her throat, swallowing as if she expected to feel evidence already of her infection.

"You would destroy me, Edmund?" she asked, as though she genuinely found it difficult to believe.

"I would destroy you all," he told her. "I would bring disaster, turn the world upside down, to end your rule. . . . We cannot allow you to stamp out learning itself to preserve your empire forever. Order must be fought with chaos, and chaos is come, my lady."

When she tried to rise from the bed, he reached out to restrain her, and though there was no power left in him, she allowed herself to be checked. The coverlet fell away from her, to expose her breasts as she sat upright.

"The boy will die for this, Master Cordery," she said. "His mother, too."

"They're gone," he told her. "Noell went from your table to the custody of the society that I serve. By now they're beyond your reach. The archduke will never catch them."

She stared at him, and now he could see the beginnings of hate and fear in her stare.

"You came here last night to bring me poisoned blood," she said. "In the hope that this new disease might kill even me, you condemned yourself to death. What did you do, Edmund?"

He reached out again to touch her arm, and was pleased to see her flinch and draw away: that he had become dreadful.

"Only vampires live forever," he told her hoarsely. "But anyone may drink blood, if they have the stomach for it. I took full measure from my two sick rats . . . and I pray to God that the seed of this fever is raging in my blood . . . and in my semen, too. You, too, have received full measure, my lady . . . and you are in God's hands now like any common mortal. I cannot know for sure whether you will catch the plague, or whether it will kill you, but I—an unbeliever—am not ashamed to pray. Perhaps you could pray, too, my lady, so that we may know how the Lord favors one unbeliever over another."

She looked down at him, her face gradually losing the expressions that had tugged at her features, becoming masklike in its steadiness.

"You could have taken our side, Edmund. I trusted you, and I could have made the archduke trust you, too. You could have become a vampire. We could have shared the centuries, you and I."

This was dissimulation, and they both knew it. He had been her lover, and had ceased to be, and had grown older for so many years that now she remembered him as much in his son as in himself. The promises were all too obviously hollow now, and she realized that she could not even taunt him with them.

From beside the bed she took up the small silver knife that she had used to let his blood. She held it now as if it were a dagger, not a delicate instrument to be used with care and love.

"I thought you still loved me," she told him. "I really did."

That, at least, he thought, might be true.

He actually put his head farther back, to expose his throat to the expected thrust. He wanted her to strike him—angrily, brutally, passionately. He had nothing more to say, and would not confirm or deny that he did still love her.

He admitted to himself now that his motives had been mixed, and that he really did not know whether it was loyalty to the Fraternity that had made him submit to this extraordinary experiment. It did not matter.

She cut his throat, and he watched her for a few long seconds while she stared at the blood gouting from the wound. When he saw her put stained fingers to her lips, knowing what she knew, he realized that after her own fashion, she still loved him.

STEVEN GOULD

Peaches for Mad Molly

In the story that follows, Steven Gould, a frequent contributor to *Analog*, takes the housing shortage to unprecedented extremes, and with uncommon skill gives us a fast-moving look at the consequences . . . and some of the very unexpected complications.

Recently married, Gould and his wife live in Bryan, Texas.

PEACHES FOR MAD MOLLY

Steven Gould

Sometime during the night the wind pulled a one-pointer off the west face of the building up around the 630th floor. I heard him screaming as he went by, very loud, like this was his last chance to voice an opinion, but it was all so sudden that he didn't know what it was. Then he hit a microwave relay off 542 . . . hard, and the chance was gone. Chunks of him landed in Buffalo Bayou forty-five seconds later.

The alligators probably liked that.

I don't know if his purchase failed or his rope broke or if the sucker just couldn't tie a decent knot. He pissed me off though, because I couldn't get back to sleep until I'd checked all four of my belay points, the ropes, and the knots. Now if he'd fallen without expressing himself, maybe?

No, I would have heard the noise as he splattered through the rods of the antennae.

Stupid one-pointer.

The next morning I woke up a lot earlier than usual because someone was plucking one of my ropes, *adagio*, thrum, thrum, like the second movement of Ludwig's seventh. It was Mad Molly.

"You awake, Bruce?" she asked.

I groaned. "I am now." My name is not Bruce. Molly, for some reason, calls everyone Bruce. "*Shto etta*, Molly?"

She was crouched on a roughing point, one of the meter cubes sticking out of the tower face to induce the micro-turbulence boundary layer. She was dressed in a brightly flowered scarlet kimono, livid green bermuda shorts, a sweatshirt, and tabi socks. Her belay line, bright orange against the gray building, stretched from around the corner to Molly's person where it vanished beneath her kimono, like a snake hiding its head.

"I got a batch to go to the Bruce, Bruce."

I turned and looked down. There was a damp wind in my face. Some low clouds had come in overnight, hiding the ground, but the tower's shadow stretched a long ways across the fluffy stuff below. "Jeeze, Molly. You know the Bruce won't be on shift for another hour." Damn, she had me doing it! "Oh, hell. I'll be over after I get dressed."

She blinked twice. Her eyes were black chips of stone in a face so seamed and browned by the sun that it was hard to tell her age. "Okay, Bruce," she said, then stood abruptly and flung herself off the cube. She dropped maybe five meters before her rope tightened her fall into an arc that swung her down and around the corner.

I let out my breath. She's not called Mad Molly for nothing.

I dressed, drank the water out of my catch basin, urinated on the clouds (seems only fair) and rolled up my bag.

Between the direct sunlight and the stuff bouncing off the clouds below the south face was blinding. I put my shades on at the corner.

Molly's nest, like a mud dauber's, hung from an industrial exhaust vent off the 611th floor. It was woven, sewed, tucked, patched, welded, snapped, zipped, and tied into creation. It looked like a wasp's nest on a piece of chrome. It did not blend in.

Her pigeon coop, about two floors lower down, blended in even less. It was made of paper, sheet plastic, wire, and it was speckled with pigeon droppings. It was where it was because only a fool lives directly under *under* defecating birds, and Molly, while mad, was not stupid.

Molly was crouched in the doorway of her nest balanced on her feet like one of her pigeons. She was staring out at nothing and muttering angrily to herself.

"What's wrong, Molly? Didn't you sleep okay?"

She glared at me. "That damn Bruce got another three of my birds yesterday."

I hooked my bag onto a beaner and hung it under her house. "What Bruce, Molly? That red tailed hawk?"

"Yeah, that Bruce. Then the other Bruce pops off last night and wakes me up so I can't get back to sleep because I'm listening for that damn hawk." She backed into her nest to let me in.

"Hawks don't hunt at night, Molly."

She flapped her arms. "So? Like maybe the vicious, son-of-a-bitchin' Bruce gets into the coop? He could kill half my birds in one night!" She started coiling one of her ropes, pulling the line with short, angry jerks. "I don't know if it's worth it anymore, Bruce. It's hot in the summer. It's freezing in the winter. The Babs are always hassling me instead of the Howlers, the Howlers keep hassling me for free birds or they'll cut me loose one night. I can't cook on cloudy days unless I want to pay an arm and a leg for fuel. I can't get fresh fruit or vegetables. That crazy social worker who's afraid of heights comes by and asks if he can help me. I say 'Yeah, get me some fresh fruit.' He brings me applications for readmittance! God, I'd kill for a fresh peach! I'd be better off back in the home!"

I shrugged. "Maybe you would, Molly. After all, you're getting on in years."

"Fat lot you know, Bruce! You crazy or something? Trade this view for six walls? Breathe that stale stuff they got in there? Give up my birds? Give up my freedom? Shit, Bruce, who the hell's side are you on anyway?"

I laughed. "Yours, Molly."

She started wrapping the pigeons and swearing under her breath.

I looked at Molly's clippings, bits of faded newsprint stuck to the wall of the tower itself. By the light coming through some of the plastic sheeting in the roof, I saw a picture of Molly on Mt. McKinley dated twenty years before. An article about her second attempt on Everest. Stories about her climbing buildings in New York, Chicago, and L.A. I looked closer at one that talked about her climbing the south face of El Capitan on her fourteenth birthday. It had the date.

I looked twice and tried to remember what day of the month it was. I had to count backwards in my head to be sure.

Tomorrow was Mad Molly's birthday.

The Bruce in question was Murry Zapata, outdoor rec guard of the south balcony on the 480th floor. This meant I had to take the birds down 131 stories, or a little over half a kilometer. And then climb back.

Even on the face of Le Bab tower, with a roughing cube or vent or external rail every meter or so, this is a serious climb. Molly's pigeons alone were not worth the trip, so I dropped five floors and went to see Lenny.

It's a real pain to climb around Lenny's because nearly every horizontal surface has a plant box or pot on it. So I rappeled down even with him and shouted over to where he was fiddling with a clump of fennel.

"Hey, Lenny. I'm making a run. You got anything for Murry?"

He straightened up. "Yeah, wait a sec." He was wearing shorts and his climbing harness and nothing else. He was brown all over. If I did that sort of thing I'd be a melanoma farm.

Lenny climbed down to his tent and disappeared inside. I worked my way over there, avoiding the plants. I smelled dirt, a rare smell up here. It was an odor rich and textured. It kicked in memories of freshly plowed fields or newly dug graves. When I got to Lenny's tent, he came out with a bag.

"What'cha got," I asked.

He shrugged. "Garlic, cumin, and anise. The weights are marked on the outside. Murry should have no trouble moving it. The Chicanos can't get enough of the garlic. Tell Murry that I'll have some of those tiny *muy caliente* chilis for him next week."

"Got it."

"By the way, Fran said yesterday to tell you she has some daisies ready to go down."

"Check. You ever grow any fruit, Lenny?"

"On these little ledges? I thought about getting a dwarf orange once but decided against it. I grow dew berries but none of them are ripe right now. No way I could grow trees. Last year I grew some cantaloupe but that's too much trouble. You need a bigger bed than I like."

"Oh, well. It was a thought." I added his bag to the pigeons in my pack. "I'll probably be late getting back."

He nodded. "Yeah, I know. Better you than me, though. Last time *I* went, the Howlers stole all my tomatoes. Watch out down below. The Howlers are claiming the entire circumference from 520 to 530."

"Oh, yeah? Just so they don't interfere with my right of eminent domain."

He shrugged. "Just be careful. I don't care if they want a cut. Like maybe a clump of garlic."

I blinked. "Nobody cuts my cargo. Nobody."

"Not even Dactyl?"

"Dactyl's never bothered me. He's just a kid."

Lenny shrugged. "He's sent his share down. You get yourself pushed off and we'll have to find someone else to do the runs. Just be careful."

"Careful is what I do best."

Fran lived around the corner, on the east face. She grew flowers, took in sewing, and did laundry. When she had the daylight for her solar panel, she watched TV.

"Why don't you live inside, Fran. You could watch TV twenty-four hours a day."

She grinned at me, a not unpleasant event. "Nah. Then I'd pork up to about a hundred kilos eating that syntha crap and not getting any exercise and I'd have to have a permit to grow even one flower in my cubicle and a dispensation for the wattage for a grow light and so on and so forth. When they put me in a coffin, I want to be dead."

"Hey, they have exercise rooms and indoor tracks and the rec balconies."

"Big deal. Shut up for a second while I see if Bob is still mad at Sue because he found out about Marilyn's connection with her mother's surgeon. When the commercial comes I'll cut and bundle some daisies."

She turned her head back to the flat screen. I looked at her blue bonnets and pansies while I waited.

"There, I was right. Marilyn is sleeping with Sue's mother. That will make everything okay." She tucked the TV in a pocket and prepared the daisies for me. "I'm going to have peonies next week." I laced the wrapped flowers on the outside of the pack to avoid crushing the petals. While I was doing that Fran moved closer. "Stop over on the way back?"

"Maybe," I said. "Of course I'll drop your script off."

She withdrew a little.

"I want to, Fran, honest. But I want to get some fresh fruit for Mad Molly's birthday tomorrow and I don't know where I'll have to go to get it."

She turned away and shrugged. I stood there for a moment, then left, irritated. When I looked back she was watching the TV again.

The Howlers had claimed ten floors and the entire circumference of the Le Bab Tower between those floors. That's an area of forty meters by 250 meters per side or 40,000 square meters total. The tower is over a kilometer on a side at the base but it tapers in stages until its only twenty meters square at three thousand meters.

Their greediness was to my advantage because there's only thirty-five or so Howlers and that's a lot of area to cover. As I rappelled down to 529 I slowly worked my way around the building. There was a bunch of them in hammocks on the south face, sunbathing. I saw one or two on the east face but most of them were on the west face. Only one person was on the north side.

I moved down to 521 on the north face well away from the one guy and doubled my longest line. It was a hundred meter blue line twelve millimeters thick. I coiled it carefully on a roughing cube after wrapping the halfway point of the rope around another roughing cube one complete circuit, each end trailing down. I pushed it close into the building so it wouldn't slip. Then I clipped my brake bars around the doubled line.

The guy at the other corner noticed me now and started working his way from roughing cube to roughing cube, curious. I kicked the rope off the cube and it fell cleanly with no snarls, no snags. He shouted. I jumped, a gloved hand on the rope where it came out of the brake bars. I did the forty meters in five jumps, a total of ten seconds. Halfway down I heard him shout for help and heard others come around the corner. At 518 I braked and swung into the building. The closest Howler was still fifteen meters or so away from my rope, but he was speeding up. I leaned against the building and flicked the right hand rope hard, sending a sinusoidal wave traveling up the line. It reached the top and the now loose rope flicked off the cube above and fell. I sat down and braced. A hundred meter rope weighs in at eight kilos and the shock of it pulling up short could have pulled me from the cube.

They shouted things after me, but none of them followed. I heard one of them call out, "Quit'cha bitchin. He's got to pass us on his way home. We'll educate him then."

All the rec guards deal. It's a good job to have if you're inside. Even things that originate inside the tower end up traveling the outside pipeline. Ain't no corridor checks out here. No TV cameras or sniffers either. The Howlers do a lot of that sort of work.

Murry is different from the other guards, though. He doesn't deal slice or spike or any of the other nasty pharmoddities, and he treats us outsiders like humans. He says he was outside once. I believe him.

"So, Murry, what's with your wife? She had that baby yet?"

"Nah. And boy is she tired of being pregnant. She's, like, out to *here*." He held his hands out. "You tell Fran I want something special when she finally dominoes. Like roses."

"Christ, Murry. You know Fran can't do roses. Not in friggin pots. Maybe day lilies. I'll ask her." I sat in my seat harness, hanging outside the cage that's around the rec balcony. Murry stood inside smelling the daisies. There were some kids kicking a soccer ball on the far side of the balcony and several adults standing at the railing looking out through the bars. Several people stared at me. I ignored them.

Murry counted out the script for the load and passed it through the bars. I zipped it in a pocket. Then he pulled out the provisions I'd ordered the last run and I dropped them, item by item, into the pack.

"You ever get any fresh fruit in there, Murry?"

"What do I look like, guy, a millionaire? The guys that get that sort of stuff live up there above 750. Hell, I once had this escort job up to 752 and while the honcho I escorted was talking to the resident, they had me wait out on this patio. This guy had apples and peaches and *cherries* for crissakes! *Cherries*!" He shook his head. 'It was weird, too. None of this cage crap." He rapped on the bars with his fist. "He had a chest high railing and that was it."

"Well of course. What with the barrier at 650 he doesn't have to worry about us. I'll bet there's lots of open balconies up that way." I paused. "Well, I gotta go. I've got a long way to climb."

"Better you than me. Don't forget to tell Fran about the special flowers."

"Right."

They were waiting for me, all the Howlers sitting on the south face, silent, intent. I stopped four stories below 520 and rested. While I rested I coiled my belay line and packed it in my pack. I sat there, fifteen kilos of supplies and climbing paraphernalia on my back, and looked out on the world.

The wind had shifted more to the southwest and was less damp than the morning air. It had also strengthened but the boundary layer created by the roughing cubes kept the really high winds out from the face of the tower.

Sometime during the day the low clouds below had broken into patches, letting the ground below show through. I perched on the roughing cube, unbelayed and contemplated the fall. 516 is just over two kilometers from the ground. That's quite a drop—though in low winds the odds were I'd smack into one of the rec balconies where the tower widened below. In a decent southerly wind you can depend on hitting the swamps instead.

What I had to do now was rough.

I had to free ascend.

No ropes, no nets, no second chances. If I lost it the only thing I had to worry about was whether or not to scream on the way down.

The Howlers were not going to leave me time for the niceties.

For the most part the Howlers were so-so climbers, but they had a few people capable of technical ascents. I had to separate the good from the bad and then out-climb the good.

I stood on the roughing cube and started off at a run, leaping two meters at a time from roughing cube to roughing cube moving sideways across the south face. Above me I heard shouts but I didn't look up. I didn't dare. The mind was blank, letting the body do the work without hindrance. The eyes saw, the body did, the mind coasted.

I slowed as I neared the corner, and stopped, nearly falling when I overbalanced, but saving myself by dropping my center of gravity.

There weren't nearly as many of them above me now. Maybe six of them had kept up with me. The others were trying to do it by the numbers, roping from point to point. I climbed two stories quickly, chimneying between a disused fractional distillation stack and a cooling tower. Then I moved around the corner and ran again.

When I stopped to move up two more stories there were only two of them above me. The other four were trying for more altitude rather than trying to keep pace horizontally.

I ran almost to the northwest corner, then moved straight up.

The first one decided to drop kick me dear Jesus through the goal posts of life. He pulled his line out, fixed it to something convenient and rappelled out with big jumps, planning, no doubt, to come swinging into me with his feet when he reached my level. I ignored him until the last minute when I let myself collapse onto a roughing cube. His feet slammed into the wall above me then rebounded out.

As he swung back out from the face I leaped after him.

His face went white. Whatever he was expecting me to do, he wasn't expecting *that*! I latched onto him like a monkey, my legs going around his waist. One of my hands grabbed his rope, the other punched with all my might into his face. I felt his jaw go and his body went slack. He released the rope below the brake bars and started sliding down the rope. I scissored him with my legs and held onto the rope with both hands. My shoulders creaked as I took the strain but he stopped sliding. Then we swung back into the wall and I sagged onto a cube astride him.

His buddy was dropping down more slowly. He was belayed but he'd seen what I'd done and wasn't going to try the airborne approach. He was still a floor or two above me so I tied his friend off so he wouldn't sleepwalk and took off sideways, running again.

I heard him shout but I didn't hear him moving. When I paused again he was bent over my friend with the broken jaw. I reached an external exhaust duct and headed for the sky as fast as I could climb.

At this point I was halfway through Howler territory. Off to my right the group that had opted for height was now moving sideways to cut me off. I kept climbing, breathing hard now but not desperate. I could climb at my current speed for another half hour without a break and I thought there was only one other outsider that could keep up that sort of pace. I wondered if he was up above.

I looked.

He was.

He wasn't on the wall.

He didn't seem to be roped on.

And he was dropping.

I tried to throw myself to the side, in the only direction I could go, but I was only partially successful. His foot caught me a glancing blow to my head and I fell three meters to the next roughing cube. I landed hard on the cube, staggered, bumped into the wall, and fell outward, off the cube. The drop was sudden, gut wrenching, and terrifying. I caught the edge of the cube with both hands, wrenching my shoulders and banging my elbow. My head ached, the sky spun in circles and I knew that there was over a kilometer of empty space beneath my feet.

Dactyl had stopped somehow, several stories below me, and, as I hung there, I could see the metallic gleam of some sort of wire, stretched taut down the face of the tower.

I chinned myself up onto the cube and traversed away from the wire, moving and climbing fast. I ignored the pain in my shoulders and the throbbing of my head and even the stomach churning fear and sudden clammy sweat.

There was a whirring sound and the hint of movement behind me. I turned around and caught the flash of gray moving up the face. I looked up.

He was waiting, up on the edge of Howler territory, just watching. Closer were the three clowns who were trying to get above me before I passed them. I eyed the gap, thought about it, and then went into overdrive. They didn't make it. I passed them before they reached the exhaust duct. For a few stories they tried to pursue and one of them even threw a grapple that fell short.

That left only Dactyl.

He was directly overhead when I reached 530. I paused and glanced down. The others had stopped and were looking up. Even the clothesliners had made it around the corner and were watching. I looked back up. Dactyl moved aside about five meters and sat down on a ledge. I climbed up even with him and sat too.

Dactyl showed up one day in the middle of Howler territory. Three Howlers took the long dive before it was decided that maybe the Howler should ignore Dactyl before there were no Howlers left. He's a loner who does a mixed bag: some free ascent, some rope work, and some fancy mech stuff.

There was something about him that made him hard to see, almost. Not really, but he did blend into the building. His nylons, his climbing shoes, his harness were gray like the roughing cube he sat on. His harness was strung with gray boxes and pouches of varying sizes, front and back, giving his torso a bulky appearance, sort of like a turtle with long arms. He was younger than I'd thought he'd be, perhaps twenty, but then I'd only seen him at a distance before now. His eyes looked straight at me, steady and hard. He wasn't sweating a bit.

"Why?" I said.

He shrugged. "Be natural, become a part of your environment. Who said that?"

"Lot's of people said that. Even I said that."

Dactyl nodded. "So, like I'm doing that thing. I'm becoming a part of the environment. One thing you should know by now, dude . . . ."

"What's that?" I asked warily.

"The environment is hostile."

I looked out, away from him. In the far distance I saw white sails in Galveston bay. I turned back. "What did I ever do to you?"

He smiled. "You take it too personal. It's more random than that. Think of me as an extra-somatic evolutionary factor. You've got to evolve. You've got to adapt. *Mano a Mano* shit like that."

I let that stew for a while. The Howlers were gathering below, inside their territory. They were discussing something with much hand waving and punctuated gestures.

"So," I finally said. "You ever walk through downtown Houston?"

He blinked, opened his mouth to say something, then closed it. Finally, almost unwillingly, he said, "On the ground? No. They eat people down there."

I shrugged. "Sometimes they do. Sometimes they don't. Last time I was in Tranquillity Park they were eating alligator tail with Siamese peanut sauce. Except when the alligators were eating them."

"Oh."

"You even been down below at all?"

"I was born inside."

"Well, don't let it bother you," I said as I stood up.

He frowned slightly. "What's that supposed to mean?"

I grinned. "It's not where you were born that matters," I said. "It's where you die."

I started climbing.

*   *   *

The first half-hour was evenly paced. He waited about a minute before he started after me and for the the next seventy floors it was as if there was an invisible fifteen meter rope stretched between us. About 600 he lowered the gap to ten meters. I picked up the pace a little, but the gap stayed the same for the next ten floors.

I was breathing hard now and feeling the burn in my thighs and arms. My clothes were soaked in sweat but my hands were dry and I was in rhythm, climbing smooth and steady.

Dactyl was also climbing fast, but jerky, his movements inefficient. The gap was still ten meters but I could tell he was straining.

I doubled my speed.

The universe contracted. There was only the wall, the next purchase, the next breath. There were no peaches, no birthdays, no flowers, and no Dactyl. There was no thought.

But there *was* pain.

My thighs went from burning to screaming. I started taking up some of the slack with my arms and they joined the chorus. I climbed through the red haze for fifteen more stories and then collapsed on a roughing cube.

The world reeled as I gasped for the first breaths. I felt incipient cramps lurking in my thighs and I wanted those muscle cells to have all the oxygen I could give them. Then, as the universe steadied, I looked down for Dactyl.

He wasn't on the north face.

Had he given up?

I didn't know and it bothered me.

Five stories above was the barrier—a black, ten meter overhang perpendicular to the face. It was perfectly smooth, made of metal, its welds ground flush. I didn't know what was above it. There were rumors about automatic lasers, armed guards, and computer monitored imaging devices. I'd worry about them when I got past that overhang.

I was two stories short of it when Dactyl appeared at the northeast corner of the building.

Above me.

It wasn't possible. I almost quit then but something made me go on. I tried to blank my mind and began running toward the west face, doing the squirrel hopping from block to block, even though my muscles weren't up to it. I almost lost it twice, once when my mind dwelt too much on how Dactyl had passed me and once when my quadriceps gave way.

I stopped at the corner, gasping, and looked back. Dactyl was working his way leisurely after me, slowly, almost labored. I ducked around and climbed again, until I was crouched on a roughing cube, the dark overhang touching my head. I peeked around the corner. Dactyl had paused, apparently resting.

I took off my pack and pulled out a thirty-meter length of two-ton-test line, a half-meter piece of ten-kilo-test monofilament, and a grapple. I tied the monofilament between the heavier line and the grapple.

I peeked around the corner again. Dactyl was moving again, but slowly, carefully. He was still two-hundred meters across the face. I dropped down two meters and stepped back around the corner. Dactyl stopped when he saw me, but I ignored him, playing out the grapple and line until it hung about fifteen meters below me. Then I started swinging it.

It was hard work, tricky, too. I didn't think I had the time to rig a quick belay before Dactyl got there. At least the grapple was light, three kilos at most, but as it swung wider and wider it threatened to pull me off at each end of its swing, especially as the corner formed by the barrier concentrated the wind somewhat.

Finally the grapple raised far enough on the swing away from the corner. As it dropped to the bottom of its swing I began pulling it in. As the moment arm decreased the grapple sped up, gaining enough speed to flip up above the edge of the overhang. I had no idea how thick the overhang was or even if there was something up there for the grapple to catch on. I held my breath.

There was a distant clinking noise as it struck something and the rope slackened. For an instant I thought it was dropping back down and I was scared because I was already off balance and I didn't know how far Dactyl was behind me. Then the rope stopped moving and the grapple didn't drop into sight.

I risked a quick look behind. Dactyl was still a hundred meters away. I took the rope and moved back around the corner, pulling the rope cautiously tight. As luck would have it, with the line pulled over, Dactyl wouldn't be able to see any part of the rope until he rounded the corner.

It took me two minutes to tie the lower end of the rope around a roughing cube and then to two more cubes for backup. Then I recklessly dropped from cube to cube until I was three stories down and hidden behind a Bernoulli exhaust vent.

He stuck his head around the corner almost immediately. Saw the dangling line and tugged it hard. The ten-kilo test line hidden above the barrier held. Dactyl clipped a beaner over the line and leaped out, almost like a flying squirrel, his hands reaching for the rope. He was halfway out before his full weight hit the rope.

The ten kilo test snapped immediately. I heard his indrawn breath, but he didn't swear. Instead, as he arched down, he tried to twist around, to get his legs between him and the face as he swung into it.

He was only partially successful, slamming hard into the corner of a roughing cube, one leg taking some of the shock. I heard the breath leave his lungs in an explosive grunt and then he was sliding down the rope toward the unattached end, grabbing weakly to stop himself, but only managing to slow the drop.

I moved like a striking snake.

I was already lower down the tower from where he'd hit the wall and took three giant strides from cube to cube to get directly beneath him. Then he was off the end of the rope and dropping free and my hand reached out, snared his climbing harness, and I flattened myself atop the cube I was on.

For the second time that day I nearly dislocated my shoulder. His weight nearly pulled me off the tower. The back of my shirt suddenly split. I heard his head crack onto the cube and he felt like a sack of dirt, lifeless, but heavy as the world.

It took some time to get him safely onto the cube and lashed in place.

It took even longer to get my second grapple up where the first one was. It seemed my first attempt was a fluke and I had to repeat the tiring process six more times before I could clip my ascenders to the rope and inchworm up it.

The building had narrowed above the barrier, to something like 150 meters per side. I was on the edge of a terrace running around the building. Unlike the recreation balconies below, it was open to the sky, uncaged, with only a chest high railing to contain its occupants. Scattered artfully across the patio were lounge chairs and greenery topped planters.

I saw a small crowd of formally dressed men and women mingling on the west terrace, sheltered from the northeast wind. Servants moved among them with trays. Cocktail hour among the rich, the influential, and the cloudy.

I pulled myself quickly over the edge and crouched behind a planter, pulling my rope in and folding my grapples.

The terrace areas unsheltered by the wind seemed to be deserted. I looked for cameras and IR reflectors and capcitance wires but I didn't see any. I couldn't see any reason for any.

Above me, the face of the tower rose another five hundred meters or so, but unlike the faces below, there were individual balconies spotted here and there among the roughing cubes. On more than one I could see growing plants, even trees.

I had more than a hundred floors to go, perhaps 400 meters.

My arms and legs were trembling. There was a sharp pain in the shoulder Dactyl had kicked, making it hard for me to lift that arm higher than my neck.

I nearly gave it up. I thought about putting down my pack, unbuckling my climbing harness, and stretching out on one of these lounge chairs. Perhaps later I'd take a drink off of one of those trays.

Then a guard would come and escort me all the way to the ground.

Besides, I could do a hundred stories standing on my head, right? Right.

The sun was completely down by the time I reached 700 but lights from the building itself gave me what I couldn't make out by feel. The balconies were fancy, sheltered from the wind by removable fairings and jutting fins. I kept my eye out for a balcony with fruit trees, just in case. I wouldn't climb all the way up to 752 if I didn't have to.

But I had to.

There were only four balconies on 752, one to each side. They were the largest private balconies I'd ever seen on the tower. Only one of them had anything resembling a garden. I spent five minutes looking over the edge at planter after planter of vegetables, flowers, shrubs, and trees. I couldn't see any lights through the glass doors leading into the building and I couldn't see any peaches.

I sighed and pulled myself over the edge for a closer look, standing upright with difficulty. My limbs were leaden, my breath still labored. I could hear my pulse thudding in my ears, and I still couldn't see any peaches.

There were some green oranges on a tree near me, but that was the closest thing to fruit I could see. I shivered. I was almost two kilometers above sea level and the sun had gone down an hour ago. My sweat soaked clothes were starting to chill.

Something was nagging me and, at first, the fatigue toxins wouldn't let me think clearly. Then an important fact swam into my attention.

I hadn't checked for alarms.

They were there, in the wall above the railing, a series of small reflectors for the I/R beams that I'd crawled through to enter the balcony.

Time to leave. Long past time. I stepped toward the railing and heard a door open behind me. I started to swing my leg up over the edge when I felt something stick me in the side. And then the universe exploded.

All the muscles on my right side convulsed spasmodically and I came down onto the concrete floor with a crash, slamming my shoulder and hip into the ground. My head was saved from the same fate by the backpack I wore.

Taser, I thought.

When I could focus, I saw the man standing about three meters away, wearing a white khaftan. He was older than I was by decades. Most of his hair was gone and his face had deep lines etched by something other than smiling. I couldn't help comparing him to Mad Molly, but it just wasn't the same. Mad Molly could be as old but she didn't look anywhere as *nasty* as this guy did.

He held the taser loosely in his right hand. In his left hand he held a drink with ice that he swirled gently around, clink, clink.

"What are you doing here, you disgusting little fly?"

His voice, as he asked the question, was vehement and acid. His expression didn't change though.

"Nothing." I tried to say it strongly, firmly, reasonably. It came out like a frog's croak.

He shot me with the taser again. I caught the glint on the wire as it sped out, tried to dodge, but too late.

I arched over the backpack, my muscles doing things I wouldn't have believed possible. My head banged sharply against the floor. Then it stopped again.

I was disoriented, the room spun. My legs decided to go into a massive cramp. I gasped out loud.

This seemed to please him.

"Who sent you? I'll know in the end. I can do this all night long."

I said quickly, "Nobody sent me. I hoped to get some peaches."

He shot me again.

I really didn't think much of this turn of events. My muscles had built up enough lactic acid without electro-convulsive induced contractions. When everything settled down again I had another bump on my head and more cramps.

He took a sip from his drink.

"You'll have to do better than that," he said. "Nobody would risk climbing the outside for peaches. Besides, there won't be peaches on that tree for another five months." He pointed the taser. "Who sent you?"

I couldn't even talk at this point. He seemed to realize this, fortunately, and waited a few moments, lowering the taser. Then he asked again, "Who sent you?"

"Get stuffed," I told him weakly.

"Stupid little man." He lifted the taser again and something smashed him in the arm, causing him to drop the weapon. He stooped to pick it up again but there was a streak of gray and the thud of full body contact as someone hit him and bowled him over onto his back.

I saw the newcomer scoop up the taser and spin sharply. The taser passed over my head and out over the railing.

It was Dactyl.

The man in the khaftan saw Dactyl's face then and said, "You!" He started to scramble to his feet. Dactyl took one sliding step forward and kicked him in the face. The man collapsed in a small heap, his khaftan making him look like a white sack with limbs sticking out.

Dactyl stood there for a moment looking down. Then he turned and walked slowly back to me.

"That was a nasty trick with the rope."

I laughed, albeit weakly. "If you weren't so lazy you would have made your own way up." I eyed him warily, but my body wasn't up to movement yet. Was he going to kick me in the face, too? Still, I had to know something. "How did you pass me down there, below the barrier? You were exhausted, I could see it."

He shrugged. "You're right. I'm lazy." He flipped a device off his back. It looked like a gun with two triggers. I made ready to jump. He pointed it up and pulled the trigger. I heard a *chunk* and something buried itself in the ceiling. He pulled the second trigger and there was a whining sound. Dactyl and gun floated off the floor. I looked closer and saw the wire.

"Cheater," I said.

He laughed and lowered himself back to the floor. "What the hell are you doing here?" he asked.

I told him.

"You're shitting me."

"No."

He laughed then and walked briskly through the door into the tower.

I struggled to stand. Made it. I was leaning against the railing when Dactyl came back through the door with a plastic two-liter container. He handed it to me. It was ice cold.

"What's this?"

"Last season's peaches. From the freezer. He always hoards them until just before the fresh ones are ready."

I stared at him. "How the hell did you know that?"

He shrugged, took the peaches out of my hand and put them in my pack. "Look, I'd get out of here before he wakes up. Not only does he have a lot nastier things than that taser, but security will do whatever he wants."

He swung up over the edge and lowered himself to arm's length. Just before he dropped completely from sight he added something which floated up with the wind.

"He's my father."

I started down the tower not too long after Dactyl. Physically I was a wreck. The taser had exhausted my muscles in a way that exercise never had. I probably wasn't in the best shape to do any kind of rope work, but Dactyl's words rang true. I didn't want anybody after me in the condition I was in, much less security.

Security is bad. They use copters and rail cars that run up and down the outside of the building. They fire rubber bullets and water cannon. Don't think this makes them humane. A person blasted off a ledge by either is going to die. Security is just careful not to damage the tower.

So, I did my descent in stages, feeling like an old man tottering carefully down a flight of stairs. Still, descent was far easier than ascent, and my rope work had me down on the barrier patio in less than ten minutes.

It was nearing midnight, actually lighter now that the quarter moon had risen, and the patio, instead of being deserted, had far more people on it than it had at sunset. A few people saw me coiling my rope after my last rappel. I ignored them, going about my business with as much *panache* as I could muster. On my way to the edge of the balcony I stopped at the buffet and built myself a sandwich.

More people began looking my way and talking. An elderly woman standing at one end of the buffet took a long look at me, then said, "Try the wontons. I think there's really pork in them."

I smiled at her. "I don't know. Pork is tricky. You never know who provided it."

Her hand stopped, a wonton halfway to her mouth, and stared at me. Then, almost defiantly, she popped it into her mouth and chewed it with relish. "Just so it's well cooked."

A white clad steward left the end of the table and walked over to a phone hanging by a door.

I took my sandwich over to the edge and set it down while I took the rope from the pack. My legs trembled slightly. The woman with the wontons followed me over after a minute.

"Here," she said, holding out a tall glass that clinked. "Ice tea."

I blinked, surprised. "Why, thank you. This is uncommonly kind."

She shrugged. "You look like you need it. Are you going to collapse right here? It would be exciting, but I'd avoid it if I were you. I think that nasty man called security."

"Do I look as bad as all that?"

"Honey, you look like death warmed over."

I finished playing out the rope and clipped on my brake-bars. "I'm afraid you're right." I took a bite out of the sandwich and chewed quickly. I washed it down with the tea. It wasn't one of Mad Molly's roast pigeons but it wasn't garbage, either.

"You'll get indigestion," the woman warned.

I smiled and took another large bite. The crowd of people staring at me was getting bigger. There was a stirring in the crowd from over by the door. I took another bite and another swig, then swung over the edge. "We must do this again, sometime," I said. "Next time, we'll dance."

I dropped into the dark, jumping out so I could swing into the building. I didn't reach it on the first swing, so I let out more rope and pumped my legs. I came within a yard of the tower and swung out again. I felt better than before but was still weak. I looked up and saw heads looking over the edge at me. Something gleamed in the moonlight.

A knife?

I reached the wall and dropped onto a roughing cube, unbalanced, unsure of my purchase. For a moment I teetered, then was able to heave myself in toward the wall, safe. I turned, to release one end of the rope, so I could snake it down from above.

I didn't have to. It fell from above, two new ends whipping through the night air.

Bastards. I almost shouted it, but it seemed better to let them think I'd fallen. Besides, I couldn't be bothered with any action so energetic. I was bone weary, tired beyond reaction.

For the next hundred stories I made like a spider with arthritis, slow careful descents with lengthy rests. After falling asleep and nearly falling off a cube, I belayed myself during all rest stops. At one point I'm sure I slept for over an hour because my muscles had set up, stiff and sore. It took me another half hour of careful motion before I was moving smoothly again.

Finally I reached Mad Molly's, moving carefully, quietly. I unloaded her supplies and the peaches and put them carefully inside her door. I could hear her snoring. Then, leaving my stash under her house as usual, I climbed down, intending to see Fran and make her breakfast.

I didn't make it to Fran's.

In the half dark before the dawn they came at me.

This is the place for a good line like "they came on me like the wolf upon the fold" or "as the piranha swarm." Forget it. I was too tired. All I know is they came at me, the Howlers did. At me, who'd been beaten, electroshocked, indigested, sliced at, and bone wearified, if there exists such a verb. I watched them come in dull amazement, which is not a suit of clothes, but an amalgam of fatigue and astonished reaction to the last straw on my camellian back.

Before I'd been hurt and felt the need to ignore it. I'd been challenged and felt the need to respond. I'd felt curiosity and felt the need to satisfy it. I'd felt fear and the need to overcome it. But I hadn't yet felt what I felt now.

I felt rage, and the need to express it.

I'm sure the first two cleared the recreation balcony, they had to. They came at me fast unbelayed and I used every bit of their momentum to heave them out. The next one, doubtless feeling clever, landed on my back and clung like a monkey. I'd passed caring, I simply threw myself to the side, aiming my back at the roughing cube two meters below. He tried, but he didn't get off in time. I'm grateful though, because the shock would have broken my back if he hadn't been there.

I don't think he cleared the rec balcony.

I ran then, but slowly, so angry that I wanted them to catch up, to let me use my fists and feet on their stubborn, malicious, stupid heads. For the next ten minutes it was a running battle only I ran out of steam before they ran out of Howlers.

I ended up backed into a cranny where a cooling vent formed a ledge some five meters deep and four meters wide, when Dactyl dropped into the midst of them, a gray blur that sent three of them for a dive and two more scrambling back around the edges.

I was over feeling mad by then and back to just feeling tired.

Dactyl looked a little tired himself. "I can't let you out of my sight for a minute, can I?" he said. "What's the matter? You get tired of their shit?"

"Right . . ." I laughed weakly. "Now I'm back to owing *you*."

"That's right, suck-foot. And I'm not going to let you forget it."

I tottered forward then and looked at the faces around us. I didn't feel so good.

"Uh, Dacty."

"Yeah."

"I think you better take a look over the edge."

He walked casually forward and took a look down, then to both sides, then up. He backed up again.

"Looks like you're going to get that chance to repay me real soon," he said.

The Howlers were out there—all of the Howlers still alive—every last one of them. In the predawn gray they were climbing steadily toward us from all sides, as thick as cannibals at a funeral. I didn't think much of our chances.

"Uh, Dactyl?"

"Yeah."

"Do you think that piton gun of yours can get us out of here?"

He shook his head. "I don't have anything to shoot into. The angles are all wrong."

"Oh."

He tilted his head then and said, "I do have a parachute."

"What?"

He showed me a gray bundle connected to the back of his climbing harness between batteries.

"You ever use it?"

"Do I look crazy?" he asked.

I took a nine meter length of my strongest line and snapped one end to my harness and the other to his.

The Howlers were starting to come over the lip.

"The answer is yes," I said.

We started running.

I took two of them off with me, and Dactyl seemed to have kicked one man right in the face. The line stretched between us pulled another one into the void. I was falling, bodies tumbling around me in the air, the recreation deck growing in size. I kept waiting for Dactyl to open the chute but we seemed to fall forever. Now I could see the broken Howlers who'd preceded us, draped on the cage work over the balcony. The wind was a shrieking banshee in my ears. The sun rose. I thought, *here I am falling to my death and the bloody sun comes up*!

In the bright light of the dawn a silken flower blossomed from Dactyl's back. I watched him float up away from me and then the chute opened with a dull boom. He jerked up away from me and there came a sudden, numbing shock. Suddenly I was dangling at the end of a three meter pendulum, tick, tick and watching four more bodies crash into the cage.

The wind took us then, far out, away from the tower, spinning slowly as we dropped. I found myself wondering if we'd land on water or land.

Getting out of the swamp, past alligators and cannibals, and through the Le Bab Security perimeter is a story in itself. It was hard, it took some time, but we did it.

While we were gone there was a shakeup in the way of things. Between my trespassing and Howlers dropping out of the sky, the Security people were riled up enough to come out and "shake off" some of the fleas. Fortunately most of the victims were Howlers.

To finish this story up neatly I would like to add that Molly liked the peaches—but she didn't.

It figures.

HARRY TURTLEDOVE

The Last Article

Science fiction is a field known for sudden rises to prominence, so it's not really surprising to look around and see how far Harry Turtledove has come, and how fast. In a handful of years (writing both as Turtledove and as Eric G. Iverson), he has become a regular in *Analog, Amazing*, and *Isaac Asimov's Science Fiction Magazine*, as well as selling to markets such as *Fantasy Book, Playboy, The Magazine of Fantasy and Science Fiction*, and *Universe*. Although he has also published many nonrelated stories, Turtledove's reputation to date rests mainly on his two popular series of magazine stories: the "Basil Argyros" series, detailing the adventures of a "magistrianoi" in an alternate Byzantine Empire, and the "Sim" series, which take place in an alternate world in which European explorers find North America inhabited by homonids—"Sims"—instead of Indians. Turtledove is just starting to make his mark at longer lengths. A novel called *Agent of Byzantium* appeared in 1987, and a tetrology called *The Videssos Cycle* was also published recently. His most recent book is the novel *A Different Flesh*. A native Californian, Turtledove has a Ph.D. in Byzantine history from U.C.L.A., and has published a scholarly translation of a ninth-century Byzantine chronicle. He lives in Canoga Park, California, with his wife and two small daughters.

In the story that follows, he takes us to the recent past for a chilling vision of What Might Have Been.

THE LAST ARTICLE

Harry Turtledove

Nonviolence is the first article of my faith. It is also the last article of my creed.

—Mohandas Gandhi

The one means that wins the easiest victory over reason: terror and force.

—Adolf Hitler, *Mein Kampf*

The tank rumbled down the Rajpath, past the ruins of the Memorial Arch, toward the India Gate. The gateway arch was still standing, although it had taken a couple of shell hits in the fighting before New Delphi fell. The Union Jack fluttered above it.

British troops lined both sides of the Rajpath, watching silently as the tank rolled past them. Their khaki uniforms were filthy and torn; many wore bandages. They had the weary, past-caring stares of beaten men, though the Army of India had fought until flesh and munitions gave out.

The India Gate drew near. A military bank, smartened up for the occasion, began to play as the tank went past. The bagpipes sounded thin and lost in the hot, humid air.

A single man stood waiting in the shadow of the gate. Field Marshal Walther Model leaned down into the cupola of the Panzer IV. "No one can match the British at ceremonies of this sort," he said to his aide.

Major Dieter Lasch laughed, a bit unkindly. "They've had enough practice, sir," he answered, raising his voice to be heard over the flatulent roar of the tank's engine.

"What is that tune?" the field marshal asked. "Does it have a meaning?"

"It's called 'The World Turned Upside Down,' " said Lasch, who had been involved with his British opposite number in planning the formal surrender. "Lord Cornwallis's army musicians played it when he yielded to the Americans at Yorktown."

"Ah, the Americans." Model was for a moment so lost in his own thoughts that his monocle threatened to slip from his right eye. He screwed it back in. The single lens was the only thing he shared with the clichéd image of a high German officer. He was no lean, hawk-faced Prussian. But his rounded features were unyielding, and his stocky body sustained the energy of his will better than the thin, dyspeptic frames of so many aristocrats. "The Americans," he repeated. "Well, that will be the next step, won't it? But enough. One thing at a time."

The panzer stopped. The driver switched off the engine. The sudden quiet was startling. Model leaped nimbly down. He had been leaping down from tanks for eight years now, since his days as a staff officer for the IV Corps in the Polish campaign.

The man in the shadows stepped forward, saluted. Flashbulbs lit his long, tired face as German photographers recorded the moment for history. The Englishman ignored cameras and cameramen alike. "Field Marshal Model," he said politely. He might have been about to discuss the weather.

Model admired his sangfroid. "Field Marshal Auchinleck," he replied, returning the salute and giving Auchinleck a last few seconds to remain his equal. Then he came back to the matter at hand. "Field Marshal, have you signed the instrument of surrender of the British Army of India to the forces of the Reich?"

"I have," Auchinleck replied. He reached into the left pocket of his battle dress, removed a folded sheet of paper. Before handing it to Model, though, he said, "I should like to request your permission to make a brief statement at this time."

"Of course, sir. You may say what you like, at whatever length you like." In victory, Model could afford to be magnanimous. He had even granted Marshal Zhukov leave to speak in the Soviet capitulation at Kuibyshev, before the marshal was taken out and shot.

"I thank you." Auchinleck stiffly dipped his head. "I will say, then, that I find the terms I have been forced to accept to be cruelly hard on the brave men who have served under my command."

"That is your privilege, sir." But Model's round face was no longer kindly, and his voice had iron in it as he replied, "I must remind you, however, that my treating with you at all under the rules of war is an act of mercy for which Berlin may yet reprimand me. When Britain surrendered in 1941, all Imperial forces were also ordered to lay down their arms. I daresay you did not expect us to come so far, but I would be within my rights in reckoning you no more than so many bandits."

A slow flush darkened Auchinleck's cheeks. "We gave you a bloody good run, for bandits."

"So you did." Model remained polite. He did not say he would ten times rather fight straight-up battles than deal with the partisans who to this day harassed the Germans and their allies in occupied Russia. "Have you anything further to add?"

"No, sir, I do not." Auchinleck gave the German the signed surrender, handed him his sidearm. Model put the pistol in the empty holster he wore for the occasion. It did not fit well; the holster was made for a Walther P38, not this man-killing brute of a Webley and Scott. That mattered little, though—the ceremony was almost over.

Auchinleck and Model exchanged salutes for the last time. The British field marshal stepped away. A German lieutenant came up to lead him into captivity.

Major Lasch waved his left hand. The Union Jack came down from the flagpole on the India Gate. The swastika rose to replace it.

Lasch tapped discreetly on the door, stuck his head into the field marshal's office. "That Indian politician is here for his appointment with you, sir."

"Oh yes. Very well, Dieter, send him in." Model had been dealing with Indian politicians even before the British surrender, and with hordes of them now that resistance was over. He had no more liking for the breed than for Russian politicians, or even German ones. No matter what pious principles they spouted, his experience was that they were all out for their own good first.

The small, frail brown man the aide showed in made him wonder. The Indian's emaciated frame and the plain white cotton loincloth that was his only garment contrasted starkly with the Victorian splendor of the Viceregal Palace from which Model was administering the Reich's new conquest. "Sit down, *Herr* Gandhi," the field marshal urged.

"I thank you very much, sir." As he took his seat, Gandhi seemed a child in an adult's chair: it was much too wide for him, and its soft, overstuffed cushions hardly sagged under his meager weight. But his eyes, Model saw, were not child's eyes. They peered with disconcerting keenness through his wire-framed spectacles as he said, "I have come to inquire when we may expect German troops to depart from our country."

Model leaned forward, frowning. For a moment he thought he had misunderstood Gandhi's Gujarati-flavored English. When he was sure he had not, he said, "Do you think perhaps we have come all this way as tourists?"

"Indeed I do not." Gandhi's voice was sharp with disapproval. "Tourists do not leave so many dead behind them."

Model's temper kindled. "No, tourists do not pay such a high price for the journey. Having come regardless of that cost, I assure you we shall stay."

"I am very sorry, sir; I cannot permit it."

"*You* cannot?" Again, Model had to concentrate to keep his monocle from falling out. He had heard arrogance from politicians before, but this scrawny old devil surpassed belief. "Do you forget I can call my aide and have you shot behind this building? You would not be the first, I assure you."

"Yes, I know that," Gandhi said sadly. "If you have that fate in mind for me, I am an old man. I will not run."

Combat had taught Model a hard indifference to the prospect of injury or death. He saw the older man possessed something of the same sort, however he had acquired it. A moment later he realized his threat had not only failed to frighten Gandhi, but had actually amused him. Disconcerted, the field marshal said, "Have you any serious issues to address?"

"Only the one I named just now. We are a nation of more than 300 million; it is no more just for Germany to rule us than for the British."

Model shrugged. "If we are able to, we will. We have the strength to hold what we have conquered, I assure you."

"Where there is no right, there can be no strength," Gandhi said. "We will not permit you to hold us in bondage."

"Do you think to threaten me?" Model growled. In fact, though, the Indian's audacity surprised him. Most of the locals had fallen over themselves, fawning on their new masters. Here, at least, was a man out of the ordinary.

Gandhi was still shaking his head, although Model saw he had still not frightened him (a man out of the ordinary indeed, thought the field marshal, who respected courage when he found it). "I make no threats, sir, but I will do what I believe to be right."

"Most noble," Model said, but to his annoyance the words came out sincere rather than with the sardonic edge he had intended. He had heard such canting phrases before, from Englishmen, from Russians, yes, and from Germans as well. Somehow, though, this Gandhi struck him as one who always meant exactly what he said. He rubbed his chin, considering how to handle such an intransigent.

A large green fly came buzzing into the office. Model's air of detachment vanished the moment he heard that malignant whine. He sprang from his seat, swatted at the fly. He missed. The insect flew around awhile longer, then settled on the arm of Gandhi's chair. "Kill it," Model told him. "Last week one of those accursed things bit me on the neck, and I still have the lump to prove it."

Gandhi brought his hand down, but several inches from the fly. Frightened, it took off. Gandhi rose. He was surprisingly nimble for a man nearing eighty. He chivied the fly out of the office, ignoring Model, who watched his performance in openmouthed wonder.

"I hope it will not trouble you again," Gandhi said, returning as calmly as if he had done nothing out of the ordinary. "I am one of those who practice ahimsa: I will do not injury to any living thing."

Model remembered the fall of Moscow, and the smell of burning bodies filling the chilly autumn air. He remembered machine guns knocking down cossack cavalry before they could close, and the screams of the wounded horses, more heartrending than any woman's. He knew of other things, too, things he had not seen for himself and of which he had no desire to learn more.

"*Herr* Gandhi," he said, "how do you propose to bend to your will someone who opposes you, if you will not use force for the purpose?"

"I have never said I will not use force, sir." Gandhi's smile invited the field marshal to enjoy with him the distinction he was making. "I will not use violence. If my people refuse to cooperate in any way with yours, how can you compel them? What choice will you have but to grant us leave to do as we will?"

Without the intelligence estimates he had read, Model would have dismissed the Indian as a madman. No madman, though, could have caused the British so much trouble. But perhaps the decadent Raj simply had not made him afraid. Model tried again. "You understand that what you have said is treason against the Reich," he said harshly.

Gandhi bowed in his seat. "You may, of course, do what you will with me. My spirit will in any case survive among my people."

Model felt his face heat. Few men were immune to fear. Just his luck, he thought sourly, to have run into one of them. "I warn you, *Herr* Gandhi, to obey the authority of the officials of the Reich, or it will be the worse for you."

"I will do what I believe to be right, and nothing else. If you Germans exert yourselves toward the freeing of India, joyfully will I work with you. If not, then I regret we must be foes."

The field marshal gave him one last chance to see reason. "Were it you and I alone, there might be some doubt as to what would happen." Not much, he thought, not when Gandhi was twenty-odd years older and thin enough to break like a stick. He fought down the irrelevance, went on, "But where, *Herr* Gandhi, is your *Wehrmacht*?"

Of all things, he had least expected to amuse the Indian again. Yet Gandhi's eyes unmistakably twinkled behind the lenses of his spectacles. "Field Marshal, I have an army, too."

Model's patience, never of the most enduring sort, wore thin all at once. "Get out!" he snapped.

Gandhi stood, bowed, and departed. Major Lasch stuck his head into the office. The field marshal's glare drove him out again in a hurry.

"Well?" Jawaharlal Nehru paced back and forth. Tall, slim, and saturnine, he towered over Gandhi without dominating him. "Dare we use the same policies against the Germans that we employed against the English?"

"If we wish our land free, dare we do otherwise?" Gandhi replied. "They will not grant our wish of their own volition. Model struck me as a man not much different from various British leaders whom we have succeeded in vexing in the past." He smiled at the memory of what passive resistance had done to officials charged with combating it.

"Very well, satyagraha it is." But Nehru was not smiling. He had less humor than his older colleague.

Gandhi teased him gently: "Do you fear another spell in prison, then?" Both men had spent time behind bars during the war, until the British released them in a last, vain effort to rally the support of the Indian people to the Raj.

"You know better." Nehru refused to be drawn, and persisted, "The rumors that come out of Europe frighten me."

"Do you tell me you take them seriously?" Gandhi shook his head in surprise and a little reproof. "Each side in any war will always paint its opponents as blackly as it can."

"I hope you are right, and that that is all. Still, I confess I would feel more at ease with what we plan to do if you found me one Jew, officer or other rank, in the army now occupying us."

"You would be hard-pressed to find any among the forces they defeated. The British have little love for Jews, either."

"Yes, but I daresay it could be done. With the Germans, they are banned by law. The English would never make such a rule. And while the laws are vile enough, I think of the tales that man Wiesenthal told, the one who came here the gods know how across Russia and Persia from Poland."

"Those I do not believe," Gandhi said firmly. "No nation could act in that way and hope to survive. Where could men be found to carry out such horrors?"

"*Azad Hind,*" Nehru said, quoting the "Free India" motto of the locals who had fought on the German side.

But Gandhi shook his head. "They are only soldiers, doing as soldiers have always done. Wiesenthal's claims are for an entirely different order of bestiality, one that could not exist without destroying the fabric of the state that gave it birth."

"I hope very much you are right," Nehru said.

Walther Model slammed the door behind him hard enough to make his aide, whose desk faced away from the field marshal's office, jump in alarm. "Enough of this twaddle for one day," Model said. "I need schnapps, to get the taste of these Indians out of my mouth. Come along if you care to, Dieter."

"Thank you, sir." Major Lasch threw down his pen, eagerly got to his feet. "I sometimes think conquering India was easier than ruling it will be."

Model rolled his eyes. "I *know* it was. I would ten times rather be planning a new campaign than sitting here bogged down in pettifogging details. The sooner Berlin sends me people trained in colonial administration, the happier I will be."

The bar might have been taken from an English pub. It was dark, quiet, and paneled in walnut; a dartboard still hung on the wall. But a German sergeant in field gray stood behind the bar, and, despite the lazily turning ceiling fan, the temperature was close to thirty-five Celsius. The one might have been possible in occupied London, the other not.

Model knocked back his first shot at a gulp. He sipped his second more slowly, savoring it. Warmth spread through him, warmth that had nothing to do with the heat of the evening. He leaned back in his chair, steepled his fingers. "A long day," he said.

"Yes, sir," Lasch agreed. "After the affrontery of that Gandhi, any day would seem a long one. I've rarely seen you so angry." Considering Model's temper, that was no small statement.

"Ah yes, Gandhi." Model's tone was reflective rather than irate; Lasch looked at him curiously. The field marshal said, "For my money, he's worth a dozen of the ordinary sort."

"Sir?" The aide no longer tried to hide his surprise.

"He is an honest man. He tells me what he thinks, and he will stick by that. I may kill him—I may have to kill him—but he and I will both know why, and I will not change his mind." Model took another sip of schnapps. He hesitated, as if unsure whether to go on. At last he did. "Do you know, Dieter, after he left I had a vision."

"Sir?" Now Lasch was alarmed.

The field marshal might have read his aide's thoughts. He chuckled wryly. "No, no, I am not about to swear off eating beefsteak and wear sandals instead of my boots, that I promise. But I saw myself as a Roman procurator, listening to the rantings of some early Christian priest."

Lasch raised an eyebrow. Such musings were unlike Model, who was usually direct to the point of bluntness and altogether materialistic—assets in the makeup of a general officer. The major cautiously sounded these unexpected depths: "How do you suppose the Roman felt, facing that kind of man?"

"Bloody confused, I suspect," Model said, which sounded more like him. "And because he and his comrades did not know how to handle such fanatics, you and I are Christians today, Dieter."

"So we are." The major rubbed his chin. "Is that a bad thing?"

Model laughed and finished his drink. "From your point of view or mine, no. But I doubt that old Roman would agree with us, any more than Gandhi agrees with me over what will happen next here. But then, I have two advantages over the dead procurator." He raised his finger; the sergeant hurried over to fill his glass.

At Lasch's nod, the young man also poured more schnapps for him. The major drank, then said, "I should hope so. We are more civilized, more sophisticated, than the Romans ever dreamed of being."

But Model was still in that fey mood. "Are we? My procurator was such a sophisticate that he tolerated anything, and never saw the danger in a foe who would not do the same. Our Christian God, though, is a jealous god who puts up with no rivals. And one who is a National Socialist serves also the *Volk*, to whom he owes sole loyalty. I am immune to Gandhi's virus in a way the Roman was not to the Christian's."

"Yes, that makes sense," Lasch agreed after a moment. "I had not thought of it in that way, but I see it is so. And what is our other advantage over the Roman procurator?"

Suddenly the field marshal looked hard and cold, much the way he had looked leading the tanks of Third Panzer against the Kremlin compound. "The machine gun," he said.

The rising sun's rays made the sandstone of the Red Fort seem even more the color of blood. Gandhi frowned and turned his back on the fortress, not caring for that thought. Even at dawn the air was warm and muggy.

"I wish you were not here," Nehru told him. The younger man lifted his trademark fore-and-aft cap, scratched his graying hair, and glanced at the crowd growing around them. "The Germans' orders forbid assemblies, and they will hold you responsible for this gathering."

"I am, am I not?" Gandhi replied. "Would you have me send my followers into a danger I do not care to face myself? How would I presume to lead them afterward?"

"A general does not fight in the front ranks," Nehru came back. "If you are lost to our cause, will we be able to go on?"

"If not, then surely the cause is not worthy, yes? Now let us be going."

Nehru threw his hands in the air. Gandhi nodded, satisfied, and worked his way toward the head of the crowd. Men and women stepped aside to let him through. Still shaking his head, Nehru followed.

The crowd slowly began to march east up Chandni Chauk, the Street of Silversmiths. Some of the fancy shops had been wrecked in the fighting, more looted afterward. But others were opening up, their owners as happy to take German money as they had been to serve the British before.

One of the proprietors, a man who had managed to stay plump even through the past year of hardship, came rushing out of his shop when he saw the procession go by. He ran to the head of the march and spotted Nehru, whose height and elegant dress singled him out.

"Are you out of your mind?" the silversmith shouted. "The Germans have banned assemblies. If they see you, something dreadful will happen."

"Is it not dreadful that they take away the liberty that properly belongs to us?" Gandhi asked. The silversmith spun round. His eyes grew wide when he recognized the man who was speaking to him. Gandhi went on, "Not only is it dreadful, it is wrong. And so we do not recognize the German's right to ban anything we may choose to do. Join us, will you?"

"Great-souled one, I—I—," the silversmith spluttered. Then his glance slid past Gandhi. "The Germans!" he squeaked. He turned and ran.

Gandhi led the procession toward the approaching squad. The Germans stamped down Chandni Chauk as if they expected the people in front of them to melt from their path. Their gear, Gandhi thought, was not that much different from what British soldiers wore: ankle boots, shorts, and open-necked tunics. But their coal-scuttle helmets gave them a look of sullen, beetle-browed ferocity the British tin hat did not convey. Even for a man of Gandhi's equanimity, it was daunting, as no doubt it was intended to be.

"Hello, my friends," he said. "Do any of you speak English?"

"I speak it, a little," one of them replied. His shoulder straps had the twin pips of a sergeant major: he was the squad leader, then. He hefted his rifle, not menacingly, Gandhi thought, but to emphasize what he was saying. "Go to your homes back. This coming together is *verboten.*"

"I am sorry, but I must refuse to obey your order," Gandhi said. "We are walking peacefully on our own street in our own city. We will harm no one, no matter what; this I promise you. But walk we will, as we wish." He repeated himself until he was sure the sergeant major understood.

The German spoke to his comrades in his own language. One of the soldiers raised his gun and with a nasty smile pointed it at Gandhi. The Indian nodded politely. The German blinked to see him unafraid. The sergeant major slapped the rifle down. One of his men had a field telephone on his back. The sergeant major cranked it, waited for a reply, spoke urgently into it.

Nehru caught Gandhi's eye. His dark, tired gaze was full of worry. Somehow that nettled Gandhi more than the Germans' arrogance in ordering about his people. He began to walk forward again. The marchers followed him, flowing around the German squad like water flowing round a boulder.

The soldier who had pointed his rifle at Gandhi shouted in alarm. He brought up the weapon again. The sergeant major barked at him. Reluctantly, he lowered it.

"A sensible man," Gandhi said to Nehru. "He sees we do no injury to him or his, and so does none to us."

"Sadly, though, not everyone is so sensible," the younger man replied, "as witness his lance corporal there. And even a sensible man may not be well inclined to us. You notice he is still on the telephone."

The phone on Field Marshal Model's desk jangled. He jumped and swore; he had left orders he was to be disturbed only for an emergency. He had to find time to work. He picked up the phone. "This had better be good," he growled without preamble.

He listened, swore again, slammed the receiver down. "*Lasch!*" he shouted.

It was his aide's turn to jump. "Sir?"

"Don't just sit there on your fat arse," the field marshal said unfairly. "Call out my car and driver, and quickly. Then belt on your sidearm and come along. The Indians are doing something stupid. Oh yes, order out a platoon and have them come after us. Up on Chandni Chauk, the trouble is."

Lasch called for the car and the troops, then hurried after Model. "A riot?" he asked as he caught up.

"No, no." Model moved his stumpy frame along so fast that the taller Lasch had to trot beside him. "Some of Gandhi's tricks, damn him."

The field marshal's Mercedes was waiting when he and his aide hurried out of the Viceregal Palace. "Chandni Chauk," Model snapped as the driver held the door open for him. After that he sat in furious silence as the powerful car roared up Irwin Road, round a third of Connaught Circle, and north on Chelmsford Road past the bombed-out railway station until, for no reason Model could see, the street's name changed to Qutb Road.

A little later the driver said, "Some kind of disturbance up ahead, sir."

"Disturbance?" Lasch echoed, leaning forward to peer through the windscreen. "It's a whole damned regiment's worth of Indians coming at us. Don't they know better than that? And what the devil," he added, his voice rising, "are so many of our men doing ambling along beside them? Don't they know they're supposed to break up this sort of thing?" In his indignation he did not notice he was repeating himself.

"I suspect they don't," Model said dryly. "Gandhi, I gather, can have that effect on people who aren't ready for his peculiar brand of stubbornness. That, however, does not include me." He tapped the driver on the shoulder. "Pull up about two hundred meters in front of the first rank of them, Joachim."

"Yes, sir."

Even before the car had stopped moving, Model jumped out of it. Lasch, hand on his pistol, was close behind, protesting, "What if one of those fanatics has a gun?"

"Then Colonel General Weidling assumes command, and a lot of Indians end up dead." Model strode toward Gandhi, ignoring the German troops who were drawing themselves to stiff, horrified attention at the sight of his field marshal's uniform. He would deal with them later. For the moment, Gandhi was more important.

He had stopped—which meant the rest of the marchers did, too—and was waiting politely for Model to approach. The German commandant was not impressed. He thought Gandhi sincere, and could not doubt his courage, but none of that mattered at all. He said harshly, "You were warned against this sort of behavior."

Gandhi looked him in the eye. They were very much of a height. "And I told you, I do not recognize your right to give such orders. This is our country, not yours, and if some of us choose to walk on our streets, we will do so."

From behind Gandhi, Nehru's glance flicked worriedly from one of the antagonists to the other. Model noticed him only peripherally; if Nehru was already afraid, he could be handled whenever necessary. Gandhi was a tougher nut. The field marshal waved at the crowd behind the old man. "You are responsible for all these people. If harm come to them, you will be to blame."

"Why should harm come to them? They are not soldiers. They do not attack your men. I told that to one of your sergeants, and he understood it, and refrained from hindering us. Surely you, sir, an educated, cultured man, can see that what I say is self-evident truth."

Model turned his head to speak to his aide in German: "If we did not have Goebbels, this would be the one for his job." He shuddered to think of the propaganda victory Gandhi would win if he got away with flouting German ordinances. The whole countryside would be boiling with partisans in a week. And he had already managed to hoodwink some Germans into letting him do it!

Then Gandhi surprised him again. *"Ich danke Ihnen, Herr Generalfeldmarschall, aber das glaube ich kein Kompliment zu sein,"* he said in slow but clear German: "I thank you, Field Marshal, but I believe that to be no compliment."

Having to hold his monocle in place helped Model keep his face straight. "Take it however you like," he said. "Get these people off the street, or they and you will face the consequences. We will do what you force us to."

"I force you to nothing. As for these people who follow, each does so of his or her own free will. We are free, and will show it, not by violence, but through firmness in truth."

Now Model listened with only half an ear. He had kept Gandhi talking long enough for the platoon he had ordered out to arrive. Half a dozen SdKfz 251 armored personnel carriers came clanking up. The men piled out of them. "Give me a firing line, three ranks deep," Model shouted. As the troopers scrambled to obey, he waved the half-tracks into position behind them, all but blocking Qutb Road. The half-tracks' commanders swiveled the machine guns at the front of the vehicles' troop compartments so they bore on the Indians.

Gandhi watched these preparations as calmly as if they had nothing to do with him. Again Model had to admire his calm. Gandhi's followers were less able to keep fear from their faces. Very few, though, used the pause to slip away. Gandhi's discipline was a long way from the military sort, but effective all the same.

"Tell them to disperse now, and we can still get away without bloodshed," the field marshal said.

"We will shed no one's blood, sir. But we will continue on our pleasant journey. Moving carefully, we will, I think, be able to get between your large lorries there." Gandhi turned to wave his people forward once more.

"You insolent—" Rage choked Model, which was as well, for it kept him from cursing Gandhi like a fishwife. To give him time to master his temper, he plucked his monocle from his eye and began polishing the lens with a silk handkerchief. He replaced the monocle, started to jam the handkerchief back into his trouser pocket, then suddenly had a better idea.

"Come, Lasch," he said, and started toward the waiting German troops. About halfway to them, he dropped the handkerchief on the ground. He spoke in loud, simple German so his men and Gandhi could both follow: "If any Indians come past this spot, I wash my hands of them."

He might have known Gandhi would have a comeback ready. "That is what Pilate said also, you will recall, sir."

"Pilate washed his hands to evade responsibility," the field marshal answered steadily; he was in control of himself again. "I accept it: I am responsible to my Führer and to the *Oberkommando-Wehrmacht* for maintaining Reichs control over India, and will do what I see fit to carry out that obligation."

For the first time since they had come to know each other, Gandhi looked sad. "I too, sir, have my responsibilities." He bowed slightly to Model.

Lasch chose that moment to whisper in his commander's ear: "Sir, what of our men over there? Had you planned to leave them in the line of fire?"

The field marshal frowned. He had planned to do just that; the wretches deserved no better, for being taken in by Gandhi. But Lasch had a point. The platoon might balk at shooting countrymen, if it came to that. "You men," Model said sourly, jabbing his marshal's baton at them, "fall in behind the armored personnel carriers, at once."

The Germans' boots pounded on the macadam as they dashed to obey. They were still all right, then, with a clear order in front of them. Something, Model thought, but not much.

He had also worried that the Indians would take advantage of the moment of confusion to press forward, but they did not. Gandhi and Nehru and a couple of other men were arguing among themselves. Model nodded once. Some of them knew he was earnest, then. And Gandhi's followers' discipline, as the field marshal had thought a few minutes ago, was not of the military sort. He could not simply issue an order and know his will would be done.

"I issue no orders," Gandhi said. "Let each man follow his conscience as he will—what else is freedom?"

"They will follow *you* if you go forward, great-souled one," Nehru replied, "and that German, I fear, means to carry out his threat. Will you throw your life away, and those of your countrymen?"

"I will not throw my life away," Gandhi said, but before the men around him could relax, he went on, "I will gladly give it, if freedom requires that. I am but one man. If I fall, others will surely carry on; perhaps the memory of me will serve to make them more steadfast."

He stepped forward.

"Oh damnation," Nehru said softly, and followed.

For all his vigor, Gandhi was far from young. Nehru did not need to nod to the marchers close by him; of their own accord, they hurried ahead of the man who had led them for so long, forming with their bodies a barrier between him and the German guns.

He tried to go faster. "Stop! Leave me my place! What are you doing?" he cried, though in his heart he understood only too well.

"This once, they will not listen to you," Nehru said.

"But they must!" Gandhi peered through eyes dimmed now by tears as well as age. "Where is that stupid handkerchief? We must be almost to it!"

"For the last time, I warn you to halt!" Model shouted. The Indians still came on. The sound of their feet, sandal-clad or bare, was like a growing murmur on the pavement, very different from the clatter of German boots. "Fools!" the field marshal muttered under his breath. He turned to his men. "Take your aim!"

The advance slowed when the rifles came up; of that Model was certain. For a moment he thought that ultimate threat would be enough to bring the marchers to their senses. But then they advanced again. The Polish calvary had shown that same reckless bravery, charging with lances and sabers and carbines against the German tanks. Model wondered whether the inhabitants of the *Reichsgeneral-gouvernement* of Poland thought the gallantry worthwhile.

A man stepped on the field marshal's handkerchief. "Fire!" Model said.

A second passed, two. Nothing happened. Model scowled at his men. Gandhi's deviltry had got into them; sneaky as a Jew, he was turning the appearance of weakness into a strange kind of strength. But then trained discipline paid its dividend. One finger tightened on a Mauser trigger. A single shot rang out. As if it were a signal that recalled the other men to their duty, they, too, began to fire. From the armored personnel carriers, the machine guns started their deadly chatter. Model heard screams above the gunfire.

The volley smashed into the front ranks of marchers at close range. Men fell. Others ran, or tried to, only to be held by the power of the stream still advancing behind them. Once begun, the Germans methodically poured fire into the column of Indians. The march dissolved into a panic-stricken mob.

Gandhi still tried to press forward. A fleeing wounded man smashed into him, splashing him with blood and knocking him to the ground. Nehru and another man immediately lay down on top of him.

"Let me up! Let me up!" he shouted.

"No," Nehru screamed in his ear. "With shooting like this, you are in the safest spot you can be. We need you, and need you alive. Now we have martyrs around whom to rally our cause."

"Now we have dead husbands and wives, fathers and mothers. Who will tend to their loved ones?"

Gandhi had no time for more protest. Nehru and the other man hauled him to his feet and dragged him away. Soon they were among their people, all running now from the German guns. A bullet struck the back of the unknown man who was helping Gandhi escape. Gandhi heard the slap of the impact, felt the man jerk. Then the strong grip on him loosened as the man fell.

He tried to tear free from Nehru. Before he could, another Indian laid hold of him. Even at that horrid moment, he felt the irony of his predicament. All his life he had championed individual liberty, and here his own followers were robbing him of his. In other circumstances, it might have been funny.

"In here," Nehru shouted. Several people had already broken down the door to a shop and, Gandhi saw a moment later, the rear exit as well. Then he was hustled into the alley behind the shop, and through a maze of lanes that reminded him of the old Delhi, which, unlike its British-designed sister city, was an Indian town through and through.

At last the nameless man with Gandhi and Nehru knocked on the back door of a tearoom. The woman who opened it gasped to recognize her unexpected guests, then pressed her hands together in front of her and stepped aside to let them in. "You will be safe here," the man said, "at least for a while. Now I must see to my own family."

"From the bottom of our hearts, we thank you," Nehru replied as the fellow hurried away. Gandhi said nothing. He was winded, battered, and filled with anguish at the failure of the march and at the suffering it had brought to so many marchers and to their kinsfolk.

The woman sat the two fugitive leaders at a small table in the kitchen, served them tea and cakes. "I will leave you now, best ones," she said gently, "lest those out front wonder why I neglect them for so long."

Gandhi left the cake on his plate. He sipped the tea. Its warmth began to restore him physically, but the wound in his spirit would never heal. "The Armritsar massacre pales beside this," he said, setting down the empty cup. "There the British panicked and opened fire. This had nothing of panic about it. Model told me what he would do, and he did it." He shook his head, still hardly believing what he had just been through.

"So he did." Nehru had gobbled his cake like a starving wolf, and ate his companion's when he saw Gandhi did not want it. His once immaculate white jacket and pants were torn, filthy, and blood-spattered; his cap sat awry on his head. But his eyes, usually so somber, were lit with a fierce glow. "And by his brutality, he has delivered himself into our hands. No one now can imagine the Germans have anything but their own interests at heart. We will gain followers all over the country. After this, not a wheel will turn in India."

"Yes, I will declare the satyagraha campaign," Gandhi said. "Noncooperation will show how we reject foreign rule, and will cost the Germans dear because they will not be able to exploit us. The combination of nonviolence and determined spirit will surely shame them into granting us our liberty."

"There—you see." Encouraged by his mentor's rally, Nehru rose and came round the table to embrace the older man. "We will triumph yet."

"So we will," Gandhi said, and sighed heavily. He had pursued India's freedom for half his long life, and this change of masters was a setback he had not truly planned for, even after England and Russia fell. The British were finally beginning to listen to him when the Germans swept them aside. Now he had to begin anew. He sighed again. "It will cost our poor people dear, though."

"Cease firing," Model said. Few good targets were left on Qutb Road; almost all the Indians in the procession were down or had run from the guns.

Even after the bullets stopped, the street was far from silent. Most of the people the German platoon had shot were alive and shrieking; as if he needed more proof, the Russian campaign had taught the field marshal how hard human beings were to kill outright.

Still, the din distressed him, and evidently Lasch as well. "We ought to put them out of their misery," the major said.

"So we should." Model had a happy inspiration. "And I know just how. Come with me."

The two men turned their backs on the carnage and walked around the row of armored personnel carriers. As they passed the lieutenant commanding the platoon, Model nodded to him and said, "Well done."

The lieutenant saluted. "Thank you, sir." The soldiers in earshot nodded at one another: nothing bucked up the odds of getting promoted like performing under the commander's eye.

The Germans behind the armored vehicles were not so proud of themselves. They were the ones who had let the march get this big and come this far in the first place. Model slapped his boot with his field marshal's baton. "You all deserve courts-martial," he said coldly, glaring at them. "You know the orders concerning native assemblies, yet there you were tagging along, more like sheepdogs than soldiers." He spat in disgust.

"But sir—," began one of them—a sergeant major, Model saw. He subsided in a hurry when Model's gaze swung his way.

"Speak," the field marshal urged. "Enlighten me—tell me what possessed you to act in the disgraceful way you did. Was it some evil spirit, perhaps? This country abounds with them, if you listen to the natives—as you all too obviously have been."

The sergeant major flushed under Model's sarcasm, but finally burst out, "Sir, it didn't look to me as if they were up to any harm, that's all. The old man heading them up swore they were peaceful, and he looked too feeble to be anything but, if you take my meaning."

Model's smile had all the warmth of a Moscow December night. "And so in your wisdom you set aside the commands you had received. The results of that wisdom you hear now.'' The field marshal briefly let himself listen to the cries of the wounded, a sound the war had taught him to screen out. ''Now then, come with me—yes, you, Sergeant Major, and the rest of your shirkers, too, or those of you who wish to avoid a court.''

As he had known they would, they all trooped after him. ''There is your handiwork,'' he said, pointing to the shambles in the street. His voice hardened. ''You are responsible for those people lying there—had you acted as you should have, you would have broken up that march long before it ever got so far or so large. Now the least you can do is give those people their release.'' He set hands on hips, waited.

No one moved. ''Sir?'' the sergeant major said faintly. He seemed to have become the group's spokesman.

Model made an impatient gesture. ''Go on, finish them. A bullet in the back of the head will quiet them once and for all.''

''In cold blood, sir?'' The sergeant major had not wanted to understand him before. Now he had no choice.

The field marshal was inexorable. ''They—and you—disobeyed Reichs commands. They made themselves liable to capital punishment the moment they gathered. You at least have the chance to atone, by carrying out this just sentence.''

''I don't think I can,'' the sergeant major muttered.

He was probably just talking to himself, but Model gave him no chance to change his mind. He turned to the lieutenant of the platoon that had broken the march. ''Place this man under arrest.'' After the sergeant major had been seized, Model turned his chill, monocled stare at the rest of the reluctant soldiers. ''Any others?''

Two more men let themselves be arrested rather than draw their weapons. The field marshal nodded to the others. ''Carry out your orders.'' He had an after-thought. ''If you find Gandhi or Nehru out there, bring them to me alive.''

The Germans moved out hesitantly. They were no *Einsatzkommandos*, and not used to this kind of work. Some looked away as they administered the first coup de grace; one missed as a result, and had his bullet ricochet off the pavement and almost hit a comrade. But as the soldiers worked their way up Qutb Road, they became quicker, more confident, and more competent. War was like that, Model thought. So soon one became used to what had been unimaginable.

After a while the flat cracks died away, but from lack of targets rather than reluctance. A few at a time, the soldiers returned to Model. ''No sign of the two leaders?'' he asked. They all shook their heads.

''Very well—dismissed. And obey your orders like good Germans henceforward.''

''No further reprisals?'' Lasch asked as the relieved troopers hurried away.

''No, let them go. They carried out their part of the bargain, and I will meet mine. I am a fair man, after all, Dieter.''

''Very well, sir.''

*   *   *

Gandhi listened with undisguised dismay as the shopkeeper babbled out his tale of horror. "This is madness!" he cried.

"I doubt Field Marshal Model, for his part, understands the principle of ahimsa," Nehru put in. Neither Gandhi nor he knew exactly where they were: a safe house somewhere not far from the center of Delphi was the best guess he could make. The men who brought the shopkeeper were masked. What one did not know, one could not tell the Germans if captured.

"Neither do you," the older man replied, which was true; Nehru had a more pragmatic nature than Gandhi. Gandhi went on, "Rather more to the point, neither do the British. And Model, to speak to, seemed no different from any high-ranking British military man. His specialty has made him harsh and rigid, but he is not stupid and does not appear unusually cruel."

"Just a simple soldier, doing his job." Nehru's irony was palpable.

"He must have gone insane," Gandhi said; it was the only explanation that made even the slightest sense of the massacre of the wounded. "Undoubtedly he will be censured when the news of this atrocity reaches Berlin, as General Dyer was by the British after Armritsar."

"Such is to be hoped." But again Nehru did not sound hopeful.

"How could it be otherwise, after such an appalling action? What government, what leaders could fail to be filled with humiliation and remorse at it?"

Model strode into the mess. The officers stood and raised their glasses in salute. "Sit, sit," the field marshal growled, using gruffness to hide his pleasure.

An Indian servant brought him a fair imitation of roast beef and Yorkshire pudding: better than they were eating in London these days, he thought. The servant was silent and unsmiling, but Model would only have noticed more about him had he been otherwise. Servants were supposed to assume a cloak of invisibility.

When the meal was done, Model took out his cigar case. The *Waffen-SS* officer on his left produced a lighter. Model leaned forward, puffed a cigar into life. "My thanks, *Brigadeführer*," the field marshal said. He had little use for SS titles of rank, but brigade commander was at least recognizably close to brigadier.

"Sir, it is my great pleasure," Jürgen Stroop declared. "You could not have handled things better. A lesson for the Indians—less than they deserve, too" (he also took no notice of the servant) "and a good one for your men as well. We train ours harshly, too."

Model nodded. He knew about SS training methods. No one denied the daring of the *Waffen-SS* divisions. No one (except the SS) denied that the *Wehrmacht* had better officers.

Stroop drank. "A lesson," he repeated in a pedantic tone that went oddly with the SS's reputation for aggressiveness. "Force is the only thing the racially inferior can understand. Why, when I was in Warsaw—"

That had been four or five years ago, Model suddenly recalled. Stroop had been a *Brigadeführer* then, too, if memory served; no wonder he was still one now, even after all the hard fighting since. He was lucky not to be a buck private. Imagine letting a pack of desperate, starving Jews chew up the finest troops in the world.

And imagine, afterward, submitting a seventy-five-page operations report bound in leather and grandiosely called "The Warsaw Ghetto Is No More." And imagine, with all that, having the crust to boast about it afterward. No wonder the man sounded like a pompous ass. He *was* a pompous ass, and an inept butcher to boot. Model had done enough butchery before today's work—anyone who fought in Russia learned all about butchery—but he had never botched it.

He did not revel in it, either. He wished Stroop would shut up. He thought about telling the *Brigadeführer* he would sooner have been listening to Gandhi. The look on the fellow's face, he thought, would be worth it. But no. One could never be sure who was listening. Better safe.

The shortwave set crackled to life. It was in a secret cellar, a tiny, dark, hot room lit only by the glow of its dial and by the red end of the cigarette in its owner's mouth. The Germans had made not turning in a radio a capital crime. Of course, Gandhi thought, harboring him was also a capital crime. That weighed on his conscience. But the man knew the risk he was taking.

The fellow (Gandhi knew him only as Lal) fiddled with the controls. "Usually we listen to the Americans," he said. "There is some hope of truth from them. But tonight you want to hear Berlin."

"Yes," Gandhi said. "I must learn what action is to be taken against Model."

"If any," Nehru added. He was once again impeccably attired in white, which made him the most easily visible object in the cellar.

"We have argued this before," Gandhi said tiredly. "No government can uphold the author of a cold-blooded slaughter of wounded men and women. The world would cry out in abhorrence."

Lal said, "That government controls too much of the world already." He adjusted the tuning knob again. After a burst of static, the strains of a Strauss waltz filled the little room. Lal grunted in satisfaction. "We are a little early yet."

After a few minutes the incongruously sweet music died away. "This is Radio Berlin's English-language channel," an announcer declared. "In a moment, the news program." Another German tune rang out: the *Horst Wessel* song. Gandhi's nostrils flared with distaste.

A new voice came over the air. "Good day. This is William Joyce." The nasal Oxonian accent was that of the archetypal British aristocrat, now vanished from India as well as England. It was the accent that flavored Gandhi's own English, and Nehru's as well. In fact, Gandhi had heard, Joyce was a New York-born rabble-rouser of Irish blood who also happened to be a passionately sincere Nazi. The combination struck the Indian as distressing.

"What did the English used to call him?" Nehru murmured. "Lord Haw-Haw?"

Gandhi waved his friends to silence. Joyce was reading the news, or what the Propaganda Ministry in Berlin wanted to present to English-speakers as the news.

Most of it was on the dull side: a trade agreement between Manchukuo, Japanese-dominated China, and Japanese-dominated Siberia; advances by German-supported French troops against American-supported French troops in a war by proxy in the African jungles. Slightly more interesting was the German warning about American interference in the East Asia Co-Prosperity Sphere.

One day soon, Gandhi thought sadly, the two mighty powers of the Old World would turn on the one great nation that stood between them. He feared the outcome. Thinking herself secure behind ocean barriers, the United States had stayed out of the European war. Now the war was bigger than Europe, and the ocean barriers no longer, but highways for her foes.

Lord Haw-Haw droned on and on. He gloated over the fate of rebels hunted down in Scotland: they were publicly hanged. Nehru leaned forward. "Now," he guessed. Gandhi nodded.

But the commentator passed on to unlikely sounding boasts about the prosperity of Europe under the New Order. Against his will, Gandhi felt anger rise in him. Were Indians too insignificant to the Reich even to be mentioned?

More music came from the radio: the first bars of the other German anthem, "*Deutschland über alles.*" William Joyce said solemnly, "And now, a special announcement from the Ministry for Administration of Acquired Territories. *Reichsminister* Reinhard Heydrich commends Field Marshal Walther Model's heroic suppression of insurrection in India, and warns that his leniency will not be repeated."

"Leniency!" Nehru and Gandhi burst out together, the latter making it into as much of a curse as he allowed himself.

As if explaining to them, the voice on the radio went on, "Henceforward, hostages will be taken at the slightest sound of disorder, and will be executed forthwith if it continues. Field Marshal Model had also placed a reward of fifty thousand rupees on the capture of the criminal revolutionary Gandhi, and twenty-five thousand on the capture of his henchman Nehru."

"*Deutschland über alles*" rang out again, to signal the end of the announcement. Joyce went on to the next piece of news. "Turn that off," Nehru said after a moment. Lal obeyed, plunging the cellar into complete darkness. Nehru surprised Gandhi by laughing. "I have never before been the henchman of a criminal revolutionary."

The older man might as well not have heard him. "They commended him," he said. "Commended!" Disbelief put the full tally of his years in his voice, which usually sounded much stronger and younger.

"What will you do?" Lal asked quietly. A match flared, dazzling in the dark, as he lit another cigarette.

"They shall not govern India in this fashion," Gandhi snapped. "Not a soul will cooperate with them from now on. We outnumber them a thousand to one; what can they accomplish without us? We shall use that to full advantage."

"I hope the price is not more than the people can pay," Nehru said.

"The British shot us down, too, and we were on our way toward prevailing," Gandhi said stoutly. As he would not have a few days before, though, he added, "So do I."

Field Marshal Model scowled and yawned at the same time. The pot of tea that should have been on his desk was nowhere to be found. His stomach growled. A plate of rolls should have been beside the teapot.

"How am I supposed to get anything done without breakfast?" he asked rhetorically (no one was in the office to hear him complain). Rhetorical complaint was not enough to satisfy him. "Lasch!" he shouted.

"Sir?" The aide came rushing in.

Model jerked his chin at the empty space on his desk where the silver tray full of good things should have been. "What's become of what's his name? Naoroji, that's it. If he's home with a hangover, he could have had the courtesy to let us know."

"I will inquire with the liaison officer for native personnel, sir, and also have the kitchen staff send you up something to eat." Lasch picked up a telephone, spoke into it. The longer he talked, the less happy he looked. When he turned back to the field marshal, his expression was a good match for the stony one Model often wore. He said, "None of the locals has shown up for work today, sir."

"What? None?" Model's frown made his monocle dig into his cheek. He hesitated. "I will feel better if you tell me some new hideous malady has broken out among them."

Lasch spoke with the liaison officer again. He shook his head. "Nothing like that, sir—or at least," he corrected himself with the caution that made him a good aide, "nothing Captain Wechsler knows about."

Model's phone rang again. It startled him; he jumped. "*Bitte?*" he growled into the mouthpiece, embarrassed at starting even though only Lash had seen. He listened. Then he growled again, in good earnest this time. He slammed the phone down. "That was our railway officer. Hardly any natives are coming into the station."

The phone rang again. "*Bitte?*" This time it was a swearword. Model snarled, cutting off whatever the man on the other end was saying, and hung up. "The damned clerks are staying out, too," he shouted at Lasch, as if it were the major's fault. "I know what's wrong with the blasted locals, by God—an overdose of Gandhi, that's what."

"We should have shot him down in that riot he led," Lasch said angrily.

"Not for lack of effort that we didn't," Model said. Now that he saw where his trouble was coming from, he began thinking like a General Staff-trained officer again. That discipline went deep in him. His voice was cool and musing as he corrected his aide: "It was no riot, Dieter. That man is a skilled agitator. Armed with no more than words, he gave the British fits. Remember that the Führer started out as an agitator, too."

"Ah, but the Führer wasn't above breaking heads to back up what he said." Lasch smiled reminiscently, and raised a fist. He was a Munich man, and wore on his sleeve the hash mark that showed party membership before 1933.

But the field marshal said, "You think Gandhi doesn't? His way is to break them from the inside out, to make his foes doubt themselves. Those soldiers who took courts rather than obey their commanding officer had their heads broken, wouldn't you say? Think of him as a Russian tank commander, say, rather than as a political agitator. He is fighting us every bit as much as the Russians did."

Lasch thought about it. Plainly he did not like it. "A coward's way of fighting."

"The weak cannot use the weapons of the strong," Model shrugged. "He does what he can, and skillfully. But I can make his backers doubt themselves, too: see if I don't."

"Sir?"

"We'll start with the railway workers. They are the most essential to have back on the job, yes? Get a list of names. Cross off every twentieth one. Send a squad to each of those homes, haul the slackers out, and shoot them in the street. If the survivors don't report tomorrow, do it again. Keep at it every day until they go back to work or no workers are left."

"Yes, sir." Lasch hesitated. At last he asked, "Are you sure, sir?"

"Have you a better idea, Dieter? We have a dozen divisions here; Gandhi has the whole subcontinent. I have to convince them in a hurry that obeying me is a better idea than obeying him. Obeying is what counts. I don't care a pfennig as to whether they love me. *Oderint, dum metuant.*"

"Sir?" The major had no Latin.

" 'Let them hate, so long as they fear.' "

"Ah," Lasch said. "Yes, I like that." He fingered his chion as he thought. "In aid of which, the Muslims hereabouts like the Hindus none too well. I daresay we could use them to help hunt Gandhi down."

"Now that *I* like," Model said. "Most of our Indian Legion lads are Muslims. They will know people, or know people who know people. And"—the field marshal chuckled cynically—"the reward will do no harm, either. Now get those feelers in motion—and if they pay off, you'll probably have earned yourself a new pip on your shoulder boards."

"Thank you very much, sir!"

"My pleasure. As I say, you'll have earned it. So long as things go as they should, I am a very easy man to get along with. Even Gandhi could, if he wanted to. He will end up having caused a lot of people to be killed because he does not."

"Yes, sir," Lasch agreed. "If only he would see that, since we have won India from the British, we will not turn around and tamely yield it to those who could not claim it for themselves."

"You're turning into a political philosopher now, Dieter?"

"Ha! Not likely." But the major looked pleased as he picked up the phone.

"My dear friend, my ally, my teacher, we are losing," Nehru said as the messenger scuttled away from this latest in a series of what were hopefully called safe houses. "Day by day, more people return to their jobs."

Gandhi shook his head, slowly, as if the motion caused him physical pain. "But they must not. Each one who cooperated with the Germans sets back the day of his own freedom."

"Each one who fails to ends up dead," Nehru said dryly. "Most men lack your courage, great-souled one. To them, that carries more weight than the other. Some are willing to resist, but would rather take up arms than the restraint of satyagraha."

"If they take up arms, they will be defeated. The British could not beat the Germans with guns and tanks and planes; how shall we? Besides, if we shoot a German here and there, we give them the excuse they need to strike at us. When one of their lieutenants was waylaid last month, their bombers leveled a village in reprisal. Against those who fight through nonviolence, they have no such justification."

"They do not seem to need one, either," Nehru pointed out.

Before Gandhi could reply to that, a man burst into the hovel where they were hiding. "You must flee!" he cried. "The Germans have found this place! They are coming. Out with me, quick! I have a cart waiting."

Nehru snatched up the canvas bag in which he carried his few belongings. For a man used to being something of a dandy, the haggard life of a fugitive came hard. Gandhi had never wanted much. Now that he had nothing, that did not disturb him. He rose calmly, followed the man who had come to warn them.

"Hurry!" the fellow shouted as they scrambled into his oxcart while the hump-backed cattle watched indifferently with their liquid brown eyes. When Gandhi and Nehru were lying in the cart, the man piled blankets and straw mats over them. He scrambled up to take the reins, saying, *"Inshallah*, we shall be safely away from here before the platoon arrives." He flicked a switch over the backs of the cattle. They lowed indignantly. The cart rattled away.

Lying in the sweltering semidarkness under the concealment the man had draped on him, Gandhi peered through chinks, trying to figure out where in Delhi he was going next. He had played the game more than once these past few weeks, though he knew doctrine said he should not. The less he knew, the less he could reveal. Unlike most men, though, he was confident he could not be made to talk against his will.

"We are using the technique the American Poe called the 'purloined letter,' I see," he remarked to Nehru. "We will be close by the German barracks. They will not think to look for us there."

The younger man frowned. "I did not know we had safe houses there," he said. Then he relaxed, as well as he could when folded into too small a space. "Of course, I do not pretend to know everything there is to know about such matters. It would be dangerous if I did."

"I was thinking much the same myself, though with me as subject of the sentence." Gandhi laughed quietly. "Try as we will, we always have ourselves at the center of things, don't we?"

He had to raise his voice to finish. An armored personnel carrier came rumbling and rattling toward them, getting louder as it approached. The silence when the driver suddenly killed the engine was a startling contrast to the previous racket. Then there was noise again, as soldiers shouted in German.

"What are they saying?" Nehru asked.

"Hush," Gandhi said absently: not from ill manners, but out of the concentration he needed to follow German at all. After a moment he resumed, "They are swearing at a black-bearded man, asking why he flagged them down."

"Why would anyone flag down German sol—" Nehru began, then stopped in abrupt dismay. The fellow who burst into their hiding place wore a bushy black beard. "Now we better get out of—" Again Nehru broke off in mid-sentence, this time because the oxcart driver was throwing off the coverings that concealed his two passengers.

Nehru started to get to his feet so he could try to scramble out and run. Too late—a rifle barrel that looked wide as a tunnel was shoved in his face as a German came dashing up to the cart. The big curved magazine said the gun was one of the automatic assault rifles that had wreaked such havoc among the British infantry. A burst would turn a man into bloody hash. Nehru sank back in despair.

Gandhi, less spry than his friend, had only sat up in the bottom of the cart. "Good day, gentlemen," he said to the Germans peering down at him. His tone took no notice of their weapons.

"Down." The word was in such gutturally accented Hindi that Gandhi hardly understood it, but the accompanying gesture with a rifle was unmistakable.

His face a mask of misery, Nehru got out of the cart. A German helped Gandhi descend. *"Danke,"* he said. The soldier nodded gruffly. He pointed the barrel of his rifle—toward the armored personnel carrier.

"My rupees!" the black-bearded man shouted.

Nehru turned on him, so quickly he almost got shot for it. "Your thirty pieces of silver, you mean," he cried.

"Ah, a British education," Gandhi murmured. No one was listening to him.

"My rupees," the man repeated. He did not understand Nehru; so often, Gandhi thought sadly, that was at the root of everything.

"You'll get them," promised the sergeant leading the German squad. Gandhi wondered if he was telling the truth. Probably so, he decided. The British had had centuries to build a network of Indian clients. Here but a matter of months, the Germans would need all they could find.

"In." The soldier with a few words of Hindi nodded to the back of the armored personnel carrier. Up close, the vehicle took on a war-battered individuality its kind had lacked when they were just big, intimidating shapes rumbling down the highway. It was bullet-scarred and patched in a couple of places, with sheets of steel crudely welded on.

Inside, the jagged lips of the bullet holes had been hammered down so they did not gouge a man's back. The carrier smelled of leather, sweat, tobacco, smokeless powder, and exhaust fumes. It was crowded, all the more so with the two Indians added to its usual contingent. The motor's roar when it started up challenged even Gandhi's equanimity.

Not, he thought with uncharacteristic bitterness, that that equanimity had done him much good.

"They are here, sir," Lasch told Model, then, at the field marshal's blank look, amplified: "Gandhi and Nehru."

Model's eyebrow came down toward his monocle. "I won't bother with Nehru. Now that we have him, take him out and give him a noodle"—army slang for a bullet in the back of the neck—"but don't waste my time over him. Gandhi, now, is interesting. Fetch him in."

"Yes, sir," the major sighed. Model smiled. Lasch did not find Gandhi interesting. Lasch would never carry a field marshal's baton, not if he lived to be ninety.

Model waved away the soldiers who escorted Gandhi into his office. Either of them could have broken the little Indian like a stick. "Have a care," Gandhi said. "If I am the desperate criminal bandit you have styled me, I may overpower you and escape."

"If you do, you will have earned it," Model retorted. "Sit, if you care to."

"Thank you." Gandhi sat. "They took Jawaharlal away. Why have you summoned me instead?"

"To talk for a while, before you join him." Model saw that Gandhi knew what he meant, and that the old man remained unafraid. Not that that would change anything, Model thought, although he respected his opponent's courage the more for his keeping it in the last extremity.

"I will talk, in the hope of persuading you to have mercy on my people. For myself I ask nothing."

Model shrugged. "I was as merciful as the circumstances of war allowed, until you began your campaign against us. Since then I have done what I needed to restore order. When it returns, I may be milder again."

"You seem a decent man," Gandhi said, puzzlement in his voice. "How can you so callously massacre people who have done you no harm?"

"I never would have, had you not urged them to folly."

"Seeking freedom is not folly."

"It is when you cannot gain it—and you cannot. Already your people are losing their stomach for—what do you call it? Passive resistance? A silly notion. A passive resister simply ends up dead, with no chance to hit back at his foe."

That hit a nerve, Model thought. Gandhi's voice was less detached as he answered, "Satyagraha strikes the oppressor's soul, not his body. You must be without honor or conscience, to fail to feel your victims' anguish."

Nettled in turn, the field marshal snapped, "I have honor. I follow the oath of obedience I swore with the army to the Führer and through him to the Reich. I need consider nothing past that."

Now Gandhi's calm was gone. "But he is a madman! What has he done to the Jews of Europe?"

"Removed them," Model said matter-of-factly; *Einsatzgruppe* B had followed Army Group Central to Moscow and beyond. "They were capitalists or Bolsheviks, and either way enemies of the Reich. When an enemy falls into a man's hands, what else is there to do but destroy him, lest he revive to turn the tables one day?"

Gandhi had buried his face in his hands. Without looking at Model, he said, "Make him a friend."

"Even the British knew better than that, or they would not have held India as long as they did," the field marshal snorted. "They must have begun to forget, though, or your movement would have got what it deserves long ago. You first made the mistake of confusing us with them long ago, by the way." He touched a fat dossier on his desk.

"When was that?" Gandhi asked indifferently. The man was beaten now, Model thought with a touch of pride: he had succeeded where a generation of degenerate, decadent Englishmen had failed. Of course, the field marshal told himself, he had beaten the British, too.

He opened the dossier, riffled through it. "Here we are," he said, nodding in satisfaction. "It was after *Kristallnacht*, eh, in 1938, when you urged the German

Jews to play at the same game of passive resistance you were using here. Had they been fools enough to try it, we would have thanked you, you know: it would have let us bag the enemies of the Reich all the more easily.''

"Yes, I made a mistake," Gandhi said. Now he was looking at the field marshal, looking at him with such fierceness that for a moment Model thought he would attack him despite advanced age and effete philosophy. But Gandhi only continued sorrowfully, ''I made the mistake of thinking I faced a regime ruled by conscience, one that could at the very least be shamed into doing that which is right.''

Model refused to be baited. "We do what is right for our *Volk*, for our Reich. We are meant to rule, and rule we do—as you see." The field marshal tapped the dossier again. "You could be sentenced to death for this earlier meddling in the affairs of the fatherland, you know, even without these later acts of insane defiance you have caused.''

"History will judge us," Gandhi warned as the field marshal rose to have him taken away.

Model smiled then. "Winners write history." He watched the two strapping German guards lead the old man off. "A very good morning's work," the field marshal told Lasch when Gandhi was gone. "What's on the menu for lunch?''

"Blood sausage and sauerkraut, I believe.''

"Ah, good. Something to look forward to." Model sat down. He went back to work.

EILEEN GUNN

Stable Strategies for Middle Management

Here's a very funny story that features one of the most bizarre career-advancement ploys that anyone is ever likely to see . . .

Eileen Gunn worked as one of the top-paid technical writers in the country for various large corporations for too many years (doubtless there is *no* resemblance between them and the company portrayed here), which is probably why it took her ten years to make her first three sales—since then she has wised up, plunged herself into decent poverty like everyone else as a free-lance SF writer, and in short order has rapidly made three *more* sales. With luck and continued nonemployment (Business Leaders of the Pacific Northwest: Don't Hire This Woman!), there will soon be a lot more, as she's not only one of the best young writers in the business, but has one of the weirdest imaginations this side of Howard Waldrop (she can occasionally be *seen* just this side of Howard Waldrop in convention photographs; he is the one wearing the Zippy The Pinhead T shirt). Her work has appeared in *Amazing, Proteus, Tales By Moonlight*, and *Isaac Asimov's Science Fiction Magazine*. She lives in Seattle, Washington, where she is eyed warily by her neighbors, and occasionally plays a Radar Angel or the S & M Fairy in the quaint nature festivals indigenous to the region.

STABLE STRATEGIES FOR MIDDLE MANAGEMENT

Eileen Gunn

Our cousin the insect has an external skeleton made of shiny brown chitin, a material that is particularly responsive to the demands of evolution. Just as bioengineering has sculpted our bodies into new forms, so evolution has shaped the early insect's chewing mouthparts into her descendants' chisels, siphons, and stilettos, and has molded from the chitin special tools—pockets to carry pollen, combs to clean her compound eyes, notches on which she can fiddle a song.

—From the popular science
program *Insect People*!

I awoke this morning to discover that bioengineering had made demands upon me during the night. My tongue had turned into a stiletto, and my left hand now contained a small chitinous comb, as if for cleaning a compound eye. Since I didn't have compound eyes, I thought that perhaps this presaged some change to come.

I dragged myself out of bed, wondering how I was going to drink my coffee through a stiletto. Was I now expected to kill my breakfast, and dispense with coffee entirely? I hoped I was not evolving into a creature whose survival depended on early-morning alertness. My circadian rhythms would no doubt keep pace with any physical changes, but my unevolved soul was repulsed at the thought of my waking cheerfully at dawn, ravenous for some wriggly little creature that had arisen even earlier.

I looked down at Greg, still asleep, the edge of our red and white quilt pulled up under his chin. His mouth had changed during the night too, and seemed to contain some sort of a long probe. Were we growing apart?

I reached down with my unchanged hand and touched his hair. It was still shiny brown, soft and thick, luxurious. But along his cheek, under his beard, I could feel patches of sclerotin, as the flexible chitin in his skin was slowly hardening to an impermeable armor.

He opened his eyes, staring blearily forward without moving his head. I could see him move his mouth cautiously, examining its internal changes. He turned his head and looked up at me, rubbing his hair slightly into my hand.

"Time to get up?" he asked. I nodded. "Oh, God," he said. He said this every morning. It was like a prayer.

"I'll make coffee," I said. "Do you want some?"

He shook his head slowly. "Just a glass of apricot nectar," he said. He unrolled his long, rough tongue and looked at it, slightly cross-eyed. "This is real interesting, but it wasn't in the catalog. I'll be sipping lunch from flowers pretty soon. That ought to draw a second glance at Duke's."

"I thought account execs were expected to sip their lunches," I said.

"Not from the flower arrangements . . ." he said, still exploring the odd shape of his mouth. Then he looked up at me and reached up from under the covers. "Come here."

It had been a while, I thought, and I had to get to work. But he did smell terribly attractive. Perhaps he was developing aphrodisiac scent glands. I climbed back under the covers and stretched my body against his. We were both developing chitinous knobs and odd lumps that made this less than comfortable. "How am I supposed to kiss you with a stiletto in my mouth?" I asked.

"There are other things to do. New equipment presents new possibilities." He pushed the covers back and ran his unchanged hands down my body from shoulder to thigh. "Let me know if my tongue is too rough."

It was not.

Fuzzy-minded, I got out of bed for the second time and drifted into the kitchen.

Measuring the coffee into the grinder, I realized that I was no longer interested in drinking it, although it was diverting for a moment to spear the beans with my stiletto. What was the damn thing for, anyhow? I wasn't sure I wanted to find out.

Putting the grinder aside, I poured a can of apricot nectar into a tulip glass. Shallow glasses were going to be a problem for Greg in the future, I thought. Not to mention solid food.

My particular problem, however, if I could figure out what I was supposed to eat for breakfast, was getting to the office in time for my ten A.M. meeting. Maybe I'd just skip breakfast. I dressed quickly and dashed out the door before Greg was even out of bed.

Thirty minutes later, I was more or less awake and sitting in the small conference room with the new marketing manager, listening to him lay out his plan for the Model 2000 launch.

In signing up for his bioengineering program, Harry had chosen specialized primate adaptation, B-E Option No. 4. He had evolved into a text-book example:

small and long-limbed, with forward-facing eyes for judging distances and long, grasping fingers to keep him from falling out of his tree.

He was dressed for success in a pin-striped three-piece suit that fit his simian proportions perfectly. I wondered what premium he paid for custom-made. Or did he patronize a ready-to-wear shop that catered especially to primates?

I listened as he leaped agilely from one ridiculous marketing premise to the next. Trying to borrow credibility from mathematics and engineering, he used wildly metaphoric bizspeak, "factoring in the need for pipeline throughout," "fine-tuning the media mix," without even cracking a smile.

Harry had been with the company only a few months, straight from business school. He saw himself as a much-needed infusion of talent. I didn't like him, but I envied his ability to root through his subconscious and toss out one half-formed idea after another. I know he felt it reflected badly on me that I didn't join in and spew forth a random selection of promotional suggestions.

I didn't think much of his marketing plan. The advertising section was a textbook application of theory with no practical basis. I had two options: I could force him to accept a solution that would work, or I could yes him to death, making sure everybody understood it was his idea. I knew which path I'd take.

"Yeah, we can do that for you," I told him. "No problem." We'd see which of us would survive and which was hurtling to an evolutionary dead end.

Although Harry had won his point, he continued to belabor it. My attention wandered—I'd heard it all before. His voice was the hum of an air conditioner, a familiar, easily ignored background noise. I drowsed and new emotions stirred in me, yearnings to float through moist air currents, to land on bright surfaces, to engorge myself with warm, wet food.

Adrift in insect dreams, I became sharply aware of the bare skin of Harry's arm, between his gold-plated watchband and his rolled-up sleeve, as he manipulated papers on the conference room table. He smelled greasily delicious, like a pepperoni pizza or a charcoal-broiled hamburger. I realized he probably wouldn't taste as good as he smelled, but I was hungry. My stiletto-like tongue was there for a purpose, and it wasn't to skewer cubes of tofu. I leaned over his arm and braced myself against the back of his hand, probing with my stylets to find a capillary.

Harry noticed what I was doing and swatted me sharply on the side of the head. I pulled away before he could hit me again.

"We were discussing the Model 2000 launch. Or have you forgotten?" he said, rubbing his arm.

"Sorry. I skipped breakfast this morning." I was embarrassed.

"Well, get your hormones adjusted, for chrissake." He was annoyed, and I couldn't really blame him. "Let's get back to the media allocation issue, if you can keep your mind on it. I've got another meeting at eleven in Building Two."

Inappropriate feeding behavior was not unusual in the company, and corporate etiquette sometimes allowed minor lapses to pass without pursuit. Of course, I could no longer hope that he would support me on moving some money out of the direct-mail budget. . . .

During the remainder of the meeting, my glance kept drifting through the open door of the conference room, toward a large decorative plant in the hall, one of those oases of generic greenery that dot the corporate landscape. It didn't look succulent exactly—it obviously wasn't what I would have preferred to eat if I hadn't been so hungry—but I wondered if I swung both ways?

I grabbed a handful of the broad leaves as I left the room and carried them back to my office. With my tongue, I probed a vein in the thickest part of a leaf. It wasn't so bad. Tasted green. I sucked them dry and tossed the husks in the wastebasket.

I was still omnivorous, at least—female mosquitoes don't eat plants. So the process wasn't complete. . . .

I got a cup of coffee, for company, from the kitchenette and sat in my office with the door closed and wondered what was happening. The incident with Harry disturbed me. Was I turning into a mosquito? If so, what the hell kind of good was that supposed to do me? The company didn't have any use for a whining loner.

There was a knock at the door, and my boss stuck his head in. I nodded and gestured him into my office. He sat down in the visitor's chair on the other side of my desk. From the look on his face, I could tell Harry had talked to him already.

Tom Samson was an older guy, pre-bioengineering. He was well versed in stimulus-response techniques, but had somehow never made it to the top job. I liked him, but then that was what he intended. Without sacrificing authority, he had pitched his appearance, his gestures, the tone of his voice, to the warm end of the spectrum. Even though I knew what he was doing, it worked.

He looked at me with what appeared to be sympathy, but was actually a practiced sign stimulus, intended to defuse any fight-or-flight response. "Is there something bothering you, Margaret?"

"Bothering me? I'm hungry, that's all. I get short-tempered when I'm hungry."

Watch it, I thought. He hasn't referred to the incident; leave it for him to bring up. I made my mind go bland and forced myself to meet his eyes. A shifty gaze is a guilty gaze.

Tom just looked at me, biding his time, waiting for me to put myself on the spot. My coffee smelt burnt, but I stuck my tongue in it and pretended to drink. "I'm just not human until I've had my coffee in the morning." Sounded phony. Shut up, I thought.

This was the opening that Tom was waiting for. "That's what I wanted to speak to you about, Margaret." He sat there, hunched over in a relaxed way, like a mountain gorilla, unthreatened by natural enemies. "I just talked to Harry Winthrop, and he said you were trying to suck his blood during a meeting on marketing strategy." He paused for a moment to check my reaction, but the neutral expression was fixed on my face and I said nothing. His face changed to project disappointment. "You know, when we noticed you were developing three distinct body segments, we had great hopes for you. But your actions just don't reflect the social and organizational development we expected."

He paused, and it was my turn to say something in my defense. "Most insects are solitary, you know. Perhaps the company erred in hoping for a termite or an ant. I'm not responsible for that."

"Now, Margaret," he said, his voice simulating genial reprimand. "This isn't the jungle, you know. When you signed those consent forms, you agreed to let the B-E staff mold you into a more useful corporate organism. But this isn't nature, this is man reshaping nature. It doesn't follow the old rules. You can truly be anything you want to be. But you have to cooperate."

"I'm doing the best I can," I said, cooperatively. "I'm putting in eighty hours a week."

"Margaret, the quality of your work is not an issue. It's your interactions with others that you have to work on. You have to learn to work as part of the group. I just cannot permit such backbiting to continue. I'll have Arthur get you an appointment this afternoon with the B-E counselor." Arthur was his secretary. He knew everything that happened in the department and mostly kept his mouth shut.

"I'd be a social insect if I could manage it," I muttered as Tom left my office. "But I've never known what to say to people in bars."

For lunch I met Greg and our friend David Detlor at a health-food restaurant that advertises fifty different kinds of fruit nectar. We'd never eaten there before, but Greg knew he'd love the place. It was already a favorite of David's, and he still has all his teeth, so I figured it would be okay with me.

David was there when I arrived, but not Greg. David works for the company too, in a different department. He, however, has proved remarkably resistant to corporate blandishment. Not only has he never undertaken B-E, he hasn't even bought a three-piece suit. Today he was wearing chewed-up blue jeans and a flashy Hawaiian shirt, of a type that was cool about ten years ago.

"Your boss lets you dress like that?" I asked.

"We have this agreement. I don't tell her she has to give me a job, and she doesn't tell me what to wear."

David's perspective on life is very different from mine. And I don't think it's just that he's in R&D and I'm in Advertising—it's more basic than that. Where he sees the world as a bunch of really neat but optional puzzles put there for his enjoyment, I see it as . . . well, as a series of SATs.

"So what's new with you guys?" he asked, while we stood around waiting for a table.

"Greg's turning into a goddamn butterfly. He went out last week and bought a dozen Italian silk sweaters. It's not a corporate look."

"He's not a corporate *guy*, Margaret."

"Then why is he having all this B-E done if he's not even going to use it?"

"He's dressing up a little. He just wants to look nice. Like Michael Jackson, you know?"

I couldn't tell whether David was kidding me or not. Then he started telling me about his music, this barbershop quartet that he sings in. They were going to dress in black leather for the next competition and sing Shel Silverstein's "Come to Me, My Masochistic Baby."

"It'll knock them on their tails," he said gleefully. "We've already got a great arrangement."

"Do you think it will win, David?" It seemed too weird to please the judges in that sort of a show.

"Who cares?" said David. He didn't look worried.

Just then Greg showed up. He was wearing a cobalt blue silk sweater with a copper green design on it. Italian. He was also wearing a pair of dangly earrings shaped like bright blue airplanes. We were shown to a table near a display of carved vegetables.

"This is great," said David. "Everybody wants to sit near the vegetables. It's where you sit to be *seen* in this place." He nodded to Greg. "I think it's your sweater."

"It's the butterfly in my personality," said Greg. "Headwaiters never used to do stuff like this for me. I always got the table next to the espresso machine."

If Greg was going to go on about the perks that come with being a butterfly, I was going to change the subject.

"David, how come you still haven't signed up for B-E?" I asked. "The company pays half the cost, and they don't ask questions."

David screwed up his mouth, raised his hands to his face, and made small, twitching, insect gestures, as if grooming his nose and eyes. "I'm doing okay the way I am."

Greg chuckled at this, but I was serious. "You'll get ahead faster with a little adjustment. Plus you're showing a good attitude, you know, if you do it."

"I'm getting ahead faster than I want to right now—it looks like I won't be able to take the three months off that I wanted this summer."

"Three months?" I was astonished. "Aren't you afraid you won't have a job to come back to?"

"I could live with that," said David calmly, opening his menu.

The waiter took our orders. We sat for a moment in a companionable silence, the self-congratulation that follows ordering high-fiber food-stuffs. Then I told them the story of my encounter with Harry Winthrop.

"There's something wrong with me," I said. "Why suck his blood? What good is that supposed to do me?"

"Well," said David, "*you* chose this schedule of treatments. Where did you want it to go?"

"According to the catalog," I said, "the No. 2 Insect Option is supposed to make me into a successful competitor for a middle-management niche, with triggerable responses that can be useful in gaining entry to upper hierarchical levels. Unquote." Of course, that was just ad talk—I didn't really expect it to do all that. "That's what I want. I want to be in charge. I want to be the boss."

"Maybe you should go back to BioEngineering and try again," said Greg. "Sometimes the hormones don't do what you expect. Look at my tongue, for instance." He unfurled it gently and rolled it back into his mouth. "Though I'm sort of getting to like it." He sucked at his drink, making disgusting slurping sounds. He didn't need a straw.

"Don't bother with it, Margaret," said David firmly, taking a cup of rosehip tea from the waiter. "Bioengineering is a waste of time and money and millions of years of evolution. If human beings were intended to be managers, we'd have evolved pin-striped body covering."

"That's cleverly put," I said, "but it's dead wrong."

The waiter brought our lunches, and we stopped talking as he put them in front of us. It seemed like the anticipatory silence of three very hungry people, but was in fact the polite silence of three people who have been brought up not to argue in front of disinterested bystanders. As soon as he left, we resumed the discussion.

"I mean it," David said. "The dubious survival benefits of management aside, bioengineering is a waste of effort. Harry Winthrop, for instance, doesn't need B-E at all. Here he is, fresh out of business school, audibly buzzing with lust for a high-level management position. Basically he's just marking time until a presidency opens up somewhere. And what gives him the edge over you is his youth and inexperience, not some specialized primate adaptation."

"Well," I said with some asperity, "he's not constrained by a knowledge of what's failed in the past, that's for sure. But saying that doesn't solve my problem, David. Harry's signed up. I've signed up. The changes are under way and I don't have any choice."

I squeezed a huge glob of honey into my tea from a plastic bottle shaped like a teddy bear. I took a sip of the tea; it was minty and very sweet. "And now I'm turning into the wrong kind of insect. It's ruined my ability to deal with Product Marketing."

"Oh, give it a rest!" said Greg suddenly. "This is *so* boring. I don't want to hear any more about corporate hugger-mugger. Let's talk about something that's fun."

I had had enough of Greg's lepidopterate lack of concentration. "Something that's *fun*? I've invested all my time and most of my genetic material in this job. This is all the goddamn fun there is."

The honeyed tea made me feel hot. My stomach itched—I wondered if I was having an allergic reaction. I scratched, and not discreetly. My hand came out from under my shirt full of little waxy scales. What the hell was going on under there? I tasted one of the scales; it was wax all right. Worker bee changes? I couldn't help myself—I stuffed the wax into my mouth.

David was busying himself with his alfalfa sprouts, but Greg looked disgusted. "That's gross, Margaret," he said. He made a face, sticking his tongue part way out. Talk about gross. "Can't you wait until after lunch?"

I was doing what came naturally, and did not dignify his statement with a response. There was a side dish of bee pollen on the table. I took a spoonful and mixed it with the wax, chewing noisily. I'd had a rough morning, and bickering with Greg wasn't making the day more pleasant.

Besides, neither he nor David has any real respect for my position in the company. Greg doesn't take my job seriously at all. And David simply does what he wants to do, regardless of whether it makes any money, for himself or anyone else. He was giving me a back-to-nature lecture, and it was far too late for that.

This whole lunch was a waste of time. I was tired of listening to them, and felt an intense urge to get back to work. A couple of quick stings distracted them both: I had the advantage of surprise. I ate some more honey and quickly waxed them over. They were soon hibernating side by side in two large octagonal cells.

I looked around the restaurant. People were rather nervously pretending not to have noticed. I called the waiter over and handed him my credit card. He signaled to several bus boys, who brought a covered cart and took Greg and David away. "They'll eat themselves out of that by Thursday afternoon," I told him. "Store them on their sides in a warm, dry place, away from direct heat." I left a large tip.

I walked back to the office, feeling a bit ashamed of myself. A couple days of hibernation weren't going to make Greg or David more sympathetic to my problems. And they'd be real mad when they got out.

I didn't use to do things like that. I used to be more patient, didn't I? More appreciative of the diverse spectrum of human possibility. More interested in sex and television.

This job was not doing much for me as a warm, personable human being. At the very least, it was turning me into an unpleasant lunch companion. Whatever had made me think I wanted to get into management anyway?

The money, maybe.

But that wasn't all. It was the challenge, the chance to do something new, to control the total effort instead of just doing part of a project. . . .

The money too, though. There were other ways to get money. Maybe I should just kick the supports out from under the damn job and start over again.

I saw myself sauntering into Tom's office, twirling his visitor's chair around and falling into it. The words "I quit" would force their way out, almost against my will. His face would show surprise—feigned, of course. By then I'd have to go through with it. Maybe I'd put my feet up on his desk. And then—

But was it possible to just quit, to go back to being the person I used to be? No, I wouldn't be able to do it. I'd never be a management virgin again.

I walked up to the employee entrance at the rear of the building. A suction device next to the door sniffed at me, recognized my scent, and clicked the door open. Inside, a group of new employees, trainees, were clustered near the door, while a personnel officer introduced them to the lock and let it familiarize itself with their pheromones.

On the way down the hall, I passed Tom's office. The door was open. He was at his desk, bowed over some papers, and looked up as I went by.

"Ah, Margaret," he said. "Just the person I want to talk to. Come in for a minute, would you." He moved a large file folder onto the papers in front of him on his desk, and folded his hands on top of them. "So glad you were passing by." He nodded toward a large, comfortable chair. "Sit down."

"We're going to be doing a bit of restructuring in the department," he began, "and I'll need your input, so I want to fill you in now on what will be happening."

I was immediately suspicious. Whenever Tom said "I'll need your input," he meant everything was decided already.

"We'll be reorganizing the whole division, of course," he continued, drawing little boxes on a blank piece of paper. He'd mentioned this at the department meeting last week.

"Now, your group subdivides functionally into two separate areas, wouldn't you say?"

"Well—"

"Yes," he said thoughtfully, nodding his head as though in agreement. "That would be the way to do it." He added a few lines and a few more boxes. From what I could see, it meant that Harry would do all the interesting stuff and I'd sweep up afterwards.

"Looks to me as if you've cut the balls out of my area and put them over into Harry Winthrop's," I said.

"Ah, but your area is still very important, my dear. That's why I don't have you actually reporting to Harry." He gave me a smile like a lie.

He had put me in a tidy little bind. After all, he was my boss. If he was going to take most of my area away from me, as it seemed he was, there wasn't much I could do to stop him. And I would be better off if we both pretended that I hadn't experienced any loss of status. That way I kept my title and my salary.

"Oh, I see." I said. "Right."

It dawned on me that this whole thing had been decided already, and that Harry Winthrop probably knew all about it. He'd probably even wangled a raise out of it. Tom had called me in here to make it look casual, to make it look as though I had something to say about it. I'd been set up.

This made me mad. There was no question of quitting now. I'd stick around and fight. My eyes blurred, unfocused, refocused again. Compound eyes! The promise of the small comb in my hand was fulfilled! I felt a deep chemical understanding of the ecological system I was now a part of. I knew where I fit in. And I knew what I was going to do. It was inevitable now, hardwired in at the DNA level.

The strength of this conviction triggered another change in the chitin, and for the first time I could actually feel the rearrangement of my mouth and nose, a numb tickling like inhaling seltzer water. The stiletto receded and mandibles jutted forth, rather like Katharine Hepburn. Form and function achieved an orgasmic synchronicity. As my jaw pushed forward, mantis-like, it also opened, and I pounced on Tom and bit his head off.

He leaped from his desk and danced headless about the office.

I felt in complete control of myself as I watched him and continued the conversation. "About the Model 2000 launch," I said. "If we factor in the demand for pipeline throughput and adjust the media mix just a bit, I think we can present a very tasty little package to Product Marketing by the end of the week."

Tom continued to strut spasmodically, making vulgar copulative motions. Was I responsible for evoking these mantid reactions? I was unaware of a sexual component in our relationship.

I got up from the visitor's chair and sat behind his desk, thinking about what had just happened. It goes without saying that I was surprised at my own actions. I mean, irritable is one thing, but biting people's heads off is quite another. But I have to admit that my second thought was, well, this certainly is a useful strategy, and should make a considerable difference in my ability to advance myself. Hell of a lot more productive than sucking people's blood.

Maybe there was something after all to Tom's talk about having the proper attitude.

And, of course, thinking of Tom, my third reaction was regret. He really had been a likeable guy, for the most part. But what's done is done, you know, and there's no use chewing on it after the fact.

I buzzed his assistant on the intercom. "Arthur," I said, "Mr. Samson and I have come to an evolutionary parting of the ways. Please have him re-engineered. And charge it to Personnel."

Now I feel an odd itching on my forearms and thighs. Notches on which I might fiddle a song?

NANCY KRESS

In Memoriam

Born in Buffalo, New York, Nancy Kress now lives with her family in Brockport, New York. She began selling her elegant and incisive stories in the mid-'70s, and has since become a frequent contributor to *IAsfm*, *F & SF*, *Omni*, and elsewhere. Her books include the novels *The Prince of Morning Bells*, *The Golden Grove*, and *The White Pipes*, and the collection *Trinity and Other Stories*. Her most recent book is the novel *An Alien Light*. Her story "Trinity" was in our Second Annual Collection; her "Out of All Them Bright Stars"—a Nebula winner—was in our Third Annual Collection.

Here she spins an eloquent and razor-sharp tale of the persistence of memory.

IN MEMORIAM

Nancy Kress

As soon as Aaron followed me into the garden, I knew he was angry. He pursed his mouth, that sweet exaggerated fullness of lips that hadn't changed since he was two years old and that looked silly on the middle-aged man he had become. But he said nothing—in itself a sign of trouble. Oh, I knew him through and through. As well as I knew his father, as well as his father had known me.

Aaron closed the door behind us and walked to the lawn chairs, skirting the tiny shrine as if it weren't there. He lowered himself gingerly into a chair.

"Be careful," I said, pointlessly. "Your back again?"

He waved this remark away; even as a little boy he had hated to have attention called to any physical problem. A skinned knee, a stiff neck, a broken wrist. I remembered. I remembered everything.

"Coffee? A splash?"

"Coffee. Come closer, I don't want to shout. You don't have your hearing field on, do you?"

I didn't. I poured him his coffee from the lawn bar and floated my chair close enough to hand it to him. Next door, Todd came out of his house, dressed in shorts and carrying a trowel. He waved cheerfully.

"I know you don't want to hear this," Aaron began—he had never been one for small talk, never one for subtlety—"but I have to say it one more time. Listen to Dr. Lorsky about the operation."

"Sugar?"

"Black. Mom—"

"Be quiet," I said, and he looked startled enough, but his surprise wasn't followed by a scowl. Aaron, who always reacted to a direct order as if to assault. I sat up straighter and peered at him. No scowl.

He took a long, deliberate sip of coffee, which was too hot for long sips. "Is there a reason you won't listen to Dr. Lorsky? A real, rational reason?" He didn't look at the shrine.

"You know the reason," I said. Thirty feet away in his side yard, Todd began to weed his flower beds, digging out the most stubborn weeds with the trowel, pulling the rest by hand. He never used a power hoe. The flowers, snapdragons and yarrow and azaleas and lemondrop marigolds, crowded together in the brief hot riot of midsummer.

Aaron waggled his fingers at the shrine he still wouldn't see. "That's not a reason!"

He was right, of course—the shrine was effect, not cause. I smiled at his perceptiveness, unable to help the sly, silly glow of a maternal pride thirty years out of date. But Aaron took the smile for something else: acquiesence, perhaps, or weakening. He put his cup on the grass and leaned forward. Earnestly—he had been such an earnest little boy, unsmiling in the face of jokes he didn't understand, putting his toys away in the exact same spots each night, presenting his teenage demands in carefully numbered lists, lecturing the other boys on their routine childish brutality.

A prig, actually.

"Mom, listen to me. I'm asking you to reconsider. That's all. For three reasons. First, because it's getting dangerous for you to live out here all alone. Despite the electronic surveillance. What if you were robbed?"

"Robbed," I said dryly. Aaron didn't catch it; I didn't really expect him to. He knew why I had bought this house, why I stayed in it. I said gently, "Your coffee's getting cold." He ignored me, pressing doggedly on, his hands gripping the arms of his chair. On the back of the left hand were two liver spots. When had that happened?

"*Second*, this business of ancestor worship or whatever it's supposed to be. This shrine. You never believed in this nonsense before. You raised me to think rationally, without superstition, and here you are planting flowers to your dead forebears unto the nth generation and meditating to them like you were some teenaged wirehead split-brain."

"We used to meditate a lot when I was a girl, before wireheads were invented," I said, to annoy him. His intensity was scaring me. "But Aaron, darling, that's not what I do here."

"What *do* you do?" he said, and immediately, I could see, regretted it. The shrine shone lustrous in the sunlight. It was a triptych of black slabs two feet high. In the late afternoon heat, the black neo-nitonol had softened into feature-lessness, but when night fell, the names would again spring into hard-etched clarity. Hundreds of tiny names, engraved close together in meticulous script, linked with the lines of generation. At the base of the triptych bloomed low flowers: violets and forget-me-nots and rosemary.

" 'There's rosemary, that's for remembrance,' " I said, but Aaron, being Aaron, didn't recognize Ophelia's line. Not a reader, my Aaron. Bytes not books. Oh, I remembered.

In the other yard, Todd's trowel clunked as it hit a buried stone.

"It isn't healthy," Aaron said. "Shrines. Ancestor worship! And in the third place, time is running out for you to have the operation. I spoke to Dr. Lorsky yesterday—"

"You spoke to my doctor without my permission—"

"—and he said your temporal lobes still scan well but he can't say how much longer that will be true. There's that cut-off point where the body just can't handle it anymore. And then the brain wipe wouldn't do you any good. It would be too late. Mom—you *know*."

I knew. The sheer weight of memory reached some critical mass. All those memories: the shade of blue of a dress worn fifty years ago, the tilt of the head of someone long dead, the sudden sharp smell of a grandmother's cabbage soup mingled with the dusty scent of an apartment razed for two decades. And each memory bringing on others, a rush of them, till the grandmother was there before you, whole. The burden and bulk of all those minute sensations over days and years and decades, triggering chemical changes in the brain which in turn trigger cellular changes, until the body cannot bear any more and breakdown accelerates. The cut-off point. It is our memories that kill us.

Aaron groped with one hand for his coffee cup, beside his chair on the grass. The crows' feet at the corners of his eyes were still tentative, like lines scratched in soft sand. He ducked his head and mumbled. "I just . . . I just don't want you to die, Mom."

I looked away. It is always, somehow, a surprise to find that an adult child still loves you.

Next door, Todd straightened from one flower bed and moved to the next. He pulled his shirt over his head and tossed it to the ground. Sweat gleamed on the muscles of his back, still hard and taut in his mid-thirties body. The shirt made a dark patch on the bright grass.

A bee buzzed up from the flowers around the black triptych and circled by my ear. Glad of the distraction, I waved it away.

"Aaron . . . I *can't*. I just can't. Be wiped."

"Even if you die for it? What point is there to that?"

I stayed silent. We had discussed it before, all of it, the whole dreary topic. But Aaron had never before looked like that. And he had never begged.

"Please, Mom. Please. You already get confused. Last week you thought that woman in the park was your dead sister. I know you're going to say it was just for a second, but that's the way it starts. Just for a second, then more and more, and then it's too late for the wipe. You say you wouldn't be 'you' anymore with a wipe—but if your memory goes and the body follows it, are you 'you' anyway? Feeble and senile? Are you still 'you' if you're dead?"

"That isn't the point," I began, but he must have seen on my face something which he thought was a softening, a wavering. He reached for my hand. His fingers were dry and hot.

"It *is* the point! Death is the point! Your body can't be made any younger, but it doesn't have to become any older. You *don't*. And you have the bodily strength, still, you have the money—Christ, it isn't as if you would be a vegetable. You'd still remember language, routines—and you'd make new memories, start over. A new life. *Life*, not death!"

I said nothing to that. Aaron could see the years of my life stretching behind me, years he wanted me to cut off as casually as paring a fingernail. He could not see the other, greater loss.

"You're wrong," I said, as gently as I could, and took my fingers from his. "I'm not refusing the wipe because I want death. I'm refusing it because too much of me has already died."

He stared at me with incomprehension. The bee I had waved away buzzed around his left ear. I saw his blue eyes flick to it and then back to me, refusing to be distracted. Linear thinking, always: was it growing up with all those computers? Such blue eyes, such a handsome man, still.

Next door Todd began to whistle. Aaron stiffened and half-turned to look for the first time over his shoulder; he had not realized Todd was there. He looked back at me. His eyes shadowed and dropped, and in that tiny sideways slide—not at all linear—I knew. I suddenly knew.

He saw it. "Mom . . . Mother . . ."

"You're going to have the wipe."

He raised the coffee cup to his mouth and drank: an automatic covering gesture, the coffee must have been cold. Repulsive. Cold coffee is repulsive.

I folded my arms across my belly and leaned forward.

He said quietly, "My back is getting worse. The migraines are back, once or twice every week. Lorsky says I'm an old forty-two, you know how much people vary. I'm not the easy-living type who forgets easily. I take things hard, I don't forget, and I don't want to die."

I said nothing.

"Mom?"

I said nothing.

"Please understand . . . please." It came out in a whisper. I said nothing. Aaron put his cup on the table and eased himself from the chair, leaning heavily on its arm and webbed back. The movement attracted Todd's attention. I saw, past the bulk of Aaron's body, the moment Todd decided to walk over and be neighborly.

"Hello, Mrs. Kinnian. Aaron."

I watched Aaron's face clench. He turned slowly.

Todd said, "Hot, isn't it? I was away for a week and my weeds just ambushed everything."

"Sailing," Aaron said carefully.

"Yes, sailing." Todd said, faintly surprised. He wiped the sweat from his eyes. "Do you sail?"

"I did. Once. When I was a kid. My father used to take me."

"You should have kept it up. Great sport. Mrs. Kinnian, can I weed those flowers for you?"

He pointed to the black triptych. I said, "No, thank you, Todd. The gardener will be around tomorrow."

"Well, if you . . . all right. Take care."

He smiled at us: a handsome blue-eyed man in his prime, ruddy with health and exercise, his face as open and clear as a child's. Beside him, Aaron looked puffy, stiff, out of shape. The skin at the back of Aaron's neck formed ridges that worked up and down above his collar.

"Take care," I said to Todd. He walked back to his weeding. Aaron turned to me. I saw his eyes.

"I'm sorry, Mom. I am . . . sorry. But I'm going to have the wipe. I'm going to do it."

"To me."

"For me."

After that there was nothing else to say. I watched Aaron walk around the flowered shrine, open the door to the house, disappear in the cool interior. There was a brief hum from the air conditioner, cut off the moment the door closed. A second door slammed; Todd, too, had gone inside his house.

I realized that I had not asked Aaron when Dr. Lorsky would do the wipe. He might not have told me. He had already been stretched as far as he would go, pulled off center by emotion and imagination, neither of which he wanted. He had never been an imaginative child, only a practical one. Coming to me in the garden with his math homework, worried about fractions, unconcerned with the flowers blooming and dying around him. I remembered.

But *he* would not.

Todd came back outside, carrying a cold drink, and returned to weeding. I watched him a while. I watched him an hour, two. I watched him after he had left and dusk began to fall over the garden. Then I struggled out of my chair—everything ached, I had been sitting too long—and picked some snapdragons. Purple, deepened by the shadows. I laid them in front of the black triptych.

When Todd and I had been married, I had carried roses: white with pink undertones at the tips of the petals, deep pink at the heart. I hadn't seen such roses in years. Maybe the strain wasn't grown anymore.

The script on the shrine had sprung out clear and hard. I touched it with one finger, tracing the names. Then I went into the house to watch TV. A brain-wipe clinic had been bombed. Elderly activists crowded in front of the camera, yelling and waving gnarled fists. They were led away by police, strong youthful men and women trying to get the old people to *behave* like old people. The unlined faces beneath their helmets looked bewildered. They *were* bewildered. Misunderstanding everything; believing that remembrance is death; getting it all backwards. Trying to make us go away as if we didn't exist. As if we never had.

MIKE RESNICK

Kirinyaga

Although we like to compliment ourselves—rather smugly—on the brightness and rationality of our tidy, shiny modern world, the Old Ways still exist—and, as the grim little story that follows suggests, perhaps they always *will*.

Mike Resnick is one of the bestselling authors in science fiction, and one of the most prolific. His many novels include *The Dark Lady, Stalking the Unicorn, Ivory*, and *Santiago*. His most recent novel was the well-received *Paradise*. He lives with his family, a whole bunch of dogs—he and his wife run a kennel—and at least one computer in Cincinnati, Ohio.

KIRINYAGA

Mike Resnick

In the beginning, Ngai lived alone atop the mountain called Kirinyaga. In the fullness of time, he created three sons, who became fathers of the Masai, the Kamba, and the Kikuyu races; and to each son he offered a spear, a bow, and a digging stick. The Masai chose the spear, and was told to tend herds on the vast savanna. The Kamba chose the bow, and was sent to the dense forests to hunt for game. But Gikuyu, the first Kikuyu, knew that Ngai loved the earth and the seasons, and chose the digging stick. To reward him for this, Ngai not only taught him the secrets of the seed and the harvest, but gave him Kirinyaga, with its holy fig tree and rich lands.

The sons and daughters of Gikuyu remained on Kirinyaga until the white man came and took their lands away; and even when the white man had been banished, they did not return, but chose to remain in the cities, wearing Western clothes and using Western machines and living Western lives. Even I, who am a *mundumugu*—a witch doctor—was born in the city. I have never seen the lion or the elephant or the rhinoceros, for all of them were extinct before my birth; nor have I seen Kirinyaga as Ngai meant it to be seen, for a bustling, overcrowded city of 3 million inhabitants covers its slopes, every year approaching closer and closer to Ngai's throne at the summit. Even the Kikuyu have forgotten its true name, and now know it only as Mount Kenya.

To be thrown out of Paradise, as were the Christian Adam and Eve, is a terrible fate, but to live beside a debased Paradise is infinitely worse. I think about them frequently, the descendants of Gikuyu who have forgotten their origin and their traditions and are now merely Kenyans, and I wonder why more of them did not join with us when we created the Eutopian world of Kirinyaga.

True, it is a harsh life, for Ngai never meant life to be easy; but it is also a satisfying life. We live in harmony with our environment; we offer sacrifices when Ngai's tears of compassion fall upon our fields and give sustenance to our crops; we slaughter a goat to thank him for the harvest.

Our pleasures are simple: a gourd of *pombe* to drink, the warmth of a *boma* when the sun has gone down, the wail of a newborn son or daughter, the footraces and spear throwing and other contests, the nightly singing and dancing.

Maintenance watches Kirinyaga discreetly, making minor orbital adjustments when necessary, assuring that our tropical climate remains constant. From time to time they have subtly suggested that we might wish to draw upon their medical expertise, or perhaps allow our children to make use of their educational facilities, but they have taken our refusal with good grace, and have never shown any desire to interfere in our affairs.

Until I strangled the baby.

It was less than an hour later that Koinnage, our paramount chief, sought me out.

"That was an unwise thing to do, Koriba," he said grimly.

"It was not a matter of choice," I replied. "You know that."

"Of course you had a choice," he responded. "You could have let the infant live." He paused, trying to control his anger and his fear. "Maintenance has never set foot on Kirinyaga before, but now they will come."

"Let them," I said with a shrug. "No law has been broken."

"We have killed a baby," he replied. "They will come, and they will revoke our charter!"

I shook my head. "No one will revoke our charter."

"Do not be too certain of that, Koriba," he warned me. "You can bury a goat alive, and they will monitor us and shake their heads and speak contemptuously among themselves about our religion. You can leave the aged and the infirm out for the hyenas to eat, and they will look upon us with disgust and call us godless heathens. But I tell you that killing a newborn infant is another matter. They will not sit idly by; they will come."

"If they do, I shall explain why I killed it," I replied calmly.

"They will not accept your answers," said Koinnage. "They will not understand."

"They will have no choice but to accept my answers," I said. "This is Kirinyaga, and they are not permitted to interfere."

"They will find a way," he said with an air of certainty. "We must apologize and tell them that it will not happen again."

"We will not apologize," I said sternly. "Nor can we promise that it will not happen again."

"Then, as paramount chief, *I* will apologize."

I stared at him for a long moment, then shrugged. "Do what you must do," I said.

Suddenly I could see the terror in his eyes.

"What will you do to me?" he asked fearfully.

"I? Nothing at all," I said. "Are you not my chief?" As he relaxed, I added: "But if I were you, I would beware of insects."

"Insects?" he repeated. "Why?"

"Because the next insect that bites you, be it spider or mosquito or fly, will surely kill you," I said. "Your blood will boil within your body, and your bones will melt. You will want to scream out your agony, yet you will be unable to utter a sound." I paused. "It is not a death I would wish on a friend," I added seriously.

"Are we not friends, Koriba?" he said, his ebon face turning an ash gray.

"I thought we were," I said. "But my friends honor our traditions. They do not apologize for them to the white man."

"I will not apologize!" he promised fervently. He spat on both his hands as a gesture of his sincerity.

I opened one of the pouches I kept around my waist and withdrew a small polished stone, from the shore of our nearby river. "Wear this around your neck," I said, handing it to him, "and it shall protect you from the bites of insects."

"Thank you, Koriba!" he said with sincere gratitude, and another crisis had been averted.

We spoke about the affairs of the village for a few more minutes, and finally he left me. I sent for Wambu, the infant's mother, and led her through the ritual of purification, so that she might conceive again. I also gave her an ointment to relieve the pain in her breasts, since they were heavy with milk. Then I sat down by the fire before my *boma* and made myself available to my people, settling disputes over the ownership of chickens and goats, and supplying charms against demons, and instructing my people in the ancient ways.

By the time of the evening meal, no one had a thought for the dead baby. I ate alone in my *boma*, as befitted my status, for the *mundumugu* always lives and eats apart from his people. When I had finished, I wrapped a blanket around my body to protect me from the cold and walked down the dirt path to where all the other *bomas* were clustered. The cattle and goats and chickens were penned up for the night, and my people, who had slaughtered and eaten a cow, were now singing and dancing and drinking great quantities of *pombe*. As they made way for me, I walked over to the caldron and took a drink of *pombe*, and then, at Kanjara's request, I slit open a goat and read its entrails and saw that his youngest wife would soon conceive, which was cause for more celebration. Finally the children urged me to tell them a story.

"But not a story of Earth," complained one of the taller boys. "We hear those all the time. This must be a story about Kirinyaga."

"All right," I said. "If you will all gather around, I will tell you a story of Kirinyaga." The youngsters all moved closer. "This," I said, "is the story of the Lion and the Hare." I paused until I was sure that I had everyone's attention, especially that of the adults. "A hare was chosen by his people to be sacrificed to a lion, so that the lion would not bring disaster to their village. The hare might have run away, but he knew that sooner or later the lion would catch him, so instead he sought out the lion and walked right up to him, and as the lion opened his mouth to swallow him, the hare said, 'I apologize, Great Lion.'

" 'For what?' asked the lion curiously.

" 'Because I am such a small meal,' answered the hare. 'For that reason, I brought honey for you as well.'

" 'I see no honey,' said the lion.

" 'That is why I apologized,' answered the hare. 'Another lion stole it from me. He is a ferocious creature, and says that he is not afraid of you.'

"The lion rose to his feet. 'Where is this other lion?' he roared.

"The hare pointed to a hole in the earth. 'Down there,' he said, 'but he will not give you back your honey.'

" 'We shall see about that!' growled the lion.

"He jumped into the hole, roaring furiously, and was never seen again, for the hare had chosen a very deep hole indeed. Then the hare went home to his people and told them that the lion would never bother them again."

Most of the children laughed and clapped their hands in delight, but the same young boy voiced his objection.

"That is not a story of Kirinyaga," he said scornfully. "We have no lions here."

"It *is* a story of Kirinyaga," I replied. "What is important about the story is not that it concerned a lion and a hare, but that it shows that the weaker can defeat the stronger if he uses his intelligence."

"What has that to do with Kirinyaga?" asked the boy.

"What if we pretend that the men of Maintenance, who have ships and weapons, are the lion, and the Kikuyu are the hares?" I suggested. "What shall the hares do if the lion demands a sacrifice?"

The boy suddenly grinned. "Now I understand! We shall throw the lion down a hole!"

"But we have no holes here," I pointed out.

"Then what shall we do?"

"The hare did not know that he would find the lion near a hole," I replied. "Had he found him by a deep lake, he would have said that a large fish took the honey."

"We have no deep lakes."

"But we do have intelligence," I said. "And if Maintenance ever interferes with us, we will use our intelligence to destroy the lion of Maintenance, just as the hare used his intelligence to destroy the lion of the fable."

"Let us think how to destroy Maintenance right now!" cried the boy. He picked up a stick and brandished it at an imaginary lion as if it were a spear and he a great hunter.

I shook my head. "The hare does not hunt the lion, and the Kikuyu do not make war. The hare merely protects himself, and the Kikuyu do the same."

"Why would Maintenance interfere with us?" asked another boy, pushing his way to the front of the group. "They are our friends."

"Perhaps they will not," I answered reassuringly. "But you must always remember that the Kikuyu have no true friends except themselves."

"Tell us another story, Koriba!" cried a young girl.

"I am an old man," I said. "The night has turned cold, and I must sleep."

"Tomorrow?" she asked. "Will you tell us another tomorrow?"

I smiled. "Ask me tomorrow, after all the fields are planted and the cattle and goats are in their enclosures and the food has been made and the fabrics have been woven."

"But girls do not herd the cattle and goats," she protested. "What if my brothers do not bring all their animals to the enclosure?"

"Then I will tell a story just to the girls," I said.

"It must be a long story," she insisted seriously, "for we work much harder than the boys."

"I will watch you in particular, little one," I replied, "and the story will be as long or as short as your work merits."

The adults all laughed, and suddenly she looked very uncomfortable, but then I chuckled and hugged her and patted her head, for it was necessary that the children learn to love their *mundumugu* as well as hold him in awe, and finally she ran off to play and dance with the other girls, while I retired to my *boma*.

Once inside, I activated my computer and discovered that a message was waiting for me from Maintenance, informing me that one of their number would be visiting me the following morning. I made a very brief reply—"Article II, Paragraph 5," which is the ordinance forbidding intervention—and lay down on my sleeping blanket, letting the rhythmic chanting of the singers carry me off to sleep.

I awoke with the sun the next morning and instructed my computer to let me know when the Maintenance ship had landed. Then I inspected my cattle and my goats—I, alone of my people, planted no crops, for the Kikuyu feed their *mundumugu*, just as they tend his herds and weave his blankets and keep his *boma* clean—and stopped by Simani's *boma* to deliver a balm to fight the disease that was afflicting his joints. Then, as the sun began warming the earth, I returned to my own *boma*, skirting the pastures where the young men were tending their animals. When I arrived, I knew the ship had landed, for I found the droppings of a hyena on the ground near my hut, and that is the surest sign of a curse.

I learned what I could from the computer, then walked outside and scanned the horizon while two naked children took turns chasing a small dog and running away from it. When they began frightening my chickens, I gently sent them back to their own *boma*, and then seated myself beside my fire. At last I saw my visitor from Maintenance, coming up the path from Haven. She was obviously uncomfortable in the heat, and she slapped futilely at the flies that circled her head. Her blonde hair was starting to turn gray, and I could tell by the ungainly way she negotiated the steep, rocky path that she was unused to such terrain. She almost lost her balance a number of times, and it was obvious that her proximity to so many animals frightened her, but she never slowed her pace, and within another ten minutes she stood before me.

"Good morning," she said.

"*Jambo, Memsaab*," I replied.

"You are Koriba, are you not?"

I briefly studied the face of my enemy; middle-aged and weary, it did not appear formidable. "I am Koriba," I replied.

"Good," she said. "My name is—"

"I know who you are," I said, for it is best, if conflict cannot be avoided, to take the offensive.

"You do?"

I pulled the bones out of my pouch and cast them on the dirt. "You are Barbara Eaton, born of Earth," I intoned, studying her reactions as I picked up the bones and cast them again. "You are married to Robert Eaton, and you have worked for Maintenance for nine years." A final cast of the bones. "You are forty-one years old, and you are barren."

"How did you know all that?" she asked with an expression of surprise.

"Am I not the *mundumugu*?"

She stared at me for a long minute. "You read my biography on your computer," she concluded at last.

"As long as the facts are correct, what difference does it make whether I read them from the bones or the computer?" I responded, refusing to confirm her statement. "Please sit down, *Memsaab* Eaton."

She lowered herself awkwardly to the ground, wrinkling her face as she raised a cloud of dust.

"It's very hot," she noted uncomfortably.

"It is very hot in Kenya," I replied.

"You could have created any climate you desired," she pointed out.

"We *did* create the climate we desired," I answered.

"Are there predators out there?" she asked, looking out over the savanna.

"A few," I replied.

"What kind?"

"Hyenas."

"Nothing larger?" she asked.

"There *is* nothing larger anymore," I said.

"I wonder why they didn't attack me?"

"Perhaps because you are an intruder," I suggested.

"Will they leave me alone on my way back to Haven?" she asked nervously, ignoring my comment.

"I will give you a charm to keep them away."

"I'd prefer an escort."

"Very well," I said.

"They're such ugly animals," she said with a shudder. "I saw them once when we were monitoring your world."

"They are very useful animals," I answered, "for they bring many omens, both good and bad."

"Really?"

I nodded. "A hyena left me an evil omen this morning."

"And?" she asked curiously.

"And here you are," I said.

She laughed. "They told me you were a sharp old man."

"They are mistaken," I replied. "I am a feeble old man who sits in front of his *boma* and watches younger men tend his cattle and goats."

"You are a feeble old man who graduated with honors from Cambridge and then acquired two postgraduate degrees from Yale," she replied.

"Who told you that?"

She smiled. "You're not the only one who reads biographies."

I shrugged. "My degrees did not help me become a better *mundumugu*," I said. "The time was wasted."

"You keep using that word. What, exactly, is *a mundumugu*?"

"You would call him a witch doctor," I answered. "But in truth the *mundumugu*, while he occasionally casts spells and interprets omens, is more a repository of the collected wisdom and traditions of his race."

"It sounds like an interesting occupation," she said.

"It is not without its compensations."

"And *such* compensations!" she said with false enthusiasm as a goat bleated in the distance and a young man yelled at it in Swahili. "Imagine having the power of life and death over an entire Eutopian world!"

So now it comes, I thought. Aloud I said: "It is not a matter of exercising power, *Memsaab* Eaton, but of maintaining traditions."

"I rather doubt that," she said bluntly.

"Why should you doubt what I say?" I asked.

"Because if it were traditional to kill newborn infants, the Kikuyu would have died out after a single generation."

"If the slaying of the infant arouses your disapproval," I said calmly, "I am surprised Maintenance has not previously asked about our custom of leaving the old and the feeble out for the hyenas."

"We know that the elderly and the infirm have consented to your treatment of them, much as we may disapprove of it," she replied. "We also know that a newborn infant could not possibly consent to its own death." She paused, staring at me. "May I ask why this particular baby was killed?"

"That *is* why you have come here, is it not?"

"I have been sent here to evaluate the situation," she replied, brushing an insect from her cheek and shifting her position on the ground. "A newborn child was killed. We would like to know why."

I shrugged. "It was killed because it was born with a terrible *thahu* upon it."

She frowned. "A *thahu*? What is that?"

"A curse."

"Do you mean that it was deformed?" she asked.

"It was not deformed."

"Then what was this curse that you refer to?"

"It was born feetfirst," I said.

"That's it?" she asked, surprised. "That's the curse?"

"Yes."

"It was murdered simply because it came out feetfirst?"

"It is not murder to put a demon to death," I explained patiently. "Our tradition tells us that a child born in this manner is actually a demon."

"You are an educated man, Koriba," she said. "How can you kill a perfectly healthy infant and blame it on some primitive tradition?"

"You must never underestimate the power of tradition, *Memsaab* Eaton," I said. "The Kikuyu turned their backs on their traditions once; the result is a mechanized, impoverished, overcrowded country that is no longer populated by Kikuyu, or Masai, or Luo, or Wakamba, but by a new, artificial tribe known only as Kenyans. We here on Kirinyaga are true Kikuyu, and we will not make that mistake again. If the rains are late, a ram must be sacrificed. If a man's veracity is questioned, he must undergo the ordeal of the *githani* trial. If an infant is born with a *thahu* upon it, it must be put to death."

"Then you intend to continue killing any children that are born feetfirst?" she asked.

"That is correct," I responded.

A drop of sweat rolled down her face as she looked directly at me and said: "I don't know what Maintenance's reaction will be."

"According to our charter, Maintenance is not permitted to interfere with us," I reminded her.

"It's not that simple, Koriba," she said. "According to your charter, any member of your community who wishes to leave your world is allowed free passage to Haven, from which he or she can board a ship to Earth." She paused. "Was that baby you killed given such a choice?"

"I did not kill a baby, but a demon," I replied, turning my head slightly as a hot breeze stirred up the dust around us.

She waited until the breeze died down, then coughed before speaking. "You do understand that not everyone in Maintenance may share that opinion?"

"What Maintenance thinks is of no concern to us," I said.

"When innocent children are murdered, what Maintenance thinks is of supreme importance to you," she responded. "I am sure you do not want to defend your practices in the Eutopian Court."

"Are you here to evaluate the situation, as you said, or to threaten us?" I asked calmly.

"To evaluate the situation," she replied. "But there seems to be only one conclusion that I can draw from the facts that you have presented to me."

"Then you have not been listening to me," I said, briefly closing my eyes as another, stronger, breeze swept past us.

"Koriba, I know that Kirinyaga was created so that you could emulate the ways of your forefathers—but surely you must see the difference between the torture of animals as a religious ritual and the murder of a human baby."

I shook my head. "They are one and the same," I replied. "We cannot change our way of life because it makes you uncomfortable. We did that once before, and within a mere handful of years, your culture had corrupted our society. With every factory we built, with every job we created, with every bit of Western technology we accepted, with every Kikuyu who converted to Christianity, we became something we were not meant to be." I stared directly into her eyes. "I am the *mundumugu*, entrusted with preserving all that makes us Kikuyu, and I will not allow that to happen again."

"There are alternatives," she said.

"Not for the Kikuyu," I replied adamantly.

"There *are*," she insisted, so intent upon what she had to say that she paid no attention to a black-and-gold centipede that crawled over her boot. "For example, years spent in space can cause certain physiological and hormonal changes in humans. You noted when I arrived that I am forty-one years old and childless. That is true. In fact, many of the women in Maintenance are childless. If you will turn the babies over to us, I am sure we can find families for them. This would effectively remove them from your society without the necessity of killing them. I could speak to my superiors about it; I think that there is an excellent chance that they would approve."

"That is a thoughtful and innovative suggestion, *Memsaab* Eaton," I said truthfully. "I am sorry that I must reject it."

"But why?" she demanded.

"Because the first time we betray our traditions, this world will cease to be Kirinyaga, and will become merely another Kenya, a nation of men awkwardly pretending to be something they are not."

"I could speak to Koinnage and the other chiefs about it," she suggested meaningfully.

"They will not disobey my instructions," I replied confidently.

"You hold that much power?"

"I hold that much respect," I answered. "A chief may enforce the law, but it is the *mundumugu* who interprets it."

"Then let us consider other alternatives."

"No."

"I am trying to avoid a conflict between Maintenance and your people," she said, her voice heavy with frustration. "It seems to me that you could at least make the effort to meet me halfway."

"I do not question your motives, *Memsaab* Eaton," I replied, "but you are an intruder representing an organization that has no legal right to interfere with our culture. We do not impose our religion or our morality upon Maintenance, and Maintenance may not impose its religion or morality upon us."

"It is not that simple."

"It is precisely that simple," I said.

"That is your last word on the subject?" she asked.

"Yes."

She stood up. "Then I think it is time for me to leave and make my report."

I stood up as well, and a shift in the wind brought the odors of the village: the scent of bananas, the smell of a fresh caldron of *pombe*, even the pungent odor of a bull that had been slaughtered that morning.

"As you wish, *Memsaab* Eaton," I said. "I will arrange for your escort." I signaled to a small boy who was tending three goats and instructed him to go to the village and send back two young men.

"Thank you," she said. "I know it's an inconvenience, but I just don't feel safe with hyenas roaming loose out there."

"You are welcome," I said. "Perhaps, while we are waiting for the men who will accompany you, you would like to hear a story about the hyena."

She shuddered involuntarily. "They are such ugly beasts!" she said distastefully. "Their hind legs seem almost deformed." She shook her head. "No, I don't think I'd be interested in hearing a story about a hyena."

"You will be interested in *this* story," I told her.

She stared at me curiously and shrugged. "All right," she said. "Go ahead."

"It is true that hyenas are deformed, ugly animals," I began, "but once, a long time ago, they were as lovely and graceful as the impala. Then one day a Kikuyu chief gave a hyena a young goat to take as a gift to Ngai, who lived atop the holy mountain Kirinyaga. The hyena took the goat between his powerful jaws and headed toward the distant mountain—but on the way he passed a settlement filled with Europeans and Arabs. It abounded in guns and machines and other wonders he had never seen before, and he stopped to look, fascinated. Finally an Arab noticed him staring intently, and asked if her, too, would like to become a civilized man—and as he opened his mouth to say that he would, the goat fell to the ground and ran away. As the goat raced out of sight, the Arab laughed and

explained that he was only joking, that of course no hyena could become a man.''
I paused for a moment, and then continued. ''So the hyena proceeded to Kirinyaga,
and when he reached the summit, Ngai asked him what had become of the goat.
When the hyena told him, Ngai hurled him off the mountaintop for having the
audacity to believe he could become a man. He did not die from the fall, but his
rear legs were crippled, and Ngai declared that from that day forward, all hyenas
would appear thus—and to remind them of the foolishness of trying to become
something that they were not, he also gave them a fool's laugh.'' I paused again,
and stared at her. ''*Memsaab* Eaton, you do not hear the Kikuyu laugh like fools,
and I will not let them become crippled like the hyena. Do you understand what
I am saying?''

She considered my statement for a moment, then looked into my eyes. ''I think
we understand each other perfectly, Koriba,'' she said.

The two young men I had sent for arrived just then, and I instructed them to
accompany her to Haven. A moment later they set off across the dry savanna,
and I returned to my duties.

I began by walking through the fields, blessing the scarecrows. Since a number
of the smaller children followed me, I rested beneath the trees more often than
was necessary, and always, whenever we paused, they begged me to tell them
more stories. I told them the tale of the Elephant and the Buffalo, and how the
Masai *elmoran* cut the rainbow with his spear so that it never again came to rest
upon the earth, and why the nine Kikuyu tribes are named after Gikuyu's nine
daughters; and when the sun became too hot, I led them back to the village.

Then, in the afternoon, I gathered the older boys about me and explained once
more how they must paint their faces and bodies for their forthcoming circumcision
ceremony. Ndemi, the boy who had insisted upon a story about Kirinyaga the
night before, sought me out privately to complain that he had been unable to slay
a small gazelle with his spear, and asked for a charm to make its flight more
accurate. I explained to him that there would come a day when he faced a buffalo
or a hyena with no charm, and that he must practice more before he came to me
again. He was one to watch, this little Ndemi, for he was impetuous and totally
without fear; in the old days, he would have made a great warrior, but on Kirinyaga
we had no warriors. If we remained fruitful and fecund, however, we would
someday need more chiefs and even another *mundumugu*, and I made up my mind
to observe him closely.

In the evening, after I ate my solitary meal, I returned to the village, for Njogu,
one of our young men, was to marry Kamiri, a girl from the next village. The
bride-price had been decided upon, and the two families were waiting for me to
preside at the ceremony.

Njogu, his face streaked with paint, wore an ostrich-feather headdress, and
looked very uneasy as he and his betrothed stood before me. I slit the throat of

a fat ram that Kamiri's father had brought for the occasion, and then I turned to Njogu.

"What have you to say?" I asked.

He took a step forward. "I want Kamiri to come and till the fields of my *shamba*," he said, his voice cracking with nervousness as he spoke the prescribed words, "for I am a man, and I need a woman to tend to my *shamba* and dig deep around the roots of my plantings, that they may grow well and bring prosperity to my house."

He spit on both his hands to show his sincerity, and then, exhaling deeply with relief, he stepped back.

I turned to Kamiri.

"Do you consent to till the *shamba* of Njogu, son of Muchiri?" I asked her.

"Yes," she said softly, bowing her head. "I consent."

I held out my right hand, and the bride's mother placed a gourd of *pombe* in it.

"If this man does not please you," I said to Kamiri, "I will spill the *pombe* upon the ground."

"Do not spill it," she replied.

"Then drink," I said, handing the gourd to her.

She lifted it to her lips and took a swallow, then handed it to Njogu, who did the same.

When the gourd was empty, the parents of Njogu and Kamiri stuffed it with grass, signifying the friendship between the two clans.

Then a cheer rose from the onlookers, the ram was carried off to be roasted, more *pombe* appeared as if by magic, and while the groom took the bride off to his *boma*, the remainder of the people celebrated far into the night. They stopped only when the bleating of the goats told them that some hyenas were nearby, and then the women and children went off to their *bomas* while the men took their spears and went into the fields to frighten the hyenas away.

Koinnage came up to me as I was about to leave.

"Did you speak to the woman from Maintenance?" he asked.

"I did," I replied.

"What did she say?"

"She said that they do not approve of killing babies who are born feetfirst."

"And what did *you* say?" he asked nervously.

"I told her that we did not need the approval of Maintenance to practice our religion," I replied.

"Will Maintenance listen?"

"They have no choice," I said. "And *we* have no choice, either," I added. "Let them dictate one thing that we must or must not do, and soon they will dictate all things. Give them their way, and Njogu and Kamiri would have recited wedding vows from the Bible or the Koran. It happened to us in Kenya; we cannot permit it to happen on Kirinyaga.''

''But they will not punish us?'' he persisted.

''They will not punish us,'' I replied.

Satisfied, he walked off to his *boma* while I took the narrow, winding path to my own. I stopped by the enclosure where my animals were kept and saw that there were two new goats there, gifts from the bride's and groom's families in gratitude for my services. A few minutes later I was asleep within the walls of my own *boma*.

The computer woke me a few minutes before sunrise. I stood up, splashed my face with water from the gourd I keep by my sleeping blanket, and walked over to the terminal.

There was a message for me from Barbara Eaton, brief and to the point:

It is the preliminary finding of Maintenance that infanticide, for any reason, is a direct violation of Kirinyaga's charter. No action will be taken for past offenses.

We are also evaluating your practice of euthanasia, and may require further testimony from you at some point in the future.

Barbara Eaton

A runner from Koinnage arrived a moment later, asking me to attend a meeting of the Council of Elders, and I knew that he had received the same message.

I wrapped my blanket around my shoulders and began walking to Koinnage's *shamba*, which consisted of his *boma* as well as those of his three sons and their wives. When I arrived, I found not only the local elders waiting for me, but also two chiefs from neighboring villages.

''Did you receive the message from Maintenance?'' demanded Koinnage, as I seated myself opposite him.

''I did.''

''I warned you that this would happen!'' he said. ''What will we do now?''

''We will do what we have always done,'' I answered calmly.

''We cannot,'' said one of the neighboring chiefs. ''They have forbidden it.''

''They have no right to forbid it,'' I replied.

''There is a woman in my village whose time is near,'' continued the chief, ''and all of the signs and omens point to the birth of twins. We have been taught that the firstborn must be killed, for one mother cannot produce two souls—but now Maintenance has forbidden it. What are we to do?''

''We must kill the firstborn,'' I said, ''for it will be a demon.''

''And then Maintenance will make us leave Kirinyaga!'' said Koinnage bitterly.

''Perhaps we could let the child live,'' said the chief. ''That might satisfy them, and then they might leave us alone.''

I shook my head. "They will not leave you alone. Already they speak about the way we leave the old and feeble out for the hyenas, as if this were some enormous sin against their God. If you give in on the one, the day will come when you must give in on the other."

"Would that be so terrible?" persisted the chief. "They have medicines that we do not possess; perhaps they could make the old young again."

"You do not understand," I said, rising to my feet. "Our society is not a collection of separate people and customs and traditions. No, it is a complex system, with all the pieces as dependent upon each other as the animals and vegetation of the savanna. If you burn the grass, you will not only kill the impala who feeds upon it, but the predator who feeds upon the impala, and the ticks and flies who live upon the predator, and the vultures and maribou storks who feed upon his remains when he dies. You cannot destroy the part without destroying the whole."

I paused to let them consider what I had said, and then continued speaking: "Kirinyaga is like the savanna. If we do not leave the old and feeble out for the hyenas, the hyenas will starve. If the hyenas starve, the grass eaters will become so numerous that there is no land left for our cattle and goats to graze. If the old and feeble do not die when Ngai decrees it, then soon we will not have enough food to go around."

I picked up a stick and balanced it precariously on my forefinger.

"This stick," I said, "is the Kikuyu people, and my finger is Kirinyaga. They are in perfect balance." I stared at the neighboring chief. "But what will happen if I alter the balance and put my finger *here*?" I asked, gesturing to the end of the stick.

"The stick will fall to the ground."

"And here?" I asked, pointing to a stop an inch away from the center.

"It will fall."

"Thus is it with us," I explained. "Whether we yield on one point or all points, the result will be the same: the Kikuyu will fall as surely as the stick will fall. Have we learned nothing from our past? We *must* adhere to our traditions; they are all that we have!"

"But Maintenance will not allow us to do so!" protested Koinnage.

"They are not warriors, but civilized men," I said, allowing a touch of contempt to creep into my voice. "Their chiefs and their *mundumugus* will not send them to Kirinyaga with guns and spears. They will issue warnings and findings and declarations, and finally, when that fails, they will go to the Eutopian Court and plead their case, and the trial will be postponed many times and reheard many more times." I could see them finally relaxing, and I smiled confidently at them. "Each of you will have died from the burden of your years before Maintenance does anything other than talk. I am your *mundumugu*; I have lived among civilized men, and I tell you that this is the truth."

The neighboring chief stood up and faced me. "I will send for you when the twins are born," he pledged.

"I will come," I promised him.

We spoke further, and then the meeting ended and the old men began wandering off to their *bomas*, while I looked to the future, which I could see more clearly than Koinnage or the elders.

I walked through the village until I found the bold young Ndemi, brandishing his spear and hurling it at a buffalo he had constructed out of dried grasses.

"*Jambo*, Koriba!" he greeted me.

"*Jambo*, my brave young warrior," I replied.

"I have been practicing, as you ordered."

"I thought you wanted to hunt the gazelle," I noted.

"Gazelles are for children," he answered. "I will slay *mbogo*, the buffalo."

"*Mbogo* may feel differently about it," I said.

"So much the better," he said confidently. "I have no wish to kill an animal as it runs away from me."

"And when will you go out to slay the fierce *mbogo*?"

He shrugged. "When I am more accurate." He smiled up at me. "Perhaps tomorrow."

I stared at him thoughtfully for a moment, and then spoke: "Tomorrow is a long time away. We have business tonight."

"What business?" he asked.

"You must find ten friends, none of them yet of circumcision age, and tell them to come to the pond within the forest to the south. They must come after the sun has set, and you must tell them that Koriba the *mundumugu* commands that they tell no one, not even their parents, that they are coming." I paused. "Do you understand, Ndemi?"

"I understand."

"Then go," I said. "Take my message to them."

He retrieved his spear from the straw buffalo and set off at a trot, young and tall and strong and fearless.

You are the future, I thought, as I watched him run toward the village. *Not Koinnage, not myself, not even the young bridegroom Njogu, for their time will have come and gone before the battle is joined. It is you, Ndemi, upon whom Kirinyaga must depend if it is to survive.*

Once before, the Kikuyu had to fight for their freedom. Under the leadership of Jomo Kenyatta, whose name has been forgotten by most of your parents, we took the terrible oath of Mau Mau, and we maimed and we killed and we committed such atrocities that finally we achieved Uhuru, for against such butchery, civilized men have no defense but to depart.

And tonight, young Ndemi, while your parents are asleep, you and your companions will meet me deep in the woods, and you in your turn and they in theirs will learn one last tradition of the Kikuyu, for I will invoke not only the strength of Ngai but also the indomitable spirit of Jomo Kenyatta. I will administer a hideous oath and force you to do unspeakable things to prove her fealty, and I will teach each of you, in turn, how to administer the oath to those who come after you.

There is a season for all things: for birth, for growth, for death. There is unquestionably a season for Utopia, but it will have to wait.

For the season of Uhuru is upon us.

BRUCE McALLISTER

The Girl Who Loved Animals

Bruce McAllister published his first story in 1963, when he was seventeen (it was *written* at the tender age of fifteen). Since then, with only a handful of stories, he has nevertheless managed to establish himself as one of the most respected writers in the business. His short fiction has appeared in *Omni, Isaac Asimov's Science Fiction Magazine, In the Field of Fire, The Magazine of Fantasy and Science Fiction*, and elsewhere. His first novel, *Humanity Prime*, was one of the original Ace Specials series. Upcoming is a new novel from Tor, and he is at work on several other novel projects. McAllister lives in Redlands, California, where he is the director of the writing program at the University of Redlands. His story "Dream Baby" was in our Fifth Annual Collection.

Here he tells the bittersweet story of a girl who loved, not wisely, but too well. . . .

THE GIRL WHO LOVED ANIMALS

Bruce McAllister

They had her on the seventeenth floor in their new hi-security unit on Figueroa and weren't going to let me up. Captain Mendoza, the one who thinks I'm the ugliest woman he's ever laid eyes on and somehow manages to take it personally, was up there with her, and no one else was allowed. Or so this young lieutenant with a fresh academy tattoo on his left thumb tries to tell me. I get up real close so the kid can hear me over the screaming media crowd in the lobby and see this infamous face of mine, and I tell him I don't think Chief Stracher will like getting a call at 0200 hours just because some desk cadet can't tell a privileged soc worker from a media rep, and how good friends really shouldn't bother each other at that time of the day anyway, am I right? It's a lie, sure, but he looks worried, and I remember why I haven't had anything done about the face I was born with. He gives me two escorts—a sleek young swatter with an infrared Ruger, and a lady in fatigues who's almost as tall as I am—and up we go. They're efficient kids. They frisk me in the elevator.

Mendoza wasn't with her. Two P.D. medics with side arms were. The girl was sitting on a sensor cot in the middle of their new glass observation room—closed-air, anti-ballistic Plexi, and the rest—and was a mess. The video footage, which four million people had seen at ten, hadn't been pixeled at all.

Their hi-sec floor cost them thirty-three million dollars, I told myself, took them three years of legislation to get, and had everything you'd ever want to keep your witness or assassin or jihad dignitary alive—CCTV, microwave eyes, pressure mats, blast doors, laser blinds, eight different kinds of gas, and, of course, Vulcan minicannons from the helipad three floors up.

I knew that Mendoza would have preferred someone more exciting than a twenty-year-old girl with a V Rating of nine point six and something strange growing inside her, but he was going to have to settle for this christening.

I asked the medics to let me in. They told me to talk into their wall grid so the new computer could hear me. The computer said something like "Yeah, she's okay," and they opened the door and frisked me again.

I asked them to leave, citing Welfare & Institutions Statute Thirty-eight. They wouldn't, citing hi-sec orders under Penal Code Seven-A. I told them to go find Mendoza and tell him I wanted privacy for the official interview.

Very nicely they said that neither of them could leave and that if I kept asking I could be held for obstruction, despite the same statute's cooperation clause. That sounded right to me. I smiled and got to work.

Her name was Lissy Tomer. She was twenty-one, not twenty. According to Records, she'd been born in the East Valley, been abused as a child by both sets of parents, and, as the old story goes, hooked up with a man who would oblige her the same way. What had kept County out of her life, I knew, was the fact that early on, someone in W&I had set her up with an easy spousal-abuse complaint and felony restraining-order option that needed only a phone call to trigger. But she'd never exercised it, though the older bruises said she should have.

She was pale and underweight and wouldn't have looked very good even without the contusions, the bloody nose and lip, the belly, and the shivering. The bloody clothes didn't help either. Neither did the wires and contact gel they had all over her for their beautiful new cot.

But there was a fragility to her—princess-in-the-fairy-tale kind—that almost made her pretty.

She flinched when I said hello, just as if I'd hit her. I wondered which had been worse—the beating or the media. He'd done it in a park and had been screaming at her when Mendoza's finest arrived, and two uniforms had picked up a couple of C's by calling it in to the networks.

She was going to get hit with a beautiful posttraumatic stress disorder sometime down the road even if things didn't get worse for her—which they would. The press wanted her badly. She was bloody, showing, and *very* visual.

"Has the fetus been checked?" I asked the side arms. If they were going to listen, they could help.

The shorter one said yes, a portable sonogram from County, and the baby looked okay.

I turned back to the girl. She was looking up at me from the cot, looking hopeful, and I couldn't for the life of me imagine what she thought I could do for her.

"I'm your new V.R. advocate, Lissy."

She nodded, keeping her hands in her lap like a good girl.

"I'm going to ask you some questions, if that's all right. The more I know, the more help I can be, Lissy. But you know that, don't you." I grinned.

She nodded again and smiled, but the lip hurt.

I identified myself, badge and department and appellation, then read her her rights under Protective Services provisions, as amended—what we in the trade call the Nhat Hanh Act. What you get and what you don't.

"First question, Lissy: Why'd you do it?" I asked it as gently as I could, flicking the hand recorder on. It was the law.

I wondered if she knew what a law was.

Her I.Q. was eighty-four, congenital, and she was a Collins psychotype, class three dependent. She'd had six years of school and had once worked for five months for a custodial service in Monterey Park. Her Vulnerability Rating, all factors factored, was a whopping nine point six. It was the rating that had gotten her a felony restraint complaint option on the marital bond, and County had assumed that was enough to protect her . . . from him.

As far as the provisions on low-I.Q. cases went, the husband had been fixed, she had a second-degree dependency on him, and an abortion in event of rape by another was standard. As far as County was concerned, she was protected, and society had exercised proper conscience. I really couldn't blame her last V.R. advocate. I'd have assumed the same.

And missed one thing.

"I like animals a lot," she said, and it made her smile. In the middle of a glass room, two armed medics beside her, the media screaming downstairs to get at her, her husband somewhere wishing he'd killed her, it was the one thing that could make her smile.

She told me about a kitten she'd once had at the housing project on Crenshaw. She'd named it Lissy and had kept it alive "all by herself." It was her job, she said, like her mother and fathers had jobs. Her second stepfather—or was it her mother's brother? I couldn't tell, and it didn't matter—had taken it away one day, but she'd had it for a month or two.

When she started living with the man who'd eventually beat her up in a park for the ten o'clock news, he let her have a little dog. He would have killed it out of jealousy in the end, but it died because she didn't know about shots. He wouldn't have paid for them anyway, and she seemed to know that. He hadn't been like that when they first met. It sounded like neurotransmitter blocks, MPHG metabolism. The new bromaine that was on the streets would do it; all the fentanyl analogs would, too. There were a dozen substances on the street that would. You saw it all the time.

She told me how she'd slept with the kitten and the little dog and, when she didn't have them anymore, with the two or three toys she'd had so long that most of their fur was worn off. How she could smell the kitten for months in her room just as if it were still there. How the dog had died in the shower. How her husband had gotten mad, hit her, and taken the thing away. But you could tell she was glad when the body wasn't there in the shower anymore.

*   *   *

"This man was watching me in the park," she said. "He always watched me."

"Why were you in the park, Lissy?"

She looked at me out of the corner of her eye and gave me a smile, the conspiratorial kind. "There's more than one squirrel in those trees. Maybe a whole family. I like to watch them."

I was surprised there were any animals at all in the park. You don't see them anymore, except for the domesticates.

"Did you talk to this man?"

She seemed to know what I was asking. She said, "I wasn't scared of him. He smiled a lot." She laughed at something, and we all jumped. "I knew he wanted to talk to me, so I pretended there was a squirrel over by him, and I fed it. He said, Did I like animals and how I could make a lot of money and help the animals of the world."

It wasn't important. A dollar. A thousand. But I had to ask.

"How much money did he tell you?"

"Nine thousand dollars. That's how much I'm going to get, and I'll be able to see it when it's born, and visit it."

She told me how they entered her, how they did it gently while she watched, the instrument clean and bright.

The fertilized egg would affix to the wall of her uterus, they'd told her, and together they would make a placenta. What the fetus needed nutritionally would pass through the placental barrier, and her body wouldn't reject it.

Her eyes looked worried now. She was remembering things—a beating, men in uniforms with guns, a man with a microphone pushed against her belly. *Had her husband hit her there? If so, how many times?* I wondered.

"Will the baby be okay?" she asked, and I realized I'd never seen eyes so colorless, a face so trusting.

"That's what the doctors say," I said, looking up at the side arms, putting it on them.

Nine thousand. More than a man like her husband would ever see stacked in his life, but he'd beaten her anyway, furious that she could get it in her own way when he'd failed again and again, furious that she'd managed to get it with the one thing he thought he owned—her body.

Paranoid somatopaths are that way.

I ought to know. I married one.

I'm thinking of the mess we've made of it, Lissy. I'm thinking of the three hundred thousand grown children of the walking wounded of an old war in Asia who walk the same way.

I'm thinking of the four hundred thousand walljackers, our living dead. I'm thinking of the zoos, the ones we don't have anymore, and what they must have been like, what little girls like Lissy Tomer must have done there on summer days.

I'm thinking of a father who went to war, came back, but was never the same again, of a mother who somehow carried us all, of how cars and smog and cement can make a childhood and leave you thinking you can change it all.

I wasn't sure, but I could guess. The man in the park was a body broker for pharmaceuticals and nonprofits, and behind him somewhere was a species resurrection group that somehow had the money. He'd gotten a hefty three hundred percent, which meant the investment was already thirty-six grand. He'd spent some of his twenty-seven paying off a few W&I people in the biggest counties, gotten a couple dozen names on high-V.R. searches, watched the best bets himself, and finally made his selection.

The group behind him didn't know how such things worked or didn't particularly care; they simply wanted consenting women of childbearing age, good health, no substance abuse, no walljackers, no suicidal inclinations; and the broker's reputation was good, and he did his job.

Somehow he'd missed the husband.

As I found out later, she was one of ten. Surrogates for human babies were a dime a dozen, had been for years. This was something else.

In a nation of two hundred eighty million, Lissy Tomer was one of ten—but in her heart of hearts she was the only one. Because a man who said he loved animals had talked to her in a park once. Because he'd said she would get a lot of money—money that ought to make a husband who was never happy, happy. Because she would get to see it when it was born and get to visit it wherever it was kept.

The odd thing was, I could understand how she felt.

I called Antalou at three A.M., got her mad but at least awake, and got her to agree we should try to get the girl out that same night—out of that room, away from the press, and into a County unit for a complete fetal check. Antalou is the kind of boss you only get in heaven. She tried, but Mendoza stonewalled her under P.C. Twenty-two, the Jorgenson clause—he was getting all the publicity he and his new unit needed with the press screaming downstairs—and we gave up at five, and I went home for a couple hours of sleep before the paperwork began.

I knew that sitting there in the middle of all that glass with two armed medics was almost as bad as the press, but what could I do, Lissy, what could I do?

I should have gone to the hotel room that night, but the apartment was closer. I slept on the sofa. I didn't look at the bedroom door, which is always locked from the outside. The nurse has a key. Some days it's easier not to think about what's in there. Some days it's harder.

I thought about daughters.

We got her checked again, this time at County Medical, and the word came back okay. Echomytic bruises with some placental bleeding, but the fetal signs were fine. I went ahead and asked whether the fetus was a threat to the mother in any case, and they laughed. No more than any human child would be, they said. All you're doing is borrowing the womb, they said. "Sure," this cocky young resident says to me, "it's low-tech all the way." I had a lot of homework to do, I realized.

Security at the hospital reported a visit by a man who was not her husband, and they didn't let him through. The same man called me an hour later. He was all smiles and wore a suit.

I told him we'd have to abort if County, under the Victims' Rights Act, decided it was best or the girl wanted it. He pointed out with a smile that the thing she was carrying was worth a lot of money to the people he represented, and they could make her life more comfortable, and we ought to protect the girl's interests.

I told him what I thought of him, and he laughed. "You've got it all wrong, Doctor."

I let it pass. He knows I'm an MPS-V.R., no Ph.D., no M.D. He probably even knows I got the degree under duress, years late, because Antalou said we needed all the paper we could get if the department was going to survive. I know what he's doing, and he knows I know.

"The people I represent are caring people, Doctor. Their cause is a good one. They're not what you're accustomed to working with, and they've retained me simply as a program consultant, a 'resource locator.' It's all aboveboard, Doctor, completely legal, I assure you. But I really don't need to tell you any of this, do I?"

"No, you don't."

I added that, legal or not, if he tried to see her again I would have him for harassment under the D.A.'s cooperation clause.

He laughed, and I knew then he had a law degree from one of the local universities. The suit was right. I could imagine him in it at the park that day.

"You may be able to pull that with the mopes and 5150's you work with on the street, Doctor, but I know the law. I'll make you a deal. I'll stay away for the next three months, as long as you look after the girl's best interests, how's that?"

I knew there was more, so I waited.

"My people will go on paying for weekly visits up to the eighth month, then daily through to term, the clinic to be designated by them. They want ultrasound, CVS, and amniotic antiabort treatments, and the diet and abstinence programs the girl's already agreed to. All you have to do is get her to her appointments, and we pay for it. Save the county some money.''

I waited.

His voice changed as I'd known it would. The way they do in the courtrooms. I'd heard it change like that a hundred times before, years of it, both sides of the aisle.

"If County can't oblige," he said, "we'll just have to try Forty-A, right?"

I told him to take a flying something.

Maybe I didn't know the law, but I knew Forty-A. In certain circles it's known simply as Fucker-Forty. Under it—the state's own legislation—he'd be able to sue the county and this V.R. advocate in particular for loss of livelihood—his and hers—and probably win after appeals.

This was the last thing Antalou or any of us needed.

The guy was still smiling.

"You've kept that face for a reason, Doctor. What do young girls think of it?"

I hung up on him.

With Antalou's help I got her into the Huntington on Normandy, a maternal unit for sedated Ward B types. Some of the other women had seen her on the news two evenings before; some hadn't. *It didn't matter*, I thought. *It was about as good a place for her to hide as possible*, I told myself. I was wrong. Everything's on computer these days, and some information's as cheap as a needle.

I get a call the next morning from the unit saying a man had gotten in and tried to kill her, and she was gone.

I'm thinking of the ones I've lost, Lissy. The tenth-generation maggot casings on the one in Koreatown, the door locked for days. The one named Consejo, the one I went with to the morgue, where they cut up babies, looking for hers. The skinny one I thought I'd saved, the way I was supposed to, but he's lying in a pool of O-positive in a room covered with the beautiful pink dust they used for prints.

Or the ones when I was a kid, East L.A., Fontana, the drugs taking them like some big machine, the snipings that always killed the ones that had nothing to do with it—the chubby ones, the ones who liked to read—the man who took Karenna and wasn't gentle, the uncle who killed his own nephews and blamed it on coyotes, which weren't there anymore, hadn't been for years.

I'm thinking of the ones I've lost, Lissy.

I looked for her all day, glad to be out of the apartment, glad to be away from a phone that might ring with a slick lawyer's face on it.

When I went back to the apartment that night to pick up another change of clothes for the hotel room, she was sitting crosslegged by the door.

"Lissy," I said, wondering how she'd gotten the address.

"I'm sorry," she said.

She had her hand on her belly, holding it not out of pain but as if it were the most comforting thing in the world.

"He wants to kill me. He says that anybody who has an animal growing in her is a devil and's got to die. He fell down the stairs. I didn't push him, I didn't."

She was crying, and the only thing I could think to do was get down and put my arms around her and try not to cry myself.

"I know, I know," I said. The symptoms were like Parkinson's, I remembered. You tripped easily.

I wasn't thinking clearly. I hadn't had more than two or three hours of sleep for three nights running, and all I could think of was getting us both inside, away from the steps, the world.

Maybe it was fatigue. Or maybe something else. I should have gotten her to a hospital. I should have called Mendoza for an escort back to his unit. What I did was get her some clothes from the bedroom, keep my eyes on the rug while I was in there, and lock the door again when I came out. She didn't ask why neither of us were going to sleep in the bedroom. She didn't ask about the lock. She just held her belly, and smiled like some Madonna.

I took two Dalmanes from the medicine cabinet, thinking they might be enough to get the pictures of what was in that room out of my head.

I don't know whether they did or not. Lissy was beside me, her shoulder pressing against me, as I got the futon and the sofa ready.

Her stomach growled, and we laughed. I said, "Who's growling? Who's growling?" and we laughed again. I asked her if she was hungry and if she could eat sandwiches. She laughed again, and I got her a fresh one from the kitchen.

She took the futon, lying on her side to keep the weight off. I took the sofa because of my long legs.

I felt something beside me in the dark. She kissed me, said "Goodnight," and I heard her nightgown whisper back into the darkness. I held it in for a while and then couldn't anymore. It didn't last long. Dalmane's a knockout.

The next day I took her to the designated clinic and waited outside for her. She was happy. The big amino needle they stuck her with didn't bother her, she said. She liked how much bigger her breasts were, she said, like a mother's should be. She didn't mind being careful about what she ate and drank. She even liked the strange V of hair growing on her abdomen, because—because it was hairy, she said, just like the thing inside her. She liked how she felt, and she wanted to know if I could see it, the glow, the one expectant mothers are supposed to have. I told her I could.

I'm thinking of a ten-year-old, the one that used to tag along with me on the median train every Saturday when I went in for caseloads while most mothers had their faces changed, or played, or mothered. We talked a lot back then, and I miss it. She wasn't going to need a lot of work on that face, I knew—maybe the ears, just a little, if she was picky. She'd gotten her father's genes. But she talked like me—like a kid from East L.A.—tough, with a smile, and I thought she was going to end up a D.A. or a showy defense type or at least an exec. That's how stupid we get. In four years she was into molecular opiates and trillazines, and whose fault was that? The top brokers roll over two billion a year in this city alone; the local *capi* net a twentieth of that, their street dealers a fourth; and God knows what the guys in the labs bring home to their families.

It's six years later, and I hear her letting herself in one morning. She's fumbling and stumbling at the front door. I get up, dreading it. What I see tells me that the drugs are nothing, nothing at all. She's running with a strange group of kids, a lot of them older. *This new thing's* a fad, I tell myself. It's like not having your face fixed—like not getting the nasal ramification modified, the mandibular thrust attended to—when you could do it easily, anytime, and cheaply, just because you want to make a point, and it's fun to goose the ones who need goosing. *That's all she's really doing, you tell yourself.*

You've seen her a couple of times like this, but you still don't recognize her. She's heavy around the chest and shoulders, which makes her breasts seem a lot smaller. Her face is heavy; her eyes are puffy, almost closed. She walks with a limp because something hurts down low. Her shoulders are bare, and they've got tattoos now, the new metallic kind, glittery and painful. She's wearing expensive pants, but they're dirty.

So you have a daughter now who's not a daughter, or she's both, boy and girl. The operation cost four grand, and you don't want to think how she got the money. Everyone's doing it, you tell yourself. But the operation doesn't take. She gets an infection, and the thing stops being fun, and six months later she's got no neurological response to some of the tissues the doctors have slapped on her, and pain in the others. It costs money to reverse. She doesn't have it. She spends it on other things, she says.

She wants money for the operation, she says, standing in front of you. You owe it to her, she says.

You try to find the ten-year-old in those eyes, and you can't.

Did you ever?

*   *   *

The call came through at six, and I knew it was County.

A full jacket—ward status, medical action, all of it—had been put through. The fetus would be aborted—"for the mother's safety . . . to prevent further exploitation by private interests . . . and physical endangerment by spouse."

Had Antalou been there, she'd have told me how County had already gotten flack from the board of supervisors, state W&I, and the attorney general's office over a V.R. like this slipping through and getting this much press. They wanted it over, done with. If the fetus were aborted, County's position would be clear —to state, the feds, and the religious groups that were starting to scream bloody murder.

It would be an abortion no one would ever complain about.

The husband was down at County holding with a pretty fibercast on his left tibia, but they weren't taking any chances. Word on two interstate conspiracies to kill the ten women had reached the D.A., and they were, they said, taking it seriously. I was, I said, glad to hear it.

Mendoza said he liked sassy women as much as the next guy, but he wanted her back in custody, and the new D.A. was screaming jurisdiction, too. Everyone wanted a piece of the ten o'clock news before the cameras lost interest and rolled on.

Society wasn't ready for it. The atavistic fears were there. You could be on trillazines, you could have an operation to be both a boy and a girl for the thrill of it, you could be a walljacker, but a mother like this, no, not yet.

I should have told someone but didn't. I took her to the zoo instead. We stood in front of the cages watching the holograms of the big cats, the tropical birds, the grass eaters of Africa—the ones that are gone. She wasn't interested in the real ones, she said—the pigeons, sparrows, coyotes, the dull hardy ones that will outlast us all. She never came here as a child, she said, and I believe it. A boyfriend at her one and only job took her once, and later, because she asked her to, so did a woman who wanted the same thing from her.

We watched the lions, the ibex, the white bears. We watched the long-legged wolf, the harp seals, the rheas. We watched the tapes stop and repeat, stop and repeat; and then she said, "Let's go," pulled at my hand, and we moved on to the most important cage of all.

There, the hologram walked back and forth looking out at us, looking through us, its red sagittal crest and furrowed brow so convincing. Alive, its name had been Mark Anthony, the plaque said. It had weighed two hundred kilos. It had lived to be ten. It wasn't one of the two whose child was growing inside her, but she seemed to know this, and it didn't matter.

"They all died the same way," she said to me. "That's what counts, Jo."
Inbred depression, I remembered reading. *Petechial hemorrhages, cirrhosis, renal failure*.

Somewhere in the nation the remaining fertilized ova were sitting frozen in a lab, as they had for thirty years. A few dozen had been removed, thawed, encouraged to divide to sixteen cells, and finally implanted that day seven months ago. Ten had taken. As they should have, naturally, apes that we are. "Sure, it could've been done back then," the cocky young resident with insubordination written all over him had said. "All you'd have needed was an egg and a little plastic tube. And, of course,"—I didn't like the way he smiled—"a woman who was willing. . . ."

I stopped her. I asked her if she knew what The Arks were, and she said no. I started to tell her about the intensive-care zoos where for twenty years the best and brightest of them, ten thousand species in all, had been kept while two hundred thousand others disappeared—the toxics, the new diseases, the land-use policies of a new world taking them one by one—how The Arks hadn't worked, how two thirds of the macrokingdom were gone now, and how the thing she carried inside her was one of them and one of the best.

She wasn't listening. She didn't need to hear it, and I knew the man in the suit had gotten his yes without having to say these things. The idea of having it inside her, hers for a little while, had been enough.

She told me what she was going to buy with the money. She asked me whether I thought the baby would end up at this zoo. I told her I didn't know but could check, and hated the lie. She said she might have to move to another city to be near it. I nodded and didn't say a thing.

I couldn't stand it. I sat her down on a bench and told her what the County was going to do to her.

When I was through she looked at me and said she'd known it would happen, it always happened. She didn't cry. I thought maybe she wanted to leave, but she shook her head.

We went through the zoo one more time. We didn't leave until dark.

"Are you out of your mind, Jo?" Antalou said.

"It's not permanent," I said.

"*Of course* it's not permanent. Everyone's been looking everywhere for her. What the hell do you think you're doing?"

I said it didn't matter, did it? The County homes and units weren't safe, and we didn't want her with Mendoza, and who'd think of a soc worker's house—a P.D. safe house maybe, but not a soc worker's because that's against policy, and everyone knows that soc workers are spineless, right?

"Sure," Antalou said. "But you didn't *tell* anybody, Jo."

"I've had some thinking to do."

Suddenly Antalou got gentle, and I knew what she was thinking. I needed downtime, maybe some psychiatric profiling done. She's a friend of mine, but she's a professional, too. The two of us go back all the way to corrections, Antalou and I, and lying isn't easy.

"Get her over to County holding immediately—that's the best we can do for her," she said finally. "And let's have lunch soon, Jo. I want to know what's going on in that head of yours."

It took me the night and the morning. They put her in the nicest hole they had and doubled the security, and when I left she cried for a long time, they told me. I didn't want to leave, but I had to get some thinking done.

When it was done, I called Antalou.

She swore at me when I was through but said she'd give it a try. It was crazy, but what isn't these days?

The County bit, but with stipulations. Postpartum wipe. New I.D. Fine, but also a fund set up out of *our* money. Antalou groaned. I said. Why not.

Someone at County had a heart, but it was our mention of Statute Forty-A, I found out later, that clinched it. They saw the thing dragging on through the courts, cameras rolling forever, and that was worse than any temporary heat from state or the feds.

So they let her have the baby. I slept in the waiting room of the maternity unit, and it took local troops as well as hospital security to keep the press away. We used a teaching hospital down south—approved by the group that was funding her—but even then the media found out and came by the droves.

We promised full access at a medically approved moment if they cooled it, which they did. The four that didn't were taken bodily from the building under one penal code section or another.

At the beginning of the second stage of labor, the infant abruptly rotates from occiput-posterior to right occiput-anterior position; descent is rapid, and a viable two-thousand-gram female is delivered without episiotomy. Interspecific Apgar scores are nine and ten at one and five minutes, respectively.

The report would sound like all the others I'd read. The only difference would be how the thing looked, and even that wasn't much.

The little head, hairless face, broad nose, black hair sticking up like some old movie comic's. Human eyes, hairless chest, skinny arms. The feet would look like hands, sure, and the skin would be a little gray, but how much was that? To the girl in the bed it wasn't anything at all.

She said she wanted me to be there, and I said sure but didn't know the real reason.

When her water broke, they told me, and I got scrubbed up, put on the green throw-aways like they said, and got back to her room quickly. The contractions had started up like a hammer.

It didn't go smoothly. The cord got hung up on the baby's neck inside, and the fetal monitor started screaming. She got scared; I got scared. They put her up on all fours to shift the baby, but it didn't work. They wheeled her to the O.R. for a C-section, which they really didn't want to do; and for two hours it was fetal signs getting better, then worse, doctors preparing for a section, then the signs somehow getting better again. Epidural block, episiotomy, some concerted forceps work, and the little head finally starts to show.

Lissy was exhausted, making little sounds. More deep breaths, a few encouraging shouts from the doctors, more pushing from Lissy, and the head was through, then the body, white as a ghost from the vernix, and someone was saying something to me in a weak voice.

"Will you cut the cord, please?"

It was Lissy.

I couldn't move. She said it again.

The doctor was waiting, the baby slick in his hands. Lissy was white as a sheet, her forehead shiny with the sweat, and she couldn't see it from where she was. "It would be special to me, Jo," she said.

One of the nurses was beside me saying how it's done all the time—by husbands and lovers, sisters and mothers and friends—but that if I was going to do it I needed to do it now, please.

I tried to remember who had cut the cord when Meg was born, and I couldn't. I could remember a doctor, that was all.

I don't remember taking the surgical steel snips, but I did. I remember not wanting to cut it—flesh and blood, the first of its kind in a long, long time—and when I finally did, it was tough, the cutting made a noise, and then it was over, the mother had the baby in her arms, and everyone was smiling.

A woman could have carried a *Gorilla gorilla beringei* to term without a care in the world a hundred, a thousand, a million years ago. The placenta would have known what to do; the blood would never have mixed. The gestation was the same nine months. The only thing stopping anyone that winter day in '97 when Cleo, the last of her kind on the face of this earth, died of renal failure in the National Zoo in DC, was the thought of carrying it.

It had taken three decades, a well-endowed resurrection group, a slick body broker, and a skinny twenty-one-year-old girl who didn't mind the thought of it.

She wants money for the operation, my daughter says to me that day in the doorway, shoulders heavy, face puffy, slurring it, the throat a throat I don't know, the voice deeper. I tell her again I don't have it, that perhaps her friends—the ones she's helped out so often when she had the money and they didn't—could help her. I say it nicely, with no sarcasm, trying not to look at where she hurts, but she knows exactly what I'm saying.

She goes for my eyes, as if she's had practice, and I don't fight back. She gets my cheek and the corner of my eye, screams something about never loving me and me never loving her—which isn't true.

She knows I know how she'll spend the money, and it makes her mad.

I don't remember the ten-year-old ever wanting to get even with anyone, but this one always does. She hurts. She wants to hurt back. If she knew, if she only knew what I'd carry for her.

I'll find her, I know—tonight, tomorrow morning, the next day or two—sitting at a walljack somewhere in the apartment, her body plugged in, the little unit with its Medusa wires sitting in her lap, her heavy shoulders hunched as if she were praying, and I'll unplug her—to show I care.

But she'll have gotten even with me, and that's what counts, and no matter how much I plead with her, promise her anything she wants, she won't try a program, she won't go with me to County—both of us, together—for help.

Her body doesn't hurt at all when she's on the wall. When you're a walljacker you don't care what kind of tissue's hanging off you, you don't care what you look like—what anyone looks like. The universe is inside. The juice is from the wall, the little unit translates, and the right places in your skull—the medulla all the way to the cerebellum, all the right centers—get played like the keys of the most beautiful synthesizer in the world. You see blue skies that make you cry. You see young men and women who make you come in your pants without your even needing to touch them. You see loving mothers. You see fathers that never leave you.

I'll know what to do. I'll flip the circuit breakers and sit in the darkness with a hand light until she comes out of it, cold-turkeying, screaming mad, and I'll say nothing. I'll tell myself once again that it's the drugs, it's the jacking, it's not her. She's dead and gone and hasn't been the little girl on that train with her hair tucked behind her ears for a long time, that this one's a lie but one I've got to keep playing.

So I walk into the bedroom, and she's there, in the chair, like always. She's got clothes on for a change and doesn't smell, and I find myself thinking how neat she looks—chic even. I don't feel a thing.

As I take a step toward the kitchen and the breaker box, I see what she's done.

I see the wires doubling back to the walljack, and I remember hearing about this from someone. It's getting common, a fad.

There are two ways to do it. You can rig it so that anyone who touches you gets ripped with a treble wall dose in a bypass. Or so that anyone who kills the electricity, even touches the wires, kills you.

Both are tamperproof. The M.E. has twenty bodies to prove it, and the guys stuck with the job downtown don't see a breakthrough for months.

She's opted for the second. Because it hurts the most.

She's starving to death in the chair, cells drying out, unless someone I.V.'s her—carefully. Even then the average expectancy is two months, I remember.

I get out. I go to a cheap hotel downtown. I dream about blackouts in big cities and bodies that move but aren't alive and about daughters. The next morning I get a glucose drip into her arm, and I don't need any help with the needle.

That's what's behind the door, Lissy.

We gave them their press conference. The doctors gave her a mild shot of pergisthan to perk her up, since she wouldn't be nursing, and she did it, held the baby in her arms like a pro, smiled though she was pale as a sheet, and the conference lasted two whole hours. Most of the press went away happy, and two of Mendoza's girls roughed up the three that tried to hide out on the floor that night. "Mendoza says hello," they said, grinning.

The floor returned to normal. I went in.

The mother was asleep. The baby was in the incubator. Three nurses were watching over them.

The body broker came with his team two days later and looked happy. Six of his ten babies had made it.

Her name is Mary McLoughlin. I chose it. Her hair is dark, and she wears it short. She lives in Chula Vista, just south of San Diego, and I get down there as often as I can, and we go out.

She doesn't remember a thing, so I was the one who had to suggest it. We go to the zoo, the San Diego Zoo, one of the biggest once. We go to the primates. We stand in front of the new exhibit, and she tells me how the real thing is so much better than the holograms, which she thinks she's seen before but isn't sure.

The baby is a year old now. They've named her Cleo, and they keep her behind glass—two or three vets in gauze masks with her at all times—safe from the air and diseases. But we get to stand there, watching her like the rest, up close, while she looks at us and clowns.

No one recognizes the dark-haired girl I'm with. The other one, the one who'd have good reason to be here, disappeared long ago, the media says. Sometimes the spotlight is just too great, they said.

"I can almost smell her, Jo," she says, remembering a dream, a vague thing, a kitten slept with. "She's not full-grown, you know."

I tell her, yes, I know.

"She's sure funny looking, isn't she."

I nod.

"Hey, I think she knows me!" She says it with a laugh, doesn't know what she's said. "Look at how she's looking at me!"

The creature is looking at her—it's looking at all of us and with eyes that aren't dumb. Looking at us, not through us.

"Can we come back tomorrow, Jo?" she asks when the crowd gets too heavy to see through.

Of course, I say. We'll come a lot, I say.

I've filed for guardianship under Statute Twenty-seven, the old W&I provisions, and if it goes through, Lissy will be moving back to L.A. with me. *I'm hetero, so it won't get kicked for exploitation, and I'm in the right field*, I think. I can't move myself, but we'll go down to the zoo every weekend. It'll be good to get away. Mendoza has asked me out, and who knows, I may say yes.

But I still have to have that lunch with Antalou, and I have no idea what I'm going to tell her.

CONNIE WILLIS

The Last of the Winnebagoes

Connie Willis lives in Greeley, Colorado, with her family. She first attracted attention as a writer in the late '70s with a number of outstanding stories for the now-defunct magazine *Galileo*, and in the subsequent few years has made a large name for herself very fast indeed. In 1982, she won two Nebula Awards, one for her superb novelette "Fire Watch," and one for her poignant short story "A Letter from the Clearys"; a few months later, "Fire Watch" went on to win her a Hugo Award as well. Her short fiction has appeared in *Isaac Asimov's Science Fiction Magazine, Omni, The Magazine of Fantasy and Science Fiction, The Berkley Showcase, The Twilight Zone Magazine, The Missouri Review*, and elsewhere. Her books include the novel *Water Witch*, written in collaboration with Cynthia Felice, and *Fire Watch*, a collection of her short fiction. Her most recent book was *Lincoln's Dreams*, her first solo novel. Upcoming is another novel in collaboration with Cynthia Felice, and a new solo novel. Her story "The Sidon in the Mirror" was in our First Annual Collection, her story "Blued Moon" was in our Second Annual Collection, and her story "Chance" was in our Fourth Annual Collection.

In the ingenious, bittersweet, and powerful story that follows, she takes us to near-future Arizona to unravel a mystery of the hidden depths of the human heart.

THE LAST OF THE WINNEBAGOES

Connie Willis

On the way out to Tempe I saw a dead jackal in the road. I was in the far left lane of Van Buren, ten lanes away from it, and its long legs were facing away from me, the squarish muzzle flat against the pavement so it looked narrower than it really was, and for a minute I thought it was a dog.

I had not seen an animal in the road like that for fifteen years. They can't get onto the divideds, of course, and most of the multiways are fenced. And people are more careful of their animals.

The jackal was probably somebody's pet. This part of Phoenix was mostly residential, and after all this time, people still think they can turn the nasty, carrion-loving creatures into pets. Which was no reason to have hit it and, worse, left it there. It's a felony to strike an animal and another one to not report it, but whoever had hit it was long gone.

I pulled the Hitori over onto the center shoulder and sat there awhile, staring at the empty multiway. I wondered who had hit it and whether they had stopped to see if it was dead.

Katie had stopped. She had hit the brakes so hard she sent the car into a skid that brought it up against the ditch, and jumped out of the jeep. I was still running toward him, floundering in the snow. We made it to him almost at the same time. I knelt beside him, the camera dangling from my neck, its broken case hanging half open.

"I hit him," Katie had said. "I hit him with the jeep."

I looked in the rearview mirror. I couldn't even see over the pile of camera equipment in the back seat with the eisenstadt balanced on top. I got out. I had come nearly a mile, and looking back, I couldn't see the jackal, though I knew now that's what it was.

"McCombe! David! Are you there yet?" Ramirez's voice said from inside the car.

I leaned in. "No," I shouted in the general direction of the phone's mike. "I'm still on the multiway."

"Mother of God, what's taking you so long? The governor's conference is at twelve, and I want you to go out to Scottsdale and do a layout on the closing of Taliesin West. The appointment's for ten. Listen, McCombe, I got the poop on the Amblers for you. They bill themselves as 'One Hundred Percent Authentic,' but they're not. Their RV isn't really a Winnebago, it's an Open Road. It *is* the last RV on the road, though, according to Highway Patrol. A man named Eldridge was touring with one, also *not* a Winnebago, a Shasta, until March, but he lost his license in Oklahoma for using a tanker lane, so this is it. Recreation vehicles are banned in all but four states. Texas has legislation in committee, and Utah has a full-divided bill coming up next month. Arizona will be next, so take lots of pictures, Davey boy. This may be your last chance. And get some of the zoo."

"What about the Amblers?" I said.

"Their name *is* Ambler, believe it or not. I ran a lifeline on them. He was a welder. She was a bank teller. No kids. They've been doing this since eighty-nine when he retired. Nineteen years. David, are you using the eisenstadt?"

We had been through this the last three times I'd been on a shoot. "I'm not *there* yet," I said.

"Well, I want you to use it at the governor's conference. Set it on his desk if you can."

I intended to set it on a desk, all right. One of the desks at the back, and let it get some nice shots of the rear ends of reporters as they reached wildly for a little clear air-space to shoot their pictures in, some of them holding their vidcams in their upstretched arms and aiming them in what they hope is the right direction because they can't see the governor at all, let it get a nice shot of one of the reporter's arms as he knocked it face-down on the desk.

"This one's a new model. It's got a trigger. It's set for faces, full-lengths, and vehicles."

So great. I come home with a hundred-frame cartridge full of passersby and tricycles. How the hell did it know when to click the shutter or which one the governor was in a press conference of eight hundred people, full-length *or* face? It was supposed to have all kinds of fancy light-metrics and computer-composition features, but all it could really do was mindlessly snap whatever passed in front of its idiot lens, just like the highway speed cameras.

It had probably been designed by the same government types who'd put the highway cameras along the road instead of overhead so that all it takes is a little speed to reduce the new side-license plates to a blur, and people go faster than ever. A great camera, the eisenstadt. I could hardly wait to use it.

"Sun-co's very interested in the eisenstadt," Ramirez said. She didn't say goodbye. She never does. She just stops talking and then starts up again later. I looked back in the direction of the jackal.

The multiway was completely deserted. New cars and singles don't use the undivided multiways much, even during rush hours. Too many of the little cars have been squashed by tankers. Usually there are at least a few obsoletes and renegade semis taking advantage of the Patrol's being on the divideds, but there wasn't anybody at all.

I got back in the car and backed up even with the jackal. I turned off the ignition but didn't get out. I could see the trickle of blood from its mouth from here. A tanker went roaring past out of nowhere, trying to beat the cameras, straddling the three middle lanes and crushing the jackal's rear half to a bloody mush. It was a good thing I hadn't been trying to cross the road. He never would have even seen me.

I started the car and drove to the nearest off-ramp to find a phone. There was one at an old 7-Eleven on McDowell.

"I'm calling to report a dead animal on the road," I told the woman who answered the Society's phone.

"Name and number?"

"It's a jackal," I said. "It's between Thirtieth and Thirty-Second on Van Buren. It's in the far right lane."

"Did you render emergency assistance?"

"There was no assistance to be rendered. It was dead."

"Did you move the animal to the side of the road?"

"No."

"Why not?" she said, her tone suddenly sharper, more alert.

Because I thought it was a dog. "I didn't have a shovel," I said, and hung up.

I got out to Tempe by eight-thirty, in spite of the fact that every tanker in the state suddenly decided to take Van Buren. I got pushed out onto the shoulder and drove on that most of the way.

The Winnebago was set up in the fairgrounds between Phoenix and Tempe, next to the old zoo. The flyer had said they would be open from nine to nine, and I had wanted to get most of my pictures before they opened, but it was already a quarter to nine, and even if there were no cars in the dusty parking lot, I was probably too late.

It's a tough job being a photographer. The minute most people see a camera, their real faces close like a shutter in too much light, and all that's left is their camera face, their public face. It's a smiling face, except in the case of Saudi terrorists or senators, but, smiling or not, it shows no real emotion. Actors, politicians, people who have their pictures taken all the time are the worst. The longer the person's been in the public eye, the easier it is for me to get great vidcam footage and the harder it is to get anything approaching a real photograph, and the Amblers had been at this for nearly twenty years. By a quarter to nine they would already have their camera faces on.

I parked down at the foot of the hill next to the clump of ocotillas and yucca where the zoo sign had been, pulled my Nikon longshot out of the mess in the back seat, and took some shots of the sign they'd set up by the multiway: "See a Genuine Winnebago. One Hundred Percent Authentic."

The Genuine Winnebago was parked longways against the stone banks of cacti and palms at the front of the zoo. Ramirez had said it wasn't a real Winnebago, but it had the identifying W with its extending stripes running the length of the RV, and it seemed to me to be the right shape, though I hadn't seen one in at least ten years.

I was probably the wrong person for this story. I had never had any great love for RV's, and my first thought when Ramirez called with the assignment was that there are some things that should be extinct, like mosquitoes and lane dividers, and RV's are right at the top of the list. They had been everywhere in the mountains when I'd lived in Colorado, crawling along in the left-hand lane, taking up two lanes even in the days when a lane was fifteen feet wide, with a train of cursing cars behind them.

I'd been behind one on Independence Pass that had stopped cold while a ten-year-old got out to take pictures of the scenery with an Instamatic, and one of them had tried to take the curve in front of my house and ended up in my ditch, looking like a beached whale. But that was always a bad curve.

An old man in an ironed short-sleeved shirt came out the side door and around to the front end and began washing the Winnebago with a sponge and a bucket. I wondered where he had gotten the water. According to Ramirez's advance work, which she'd sent me over the modem about the Winnebago, it had maybe a fifty-gallon water tank, tops, which is barely enough for drinking water, a shower, and maybe washing a dish or two, and there certainly weren't any hookups here at the zoo, but he was swilling water onto the front bumper and even over the tires as if he had more than enough.

I took a few shots of the RV standing in the huge expanse of parking lot and then hit the longshot to full for a picture of the old man working on the bumper. He had large reddish-brown freckles on his arms and the top of his bald head, and he scrubbed away at the bumper with a vengeance. After a minute he stopped and stepped back, and then called to his wife. He looked worried, or maybe just crabby. I was too far away to tell if he had snapped out her name impatiently or simply called her to come and look, and I couldn't see his face. She opened the metal side door, with its narrow louvered window, and stepped down onto the metal step.

The old man asked her something, and she, still standing on the step, looked out toward the multiway and shook her head, and then came around to the front, wiping her hands on a dishtowel, and they both stood there looking at his handiwork.

They were One Hundred Percent Authentic, even if the Winnebago wasn't, down to her flowered blouse and polyester slacks, probably also one hundred percent, and the cross-stitched rooster on the dishtowel. She had on brown leather slip-ons like I remembered my grandmother wearing, and I was willing to bet she had set her thinning white hair on bobby pins. Their bio said they were in their eighties, but I would have put them in their nineties, although I wondered if they were too perfect and therefore fake, like the Winnebago. But she went on wiping her hands on the dishtowel the way my grandmother had when she was upset, even though I couldn't see if her face was showing any emotion, and that action at least was authentic.

She apparently told him the bumper looked fine because he dropped the dripping sponge into the bucket and went around behind the Winnebago. She went back inside, shutting the metal door behind her even though it had to be already at least a hundred and ten out, and they hadn't even bothered to park under what scanty shade the palms provided.

I put the longshot back in the car. The old man came around the front with a big plywood sign. He propped it against the vehicle's side. "The Last of the Winnebagos," the sign read in somebody's idea of what Indian writing should look like. "See a vanishing breed. Admission—Adults—$8.00, Children under twelve—$5.00 Open 9 A.M. to Sunset." He strung up a row of red and yellow flags, and then picked up the bucket and started toward the door, but halfway there he stopped and took a few steps down the parking lot to where I thought he probably had a good view of the road, and then went back, walking like an old man, and took another swipe at the bumper with the sponge.

"Are you done with the RV yet, McCombe?" Ramirez said on the car phone.

I slung the camera into the back. "I just got here. Every tanker in Arizona was on Van Buren this morning. Why the hell don't you have me do a piece on abuses of the multiway system by water-haulers?"

"Because I want you to get to Tempe alive. The governor's press conference has been moved to one, so you're okay. Have you used the eisenstadt yet?"

"I told you, I just got here. I haven't even turned the damned thing on."

"You don't turn it on. It self-activates when you set it bottom down on a level surface."

Great. It had probably already shot its 100-frame cartridge on the way here.

"Well, if you don't use it on the Winnebago, make sure you use it at the governor's conference," she said. "By the way, have you thought any more about moving to investigative?"

That was why Sun-co was really so interested in the eisenstadt. It had been easier to send a photographer who could write stories than it had to send a photographer and a reporter, especially in the little one-seater Hitoris they were ordering now, which was how I got to be a photojournalist. And since that had worked out so well, why send either? Send an eisenstadt and a DAT deck and you won't need an Hitori and way-mile credits to get them there. You can send them through the mail. They can sit unnoticed on the old governor's desk, and after a while somebody in a one-seater who wouldn't have to be either a photographer *or* a reporter can sneak in to retrieve them and a dozen others.

"No," I said, glancing back up the hill. The old man gave one last swipe to the front bumper and then walked over to one of the zoo's old stone-edged planters and dumped the bucket in on a tangle of prickly pear, which would probably think it was a spring shower and bloom before I made it up the hill. "Look, if I'm going to get any pictures before the touristas arrive, I'd better go."

"I wish you'd think about it. And use the eisenstadt this time. You'll like it once you try it. Even *you'll* forget it's a camera."

"I'll bet," I said. I looked back down the multiway. Nobody at all was coming now. Maybe that was what all the Amblers' anxiety was about—I should have asked Ramirez what their average daily attendance was and what sort of people used up credits to come this far out and see an old beat-up RV. The curve into Tempe alone was three point two miles. Maybe nobody came at all. If that was the case, I might have a chance of getting some decent pictures. I got in the Hitori and drove up the steep drive.

"Howdy," the old man said, all smiles, holding out his reddish-brown freckled hand to shake mine. "Name's Jake Ambler. And this here's Winnie," he said, patting the metal side of the RV, "Last of the Winnebagos. Is there just the one of you?"

"David McCombe," I said, holding out my press pass. "I'm a photographer. Sun-co. Phoenix *Sun*, Tempe-Mesa *Tribune*, Glendale *Star*, and affiliated stations. I was wondering if I could take some pictures of your vehicle?" I touched my pocket and turned the taper on.

"You bet. We've always cooperated with the media, Mrs. Ambler and me. I was just cleaning old Winnie up," he said. "She got pretty dusty on the way down from Globe." He didn't make any attempt to tell his wife I was there, even though she could hardly avoid hearing us, and she didn't open the metal door again. "We been on the road now with Winnie for almost twenty years. Bought her in 1989 in Forest City, Iowa, where they were made. The wife didn't want to buy her, didn't know if she'd like traveling, but now she's the one wouldn't part with it."

He was well into his spiel now, an open, friendly, I-have-nothing-to-hide expression on his face that hid everything. There was no point in taking any stills, so I got out the vidcam and shot the TV footage while he led me around the RV.

"This up here," he said, standing with one foot on the flimsy metal ladder and patting the metal bar around the top, "is the luggage rack, and this is the holding tank. It'll hold thirty gallons and has an automatic electric pump that hooks up to any waste hookup. Empties in five minutes, and you don't even get your hands dirty." He held up his fat pink hands palms forward as if to show me. "Water tank," he said, slapping a silver metal tank next to it. "Holds forty gallons, which is plenty for just the two of us. Interior space is a hundred fifty cubic feet with six feet four of headroom. That's plenty even for a tall guy like yourself.''

He gave me the whole tour. His manner was easy, just short of slap-on-the-back hearty, but he looked relieved when an ancient VW bug came chugging catty-cornered up through the parking lot. He must have thought they wouldn't have any customers either.

A family piled out, Japanese tourists, a woman with short black hair, a man in shorts, two kids. One of the kids had a ferret on a leash.

"I'll just look around while you tend to the paying customers," I told him.

I locked the vidcam in the car, took the longshot, and went up toward the zoo. I took a wide-angle of the zoo sign for Ramirez. I could see it now—she'd run a caption like, "The old zoo stands empty today. No sound of lion's roar, of elephant's trumpeting, of children's laughter, can be heard here. The old Phoenix Zoo, last of its kind, while just outside its gates stands yet another last of its kind. Story on page 10." Maybe it would be a good idea to let the eisenstadts and the computers take over.

I went inside. I hadn't been out here in years. In the late eighties there had been a big flap over zoo policy. I had taken the pictures, but I hadn't covered the story since there were still such things as reporters back then. I had photographed the cages in question and the new zoo director who had caused all the flap by stopping the zoo's renovation project cold and giving the money to a wildlife protection group.

"I refuse to spend money on cages when in a few years we'll have nothing to put in them. The timber wolf, the California condor, the grizzly bear, are in imminent danger of becoming extinct, and it's our responsibility to save them, not make a comfortable prison for the last survivors."

The Society had called him an alarmist, which just goes to show you how much things can change. Well, he was an alarmist, wasn't he? The grizzly bear isn't extinct in the wild—it's Colorado's biggest tourist draw, and there are so many whooping cranes Texas is talking about limited hunting.

In all the uproar, the zoo had ceased to exist, and the animals all went to an even more comfortable prison in Sun City—sixteen acres of savannah land for the zebras and lions, and snow manufactured daily for the polar bears.

They hadn't really been cages, in spite of what the zoo director said. The old capybara enclosure, which was the first thing inside the gate, was a nice little meadow with a low stone wall around it. A family of prairie dogs had taken up residence in the middle of it.

I went back to the gate and looked down at the Winnebago. The family circled the Winnebago, the man bending down to look underneath the body. One of the kids was hanging off the ladder at the back of the RV. The ferret was nosing around the front wheel Jake Ambler had so carefully scrubbed down, looking like it was about ready to lift its leg, if ferrets do that. The kid yanked on its leash and then picked it up in his arms. The mother said something to him. Her nose was sunburned.

Katie's nose had been sunburned. She had had that white cream on it, that skiers used to use. She was wearing a parka and jeans and bulky pink-and-white moonboots that she couldn't run in, but she still made it to Aberfan before I did. I pushed past her and knelt over him.

"I hit him," she said bewilderedly. "I hit a dog."

"Get back in the jeep, damn it!" I shouted at her. I stripped off my sweater and tried to wrap him in it. "We've got to get him to the vet."

"Is he dead?" Katie said, her face as pale as the cream on her nose.

"No!" I had shouted. "No, he isn't dead."

The mother turned and looked up toward the zoo, her hand shading her face. She caught sight of the camera, dropped her hand, and smiled, a toothy, impossible smile. People in the public eye are the worst, but even people having a snapshot taken close down somehow, and it isn't just the phony smile. It's as if that old superstition is true, and cameras do really steal the soul.

I pretended to take her picture and then lowered the camera. The zoo director had put up a row of tombstone-shaped signs in front of the gate, one for each endangered species. They were covered with plastic, which hadn't helped much. I wiped the streaky dust off the one in front of me. "Canis latrans," it said, with two green stars after it. "Coyote. North American wild dog. Due to large-scale poisoning by ranchers, who saw it as a threat to cattle and sheep, the coyote is nearly extinct in the wild." Underneath there was a photograph of a ragged coyote sitting on its haunches and an explanation of the stars. Blue—endangered species. Yellow—endangered habitat. Red—extinct in the wild.

After Misha died, I had come out here to photograph the dingo and the coyotes and the wolves, but they were already in the process of moving the zoo, so I couldn't get any pictures, and it probably wouldn't have done any good. The coyote in the picture had faded to a greenish-yellow and its yellow eyes were almost white, but it stared out of the picture looking as hearty and unconcerned as Jake Ambler, wearing its camera face.

The mother had gone back to the bug and was herding the kids inside. Mr. Ambler walked the father back to the car, shaking his shining bald head, and the man talked some more, leaning on the open door, and then got in and drove off. I walked back down.

If he was bothered by the fact that they had only stayed ten minutes and that, as far as I had been able to see, no money had changed hands, it didn't show in his face. He led me around to the side of the RV and pointed to a chipped and faded collection of decals along the painted bar of the W. "These here are the states we've been in." He pointed to the one nearest the front. "Every state in the Union, plus Canada and Mexico. Last state we were in was Nevada."

Up this close it was easy to see where he had painted out the name of the original RV and covered it with the bar of red. The paint had the dull look of un-authenticity. He had covered up the "Open Road" with a burnt-wood plaque that read, "The Amblin' Amblers."

He pointed at a bumper sticker next to the door that said, "I got lucky in Vegas at Caesar's Palace," and had a picture of a naked showgirl. "We couldn't find a decal for Nevada. I don't think they make them anymore. And you know something else you can't find? Steering wheel covers. You know the kind. That keep the wheel from burning your hands when it gets hot?"

"Do you do all the driving?" I asked.

He hesitated before answering, and I wondered if one of them didn't have a license. I'd have to look it up in the lifeline. "Mrs. Ambler spells me sometimes, but I do most of it. Mrs. Ambler reads the map. Damn maps nowadays are so hard to read. Half the time you can't tell what kind of road it is. They don't make them like they used to."

We talked for a while more about all the things you couldn't find a decent one of anymore and the sad state things had gotten in generally, and then I announced I wanted to talk to Mrs. Ambler, got the vidcam and the eisenstadt out of the car, and went inside the Winnebago.

She still had the dishtowel in her hand, even though there couldn't possibly be space for that many dishes in the tiny RV. The inside was even smaller than I had thought it would be, low enough that I had to duck and so narrow I had to hold the Nikon close to my body to keep from hitting the lens on the passenger seat. It felt like an oven inside, and it was only nine o'clock in the morning.

I set the eisenstadt down on the kitchen counter, making sure its concealed lens was facing out. If it would work anywhere, it would be here. There was basically nowhere for Mrs. Ambler to go that she could get out of range. There was nowhere I could go either, and sorry, Ramirez, there are just some things a live photographer can do better than a preprogrammed one, like stay out of the picture.

"This is the galley," Mrs. Ambler said, folding her dishtowel and hanging it from a plastic ring on the cupboard below the sink with the cross-stitch design showing. It wasn't a rooster after all. It was a poodle wearing a sunbonnet and carrying a basket. "Shop on Wednesday," the motto underneath said.

"As you can see, we have a double sink with a hand-pump faucet. The refrigerator is LP-electric and holds four cubic feet. Back here is the dinette area. The table folds up into the rear wall, and we have our bed. And this is our bathroom."

She was as bad as her husband. "How long have you had the Winnebago?" I said to stop the spiel. Sometimes, if you can get people talking about something besides what they intended to talk about, you can disarm them into something like a natural expression.

"Nineteen years," she said, lifting up the lid of the chemical toilet. "We bought it in 1989. I didn't want to buy it—I didn't like the idea of selling our house and going gallivanting off like a couple of hippies, but Jake went ahead and bought it, and now I wouldn't trade it for anything. The shower operates on a forty-gallon pressurized water system." She stood back so I could get a picture of the shower stall, so narrow you wouldn't have to worry about dropping the soap. I dutifully took some vidcam footage.

"You live here full-time then?" I said, trying not to let my voice convey how impossible that prospect sounded. Ramirez had said they were from Minnesota. I had assumed they had a house there and only went on the road for part of the year.

"Jake says the great outdoors is our home," she said. I gave up trying to get a picture of her and snapped a few high-quality detail stills for the papers: the "Pilot" sign taped on the dashboard in front of the driver's seat, the crocheted granny-square afghan on the uncomfortable-looking couch, a row of salt and pepper shakers in the back windows—Indian children, black scottie dogs, ears of corn.

"Sometimes we live on the open prairies and sometimes on the seashore," she said. She went over to the sink and hand-pumped a scant two cups of water into a little pan and set it on the two-burner stove. She took down two turquoise melmac cups and flowered saucers and a jar of freeze-dried and spooned a little into the cups. "Last year we were in the Colorado Rockies. We can have a house on a lake or in the desert, and when we get tired of it, we just move on. Oh, my, the things we've seen."

I didn't believe her. Colorado had been one of the first states to ban recreational vehicles, even before the gas crunch and the multiways. It had banned them on the passes first and then shut them out of the national forests, and by the time I left they weren't even allowed on the interstates.

Ramirez had said RV's were banned outright in forty-seven states. New Mexico was one, Utah had heavy restricks, and daytime travel was forbidden in all the western states. Whatever they'd seen, and it sure wasn't Colorado, they had seen it in the dark or on some unpatrolled multiway, going like sixty to outrun the cameras. Not exactly the footloose and fancy-free life they tried to paint.

The water boiled. Mrs. Ambler poured it into the cups, spilling a little on the turquoise saucers. She blotted it up with the dishtowel. "We came down here because of the snow. They get winter so early in Colorado."

"I know," I said. It had snowed two feet, and it was only the middle of September. Nobody even had their snow tires on. The aspens hadn't turned yet, and some of the branches broke under the weight of the snow. Katie's nose was still sunburned from the summer.

"Where did you come from just now?" I asked her.

"Globe," she said, and opened the door to yell to her husband. "Jake! Coffee!" She carried the cups to the table-that-converts-into-a-bed. "It has leaves that you can put in it so it seats six," she said.

I sat down at the table so she was on the side where the eisenstadt could catch her. The sun was coming in through the cranked-open back windows, already hot. Mrs. Ambler got onto her knees on the plaid cushions and let down a woven cloth shade, carefully, so it wouldn't knock the salt and pepper shakers off.

There were some snapshots stuck up between the ceramic ears of corn. I picked one up. It was a square Polaroid from the days when you had to peel off the print and glue it to a stiff card: The two of them, looking exactly the way they did now, with that friendly, impenetrable camera smile, were standing in front of a blur of orange rock—the Grand Canyon? Zion? Monument Valley? Polaroid had always chosen color over definition. Mrs. Ambler was holding a little yellow blur in her arms that could have been a cat but wasn't. It was a dog.

"That's Jake and me at Devil's Tower," she said, taking the picture away from me. "And Taco. You can't tell from this picture, but she was the cutest little thing. A chihuahua." She handed it back to me and rummaged behind the salt and pepper shakers. "Sweetest little dog you ever saw. This will give you a better idea."

The picture she handed me was considerably better, a matte print done with a decent camera. Mrs. Ambler was holding the chihuahua in this one, too, standing in front of the Winnebago.

"She used to sit on the arm of Jake's chair while he drove and when we came to a red light she'd look at it, and when it turned green she'd bark to tell him to go. She was the smartest little thing."

I looked at the dog's flaring, pointed ears, its bulging eyes and rat's snout. The dogs never come through. I took dozens of pictures, there at the end, and they might as well have been calendar shots. Nothing of the real dog at all. I decided it was the lack of muscles in their faces—they could not smile, in spite of what their owners claimed. It is the muscles in the face that make people leap across the years in pictures. The expressions on dogs' faces were what breeding had fastened on them—the gloomy bloodhound, the alert collie, the rakish mutt —and anything else was wishful thinking on the part of the doting master, who would also swear that a color-blind chihuahua with a brain pan the size of a Mexican jumping bean could tell when the light changed.

My theory of the facial muscles doesn't really hold water, of course. Cats can't smile either, and they come through. Smugness, slyness, disdain—all of those expressions come through beautifully, and they don't have any muscles in their faces either, so maybe it's love that you can't capture in a picture because love was the only expression dogs were capable of.

I was still looking at the picture. "She is a cute little thing," I said and handed it back to her. "She wasn't very big, was she?"

"I could carry Taco in my jacket pocket. We didn't name her Taco. We got her from a man in California that named her that," she said, as if she could see herself that the dog didn't come through in the picture. As if, had she named the dog herself, it would have been different. Then the name would have been a more real name, and Taco would have, by default, become more real as well. As if a name could convey what the picture didn't—all the things the little dog did and was and meant to her.

Names don't do it either, of course. I had named Aberfan myself. The vet's assistant, when he heard it, typed it in as Abraham.

"Age?" he had said calmly, even though he had no business typing all this into a computer, he should have been in the operating room with the vet.

"You've got that in there, damn it," I shouted.

He looked calmly puzzled. "I don't know any Abraham . . ."

"Aberfan, damn it. Aberfan!"

"Here it is," the assistant said imperturbably.

Katie, standing across the desk, looked up from the screen. "He had the newparvo and lived through it?" she said bleakly.

"He had the newparvo and lived through it," I said, "until you came along."

"I had an Australian shepherd," I told Mrs. Ambler.

Jake came into the Winnebago, carrying the plastic bucket. "Well, it's about time," Mrs. Ambler said. "Your coffee's getting cold."

"I was just going to finish washing off Winnie," he said. He wedged the bucket into the tiny sink and began pumping vigorously with the heel of his hand. "She got mighty dusty coming down through all that sand."

"I was telling Mr. McCombe here about Taco," she said, getting up and taking him the cup and saucer. "Here, drink your coffee before it gets cold."

"I'll be in in a minute," he said. He stopped pumping and tugged the bucket out of the sink.

"Mr. McCombe had a dog," she said, still holding the cup out to him. "He had an Australian shepherd. I was telling him about Taco."

"He's not interested in that," Jake said. They exchanged one of those warning looks that married couples are so good at. "Tell him about the Winnebago. That's what he's here for."

Jake went back outside. I screwed the longshot's lens cap on and put the vidcam back in its case. She took the little pan off the miniature stove and poured the coffee back into it. "I think I've got all the pictures I need," I said to her back.

She didn't turn around. "He never liked Taco. He wouldn't even let her sleep on the bed with us. Said it made his legs cramp. A little dog like that that didn't weigh anything."

I took the longshot's lens cap back off.

"You know what we were doing the day she died? We were out shopping. I didn't want to leave her alone, but Jake said she'd be fine. It was ninety degrees that day, and he just kept on going from store to store, and when we got back she was dead.'' She set the pan on the stove and turned on the burner. ''The vet said it was the newparvo, but it wasn't. She died from the heat, poor little thing.''

I set the Nikon down gently on the formica table and estimated the settings.

''When did Taco die?'' I asked her, to make her turn around.

''Ninety,'' she said. She turned back to me, and I let my hand come down on the button in an almost soundless click, but her public face was still in place: apologetic now, smiling, a little sheepish. ''My, that was a long time ago.''

I stood up and collected my cameras. ''I think I've got all the pictures I need,'' I said again. ''If I don't, I'll come back out.''

''Don't forget your briefcase,'' she said, handing me the eisenstadt. ''Did your dog die of the newparvo, too?''

''He died fifteen years ago,'' I said. ''In ninety-three.''

She nodded understandingly. ''The third wave,'' she said.

I went outside. Jake was standing behind the Winnebago, under the back window, holding the bucket. He shifted it to his left hand and held out his right hand to me. ''You get all the pictures you needed?'' he asked.

''Yeah,'' I said. ''I think your wife showed me about everything.'' I shook his hand.

''You come on back out if you need any more pictures,'' he said, and sounded, if possible, even more jovial, open-handed, friendly than he had before. ''Mrs. Ambler and me, we always cooperate with the media.''

''Your wife was telling me about your chihuahua,'' I said, more to see the effect on him than anything else.

''Yeah, the wife still misses that little dog after all these years,'' he said, and he looked the way she had, mildly apologetic, still smiling. ''It died of the newparvo. I told her she ought to get it vaccinated, but she kept putting it off.'' He shook his head. ''Of course, it wasn't really her fault. You know whose fault the newparvo really was, don't you?''

Yeah, I knew. It was the communists' fault, and it didn't matter that all their dogs had died, too, because he would say their chemical warfare had gotten out of hand or that everybody knows commies hate dogs. Or maybe it was the fault of the Japanese, though I doubted that. He was, after all, in a tourist business. Or the Democrats or the atheists or all of them put together, and even that was One Hundred Percent Authentic—portrait of the kind of man who drives a Winnebago—but I didn't want to hear it. I walked over to the Hitori and slung the eisenstadt in the back.

''You know who really killed your dog, don't you?'' he called after me.

''Yes,'' I said, and got in the car.

I went home, fighting my way through a fleet of red-painted water tankers who weren't even bothering to try to outrun the cameras and thinking about Taco. My grandmother had had a chihuahua. Perdita. Meanest dog that ever lived. Used to lurk behind the door waiting to take Labrador-sized chunks out of my leg. And my grandmother's. It developed some lingering chihuahuan ailment that made it incontinent and even more ill-tempered, if that was possible.

Toward the end, it wouldn't even let my grandmother near it, but she refused to have it put to sleep and was unfailingly kind to it, even though I never saw any indication that the dog felt anything but unrelieved spite toward her. If the newparvo hadn't come along, it probably would still have been around making her life miserable.

I wondered what Taco, the wonder dog, able to distinguish red and green at a single intersection, had really been like, and if it had died of heat prostration. And what it had been like for the Amblers, living all that time in a hundred and fifty cubic feet together and blaming each other for their own guilt.

I called Ramirez as soon as I got home, breaking in without announcing myself, the way she always did. "I need a lifeline," I said.

"I'm glad you called," she said. "You got a call from the Society. And how's this as a slant for your story? 'The Winnebago and the Winnebagos.' They're an Indian tribe. In Minnesota, I think—why the hell aren't you at the governor's conference?"

"I came home," I said. "What did the Society want?"

"They didn't say. They asked for your schedule. I told them you were with the governor in Tempe. Is this about a story?"

"Yeah."

"Well, you run a proposal past me before you write it. The last thing the paper needs is to get in trouble with the Society."

"The lifeline's for Katherine Powell." I spelled it.

She spelled it back to me. "Is she connected with the Society story?"

"No."

"Then what is she connected with? I've got to put something on the request-for-info."

"Put down background."

"For the Winnebago story?"

"Yes," I said. "For the Winnebago story. How long will it take?"

"That depends. When do you plan to tell me why you ditched the governor's conference? *And* Taliesin West. Jesus Maria, I'll have to call the *Republic* and see if they'll trade footage. I'm sure they'll be thrilled to have shots of an extinct RV. That is, assuming you got any shots. You did make it out to the zoo, didn't you?"

"Yes. I got vidcam footage, stills, the works. I even used the eisenstadt."

"Mind sending your pictures in while I look up your old flame, or is that too much to ask? I don't know how long this will take. It took me two days to get clearance on the Amblers. Do you want the whole thing—pictures, documentation?"

"No. Just a resume. And a phone number."

She cut out, still not saying goodbye. If phones still had receivers, Ramirez would be a great one for hanging up on people. I highwired the vidcam footage and the eisenstadts in to the paper and then fed the eisenstadt cartridge into the developer. I was more than a little curious about what kind of pictures it would take, in spite of the fact that it was trying to do me out of a job. At least it used high-res film and not some damn two hundred thousand-pixel TV substitute. I didn't believe it could compose, and I doubted if the eisenstadt would be able to do foreground-background either, but it might, under certain circumstances, get a picture I couldn't.

The doorbell rang. I answered the door. A lanky young man in a Hawaiian shirt and baggies was standing on the front step, and there was another man in a Society uniform out in the driveway.

"Mr. McCombe?" he said, extending a hand. "Jim Hunter. Humane Society."

I don't know what I'd expected—that they wouldn't bother to trace the call? That they'd let somebody get away with leaving a dead animal on the road?

"I just wanted to stop by and thank you on behalf of the Society for phoning in that report on the jackal. Can I come in?"

He smiled, an open, friendly, smug smile, as if he expected me to be stupid enough to say, "I don't know what you're talking about," and slam the screen door on his hand.

"Just doing my duty," I said, smiling back at him.

"Well, we really appreciate responsible citizens like you. It makes our job a whole lot easier." He pulled a folded readout from his shirt pocket. "I just need to double-check a couple of things. You're a reporter for Sunco, is that right?"

"Photo-journalist," I said.

"And the Hitori you were driving belongs to the paper?"

I nodded.

"It has a phone. Why didn't you use it to make the call?"

The uniform was bending over the Hitori.

"I didn't realize it had a phone. The paper just bought the Hitoris. This is only the second time I've had one out."

Since they knew the paper had had phones put in, they also knew what I'd just told them. I wondered where they'd gotten the info. Public phones were supposed to be tap-free, and if they'd read the license number off one of the cameras, they wouldn't know who'd had the car unless they'd talked to Ramirez, and if they'd talked to her, she wouldn't have been talking blithely about the last thing she needed being trouble with the Society.

"You didn't know the car had a phone," he said, "so you drove to—" He consulted the readout, somehow giving the impression he was taking notes. I'd have bet there was a taper in the pocket of that shirt. "—The 7-Eleven at McDowell and Fortieth Street, and made the call from there. Why didn't you give the Society rep your name and address?"

"I was in a hurry," I said. "I had two assignments to cover before noon, the second out in Scottsdale."

"Which is why you didn't render assistance to the animal either. Because you were in a hurry."

You bastard, I thought. "No," I said. "I didn't render assistance because there wasn't any assistance to be rendered. The—it was dead."

"And how did you know that, Mr. McCombe?"

"There was blood coming out of its mouth," I said.

I had thought that that was a good sign, that he wasn't bleeding anywhere else. The blood had come out of Aberfan's mouth when he tried to lift his head, just a little trickle, sinking into the hard-packed snow. It had stopped before we even got him into the car. "It's all right, boy," I told him. "We'll be there in a minute."

Katie started the jeep, killed it, started it again, backed it up to where she could turn around.

Aberfan lay limply across my lap, his tail against the gear shift. "Just lie still, boy," I said. I patted his neck. It was wet, and I raised my hand and looked at the palm, afraid it was blood. It was only water from the melted snow. I dried his neck and the top of his head with the sleeve of my sweater.

"How far is it?" Katie said. She was clutching the steering wheel with both hands and sitting stiffly forward in the seat. The windshield wipers flipped back and forth, trying to keep up with the snow.

"About five miles," I said, and she stepped on the gas pedal and then let up on it again as we began to skid. "On the right side of the highway."

Aberfan raised his head off my lap and looked at me. His gums were gray, and he was panting, but I couldn't see any more blood. He tried to lick my hand. "You'll make it, Aberfan," I said. "You made it before, remember?"

"But you didn't get out of the car and go check, to make sure it was dead?" Hunter said.

"No."

"And you don't have any idea who hit the jackal?" he said, and made it sound like the accusation it was.

"No."

He glanced back at the uniform, who had moved around the car to the other side. "Whew," Hunter said, shaking his Hawaiian collar, "it's like an oven out here. Mind if I come in?" which meant the uniform needed more privacy. Well, then, by all means, give him more privacy. The sooner he sprayed print-fix on the bumper and tires and peeled off the incriminating traces of jackal blood that weren't there and stuck them in the evidence bags he was carrying in the pockets of that uniform, the sooner they'd leave. I opened the screen door wider.

"Oh, this is great," Hunter said, still trying to generate a breeze with his collar. "These old adobe houses stay so cool." He glanced around the room at the developer and the enlarger, the couch, the dry-mounted photographs on the wall. "You don't have any idea who might have hit the jackal?"

"I figure it was a tanker," I said. "What else would be on Van Buren that time of morning?"

I was almost sure it had been a car or a small truck. A tanker would have left the jackal a spot on the pavement. But a tanker would get a license suspension and two weeks of having to run water into Santa Fe instead of Phoenix, and probably not that. Rumor at the paper had it the Society was in the water board's pocket. If it was a car, on the other hand, the Society would take away the car and stick its driver with a prison sentence.

"They're all trying to beat the cameras," I said. "The tanker probably didn't even know it'd hit it."

"What?" he said.

"I said, it had to be a tanker. There isn't anything else on Van Buren during rush hour."

I expected him to say, "Except for you," but he didn't. He wasn't even listening. "Is this your dog?" he said.

He was looking at the photograph of Perdita. "No," I said. "That was my grandmother's dog."

"What is it?"

A nasty little beast. And when it died of the newparvo, my grandmother had cried like a baby. "A chihuahua."

He looked around at the other walls. "Did you take all these pictures of dogs?" His whole manner had changed, taking on a politeness that made me realize just how insolent he had intended to be before. The one on the road wasn't the only jackal around.

"Some of them," I said. He was looking at the photograph next to it. "I didn't take that one."

"I know what this one is," he said, pointing at it. "It's a boxer, right?"

"An English bulldog," I said.

"Oh, right. Weren't those the ones that were exterminated? For being vicious?"

"No," I said.

He moved on to the picture over the developer, like a tourist in a museum. "I bet you didn't take this one either," he said, pointing at the high shoes, the old-fashioned hat on the stout old woman holding the dogs in her arms.

"That's a photograph of Beatrix Potter, the English children's author," I said. "She wrote *Peter Rabbit*."

He wasn't interested. "What kind of dogs are those?"

"Pekingese."

"It's a great picture of them."

It is, in fact, a terrible picture of them. One of them has wrenched his face away from the camera, and the other sits grimly in her owner's hand, waiting for its chance. Obviously neither of them liked having its picture taken, though you can't tell that from their expressions. They reveal nothing in their little flat-nosed faces, in their black little eyes.

Beatrix Potter, on the other hand, comes through beautifully, in spite of the attempt to smile for the camera and the fact that she must have had to hold onto the Pekes for dear life, or maybe because of that. The fierce, humorous love she felt for her fierce, humorous little dogs is all there in her face. She must never, in spite of *Peter Rabbit* and its attendant fame, have developed a public face. Everything she felt was right there, unprotected, unshuttered. Like Katie.

"Are any of these your dog?" Hunter asked. He was standing looking at the picture of Misha that hung above the couch.

"No," I said.

"How come you don't have any pictures of your dog?" he asked, and I wondered how he knew I had had a dog and what else he knew.

"He didn't like having his picture taken."

He folded up the readout, stuck it in his pocket, and turned around to look at the photo of Perdita again. "He looks like he was a real nice little dog," he said.

The uniform was waiting on the front step, obviously finished with whatever he had done to the car.

"We'll let you know if we find out who's responsible," Hunter said, and they left. On the way out to the street the uniform tried to tell him what he'd found, but Hunter cut him off. The suspect has a house full of photographs of dogs, therefore he didn't run over a poor facsimile of one on Van Buren this morning. Case closed.

I went back over to the developer and fed the eisenstadt film in. "Positives, one two three order, five seconds," I said, and watched as the pictures came up on the developer's screen. Ramirez had said the eisenstadt automatically turned on whenever it was set upright on a level surface. She was right. It had taken a half-dozen shots on the way out to Tempe. Two shots of the Hitori it must have taken when I set it down to load the car, open door of same with prickly pear in the foreground, a blurred shot of palm trees and buildings with a minuscule, sharp-focused glimpse of the traffic on the expressway. Vehicles and people. There was a great shot of the red tanker that had clipped the jackal and ten or so of the yucca I had parked next to at the foot of the hill.

It had gotten two nice shots of my forearm as I set it down on the kitchen counter of the Winnebago and some beautifully composed still lifes of Melmac with Spoons. Vehicles and people. The rest of the pictures were dead losses: my back, the open bathroom door, Jake's back, and Mrs. Ambler's public face.

Except the last one. She had been standing right in front of the eisenstadt, looking almost directly into the lens. "When I think of that poor thing, all alone," she had said, and by the time she turned around she had her public face back on, but for a minute there, looking at what she thought was a briefcase and remembering, there she was, the person I had tried all morning to get a picture of.

I took it into the living room and sat down and looked at it awhile.

"So you knew this Katherine Powell in Colorado," Ramirez said, breaking in without preamble, and the highwire slid silently forward and began to print out the lifeline. "I always suspected you of having some deep dark secret in your past. Is she the reason you moved to Phoenix?"

I was watching the highwire advance the paper. Katherine Powell. 4628 Dutchman Drive, Apache Junction. Forty miles away.

"Holy Mother, you were really cradle-robbing. According to my calculations, she was seventeen when you lived there."

Sixteen.

"Are you the owner of the dog?" the vet had asked her, his face slackening into pity when he saw how young she was.

"No," she said. "I'm the one who hit him."

"My God," he said. "How old are you?"

"Sixteen," she said, and her face was wide open. "I just got my license."

"Aren't you even going to tell me what she has to do with this Winnebago thing?" Ramirez said.

"I moved down here to get away from the snow," I said, and cut out without saying goodbye.

The lifeline was still rolling silently forward. Hacker at Hewlett-Packard. Fired in ninety-nine, probably during the unionization. Divorced. Two kids. She had moved to Arizona five years after I did. Management programmer for Toshiba. Arizona driver's license.

I went back to the developer and looked at the picture of Mrs. Ambler. I had said dogs never came through. That wasn't true. Taco wasn't in the blurry snapshots Mrs. Ambler had been so anxious to show me, in the stories she had been so anxious to tell. But she was in this picture, reflected in the pain and love and loss on Mrs. Ambler's face. I could see her plain as day, perched on the arm of the driver's seat, barking impatiently when the light turned green.

I put a new cartridge in the eisenstadt and went out to see Katie.

I had to take Van Buren—it was almost four o'clock, and the rush hour would have started on the divideds—but the jackal was gone anyway. The Society is efficient. Like Hitler and his Nazis.

"Why don't you have any pictures of your dog?" Hunter had asked. The question could have been based on the assumption that anyone who would fill his living room with photographs of dogs must have had one of his own, but it wasn't. He had known about Aberfan, which meant he'd had access to my lifeline, which meant all kinds of things. My lifeline was privacy-coded, so I had to be notified before anybody could get access, except, it appeared, the Society. A reporter I knew at the paper, Dolores Chiwere, had tried to do a story a while back claiming that the Society had an illegal link to the lifeline banks, but she hadn't been able to come up with enough evidence to convince her editor. I wondered if this counted.

The lifeline would have told them about Aberfan but not about how he died. Killing a dog wasn't a crime in those days, and I hadn't pressed charges against Katie for reckless driving or even called the police.

"I think you should," the vet's assistant had said. "There are less than a hundred dogs left. People can't just go around killing them."

"My God, man, it was snowing and slick," the vet had said angrily, "and she's just a kid."

"She's old enough to have a license," I said, looking at Katie. She was fumbling in her purse for her driver's license. "She's old enough to have been on the roads."

Katie found her license and gave it to me. It was so new it was still shiny. Katherine Powell. She had turned sixteen two weeks ago.

"This won't bring him back," the vet had said, and taken the license out of my hand and given it back to her. "You go on home now."

"I need her name for the records," the vet's assistant had said.

She had stepped forward. "Katie Powell," she had said.

"We'll do the paperwork later," the vet had said firmly.

They never did do the paperwork, though. The next week the third wave hit, and I suppose there hadn't seemed any point.

I slowed down at the zoo entrance and looked up into the parking lot as I went past. The Amblers were doing a booming business. There were at least five cars and twice as many kids clustered around the Winnebago.

"Where the hell are you?" Ramirez said. "And where the hell are your pictures? I talked the *Republic* into a trade, but they insisted on scoop rights. I need your stills now!"

"I'll send them in as soon as I get home," I said. "I'm on a story."

"The hell you are! You're on your way out to see your old girlfriend. Well, not on the paper's credits, you're not."

"Did you get the stuff on the Winnebago Indians?" I asked her.

"Yes. They were in Wisconsin, but they're not anymore. In the mid-seventies there were sixteen hundred of them on the reservation and about forty-five hundred altogether, but by 1990, the number was down to five hundred, and now they don't think there are any left, and nobody knows what happened to them."

I'll tell you what happened to them, I thought. Almost all of them were killed in the first wave, and people blamed the government and the Japanese and the ozone layer, and after the second wave hit, the Society passed all kinds of laws to protect the survivors, but it was too late, they were already below the minimum survival population limit, and then the third wave polished off the rest of them, and the last of the Winnebagos sat in a cage somewhere, and if I had been there I would probably have taken his picture.

"I called the Bureau of Indian Affairs," Ramirez said, "and they're supposed to call me back, and you don't give a damn about the Winnebagos. You just wanted to get me off the subject. What's this story you're on?"

I looked around the dashboard for an exclusion button.

"What the hell is going on, David? First you ditch two big stories, now you can't even get your pictures in. Jesus, if something's wrong, you can tell me. I want to help. It has something to do with Colorado, doesn't it?"

I found the button and cut her off.

Van Buren got crowded as the afternoon rush spilled over off the divideds. Out past the curve, where Van Buren turns into Apache Boulevard, they were putting in new lanes. The cement forms were already up on the eastbound side, and they were building the wooden forms up in two of the six lanes on my side.

The Amblers must have just beaten the workmen, though at the rate the men were working right now, leaning on their shovels in the hot afternoon sun and smoking stew, it had probably taken them six weeks to do this stretch.

Mesa was still open multiway, but as soon as I was through downtown, the construction started again, and this stretch was nearly done—forms up on both sides and most of the cement poured. The Amblers couldn't have come in from Globe on this road. The lanes were barely wide enough for the Hitori, and the tanker lanes were gated. Superstition is full-divided, and the old highway down from Roosevelt is, too, which meant they hadn't come in from Globe at all. I wondered how they had come in—probably in some tanker lane on a multiway.

"Oh, my, the things we've seen," Mrs. Ambler had said. I wondered how much they'd been able to see skittering across the dark desert like a couple of kangaroo mice, trying to beat the cameras.

The roadworkers didn't have the new exit signs up yet, and I missed the exit for Apache Junction and had to go halfway to Superior, trapped in my narrow, cement-sided lane, till I hit a change-lanes and could get turned around.

Katie's address was in Superstition Estates, a development pushed up as close to the base of Superstition Mountain as it could get. I thought about what I would say to Katie when I got there. I had said maybe ten sentences altogether to her, most of them shouted directions, in the two hours we had been together. In the jeep on the way to the vet's I had talked to Aberfan, and after we got there, sitting in the waiting room, we hadn't talked at all.

It occurred to me that I might not recognize her. I didn't really remember what she looked like—only the sunburned nose and that terrible openness, and now, fifteen years later, it seemed unlikely that she would have either of them. The Arizona sun would have taken care of the first, and she had gotten married and divorced, been fired, had who knows what else happen to her in fifteen years to close her face. In which case, there had been no point in my driving all the way out here. But Mrs. Ambler had had an almost impenetrable public face, and you could still catch her off-guard. If you got her talking about the dogs. If she didn't know she was being photographed.

Katie's house was an old-style passive solar, with flat black panels on the roof. It looked presentable, but not compulsively neat. There wasn't any grass—tankers won't waste their credits coming this far out, and Apache Junction isn't big enough to match the bribes and incentives of Phoenix or Tempe—but the front yard was laid out with alternating patches of black lava chips and prickly pear. The side yard had a parched-looking palo verde tree, and there was a cat tied to it. A little girl was playing under it with toy cars.

I took the eisenstadt out of the back and went up to the front door and rang the bell. At the last moment, when it was too late to change my mind, walk away, because she already opening the screen door, it occurred to me that she might not recognize me, that I might have to tell her who I was.

Her nose wasn't sunburned, and she had put on the weight a sixteen-year-old puts on to get to be thirty, but otherwise she looked the same as she had that day in front of my house. And her face hadn't completely closed. I could tell, looking at her, that she recognized me and that she had known I was coming. She must have put a notify on her lifeline to have them warn her if I asked her whereabouts. I thought about what that meant.

She opened the screen door a little, the way I had to the Humane Society. "What do you want?" she said.

I had never seen her angry, not even when I turned on her at the vet's. "I wanted to see you," I said.

I had thought I might tell her I had run across her name while I was working on a story and wondered if it was the same person or that I was doing a piece on the last of the passive solars. "I saw a dead jackal on the road this morning," I said.

"And you thought I killed it?" she said. She tried to shut the screen door.

I put out my hand without thinking to stop her. "No," I said. I took my hand off the door. "No, of course I don't think that. Can I come in? I just want to talk to you."

The little girl had come over, clutching her toy cars to her pink T-shirt, and was standing off to the side, watching curiously.

"Come on inside, Jana," Katie said, and opened the screen door a fraction wider. The little girl scooted through. "Go on in the kitchen," she said. "I'll fix you some Kool-Aid." She looked up at me. "I used to have nightmares about your coming. I'd dream that I'd go to the door and there you'd be."

"It's really hot out here," I said and knew I sounded like Hunter. "Can I come in?"

She opened the screen door all the way. "I've got to make my daughter something to drink," she said, and led the way into the kitchen, the little girl dancing in front of her.

"What kind of Kool-Aid do you want?" Katie asked her, and she shouted, "Red!"

The kitchen counter faced the stove, refrigerator, and water cooler across a narrow aisle that opened out into an alcove with a table and chairs. I put the eisenstadt down on the table and then sat down myself so she wouldn't suggest moving into another room.

Katie reached a plastic pitcher down from one of the shelves and stuck it under the water tank to fill it. Jana dumped her cars on the counter, clambered up beside them, and began opening the cupboard doors.

"How old's your little girl?" I asked.

Katie got a wooden spoon out of the drawer next to the stove and brought it and the pitcher over to the table. "She's four," she said. "Did you find the Kool-Aid?" she asked the little girl.

"Yes," the little girl said, but it wasn't Kool-Aid. It was a pinkish cube she peeled a plastic wrapping off of. It fizzed and turned a thinnish red when she dropped it in the pitcher. Kool-Aid must have become extinct, too, along with Winnebagos and passive solar. Or else changed beyond recognition. Like the Humane Society.

Katie poured the red stuff into a glass with a cartoon whale on it.

"Is she your only one?" I asked.

"No, I have a little boy," she said, but warily, as if she wasn't sure she wanted to tell me, even though if I'd requested the lifeline I already had access to all this information. Jana asked if she could have a cookie and then took it and her Kool-Aid back down the hall and outside. I could hear the screen door slam.

Katie put the pitcher in the refrigerator and leaned against the kitchen counter, her arms folded across her chest. "What do you want?"

She was just out of range of the eisenstadt, her face in the shadow of the narrow aisle.

"There was a dead jackal on the road this morning," I said. I kept my voice low so she would lean forward into the light to try and hear me. "It'd been hit by a car, and it was lying funny, at an angle. It looked like a dog. I wanted to talk to somebody who remembered Aberfan, somebody who knew him."

"I didn't know him," she said. "I only killed him, remember? That's why you did this, isn't it, because I killed Aberfan?"

She didn't look at the eisenstadt, hadn't even glanced at it when I set it on the table, but I wondered suddenly if she knew what I was up to. She was still carefully out of range. And what if I said to her, "That's right. That's why I did this, because you killed him, and I didn't have any pictures of him. You owe me. If I can't have a picture of Aberfan, you at least owe me a picture of you remembering him."

Only she didn't remember him, didn't know anything about him except what she had seen on the way to the vet's, Aberfan lying on my lap and looking up at me, already dying. I had had no business coming here, dredging all this up again. No business.

"At first I thought you were going to have me arrested," Katie said, "and then after all the dogs died, I thought you were going to kill me."

The screen door banged. "Forgot my cars," the little girl said and scooped them into the tail of her T-shirt. Katie tousled her hair as she went past, and then folded her arms again.

" 'It wasn't my fault,' I was going to tell you when you came to kill me," she said. " 'It was snowy. He ran right in front of me. I didn't even see him.' I looked up everything I could find about newparvo. Preparing for the defense. How it mutated from parvovirus and from cat distemper before that and then kept on mutating, so they couldn't come up with a vaccine. How even before the third wave they were below the minimum survival population. How it was the fault of the people who owned the last survivors because they wouldn't risk their dogs to breed them. How the scientists didn't come up with a vaccine until only the jackals were left. 'You're wrong,' I was going to tell you. 'It was the puppy mill owners' fault that all the dogs died. If they hadn't kept their dogs in such unsanitary conditions, it never would have gotten out of control in the first place.' I had my defense all ready. But you'd moved away."

Jana banged in again, carrying the empty whale glass. She had a red smear across the whole lower half of her face. "I need some more," she said, making "some more" into one word. She held the glass in both hands while Katie opened the refrigerator and poured her another glassful.

"Wait a minute, honey," she said. "You've got Kool-Aid all over you," and bent to wipe Jana's face with a paper towel.

Katie hadn't said a word in her defense while we waited at the vet's, not, "It was snowy," or, "He ran right out in front of me," or, "I didn't even see him." She had sat silently beside me, twisting her mittens in her lap, until the vet came out and told me Aberfan was dead, and then she had said, "I didn't know there were any left in Colorado. I thought they were all dead."

And I had turned to her, to a sixteen-year-old not even old enough to know how to shut her face, and said, "Now they all are. Thanks to you."

"That kind of talk isn't necessary," the vet had said warningly.

I had wrenched away from the hand he tried to put on my shoulder. "How does it feel to have killed one of the last dogs in the world?" I shouted at her. "How does it feel to be responsible for the extinction of an entire species?"

The screen door banged again. Katie was looking at me, still holding the reddened paper towel.

"You moved away," she said, "and I thought maybe that meant you'd forgiven me, but it didn't, did it?" She came over to the table and wiped at the red circle the glass had left. "Why did you do it? To punish me? Or did you think that's what I'd been doing the last fifteen years, roaring around the roads murdering animals?"

"What?" I said.

"The Society's already been here."

"The Society?" I said, not understanding.

"Yes," she said, still looking at the red-stained towel. "They said you had reported a dead animal on Van Buren. They wanted to know where I was this morning between eight and nine A.M."

I nearly ran down a roadworker on the way back into Phoenix. He leaped for the still-wet cement barrier, dropping the shovel he'd been leaning on all day, and I ran right over it.

The Society had already been there. They had left my house and gone straight to hers. Only that wasn't possible, because I hadn't even called Katie then. I hadn't even seen the picture of Mrs. Ambler yet. Which meant they had gone to see Ramirez after they left me, and the last thing Ramirez and the paper needed was trouble with the Society.

"I thought it was suspicious when he didn't go to the governor's conference," she had told them, "and just now he called and asked for a lifeline on this person here. Katherine Powell. 4628 Dutchman Drive. He knew her in Colorado."

"Ramirez!" I shouted at the car phone. "I want to talk to you!" There wasn't any answer.

I swore at her for a good ten miles before I remembered I had the exclusion button on. I punched it off. "Ramirez, where the hell are you?"

"I could ask you the same question," she said. She sounded even angrier than Katie, but not as angry as I was. "You cut me off, you won't tell me what's going on."

"So you decided you had it figured out for yourself, and you told your little theory to the Society."

"What?" she said, and I recognized that tone, too. I had heard it in my own voice when Katie told me the Society had been there. Ramirez hadn't told anybody anything, she didn't even know what I was talking about, but I was going too fast to stop.

"You told the Society I'd asked for Katie's lifeline, didn't you?" I shouted.

"No," she said. "I didn't. Don't you think it's time you told me what's going on?"

"Did the Society come see you this afternoon?"

"No. I told you. They called this morning and wanted to talk to you. I told them you were at the governor's conference."

"And they didn't call back later?"

"No. Are you in trouble?"

I hit the exclusion button. "Yes," I said. "Yes, I'm in trouble."

Ramirez hadn't told them. Maybe somebody else at the paper had, but I didn't think so. There had after all been Dolores Chiwere's story about them having illegal access to the lifelines. "How come you don't have any pictures of your dog?" Hunter had asked me, which meant they'd read my lifeline, too. So they knew we had both lived in Colorado, in the same town, when Aberfan died.

"What did you tell them?" I had demanded of Katie. She had been standing there in the kitchen still messing with the Kool-Aid-stained towel, and I had wanted to yank it out of her hands and make her look at me. "What did you tell the Society?"

She looked up at me. "I told them I was on Indian School Road, picking up the month's programming assignments from my company. Unfortunately, I could just as easily have driven in on Van Buren."

"About Aberfan!" I shouted. "What did you tell them about Aberfan?"

She looked steadily at me. "I didn't tell them anything. I assumed you'd already told them."

I had taken hold of her shoulders. "If they come back, don't tell them anything. Not even if they arrest you. I'll take care of this. I'll . . ."

But I hadn't told her what I'd do because I didn't know. I had run out of her house, colliding with Jana in the hall on her way in for another refill, and roared off for home, even though I didn't have any idea what I would do when I got there.

Call the Society and tell them to leave Katie alone, that she had nothing to do with this? That would be even more suspicious than everything else I'd done so far, and you couldn't get much more suspicious than that.

I had seen a dead jackal on the road (or so I said), and instead of reporting it immediately on the phone right there in my car, I'd driven to a convenience store two miles away. I'd called the Society, but I'd refused to give them my name and number. And then I'd canceled two shoots without telling my boss and asked for the lifeline of one Katherine Powell, whom I had known fifteen years ago and who could have been on Van Buren at the time of the accident.

The connection was obvious, and how long would it take them to make the connection that fifteen years ago was when Aberfan had died?

Apache was beginning to fill up with rush hour overflow and a whole fleet of tankers. The overflow obviously spent all their time driving dividers—nobody bothered to signal that they were changing lanes. Nobody even gave an indication that they knew what a lane was. Going around the curve from Tempe and onto Van Buren they were all over the road. I moved over into the tanker lane.

My lifeline didn't have the vet's name on it. They were just getting started in those days, and there was a lot of nervousness about invasion of privacy. Nothing went online without the person's permission, especially not medical and bank records, and the lifelines were little more than puff bios: family, occupation, hobbies, pets. The only things on the lifeline besides Aberfan's name was the date of his death and my address at the time, but that was probably enough. There were only two vets in town.

The vet hadn't written Katie's name down on Aberfan's record. He had handed her driver's license back to her without even looking at it, but Katie had told her name to the vet's assistant. He might have written it down. There was no way I could find out. I couldn't ask for the vet's lifeline because the Society had access to the lifelines. They'd get to him before I could. I could maybe have the paper get the vet's records for me, but I'd have to tell Ramirez what was going on, and the phone was probably tapped, too. And if I showed up at the paper, Ramirez would confiscate the car. I couldn't go there.

Wherever the hell I was going, I was driving too fast to get there. When the tanker ahead of me slowed down to ninety, I practically climbed up his back bumper. I had gone past the place where the jackal had been hit without ever seeing it. Even without the traffic, there probably hadn't been anything to see. What the Society hadn't taken care of, the overflow probably had, and anyway, there hadn't been any evidence to begin with. If there had been, if the cameras had seen the car that hit it, they wouldn't have come after me. And Katie.

The Society couldn't charge her with Aberfan's death—killing an animal hadn't been a crime back then—but if they found out about Aberfan they would charge her with the jackal's death, and it wouldn't matter if a hundred witnesses, a hundred highway cameras had seen her on Indian School Road. It wouldn't matter if the print-fix on her car was clean. She had killed one of the last dogs, hadn't she? They would crucify her.

I should never have left Katie. "Don't tell them anything," I had told her, but she had never been afraid of admitting guilt. When the receptionist had asked her what had happened, she had said, "I hit him," just like that, no attempt to make excuses, to run off, to lay the blame on someone else.

I had run off to try to stop the Society from finding out that Katie had hit Aberfan, and meanwhile the Society was probably back at Katie's, asking her how she'd happened to know me in Colorado, asking her how Aberfan died.

I was wrong about the Society. They weren't at Katie's house. They were at mine, standing on the porch, waiting for me to let them in.

"You're a hard man to track down," Hunter said.

The uniform grinned. "Where you been?"

"Sorry," I said, fishing my keys out of my pocket. "I thought you were all done with me. I've already told you everything I know about the incident."

Hunter stepped back just far enough for me to get the screen door open and the key in the lock. "Officer Segura and I just need to ask you a couple more questions."

"Where'd you go this afternoon?" Segura asked.

"I went to see an old friend of mine."

"Who?"

"Come on, come on," Hunter said. "Let the guy get in his own front door before you start badgering him with a lot of questions."

I opened the door. "Did the cameras get a picture of the tanker that hit the jackal?" I asked.

"Tanker?" Segura said.

"I told you," I said, "I figure it had to be a tanker. The jackal was lying in the tanker lane." I led the way into the living room, depositing my keys on the computer and switching the phone to exclusion while I talked. The last thing I needed was Ramirez bursting in with, "What's going on? Are you in trouble?"

"It was probably a renegade that hit it, which would explain why he didn't stop." I gestured at them to sit down.

Hunter did. Segura started for the couch and then stopped, staring at the photos on the wall above it. "Jesus, will you look at all the dogs!" he said. "Did you take all these pictures?"

"I took some of them. That one in the middle is Misha."

"The last dog, right?"

"Yes," I said.

"No kidding. The very last one."

No kidding. She was being kept in isolation at the Society's research facility in St. Louis when I saw her. I had talked them into letting me shoot her, but it had to be from outside the quarantine area. The picture had an unfocused look that came from shooting it through a wire mesh-reinforced window in the door, but I wouldn't have done any better if they'd let me inside. Misha was past having any expression to photograph. She hadn't eaten in a week at that point. She lay with her head on her paws, staring at the door, the whole time I was there.

"You wouldn't consider selling this picture to the Society, would you?"

"No, I wouldn't."

He nodded understandingly. "I guess people were pretty upset when she died."

Pretty upset. They had turned on anyone who had anything to do with it—the puppy mill owners, the scientists who hadn't come up with a vaccine, Misha's vet—and a lot of others who hadn't. And they had handed over their civil rights to a bunch of jackals who were able to grab them because everybody felt so guilty. Pretty upset.

"What's this one?" Segura asked. He had already moved on to the picture next to it.

"It's General Patton's bull terrier Willie."

They fed and cleaned up after Misha with those robot arms they used to use in the nuclear plants. Her owner, a tired-looking woman, was allowed to watch her through the wire-mesh window but had to stay off to the side because Misha flung herself barking against the door whenever she saw her.

"You should make them let you in," I had told her. "It's cruel to keep her locked up like that. You should make them let you take her back home."

"And let her get the newparvo?" she said.

There was nobody left for Misha to get the newparvo from, but I didn't say that. I set the light readings on the camera, trying not to lean into Misha's line of vision.

"You know what killed them, don't you?" she said. "The ozone layer. All those holes. The radiation got in and caused it."

It was the communists, it was the Mexicans, it was the government. And the only people who acknowledged their guilt weren't guilty at all.

"This one here looks kind of like a jackal," Segura said. He was looking at a picture I had taken of a German shepherd after Aberfan died. "Dogs were a lot like jackals, weren't they?"

"No," I said, and sat down on the shelf in front of the developer's screen, across from Hunter. "I already told you everything I know about the jackal. I saw it lying in the road, and I called you."

"You said when you saw the jackal it was in the far right lane," Hunter said.

"That's right."

"And you were in the far left lane?"

"I was in the far left lane."

They were going to take me over my story, point by point, and when I couldn't remember what I'd said before, they were going to say, "Are you sure that's what you saw, Mr. McCombe? Are you sure you didn't see the jackal get hit? Katherine Powell hit it, didn't she?"

"You told us this morning you stopped, but the jackal was already dead. Is that right?" Hunter asked.

"No," I said.

Segura looked up. Hunter touched his hand casually to his pocket and then brought it back to his knee, turning on the taper.

"I didn't stop for about a mile. Then I backed up and looked at it, but it was dead. There was blood coming out of its mouth."

Hunter didn't say anything. He kept his hands on his knees and waited—an old journalist's trick, if you wait long enough, they'll say something they didn't intend to, just to fill the silence.

"The jackal's body was at a peculiar angle," I said, right on cue. "The way it was lying, it didn't look like a jackal. I thought it was a dog." I waited till the silence got uncomfortable again. "It brought back a lot of terrible memories," I said. "I wasn't even thinking. I just wanted to get away from it. After a few minutes I realized I should have called the Society, and I stopped at the 7-Eleven."

I waited again, till Segura began to shoot uncomfortable glances at Hunter, and then started in again. "I thought I'd be okay, that I could go ahead and work, but after I got to my first shoot, I knew I wasn't going to make it, so I came home.'' Candor. Openness. If the Amblers can do it, so can you. "I guess I was still in shock or something. I didn't even call my boss and have her get somebody to cover the governor's conference. All I could think about was—'' I stopped and rubbed my hand across my face. "I needed to talk to somebody. I had the paper look up an old friend of mine, Katherine Powell.''

I stopped, I hoped this time for good. I had admitted lying to them and confessed to two crimes: leaving the scene of the accident and using press access to get a lifeline for personal use, and maybe that would be enough to satisfy them. I didn't want to say anything about going out to see Katie. They would know she would have told me about their visit and decide this confession was an attempt to get her off, and maybe they'd been watching the house and knew it anyway, and this was all wasted effort.

The silence dragged on. Hunter's hands tapped his knees twice and then subsided. The story didn't explain why I'd picked Katie, who I hadn't seen in fifteen years, who I knew in Colorado, to go see, but maybe, maybe they wouldn't make the connection.

"This Katherine Powell,'' Hunter said, "you knew her in Colorado, is that right?''

"We lived in the same little town.''

We waited.

"Isn't that when your dog died?'' Segura said suddenly. Hunter shot him a glance of pure rage, and I thought, it isn't a taper he's got in that shirt pocket. It's the vet's records, and Katie's name is on them.

"Yes,'' I said. "He died in September of eighty-nine.''

Segura opened his mouth.

"In the third wave?'' Hunter asked before he could say anything.

"No,'' I said. "He was hit by a car.''

They both looked genuinely shocked. The Amblers could have taken lessons from them. "Who hit it?'' Segura asked, and Hunter leaned forward, his hand moving reflexively toward his pocket.

"I don't know,'' I said. "It was a hit and run. Whoever it was just left him lying there in the road. That's why when I saw the jackal, it . . . that was how I met Katherine Powell. She stopped and helped me. She helped me get him into her car, and we took him to the vet's, but it was too late.''

Hunter's public face was pretty indestructible, but Segura's wasn't. He looked surprised and enlightened and disappointed all at once.

"That's why I wanted to see her,'' I said unnecessarily.

"Your dog was hit on what day?'' Hunter asked.

"September thirtieth.''

"What was the vet's name?''

He hadn't changed his way of asking the questions, but he no longer cared what the answers were. He had thought he'd found a connection, a cover-up, but here we were, a couple of dog lovers, a couple of good Samaritans, and his theory had collapsed. He was done with the interview, he was just finishing up, and all I had to do was be careful not to relax too soon.

I frowned. "I don't remember his name. Cooper, I think."

"What kind of car did you say hit your dog?"

"I don't know," I said, thinking, not a jeep. Make it something besides a jeep. "I didn't see him get hit. The vet said it was something big, a pickup maybe. Or a Winnebago."

And I knew who had hit the jackal. It had all been right there in front of me —the old man using up their forty-gallon water supply to wash the bumper, the lies about their coming in from Globe—only I had been too intent on keeping them from finding out about Katie, on getting the picture of Aberfan, to see it. It was like the damned parvo. When you had it licked in one place, it broke out somewhere else.

"Were there any identifying tire tracks?" Hunter said.

"What?" I said. "No. It was snowing that day." It had to show in my face, and he hadn't missed anything yet. I passed my hand over my eyes. "I'm sorry. These questions are bringing it all back."

"Sorry," Hunter said.

"Can't we get this stuff from the police report?" Segura asked.

"There wasn't a police report," I said. "It wasn't a crime to kill a dog when Aberfan died."

It was the right thing to say. The look of shock on their faces was the real thing this time, and they looked at each other in disbelief instead of at me. They asked a few more questions and then stood up to leave. I walked them to the door.

"Thank you for your cooperation, Mr. McCombe," Hunter said. "We appreciate what a difficult experience this has been for you."

I shut the screen door between us. The Amblers would have been going too fast, trying to beat the cameras because they weren't even supposed to be on Van Buren. It was almost rush hour, and they were in the tanker lane, and they hadn't even seen the jackal till they hit it, and then it was too late. They had to know the penalty for hitting an animal was jail and confiscation of the vehicle, and there wasn't anybody else on the road.

"Oh, one more question," Hunter said from halfway down the walk. "You said you went to your first assignment this morning. What was it?"

Candid. Open. "It was out at the old zoo. A sideshow kind of thing."

I watched them all the way out to their car and down the street. Then I latched the screen, pulled the inside door shut, and locked it, too. It had been right there in front of me—the ferret sniffing the wheel, the bumper, Jake anxiously watching the road. I had thought he was looking for customers, but he wasn't. He was expecting to see the Society drive up. "He's not interested in that," he had said when Mrs. Ambler said she had been telling me about Taco. He had listened to our whole conversation, standing under the back window with his guilty bucket, ready to come back in and cut her off if she said too much, and I hadn't tumbled to any of it. I had been so intent on Aberfan I hadn't even seen it when I looked right through the lens at it. And what kind of an excuse was that? Katie hadn't even tried to use it, and she was learning to drive.

I went and got the Nikon and pulled the film out of it. It was too late to do anything about the eisenstadt pictures or the vidcam footage, but I didn't think there was anything in them. Jake had already washed the bumper by the time I'd taken those pictures.

I fed the longshot film into the developer. "Positives, one two three order, fifteen seconds," I said, and waited for the image to come on the screen.

I wondered who had been driving. Jake, probably. "He never liked Taco," she had said, and there was no mistaking the bitterness in her voice. "I didn't want to buy the Winnebago."

They would both lose their licenses, no matter who was driving, and the Society would confiscate the Winnebago. They would probably not send two octogenarian specimens of Americana like the Amblers to prison. They wouldn't have to. The trial would take six months, and Texas already had legislation in committee.

The first picture came up. A light-setting shot of an ocotillo.

Even if they got off, even if they didn't end up taking away the Winnebago for unauthorized use of a tanker lane or failure to purchase a sales tax permit, the Amblers had six months left at the outside. Utah was all ready to pass a full-divided bill, and Arizona would be next. In spite of the road crews' stew-slowed pace, Phoenix would be all-divided by the time the investigation was over, and they'd be completely boxed in. Permanent residents of the zoo. Like the coyote.

A shot of the zoo sign, half-hidden in the cactus. A close-up of the Amblers' balloon-trailing sign. The Winnebago in the parking lot.

"Hold," I said. "Crop." I indicated the areas with my finger. "Enlarge to full screen."

The longshot takes great pictures, sharp contrast, excellent detail. The developer only had a five hundred thousand-pixel screen, but the dark smear on the bumper was easy to see, and the developed picture would be much clearer. You'd be able to see every splatter, every grayish-yellow hair. The Society's computers would probably be able to type the blood from it.

"Continue," I said, and the next picture came on the screen. Artsy shot of the Winnebago and the zoo entrance. Jake washing the bumper. Red-handed.

Maybe Hunter had bought my story, but he didn't have any other suspects, and how long would it be before he decided to ask Katie a few more questions? If he thought it was the Amblers, he'd leave her alone.

The Japanese family clustered around the waste-disposal tank. Closeup of the decals on the side. Interiors—Mrs. Ambler in the gallery, the upright-coffin shower stall, Mrs. Ambler making coffee.

No wonder she had looked that way in the eisenstadt shot, her face full of memory and grief and loss. Maybe in the instant before they hit it, it had looked like a dog to her, too.

All I had to do was tell Hunter about the Amblers, and Katie was off the hook. It should be easy. I had done it before.

"Stop," I said to a shot of the salt-and-pepper collection. The black and white scottie dogs had painted, red-plaid bows and red tongues. "Expose," I said. "One through twenty-four."

The screen went to question marks and started beeping. I should have known better. The developer could handle a lot of orders, but asking it to expose perfectly good film went against its whole memory, and I didn't have time to give it the step-by-steps that would convince it I meant what I said.

"Eject," I said. The scotties blinked out. The developer spat out the film, rerolled into its protective case.

The doorbell rang. I switched on the overhead and pulled the film out to full length and held it directly under the light. I had told Hunter an RV hit Aberfan, and he had said on the way out, almost an afterthought, "That first shoot you went to, what was it?" And after he left, what had he done, gone out to check on the sideshow kind of thing, gotten Mrs. Ambler to spill her guts? There hadn't been time to do that and get back. He must have called Ramirez. I was glad I had locked the door.

I turned off the overhead. I rerolled the film, fed it back into the developer, and gave it a direction it could handle. "Permanganate bath, full strength, one through twenty-four. Remove one hundred per cent emulsion. No notify."

The screen went dark. It would take the developer at least fifteen minutes to run the film through the bleach bath, and the Society's computers could probably enhance a picture out of two crystals of silver and thin air, but at least the detail wouldn't be there. I unlocked the door.

It was Katie.

She held up the eisenstadt. "You forgot your briefcase," she said.

I stared blankly at it. I hadn't even realized I didn't have it. I must have left it on the kitchen table when I went tearing out, running down little girls and stewed roadworkers in my rush to keep Katie from getting involved. And here she was, and Hunter would be back any minute, saying, "That shoot you went on this morning, did you take any pictures?"

"It isn't a briefcase," I said.

"I wanted to tell you," she said, and stopped. "I shouldn't have accused you of telling the Society I'd killed the jackal. I don't know why you came to see me today, but I know you're not capable of—"

"You have no idea what I'm capable of," I said. I opened the door enough to reach for the eisenstadt. "Thanks for bringing it back. I'll get the paper to reimburse your way-mile credits."

Go home. Go home. If you're here when the Society comes back, they'll ask you how you met me, and I just destroyed the evidence that could shift the blame to the Amblers. I took hold of the eisenstadt's handle and started to shut the door.

She put her hand on the door. The screen door and the fading light made her look unfocused, like Misha. "Are you in trouble?"

"No," I said. "Look, I'm very busy."

"Why did you come to see me?" she asked. "Did you kill the jackal?"

"No," I said, but I opened the door and let her in.

I went over to the developer and asked for a visual status. It was only on the sixth frame. "I'm destroying evidence," I said to Katie. "I took a picture this morning of the vehicle that hit it, only I didn't know it was the guilty party until a half an hour ago." I motioned for her to sit down on the couch. "They're in their eighties. They were driving on a road they weren't supposed to be on, in an obsolete recreation vehicle, worrying about the cameras and the tankers. There's no way they could have seen it in time to stop. The Society won't see it that way, though. They're determined to blame somebody, anybody, even though it won't bring them back."

She set her canvas carryit and the eisenstadt down on the table next to the couch. "The Society was here when I got home," I said. "They'd figured out we were both in Colorado when Aberfan died. I told them it was a hit and run, and you'd stopped to help me. They had the vet's records, and your name was on them."

I couldn't read her face. "If they come back, you tell them that you gave me a ride to the vet's." I went back to the developer. The longshot film was done. "Eject," I said, and the developer spit it into my hand. I fed it into the recycler.

"McCombe! Where the hell are you?" Ramirez's voice exploded into the room, and I jumped and started for the door, but she wasn't there. The phone was flashing. "McCombe! This is important!"

Ramirez was on the phone and using some override I didn't even know existed. I went over and pushed it back to access. The lights went out. "I'm here," I said.

"You won't believe what just happened!" She sounded outraged. "A couple of terrorist types from the Society just stormed in here and confiscated the stuff you sent me!"

All I'd sent her was the vidcam footage and the shots from the eisenstadt, and there shouldn't have been anything on those. Jake had already washed the bumper. "What stuff?" I said.

"The prints from the eisenstadt!" she said, still shouting. "Which I didn't have a chance to look at when they came in because I was too busy trying to work a trade on your governor's conference, not to mention trying to track you down! I had hardcopies made and sent the originals straight down to composing with your vidcam footage. I finally got to them half an hour ago, and while I'm sorting through them, this Society creep just grabs them away from me. No warrants, no 'would you mind?,' nothing. Right out of my hand. Like a bunch of—''

"Jackals," I said. "You're sure it wasn't the vidcam footage?" There wasn't anything in the eisenstadt shots except Mrs. Ambler and Taco, and even Hunter couldn't have put that together, could he?

"Of course I'm sure," Ramirez said, her voice bouncing off the walls. "It was one of the prints from the eisenstadt. I never even saw the vidcam stuff. I sent it straight to composing. I told you."

I went over to the developer and fed the cartridge in. The first dozen shots were nothing, stuff the eisenstadt had taken from the back seat of the car. "Start with frame ten," I said. "Positives. One two three order. Five seconds."

"What did you say?" Ramirez demanded.

"I said, did they say what they were looking for?"

"Are you kidding? I wasn't even there as far as they were concerned. They split up the pile and started through them on *my* desk."

The yucca at the foot of the hill. More yucca. My forearm as I set the eisenstadt down on the counter. My back.

"Whatever it was they were looking for, they found it," Ramirez said.

I glanced at Katie. She met my gaze steadily, unafraid. She had never been afraid, not even when I told her she had killed all the dogs, not even when I showed up on her doorstep after fifteen years.

"The one in the uniform showed it to the other one," Ramirez was saying, "and said, 'You were wrong about the woman doing it. Look at this.' "

"Did you get a look at the picture?"

Still life of cups and spoons. Mrs. Ambler's arm. Mrs. Ambler's back.

"I tried. It was a truck of some kind."

"A truck? Are you sure? Not a Winnebago?"

"A truck. What the hell is going on over there?"

I didn't answer. Jake's back. Open shower door. Still life with Sanka. Mrs. Ambler remembering Taco.

"What woman are they talking about?" Ramirez said. "The one you wanted the lifeline on?"

"No," I said. The picture of Mrs. Ambler was the last one on the cartridge. The developer went back to the beginning. Bottom half of the Hitori. Open car door. Prickly pear. "Did they say anything else?"

"The one in uniform pointed to something on the hardcopy and said, 'See. There's his number on the side. Can you make it out?' "

Blurred palm trees and the expressway. The tanker hitting the jackal.

"Stop," I said. The image froze.

"What?" Ramirez said.

It was a great action shot, the back wheels passing right over the mess that had been the jackal's hind legs. The jackal was already dead, of course, but you couldn't see that or the already drying blood coming out of its mouth because of the angle. You couldn't see the truck's license number either because of the speed the tanker was going, but the number was there, waiting for the Society's computers. It looked like the tanker had just hit it.

"What did they do with the picture?" I asked.

"They took it into the chief's office. I tried to call up the originals from composing, but the chief had already sent for them *and* your vidcam footage. Then I tried to get you, but I couldn't get past your damned exclusion."

"Are they still in there with the chief?"

"They just left. They're on their way over to your house. The chief told me to tell you he wants 'full cooperation,' which means hand over the negatives and any other film you just took this morning. He told *me* to keep my hands off. No story. Case closed."

"How long ago did they leave?"

"Five minutes. You've got plenty of time to make me a print. Don't highwire it. I'll come pick it up."

"What happened to, 'The last thing I need is trouble with the Society'?"

"It'll take them at least twenty minutes to get to your place. Hide it somewhere the Society won't find it."

"I can't," I said, and listened to her furious silence. "My developer's broken. It just ate my longshot film," I said, and hit the exclusion button again.

"You want to see who hit the jackal?" I said to Katie, and motioned her over to the developer. "One of Phoenix's finest."

She came and stood in front of the screen, looking at the picture. If the Society's computers were really good, they could probably prove the jackal was already dead, but the Society wouldn't keep the film long enough for that. Hunter and Segura had probably already destroyed the highwire copies. Maybe I should offer to run the cartridge sheet through the permanganate bath for them when they got here, just to save time.

I looked at Katie. "It looks guilty as hell, doesn't it?" I said. "Only it isn't." She didn't say anything, didn't move. "It would have killed the jackal if it had hit it. It was going at least ninety. But the jackal was already dead."

She looked across at me.

"The Society would have sent the Amblers to jail. It would have confiscated the house they've lived in for fifteen years for an accident that was nobody's fault. They didn't even see it coming. It just ran right out in front of them."

Katie put her hand up to the screen and touched the jackal's image.

"They've suffered enough," I said, looking at her. It was getting dark. I hadn't turned on any lights, and the red image of the tanker made her nose look sunburned.

"All these years she's blamed him for her dog's death, and he didn't do it," I said. "A Winnebago's a hundred square feet on the inside. That's about as big as this developer, and they've lived inside it for fifteen years, while the lanes got narrower and the highways shut down, hardly enough room to breathe, let alone live, and her blaming him for something he didn't do."

In the ruddy light from the screen she looked sixteen.

"They won't do anything to the driver, not with the tankers hauling thousands of gallons of water into Phoenix every day. Even the Society won't run the risk of a boycott. They'll destroy the negatives and call the case closed. And the Society won't go after the Amblers," I said. "Or you."

I turned back to the developer. "Go," I said, and the image changed. Yucca. Yucca. My forearm. My back. Cups and spoons.

"Besides," I said. "I'm an old hand at shifting the blame." Mrs. Ambler's arm. Mrs. Ambler's back. Open shower door. "Did I ever tell you about Aberfan?"

Katie was still watching the screen, her face pale now from the light blue one hundred percent formica shower stall.

"The Society already thinks the tanker did it. The only one I've got to convince is my editor." I reached across to the phone and took the exclusion off. "Ramirez," I said, "wanta go after the Society?"

Jake's back. Cups, spoons, and Sanka.

"I did," Ramirez said in a voice that could have frozen the Salt River, "but your developer was broken, and you couldn't get me a picture."

Mrs. Ambler and Taco.

I hit the exclusion button again and left my hand on it. "Stop," I said. "Print." The screen went dark, and the print slid out into the tray. "Reduce frame. Permanganate bath by one per cent. Follow on screen." I took my hand off. "What's Dolores Chiwere doing these days, Ramirez?"

"She's working investigative. Why?"

I didn't answer. The picture of Mrs. Ambler faded a little, a little more.

"The Society *does* have a link to the lifelines!" Ramirez said, not quite as fast as Hunter, but almost. "That's why you requested your old girlfriend's line, isn't it? You're running a sting."

I had been wondering how to get Ramirez off Katie's trail, and she had done it herself, jumping to conclusions just like the Society. With a little effort, I could convince Katie, too: Do you know why I really came to see you today? To catch the Society. I had to pick somebody the Society couldn't possibly know about from my lifeline, somebody I didn't have any known connection with.

Katie watched the screen, looking like she already half-believed it. The picture of Mrs. Ambler faded some more. Any known connection.

"Stop," I said.

"What about the truck?" Ramirez demanded. "What does it have to do with this sting of yours?"

"Nothing," I said. "And neither does the water board, which is an even bigger bully than the Society. So do what the chief says. Full cooperation. Case closed. We'll get them on lifeline tapping."

She digested that, or maybe she'd already hung up and was calling Dolores Chiwere. I looked at the image of Mrs. Ambler on the screen. It had faded enough to look slightly overexposed but not enough to look tampered with. And Taco was gone.

I looked at Katie. "The Society will be here in another fifteen minutes," I said, "which gives me just enough time to tell you about Aberfan." I gestured at the couch. "Sit down."

She came and sat down. "He was a great dog," I said. "He loved the snow. He'd dig through it and toss it up with his muzzle and snap at the snowflakes, trying to catch them."

Ramirez had obviously hung up, but she would call back if she couldn't track down Chiwere. I put the exclusion back on and went over to the developer. The image of Mrs. Ambler was still on the screen. The bath hadn't affected the detail that much. You could still see the wrinkles, the thin white hair, but the guilt, or blame, the look of loss and love, was gone. She looked serene, almost happy.

"There are hardly any good pictures of dogs," I said. "They lack the necessary muscles to take good pictures, and Aberfan lunged at you as soon as he saw the camera."

I turned the developer off. Without the light from the screen, it was almost dark in the room. I turned on the overhead.

"There were less than a hundred dogs left in the United States, and he'd already had the newparvo once and nearly died. The only pictures I had of him had been taken when he was asleep. I wanted a picture of Aberfan playing in the snow."

I leaned against the narrow shelf in front of the developer's screen. Katie looked the way she had at the vet's, sitting there with her hands clenched, waiting for me to tell her something terrible.

"I wanted a picture of him playing in the snow, but he always lunged at the camera," I said, "so I let him out in the front yard, and then I sneaked out the side door and went across the road to some pine trees where he wouldn't be able to see me. But he did."

"And he ran across the road," Katie said. "And I hit him."

She was looking down at her hands. I waited for her to look up, dreading what I would see in her face. Or not see.

"It took me a long time to find out where you'd gone," she said to her hands. "I was afraid you'd refuse me access to your lifeline. I finally saw one of your pictures in a newspaper, and I moved to Phoenix, but after I got here I was afraid to call you for fear you'd hang up on me.''

She twisted her hands the way she had twisted her mittens at the vet's. ''My husband said I was obsessed with it, that I should have gotten over it by now, everybody else had, that they were only dogs anyway.'' She looked up, and I braced my hands against the developer. ''He said forgiveness wasn't something somebody else could give you, but I didn't want you to forgive me exactly. I just wanted to tell you I was sorry.''

There hadn't been any reproach, any accusation in her face when I told her she was responsible for the extinction of a species that day at the vet's, and there wasn't now. Maybe she didn't have the facial muscles for it, I thought bitterly.

''Do you know why I came to see you today?'' I said angrily. ''My camera broke when I tried to catch Aberfan. I didn't get any pictures.'' I grabbed the picture of Mrs. Ambler out of the developer's tray and flung it at her. ''Her dog died of newparvo. They left it in the Winnebago, and when they came back, it was dead.''

''Poor thing,'' she said, but she wasn't looking at the picture. She was looking at me.

''She didn't know she was having her picture taken. I thought if I got you talking about Aberfan, I could get a picture like that of you.''

And surely now I would see it, the look I had really wanted when I set the eisenstadt down on Katie's kitchen table, the look I still wanted, even though the eisenstadt was facing the wrong way, the look of betrayal the dogs had never given us. Not even Misha. Not even Aberfan. How does it feel to be responsible for the extinction of an entire species?

I pointed at the eisenstadt. ''It's not a briefcase. It's a camera. I was going to take your picture without your even knowing it.''

She had never known Aberfan. She had never known Mrs. Ambler either, but in that instant before she started to cry she looked like both of them. She put her hand up to her mouth. ''Oh,'' she said, and the love, the loss was there in her voice, too. ''If you'd had it then, it wouldn't have happened.''

I looked at the eisenstadt. If I had had it, I could have set it on the porch and Aberfan would never have even noticed it. He would have burrowed through the snow and tossed it up with his nose, and I could have thrown snow up in big glittering sprays that he would have leaped at, and it never would have happened. Katie Powell would have driven past, and I would have stopped to wave at her, and she, sixteen years old and just learning to drive, would maybe even have risked taking a mittened hand off the steering wheel to wave back, and Aberfan would have wagged his tail into a blizzard and then barked at the snow he'd churned up.

He wouldn't have caught the third wave. He would have lived to be an old dog, fourteen or fifteen, too old to play in the snow any more, and even if he had been the last dog in the world I would not have let them lock him up in a cage, I would not have let them take him away. If I had had the eisenstadt.

No wonder I hated it.

It had been at least fifteen minutes since Ramirez called. The Society would be here any minute. "You shouldn't be here when the Society comes," I said, and Katie nodded and smudged the tears off her cheeks and stood up, reaching for her carryit.

"Do you ever take pictures?" she said, shouldering the carryit. "I mean, besides for the papers?"

"I don't know if I'll be taking pictures for them much longer. Photojournalists are becoming an extinct breed."

"Maybe you could come take some pictures of Jana and Kevin. Kids grow up so fast, they're gone before you know it."

"I'd like that," I said. I opened the screen door for her and looked both ways down the street at the darkness. "All clear," I said, and she went out. I shut the screen door between us.

She turned and looked at me one last time with her dear, open face that even I hadn't been able to close. "I miss them," she said.

I put my hand up to the screen. "I miss them, too."

I watched her to make sure she turned the corner and then went back in the living room and took down the picture of Misha. I propped it against the developer so Segura would be able to see it from the door. In a month or so, when the Amblers were safely in Texas and the Society had forgotten about Katie, I'd call Segura and tell him I might be willing to sell it to the Society, and then in a day or so I'd tell him I'd changed my mind. When he came out to try to talk me into it, I'd tell him about Perdita and Beatrix Potter, and he would tell me about the Society.

Chiwere and Ramirez would have to take the credit for the story—I didn't want Hunter putting anything else together—and it would take more than one story to break them, but it was a start.

Katie had left the print of Mrs. Ambler on the couch. I picked it up and looked at it a minute and then fed it into the developer. "Recycle," I said.

I picked up the eisenstadt from the table by the couch and took the film cartridge out. I started to pull the film out to expose it, and then shoved it into the developer instead and turned it on. "Positives, one two three order, five seconds."

I had apparently set the camera on its activator again—there were ten shots or so of the back seat of the Hitori. Vehicles and people. The pictures of Katie were all in shadow. There was a Still Life of Kool-Aid Pitcher with Whale Glass and another one of Jana's toy cars, and some near-black frames that meant Katie had laid the eisenstadt face-down when she brought it to me.

"Two seconds," I said, and waited for the developer to flash the last shots so

I could make sure there wasn't anything else on the cartridge and then expose it before the Society got here. All but the last frame was of the darkness that was all the eisenstadt could see lying on its face. The last one was of me.

The trick in getting good pictures is to make people forget they're being photographed. Distract them. Get them talking about something they care about.

"Stop," I said, and the image froze.

Aberfan was a great dog. He loved to play in the snow, and after I had murdered him, he lifted his head off my lap and tried to lick my hand.

The Society would be here any minute to take the longshot film and destroy it, and this one would have to go, too, along with the rest of the cartridge. I couldn't risk Hunter's being reminded of Katie. Or Segura taking a notion to do a print-fix and peel on Jana's toy cars.

It was too bad. The eisenstadt takes great pictures. "Even you'll forget it's a camera," Ramirez had said in her spiel, and that was certainly true. I was looking straight into the lens.

And it was all there, Misha and Taco and Perdita and the look he gave me on the way to the vet's while I stroked his poor head and told him it would be all right, that look of love and pity I had been trying to capture all these years. The picture of Aberfan.

The Society would be here any minute. "Eject," I said, and cracked the cartridge open, and exposed it to the light.

LEWIS SHINER

Love in Vain

Lewis Shiner is widely regarded as one of the most exciting new SF writers of the '80s. His stories have appeared in *The Magazine of Fantasy and Science Fiction, Omni, Oui, Shayol, Isaac Asimov's Science Fiction Magazine, The Twilight Zone Magazine, Wild Cards*, and elsewhere. His books include *Frontera* and the critically acclaimed *Deserted Cities of the Heart*. Upcoming is a new novel, *Slam*. His story "Twilight Time" was in our Second Annual Collection; his story "The War at Home" was in our Third Annual Collection; his story "Jeff Beck" was in our Fourth Annual Collection. Shiner lives in Austin, Texas, with his wife Edith.

In the brutal, brilliant story that follows, he teaches us some things we may *not* want to learn about the old cold creatures that still exist deep inside us all.

LOVE IN VAIN

Lewis Shiner

For James Ellroy

I remember the room: whitewashed walls, no windows, a map of the U.S. on my left as I came in. There must have been a hundred pins with little colored heads stuck along the interstates. By the other door was a wooden table, the top full of scratches and coffee rings. Charlie was already sitting on the far side of it.

They called it Charlie's "office" and a Texas Ranger named Gonzales had brought me back there to meet him. "Charlie?" Gonzales said. "This here's Dave McKenna, from the D.A. up in Dallas?"

"Morning," Charlie said. I could see details, but they didn't seem to add up to anything. His left eye, the glass one, drooped a little, and his teeth were brown and ragged. He had on jeans and a plaid short-sleeved shirt and he was shaved clean. His hair was damp and combed straight back. His sideburns had gray in them and came to the bottom of his ears.

I had some files and a notebook in my right hand so I wouldn't have to shake with him. He didn't offer. "You looking to close you up some cases?" he said.

I had to clear my throat. "Well, we thought we might give it a try." I sat down in the other chair.

He nodded and looked at Gonzales. "Ernie? You don't suppose I could have a little more coffee?"

Gonzales had been leaning against the wall by the map, but he straightened right up and said, "Sure thing, Charlie." He brought in a full pot of coffee from the other room and set it on the table. Charlie had a styrofoam cup that looked like it could hold about a quart. He filled it up and then added three packets of sugar and some powdered cream substitute.

"How about you?" Charlie said.

"No," I said. "Thanks."

"You don't need to be nervous," Charlie said. His breath smelled of coffee and cigarettes. When he wasn't talking, his mouth relaxed into an easy smile. You didn't have to see anything menacing in it. It was the kind of smile you could see from any highway in Texas, looking out at you from a porch or behind a gas pump, waiting for you to drive on through.

I took out a little pocket-sized cassette recorder. "Would it be okay if I taped this?"

"Sure, go ahead."

I pushed the little orange button on top. "March 27, Williamson County Jail. Present are Sergeant Ernesto Gonzales and Charles Dean Harris."

"Charlie," he said.

"Pardon?"

"Nobody ever calls me Charles."

"Right," I said. "Okay."

"I guess maybe my mother did sometimes. Always sounded wrong somehow." He tilted his chair back against the wall. "You don't suppose you could back that up and do it over?"

"Yeah, okay, fine." I rewound the tape and went through the introduction again. This time I called him Charlie. Twenty-five years ago he'd stabbed his mother to death. She'd been his first.

It had taken me three hours to drive from Dallas to the Williamson County Jail in Georgetown, a straight shot down Interstate 35. I'd left a little before eight that morning. Alice was already at work and I had to get Jeffrey off to school. The hardest part was getting him away from the television.

He was watching MTV. They were playing the Heart video where the blonde guitar player wears the low-cut golden prom dress. Every time she moved, her magnificent breasts seemed to hesitate before they went along, like they were proud, willful animals, just barely under her control.

I turned the TV off and swung Jeffrey around a couple of times and sent him out for the bus. I got together the files I needed and went into the bedroom to make the bed. The covers were turned back on both sides, but the middle was undisturbed. Alice and I hadn't made love in six weeks. And counting.

I walked through the house, picking up Jeffrey's Masters of the Universe toys. I saw that Alice had loaded up the mantel again with framed pictures of her brothers and parents and the dog she'd had as a little girl. For a second it seemed like the entire house was buried in all this crap that had nothing to do with me —dolls and vases and doilies and candles and baskets on every inch of every flat surface she could reach. You couldn't walk from one end of a room to the other without running into a Victorian chair or secretary or umbrella stand, couldn't see the floors for the flowered rugs.

I locked up and got in the car and took the LBJ loop all the way around town. The idea was to avoid traffic. I was kidding myself. Driving in Dallas is a kind of contest; if somebody manages to pull in front of you he's clearly got a bigger dick than you do. Rather than let this happen it's better that one of you die.

I was in traffic the whole way down, through a hundred and seventy miles of Charlie Dean Harris country: flat, desolate grasslands with an occasional bridge or culvert where you could dump a body. Charlie had wandered and murdered all over the South, but once he found I-35 he was home to stay.

I opened one of the folders and rested it against the edge of the table so Charlie wouldn't see my hand shaking. "I've got a case here from 1974. A Dallas girl on her way home from Austin for spring break. Her name was Carol, uh, Fairchild. Black hair, blue eyes. Eighteen years old."

Charlie was nodding. "She had braces on her teeth. Would have been real pretty without 'em."

I looked at the sheet of paper in the folder. Braces, it said. The plain white walls seemed to wobble a little. "Then you remember her."

"Yessir, I suppose I do. I killed her." He smiled. It looked like a reflex, something he didn't even know he was doing. "I killed her to have sex with her."

"Can you remember anything else?"

He shrugged. "It was just to have sex, that's all. I remember when she got in the car. She was wearing a T-shirt, one of them man's T-shirts, with the straps and all." He dropped the chair back down and put his elbows on the table. "You could see her titties," he said, explaining.

I wanted to pull away but I didn't. "Where was this?"

He thought for a minute. "Between here and Round Rock, right there off the Interstate."

I looked down at my folder again. Last seen wearing navy tank top, blue jeans. "What color was the T-shirt?"

"Red," he said. "She would have been strangled. With a piece of electrical wire I had there in the car. I had supposed she was a prostitute, dressed the way she was and all. I asked her to have sex and she said she would, so I got off the highway and then she didn't want to. So I killed her and I had sex with her."

Nobody said anything for what must have been at least a minute. I could hear a little scratching noise as the tape moved inside the recorder. Charlie was looking straight at me with his good eye. "I wasn't satisfied," he said.

"What?"

"I wasn't satisfied. I had sex with her but I wasn't satisfied."

"Listen, you don't have to tell me . . ."

"I got to tell it all," he said.

"I don't want to hear it," I said. My voice came out too high, too loud. But Charlie kept staring at me.

"It don't matter," he said. "I still got to tell it. I got to tell it all. I can't live with the terrible things I did. Jesus says that if I tell everything I can be with Betsy when this is all over." Betsy was his common-law wife. He'd killed her, too, after living with her since she was nine. The words sounded like he'd been practicing them, over and over.

"I'll take you to her if you want," he said.

"Betsy . . .?"

"No, your girl there. Carol Fairchild. I'll take you where I buried her." He wasn't smiling anymore. He had the sad, earnest look of a laundromat bum telling you how he'd lost his oil fortune up in Oklahoma.

I looked at Gonzales. "We can set it up for you if you want," he said. "Sheriff'll have to okay it and all, but we could prob'ly do it first thing tomorrow."

"Okay," I said. "That'd be good."

Charlie nodded, drank some coffee, lit a cigarette. "Well, fine," he said. "You want to try another?"

"No," I said. "Not just yet."

"Whatever," Charlie said. "You just let me know."

Later, walking me out, Gonzales said, "Don't let Charlie get to you. He wants people to like him, you know? So he figures out what you want him to be, and he tries to be that for you."

I knew he was trying to cheer me up. I thanked him and told him I'd be back in the morning.

I called Alice from Jack's office in Austin, thirty miles farther down I-35. "It's me," I said.

"Oh," she said. She sounded tired. "How's it going?"

I didn't know what to tell her. "Fine," I said. "I need to stay over another day or so."

"Okay," she said.

"Are you okay?"

"Fine," she said.

"Jeffrey?"

"He's fine."

I watched thirty seconds tick by on Jack's wall clock. "Anything else?" she said.

"I guess not." My eyes stung and I reflexively shaded them with my free hand. "I'll be at Jack's if you need me."

"Okay," she said. I waited a while longer and then put the phone back on the hook.

Jack was just coming out of his office. "Oh-oh," he said.

It took a couple of breaths to get my throat to unclench. "Yeah," I said.

"Bad?"

"Bad as it could be, I guess. It's over, probably. I mean, I think it's over, but how do you know?"

"You don't," Jack said. His secretary, a good-looking Chicana named Liz, typed away on her word processor and tried to act like she wasn't having to listen to us. "You just after a while get fed up and you say fuck it. You want to get a burger or what?"

Jack and I went to U.T. law school together. He was losing his hair and putting on weight but he wouldn't do anything about it. Jogging was for assholes. He would rather die fat and keep his self-respect.

He'd been divorced two years now and was always glad to fold out the couch for me. It had been a while. After Jeffrey was born, Alice and I had somehow lost touch with all our friends, given up everything except work and TV. "I've missed this," I said.

"Missed what?"

"Friends," I said. We were in a big prairie-style house north of campus that had been fixed up with a kitchen and bar and hanging plants. I was full, but still working on the last of the batter-dipped french fries.

"Not my fault, you prick. You're the one dropped down to Christmas cards."

"Yeah, well . . ."

"Forget it. How'd it go with Charlie Dean?"

"Unbelievable," I said. "I mean, really. He confessed to everything. Had details. Even had a couple wrong, enough to look good. But the major stuff was right on."

"So that's great. Isn't it?"

"It was a setup. The name I gave him was a fake. No such person, no such case."

"I don't get it."

"Jack, the son of a bitch has confessed to something like three thousand murders. It ain't possible. So they wanted to catch him lying."

"With his pants down, so to speak."

"Same old Jack."

"You said he had details."

"That's the creepy part. He knew she was supposed to have braces. I had it in the phony-case file, but he brought it up before I could say anything about it."

"Lucky guess."

"No. It was too creepy. And there's all this shit he keeps telling you. Things you wish you'd never heard, you know what I mean?"

"I know exactly what you mean," Jack said. "When I was in junior high I saw a bum go in the men's room at the bus station with a loaf of bread. I told this friend of mine about it and he says the bum was going in there to wipe all the dried piss off the toilets with the bread and then eat it. For the protein. Said it happens all the time."

"Jesus *Christ*, Jack."

"See? I know what you're talking about. There's things you don't want in your head. Once they get in there, you're not the same anymore. I can't eat white bread to this day. Twenty years, and I still can't touch it."

"You asshole." I pushed my plate away and finished my Corona. "Christ, now the beer tastes like piss."

Jack pointed his index finger at me. "You will never be the same," he said.

You could never tell how much Jack had been drinking. He said it was because he didn't let on when he was sober. I always thought it was because there was something in him that was meaner than the booze and together they left him just about even.

It was a lot of beers later that Jack said, "What was the name of that bimbo in high school you used to talk about? Your first great love or some shit? Except she never put out for you?"

"Kristi," I said. "Kristi Spector."

"Right!" Jack got up and started walking around the apartment. It wasn't too long of a walk. "A name like that, how could I forget? I got her off a soliciting rap two months ago."

"Soliciting?"

"There's a law in Texas against selling your pussy. Maybe you didn't know that."

"Kristi Spector, my God. Tell me about it."

"She's a stripper, son. Works over at the Yellow Rose. This guy figured if she'd show her tits in public he could have the rest in his car. She didn't, he called the pigs. Said she made lewd advances. Crock of shit, got thrown out of court."

"How's she look?"

"Not too goddamn bad. I wouldn't have minded taking my fee in trade, but she didn't seem to get the hint." He stopped. "I got a better idea. Let's go have a look for ourselves."

"Oh, no," I said.

"Oh, yes. She remembers you, man. She says you were 'sweet.' Come on, get up. We're going to go look at some tits."

The place was bigger inside than I expected, the ceilings higher. There were two stages and a runway behind the second one. There were stools right up by the stages for the guys that wanted to stick dollar bills in the dancers' G-strings and four-top tables everywhere else.

I should have felt guilty but I wasn't thinking about Alice at all. The issue here was sex, and Alice had written herself out of that part of my life. Instead I was thinking about the last time I'd seen Kristi.

It was senior year in high school. The director of the drama club, who was from New York, had invited some of us to a "wild" party. It was the first time I'd seen men in dresses. I'd locked myself in the bathroom with Kristi to help her take her bra off. I hadn't seen her in six months. She'd just had an abortion; the father could have been one of a couple of guys. Not me. She didn't want to spoil what we had. It was starting to look to me like there wasn't much left to spoil. That had been eighteen years ago.

The D.J. played something by Pat Benatar. The music was loud enough to give you a kind of mental privacy. You didn't really have to pay attention to anything but the dancers. At the moment it seemed like just the thing. It had been an ugly day and there was something in me that was comforted by the sight of young, good-looking women with their clothes off.

"College town," Jack said, leaning toward me so I could hear him. "Lots of local talent."

A tall blonde on the north stage unbuttoned her long-sleeved white shirt and let it hang open. Her breasts were smooth and firm and pale. Like the others, she had something on the point of her nipples that made a small, golden flash every time one caught the light.

"See anybody you know?"

"Give me a break," I shouted over the music. "You saw her a couple months ago. It's been almost twenty years for me. I may not even recognize her." A waitress came by, wearing black leather jeans and a red tank top. For a second I could hear Charlie's voice telling me about her titties. I rubbed the sides of my head and the voice went away. We ordered beers, but when they came my stomach was wrapped around itself and I had to let mine sit.

"It's got to be weird to do this for a living," I said in Jack's ear.

"Bullshit," Jack said. "You think they're not getting off on it?"

He pointed to the south stage. A brunette in high heels had let an overweight man in sideburns and a western shirt tuck a dollar into the side of her bikini bottoms. He talked earnestly to her with just the start of an embarrassed smile. She had to keep leaning closer to hear him. Finally she nodded and turned around. She bent over and grabbed her ankles. His face was about the height of the backs of her knees. She was smiling like she'd just seen somebody else's baby do something cute. After a few seconds she stood up again and the man went back to his table.

"What was that about?" I asked Jack.

"Power, man," he said. "God, I love women. I just love 'em."

"Your problem is you don't know the difference between love and sex."

"Yeah? What is it? Come on, I want to know." The music was too loud to argue with him. I shook my head. "See? You don't know either."

The brunette pushed her hair back with both hands, chin up, fingers spread wide, and it reminded me of Kristi. The theatricality of it. She'd played one of Tennessee Williams's affected Southern bitches once and it had been almost too painful to watch. Almost.

"Come on," I said, grabbing Jack's sleeve. "It's been swell, but let's get out of here. I don't need to see her. I'm better off with the fantasy."

Jack didn't say anything. He just pointed with his chin to the stage behind me.

She had on a leopard skin leotard. She had been a dark blonde in high school but now her hair was brown and short. She'd put on a little weight, not much. She stretched in front of the mirrored wall and the D.J. played the Pretenders.

I felt this weird, possessive kind of pride, watching her. That and lust. I'd been married for eight years and the worst thing I'd ever done was kiss an old girlfriend on New Year's Eve and stare longingly at the pictures in *Playboy*. But this was real, this was happening.

The song finished and another one started and she pulled one strap down on the leotard. I remembered the first time I'd seen her breasts. I was fifteen. I'd joined a youth club at the Unitarian Church because she went there Sunday afternoons. Sometimes we would skip the program and sneak off into the deserted Sunday school classrooms and there, in the twilight, surrounded by crayon drawings on manila paper, she would stretch out on the linoleum and let me lie on top of her and feel the maddening pressure of her pelvis and smell the faint, clinically erotic odor of peroxide in her hair.

She showed me her breasts on the golf course next door. We had jumped the fence and we lay in a sand trap so no one would see us. There was a little light from the street, but not enough for real color. It was like a black-and-white movie when I played it back in my mind.

They were fuller now, hung a little lower and flatter, but I remembered the small, pale nipples. She pulled the other strap down, turned her back, rotating her hips as she stripped down to a red G-string. Somebody held a dollar out to her. I wanted to go over there and tell him that I knew her.

Jack kept poking me in the ribs. "Well? Well?"

"Be cool," I said. I had been watching the traffic pattern and I knew that after the song she would take a break and then get up on the other stage. It took a long time, but I wasn't tense about it. I'm just going to say hi, I thought. And that's it.

The song was over and she walked down the stairs at the end of the stage, throwing the leotard around her shoulders. I got up, having a little trouble with the chair, and walked over to her.

"Kristi," I said. "It's Dave McKenna."

"Oh, my *God*!" She was in my arms. Her skin was hot from the lights and I could smell her deodorant. I was suddenly dizzy, aware of every square inch where our bodies were touching. "Do you still hate me?" she said, pulling away.

"What?" There was so much I'd forgotten. The twang in her voice. The milk chocolate color of her eyes. The beauty mark over her right cheekbone. The flirtatious look up through the lashes that now had a desperate edge to it.

"The last time I saw you you called me a bitch. It was after that party at your teacher's house."

"No, I . . . believe me, it wasn't like . . ."

"Listen, I'm on again," she said. "Where are you?"

"We're right over there."

"Oh, Christ, you didn't bring your wife with you? I heard you were married."

"No, it's . . ."

"I got to run, sugar, wait for me."

I went back to the table.

"You rascal," Jack said. "Why didn't you just slip it to her on the spot?"

"Shut up, Jack, will you?"

"Ooooh, touchy."

I watched her dance. She was no movie star. Her face was a little hard and even the heavy makeup didn't hide all the lines. But none of that mattered. What mattered was the way she moved, the kind of puckered smile that said yes, I want it too.

She sat down with us when she was finished. She seemed to be all hands, touching me on the arm, biting on a fingernail, gesturing in front of her face.

She was dancing three times a week, which was all they would schedule her for anymore. The money was good and she didn't mind the work, especially here where it wasn't too rowdy. Jack raised his eyebrows at me to say, see? She got by with some modeling and some "scuffling," which I assumed meant turning tricks. Her mother was still in Dallas and had sent Kristi clippings the couple of times I got my name in the paper.

"She always liked me," I said.

"She liked you the best of all of them. You were a gentleman."

"Maybe too much of one."

"It was why I loved you." She was wearing the leotard again but she might as well have been naked. I was beginning to be afraid of her so I reminded myself that nothing had happened yet, nothing *had* to happen, that I wasn't committed to anything. I pushed my beer over to her and she drank about half of it. "It gets hot up there," she said. "You wouldn't believe. Sometimes you think you're going to pass out, but you got to keep smiling."

"Are you married?" I asked her. "Were you ever?"

"Once. It lasted two whole months. The shitheel knocked me up and then split."

"What happened?"

"I kept the kid. He's four now."

"What's his name?"

"Stoney. He's a cute little bastard. I got a neighbor watches him when I'm out, and I do the same for hers. He keeps me going sometimes." She drank the rest of the beer. "What about you?"

"I got a little boy too. Jeffrey. He's seven."

"Just the one?"

"I don't think the marriage could handle more than one kid," I said.

"It's an old story," Jack said. "If your wife put you through law school, the marriage breaks up. It just took Dave a little longer than most."

"You're getting divorced?" she asked.

"I don't know. Maybe." She nodded. I guess she didn't need to ask for details. Marriages come apart every day.

"I'm on again in a little," she said. "Will you still be here when I get back?" She did what she could to make it sound casual.

"I got an early day tomorrow," I said.

"Sure. It was good to see you. Real good."

The easiest thing seemed to be to get out a pen and an old business card. "Give me your phone number. Maybe I can get loose another night."

She took the pen but she kept looking at me. "Sure," she said.

"You're an idiot," Jack said. "Why didn't you go home with her?"

I watched the streetlights. My jacket smelled like cigarettes and my head had started to hurt.

"That gorgeous piece of ass says to you, 'Ecstasy?' and Dave says, 'No thanks.' What the hell's the matter with you? Alice make you leave your dick in the safe-deposit box?"

"Jack," I said, "will you shut the fuck up?" The card with her number on it was in the inside pocket of the jacket. I could feel it there, like a cool fingernail against my flesh.

Jack went back to his room to crash a little after midnight. I couldn't sleep. I put on the headphones and listened to Robert Johnson, "King of the Delta Blues Singers." There was something about his voice. He had this deadpan tone that sat down and told you what was wrong like it was no big deal. Then the voice would crack and you could tell it was a hell of a lot worse than he was letting on.

They said the devil himself had tuned Johnson's guitar. He died in 1938, poisoned by a jealous husband. He'd made his first recordings in a hotel room in San Antonio, just another seventy miles on down I-35.

Charlie and Gonzales and I took my car out to what Gonzales called the "site." The sheriff and a deputy were in a brown county station wagon behind us. Charlie sat on the passenger side and Gonzales was in the back. Charlie could have opened the door at a stoplight and been gone. He wasn't even in handcuffs. Nobody said anything about it.

We got on I-35 and Charlie said, "Go on south to the second exit after the caves." The Inner Space Caverns were just south of Georgetown, basically a single long, unspectacular tunnel that ran for miles under the highway. "I killed a girl there once. When they turned off the lights."

I nodded but I didn't say anything. That morning, before I went in to the "office," Gonzales had told me that it made Charlie angry if you let on that you didn't believe him. I was tired, and hung over from watching Jack drink, and I didn't really give a damn about Charlie's feelings.

I got off at the exit and followed the access road for a while. Charlie had his eyes closed and seemed to be thinking hard.

"Having trouble?" I asked him.

"Nah," he said. "Just didn't want to take you to the wrong one." I looked at him and he started laughing. It was a joke. Gonzales chuckled in the back seat and there was this cheerful kind of feeling in the car that made me want to pull over and run away.

"Nosir," Charlie said, "I sure don't suppose I'd want to do that." He grinned at me and he knew what I was thinking, he could see the horror right there on my face. He just kept smiling. Come on, I could hear him saying. Loosen up. Be one of the guys.

I wiped the sweat from my hands onto my pant legs. Finally he said, "There's a dirt road a ways ahead. Turn off on it. It'll go over a hill and then across a cattle grating. After the grating is a stand of trees off to the left. You'll want to park up under 'em."

How can he be doing this? I thought. He's got to know there's nothing there. Or does he? When we don't turn anything up, what's he going to do? Are they going to wish they'd cuffed him after all? The sheriff knew what I was up to, but none of the others did. Would Gonzales turn on me for betraying Charlie?

The road did just what Charlie said it would. We parked the cars under the trees and the deputy and I got shovels out of the sheriff's trunk. The trees were oaks and their leaves were tiny and very pale green.

"It would be over here," Charlie said. He stood on a patch of low ground, covered with clumps of Johnson grass. "Not too deep."

He was right. She was only about six or eight inches down. The deputy had a body bag and he tried to move her into it, but she kept coming apart. There wasn't much left but a skeleton and a few rags.

And the braces. Still shining, clinging to the teeth of the skull like a metal smile.

*   *   *

On the way back to Georgetown we passed a woman on the side of the road. She was staring into the hood of her car. She looked like she was about to cry. Charlie turned all the way around in his seat to watch her as we drove by.

"There's just victims ever'where," Charlie said. There was a sadness in his voice I didn't believe. "The highway's full of 'em. Kids, hitchhikers, waitresses . . . You ever pick one up?"

"No," I said, but it wasn't true. It was in Dallas, I was home for spring break. It was the end of the sixties. She had on a green dress. Nothing happened. But she had smiled at me and put one arm up on the back of the seat. I was on the way to my girlfriend's house and I let her off a few blocks away. And that night, when I was inside her, I imagined my girlfriend with the hitchhiker's face, with her blonde hair and freckles, her slightly coarse features, the dots of sweat on her upper lip.

"But you thought about it," Charlie said. "Didn't you?"

"Listen," I said. "I got a job to do. I just want to do it and get out of here, okay?"

"I know what you're saying," Charlie said. "Jesus forgives me, but I can't ask that of nobody else. I was just trying to get along, that's all. That's all any of us is ever trying to do."

I called Dallas collect from the sheriff's phone. He gave me a private room where I could shout if I had to. The switchboard put me through to Ricky Slatkin, the head of my department.

"Dave, will you for Chrissake calm down. It's a coincidence. That's all. Forensics will figure out who this girl is and we'll put another 70 or 80 years on Charlie's sentence. Maybe give him another death penalty. What the hell, right? Meanwhile we'll give him another ringer."

"You give him one. I want out of this. I am fucking terrified."

"I, uh, understand you're under some stress at home these days."

"I am not at home. I'm in Georgetown, in the Williamson County Jail, and I am under some fucking stress right here. Don't you understand? He *thought* this dead girl into existence."

"What, Charlie Dean Harris is God now, is that it? Come on, Dave. Go out and have a few beers and by tomorrow it'll all make sense to you."

"He's evil, Jack," I said. We were back at his place after a pizza at Conan's. Jack had ordered a pitcher of beer and drunk it all himself. "I didn't use to believe in it, but that was before I met Charlie."

He had a women's basketball game on TV, the sound turned down to a low hum. "That's horseshit," he said. His voice was too loud. "Horseshit, Christian horseshit. They want you to believe that Evil has got a capital *E* and it's sitting over there in the corner, see it? Horseshit. Evil isn't a thing. It's something that's *not* there. It's an absence. The lack of the thing that stops you from doing whatever you damn well please.''

He chugged half a beer. ''Your pal Charlie ain't evil. He's just damaged goods. He's just like you or me but something died in him. You know what I'm talking about. You've felt it. First it goes to sleep and then it dies. You know when you stand up in court and try to get a rapist off when you know he did it. You tell yourself that it's part of the game, you try to give the asshole the benefit of the doubt, hell, somebody's got to do it, right? You try to believe the girl is just some slut that changed her mind, but you can smell it. Something inside you starting to rot.''

He finished the beer and threw it at a paper sack in the corner. It hit another bottle inside the sack and shattered. ''Then you go home and your wife's got a goddamn headache or her period or she's asleep in front of the TV or she's not in the goddamn mood and you just want to beat the . . .'' His right fist was clenched up so tight the knuckles were a shiny yellow. His eyes looked like open sores. He got up for another beer and he was in the kitchen for a long time.

When he came back I said, ''I'm going out.'' I said it without giving myself a chance to think about it.

''Kristi,'' Jack said. He had a fresh beer and was all right again.

''Yeah.''

''You bastard! Can I smell your fingers when you get back?''

''Fuck you, Jack.''

''Oh no, save it for her. She's going to use you up, you lucky bastard.''

I called her from a pay phone and she gave me directions. She was at the Royal Palms Trailer Park, near Bergstrom Air Force Base on the south end of town. It wasn't hard to find. They even had a few palm trees. There were rural-type galvanized mailboxes on posts by the gravel driveways. I found the one that said Spector and parked behind a white Dodge with six-figure mileage.

The temperature was in the sixties but I was shaking. My shoulders kept trying to crawl up around my neck. I got out of the car. I couldn't feel my feet. Asshole, I told myself. I don't want to hear about your personal problems. You better enjoy this or I'll kill you.

I knocked on the door and it made a kind of mute rattling sound. Kristi opened it. She was wearing a plaid bathrobe, so old I couldn't tell what the colors used to be. She stood back to let me in and said, ''I didn't think you'd call.''

''But I did,'' I said. The trailer was tiny—a living room with a green sofa and a 19-inch color TV, a kitchen the size of a short hall, a single bedroom behind it, the door open, the bed unmade. A blond-haired boy was asleep on the sofa, wrapped in an army blanket. The shelf above him was full of plays—Albee,

Ionesco, Tennessee Williams. The walls were covered with photographs in dime-store frames.

A couple of them were from the drama club; one even had me in it. I was sixteen and looked maybe nine. My hair was too long in front, my chest was sucked in, and I had a stupid smirk on my face. I was looking at Kristi. Who would want to look at anything else? She had on cutoffs that had frayed up past the crease of her thighs. Her shirt was unbuttoned and tied under her breasts. Her head was back and she was laughing. I'd always been able to make her laugh.

"You want a drink?" she whispered.

"No," I said. I turned to look at her. We weren't either of us laughing now. I reached for her and she glanced over at the boy and shook her head. She grabbed the cuff of my shirt and pulled me gently back toward the bedroom.

It smelled of perfume and hand lotion and a little of mildew. The only light trickled in through heavy, old-fashioned venetian blinds. She untied the bathrobe and let it fall. I kissed her and her arms went around my neck. I touched her shoulder blades and her hair and her buttocks and then I got out of my clothes and left them in a pile on the floor. She ran on tiptoes back to the front of the trailer and locked and chained the door. Then she came back and shut the bedroom door and lay down on the bed.

I lay down next to her. The smell and feel of her was wonderful, and at the same time it was not quite real. There were too many unfamiliar things and it was hard to connect to the rest of my life.

Then I was on my knees between her legs, gently touching her. Her arms were spread out beside her, tangled in the sheets, her hips moving with pleasure. Only once, in high school, had she let me touch her there, in the back seat of a friend's car, her skirt up around her hips, panties to her knees, and before I had recovered from the wonder of it she had pulled away.

But that was eighteen years ago and this was now. There had been a lot of men touching her since then, maybe hundreds. But that was all right. I lay on top of her and she guided me inside. She tried to say something, maybe it was only my name, but I put my mouth over hers to shut her up. I put both my arms around her and closed my eyes and let the heat and pleasure run up through me.

When I finished and we rolled apart she lay on top of me, pinning me to the bed. "That was real sweet," she said.

I kissed her and hugged her because I couldn't say what I was thinking. I was thinking about Charlie, remembering the earnest look on his face when he said, "It was just to have sex, that's all."

She was wide awake and I was exhausted. She complained about the state cutting back on aid to single parents. She told me about the tiny pieces of tape she had to wear on the ends of her nipples when she danced, a weird Health

Department regulation. I remembered the tiny golden flashes and fell asleep to the memory of her dancing.

Screaming woke me up. Kristi was already out of bed and headed for the living room. "It's just Stoney," she said, and I lay back down.

I woke up again a little before dawn. There was an arm around my waist but it seemed much too small. I rolled over and saw that the little boy had crawled into bed between us.

I got up without moving him and went to the bathroom. There was no water in the toilet; when I pushed the handle a trap opened in the bottom of the bowl and a fine spray washed the sides. I got dressed, trying not to bump into anything. Kristi was asleep on the side of the bed closest to the door, her mouth open a little. Stoney had burrowed into the middle of her back.

I was going to turn around and go when a voyeuristic impulse made me open the drawer of her nightstand. Or maybe I subconsciously knew what I'd find. There was a Beeline book called *Molly's Sexual Follies*, a tube of KY, a box of Ramses lubricated condoms, a few used Kleenex. An emery board, a finger puppet, one hoop earring. A short-barreled Colt .32 revolver.

I got to the jail at nine in the morning. The woman at the visitor's window recognized me and buzzed me back. Gonzales was at his desk. He looked up when I walked in and said, "I didn't know you was coming in today."

"I just had a couple of quick questions for Charlie," I said. "Only take a second."

"Did you want to use the office . . . ?"

"No, no point. If I could just talk to him in his cell for a couple of minutes, that would be great."

Gonzales got the keys. Charlie had a cell to himself, five by ten feet, white-painted bars on the long wall facing the corridor. There were Bibles and religious tracts on his cot, a few paintings hanging on the wall. "Maybe you can get Charlie to show you his pictures," Gonzales said. A stool in the corner had brushes and tubes of paint on the top.

"You painted these?" I asked Charlie. My voice sounded fairly normal, all things considered.

"Yessir, I did."

"They're pretty good." They were landscapes with trees and horses, but no people.

"Thank you kindly."

"You can just call for me when you're ready," Gonzales said. He went out and locked the door.

"I thought you'd be back," Charlie said. "Was there something else you wanted to ask me?" He sat on the edge of the cot, forearms on his knees.

I didn't say anything. I took the Colt out of the waistband of my pants and pointed it at him. I'd already looked it over on the drive up and there were bullets in all six cylinders. My hand was shaking so I steadied it with my left and fired all six rounds into his head and chest.

I hadn't noticed all the background noises until they stopped, the typewriters and the birds and somebody singing upstairs. Charlie stood up and walked over to where I was standing. The revolver clicked on an empty shell.

"You can't get rid of me that easy," Charlie said with his droopy-eyed smile. "I been around too long. I was Springheeled Jack and Richard Speck. I was Ted Bundy and that fella up to Seattle they never caught." The door banged open at the end of the hall. "You can't never get rid of me because I'm *inside* you."

I dropped the gun and locked my hands behind my head. Gonzales stuck his head around the corner. He was squinting. He had his gun out and he looked terrified. Charlie and I stared back at him calmly.

"It's okay, Ernie," Charlie said. "No harm done. Mr. McKenna was just having him a little joke."

Charlie told Gonzales the gun was loaded with blanks. They had to believe him because there weren't any bullet holes in the cell. I told them I'd bought the gun off a defendant years ago, that I'd had it in the car.

They called Dallas and Ricky asked to talk to me. "There's going to be an inquest," he said. "No way around it."

"Sure there is," I said. "I quit. I'll send it to you in writing. I'll put it in the mail today. Express."

"You need some help, Dave. You understand what I'm saying to you here? *Professional* help. Think about it. Just tell me you'll think about it."

Gonzales was scared and angry and wanted me charged with smuggling weapons into the jail. The sheriff knew it wasn't worth the headlines and by suppertime I was out.

Jack had already heard about it through some kind of legal grapevine. He thought it was funny. We skipped dinner and went down to the bars on Sixth Street. I couldn't drink anything. I was afraid of going numb, or letting down my guard. But Jack made up for me. As usual.

"Kristi called me today," Jack said. "I told her I didn't know but what you might be going back to Dallas today. Just a kind of feeling I had."

"I'm not going back," I said. "But it was the right thing to tell her."

"Not what it was cracked up to be, huh?"

"Oh yeah," I said. "That and much, much more."

For once he let it go. "You mean you're not going back tonight or not going back period?"

"Period," I said. "My job's gone, I pissed that away this morning. I'll get something down here. I don't care what. I'll pump gas. I'll fucking wait tables. You can draw up the divorce papers and I'll sign them."

"Just like that?"

"Just like that."

"What's Alice going to say?"

"I don't know if she'll even notice. She can have the goddamn house and her car and the savings. All of it. All I want is some time with Jeffrey. As much as I can get. Every week if I can."

"Good luck."

"I've got to have it. I don't want him growing up screwed up like the rest of us. I've got stuff I've got to tell him. He's going to need help. All of us are. Jack, goddamn it, are you listening to me?"

He wasn't. He was staring at the Heart video on the bar's big-screen TV, at the blonde guitarist. "Look at that," Jack said. "Sweet suffering Jesus. Couldn't you just fuck that to death?"

JUDITH MOFFETT

The Hob

Here's a compassionate, lyrical, and compelling look behind one of the oldest bits of English folklore.

Although Judith Moffett is the author of two books of poetry, a book of criticism, and a book of translations from the Swedish, she made her first professional fiction sale in 1986. Since then, she has won the John W. Campbell Award as Best New Writer of 1987, and the Theodore Sturgeon Award for her story "Surviving," and her first novel *Pennterra* was released to critical acclaim. She has since completed a second novel. Born in Louisville, Kentucky, she now lives with her husband in Wallingford, Pennsylvania, and teaches a science-fiction course and a graduate course in twentieth-century American poetry at the University of Pennsylvania. She has also taught for four summers at the prestigious Breadloaf Writers' Conference, and was given a National Endowment for the Arts Creative Writing Fellowship Grant for her poetry—which she then used to finance the writing of her first novel.

THE HOB

Judith Moffett

1

Elphi was the first of them to wake that spring, which meant he was the first to catch, almost at once, the faint whiff of corruption. Feeling ghastly, as always upon just emerging from hibernation, he dragged himself out of his bunk to go and see which of the remnant of elderly hobs had died during the winter.

He tottered round the den in darkness, unable as yet to manage the coordination required to strike a light. Nor did he really require one. Hobs were nocturnal. Besides, this group had been overwintering in the same den for nearly a hundred years.

Tarn Hole and Hasty Bank lay together, deep in sleep. Hodge Hob seemed all right . . . and Broxa . . . and Scugdale. . . . Ah. Woof Howe Hob was the dead one. Elphi checked on Hart Hall, just to make sure there had been only one death, then wobbled back to his own bed to think.

They would have to get Woof Howe out of the den: he thrust that thought, and the necessity for fast action, into the forefront of his mind to blank out the yawning hollowness, the would-be grief. Every decade or two, now, another of them was lost. The long exile seemed to be coming inexorably to an end, not by rescue as they had gone on expecting for so long, but by slow attrition. Only seven were left of the fifteen stranded in this place, and soon there would be none.

Elphi rolled out again; these thoughts were unproductive, as they had ever been. He needed a drink and a meal.

The great stone that had sealed the den all winter posed a problem. By human standards the hobs were prodigiously strong for their size, even in great age, but Elphi—feeble after his months-long fast—would ordinarily not have attempted to move the stone unaided. But he managed it, finally, and poked his head with due caution out into the world.

Outside it was early April on the heather moors of North Yorkshire. Weak as he was, Elphi shuddered with pleasure as the fresh moorland wind blew into his face. The wind was strong, and fiercely cold, but cold had never bothered the hobs and it was not for warmth's sake that Elphi doubled back down the ladder to fetch forth something to wrap around himself, something that would deceive the eyes of any unlikely walker still on the tops in the last few hours of light. That done, he dragged the heavy stone back across the hole, sealing in the scent of death, and set off on all fours stiffly through the snow-crusted heather.

He followed a sheep-track, keeping a weather eye out as he trotted along for any farmer who might be gathering his moor ewes to bring them down "inside" for lambing now. Those years when the hobs slept a bit later than usual they sometimes found their earliest forays cramped by the presence of farmers and dogs, neither of which could be easily fooled by their disguise. When that happened they were forced to be nocturnal indeed.

But the sheep Elphi saw had a week to go at least before they would be gathered in, and he began to relax. Walkers were always fairly few at this uncomfortable season, and the archeologists who had been working at the prehistoric settlement sites on Danby Rigg the previous summer were not in evidence there now. Perhaps getting rid of old Woof Howe would not be quite so difficult as he had feared— not like the year they had woken in mid-April to find Kempswithen dead and the tops acrawl with men and dogs for days. The only humans he was at all likely to encounter this late afternoon would be hauling hay up to their flocks, and since their tractors and pickups made a din that carried for miles in the open landscape he had no fear of being caught napping.

The local dogs all knew about the hobs, of course, as they knew about the grouse and hares, but they rarely came on the tops unless they were herding sheep, and when they were herding sheep they generally stuck to business. The problem dogs were those the walkers allowed to run loose, whether under good voice control or no. *They* could be really troublesome. In August and September, when the heather turned the moorland into a shag carpet of purple flowers forty miles wide and a tidal wave of tourists came pouring up to see and photograph them, the hobs never showed their noses aboveground by day at all. But it was a bother, despite their perfect ease at getting about in the dark; for except from November to April hobs didn't do a lot of sleeping, and they always had more than enough essential work to see to. Then there was the grouse shooting, which started every year on August twelfth and went on till long after Elphi and his companions had gone to ground for the winter. . . .

Of course, the horde of August visitors was also a great boon. All summer the hobs picked up a stream, steady but relatively thin, of useful stuff dropped or forgotten by visitors. August brought the flood, and the year's bonanza: bandanas, wool socks, chocolate bars, granola bars, small convenient pads of paper, pencils and pens, maps, rubber bands, safety pins, lengths of nylon cord, fourteen Swiss Army knives in fifteen years, guidebooks, comic books, new batteries for the transistors (three) and the electric torches (five). Every night in summer they would all be out scavenging the courses of the long-distance footpaths, the Lyke Wake Walk and the Cleveland Way, each with a big pouch to carry home the loot in.

Earlier and later in the year, however, they were forced to spend more time hunting, and hunting a meal was Elphi's first priority now. Luckily he and his people could digest just about anything they could catch (or they would not have been able to survive here at all). They were partial to dale-dwelling rabbit and spring lamb, and had no objection to road-killed ewe when they could get it; but as none of these was available at the moment, Elphi settled for a grouse he happened to start: snapped its neck, dismembered it, and ate it raw on the spot, hungrily but neatly, arranging the feathers to look like a fox kill (and counting on a real fox to come and polish off the bones he left behind).

Satisfied, his head clearer, Elphi trotted another mile to a stream, where he washed the blood off his hands and had his first drink in more than four months. He had begun to move better now. His hands and broad feet shod in sheepskin with the fleece side out settled into their long habit of brushing through the old snow without leaving identifiable tracks. Still on all fours, he picked up speed.

Now then: what were they to do with Woof Howe Hob so that no human could possibly discover that he had ever existed?

Burning would be best. But fire on the moors in April was a serious thing; a fire would be noticed and investigated. The smoke could be seen a long way, and the Park rangers were vigilant. Unless a convenient mist were to cover the signs . . . but the hobs almost never, on principle, risked a fire, and in any case there were far too few stored peats in the den to burn a body, even a hob's small body. Elphi suddenly *saw* Woof Howe on a heap of smouldering peats and his insides shriveled. He forced the picture away.

They would have to find someplace to bury Woof Howe where nobody would dig him up. But where? He cursed himself and all the rest, his dead friend included, for having failed to work out in advance a strategy for dealing with a problem so certain to occur. Their shrinking from it had condemned one of their number— himself, as it turned out—to solving it alone if none of the others woke up before something had to be done.

Elphi thought resentfully of the past century and a half—of the increasing complications the decades had added to his life. In the old days nobody would have fussed over a few odd-looking bones, unless they'd been human bones. In the old days people hadn't insisted on figuring everything out. People had accepted that the world was full of wonders and mysteries; but nowadays the living hobs' continued safety depended on making the remains of their dead comrades disappear absolutely. They'd managed it with Kempswithen, rather gruesomely, by cutting him into very small bits quite unrecognizable as humanoid, and distributing these by night over four hundred square miles of open moorland. None of them would care to go through that again, unless there were positively no other way.

Elphi thought about that while he gazed out above the stream bed and the afternoon wore gradually on. The air was utterly clear. Far off to northwestward the peak of Roseberry Topping curled down like the tip of a soft ice-cream cone (Elphi knew this, having seen a drawing of one in a newspaper a hiker had thrown away); and all between Roseberry Topping and Westerdale Moor, where he now risked standing upright for a moment to look, swept the bristly, shaggy, snowy heath, mile after mile of it, swelling and falling, a frozen sea of bleakness that was somehow at the same time achingly beautiful. White snow had powdered over an underlayer of russet—that was dead bracken at the moor's edge—and the powdered bracken lent a pinkish tint to the whole wide scene. The snow ended roughly where the patchwork fields and pastures of Danby Dale and Westerdale began, and among these, scattered down the dales, were tiny clumps of stone farm buildings.

Elphi had spent the first, best two centuries of his exile down there, on a couple of farms in Danby Dale and Great Fryup Dale. These dales, and the sweep of bleakness above them, made up the landscape of most of his extremely long life; he could scarcely remember, anymore, when he had had anything else to look at. However truly he yearned for rescue with one facet of his soul, he beheld these dales with a more immediate yearning, and the moors themselves he loved with a surprising passion. All the hobs did or had, except Hob o' t' Hurst and Tarn Hole Hob. Woof Howe had loved them too, as much as any.

Elphi drew in the pure icy air, and turned once around completely to view the whole great circle of which he was the center, noting without concern as he turned that a wall of mist had begun to drift toward him off the sea. Then he dropped down, and was again a quadruped with a big problem.

They might *expose* Woof Howe, he thought suddenly—scatter the pieces in that way. It would be risky, but possible if the right place could be found, and if the body could be hidden during the day. Elphi set off northwestward, moving very rapidly now that the kinks were out of his muscles, instinctively finding a way of least resistance between stiff scratchy twigs of heather. He meant to check out a place or three for suitability before getting on back to the den to see if anybody else was awake.

Jenny Shepherd, as she tramped along, watched the roke roll toward her with almost as little concern. Years ago on her very first walking tour of Yorkshire, Jenny, underequipped and uncertain of her route, had lost her way in a thick dripping fog long and late enough to realize exactly how much danger she might have been in. But the footpath across Great and Little Hograh Moors was plain, though wetter than it might have been, a virtual gully cut through the slight snow and marked with cairns, and having crossed it more than once before Jenny knew exactly where she was. Getting to the hostel would not be too difficult even in the dark, and anyway she was equipped today to deal with any sort of weather.

In order to cross a small stone bridge the path led steeply down into a stream bed. Impulsively Jenny decided to take a break there, sheltered somewhat from the wind's incessant keening, before the roke should swallow her up. She shrugged off her backpack, leaned it upright against the bridge, and pulled out one insulating pad of blue foam to sit on and another to use as a backrest, a thermos, a small packet of trail gorp, half a sandwich in a baggie, a space blanket, and a voluminous green nylon poncho. She was dressed already in coated nylon rain pants over pile pants over soft woolen longjohns, plus several thick sweaters and a parka, but the poncho would help keep out the wet and wind and add a layer of insulation.

Jenny shook out the space blanket and wrapped herself up in it, shiny side inward. Then she sat, awkward in so much bulkiness, and adjusted the foam rectangles behind and beneath her until they felt right. The thermos was still half full of tea; she unscrewed the lid and drank from it directly, replacing the lid after each swig to keep the cold out. There were ham and cheese in the sandwich and unsalted peanuts, raisins, and chunks of plain chocolate in the gorp.

Swathed in her space blanket, propped against the stone buttress of the bridge, Jenny munched and guzzled, one glove off and one glove on, in a glow of the well-being that ensues upon vigorous exercise in the cold, pleasurable fatigue, solitude, simple creature comforts, and the smug relish of being on top of a situation that would be too tough for plenty of other people (her own younger self, for one). The little beck poured noisily beneath the bridge's span and down toward the dale and the trees below; the wind blew, but not on Jenny. She sat there tucked into the landscape, in a daze of pure contentment.

The appearance overhead of the first wispy tendrils of mist merely deepened her sense of comfort, and she sat on, knowing it would very soon be time to pack up and go but reluctant to bring the charm of the moment to a close.

A sheep began to come down the stream bed above where Jenny sat, a blackface ewe, one of the mountain breeds—Swaledale, would it be? Or Herdwick? No, Herdwicks were a Lake District breed. With idle interest she watched it scramble down jerkily, at home here, not hurrying and doubtless as cozy in its poncho of dirty fleece as Jenny was herself in her Patagonia pile. She watched it lurch toward her, knocking the stones in its descent—and abruptly found herself thinking of the albino deer in the park at home in Pennsylvania: how when glimpsed it had seemed half-deer, half-goat, with a deer's tail that lifted and waved as it walked or leapt away, and a prick-eared full-face profile exactly like the other deer's; yet it had moved awkwardly on stubby legs and was the wrong color, grayish-white with mottling on the back.

This sheep reminded her somehow of the albino deer, an almost-but-not-quite right sort of sheep. Jenny had seen a lot of sheep, walking the English uplands. Something about this one was definitely funny. Were its legs too *thick*? Did it move oddly? With the fog swirling more densely every second it was hard to say just *what* the thing looked like. She strained forward, trying to see.

For an instant the mist thinned between them, and she perceived with a shock that the sheep was *carrying something in its mouth.*

At Jenny's startled movement the ewe swung its dead flat eyes upon her—froze—whirled and plunged back up the way it had come. As it wheeled it emitted a choked high wheeze, perhaps sheeplike, and dropped its bundle.

Jenny pushed herself to her feet, dis-cocooned herself from the space blanket, and clambered up the steep streambed. The object the sheep had dropped had rolled into the freezing water; she thrust in her ungloved right hand—gritting her teeth—and pulled it out. The thing was a dead grouse with a broken neck.

Now Jenny Shepherd, despite her name, was extremely ignorant of the personal habits of sheep. But they were grazing animals, not carnivores—even a baby knew that. Maybe the sheep had found the dead grouse and picked it up. Sheep might very well do that sort of thing, pick up carrion and walk around with it, for all Jenny knew. But she shivered, heaved the grouse back into the water and stuck her numb wet hand inside her coat. Maybe sheep *did* do that sort of thing; but she had the distinct impression that something creepy had happened, and her mood was spoiled.

Nervously now she looked at her watch. Better get a move on. She slipped and slid down to the bridge and repacked her pack in haste. There were four or five miles of open moor yet to be crossed before she would strike a road, and the fog was going to slow her down some. Before heaving the pack back on Jenny unzipped one of its outside pockets and took out a flashlight.

Elphi crashed across the open moor, beside himself. How *could* he have been so careless? Failing to spot the walker was bad enough, yet if he had kept his head all would have been well; nobody can swear to what they see in a fog with twilight coming on. But dropping the grouse, that was unpardonable. For a hundred and fifty years the success of the concealment had depended on unfaltering vigilance and presence of mind, and he had demonstrated neither. That he had just woken up from the winter's sleep, that his mind was burdened with trouble and grief, that walkers on the moors were scarcer than sunshine at this month and hour—none of it excused his incredible clumsiness. Now he had not one big problem to deal with, but two.

The old fellow groaned and swung his head from side to side, but there was no help for what he had to do. He circled back along the way he'd come so as to intersect the footpath half a mile or so east of the bridge. The absence of boot tracks in the snow there had to mean that the walker was heading in this direction, toward Westerdale, and would presently pass by.

He settled himself in the heather to wait; and minutes later, when the dark shape bulked out of the roke, he stepped upright into the path and blocked it. Feeling desperately strange, for he had not spoken openly to a human being in nearly two centuries, Elphi said hoarsely: "Stop reet theear, lad, an' don't tha treea ti run," and when a loud, startled *Oh*! burst from the walker, "Ah'll deea thee nae ho't, but thoo mun cum wiv me noo." His Yorkshire dialect was as thick as clotted cream.

The walker in its flapping garment stood rigid in the path before him. "What—I don't—I can't understand what you're *saying*!"

A woman! And an American! Elphi knew an American accent when he heard one, from the wireless, but he had *never* spoken with an American in all his life—nor with *any* sort of woman, come to that. What would an American woman be *doing* up here at this time of year, all on her own? But he pulled his wits together and replied carefully, "Ah said, ye'll have to cum wiv me. Don't be frighted, an' don't try to run off. No harm will cum ti ye."

The woman, panting and obviously badly frightened despite his words, croaked, "What in God's name *are* you?"

Elphi imagined the small, naked, elderly, hair-covered figure he presented, with his large hands and feet and bulging, knobby features, the whole wrapped up in a dirty sheepskin, and said hastily, "Ah'll tell ye that, aye, but nut noo. We's got a fair piece of ground ti kivver."

Abruptly the walker unfroze. She made some frantic movements beneath her huge garment and a bulky pack dropped out onto the ground, so that she instantly appeared both much smaller and much more maneuverable. Elphi made himself ready to give chase, but instead of fleeing she asked, "Have you got a gun?"

"A *gun* saidst 'ee?" It was Elphi's turn to be startled. "Neea, but iv thoos's na—if ye won't gang on yer own feet Ah'll bring thee along masen. Myself, that's to say. But Ah'd rather not, t'would be hard on us both. Will ye cum then?"

"This is *crazy*! No, dammit!" The woman eyed Elphi blocking the trail, then glanced down at her pack, visibly figuring the relative odds of getting past him with or without it. Suddenly, dragging the pack by one shoulder strap, she was advancing upon him. "Get out of the way!"

At this Elphi groaned and swung his head. "Mistress, tha mun cum, and theear's an end," he exclaimed desperately, and darting forward he gripped her wrist in his large knobbly sheepskin-padded hand. "Noo treea if tha can break loose."

But the woman refused to struggle, and in the end Elphi had no choice but to yank her off her feet and along the sloppy footpath for a hundred yards or so, ignoring the noises she made. He left her sitting in the path rubbing her wrist, and went back for the pack, which he shouldered himself. Then, without any more talk, they set off together into the fog.

By the time they arrived at the abandoned jet mine which served the hobs for a winter den, Jenny's tidy mind had long since shut itself down. Fairly soon she had stopped being afraid of Elphi, but the effort of grappling with the disorienting strangeness of events was more than her brain could manage. She was hurt and exhausted, and more than exhausted. Already, when Elphi in his damp fleece had reared up before her in the fog and blocked her way, she had had a long day. These additional hours of bushwhacking blindly through the tough mist-soaked heather in the dark had drained her of all purpose and thought beyond that of surviving the march.

Toward the end, as it grew harder and harder for her to lift her peat-clogged boots clear of the heather, she'd kept tripping and falling down. Whenever that happened her odd, dangerous little captor would help her up quite gently, evidently with just a tiny fraction of his superhuman strength.

Earlier, she had remembered seeing circus posters in the Middlesbrough station while changing from her London train; maybe, she'd thought, the little man was a clown or "circus freak" who had run off into the hills. But that hadn't seemed very probable; and later, when another grouse exploded under their feet like a feathered grenade, and the dwarf had pounced in a flash upon it and broken its neck—a predator that efficient—she'd given the circus idea up for a more terrifying one: maybe he was an escaped inmate of a mental hospital. Yet Elphi himself, in spite of everything, was somehow unterrifying.

But Jenny had stopped consciously noticing and deciding things about him quite a long while before they got where they were going; and when she finally heard him say "We's heear, lass," and saw him bend to ease back the stone at the entrance to the den, her knees gave way, and she flopped down sideways into the vegetation.

She awoke to the muted sound of a radio.

She lay on a hard surface, wrapped snugly in a sheepskin robe, smelly and heavy but marvelously warm. For some moments she basked in the comforting warmth, soothed by the normalness of the radio's voice; but quite soon she came fully awake and knew—with a sharp jolt of adrenalin—what had happened and where she must be now.

Jenny lay in what appeared to be a small cave, feebly lit by a stubby white "emergency" candle—one of her own, in fact. The enclosure was stuffy but not terribly so, and the candle burned steadily where it stood on a rough bench or table, set in what looked to be (and was) an aluminum pie-plate of the sort snack pies are sold in. The radio was nowhere in sight.

Someone had undressed her; she was wearing her sheet sleeping bag for a nightie and nothing else.

Tensely Jenny turned her head and struggled to take mental possession of the situation. The cave was lined with bunks like the one in which she lay, and in each of these she could just make out . . . forms. Seven of them, all evidently deep in sleep (or cold storage?) and, so far as she could tell, all creatures like the one that had kidnapped her. As she stared Jenny began to breathe in gasps again, and the fear which had faded during the march returned in full strength. *What was this place? What was going to happen to her? What the hell was it all about?*

The first explanation that occurred to her was also the most menacing: that she had lost her own mind, that her unfinished therapeutic business had finally caught up with her. If the little man had not escaped from an institution, then maybe she was on her own way to one. In fact Jenny's record of mental stability, while not without an average number of weak points, contained no hint of anything like hallucinations or drug-related episodes. But in the absence of a more obvious explanation her confidence on this score was just shaky enough to give weight and substance to such thoughts.

To escape them (and the panic they engendered) Jenny applied herself desperately to solving some problems both practical and pressing. It was cold in the cave; she could see her breath. Her bladder was bursting. A ladder against one wall disappeared into a hole in the ceiling, and as the cave appeared to have no other entryway she supposed the ladder must lead to the outside world, where now for several reasons she urgently wished to be. She threw off the robe and wriggled out of the sleeping-bag—catching her breath at the pain from dozens of sore muscles and bruises—and crippled across the stone floor barefoot; but the hole was black as night and airless, not open, at the top. Jenny was a prisoner, naked and in need.

Well, then, find something—a bucket, a pan, anything! Poking about, in the nick of time she spotted her backpack in the shadows of the far wall. In it was a pail of soft plastic meant for carrying water, which Jenny frantically grubbed out and relieved herself into. Half-full, the pail held its shape and could be stood, faintly steaming, against the wall. Shuddering violently, she then snatched bundles of clothes and food out of the pack and rushed back into bed. In point of fact there wasn't all that much in the way of extra clothing: one pair of woolen boot socks, clean underwear, slippers, a cotton turtleneck, and a spare sweater. No pants, no shoes, no outerwear; she wouldn't get far over the open moor without any of those. Still, she gratefully pulled on what she found and felt immensely better; nothing restores a sense of confidence in one's mental health, and some sense of control over one's situation, like dealing effectively with a few basic needs. Thank God her kidnapper had brought the pack along!

Next Jenny got up again and climbed to the top of the ladder; but the entrance was closed by a stone far too heavy to move.

The radio sat in a sort of doorless cupboard, a tiny transistor in a dimpled red plastic case. BOOTS THE CHEMIST was stamped on the front in gold, and a wire ran from the extended tip of its antenna along one side of the ladder, up the hole. Jenny brought it back into bed with her, taking care not to disconnect the wire.

She was undoing the twisty on her plastic bag of food when there came a scraping, thumping noise from above and a shaft of daylight shot down the hole. Then it was dark again, and legs—whitish hair-covered legs—and the back of a gray fleece came into view. Frozen where she sat, Jenny waited, heart thumping.

The figure that turned to face her at the bottom of the ladder looked by candlelight exactly like a very old, very small gnome of a man, covered with hair —crown, beard, body and all—save for his large hands and feet in pads of fleece. But this was a superficial impression. The arms were longer and the legs shorter than they should have been; and Jenny remembered how this dwarf had ranged before her on four limbs in the fog, looking as much like a sheep as he now looked like a man. She thought again of the albino deer.

They contemplated one another. Gradually, outlandish as he looked, Jenny's fear drained away again and her pulse rate dropped back to normal. Then the dwarf seemed to smile. "It's a bright morning, the roke's burned off completely," he said, in what was almost BBC English with only the faintest trace of Yorkshire left in the vowels.

Jenny said, calmly enough, "Look: I don't understand any of this. First of all I want to know if you're going to let me go."

She got an impression of beaming and nodding. "Oh yes indeed!"

"When?"

"This afternoon. Your clothes should be dry in time, I've put them out in the sun. It's a rare bit of luck, our getting a sunny morning." He unfastened the sheepskin as he spoke and hung it from a peg next to a clump of others, then slipped off his moccasins and mitts and put them on the shelf where the radio had stood. Except for his hair he wore nothing.

Abruptly Jenny's mind skittered away, resisting this strangeness. She shut her eyes, unafraid of the hairy creature but overwhelmed by the situation in which he was the central figure. "Won't you please explain to me what's going on? Who are you? Who are *they*? What is this place? Why did you make me come here? Just—what's going *on*?" Her voice went up steeply, near to breaking.

"Yes, I'll tell you all about it now, and when you've heard me out I hope you'll understand what happened yesterday—why it was necessary." He dragged a stool from under the table and perched on it, then quickly hopped up again. "Now, have you enough to eat? I'm afraid we've nothing at all to offer a guest at this time of year, apart from the grouse—but we can't make any sort of fire in this clear weather and I very much doubt you'd enjoy eating her raw. I brought her back last night in case anyone else was awake and hungry, which they're unfortunately not . . . but let me see: I've been through your pack quite thoroughly, I'm afraid, and I noticed some packets of dehydrated soup and tea and so forth;

now suppose we were to light several more of these excellent candles and bunch them together, couldn't we boil a little pot of water over the flames? I expect you're feeling the cold.'' As he spoke the old fellow bustled about—rummaged in the pack for pot and candles, filled the pot half full of water from Jenny's own canteen, lit the candles from the burning one, and arranged supports for the pot to rest on while the water heated. He moved with a speed and economy that were so remarkable as to be almost funny, a cartoon figure whisking about the cave. ''There now! You munch a few biscuits while we wait, and I'll do my best to begin to clear up the mystery.''

Jenny had sat mesmerized while her abductor rattled on, all the time dashing to and fro. Now she took tea, sugar, dried milk, two envelopes of Knorr's oxtail soup, and a packet of flat objects called Garibaldis here in England but raisin cookies by Nabisco (and squashed-fly biscuits by the children in *Swallows and Amazons*). She was famished, and lulled into calmness as the old fellow contrived to sound more and more like an Oxbridge don providing a student with fussy hospitality in his rooms in college. She had not forgotten the sensation of being dragged as by a freight train along the footpath, but was willing to set the memory aside. ''What became of your accent? Last night I could barely understand you —or are you the same one that brought me in?''

''Oh aye, that was me. As I said, none of the others is awake.'' He glanced rather uneasily at the row of shadowy cots. ''Though it's getting to be high time they were. Actually, what's happened is that most of the time you were sleeping, I've been swotting up on my Standard English. I used the wireless, you see. Better switch it off now, actually, if you don't mind,'' he added. ''Our supply of batteries is very, ah, irregular and where should *we* be now if there hadn't been any left last night, eh?'' Silently Jenny clicked off the red radio and handed it to him, and he tucked it carefully back into its cubby. Then he reseated himself upon the stool, looking expectant.

Jenny swallowed half a biscuit and objected, ''How can you totally change your accent and your whole style of speaking in one night, just by listening to the radio? It's not possible.''

''Not for you, of course not, no, no. But we're *good* at languages, you see. Very, very good; it's the one thing in us that our masters valued most.''

At this Jenny's wits reeled again, and she closed her eyes and gulped hard against nausea, certain that unless some handle on all this weirdness were provided *right away* she might start screaming helplessly and not be able to stop. She *could not* go on chatting with this Santa's elf for another second. Jenny Shepherd was a person who was never comfortable unless she felt she understood things; to understand is, to some extent, to have control over. ''Please,'' she pleaded, ''just tell me who or what you are and what's happening here. Please.''

At once the old fellow jumped up again. ''If I may—'' he murmured apologetically and peered again into the treasure trove of Jenny's backpack. ''I couldn't

help noticing that you're carrying a little book I've seen before—yes, here it is.''
He brought the book back to the table and the light: the Dalesman paperback
guide to the Cleveland Way. Swiftly finding the page he wanted he passed the
book over to Jenny, who got up eagerly from the bed, holding the robe around
her, to read by candlelight:

> The Cleveland area is extremely rich in folklore which goes back to Scandinavian
> sources and often very much further. Perhaps the hobs, those strange hairy little
> men who did great deeds—sometimes mischievous, sometimes helpful—were
> in some way a memory of those ancient folk who lingered on in parts of the
> moors almost into historic times. In the years between 1814 and 1823 George
> Calvert gathered together stories still remembered by old people. He lists 23
> "Hobmen that were commonly held to live hereabout," including the famous
> Farndale Hob, Hodge Hob of Bransdale, Hob of Tarn Hole, Dale Town Hob
> of Hawnby, and Hob of Hasty Bank. Even his list misses out others which are
> remembered, such as Hob Hole Hob of Runswick who was supposed to cure
> the whooping cough. Calvert also gives a list of witches. . . .

But this was no help, it made things worse! "You're telling me you're a *hob*?"
she blurted, aghast. What nightmarish fantasy was this? "Hob . . . as in hobbit?"
However dearly Jenny might love Tolkien's masterpiece, the idea of having spent
the night down a hobbit-hole—in the company of seven dwarves!—was completely unacceptable. In the real world hobbits and dwarves must be strictly
metaphorical, and Jenny preferred to live in the real world all the time.

The odd creature continued to watch her. "Hob as in hobbit? Oh, very likely.
Hob as in hobgoblin, most assuredly—but as to whether *we* are hobs, the answer
is yes and no.'' He took the book from her and laid it on the table. "Sit down,
my dear, and bundle up again; and shall I pour out?'' for the water had begun to
sizzle against the sides of the little pot.

"What did you mean, yes *and* no?'' Jenny asked a bit later, sitting up in bed
with a steaming Sierra Club cup of soup balanced in her lap and a plastic mug
of tea in her hands, and thinking: This better be good.

"First, may I pour myself a cup? It's a long story,'' he said, "and it's best to
begin at the beginning. My name is Elphi, by the way.

"At least the dale folk called me Elphi until I scarcely remembered my true
name, and it was the same with all of us—we took the names they gave us and
learnt to speak their language so well that we spoke no other even amongst
ourselves.

"This is the whole truth, though you need not believe it. My friends and myself
were in service aboard an exploratory vessel from another star. Hear me out,''
for Jenny had made an impatient movement, "I said you need not believe what
I tell you. The ship called here, at Earth, chiefly for supplies but also for infor-

mation. Here, of course, we knew already that only one form of life had achieved mastery over nature. Often that is the case, but on my world there were two, and one subordinate to the other. Our lords the Gafr were physically larger than we, and technologically gifted as we were not, and also they did not hibernate; that gave them an advantage, though their lives were shorter (and that gave *us* one). We think the Gafr had been with us, and over us, from the first, when we both were still more animal than thinking thing. Our development, you see, went hand in hand with theirs but their gift was mastery and ours was service—always, from our prehistory.

"And from our prehistory our lives were intertwined with theirs, for we were of great use to one another. As I've said, we Hefn are very good with languages, at speaking and writing them—and also we are stronger for our size than they, and quicker in every way, though I would have to say less clever. I've often thought that if the Neanderthal people had lived on into modern times their relations with *you* might have developed in a similar way . . . but the Gafr are far less savage than you, and never viewed us as competitors, so perhaps I'm wrong. We are very much less closely related than you and the Neanderthal people."

"How come you know so much about the Neanderthalers?" Jenny interrupted to ask.

"From the wireless, my dear! The wireless keeps us up to date. We would be at a sad disadvantage without it, don't you agree?

"So the Gafr—"

"How would you spell that?"

"G, A, F, R. One F, not two, and no E. The Gafr built the starships and we went to work aboard them. It was our life, to be their servants and dependents. You should understand that they never were cruel. Neither we nor they could imagine an existence without the other, after so many eons of relying upon one another.

"Except that aboard my ship, for no reason I can now explain, a few of us became dissatisfied, and demanded that we be given responsibilities of our own. Well, you know, it was as if the sheepdogs hereabouts were one day to complain to the farmers that from now on they wanted flocks of their own to manage, with the dipping and tupping and shearing and lambing and all the rest. Our lords were as dumbfounded as these farmers would be—a talking dog, you see. When we couldn't be reasoned or scolded out of our notion, and it began to interfere with the smooth functioning of the ship, the Gafr decided to put us off here for a while to think things over. They were to come back for us as soon as we'd had time to find out what running our own affairs without them would be like. That was a little more than three hundred and fifty years ago."

Jenny's mouth fell open; she had been following intently. "Three hundred and fifty of your years, you mean?"

"No, of yours. We live a *long* time. To human eyes we appeared very old men when still quite young, but now we are old indeed—and look it too, I fear.

"Well, they put fifteen of us off here, in Yorkshire, and some dozen others in Scandinavia somewhere. I often wonder if any of that group has managed to keep alive, or whether the ship came back for them but not for us—but there's no knowing.

"It was early autumn; we supposed they meant to fetch us off before winter, for they knew the coming of hard winter would put us to sleep. They left us well supplied and went away, and we all had plenty of time to find life without the Gafr as difficult—psychologically, I suppose you might say—as they could possibly have wished. Oh yes! We waited, very chastened, for the ship to return. But the deep snows came and finally we had to go to earth, and when we awoke the following spring we were forced to face the likelihood that we were stranded here.

"A few found they could not accept a life in this alien place without the Gafr to direct their thoughts and actions; they died in the first year. But the rest of us, though nearly as despairing, preferred life to death—and we said to one another that the ship might yet return.

"When we awoke from our first winter's sleep, the year was 1624. In those days the high moors were much as you see them now, but almost inaccessible to the world beyond them. The villages were linked by a few muddy cart tracks and stone pannier trods across the tops. No one came up here but people that had business here, or people crossing from one dale into another: farmers, poachers, panniermen, Quakers later on . . . the farmers would come up by turf road from their own holdings to gather bracken for stock bedding, and to cut turf and peat for fuel, and ling—that's what they call the heather hereabouts, you know—for kindling and thatching. They burned off the old ling to improve the grazing, and took away the burned stems for kindling. And they came after bilberries in late summer, and to bring hay to their sheep on the commons in winter, as some still do. But nobody came from outside, passing through from one distant place to another, and the local people were an ignorant, superstitious lot as the world judges such things, shut away up here. They would sit about the hearth of an evening, whole families together, and retell the old tales. And we would hang about the eaves, listening.

"All that first spring we spied out the dales farms, learnt the language and figured our chances. Some of us wanted to go to the dalesmen with our story and ask to be taken into service, for it would have comforted us to serve a good master again. But others—I was one—said such a course was as dangerous as it was useless, for we would not have been believed and the Church would have had us hunted down for devil's spawn.

"Yet we all yearned and hungered so after direction and companionship that we skulked about the farms despite the risk, watching how the men and milkmaids worked. We picked up the knack of it easily enough, of milking and churning and threshing and stacking—the language of farm labor as you might say!—and by and by we began to lend a hand, at night, when the house was sleeping— serving *in secret*, you see. We asked ourselves, would the farmers call us devil's spawn for *that*? and thought it a fair gamble. We'd thresh out the corn, and then we'd fill our pouches with barley and drink the cat's cream off the doorstep for our pay.

"At least we thought it was the cat's cream. But one night in harvesttime, one of us—Hart Hall it was—heard the farmer tell his wife, 'Mind tha leaves t'bate o' cream for t'hob. He deeas mair i' yah neet than a' t'men deea iv a day.' That's how we learnt that the people were in no doubt about who'd been helping them.

"We could scarcely believe our luck. Of course we'd heard talk of witches and fairies, very superstitious they were in those days, and now and again one would tell a tale of little men called hobmen, part elf, part goblin as it seemed, sometimes kind and sometimes tricksy. They'd put out a bowl of cream for the hob, for if they forgot, the hob would make trouble for them, and if they remembered he would use them kindly."

"That was a common practice in rural Scandinavia too—to set out a bowl of porridge for the *tomte*," Jenny put in."

"Aye? Well, well . . . no doubt the cats and foxes got the cream, before *we* came! Well, we put together every scrap we could manage to overhear about the hobmen, and the more we heard the more our way seemed plain. By great good fortune we looked the part. We *are* man-like, more or less, though we go as readily upon four feet as two, and stood a good deal smaller than the ordinary human even in those days when men were not so tall as now, and that meant no great harm would come of it should we happen to be seen. That was important. There hadn't been so many rumors of hobbish helpfulness in the dales for a very long time, and as curiosity grew we were spied upon in our turn—but I'm getting ahead of my tale.

"By the time a few years had passed we'd settled ourselves all through these dales. Certain farmsteads and local spots were spoken of as being 'haunted bi t'hob'; well, one way and another we found out where they were and one of us would go and live there, and carry on according to tradition. Not all of us did that, now—some just found a farm they liked and moved in. But for instance it was believed that a certain hob, that lived in a cave at Runswick up on the coast, could cure what they called t'kink-cough, so one of us went on up there to be Hob Hole Hob, and when the mothers would bring their sick children and call to him to cure them, he'd do what he could."

"What *could* he do, though?"

"Not a great deal, but more than nothing. He could make them more comfortable, and unless a child was very ill, he could make it more likely that they would recover.''

"How? Herbs and potions?''

"No, not at all—merely the power of suggestion. But quite effective, oh aye.

"There was a tradition too of a hob in Farndale that was the troublesome sort, and as it seemed wisest not to neglect that mischievous side of our ledger altogether, once in a while we would send somebody over there to let out the calves and spill the milk and put a cart on the barn roof, and generally make a nuisance of himself. It kept the old beliefs alive, you see. It wouldn't have done for people to start thinking the hobs had all got good as gold, we had the sense to see that. The dalesfolk used to say, 'Gin t'hobman takes ti yan, ya'r yal reet i' t'lang run, but deea he tak agin' 'ee 'tis anither story!' We wanted them to go right on saying that.

"But we did take to them—aye, we did indeed, though the Gafr and the dalesmen were so unlike. The Yorkshire farmer of those times for all his faults was what they call the salt of the earth. They made us good masters, and we served them well for nigh on two hundred years.''

Jenny wriggled and leaned toward Elphi, raptly attending. "Did any of you ever *talk* with humans, face to face? Did you ever have any human friends, that you finally told the truth to?''

"No, my dear. We have no friends among humans in the sense you mean, though we befriended a few in particular. Nor did we often speak with humans. We thought it vital to protect and preserve their sense of us as magical and strange—supernatural, in fact. But now and again it would happen.

"I'll tell you of one such occasion. For many and many a year my home was at Hob Garth near Great Fryup Dale, where a family called Stonehouse had the holding. There was a Thomas Stonehouse once, that lived there and kept sheep.

"Now, the time I'm speaking of would have been about 1760 or thereabouts, when Tommy was beginning to get on a bit in years. Somehow he fell out with a neighbor of his called Matthew Bland, an evil-tempered fellow he was, and one night I saw Bland creep along and break the hedge, and drive out Tommy's ewes. Tommy was out all the next day in the wet, trying to round them up, but without much luck for he only found five out of the forty, and so I says to myself: here's a job for Hob. The next morning all forty sheep were back in the field and the hedge patched up with new posts and rails.

"Well! but that wasn't all: when I knew Tommy to be laid up with a cold, and so above suspicion himself, I nipped along and let Bland's cattle loose. A perfectly hobbish piece of work that was! Old Bland, he was a full fortnight rounding them up. Of course, at the time the mischief was done Tommy had been in his bed with chills and a fever, and everybody knew it; but Bland came and broke the new fence anyway and let the sheep out again—he was that furious, he had to do something.

"As Tommy was still too ill to manage, his neighbors turned out to hunt the sheep for him. But the lot of 'em had wandered up onto the tops in a roke like the one we had yesterday evening, and none could be found at all. All the same, that night Hob rounded them up and drove them home, and repaired the fence again. Bear in mind, my dear, that such feats as the farmers deemed prodigious were simple enough for us, for we have excellent sight in the dark, and great strength in the low gravity here, and are quick on our feet, whether four or two.

"Now, four of Tommy's ewes had fallen into a quarry in the roke and broken their necks, and never came home again. When he was well enough he walked out to the field to see what was left of the flock and cut some hay for it—this was early spring, I remember, just about this time. We'd waked sooner than usual that year, which was a bit of luck for Tommy. I saw him heading up there, and followed. And when I knew him to be grieving over the four lost ewes I accosted him in the road and said not to fret any more, that the sheep would be accounted for and then some at lambing time—for I knew that most were carrying twins, and I meant to help with the lambing as well, to see that as many as possible would live.

"He took me then for an old man, a bit barmy though kindly intentioned. But later, when things turned out the way I'd said, it was generally talked of—how there was no use Matthew Bland trying to play tricks on Tommy Stonehouse, for the hobman had befriended him, and when t'hobman taks ti yan . . . aye, it was a bit of luck for Tommy that we woke early that spring.

"But to speak directly to a farmer so, that was rare. More often the farmer took the initiative upon himself, or his wife or children or servants did, by slipping out to spy upon us at work, or by coming to beg a cure. There was talk of a hob that haunted a cave in the Mulgrave Woods, for instance. People would put their heads in and shout 'Hob-thrush Hob! Where is thoo?' and the hob was actually meant to reply—and the dear knows how *this* tradition began—'Ah's tyin' on mah lef' fuit shoe, An' Ah'll be wiv thee—noo!' Well, we didn't go as far as that, but once in a while one of us might slip up there for a bit so's to be able to shout back if anyone called into the cave. Most often it was children.

"Mostly, people weren't frightened of t'hob. But as I've said, we thought it as well to keep the magic bright. There was one old chap, name of Gray, with a farm over in Bransdale; he married himself a new wife who couldn't or wouldn't remember to put out the jug of cream at bedtime as the old wife had always done. Well, Hodge Hob, that had helped that family for generations, he pulled out of there and never went back. And another time a family called Oughtred, that farmed over near Upleatham, lost *their* hob because he died. That was Hob Hill Hob, that missed his step and broke his neck in a mine shaft, the first of us all to go out since the very beginning. Well, Kempswithen overheard the Oughtreds discussing it—whyever had the hob gone away?—and they agreed it must have been because one of the workmen had hung his coat on the winnowing machine and forgot it, and the hobman had thought it was left there for *him*—for everyone knew you mustn't offer clothes to fairies and such or they'll take offense.

"Well! We'd been thinking another of us might go and live at Hob Hill Farm, but after that we changed our minds. And when a new milkmaid over at Hart Hall spied on Hart Hall Hob and saw him flailing away at the corn one night without a stitch on, and made him a shirt to wear, and left it in the barn, we knew he'd have to leave there too, and he did. One curious thing: the family at Hart Hall couldn't decide whether the hob had been offended because he'd been given the shirt at all, or because it had been cut from coarse cloth instead of fine linen! We know, because they fretted about it for months, and sacked the girl.

"At all events we'd make the point now and then that you mustn't offend the hob or interfere with him or get too close and crowd him, and so we made out pretty well. Still hoping for rescue, you know, but content enough on the whole. We were living all through the dales, north and south, the eleven of us who were left alive—at Runswick, Great Fryup, Commondale, Kempswithen, Hasty Bank, Scugdale, Farndale, Hawnby, Broxa . . . Woof Howe . . . and we'd visit a few in-between places that were said to be haunted by t'hob, like the Mulgrave Cave and Obtrush Rook above Farndale. It was all right.

"But after a longish time things began to change.

"This would be perhaps a hundred and fifty years ago, give or take a couple of decades. Well, I don't know just how it was, but bit by bit the people hereabouts began to be less believing somehow, less sure their grandfathers had really seen the fairies dance on Fairy Cross Plain, or that Obtrush Rook was really and truly haunted by the hobman. And by and by we began to feel that playing hob i' t'hill had ceased to be altogether safe. Even in these dales there were people now that wanted explanations for things, and that weren't above poking their noses into our affairs.

"And so, little by little, we began to withdraw from the farms. For even though we were no longer afraid of being taken for Satan's imps and hunted down, concealment had been our way of getting by for such a very long time that we preferred to go on the same way. But for the first time in many long years we often found ourselves thinking of the ship again and wishing for its return. But I fear the ship was lost.

"Gradually, then, we drew back out of the dales to the high moortops, moved into the winter dens we'd been using right along, and set ourselves to learning how to live up here entirely—to catch grouse and hares, and find eggs and berries, instead of helping ourselves to the farmer's stores. Oh, we were good hunters and we loved these moors already, but still it was a hard and painful time, almost a second exile. I remember how I once milked a ewe—thinking to get some cream—only to find that it was the jug set out for me by the farmer's wife that I wanted and missed, for that was a symbol of my service to a master that respected what I did for him; but a worse time was coming.

"There were mines on the moors since there were people in the land at all, but not so very long after we had pulled back up out of the dales altogether, ironstone began to be mined in Rosedale on a larger scale than ever before, and they built a railroad to carry the ore right round the heads of Rosedale and Farndale and down to Battersby Junction. I daresay you know the right of way now as a footpath, my dear, for part of it lies along the route of the Lyke Wake Walk. But in the middle of the last century men came pouring onto the high moors to build the railroad. Some even lived up here, in shacks, while the work was ongoing. And more men poured across the moors from the villages all round about, to work in the Rosedale pits, and then there was no peace at all for us, and no safety.

"That was when we first were forced to go about by day in sheepskin.

"It was Kempswithen's idea, he was a clever one! The skins weren't too difficult to get hold of, for sheep die of many natural causes, and also they are easily killed, though we never culled more than a single sheep from anyone's flock, and then always an old ewe or a lame one, of little value. It went against the grain to rob the farmers at all, but without some means of getting about by daylight we could not have managed. The ruse worked well, for nearly all the railroad workers and miners came here from outside the dales, and were unobservant about the ways of sheep, and we were careful.

"But the noise and smoke and peacelessness drove us away from our old haunts onto the bleakest part of the high moors where the fewest tracks crossed. We went out there and dug ourselves in.

"It was a dreary time. And the mines had scarcely been worked out and the railroad dismantled when the Second War began, and there were soldiers training on Rudland Rigg above Farndale, driving their tanks over Obtrush Rook till they had knocked it to bits, and over Fylingdales Moor, where we'd gone to escape the miners and the trains."

"Fylingdales, where the Early Warning System is now?"

"Aye, that's the place. During the war a few planes made it up this far, and some of the villages were hit. We slept through a good deal of that, luckily— we'd found this den by then, you see, an old jet working that a fox had opened. But it was uneasy sleep, it did us little good. Most particularly, it was not good for us to be of no use to any master—that began to do us active harm, and we were getting old. Two of us died before the war ended, another not long after. And still the ship did not return."

Something had been nagging at Jenny. "Couldn't you have reproduced yourselves after you came up here? You know—formed a viable community of hobs in hiding. Kept your spirits up."

"No, my dear. Not in this world. It wasn't possible, we knew it from the first, you see."

"Why wasn't it possible?" But Elphi firmly shook his head; this was plainly a subject he did not wish to pursue. Perhaps it was too painful. "Well, so now there are only eight of you?"

"Seven," said Elphi. "When I woke yesterday Woof Howe was dead. I'd been wondering what in the world to do with him when I so stupidly allowed you to see me."

Jenny threw the shadowed bunks a startled glance, wondering which contained a corpse. But something else disturbed her more. "You surely can't mean to say that in the past hundred and fifty years not one of you has ever been caught off-guard, until yesterday!"

Elphi gave the impression of smiling, though he did not really smile. "Oh, no, my dear. One or another of us has been caught napping a dozen times or more, especially in the days since the Rosedale mines were opened. Quite a few folk have sat just where you're sitting and listened, as you've been listening, to much the same tale I've been telling *you*. Dear me, yes! Once we rescued eight people from a train stalled in a late spring snowstorm, and we've revived more than one walker in the last stages of hypothermia—that's besides the ones who took us by surprise."

His ancient face peered up at her through scraggly white hair, and Jenny's apprehension grew. "And none of them ever told? It's hard to believe."

"My dear, none of them has ever remembered a thing about it afterwards! Would we take such trouble to keep ourselves hidden, only to tell the whole story to any stranger that happens by? No indeed. It passes the time and entertains our guests, but they always forget. As will you, I promise—but you'll be safe as houses. Your only problem will be accounting for the lost day."

Jenny had eaten every scrap of her emergency food and peed the plastic pail nearly full, and now she huddled under her sheepskin robe by the light of a single fresh candle, waiting for Elphi to come back. He had refused to let her climb up to empty her own slops and fetch back her own laundry. "I'm sorry, my dear, but there's no roke today—that's the difficulty. If ever you saw this place again you would remember it—and besides, you know, it's no hardship for me to do you a service." So she waited, a prisoner beneath the heavy doorway stone, desperately trying to think of a way to prevent Elphi from stealing back her memories of him.

Promising not to tell anybody, ever, had had no effect. ("They all promise, you know, but how can we afford the risk? Put yourself in my place.") She cudgeled her wits: what could she offer him in exchange for being allowed to remember all this? Nothing came. The things the hobs needed—a different social order on Earth, the return of the Gafr ship, the Yorkshire of three centuries ago —were all beyond her power to grant.

Jenny found she believed Elphi's tale entirely: that he had come to Earth from another world, that he would not harm her in any way, that he could wipe the experience of himself from her mind—as effortlessly as she might wipe a chalk-board with a wet rag—by "the power of suggestion," just as Hob Hole Hob had "cured" the whooping cough by the power of suggestion. Somewhere in the course of the telling both skepticism and terror had been neutralized by a conviction that the little creature was speaking the unvarnished truth. She had welcomed this conviction. It was preferable to the fear that she had gone stark raving mad; but above and beyond all that she did believe him.

And all at once she had an idea that just might work. At least it seemed worth trying; she darted across the stone floor and scrabbled frantically in a pocket of her pack. There was just enough time. She burrowed back beneath the sheepskin robe where Elphi had left her with only seconds to spare.

The old hob backed down the ladder with her pail flopping from one hand and her bundle of clothes clutched in the opposite arm, and this time he left the top of the shaft open to the light and cold and the wuthering of the wind. He had tied his sheepskin on again. "Time to suit up now, I think—we want to set you back in the path at the same place and time of day." He scanned the row of sleepers anxiously and seemed to sigh.

Jenny's pile pants and wool socks were nearly dry, her sweaters, longjohns, and boots only dampish. She threw off the sheepskins and began to pull on the many layers of clothing one by one. "I was wondering," she said as she dressed, "I wanted to ask you, how could the hobs just *leave* a farm where they'd been in secret service for maybe a hundred years?"

Elphi's peculiar flat eyes peered at her mildly. "Our bond was to the serving, you see. There were always other farms where extra hands were needed. What grieved us was to leave the dales entirely."

No bond to the people they served, then; no friendship, just as he had said. But all the same—"Why couldn't you come out of hiding now? I know it could be arranged! People all over the world would give anything to know about you!"

Elphi seemed both amused and sad. "No, my dear. Put it out of your mind. First, because we must wait here so long as any of us is left alive, in case the ship should come. Second, because we love these moors and would not leave them. Third, because here on Earth we have always served in secret, and have got too old to care to change our ways. Fourth, because if people knew about us we would never again be given a moment's peace. Surely you know that's so."

He was right about the last part anyway; people would never leave them alone, even if the other objections could be answered. Jenny herself didn't want to leave Elphi alone. It was no use.

As she went to mount the ladder the old hob moved to grasp her arm. "I'm afraid I must ask you to wear this," he said apologetically. "You'll be able to see, but not well. Well enough to walk. Not well enough to recognize this place again." And reaching up he slipped a thing like a deathcap over her head and fastened it loosely but firmly around her neck. "The last person to wear this was a shopkeeper from Bristol. Like you, he saw more than he should have seen, and was our guest for a little while one summer afternoon."

"When was that? Recently?"

"Between the wars, my dear."

Jenny stood, docile, and let him do as he liked with her. As he stepped away, "Which was the hob that died?" she asked through the loose weave of the cap.

There was a silence. "Woof Howe Hob."

"What *will* you do with him?"

Another silence, longer this time. "I don't quite know . . . I'd hoped some of the rest would wake up, but the smell . . . it's beginning to trouble me too much to wait. I don't imagine you can detect it."

"Can't you just wake them up?"

"No, they must wake in their own time, more's the pity."

Jenny drew a deep breath. "Why not let *me* help you, then, since there's no one else?"

An even longer silence ensued, and she began to hope. But "You can help me *think* if you like, as we walk along," Elphi finally said, "I don't deny I should be grateful for a useful idea or two, but I must have you on the path by late this afternoon, come what may." And he prodded his captive up the ladder.

Above ground, conversation was instantly impossible. After the den's deep silence the incessant wind seemed deafening. This time Jenny was humping the pack herself, and with the restricted sight and breathing imposed by the cap she found just walking quite difficult enough; she was too sore (and soon too winded) to argue anymore.

After a good long while Elphi said this was far enough, that the cap could come off now and they could have a few minutes' rest. There was nothing to sit on, only heather and a patch of bilberry, so Jenny took off her pack and sat on that, wishing she hadn't eaten every last bit of her supplies. It was a beautiful day, the low sun brilliant on the shaggy, snowy landscape, the sky deep and blue, the tiers of hills crisp against one another.

Elphi ran on a little way, scouting ahead. From a short distance, with just his back and head showing above the vegetation, it was astonishing how much he really did move and look like a sheep. She said as much when he came back. "Oh aye, it's a good and proven disguise, it's saved us many a time. Mind you, the farmers are hard to fool. They know their own stock, and they know where theirs and everyone else's ought to be—the flocks are heafed on the commons and don't stray much. 'Heafed,' that means they stick to their own bit of grazing. So we've got to wear a fleece with a blue mark on the left flank if we're going one way and a fleece with red on the shoulder if we're going another, or we'll call attention to ourselves and that's the last thing we want."

"Living *or* dead," said Jenny meaningfully.

"Aye." He gave her a sharp glance. "You've thought of something?"

"Well, all these abandoned mines and quarries, what about putting Woof Howe at the bottom of one of those, under a heap of rubble?"

Elphi said, "There's fair interest in the old iron workings. We decided against mines when we lost Kempswithen."

"What did you do with *him*? You never said."

"Nothing we should care to do again." Elphi seemed to shudder.

"Haven't I heard," said Jenny slowly, "that fire is a great danger up here in early spring? There was a notice at the station, saying that when the peat gets really alight it'll burn for weeks."

"We couldn't do that!" He seemed truly shocked. "Nay, such fires are dreadful things! Nothing at all will grow on the burned ground for fifty years and more."

"But they burn off the old heather, you told me so yourself."

"Controlled burning that is, closely watched."

"Oh." They sat silent for a bit, while Jenny thought and Elphi waited. "Well, what about this: I know a lot of bones and prehistoric animals, cave bears and Irish elk and so on—*big* animals—were found in a cave at the edge of the Park somewhere, but there haven't been any finds like that on the moors because the acid in the peat completely decomposes everything. I was reading an article about it. Couldn't you bury your friend in a peat bog?"

Elphi pondered this with evident interest. "Hmmm. It might be possible at that—nowadays it might. Nobody cuts the deep peat for fuel anymore, and bog's poor grazing land. Walkers don't want to muck about in a bog. About the only chaps who like a bog are the ones that come to look at wildflowers, and it's too early for them to be about."

"Are there any bogs inside the fenced-off part of Fylingdales, the part that's closed to the public?"

Elphi groaned softly, swinging his head. "Ach, Woof Howe did hate it so, skulking in that dreary place. But still, the flowers would have pleased him."

"Weren't there some rare plants found recently inside the fence, because the sheep haven't been able to graze them down in there?"

"Now, that's true," Elphi mused. "They wouldn't disturb the place where the bog rosemary grows. I've heard them going on about the bog rosemary and the marsh andromedas over around May Moss." He glanced at the sun. "Well, I'm obliged to you, my dear. And now we'd best be off. Time's getting on. And I want you to get out your map, and put on your rain shawl now."

"My what?"

"The green hooded thing you were wearing over your other clothes when I found you."

"Oh, the poncho." She dug this out, heaved and hoisted the pack back on and belted it, then managed to haul the poncho on and down over pack and all despite the whipping of the wind, and to snap the sides together. All this took time, and Elphi was fidgeting before she finished. She faced him, back to the wind. "Since I helped solve your problem, how about helping me with mine?"

"And what's that?"

"I want to remember all this, and come back and see you again."

This sent Elphi off into a great fit of moaning and head-swinging. Abruptly he stopped and stood, rigidly upright. "Would you force me to lie to you? What you ask cannot be given, I've told you why."

"I *swear* I wouldn't tell anybody!" But when this set off another groaning fit Jenny gave up. "All right. Forget it. Where is it you're taking me?"

Elphi sank to all fours, trembling a little, but when he spoke his voice sounded ordinary. "To the track across Great Hograh, where we met. Just over there, do you see? The line of cairns?" And sure enough, there on the horizon was a row of tiny cones. "You walk before me now, straight as you can, till you strike the path."

Jenny, map in hand and frustration in heart, obediently started to climb toward the ridge, lifting her boots high and clear of the snow-dusted heather. The wind was now at her back. Where a sheep-track went the right way she followed it until it wandered off-course, then cast about for another; and in this way she climbed at last onto the narrow path. She stopped to catch her breath and admire the view, then headed east, toward the Youth Hostel at Westerdale Hall, with the sun behind her.

For a couple of miles after that Jenny thought of nothing at all except the strange beauty of the scenery, her general soreness and tiredness, and the hot, bad dinner she would get in Westerdale. Then, with a slight start, she wondered when the fog had cleared, and why she hadn't noticed. She pulled off the flapping poncho—dry already!—rolled it up, reached behind to stuff it under the pack flap, then retrieved her map in its clear plastic cover from between her knees and consulted it. If that slope directly across the dale was Kempswithen, then she must be about *here*, and so would strike the road into Westerdale quite soon. She would be at the hostel in, oh, maybe an hour, and have a hot bath—hot wash, anyway, the hostel probably wouldn't have such a thing as a bathtub, they hardly ever did—and the biggest dinner she could buy.

"This is our off-season. You're in luck," said the hostel warden. "We were expecting you yesterday. In summer there wouldn't have been a bed in the place, but we're not fully booked tonight so not to worry. Will you be wanting supper?"

"I booked for the fifth," said Jenny a bit severely. "I'm quite sure, because the fifth is my sister's birthday."

"Right. But the fifth was yesterday; this is the sixth." He put his square finger on a wall calendar hanging behind him. "Thursday, April the sixth. All right?"

"It's Wednesday the fifth," said Jenny patiently, wondering how this obvious flake had convinced the Youth Hostel Association to hire him for a position of responsibility. She held out her wrist so he could read the day and date.

He glanced at the watch. "As a matter of fact it says Thursday the sixth. But it's quite all right, you'll get a bed. Now what about supper, yes or no? There's people waiting to sign in."

Jenny stared at the little squares on the face of her watch and felt her own face begin to burn. "Sorry, I guess I made a mistake. Ah—yes, please, I definitely do want supper." A couple of teenage boys, waiting in the queue behind her, were looking at her strangely; she fumbled out of her boots, slung them into the bootrack, hoisted up her pack, and with all the dignity she could summon up proceeded toward the dormitory she'd been assigned to.

Safe in the empty dorm she picked a bed and sat on it, dumping her pack on the floor beside her. "I left Cambridge on the third," she said aloud. "I stayed two nights in York. I got on the Middlesbrough train this morning, changed there for Whitby, got off at Kildale, and walked over the tops to Westerdale. How and where in tarnation did I manage to lose a day?"

On impulse she got out her seat ticket for the Inter-City train. The seat had been booked for the third. The conductor had looked at and punched the ticket. Nobody else had tried to sit in the same seat. There could be no reasonable likelihood of a mistake about the day.

Yet her watch, which two days ago had said Monday, April 3, now said Thursday, April 6. Where could the missing day have gone?

But there was no one to tell her, and the room was cold. Jenny came back to the present: she needed hot water, food, clean socks, her slippers, and (for later) several more blankets on her bed. She wrestled her pack around, opened it, and pulled out her towel and soap box; but her spare pair of boot socks was no longer clean. In fact, it had obviously been worn hard. Both socks were foot-shaped, stuck full of little twiglets of heather, and just slightly damp.

The prickly bits of heather made Jenny realize that the socks she was wearing were prickly as well. She stuck a finger down inside the prickliest sock to work the bits of heather loose, giving this small practical problem all her attention so as to hold panic at bay.

The prickle in her right sock was not heather, but a small piece of paper folded up tight. Hands shaking, Jenny opened the scrap of paper and spread it flat on her thigh. It was a Lipton teabag wrapper, scribbled over with a pen on the non-printed side, in her own handwriting. The scribble said:

hob called ELFY (?)—caught me in fog, made me come home with him— disguised as *sheep*—lives in hole with 6 others—*hobs are aliens*—he'll make me forget but TRY TO REMEMBER—Danby High Moor?/Bransdale?/ Farndale?—KEEP TRYING, DON'T GIVE UP!!!

These words, obviously penned in frantic haste, meant nothing whatever to Jenny. What was a hob? Yet she had written this herself, no question.

Her mind did a slow cartwheel. The sixth of April. Thursday, not Wednesday.

Jenny folded up the scrap of paper and stowed it carefully in her wallet. Methodically then she went through the pack. The emergency food packet had gone, vanished. So had the flashlight, and the candles. The spare shirt and underwear that ought to have been fresh were not. Her little aluminum mess kit pot, carefully soaped for easy cleaning through so many years of camping trips, had been blackened with smoke on the bottom.

Something inexplicable had happened and Jenny had forgotten what it was— been made to forget, apparently; and to judge by this message from out of the lost day she had considered it well worth remembering.

All right then, she decided, hunched aching and grubby on a hard bed in that cold, empty room, the thing to do was to follow instructions and not give up. Trust her own judgment. Keep faith with herself, even if it took years.

It did take years, but Jenny never gave up. She returned as often to the North York Moors National Park as summers, semester breaks, and sabbaticals permitted, coming to know Danby High Moor, and Bransdale and Farndale, and *their* moors, as well as a foreign visitor could possibly know them in every season; and each visit made her love that rugged country better. In time she became a regular guest at a farm in Danby Dale that did bed-and-breakfast for people on holiday, and never again needed to sleep in Westerdale Hall.

The wish to unriddle the mystery of the missing April 5 retained its strength and importance without, luckily, becoming obsessive, and this fact confirmed Jenny's instinctive sense that when she had scribbled that note to herself she had been afraid only of forgetting, not of the thing to be forgotten. She wanted the lost memories back, not in order to confront and exorcise them, but to repossess something of value that rightfully belonged to her.

But Elphi's powers of suggestion were exceptional. Try as she might, Jenny could not recapture what had happened. Diligent research did uncover a great deal of information about hobs (including the correct spelling of Elphi's name, for he had been famous in his day). And Jenny also made it her business to learn what she could about people who believed themselves to have been captured and examined by aliens (for instance, they are drawn back again and again to the scene of the close encounter). Many of these people had clearly been traumatized, and were afterwards tormented by their inability to remember what had happened to them. Following their example, in case it might help, Jenny eventually sat through a few sessions with a hypnotist; but whether because her participation was half-hearted or because Elphi's skills were of a superior sort, she could remember nothing.

None of Jenny's efforts, in fact, produced the results she actively desired and sought. They did have the wholly unlooked-for result of finding her a husband, and a new and better home.

Frank Flintoft at forty-eight had flyaway white hair and a farmer's stumping gait, but also wide-awake blue eyes in a curiously innocent face. His parents were very old friends of John and Rita Dowson, whose farm in Danby Dale had become Jenny's hob-hunting base in Yorkshire. Frank had grown up on his family's farm in Westerdale, gone off to Cambridge on a scholarship, then returned to take a lease on a place near Swainby, just inside the Park boundary, and settle down to breeding blackface sheep.

The Dowsons had spoken of this person to Jenny with a mixture of admiration and dubiety. A local boy that went away to University rarely came back. Frank *had* come back—but with Ideas, and also with a young bride who had left for London before the first year was out; and the Dowsons frowned upon divorce. Frank would use no chemicals, not even to spray his bracken, which put John Dowson's back up. For another thing, he went in for amateur archeology—with the blessing of the County Archeologists for half the North Riding—and was known to the Archeology Departments at the Universities of York and Leeds. And with it all, more often than not Frank's Swaledale gimmer lambs took Best of Breed at the annual Danby Show.

This paragon and Jenny were introduced on one of her summer junkets. The two hit it off immediately, saw a lot of each other whenever Jenny was in Yorkshire, but were not quick to marry. Frank had first to convince himself that Jenny truly loved the moor country for its own sake, and could be trusted not to leave it, before he was prepared to risk a second marriage; but Jenny, to her own surprise, felt wholly willing to exchange her old life for Frank, a Yorkshire sheep farm at the moors' edge, with a two hundred-year-old stone farmhouse, and part-time teaching at York University.

Not until six months after the wedding did Jenny tell her husband about the hob named Elphi. They had finished their evening meal and were sitting at the kitchen table before the electric fire, and at a certain point in the bizarre narrative Frank put his thick hand over hers. "I've heard of Elphi myself," he said thoughtfully when she had finished. "Well, and so that's what really brought you back here, year after year . . . you've still got the note you wrote yourself, I expect." Jenny had had the teabag wrapper laminated, years before. Wordless she went to her room to fetch it, and wordless he read what she had written there.

"Can *you* suggest an explanation?" she finally asked.

Frank shook his head. "But I know one thing. Ancient places have got lives of their own. There's 3,500 years of human settlement on these moors, love. When I'm working on one of the ancient sites I often feel anything at all might happen up there. Almost anything," he amended; "I'm not happy thinking of the hobs as spacemen from somewhere else—I've been hearing tales of Hob all my life, you know. He belongs to our own folklore. I'd prefer to find an explanation closer to home.''

''Well anyway, then, you won't think me barmy to go on trying to solve the mystery? It's the one *truly* extraordinary thing that ever happened to me,'' she added apologetically.

Frank grinned and shook his head again. ''You didn't by any chance marry me for convenience, did you—in order to get on with the search?''

''Not *only* for that,'' said Jenny in relief, and hugged her tolerant and broad-minded husband.

But more years went by, and gradually she forgot to think about Elphi at all. Her quest had brought her a life which suited her so perfectly, and absorbed her so entirely, that in the end there was too little dissatisfaction left in Jenny to fuel the search for a solution to the puzzle.

One early summer morning, five years after she had come to live with Frank, the two of them—as they frequently did—took the Land Rover and a hamper of sandwiches up to the tops, for a day of archeology and botanizing. Over a period of several months Frank had been surveying several minor Bronze Age sites between Nab Farm and Blakey Topping, just outside the southern boundary of the four-square-mile forbidden zone of the Early Warning System on Fyling-dales Moor. Private land within the Park was thickly strewn with these ancient sites, mostly cairns and field systems. Many had still not been officially identified, and quite a few of the landowners were unaware of their existence. The Park Committee were only too happy to accept Frank's skilled, and free, assistance with the mapping and recording of the less important sites, and Frank enjoyed the work. But the painstaking patience it required was more in his line than Jenny's; she preferred to poke about in the bogland of Nab Farm and nearby May Moss.

On this day she left Frank setting up his equipment under a gray ceiling of cloud, and hiked off briskly through a spur of afforested land to see whether the marsh andromeda had bloomed. An hour and a half later she reappeared, stumbling and panting, to drag a startled Frank away from his work, back through the narrow bit of pine plantation to the stretch of bog she had been scanning for rare plants. Something—perhaps a dog, or a trail bike—had gouged a large messy hole in the peat; and inside the hole, just visible above dark water, what looked like a hand and part of an arm had been exposed. The arm appeared to be covered with long hair.

Frank stepped back hastily, yanking his Wellington boot out of the muck with a rude noise. ''One of us had better go after the police.''

''No,'' said Jenny, still panting. ''*We've* got to dig him out. Never mind why, just help me do it.'' Already she was pulling her anorak over her head and rolling up her sleeves.

There were no flies on Frank Flintoft. After one hard look at his wife he began unbuttoning his own jacket.

Apart from a few sheep scattered across the long slopes of moor there was no one to see them delving in the bog. In twenty minutes, using a pocketknife, a plastic trowel, and their bare hands, they had exposed a small body. The body had been laid on its back in a shallow grave, not shrouded or even clothed except in the long, shaggy hair, stained a dark brown by the peaty water, that covered him completely.

While they labored to clear the face, scooping up double handfuls of mucky peat and throwing them out of the hole, Jenny abruptly began to cry silently; and when the body lay wholly uncovered, and they had poured a canteen of water over it to wash it a little cleaner, Frank stood and gazed soberly, then put his arm around Jenny and said gently, "Elphi, I presume."

Jenny took no notice of the tears that continued to streak her filthy face, except to wipe her nose on her sleeve. "No, it's another hob, called Woof Howe." And there at the graveside she began to tell Frank the story which had fallen upon her, entire and clear in every detail, as soon as their digging had revealed the corpse's form. "I'm pretty sure he meant to bury Woof Howe in the bog over there, on the grounds of the EWS," she finished. "The fence must have been too much for him—imagine trying to get in there carrying a body, all by yourself, no matter *how* strong you were." The moor wind blew upon them, stirring the reeds around the grave; Jenny shivered and leaned against Frank.

"Or I suppose this could be one of the other hobs, that died later on—Elphi himself, possibly."

"Un-uh, not Elphi," said Jenny. She spoke in a dazed way, obviously somewhat in shock, and Frank gave her a concerned look. "I really thought the acid in the peat would decompose soft tissue fast—that's what I told him, I'd actually read it somewhere—but I hadn't heard then about the bog people of Ireland and Denmark, that were preserved for thousands of years in peat bogs."

"Ah. And so the result was just the opposite of what you intended."

"It looks that way, doesn't it." She stared down at the dead face. "I'm glad and sorry both."

"But mostly glad?"

"I guess so."

"Well," said Frank, "what shall we do about it then? Notify the police after all, or the Moors Centre?"

"No." Jenny roused herself and stood on her own feet. "We'll just bury him again, and try to make it look like this spot had never been touched."

Frank started, but swallowed his objections. "Sure that's what you want?"

Jenny stated flatly, "Elphi wouldn't trust me to keep his secret. I'm going to prove he was wrong. We'll just cover Woof Howe up again, and smooth out the mud, and leave him in peace."

"It's been over fifteen years, love," Frank could not help protesting. "The other hobs could all be dead by now."

"I know, but what if they're not?"

Sighing, Frank gave in. "But we'll take his picture first at least, all right? *I*'d quite like to have one."

"Okay, I guess that can't do any harm." So, having wiped the mud off his hands as best he could, Frank snapped several pictures with Jenny's camera, with its close-up lens for photographing wildflowers, before beginning to push the peat back into the hole containing the perfectly preserved body of Woof Howe Hob.

In a fortnight's time the reeds had reestablished themselves upon the grave; in another month nobody could have said for certain just where the bog at May Moss had been disturbed. No one's curiosity was aroused and no inquiries were made; and that would have been the end of the matter, except for this:

About the time the sedge was growing tall again above Woof Howe, Frank stood in the kitchen door and called to Jenny, "What in the name of sanity possessed you to try mucking out the chicken coop all on your own?" He sounded quite cross, for him.

Jenny came into the kitchen carrying a book. "Is this a clever way of shaming me into action? You know I've had the bloody chicken coop on my conscience for weeks, but if anybody's been mucking it out it wasn't me."

"Come and see." Frank led her through the gathering dusk, across the barn-yard. There stood the coop, its floor scraped down to the wood and spread with clean straw. The hens clucked about contentedly in their yard. The manure-filled rubbish had been raked into a tidy heap for composting. Jenny stared flabber-gasted.

"Do you actually mean to say," said Frank, "that this isn't your doing?"

"It ought to be, but it's not."

They walked slowly back toward the house, arms about each other, trying to puzzle it out.

"Maybe Billy Davies dropped by after school, thinking to earn a few pounds and surprise us," Frank suggested. "I've paid him to muck out the pigs, and the barn, and he knows about composting . . . but it doesn't seem his style somehow."

"I guess it could have been John, or Peter," Jenny said doubtfully. "Though why either of them would take it upon himself . . . and the only person I've actually *spoken* to about wanting to get around to the job is you. Did you mention it to anybody?"

The thought struck each of them at the same instant.

"Waaaaaaait a minute—" said Frank, and "Good God, you don't think—" said Jenny; and both were speechless, staring at one another.

Frank found his voice first. "Now, if they're *not* all dead—"

Jenny interrupted: "Frank! What if one of the sheep on the commons, that day at May Moss—wasn't a sheep!"

His eyes opened wide. "Wasn't a sheep? You mean—and followed us here somehow, found out who you were, and where we lived?"

"Is that possible? Could they do it? What if they could!"

"*You* said it wasn't him in the grave, you were sure of it."

"I still am. It wasn't him."

"Well then, who else would muck out a chicken coop without being asked, tell me that!"

By now they were laughing and clutching at each other, almost dancing. Abruptly Jenny broke free and ran up the kitchen steps. She snatched a stoneware jug down from a shelf, filled it to the brim with cream from the crock in the fridge, and set the jug on the top step, careful not to spill a drop.

BRUCE STERLING

Our Neural Chernobyl

One of the major new talents to enter SF in recent years, Bruce Sterling sold his first story in 1976, and has since sold stories to *Universe, Omni, The Magazine of Fantasy and Science Fiction, The Last Dangerous Visions, Lone Star Universe,* and elsewhere. He has attracted special acclaim in the last few years for a series of stories set in his exotic Shaper/Mechanist future, a complex and disturbing future where warring political factions struggle to control the shape of human destiny, and the nature of humanity itself. His story "Cicada Queen" was in our First Annual Collection; his "Sunken Gardens" was in our Second Annual Collection; his "Green Days in Brunei" and "Diner in Audoghast" were in our Third Annual Collection; his "The Beautiful and the Sublime" was in our Fourth Annual Collection; his "Flowers Of Edo" was in our Fifth Annual Collection. His books include the novels *The Artificial Kid, Involution Ocean,* and *Schismatrix,* a novel set in the Shaper/Mechanist future: and, as editor, *Mirrorshades: The Cyberpunk Anthology.* His most recent novel was *Islands in the Net.* Upcoming is another novel, *The Difference Engine,* in collaboration with William Gibson.

In the compact little story that follows, packed with enough new ideas to last most writers for a 400-page novel, he shows us that even the smallest actions can have large, and often totally unexpected, consequences.

OUR NEURAL CHERNOBYL

Bruce Sterling

The late twentieth century, and the early years of our own millennium, form, in retrospect, a single era. This was the Age of the Normal Accident, in which people cheerfully accepted technological risks that today would seem quite insane.

Chernobyls were astonishingly frequent during this footloose, not to say criminally negligent, period. The nineties, with their rapid spread of powerful industrial technologies to the developing world, were a decade of frightening enormities, including the Djakarta supertanker spill, the Lahore meltdown, and the gradual but devastating mass poisonings from tainted Kenyan contraceptives.

Yet none of these prepared humankind for the astonishing global effects of biotechnology's worst disaster: the event that has come to be known as the "neural chernobyl."

We should be grateful, then, that such an authority as the Nobel prize-winning systems neurochemist Dr. Felix Hotton should have turned his able pen to the history of *Our Neural Chernobyl* (Bessemer, December 2056, $499.95). Dr. Hotton is uniquely qualified to give us this devastating reassessment of the past's wrongheaded practices. For Dr. Hotton is a shining examplar of the new "Open-Tower Science," that social movement within the scientific community that arose in response to the New Luddism of the teens and twenties.

Such pioneering Hotton papers as "The Locus Coeruleus Efferent Network: What in Heck Is It There For?" and "My Grand Fun Tracing Neural Connections with Tetramethylbenzidine" established this new, relaxed, and triumphantly subjective school of scientific exploration.

Today's scientist is a far cry from the white-coated sociopath of the past. Scientists today are democratized, media-conscious, fully integrated into the mainstream of modern culture. Today's young people, who admire scientists with a devotion once reserved for pop stars, can scarcely imagine the situation otherwise.

But in chapter 1, "The Social Roots of Gene-Hacking," Dr. Hotton brings turn-of-the-century attitudes into startling relief. This was the golden age of applied biotech. Anxious attitudes toward "genetic tampering" changed rapidly when the terrifying AIDS pandemic was finally broken by recombinant DNA research.

It was during this period that the world first became aware that the AIDS retrovirus was a fantastic blessing in a particularly hideous disguise. This disease, which dug itself with horrible, virulent cunning into the very genetic structure of its victims, proved a medical marvel when finally broken to harness. The AIDS virus's RNA transcriptase system proved an able workhorse, successfully carrying healing segments of recombinant DNA into sufferers from myriad genetic defects. Suddenly one ailment after another fell to the miracle of RNA tanscriptase techniques: sickle-cell anemia, cystic fibrosis, Tay-Sachs disease—literally hundreds of syndromes now only an unpleasant memory.

As billions poured into the biotech industry, and the instruments of research were simplified and streamlined, an unexpected dynamic emerged: the rise of "gene-hacking." As Dr. Hotton points out, the situation had a perfect parallel in the 1970s and 1980s in the subculture of computer hacking. Here again was an enormously powerful technology suddenly within the reach of the individual.

As biotech startup companies multiplied, becoming ever smaller and more advanced, a hacker subculture rose around this "hot technology" like a cloud of steam. These ingenious, anomic individuals, often led into a state of manic self-absorption by their ability to dice with genetic destiny, felt no loyalty to social interests higher than their own curiosity. As early as the 1980s, devices such as high-performance liquid chromotographs, cell-culture systems, and DNA sequencers were small enough to fit into a closet or attic. If not bought from junkyards, diverted, or stolen outright, they could be reconstructed from off-the-shelf parts by any bright and determined teenager.

Dr. Hotton's second chapter explores the background of one such individual: Andrew ("Bugs") Berenbaum, now generally accepted as the perpetrator of the neural chernobyl.

Bugs Berenbaum, as Dr. Hotton convincingly shows, was not much different from a small horde of similar bright young misfits surrounding the genetic establishments of North Carolina's Research Triangle. His father was a semisuccessful free-lance programmer, his mother a heavy marijuana user whose life centered around her role as "Lady Anne of Greengables" in Raleigh's Society for Creative Anachronism.

Both parents maintained a flimsy pretense of intellectual superiority, impressing upon Andrew the belief that the family's sufferings derived from the general stupidity and limited imagination of the average citizen. And Berenbaum, who showed an early interest in such subjects as math and engineering (then considered markedly unglamorous), did suffer some persecution from peers and schoolmates. At fifteen he had already drifted into the gene-hacker subculture, accessing gossip and learning "the scene" through computer bulletin boards and all-night beer-and-pizza sessions with other would-be pros.

At twenty-one, Berenbaum was working a summer internship with the small Raleigh firm of CoCoGenCo, a producer of specialized biochemicals. CoCo-GenCo, as later congressional investigations proved, was actually a front for the California "designer drug" manufacturer and smuggler Jimmy ("Screech") McCarley. McCarley's agents within CoCoGenCo ran innumerable late-night "research projects" in conditions of heavy secrecy. In reality, these "secret projects" were straight production runs of synthetic cocaine, beta-phenethylamine, and sundry tailored variants of endorphin, a natural antipain chemical ten thousand times more potent than morphine.

One of McCarley's "black hackers," possibly Berenbaum himself, conceived the sinister notion of "implanted dope factories." By attaching the drug-producing genetics directly into the human genome, it was argued, abusers could be "wet-wired" into permanent states of intoxication. The agent of fixation would be the AIDS retrovirus, whose RNA sequence was a matter of common knowledge and available on dozens of open scientific databases. The one drawback to the scheme was, of course, that the abuser would "burn out like a shitpaper moth in a klieg light," to use Dr. Hotton's memorable phrase.

Chapter 3 is rather technical. Given Dr. Hotton's light and popular style, it makes splendid reading. Dr. Hotton attempts to reconstruct Berenbaum's crude attempts to rectify the situation through gross manipulation of the AIDS RNA transcriptase. What Berenbaum sought, of course, was a way to shut off and start up the transcriptase carrier, so that the internal drug factory could be activated at will. Berenbaum's custom transcriptase was designed to react to a simple user-induced trigger—probably D, 1, 2, 5-phospholytic gluteinase, a fractionated component of "Dr. Brown's Celery Soda," as Hotton suggests. This harmless beverage was a favorite quaff of gene-hacker circles.

Finding the coca-production genomes too complex, Berenbaum (or perhaps a close associate, one Richard ["Sticky"] Ravetch) switched to a simpler payload: the just-discovered genome for mammalian dendritic growth factor. Dendrites are the treelike branches of brain cells, familiar to every modern schoolchild, which provide the mammalian brain with its staggering webbed complexity. It was theorized at the time that DG factor might be the key to vastly higher states of human intelligence. It is to be presumed that Berenbaum and Ravetch had both dosed themselves with it. As many modern victims of the neural chernobyl can testify, it does have an effect. Not precisely the one that the CoCoGenCo zealots envisioned, however.

While under the temporary maddening elation of dendritic "branch-effect," Berenbaum made his unfortunate breakthrough. He succeeded in providing his model RNA transcriptase with a trigger, but a trigger that made the transcriptase itself far more virulent than the original AIDS virus itself. The stage was set for disaster.

It is at this point that one must remember the social attitudes that bred the soul-threatening isolation of the contemporary scientific worker. Dr. Hotton is quite pitiless in his psychoanalysis of the mental mind-set of his predecessors. The supposedly "objective worldview" of the sciences is now quite properly seen as a form of mental brainwashing, deliberately stripping its victims of the full spectrum of human emotion and response. Under such conditions, Berenbaum's reckless act becomes almost pitiable; it was a convulsive overcompensation for years of emotional starvation. Without consulting his superiors, who might have shown more discretion, Berenbaum began offering free samples of his new wetwares to anyone willing to shoot them up.

There was a sudden brief plague of eccentric genius in Raleigh, before the now-well-known symptoms of "dendritic crash" took over, and plunged the experimenters into vision-riddled, poetic insanity. Berenbaum himself committed suicide well before the full effects were known. And the full effects, of course, were to go far beyond even this lamentable human tragedy.

Chapter 4 becomes an enthralling detective story as the evidence slowly mounts.

Even today the term "Raleigh collie" has a special ring for dog fanciers, many of whom have forgotten its original derivation. These likable, companionable, and disquietingly intelligent pets were soon transported all over the nation by eager buyers and breeders. Once it had made the jump from human host to canine, Berenbaum's transcriptase derivative, like the AIDS virus itself, was passed on through the canine maternal womb. It was also transmitted through canine sexual intercourse and, via saliva, through biting and licking.

No dendritically enriched "Raleigh collie" would think of biting a human being. On the contrary, these loyal and well-behaved pets have even been known to right spilled garbage cans and replace their trash. Neural chernobyl infections remain rare in humans. But they spread through North America's canine population like wildfire, as Dr. Hotton shows in a series of cleverly designed maps and charts.

Chapter 5 offers us the benefit of hindsight. We are now accustomed to the idea of many different modes of "intelligence." There are, for instance, the various types of computer Artificial Intelligence, which bear no real relation to human "thinking." This was not unexpected—but the diverse forms of animal intelligence can still astonish in their variety.

The variance between *Canis familiaris* and his wild cousin, the coyote, remains unexplained. Dr. Hotton makes a good effort, basing his explication on the coyote neural mapping of his colleague, Dr. Reyna Sanchez of Los Alamos National Laboratory. It does seem likely that the coyote's more fully reticulated basal commissure plays a role. At any rate, it is now clear that a startling advanced form of social organization has taken root among the nation's feral coyote population, with the use of elaborate coded barks, "scent-dumps," and specialized roles in hunting and food storage. Many of the nation's ranchers have now taken to the "protection system," in which coyote packs are "bought off" with slaughtered, barbecued livestock and sacks of dog treats. Persistent reports in Montana,

Idaho, and Saskatchewan insist that coyotes have been spotted wearing cast-off clothing during the worst cold of winter.

It is possible that the common household cat was infected even earlier than the dog. Yet the effects of heightened cat intelligence are subtle and difficult to specify. Notoriously reluctant lab subjects, cats in their infected states are even sulkier about running mazes, solving trick boxes, and so on, preferring to wait out their interlocutors with inscrutable feline patience.

It has been suggested that some domestic cats show a heightened interest in television programs. Dr. Hotton casts a skeptical light on this, pointing out (rightly, as this reviewer thinks) that cats spend most of their waking hours sitting and staring into space. Staring at the flickering of a television is not much more remarkable than the hearthside cat's fondness for the flickering fire. It certainly does not imply "understanding" of a program's content. There are, however, many cases where cats have learned to paw-push the buttons of remote-control units. Those who keep cats as mousers have claimed that some cats now torture birds and rodents for longer periods, with greater ingenuity, and in some cases with improvised tools.

There remains, however, the previously unsuspected connection between advanced dendritic branching and manual dexterity, which Dr. Hotton tackles in his sixth chapter. This concept has caused a revolution in paleoanthropology. We are now forced into the uncomfortable realization that *Pithecanthropus robustus*, formerly dismissed as a large-jawed, vegetable-chewing ape, was probably far more intelligent than *Homo sapiens*. CAT scans of the recently discovered Tanzanian fossil skeleton, nicknamed "Leonardo," reveal a *Pithecanthropus* skull-ridge obviously rich with dendritic branching. It has been suggested that the pithecanthropoids suffered from a heightened "life of the mind" similar to the life-threatening, absentminded genius of terminal neural chernobyl sufferers. This yields the uncomfortable theory that nature, through evolution, has imposed a "primate stupidity barrier" that allows humans, unlike *Pithecanthropus*, to get on successfully with the dumb animal business of living and reproducing.

But the synergetic effects of dendritic branching and manual dexterity are clear in a certain nonprimate species. I refer, of course, to the well-known "chernobyl jump" of *Procyon lotor*, the American raccoon. The astonishing advances of the raccoon, and its Chinese cousin the panda, occupy the entirety of chapter 8.

Here Dr. Hotton takes the so-called "modern view," from which I must dissociate myself. I, for one, find it intolerable that large sections of the American wilderness should be made into "no-go areas" by the vandalistic activities of our so-called "striped-tailed cousins." Admittedly, excesses may have been committed in early attempts to exterminate the verminous, booming population of these masked bandits. But the damage to agriculture has been severe, and the history of kamikaze attacks by self-infected rabid raccoons is a terrifying one.

Dr. Hotton holds that we must now "share the planet with a fellow civilized species.'' He bolsters his argument with hearsay evidence of "raccoon culture" that to me seems rather flimsy. The woven strips of bark known as "raccoon wampum" are impressive examples of animal dexterity, but to my mind it remains to be proven that they are actually "money." And their so-called "pictographs" seem little more than random daubings. The fact remains that the raccoon population continues to rise exponentially, with raccoon bitches whelping massive litters every spring. Dr. Hotton, in a footnote, suggests that we can relieve crowding pressure by increasing the human presence in space. This seems a farfetched and unsatisfactory scheme.

The last chapter is speculative in tone. The prospect of intelligent rats is grossly repugnant; so far, thank God, the tough immune system of the rat, inured to bacteria and filth, has rejected retroviral invasion. Indeed, the feral cat population seems to be driving these vermin toward extinction. Nor have opossums succumbed; indeed, marsupials of all kinds seem immune, making Australia a haven of a now-lost natural world. Whales and dolphins are endangered species; they seem unlikely to make a comeback even with the (as-yet-unknown) cetacean effects of chernobyling. And monkeys, which might pose a very considerable threat, are restricted to the few remaining patches of tropical forest and, like humans, seem resistant to the disease.

Our neural chernobyl has bred a folklore all its own. Modern urban folklore speaks of "ascended masters," a group of chernobyl victims able to survive the virus. Supposedly, they "pass for human," forming a hidden counterculture among the normals, or "sheep." This is a throwback to the dark tradition of Luddism, and the popular fears once projected onto the dangerous and reckless "priesthood of science" are now transferred to these fairy tales of supermen. This psychological transference becomes clear when one hears that these "ascended masters" specialize in advanced scientific research of a kind now frowned upon. The notion that some fraction of the population has achieved physical immortality, and hidden it from the rest of us, is utterly absurd.

Dr. Hotton, quite rightly, treats this paranoid myth with the contempt it deserves.

Despite my occasional reservations, this is a splendid book, likely to be the definitive work on this central phenomenon of modern times. Dr. Hotton may well hope to add another Pulitzer to his list of honors. At ninety-five, this grand old man of modern science has produced yet another stellar work in his rapidly increasing oeuvre. His many readers, like myself, can only marvel at his vigor and clamor for more.

for Greg Bear

ROBERT SILVERBERG

House of Bones

We usually think of our neolithic ancesters as primitive and brutish, but as the slyly fascinating story that follows suggests, if we could actually meet them, we might be surprised. . . .

Robert Silverberg is one of the most famous SF writers of modern times, with dozens of novels, anthologies, and collections to his credit. Silverberg has won five Nebula Awards and three Hugo Awards. His novels include *Dying Inside*, *Lord Valentine's Castle*, *The Book of Skulls*, *Downward to the Earth*, *Tower of Glass*, *The World Inside*, *Born with the Dead*, and *Shadrach in the Furnace*. His collections include *Unfamiliar Territory*, *Capricorn Games*, *Majipoor Chronicles*, *The Best of Robert Silverberg*, *At the Conglomeroid Cocktail Party*, and *Beyond the Safe Zone*. His most recent books are the novels *Tom O' Bedlam*, *Star of Gypsies*, and *At Winter's End*. For many years he edited the prestigious anthology series *New Dimensions*, and has recently, along with his wife, Karen Haber, taken over the editing of the *Universe* anthology series. His story "Multiples" was in our First Annual Collection; "The Affair" was in our Second Annual Collection; "Sailing to Byzantium"—which won a Nebula Award in 1986—was in our Third Annual Collection; "Against Babylon" was in our Fourth Annual Collection; and "The Pardoner's Tale" was in our Fifth Annual Collection. He lives in Oakland, California.

HOUSE OF BONES

Robert Silverberg

After the evening meal Paul starts tapping on his drum and chanting quietly to himself, and Marty picks up the rhythm, chanting too. And then the two of them launch into that night's installment of the tribal epic, which is what happens, sooner or later, every evening.

It all sounds very intense but I don't have a clue to the meaning. They sing the epic in the religious language, which I've never been allowed to learn. It has the same relation to the everyday language, I guess, as Latin does to French or Spanish. But it's private, sacred, for insiders only. Not for the likes of me.

"Tell it, man!" B.J. yells. "Let it roll!" Danny shouts.

Paul and Marty are really getting into it. Then a gust of fierce stinging cold whistles through the house as the reindeer-hide flap over the doorway is lifted, and Zeus comes stomping in.

Zeus is the chieftain. Big burly man, starting to run to fat a little. Mean-looking, just as you'd expect. Heavy black beard streaked with gray and hard, glittering eyes that glow like rubies in a face wrinkled and carved by windburn and time. Despite the Paleolithic cold, all he's wearing is a cloak of black fur, loosely draped. The thick hair on his heavy chest is turning gray too. Festoons of jewelry announce his power and status: necklaces of seashells, bone beads, and amber, a pendant of yellow wolf teeth, an ivory headband, bracelets carved from bone, five or six rings.

Sudden silence. Ordinarily when Zeus drops in at B.J.'s house it's for a little roistering and tale-telling and butt-pinching, but tonight he has come without either of his wives, and he looks troubled, grim. Jabs a finger toward Jeanne.

"You saw the stranger today? What's he like?"

There's been a stranger lurking near the village all week, leaving traces everywhere—footprints in the permafrost, hastily covered-over campsites, broken flints, scraps of charred meat. The whole tribe's keyed. Strangers aren't common. I was the last one, a year and a half ago. God only knows why they took me in:

because I seemed so pitiful to them, maybe. But the way they've been talking, they'll kill this one on sight if they can. Paul and Marty composed a Song of the Stranger last week and Marty sang it by the campfire two different nights. It was in the religious language so I couldn't understand a word of it. But it sounded terrifying.

Jeanne is Marty's wife. She got a good look at the stranger this afternoon, down by the river while netting fish for dinner. "He's short," she tells Zeus. "Shorter than any of you, but with big muscles, like Gebravar." Gebravar is Jeanne's name for me. The people of the tribe are strong, but they didn't pump iron when they were kids. My muscles fascinate them. "His hair is yellow and his eyes are gray. And he's ugly. Nasty. Bighead, big flat nose. Walks with his shoulders hunched and his head down." Jeanne shudders. "He's like a pig. A real beast. A goblin. Trying to steal fish from the net, he was. But he ran away when he saw me."

Zeus listens, glowering, asking a question now and then—did he say anything, how was he dressed, was his skin painted in any way. Then he turns to Paul.

"What do you think he is?"

"A ghost," Paul says. These people see ghosts everywhere. And Paul, who is the bard of the tribe, thinks about them all the time. His poems are full of ghosts. He feels the world of ghosts pressing in, pressing in. "Ghosts have gray eyes," he says. "This man has gray eyes."

"A ghost, maybe, yes. But what kind of ghost?"

"What *kind*?"

Zeus glares. "You should listen to your own poems," he snaps. "Can't you see it? This is a Scavenger Folk man prowling around. Or the ghost of one."

General uproar and hubbub at that.

I turn to Sally. Sally's my woman. I still have trouble saying that she's my wife, but that's what she really is. I call her Sally because there once was a girl back home who I thought I might marry, and that was her name, far from here in another geological epoch.

I ask Sally who the Scavenger Folk are.

"From the old times," she says. "Lived here when we first came. But they're all dead now. They—"

That's all she gets a chance to tell me. Zeus is suddenly looming over me. He's always regarded me with a mixture of amusement and tolerant contempt, but now there's something new in his eye. "Here is something you will do for us," he says to me. "It takes a stranger to find a stranger. This will be your task. Whether he is a ghost or a man, we must know the truth. So you, tomorrow: you will go out and you will find him and you will take him. Do you understand? At first light you will go to search for him, and you will not come back until you have him."

I try to say something, but my lips don't want to move. My silence seems good enough for Zeus, though. He smiles and nods fiercely and swings around, and goes stalking off into the night.

They all gather around me, excited in that kind of animated edgy way that comes over you when someone you know is picked for some big distinction. I can't tell whether they envy me or feel sorry for me. B.J. hugs me, Danny punches me in the arm, Paul runs up a jubilant-sounding number on his drum. Marty pulls a wickedly sharp stone blade about nine inches long out of his kit-bag and presses it into my hand.

"Here. You take this. You may need it."

I stare at it as if he had handed me a live grenade.

"Look," I say. "I don't know anything about stalking and capturing people."

"Come *on*," B.J. says. "What's the problem?"

B.J. is an architect. Paul's a poet. Marty sings, better than Pavarotti. Danny paints and sculpts. I think of them as my special buddies. They're all what you could loosely call Cro-Magnon men. I'm not. They treat me just like one of the gang, though. We five, we're some bunch. Without them I'd have gone crazy here. Lost as I am, cut off as I am from everything I used to be and know.

"You're strong and quick," Marty says. "You can do it."

"And you're pretty smart, in your crazy way," says Paul. "Smarter than *he* is. We aren't worried at all."

If they're a little condescending sometimes, I suppose I deserve it. They're highly skilled individuals, after all, proud of the things they can do. To them I'm a kind of retard. That's a novelty for me. I used to be considered highly skilled too, back where I came from.

"You go with me," I say to Marty. "You and Paul both. I'll do whatever has to be done but I want you to back me up."

"No," Marty says. "You do this alone."

"B.J.? Danny?"

"No," they say. And their smiles harden, their eyes grow chilly. Suddenly it doesn't look so chummy around here. We may be buddies but I have to go out there by myself. Or I may have misread the whole situation and we aren't such big buddies at all. Either way this is some kind of test, some rite of passage maybe, an initiation. I don't know. Just when I think these people are exactly like us except for a few piddling differences of customs and languages, I realize how alien they really are. Not savages, far from it. But they aren't even remotely like modern people. They're something entirely else. Their bodies and their minds are pure *Homo sapiens* but their souls are different from ours by 20,000 years.

To Sally I say, "Tell me more about the Scavenger Folk."

"Like animals, they were," she says. "They could speak but only in grunts and belches. They were bad hunters and they ate dead things that they found on the ground, or stole the kills of others."

"They smelled like garbage," says Danny. "Like an old dump where everything was rotten. And they didn't know how to paint or sculpt."

"This was how they screwed," says Marty, grabbing the nearest woman, pushing her down, pretending to hump her from behind. Everyone laughs, cheers, stamps his feet.

"And they walked like this," says B.J., doing an ape-shuffle, banging his chest with his fists.

There's a lot more, a lot of locker-room stuff about the ugly shaggy stupid smelly disgusting Scavenger Folk. How dirty they were, how barbaric. How the pregnant women kept the babies in their bellies twelve or thirteen months and they came out already hairy, with a full mouth of teeth. All ancient history, handed down through the generations by bards like Paul in the epics. None of them has ever actually seen a Scavenger. But they sure seem to detest them.

"They're all dead," Paul says. "They were killed in the migration wars long ago. That has to be a ghost out there."

Of course I've guessed what's up. I'm no archaeologist at all—West Point, fourth generation. My skills are in electronics, computers, time-shift physics. There was such horrible political infighting among the archaeology boys about who was going to get to go to the past that in the end none of them went and the gig wound up going to the military. Still, they sent me here with enough crash-course archaeology to be able to see that the Scavengers must have been what we call the Neanderthals, that shambling race of also-rans that got left behind in the evolutionary sweepstakes.

So there really had been a war of extermination between the slow-witted Scavengers and clever *Homo sapiens* here in Ice Age Europe. But there must have been a few survivors left on the losing side, and one of them, God knows why, is wandering around near this village.

Now I'm supposed to find the ugly stranger and capture him. Or kill him, I guess. Is that what Zeus wants from me? To take the stranger's blood on my head? A very civilized tribe, they are, even if they do hunt huge woolly elephants and build houses out of their whitened bones. Too civilized to do their own murdering, and they figure they can send me out to do it for them.

"I don't think he's a Scavenger," Danny says. "I think he's from Naz Glesim. The Naz Glesim people have gray eyes. Besides, what would a ghost want with fish?"

Naz Glesim is a land far to the northeast, perhaps near what will someday be Moscow. Even here in the Paleolithic the world is divided into a thousand little nations. Danny once went on a great solo journey through all the neighboring lands: he's a kind of tribal Marco Polo.

"You better not let the chief hear that," B.J. tells him. "He'll break your balls. Anyway, the Naz Glesim people aren't ugly. They look just like us except for their eyes."

"Well, there's that," Danny concedes. "But I still think—"

Paul shakes his head. That gesture goes way back, too. "A Scavenger ghost," he insists.

B.J. looks at me. "What do you think, Pumangiup?" That's his name for me.

"Me?" I say. "What do I know about these things?"

"You come from far away. You ever see a man like that?"

"I've seen plenty of ugly men, yes." The people of the tribe are tall and lean, brown hair and dark shining eyes, wide faces, bold cheekbones. If they had better teeth they'd be gorgeous. "But I don't know about this one. I'd have to see him."

Sally brings a new platter of grilled fish over. I run my hand fondly over her bare haunch. Inside this house made of mammoth bones nobody wears very much clothing, because the structure is well insulated and the heat builds up even in the dead of winter. To me Sally is far and away the best-looking woman in the tribe, high firm breasts, long supple legs, alert, inquisitive face. She was the mate of a man who had to be killed last summer because he became infested with ghosts. Danny and B.J. and a couple of the others bashed his head in, by way of a mercy killing, and then there was a wild six-day wake, dancing and wailing around the clock. Because she needed a change of luck they gave Sally to me, or me to her, figuring a holy fool like me must carry the charm of the gods. We have a fine time, Sally and I. We were two lost souls when we came together, and together we've kept each other from tumbling even deeper into the darkness.

"You'll be all right," B.J. says. "You can handle it. The gods love you."

"I hope that's true," I tell him.

Much later in the night Sally and I hold each other as though we both know that this could be our last time. She's all over me, hot, eager. There's no privacy in the bone-house and the others can hear us, four couples and I don't know how many kids, but that doesn't matter. It's dark. Our little bed of fox pelts is our own little world.

There's nothing esoteric, by the way, about these people's style of lovemaking. There are only so many ways that a male human body and a female human body can be joined together, and all of them, it seems, had already been invented by the time the glaciers came.

At dawn, by first light, I am on my way, alone, to hunt the Scavenger man. I rub the rough strange wall of the house of bones for luck, and off I go.

The village stretches for a couple of hundred yards along the bank of a cold, swiftly flowing river. The three round bone-houses where most of us live are arranged in a row, and the fourth one, the long house that is the residence of Zeus and his family and also serves as the temple and house of parliament, is just beyond them. On the far side of it is the new fifth house that we've been building this past week. Farther down, there's a workshop where tools are made and hides are scraped, and then a butchering area, and just past that there's an immense garbage dump and a towering heap of mammoth bones for future construction projects.

A sparse pine forest lies east of the village, and beyond it are the rolling hills and open plains where the mammoths and rhinos graze. No one ever goes into the river, because it's too cold and the current is too strong, and so it hems us in like a wall on our western border. I want to teach the tribesfolk how to build kayaks one of these days. I should also try to teach them how to swim, I guess. And maybe a few years further along I'd like to see if we can chop down some trees and build a bridge. Will it shock the pants off them when I come out with all this useful stuff? They think I'm an idiot, because I don't know about the different grades of mud and frozen ground, the colors of charcoal, the uses and qualities of antler, bone, fat, hide, and stone. They feel sorry for me because I'm so limited. But they like me all the same. And the gods *love* me. At least B.J. thinks so.

I start my search down by the riverfront, since that's where Jeanne saw the Scavenger yesterday. The sun, at dawn on this Ice Age autumn morning, is small and pale, a sad little lemon far away. But the wind is quiet now. The ground is still soft from the summer thaw, and I look for tracks. There's permafrost five feet down, but the topsoil, at least, turns spongy in May and gets downright muddy by July. Then it hardens again and by October it's like steel, but by October we live mostly indoors.

There are footprints all over the place. We wear leather sandals, but a lot of us go barefoot much of the time, even now, in forty-degree weather. The people of the tribe have long, narrow feet with high arches. But down by the water near the fishnets I pick up a different spoor, the mark of a short, thick, low-arched foot with curled-under toes. It must be my Neanderthal. I smile. I feel like Sherlock Holmes. "Hey, look, Marty," I say to the sleeping village. "I've got the ugly bugger's track. B.J.? Paul? Danny? You just watch me. I'm going to find him faster than you could believe."

Those aren't their actual names. I just call them that, Marty, Paul, B.J., Danny. Around here everyone gives everyone else his own private set of names. Marty's name for B.J. is Ungklava. He calls Danny Tisbalalak and Paul is Shibgamon. Paul calls Marty Dolibog. His name for B.J. is Kalamok. And so on all around the tribe, a ton of names, hundreds and hundreds of names for just forty or fifty people. It's a confusing system. They have reasons for it that satisfy them. You learn to live with it.

A man never reveals his true name, the one his mother whispered when he was born. Not even his father knows that, or his wife. You could put hot stones between his legs and he still wouldn't tell you that true name of his, because that'd bring every ghost from Cornwall to Vladivostok down on his ass to haunt him. The world is full of angry ghosts, resentful of the living, ready to jump on anyone who'll give them an opening and plague him like leeches, like bedbugs, like every malign and perverse bloodsucking pest rolled into one.

We are somewhere in western Russia, or maybe Poland. The landscape suggests that: flat, bleak, a cold grassy steppe with a few oaks and birches and pines here and there. Of course a lot of Europe must look like that in this glacial epoch. But the clincher is the fact that these people build mammoth-bone houses. The only place that was ever done was Eastern Europe, so far as anybody down the line knows. Possibly they're the oldest true houses in the world.

What gets me is the immensity of this prehistoric age, the spans of time. It goes back and back and back and all of it is alive for these people. We think it's a big deal to go to England and see a cathedral a thousand years old. They've been hunting on this steppe thirty times as long. Can you visualize 30,000 years? To you, George Washington lived an incredibly long time ago. George is going to have his 300th birthday very soon. Make a stack of books a foot high and tell yourself that that stands for all the time that has gone by since George was born in 1732. Now go on stacking up the books. When you've got a pile as high as a ten-story building, that's 30,000 years.

A stack of years almost as high as that separates me from you, right this minute. In my bad moments, when the loneliness and the fear and the pain and the remembrance of all that I have lost start to operate on me, I feel that stack of years pressing on me with the weight of a mountain. I try not to let it get me down. But that's a hell of a weight to carry. Now and then it grinds me right into the frozen ground.

The flat-footed track leads me up to the north, around the garbage dump, and toward the forest. Then I lose it. The prints go round and round, double back to the garbage dump, then to the butchering area, then toward the forest again, then all the way over to the river. I can't make sense of the pattern. The poor dumb bastard just seems to have been milling around, foraging in the garbage for anything edible, then taking off again but not going far, checking back to see if anything's been caught in the fishnet, and so on. Where's he sleeping? Out in the open, I guess. Well, if what I heard last night is true, he's as hairy as a gorilla; maybe the cold doesn't bother him much.

Now that I've lost the trail, I have some time to think about the nature of the mission, and I start getting uncomfortable.

I'm carrying a long stone knife. I'm out here to kill. I picked the military for my profession a long time ago, but it wasn't with the idea of killing anyone, and certainly not in hand-to-hand combat. I guess I see myself as a representative of civilization, somebody trying to hold back the night, not as anyone who would go creeping around planning to stick a sharp flint blade into some miserable solitary tramp.

But I might well be the one that gets killed. He's wild, he's hungry, he's scared, he's primitive. He may not be very smart, but at least he's shrewd enough to have made it to adulthood, and he's out here earning his living by his wits and his strength. This is his world, not mine. He may be stalking me even while I'm stalking him, and when we catch up with each other he won't be fighting by any rules I ever learned. A good argument for turning back right now.

On the other hand if I come home in one piece with the Scavenger still at large, Zeus will hang my hide on the bone-house wall for disobeying him. We may all be great buddies here but when the chief gives the word, you hop to it or else. That's the way it's been since history began and I have no reason to think it's any different back here.

I simply have to kill the Scavenger. That's all there is to it.

I don't want to get killed by a wild man in this forest, and I don't want to be nailed up by a tribal court-martial either. I want to live to get back to my own time. I still hang on to the faint chance that the rainbow will come back for me and take me down the line to tell my tale in what I have already started to think of as the future. I want to make my report.

The news I'd like to bring you people up there in the world of the future is that these Ice Age folk don't see themselves as primitive. They know, they absolutely *know*, that they're the crown of creation. They have a language—two of them, in fact—they have history, they have music, they have poetry, they have technology, they have art, they have architecture. They have religion. They have laws. They have a way of life that has worked for thousands of years, that will go on working for thousands more. You may think it's all grunts and war clubs back here, but you're wrong. I can make this world real to you, if I could only get back there to you.

But even if I can't ever get back, there's a lot I want to do here. I want to learn that epic of theirs and write it down for you to read. I want to teach them about kayaks and bridges, and maybe more. I want to finish building the bone-house we started last week. I want to go on horsing around with my buddies B.J. and Danny and Marty and Paul. I want Sally. Christ, I might even have kids by her, and inject my own futuristic genes into the Ice Age gene pool.

I don't want to die today trying to fulfill a dumb murderous mission in this cold bleak prehistoric forest.

The morning grows warmer, though not warm. I pick up the trail again, or think I do, and start off toward the east and north, into the forest. Behind me I hear the sounds of laughter and shouting and song as work gets going on the new house, but soon I'm out of earshot. Now I hold the knife in my hand, ready for anything. There are wolves in here, as well as a frightened half man who may try to kill me before I can kill him.

I wonder how likely it is that I'll find him. I wonder how long I'm supposed to stay out here, too—a couple of hours, a day, a week?—and what I'm supposed to use for food, and how I keep my ass from freezing after dark, and what Zeus will say or do if I come back empty-handed.

I'm wandering around randomly now. I don't feel like Sherlock Holmes any longer.

Working on the bone-house, that's what I'd rather be doing now. Winter is coming on and the tribe has grown too big for the existing four houses. B.J. directs the job and Marty and Paul sing and chant and play the drum and flute, and about seven of us do the heavy labor.

"Pile those jawbones chin down," B.J. will yell, as I try to slip one into the foundation the wrong way around. "*Chin down*, bozo! That's better." Paul bangs out a terrific riff on the drum to applaud me for getting it right the second time. Marty starts making up a ballad about how dumb I am, and everyone laughs. But it's loving laughter. "Now that backbone over there," B.J. yells to me. I pull a long string of mammoth vertebrae from the huge pile. The bones are white, old bones that have been lying around a long time. They're dense and heavy. "Wedge it down in there good! Tighter! Tighter!" I huff and puff under the immense weight of the thing, and stagger a little, and somehow get it where it belongs, and jump out of the way just in time as Danny and two other men come tottering toward me carrying a gigantic skull.

The winter-houses are intricate and elaborate structures that require real ingenuity of design and construction. At this point in time B.J. may well be the best architect the world has ever known. He carries around a piece of ivory on which he has carved a blueprint for the house, and makes sure everybody weaves the bones and skulls and tusks into the structure just the right way. There's no shortage of construction materials. After 30,000 years of hunting mammoths in this territory, these people have enough bones lying around to build a city the size of Los Angeles.

The houses are warm and snug. They're round and domed, like big igloos made out of bones. The foundation is a circle of mammoth skulls with maybe a hundred mammoth jawbones stacked up over them in fancy herringbone patterns to form the wall. The roof is made of hides stretched over enormous tusks mounted overhead as arches. The whole thing is supported by a wooden frame and smaller bones are chinked in to seal the openings in the walls, plus a plastering of red clay. There's an entranceway made up of gigantic thighbones set up on end. It may all sound bizarre but there's a weird kind of beauty to it and you have no idea, once you're inside, that the bitter winds of the Pleistocene are howling all around you.

The tribe is seminomadic and lives by hunting and gathering. In the summer, which is about two months long, they roam the steppe, killing mammoths and rhinos and musk oxen, and bagging up berries and nuts to get them through the winter. Toward what I would guess is August the weather turns cold and they start to head for their village of bone-houses, hunting reindeer along the way. By the time the really bad weather arrives—think Minnesota-and-a-half—they're settled in for the winter with six months' worth of meat stored in deep-freeze pits in the permafrost. It's an orderly, rhythmic life. There's a real community here. I'd be willing to call it a civilization. But—as I stalk my human prey out here in the cold—I remind myself that life here is harsh and strange. Alien. Maybe I'm doing all this buddy-buddy nickname stuff simply to save my own sanity, you think? I don't know.

If I get killed out here today the thing I'll regret most is never learning their secret religious language and not being able to understand the big historical epic that they sing every night. They just don't want to teach it to me. Evidently it's something outsiders aren't meant to understand.

The epic, Sally tells me, is an immense account of everything that's ever happened: the *Iliad* and the *Odyssey* and the *Encyclopaedia Britannica* all rolled into one, a vast tale of gods and kings and men and warfare and migrations and vanished empires and great calamities. The text is so big and Sally's recounting of it is so sketchy that I have only the foggiest idea of what it's about, but when I hear it I want desperately to understand it. It's the actual history of a forgotten world, the tribal annals of thirty millennia, told in a forgotten language, all of it as lost to us as last year's dreams.

If I could learn it and translate it I would set it all down in writing so that maybe it would be found by archaeologists thousands of years from now. I've been taking notes on these people already, an account of what they're like and how I happen to be living among them. I've made twenty tablets so far, using the same clay that the tribe uses to make its pots and sculptures, and firing it in the same beehive-shaped kiln. It's a godawful slow job writing on slabs of clay with my little bone knife. I bake my tablets and bury them in the cobblestone floor of the house. Somewhere in the twenty-first or twenty-second century a Russian archaeologist will dig them up and they'll give him one hell of a jolt. But of their history, their myths, their poetry, I don't have a thing, because of the language problem. Not a damned thing.

Noon has come and gone. I find some white berries on a glossy-leaved bush and, after only a moment's hesitation, gobble them down. There's a faint sweetness there. I'm still hungry even after I pick the bush clean.

If I were back in the village now, we'd have knocked off work at noon for a lunch of dried fruit and strips of preserved reindeer meat, washed down with mugs of mildly fermented fruit juice. The fermentation is accidental, I think, an artifact of their storage methods. But obviously there are yeasts here and I'd like to try to invent wine and beer. Maybe they'll make me a god for that. This year I invented writing, but I did it for my sake and not for theirs and they aren't much interested in it. I think they'll be more impressed with beer.

A hard, nasty wind has started up out of the east. It's September now and the long winter is clamping down. In half an hour the temperature has dropped fifteen degrees, and I'm freezing. I'm wearing a fur parka and trousers, but that thin icy wind cuts right through. And it scours up the fine dry loose topsoil and flings it in our faces. Someday that light yellow dust will lie thirty feet deep over this village, and over B.J. and Marty and Danny and Paul, and probably over me as well.

Soon they'll be quitting for the day. The house will take eight or ten more days to finish, if early-season snowstorms don't interrupt. I can imagine Paul hitting the drum six good raps to wind things up and everybody making a run for indoors, whooping and hollering. These are high-spirited guys. They jump and shout and sing, punch each other playfully on the arms, brag about the goddesses they've screwed and the holy rhinos they've killed. Not that they're kids. My guess is that they're twenty-five, thirty years old, senior men of the tribe. The life expectancy here seems to be about forty-five. I'm thirty-four. I have a grand-mother alive back in Illinois. Nobody here could possibly believe that. The one I call Zeus, the oldest and richest man in town, looks to be about fifty-three, probably is younger than that, and is generally regarded as favored by the gods because he's lived so long. He's a wild old bastard, still full of bounce and vigor. He lets you know that he keeps those two wives of his busy all night long, even at his age. These are robust people. They lead a tough life, but they don't know that, and so their souls are buoyant. I definitely will try to turn them on to beer next summer, if I last that long and if I can figure out the technology. This could be one hell of a party town.

Sometimes I can't help feeling abandoned by my own time. I know it's irra-tional. It has to be just an accident that I'm marooned here. But there are times when I think the people up there in 2013 simply shrugged and forgot about me when things went wrong, and it pisses me off tremendously until I get it under control. I'm a professionally trained hard-ass. But I'm 20,000 years from home and there are times when it hurts more than I can stand.

Maybe beer isn't the answer. Maybe what I need is a still. Brew up some stronger stuff than beer, a little moonshine to get me through those very black moments when the anger and the really heavy resentment start breaking through.

In the beginning the tribe looked on me, I guess, as a moron. Of course I was in shock. The time trip was a lot more traumatic than the experiments with rabbits and turtles had led us to think.

There I was, naked, dizzy, stunned, blinking and gaping, retching and puking. The air had a bitter acid smell to it—who expected that, that the air would smell different in the past?—and it was so cold it burned my nostrils. I knew at once that I hadn't landed in the pleasant France of the Cro-Magnons but in some harsher, bleaker land far to the east. I could still see the rainbow glow of the Zeller ring, but it was vanishing fast, and then it was gone.

The tribe found me ten minutes later. That was an absolute fluke. I could have wandered for months, encountering nothing but reindeer and bison. I could have frozen; I could have starved. But no, the men I would come to call B.J. and Danny and Marty and Paul were hunting near the place where I dropped out of the sky and they stumbled on me right away. Thank God they didn't see me arrive. They'd have decided that I was a supernatural being and would have expected miracles from me, and I can't do miracles. Instead they simply took me for some poor dope who had wandered so far from home that he didn't know where he was, which after all was essentially the truth.

I must have seemed like one sad case. I couldn't speak their language or any other language they knew. I carried no weapons. I didn't know how to make tools out of flints or sew a fur parka or set up a snare for a wolf or stampede a herd of mammoths into a trap. I didn't know anything, in fact, not a single useful thing. But instead of spearing me on the spot they took me to their village, fed me, clothed me, taught me their language. Threw their arms around me and told me what a great guy I was. They made me one of them. That was a year and a half ago. I'm a kind of holy fool for them, a sacred idiot.

I was supposed to be here just four days and then the Zeller Effect rainbow would come for me and carry me home. Of course within a few weeks I realized that something had gone wonky at the uptime end, that the experiment had malfunctioned and that I probably wasn't ever going to get home. There was that risk all along. Well, here I am, here I stay. First came stinging pain and anger and I suppose grief when the truth finally caught up with me. Now there's just a dull ache that won't go away.

In early afternoon I stumble across the Scavenger Man. It's pure dumb luck. The trail has long since given out—the forest floor is covered with soft pine duff here, and I'm not enough of a hunter to distinguish one spoor from another in that—and I'm simply moving aimlessly when I see some broken branches, and then I get a whiff of burning wood, and I follow that scent twenty or thirty yards over a low rise and there he is, hunkered down by a hastily thrown-together little hearth roasting a couple of ptarmigans on a green spit. A scavenger he may be, but he's a better man than I am when it comes to skulling ptarmigans.

He's really ugly. Jeanne wasn't exaggerating at all.

His head is huge and juts back a long way. His mouth is like a muzzle and his chin is hardly there at all and his forehead slopes down to huge brow ridges like an ape's. His hair is like straw, and it's all over him, though he isn't really shaggy, no hairier than a lot of men I've known. His eyes are gray, yes, and small, deep-set. He's built low and thick, like an Olympic weight lifter. He's wearing a strip of fur around his middle and nothing else. He's an honest-to-God Neanderthal, straight out of the textbooks, and when I see him a chill runs down my spine as though up till this minute I had never really believed that I had traveled 20,000 years in time and now, holy shit, the whole concept has finally become real to me.

He sniffs and gets my wind, and his big brows knit and his whole body goes tense. He stares at me, checking me out, sizing me up. It's very quiet here and we are primordial enemies, face to face with no one else around. I've never felt anything like that before.

We are maybe twenty feet from each other. I can smell him and he can smell me, and it's the smell of fear on both sides. I can't begin to anticipate his move. He rocks back and forth a little, as if getting ready to spring up and come charging, or maybe bolt off into the forest.

But he doesn't do that. The first moment of tension passes and he eases back. He doesn't try to attack, and he doesn't get up to run. He just sits there in a kind of patient, tired way, staring at me, waiting to see what I'm going to do. I wonder if I'm being suckered, set up for a sudden onslaught.

I'm so cold and hungry and tired that I wonder if I'll be able to kill him when he comes at me. For a moment I almost don't care.

Then I laugh at myself for expecting shrewdness and trickery from a Neanderthal man. Between one moment and the next all the menace goes out of him for me. He isn't pretty but he doesn't seem like a goblin, or a demon, just an ugly thick-bodied man sitting alone in a chilly forest.

And I know that sure as anything I'm not going to try to kill him, not because he's so terrifying but because he isn't.

"They sent me out here to kill you," I say, showing him the flint knife.

He goes on staring. I might just as well be speaking Engish, or Sanskrit.

"I'm not going to do it," I tell him. "That's the first thing you ought to know. I've never killed anyone before and I'm not going to begin with a complete stranger. Okay? Is that understood?"

He says something now. His voice is soft and indistinct, but I can tell that he's speaking some entirely other language.

"I can't understand what you're telling me," I say, "and you don't understand me. So we're even."

I take a couple of steps toward him. The blade is still in my hand. He doesn't move. I see now that he's got no weapons and even though he's powerfully built and could probably rip my arms off in two seconds, I'd be able to put the blade into him first. I point to the north, away from the village, and make a broad sweeping gesture. "You'd be wise to head off that way," I say, speaking very slowly and loudly, as if that would matter. "Get yourself out of the neighborhood. They'll kill you otherwise. You understand? *Capisce? Verstehen Sie?* Go. Scat. Scram. I won't kill you, but they will."

I gesture some more, vociferously pantomiming his route to the north. He looks at me. He looks at the knife. His enormous cavernous nostrils widen and flicker. For a moment I think I've misread him in the most idiotically naive way, that he's been simply biding his time getting ready to jump me as soon as I stop making speeches.

Then he pulls a chunk of meat from the bird he's been roasting, and offers it to me.

"I come here to kill you, and you give me lunch?"

He holds it out. A bribe? Begging for his life?

"I can't," I say. "I came here to kill you. Look, I'm just going to turn around and go back, all right? If anybody asks, I never saw you." He waves the meat at me and I begin to salivate as though it's pheasant under glass. But no, no, I can't take his lunch. I point to him, and again to the north, and once more indicate that he ought not to let the sun set on him in this town. Then I turn and start to walk away, wondering if this is the moment when he'll leap up and spring on me from behind and choke the life out of me.

I take five steps, ten, and then I hear him moving behind me.

So this is it. We really are going to fight.

I turn, my knife at the ready. He looks down at it sadly. He's standing there with the piece of meat still in his hand, coming after me to give it to me anyway.

"Jesus," I say. "You're just lonely."

He says something in that soft blurred language of his and holds out the meat. I take it and bolt it down fast, even though it's only half-cooked—dumb Neanderthal!—and I almost gag. He smiles. I don't care what he looks like, if he smiles and shares his food then he's human by me. I smile too. Zeus is going to murder me. We sit down together and watch the other ptarmigan cook, and when it's ready we share it, neither of us saying a word. He has trouble getting a wing off, and I hand him my knife, which he uses in a clumsy way and hands back to me.

After lunch I get up and say, "I'm going back now. I wish to hell you'd head off to the hills before they catch you."

And I turn, and go.

And he follows me like a lost dog who has just adopted a new owner.

So I bring him back to the village with me. There's simply no way to get rid of him short of physically attacking him, and I'm not going to do that. As we emerge from the forest a sickening wave of fear sweeps over me. I think at first it's the roast ptarmigan trying to come back up, but no, it's downright terror, because the Scavenger is obviously planning to stick with me right to the end, and the end is not going to be good. I can see Zeus' blazing eyes, his furious scowl. The thwarted Ice Age chieftain in a storm of wrath. Since I didn't do the job, they will. They'll kill him and maybe they'll kill me too, since I've revealed myself to be a dangerous moron who will bring home the very enemy he was sent out to eliminate.

"This is dumb," I tell the Neanderthal. "You shouldn't be doing this."

He smiles again. You don't understand shit, do you, fellow?

We are past the garbage dump now, past the butchering area. B.J. and his crew are at work on the new house. B.J. looks up when he sees me and his eyes are bright with surprise.

He nudges Marty and Marty nudges Paul, and Paul taps Danny on the shoulder. They point to me and to the Neanderthal. They look at each other. They open their mouths but they don't say anything. They whisper, they shake their heads. They back off a little, and circle around us, gaping, staring.

Christ. Here it comes.

I can imagine what they're thinking. They're thinking that I have really screwed up. That I've brought a ghost home for dinner. Or else an enemy that I was supposed to kill. They're thinking that I'm an absolute lunatic, that I'm an idiot, and now they've got to do the dirty work that I was too dumb to do. And I wonder if I'll try to defend the Neanderthal against them, and what it'll be like if I do. What am I going to do, take them all on at once? And go down swinging as my four sweet buddies close in on me and flatten me into the permafrost? I will. If they force me to it, by God I will. I'll go for their guts with Marty's long stone blade if they try anything on the Neanderthal, or on me.

I don't want to think about it. I don't want to think about any of this.

Then Marty points and claps his hands and jumps about three feet in the air.

"Hey!" he yells. "Look at that! He brought the ghost back with him!"

And then they move in on me, just like that, the four of them, swarming all around me, pressing close, pummeling hard. There's no room to use the knife. They come on too fast. I do what I can with elbows, knees, even teeth. But they pound on me from every side, open fists against my ribs, sides of hands crashing against the meat of my back. The breath goes from me and I come close to toppling as the pain breaks out all over me at once. I need all of my strength, and then some, to keep from going down under their onslaught, and I think, this is a dumb way to die, beaten to death by a bunch of berserk cave men in 20,000 B.C.

But after the first few wild moments things become a bit quieter and I get myself together and manage to push them back from me a little way, and I land a good one that sends Paul reeling backward with blood spouting from his lip, and I whirl toward B.J. and start to take him out, figuring I'll deal with Marty on the rebound. And then I realize that they aren't really fighting with me anymore, and in fact that they never were.

It dawns on me that they were smiling and laughing as they worked me over, that their eyes were full of laughter and love, that if they had truly wanted to work me over it would have taken the four of them about seven and a half seconds to do it.

They're just having fun. They're playing with me in a jolly roughhouse way.

They step back from me. We all stand there quietly for a moment, breathing hard, rubbing our cuts and bruises. The thought of throwing up crosses my mind and I push it away.

"You brought the ghost back," Marty says again.

"Not a ghost," I say. "He's real."

"Not a ghost?"

"Not a ghost, no. He's live. He followed me back here."

"Can you believe it?" B.J. cries. "Live! Followed him back here! Just came marching right in here with him!" He turns to Paul. His eyes are gleaming and for a second I think they're going to jump me all over again. If they do I don't think I'm going to be able to deal with it. But he says simply, "This has to be a song by tonight. This is something special."

"I'm going to get the chief," says Danny, and runs off.

"Look, I'm sorry," I say. "I know what the chief wanted. I just couldn't do it."

"Do what?" B.J. asks. "What are you talking about?" says Paul.

"Kill him," I say. "He was just sitting there by his fire, roasting a couple of birds, and he offered me a chunk, and—"

"*Kill* him?" B.J. says. "You were going to kill him?"

"Wasn't that what I was supposed—"

He goggles at me and starts to answer, but just then Zeus comes running up, and pretty much everyone else in the tribe, the women and the kids too, and they sweep up around us like the tide. Cheering, yelling, dancing, pummeling me, laughing, shouting in that cheerful bone-smashing way of theirs. Forming a ring around the Scavenger Man and throwing their hands in the air. It's a jubilee. Even Zeus is grinning. Marty begins to sing and Paul gets going on the drum. And Zeus comes over to me and embraces me like the big old bear that he is.

"I had it all wrong, didn't I?" I say later to B.J. "You were all just testing me, sure. But not to see how good a hunter I am."

He looks at me without any comprehension at all and doesn't answer. B.J., with that crafty architect's mind of his that takes in everything.

"You wanted to see if I was really human, right? If I had compassion, if I could treat a lost stranger the way I was treated myself."

Blank stares. Deadpan faces.

"Marty? Paul?"

They shrug. Tap their foreheads: the timeless gesture, ages old.

Are they putting me on? I don't know. But I'm certain that I'm right. If I had killed the Neanderthal they almost certainly would have killed me. That must have been it. I need to believe that that was it. All the time that I was congratulating them for not being the savages I had expected them to be, they were wondering how much of a savage *I* was. They had tested the depth of my humanity; and I had passed. And they finally see that I'm civilized too.

At any rate the Scavenger Man lives with us now. Not as a member of the tribe, of course, but as a sacred pet of some sort, a tame chimpanzee, perhaps. He may very well be the last of his kind, or close to it; and though the tribe looks upon him as something dopey and filthy and pathetic, they're not going to do him any harm. To them he's a pitiful bedraggled savage who'll bring good luck if he's treated well. He'll keep the ghosts away. Hell, maybe that's why they took me in, too.

As for me, I've given up what little hope I had of going home. The Zeller rainbow will never return for me, of that I'm altogether sure. But that's all right. I've been through some changes. I've come to terms with it.

We finished the new house yesterday and B.J. let me put the last tusk in place, the one they call the ghost-bone, that keeps dark spirits outside. It's apparently a big honor to be the one who sets up the ghost-bone. Afterward the four of them sang the Song of the House, which is a sort of dedication. Like all their other songs, it's in the old language, the secret one, the sacred one. I couldn't sing it with them, not having the words, but I came in with oom-pahs on the choruses and that seemed to go down pretty well.

I told them that by the next time we need to build a house, I will have invented beer, so that we can all go out when it's finished and get drunk to celebrate properly.

Of course they didn't know what the hell I was talking about, but they looked pleased anyway.

And tomorrow, Paul says, he's going to begin teaching me the other language. The secret one. The one that only the members of the tribe may know.

GEORGE ALEC EFFINGER

Schrödinger's Kitten

Every moment of every day a thousand possible futures die unborn around us, a thousand corners not turned, a thousand roads not taken. Sometimes the *uncertainty* of it all may get to us—but sometimes that very uncertainty may prove to be the finest thing of all. . . .

Perhaps *the* hot young writer of the '70s (he became a full-time writer in 1971), George Alec Effinger has subsequently maintained a reputation as one of the most creative innovators in SF, and one of the genre's finest short-story writers. His short work has appeared everywhere, from *Playboy* to *Haunt of Horror*. His first novel, *What Entropy Means to Me* (recently re-released), is considered a cult classic in some circles, and his most recent, and most popular, novel, the gritty and fascinating *When Gravity Fails*, was a prime contender for a 1987 Hugo Award. His many other books include the novels *The Wolves of Memory*, *The Bird of Time, Those Gentle Voices*, and *Utopia 3*, and the collections *Mixed Feelings, Irrational Numbers*, and *Idle Pleasures*. Upcoming is *A Fire in the Sun*, another book set in the evocative *milieu* of *When Gravity Fails*—as is "Schrödinger's Kitten."

SCHRÖDINGER'S KITTEN

George Alec Effinger

The clean crescent moon that began the new month hung in the western sky across from the alley. Jehan was barely twelve years old, too young to wear the veil, but she did so anyway. She had never before been out so late alone. She heard the sounds of celebration far away, the three-day festival marking the end of the holy month of Ramadan. Two voices sang drunkenly as they passed the alley; two others loudly and angrily disputed the price of some honey cakes. The laughter and the shouting came to Jehan as if from another world. In the past, she'd always loved the festival of Îd-el-Fitr; she took no part in the festivities now, though, and it seemed somehow odd to her that anyone else still could. Soon she gave it all no more of her attention. This year she must keep a meeting more important than any holiday. She sighed, shrugging: The festival would come around again next year. Tonight, with only the silver moon for company, she shivered in her blue-black robe.

Jehan Fatima Ashûfi stepped back a few feet deeper into the alley, farther out of the light. All along the street, people who would otherwise never be seen in this quarter were determinedly amusing themselves. Jehan shivered again and waited. The moment she longed for would come at dawn. Even now the sky was just dark enough to reveal the moon and the first impetuous stars. In the Islamic world, night began when one could no longer distinguish a white thread from a black one; it was not yet night. Jehan clutched her robe closely to her with her left hand. In her right hand, hidden by her long sleeve, was the keen-edged, gleaming, curved blade she had taken from her father's room.

She was hungry and wished she had money to buy something to eat, but she had none. In the Budayeen there were many girls her age who already had ways of getting money of their own; Jehan was not one of them. She glanced about and saw only the filth-strewn, damp, and muddy paving stones. The reek of the alley disgusted her. She was bored and lonely and afraid. Then, as if her whole sordid world suddenly dissolved into something else, something wholly foreign, she saw more.

*   *   *

Jehan Ashûfi was twenty-six years old. She was dressed in a conservative dark gray woolen suit, cut longer and more severely than fashion dictated but appropriate for a bright young physicist. She affected no jewelry and wore her black hair in a long braid down her back. She took a little effort each morning to look as plain as possible while she was accompanying her eminent teacher and adviser. That had been Heisenberg's idea: In these days who believed a beautiful woman could also be a highly talented scientist? Jehan soon learned that her wish of being inconspicuous was in vain. Her dark skin and her accent marked her as a foreigner. She was clearly not European. Possibly she had Levantine blood. Most who met her thought she was probably a Jew. This was Göttingen, Germany, and it was 1925.

The brilliant Max Born, who had first used the expression *quantum mechanics* in a paper written two years before, was leading a meeting of the university's physicists. They were discussing Max Planck's latest proposals concerning his own theories of radiation. Planck had developed some basic ideas in the emerging field of quantum physics, yet he had used classical Newtonian mechanics to describe the interactions of light and matter. It was clear that this approach was inadequate, but as yet there was no better system. At the Göttingen conference, Pascual Jordan rose to introduce a compromise solution; but before Born, the department chairman, could reply, Werner Heisenberg fell into a violent fit of sneezing.

"Are you all right, Werner?" asked Born.

Heisenberg merely waved a hand. Jordan attempted to continue, but again Heisenberg began sneezing. His eyes were red, and tears crept down his face. He was in obvious distress. He turned to his graduate assistant. "Jehan," he said, "please make immediate arrangements; I must get away. It's my damned hay fever. I want to leave at once."

One of the others at the meeting objected. "But the colloquium—"

Heisenberg was already on his feet. "You can tell Planck to go straight to hell and to take De Broglie and his matter waves with him. The same goes for Bohr and his goddamn jumping electrons. I can't stand any more of this." Heisenberg took a few shaky steps and left the room. Jehan stayed behind to make a few notations in her journal. Then she followed Heisenberg back to their apartments.

There were no minarets in the Budayeen, but in the city all around the walled quarter there were many mosques. From the tall, ancient towers, strong voices called the faithful to morning devotions. "Come to prayer, come to prayer! Prayer is better than sleep!"

Leaning against a grimy wall, Jehan heard the chanted cries of the muezzins, but she paid them no mind. She stared at the dead body at her feet, the body of a boy a few years older than she, someone she had seen about the Budayeen but whom she did not know by name. She still held the bloody knife that had killed him.

In a short while three men pushed their way through a crowd that had formed at the mouth of the alley. The three men looked down solemnly at Jehan. One was a police officer; one was a qadi, who interpreted the ancient Islamic commandments as they applied to modern life; and the third was an imam, a prayer leader who had hurried from a small mosque not far from the east gate of the Budayeen. Within the walls the pickpockets, whores, thieves, and cut-throats could do as they liked to each other. A death in the Budayeen didn't attract much attention in the rest of the city.

The police officer was tall and heavily built, with a thick black mustache and sleepy eyes. He was curious only because he had watched over the Budayeen for fifteen years, and he had never investigated a murder by a girl so young.

The qadi was young, clean-shaven, and quite plainly deferring to the imam. It was not yet clear to those in attendance if this matter should be the responsibility of the civil or the religious authorities.

The imam was tall, taller even than the police officer, but thin and narrow shouldered; yet it was not asceticism that made him so slight. He was well-known for two things: his common sense concerning the conflicts of everyday affairs and the high degree of earthly pleasures he permitted himself. He, too, was puzzled and curious. He wore a short, grizzled gray beard, and his soft brown eyes were all but hidden within the reticulation of wrinkles that had slowly etched his face. Like the police officer, the imam had once worn a brave black mustache, but the days of fierceness had long since passed for him. Now he appeared decent and kindly. In truth, he was neither; but he found it useful to cultivate that reputation.

"O my daughter," he said in his hoarse voice. He was very upset. He much preferred explicating obscure passages of the glorious Qur'an to viewing such tawdry matters as blatant dead bodies in the nearby streets.

Jehan looked up at him, but she said nothing. She looked back down at the unknown boy she had killed.

"O my daughter," said the imam, "tell me, was it thou who hath slain this child?"

Jehan looked back calmly at the old man. She was concealed beneath her kerchief, veil, and robe; all that was visible of her were her dark eyes and the long thin fingers that held the knife. "Yes, O Wise One," she said, "I killed him."

The police officer glanced at the qadi.

"Prayest thou to Allah?" asked the imam. If this hadn't been the Budayeen, he wouldn't have needed to ask.

"Yes," said Jehan. And it was true. She had prayed on several occasions in her lifetime, and she might yet pray again sometime.

"And knowest thou there is a prohibition against taking of human life that Allah hath made sacred?"

"Yes, O Wise One."

"And knowest thou further that Allah hath set a penalty upon those who breaketh this law?"

"Yes, I know."

"Then, O my daughter, tell us why thou hath brought low this poor boy."

Jehan tossed the bloody knife to the stone-paved alley. It rang noisily and then came to rest against one leg of the corpse. "I killed him because he would do me harm in the future," she said.

"He threatened you?" asked the qadi.

"No, O Respected One."

"Then—"

"Then how art thou certain that he would do thee harm?" the imam finished.

Jehan shrugged. "I have seen it many times. He would throw me to the ground and defile me. I have seen the visions."

A murmur grew from the crowd still cluttering the mouth of the alley behind Jehan and the three men. The imam's shoulders slumped. The police officer waited patiently. The qadi looked discouraged. "Then he didst not offer thee harm this morning?" said the imam.

"No."

"Indeed, as thou sayest, he hath *never* offered thee harm?"

"No. I do not know him. I have never spoken with him."

"Yet," said the qadi, clearly unhappy, "you murdered him because of what you have seen? As in a dream?"

"As in a dream, O Respected One, but more truly as in a vision."

"A dream," muttered the imam. "The Prophet, mayest blessings be on his name and peace, didst offer no absolution for murder provoked only by dreams."

A woman in the crowd cried out, "But she is only twelve years old!"

The imam turned and pushed his way through the rabble.

"Sergeant," said the qadi, "this young girl is now in your custody. The Straight Path makes our duty clear."

The police officer nodded and stepped forward. He bound the young girl's wrists and pushed her forward through the alley. The crowd of fellahin parted to make way for them. The sergeant led Jehan to a small, dank cell until she might have a hearing. A panel of religious elders would judge her according to Shari'a, the contemporary code of laws derived from the ancient and noble Qur'an. Jehan did not suffer in her noxious cell. A lifetime in the Budayeen had made her familiar with deprivation. She waited patiently for whatever outcome Allah intended.

She did not wait long. She was given another brief hearing, during which the council asked her many of the same questions the imam had asked. She answered them all without hesitation. Her judges were saddened but compelled to render their verdict. They gave her an opportunity to change her statement, but she refused. At last the senior member of the panel stood to face her. "O young one," he said in the most reluctant of voices, "the Prophet, blessings be on his name and peace, said, 'Whoso slayeth a believer, his reward is hell forever.' And elsewhere, 'Who killeth a human being for other than manslaughter or corruption in the earth, it shall be as if he killed all mankind.' Therefore, if he whom you slew had purposed corruption upon you, your act would have been justified. Yet you deny this. You rely on your dreams, your visions. Such insubstantial defense cannot persuade this council otherwise than that you are guilty. You must pay the penalty as it is written. It shall be exacted tomorrow morning just before sunrise."

Jehan's expression did not change. She said nothing. Of her many visions, she had witnessed this particular scene before also. Sometimes, as now, she was condemned; sometimes she was freed. That evening she ate a good meal, a better meal than most she had taken before in her life of poverty. She slept the night, and she was ready when the civil and religious officials came for her in the morning. An imam of great repute spoke to her at length, but Jehan did not listen carefully. The remaining acts and motions of her life seemed mechanically ordered, and she did not pay great heed to them. She followed where she was led, she responded dully when pressed for a reply, and she climbed the platform set up in the courtyard of the great Shimaal Mosque.

"Dost thou feel regret?" asked the imam, laying a gentle hand on her shoulder.

Jehan was made to kneel with her head on the block. She shrugged. "No," she said.

"Dost thou feel anger, O my daughter?"

"No."

"Then mayest Allah in His mercy grant thee peace." The imam stepped away. Jehan had no view of the headsman, but she heard the collective sigh of the onlookers as the great ax lifted high in the first faint rays of dawn, and then the blade fell.

Jehan shuddered in the alley. Watching her death always made her exceptionally uneasy. The hour wasn't much later; the fifth and final call to prayer had sounded not long before, and now it was night. The celebration continued around her more intensely than before. That her intended deed might end on the headsman's block did not deter her. She grasped the knife tightly, wishing that time would pass more swiftly, and she thought of other things.

By the end of May 1925 they were settled in a hotel on the tiny island of Helgoland some fifty miles from the German coast. Jehan relaxed in a comfortably furnished room. The landlady made her husband put Heisenberg's and Jehan's luggage in the best and most expensive room. Heisenberg had every hope of ridding himself of his allergic afflictions. He also intended to make some sense of the opaque melding of theories and countertheories put forward by his colleagues back in Göttingen. Meanwhicle the landlady gave Jehan a grim and glowering look at their every meeting but said nothing. The Herr Doktor himself was too preoccupied to care for anything as trivial as propriety, morals, the reputation of this Helgoland retreat, or Jehan's peace of mind. If anyone raised eyebrows over the arrangement, Heisenberg certainly was blithely unaware; he walked around as if he were insensible to everything but the pollen count and the occasional sheer cliffs over which he sometimes came close to tumbling.

Jehan was mindful of the old woman's disapproval. Jehan, however, had lived a full, harsh life in her twenty-six years, and a raised eyebrow rated very low on her list of things to be concerned about. She had seen too many people abandoned to starvation, too many people dispossessed and reduced to beggary, too many outsiders slain in the name of Allah, too many maimed or beheaded through the convoluted workings of Islamic justice. All these years Jehan had kept her father's bloodied dagger, packed now beneath her shetland wool sweaters and still as deadly as ever.

Heisenberg's health improved on the island, and there was a beautiful view of the sea from their room. His mood brightened quickly. One morning, while walking along the shoreline with him, Jehan read a passage from the glorious Qur'an. "This sura is called 'The Earthquake,' " she said. " 'In the name of Allah, the Beneficent, the Merciful. When Earth is shaken with her final earthquake, and Earth yields up her burdens and man saith: What aileth her? That day she will relate her chronicles, because thy Lord inspireth her. That day mankind will issue forth in separate groups to be shown their deeds. And whoso doeth good an atom's weight will see it then. And whoso doeth ill an atom's weight will see it then.' "

And Jehan wept, knowing that however much good she might do, it could never outweigh the wrongs she had already performed. But Heisenberg only stared out over the gray, tumbling waves of the ocean. He did not listen closely to the sacred verses, yet a few of Jehan's words struck him. " 'And whoso doeth good an atom's weight will see it then,' " he said, emphasizing the single word. There was a small, hesitant smile quivering at the corners of his mouth. Jehan put her arm around him to comfort him because he seemed chilled, and she led him back to the hotel. The weather had turned colder, and the air was misty with sea spray; together they listened to the cries of the herring gulls as the birds dived for fish or hovered screeching over the strip of beach. Jehan thought of what she'd read, of the end of the world. Heisenberg thought only of its beginning, and its still closely guarded secrets.

They liked their daily peaceful walk about the island. Now, more than ever before, Jehan carried with her a copy of the Qur'an, and she often read short verses to him. So different from the biblical literature he'd heard all his life,

Heisenberg let the Islamic scriptures pass without comment. Yet it seemed to him that certain specific images offered their meanings to him alone.

Jehan saw at last that he was feeling well. Heisenberg took up again full-time the tangled knot that was the current state of quantum physics. It was both his vocation and his means of relaxation. He told Jehan the best scientific minds in the world were frantically working to cobble together a slipshod mathematical model, one that might account for all the observed data. Whatever approach they tried, the data would not fit together. *He*, however, would find the key; he was that confident. He wasn't quite sure how he'd do it, but, of course, he hadn't yet really applied himself thoroughly to the question.

Jehan was not amused. She read to him: " 'Hast thou not seen those who pretend that they believe in that which is revealed unto thee and that which was revealed before thee, how they would go for judgment in their disputes to false deities when they have been ordered to abjure them? Satan would lead them far astray.' "

Heisenberg laughed heartily. "Your Allah isn't just talking about Göttingen there," he said. "He's got Bohr in mind, too, and Einstein in Berlin."

Jehan frowned at his impiety. It was the irreverence and ignorant ridicule of the kaffir, the unbeliever. She wondered if the old religion that had never truly had any claim on her was yet still part of her. She wondered how she'd feel after all these years, walking the narrow, crowded, clangorous ways of the Budayeen again. "You mustn't speak that way," she said at last.

"Hmm?" said Heisenberg. He had already forgotten what he'd said to her.

"Look out there," said Jehan. "What do you see?"

"The ocean," said Heisenberg. "Waves."

"Allah created those waves. What do *you* know about that?"

"I could determine their frequency. I could measure their amplitude."

"Measure!" cried Jehan. Her own long years of scientific study were suddenly overshadowed by an imagined insult to her heritage. "Look here," she demanded. "A handful of sand. Allah created this sand. What do *you* know about it?"

Heisenberg couldn't see what Jehan was trying to tell him. "With the proper instruments," he said, a little afraid of offending her, "in the proper setting, I could take a single grain of sand and tell you—" His words broke off suddenly. He got to his feet slowly, like an old man. He looked first at the sea, then down at the shore, then back out at the water. "Waves," he murmured, "particles, it makes no difference. All that counts is what we can actually measure. We can't measure Bohr's orbits, because they don't really *exist*! So the spectral lines we see are caused by transitions between two states. Pairs of states, yes; but that will mean a new form of mathematical expression just to describe them, referencing tables listing every possible—"

"Werner." Jehan knew that he was now lost to her.

"Just the computations alone will take days, if not weeks."

"Werner, *listen* to me. This island is so small, you can throw a stone from one end to the other. I'm not going to sit on this freezing beach or up on your bleak and dreary cliff while you make your brilliant breakthrough, whatever it is. I'm saying good-bye."

"What? Jehan?" Heisenberg blinked and returned to the tangible world.

She couldn't face him any longer. She was pouring one handful of sand through the fingers of her other hand.

It came suddenly to her mind then: If you had no water to perform the necessary ablution before prayer in the direction of Mecca, you were permitted to wash with clean sand instead. She began to weep. She couldn't hear what Heisenberg was saying to her—if indeed he was.

It was a couple of hours later in the alley now, and it was getting even colder. Jehan wrapped herself in her robe and paced back and forth.

She'd had visions of this particular night for four years, glimpses of the possible ways that it might conclude. Sometimes the young man saw her in the alley shortly after dawn, sometimes he didn't. Sometimes she killed him, sometimes she didn't. And, of course, there was the open question of whether her actions would lead to her freedom or to her execution.

When she'd had the first vision, she hadn't known what was happening or what she was seeing. She knew only the fear and the pain and the terror. The boy threw her roughly to the ground, ripped her clothing, and raped her. Then the vision passed. Jehan told no one about it; her family would have thought her insane. About three months later, the vision returned; only this time it was different in subtle ways. She was in the alley as before, but this time she smiled and gestured to the boy, inviting him. He smiled in return and followed her deeper into the alley. When he put his hand on her shoulder, she drew her father's dagger and plunged it into the boy's belly. That was as much as the vision showed her then. It terrified her even more than the rape scene had.

As time passed, the visions took on other forms. She was certain now that she was not always watching *her* future, *the* future, but rather a future, each as likely to come to pass as the others. Not all the visions could possibly be true. In some of them, she saw herself living into her old age in the city, right here in this filthy quarter of the Budayeen. In others she moved about strange places that didn't seem Islamic at all, and she spoke languages definitely not Arabic. She did not know if these conflicting visions were trying to tell her or warn her of something. Jehan prayed to know which of these versions she must actually live through. Soon after, as if to reward her for her faith, she began to have less violent visions: She could look into the future a short way and find lost objects or warn against unlucky travel plans or predict the rise and fall of crop prices. The neighbors, at first amused, began to be afraid of her. Jehan's mother counseled her never to speak of these "dreams" to anyone, or else Jehan might be locked away in some horrible institution. Jehan never told her father about her visions, because Jehan never told her father about anything. In that family, as in the others of the Budayeen—and the rest of the city, for that matter—the father did not concern himself very much with his daughters. His sons were his pride, and he had three strong sons whom he firmly believed would someday vastly increase the Ashûfi prestige and wealth. Jehan knew he was wrong, because she'd already seen what would become of the sons—two would be killed in wars against the Jews; the third would be a coward, a weakling, and a fugitive in the United States. But Jehan said nothing.

A vision: It was just past dawn. The young man—whose name Jehan never learned—was walking down the stone-paved street toward her alley. Jehan knew it without even peering out. She took a deep breath. She walked a few steps toward the street, looked left, and caught his eye. She made a brief gesture, turned her back, and went deeper into the shadowy seclusion of the alley. She was certain that he would follow her. Her stomach ached and rumbled, and she was shaking with nervous exhaustion. When the young man put his hand on her shoulder, murmuring indecent suggestions, her hand crept toward the concealed knife, but she did not grasp it. He threw her down roughly, clawed off her clothing, and raped her. Then he left her there. She was almost paralyzed, crying and cursing on the wet, foul-smelling stones. She was found sometime later by two women who took her to a doctor. Their worst fears were confirmed: Her honor had been ravaged irredeemably. Her life was effectively over, in the sense of becoming a normal adult female in that Islamic community. One of the women returned to Jehan's house with her, to tell the news to Jehan's mother, who must still tell Jehan's father. Jehan hid in the room she shared with her sisters. She heard the violent breaking of furniture and shrill obscenity of her father. There was nothing more to be done. Jehan did not know the name of her assailant. She was ruined, less than worthless. A young woman no longer a virgin could command no bride price. All those years of supporting a worthless daughter in the hopes of recovering the investment in the marriage contract—all vanished now. It was no surprise that Jehan's father felt betrayed and the father of a witless creature. There was no sympathy for Jehan; the actual story, whatever it might be, could not alter the facts. She had only the weeping of her sisters and her mother. From that morning on, Jehan was permanently repudiated and cast out from her house. Jehan's father and three brothers would not even look at her or offer her their farewells.

The years passed ever more quickly. Jehan became a woman of the streets. For a time, because of her youth and beauty, she earned a good living. Then as the decades left their unalterable blemishes upon her, she found it difficult even to earn enough for a meal and a room to sleep in. She grew older, more bitter, and filled with self-loathing. Did she hate her father and the rest of her family?

No, her fate had been fixed by the will of Allah, however impossible it was for her to comprehend it, or else by her own timidity in the single moment of choice and destiny in the alley so many years before. She could not say. Whatever the answer, she could not benefit now from either insight or wisdom. Her life was as it was, according to the inscrutable designs of Allah the Merciful. Her understanding was not required.

Eventually she was found dead, haggard and starved, and her corpse was contorted and huddled for warmth coincidentally in the same alley where the young man had so carelessly despoiled any chance Jehan had for happiness in this world. After she died, there was no one to mourn her. Perhaps Allah the Beneficent took pity on her, showing mercy to her who had received little enough mercy from her neighbors while she lived among them. It had always been a cold place for Jehan.

For a while estranged from Heisenberg, Jehan worked with Erwin Schrödinger in Zurich. At first Schrödinger's ideas confused her because they went against many of Heisenberg's basic assumptions. For the time being, Heisenberg rejected any simple picture of what the atom was like, any model at all. Schrödinger, older and more conservative than the Göttingen group, wanted to explain quantum phenomena without new mathematics and elusive imagery. He treated the electron as a wave function but a different sort of wave than De Broglie's. The properties of waves in the physical world were well-known and without ambiguity. Yet when Schrödinger calculated how a change in energy level affected his electron wave, his solutions didn't agree with observed data.

"What am I overlooking?" he asked.

Jehan shook her head. "Where I was born they say, 'Don't pour away the water in your canteen because of a mirage.'"

Schrödinger rubbed his weary eyes. He glanced down at the sheaf of papers he held. "How can I tell if this water is worth keeping or something that belongs in a sewer?" Jehan had no reply to that, and Schrödinger set his work aside, unsatisfied. A few months later several papers showed that after taking into account the relativistic effects, Schrödinger's calculations agreed remarkably well with experimental results after all.

Schrödinger was pleased. "I knew in my heart that quantum physics would prove to be a sane world, not a realm populated by phantoms and governed by ghost forces."

"It seems unreal to me now," said Jehan. "If you say the electron is a wave, you are saying it is a phantom. In the ocean, it is the water that is the wave. As for sound, it is the air that carries the wave. What exists to be a wave in your equations?"

"It is a wave of probability," Bohr says. "I do not wholly understand that yet myself," he said, "but my equations explain too many things to be illusions."

"Sir," said Jehan, frowning, "it may be that in this case the mirage is in your canteen and not before you in the desert."

Schrödinger laughed. "That might be true. I may yet have to abandon my mental pictures, but I will not abandon my mathematics."

It was a breathless afternoon in the city. The local Arabs didn't seem to be bothered by the heat, but the small party of Europeans was beginning to suffer. Their cruise ship had put ashore at the small port, and a tour had been arranged to the city some fifty miles to the south. Two hours later the travelers concluded that the expedition had been a mistake.

Among them was David Hilbert, the German mathematician, a lecturer at Göttingen since 1895. He was accompanied by his wife, Käthe, and their maid, Clärchen. At first they were quite taken by the strangeness of the city, by the foreign sights and sounds and smells; but after a short time, their senses were glutted with newness, and what had at first been exotic was now only deplorable. As they moved slowly through the bazaars, shaded ineffectually by awnings or meager arcades of sticks, they longed for the whisper of a single cool breeze. Arab men dressed in long white *gallebeyas* cried out shrilly, all the while glaring at the Europeans. It was impossible to tell what the Arabs were saying. Some dragged little carts loaded with filthy cups and pots—water? Tea? Lemonade? It made no difference. Cholera lingered at every stall; every beggar offered typhus as he clutched at sleeves.

Hilbert's wife fanned herself weakly. She was almost overcome and near collapse. Hilbert looked about desperately. "David," murmured the maid Clärchen, the only one of Hilbert's amours Frau Hilbert could tolerate, "we have come far enough."

"I know," he said, "but I see nothing—nowhere—"

"There are some ladies and gentlemen in that place. I think it's an eating place. Leave Käthe with me there and find a taxi. Then we shall go back to the boat."

Hilbert hesitated. He couldn't bear to leave the two unprotected women in the midst of this frantic heathen marketplace. Then he saw how pale his wife had become, how her eyelids drooped, how she swayed against Clärchen's shoulder. He nodded. "Let me help," he said. Together they got Frau Hilbert to the restaurant, where it was no cooler but at least the ceiling fans created a fiction of fresh air. Hilbert introduced himself to a well-dressed man who was seated at a table with his family, a wife and four children. The mathematician tried three languages before he was understood. He explained the situation, and the gentleman and his wife both assured Hilbert that he need not worry. Hilbert ran out to find a taxi.

He was soon lost. There were no streets here, not in the European sense of the word. Narrow spaces between buildings became alleys, opened into small squares, closed again; other narrow passages led off in twisting, bewildering directions. Hilbert found himself back at a souk; he thought at first it was where he'd begun and looked for the restaurant, but he was wrong. This was another souk entirely; there were probably hundreds in the city. He was beginning to panic. Even if he managed to find a taxi, how could he direct it back to where his wife and Clärchen waited?

A man's hand plucked at him. Hilbert tried to shrug the long fingers away. He looked into the face of a lean, hollowcheeked man in a striped robe and a blue knitted cap. The Arab kept repeating a few words, but Hilbert could make no sense of them. The Arab took him by the arm and half-led, half-shoved Hilbert through the crowd. Hilbert let himself be guided. They crossed through two bazaars, one of tinsmiths and one of poultry dressers. They entered a stone-paved street and emerged into an immense square. On the far side of the square was a huge, many-towered mosque, built of pink stone. Hilbert's first impression was awe; it was as lovely an edifice as the Taj. Then his guide was pushing him again through the throng or hurrying in front to hew a path for Hilbert. The square was jammed and choked with people. Soon Hilbert could see why—a platform had been erected in the center, and on it stood a man with what could only be an executioner's ax. Hilbert felt his stomach sicken. His Arab guide had thrust aside everyone in their way until Hilbert stood at the foot of the platform. He saw uniformed police and a bearded old man leading out a young girl. The crowd parted to allow them by. The girl was stunningly lovely. Hilbert looked into her huge, dark eyes—''like the eyes of a gazelle,'' he remembered from reading Omar Khayyám—and glimpsed her slender form undisguised by her modest garments. As she mounted the steps, she looked down directly at him again. Hilbert felt his heart lurch; he felt a tremendous shudder. Then she looked away.

The Arab guide screamed in Hilbert's ear. It meant nothing to the mathematician. He watched in horror as Jehan knelt, as the headsman raised his weapon of office. When the fierce, bellowing cry went up from the crowd, Hilbert noticed that his suit was now spattered with small flecks of red. The Arab screamed at him again and tightened his grip on Hilbert's arm until Hilbert complained. The Arab did not release him. With his other hand, Hilbert took out his wallet. The Arab smiled. Above him, Hilbert watched several men carry away the body of the decapitated girl.

The Arab guide did not let him go until he'd paid an enormous sum.

Perhaps another hour had passed in the alley. Jehan had withdrawn to the darkest part and sat in a damp corner with her legs drawn up, her head against the rough brick wall. If she could sleep, she told herself, the night would pass more quickly; but she would not sleep, she would fight it if drowsiness threatened. What if she should slip into slumber and waken in the late morning, her peril and her opportunity both long since lost? Her only companion, the crescent moon, had abandoned her; she looked up at fragments of constellations, stars familiar enough in their groups but indistinguishable now as individuals. How different from people, where the opposite was true. She sighed; she was not a profound person, and it did not suit her to have profound thoughts. These must not truly be profound thoughts, she decided; she was merely deluded by weariness. Slowly she let her head fall forward. She crossed her arms on her knees and cradled her head. The greater part of the night had already passed, and only silence came from the street. There were perhaps only three more hours until dawn. . . .

Soon Schrödinger's wave mechanics was proved to be equivalent to Heisenberg's matrix mechanics. It was a validation of both men's work and of the whole field of quantum physics as well. Eventually Schrödinger's simplistic wave picture of the electron was abandoned, but his mathematical laws remained undisputed. Jehan remembered Schrödinger predicting that he might need to take just that step.

Jehan had at last returned to Göttingen and Heisenberg. He had "forgiven her petulance." He welcomed her gladly, because of his genuine feelings for her and because he had much work to do. He had just formally developed what came to be known as the Heisenberg uncertainty principle. This was the first indication that the impartial observer could not help but play an essential, active role in the universe of subatomic particles. Jehan grasped Heisenberg's concept readily. Other scientists thought Heisenberg was merely making a trivial criticism of the limitations of their experiments or the quality of their observations. It was more profound than that. Heisenberg was saying that one can never hope to know both the position and momentum of an electron at the same time under *any* circumstances. He had destroyed forever the assumption of the impartial observer.

"To observe is to disturb," said Heisenberg. "Newton wouldn't have liked any of this at all."

"Einstein still doesn't like it right this very minute," said Jehan.

"I wish I had a mark for every time he's made that sour 'God doesn't play dice with the universe' comment."

"That's just the way he sees a 'wave of probability.' The path of the electron can't be known unless you look; but once you look, you change the information."

"So maybe God doesn't play dice with the universe," said Heisenberg. "He plays vingt-et-un, and if He does not have an extra ace up His sleeve, He creates one—first the sleeve, then the ace. And He turns over more natural twenty-ones than is statistically likely. Hold on, Jehan! I'm not being sacrilegious. I'm not saying that God cheats. Rather, He invented the rules of the game, and He *continues* to invent them; and this gives Him a rather large advantage over poor physicists and their lagging understanding. We are like peasants watching the card tricks of someone who may be either genius or charlatan."

Jehan pondered this metaphor. "At the Solvay conference, Bohr introduced his complementarity idea, that an electron was a wave function until it was detected, and then the wave function collapsed to a point, and you knew where the electron was. Then it was a particle. Einstein didn't like that, either.''

"That's God's card trick," said Heisenberg, shrugging.

"Well, the noble Qur'an says, 'They question thee about strong drink and games of chance. Say: In both is great sin, and some usefulness for men; but the sin of them is greater than their usefulness.' ''

"Forget dice and cards, then," said Heisenberg with a little smile. "What kind of game *would* it be appropriate for Allah to play against us?"

"Physics," said Jehan, and Heisenberg laughed.

"And knowest thou there is a prohibition against taking of human life that Allah hath made sacred?"

"Yes, O Wise One."

"And knowest thou further that Allah hath set a penalty upon those who breaketh this law?"

"Yes, I know."

"Then, O my daughter, tell us why thou hath brought low this poor boy."

Jehan tossed the bloody knife to the stone-paved alley. It rang noisily and then came to rest against one leg of the corpse. "I was celebrating the Îd-el-Fitr," she said. "This boy followed me, and I became afraid. He made filthy gestures and called out terrible things. I hurried away, but he ran after me. He grabbed me by the shoulders and pressed me against a wall. I tried to escape, but I could not. He laughed at my fear, then he struck me many times. He dragged me along through the narrowest of streets, where there were not many to witness; and then he pulled me into this vile place. He told me that he intended to defile me, and he described what he would do in foul detail. It was then that I drew my father's dagger and stabbed him. I have spent the night in horror of his intentions and of my deed, and I have prayed to Allah for forgiveness."

The imam put a trembling hand on Jehan's cheek. "Allah is All-Wise and All-Forgiving, O my daughter. Alloweth me to return with thee to thy house, where I may put the hearts of thy parents at ease."

Jehan knelt at the imam's feet. "All thanks be to Allah," she murmured.

"Allah be praised," said the imam, the police officer, and the qadi together.

More than a decade later, when Jehan had daughters of her own, she told them this story. But in those latter days children did not heed the warnings of their parents, and the sons and daughters of Jehan and her husband did many foolish things.

Dawn slipped even into the narrow alleyway where Jehan waited. She was very sleepy and hungry, but she stood up and took a few wobbling steps. Her muscles had become cramped, and she could hear her heart beating in her ears.

Jehan steadied herself with one hand on the brick wall. She went slowly to the mouth of the alley and peered out. There was no one in sight. The boy was coming neither from the left nor the right. Jehan waited until several other people appeared, going about the business of the new day. Then she hid the dagger in her sleeve once more and departed from the alley. She hurried back to her father's house. Her mother would need her to help make breakfast.

Jehan was in her early forties now, her black hair cut short, her eyes framed by clumsy spectacles, her beauty stolen by care, poor diet, and sleeplessness. She wore a white lab coat and carried a clipboard, as much a part of her as her title, Fräulein Professor Doktor Ashûfi. This was not Göttingen any longer; it was Berlin, and a war was being lost. She was still with Heisenberg. He had protected her until her own scientific credentials became protection of themselves. At that point, the Nazi officials were compelled to make her an "honorary" Aryan, as they had the Jewish physicists and mathematicians whose cooperation they needed. It had been only Jehan's long-standing loyalty to Heisenberg himself that kept her in Germany at all. The war was of little concern to her; these were not her people, but neither were the British, the French, the Russians, or the Americans. Her only interest was in her work, in the refinement of physics, in the unending anticipation of discovery.

She was glad, therefore, when the German atomic bomb project was removed from the control of the German army and given to the Reich Research Council. One of the first things to be done was the calling of a research conference at the Kaiser Wilhelm Institute of Physics in Berlin. The conference would be conducted under the tightest security; no preliminary list of topics would be released in advance, so that no foreign agents might see such terms as *fission cross sections* and *isotope enrichment*, leading to speculation on the long-term goals of these physicists.

At the same time, the Reich Research Council decided to hold a second conference for the benefit of the government's highest officials on the same day. The idea was that the scientists speaking at the Kaiser Wilhelm Institute's meeting could present short, elementary summaries of their work in plain language so that the political and military leaders could be briefed on the progress that was being made toward a nuclear weapon. Then, following the laymen's presentation, the physicists could gather and discuss the same matters in their more technical jargon.

Heisenberg thought it was a good idea. It was 1942, and material, political support, and funding were getting more difficult to find. The army wanted to put all available research resources into the rocketry program; they argued that the nuclear experiments were not showing sufficient success. Heisenberg was a theoretical physicist, not an engineer; he could not find a way to tell the council that the development of the uranium bomb must necessarily be slow and methodical.

Each new step forward in theory had to be tested carefully, and each experiment was expensive in both time and money. The Reich, however, cared only for positive results.

One evening Jehan was alone in an administrative office of the Reich Research Council, typing her proposal for an important test of their isotope-separation technique. She saw on the desk two stacks of papers. One stack listed the simple synopses the physicists had prepared for the Reich ministers who had little or no background in science. She took those papers and hid them in her briefcase. The second stack was the secret agenda for the physicists' own meeting: "Nuclear Physics as a Weapon," by Professor Dr. Schumann; "The Fission of the Uranium Atom," by Professor Dr. Hahn; "The Theoretical Basis for the Production of Energy from the Fission of Uranium," by Heisenberg; and so on. Each person attending the technical seminar would be given a program after he entered the lecture hall, and he would be required to sign for it. Jehan thought for a long while in the quiet office. She remembered her wretched childhood. She recalled her arrival in Europe and the people she had come to know, the life she had come to lead here. She thought about how Germany had changed while she hid in her castle of scientific abstractions, uninvolved with the outside world. At last she thought about what this new Germany might do with the uranium bomb. She knew exactly what she must do.

It took her only a few moments to take the highly technical agendas and drop them into the already-addressed envelopes to be sent to the Third Reich's leaders. She had guaranteed that the brief introductory discussion would be attended by no one. Jehan could easily imagine the response the unintelligible scientific papers would get from the political and military leaders—curt, polite regrets that they would not be in Berlin on that day, or that their busy schedules prevented them from attending. It was all so easy. The Reich's rulers did not hear the talks, and they did not learn how close Germany was to developing an atomic bomb. Never again was there any hope that such a weapon could be built in time to save the Reich—all because the wrong invitations had been slipped into a few envelopes.

Jehan awoke from a dream and saw that the night had grown very old. It would not be long before the sun began to flood the sky with light. Soon she would have a resolution to her anxiety. She would learn if the boy would come to the alley or stay away. She would learn if he would rape her or if she would find the courage to defend herself. She would learn if she would be judged guilty or innocent of murder. She would be granted a glimpse of the outcome to all things that concerned her.

Nevertheless, she was so tired, hungry, and uncomfortable that she was tempted to give up her vigil. The urge to go home was strong. Yet she had always believed that her visions were gifts granted by Allah, and it might offend Him to ignore the clear warnings. For Allah's sake, as well as her own, she reluctantly chose to wait out the rest of the dying night. She had seen so many visions since last evening—more than on any other day of her life—some new, some familiar from years past. It was, in a small, human way, almost comparable to the Night of Power that was bestowed upon the Prophet, may Allah's blessings be on him and peace. Then Jehan felt guilty and blasphemous for comparing herself to the Messenger that way.

She got down on her knees and faced toward Mecca and addressed a prayer to Allah, reciting one of the later suras from the glorious Qur'an, the one called "The Morning Hours," which seemed particularly relevant to her situation. " 'In the name of Allah, the Beneficent, the Merciful. By the morning hours, and by the night when it is stillest, thy Lord hath not forsaken thee nor doth He hate thee, and verily the latter portion will be better for thee than the former, and verily thy Lord will give unto thee so that thou wilt be content. Did He not find thee an orphan and protect thee? Did He not find thee wandering and direct thee? Did He not find thee destitute and enrich thee? Therefore the orphan oppress not, therefore the beggar drive not away, therefore of the bounty of thy Lord be thy discourse.' " When she finished praying, she stood up and leaned against the wall. She wondered if that sura prophesied that soon she'd be an orphan. She hoped that Allah understood that she never intended anything awful to happen to her parents. Jehan was willing to suffer whatever consequences Allah willed, but it didn't seem fair for her mother and father to have to share them with her. She shivered in the damp, cold air and gazed up to see if there was yet any brightening of the sky. She pretended that already the stars were beginning to disappear.

The square was jammed and choked with people. Soon Hilbert could see why—a platform had been erected in the center, and on it stood a man with what could only be an executioner's ax. Hilbert felt his stomach sicken. His Arab guide had thrust aside everyone in their way until Hilbert stood at the very foot of the platform. He saw uniformed police and a bearded old man leading out a young girl. The crowd parted to allow them by. The girl was stunningly lovely. Hilbert looked into her huge, dark eyes—"like the eyes of a gazelle," he remembered from reading Omar Khayyám—and glimpsed her slender form undisguised by her modest garments. As she mounted the steps, she looked down directly at him again. Hilbert felt his heart lurch; he felt a tremendous shudder. Then she looked away.

The Arab guide screamed in Hilbert's ear. It meant nothing to the mathematician. He watched in horror as Jehan knelt, as the headsman raised his weapon of office. Hilbert shouted. His guide tightened his grip on the outsider's arm, but Hilbert lashed out in fury and threw the man into a group of veiled women. In the confusion, Hilbert ran up the steps of the scaffold. The imam and the police officers looked at him angrily. The crowd began to shout fiercely at this interruption, this desecration by a European kaffir, an unbeliever. Hilbert ran to the police. "You must stop this!" he cried in German. They did not understand him and tried to heave him off the platform. "Stop!" he screamed in English.

One of the police officers answered him. "It cannot be stopped," he said gruffly. "The girl committed murder. She was found guilty, and she cannot pay the blood price to the victim's family. She must die instead."

"Blood price!" cried Hilbert. "That's barbarous! You would kill a young girl just because she is poor? Blood price! *I'll* pay your goddamn blood price! How much is it?"

The policeman conferred with the others and then went to the imam for guidance. Finally the English-speaking officer returned. "Four hundred *kiam*."

Hilbert took out his wallet with shaking hands. He counted out the money and handed it with obvious disgust to the policeman. The imam cried a declaration in his weak voice. The words were passed quickly through the crowd, and the onlookers grew more enraged at this spoiling of their morning's entertainment. "Take her and go quickly," said the police officer. "We cannot protect you, and the crowd is becoming furious."

Hilbert nodded. He grasped Jehan's thin wrist and pulled her along after him. She questioned him in Arabic, but he could not reply. As he struggled through the menacing crowd, they were struck again and again by stones. Hilbert wondered what he had done, if he and the girl would get out of the mosque's courtyard alive. His fondness for young women—it was an open joke in Göttingen—had that been all that had motivated him? Had he unconsciously decided to rescue the girl and take her back to Germany? Or was it something more laudable? He would never know. He shocked himself: While he tried to shield himself and the girl from the vicious blows of the crowd, he thought only of how he might explain the girl to his wife, Käthe, and Clärchen, his mistress.

In 1957 Jehan Fatima Ashûfi was fifty-eight years old and living in Princeton, New Jersey. By coincidence, Albert Einstein had come here to live out the end of his life, and before he died in 1955 they had many pleasant afternoons at his house. In the beginning, Jehan wanted to discuss quantum physics with Einstein; she even told him Heisenberg's answer to Einstein's objection to God playing dice with the universe. Einstein was not very amused, and from then on their conversation concerned only nostalgic memories of the better days in Germany, before the advent of the National Socialists.

This afternoon, however, Jehan was sitting in a Princeton lecture hall, listening to a young man read a remarkable paper, his Ph.D. thesis. His name was Hugh Everett, and what he was saying was that there was an explanation for all the paradoxes of the quantum world, a simple but bizarre way of looking at them. His new idea included the Copenhagen interpretation and explained away all the objections that might be raised by less open-minded physicists. He stated first of all that quantum mechanics provided predictions that were invariably correct when measured against experimental data. Quantum physics *had* to be consistent and valid, there was no longer any doubt. The trouble was that quantum theory was beginning to lead to unappetizing alternatives.

Schrödinger's cat paradox—in which the cat in the box was merely a quantum wave function, not alive and not dead, until an observer looked to see which state the cat was in—was eliminated. Everett showed that the cat was no mere ghostly wave function. Everett said that wave functions do not "collapse," choosing one alternative or the other. He said that the process of observation chose one reality, but the other reality existed in its own right, just as "real" as our world. Particles do not choose at random which path to take—they take every path, in a separate, newly branched world for each option. Of course, at the particle level, this meant a huge number of branchings occurring at every moment.

Jehan knew this almost-metaphysical idea would find a chilly reception from most physicists, but she had special reasons to accept it eagerly. It explained her visions. She glimpsed the particular branch that would be "real" for her and also those that would be "real" for other versions of her, her own duplicates living on the countless parallel worlds. Now, as she listened to Everett, she smiled. She saw another young man in the audience, wearing a T-shirt that said, WIGNER: DO YOU THINK YOUR FRIEND COULD FEED MY CAT? HEISENBERG WASN'T SURE. THANKS, SCHRÖDINGER. She found that very amusing.

When Everett finished reading, Jehan felt good. It wasn't peace she felt; it was more like the release one feels after an argument that had been brewing for a long while. Jehan thought back over the turns and sidetracks she had taken since that dawn in the alley in the Budayeen. She smiled again, sadly, took a deep breath, and let it out. How many things she had done, how many things had happened to her! They had been long, strange lives. The only question that still remained was, How many uncountable futures did she still have to devise, to fabricate from the immaterial resources of this moment? As she sat there—in some worlds— Jehan knew the futures went on without her willing them to, needing nothing of her permission. She was not cautious of when tomorrow came but *which* tomorrow came.

Jehan saw them all, but she still understood nothing. She thought, *The Chinese say that a journey of a thousand li begins with a single step. How shortsighted that is! A* thousand *journeys of a thousand li begin with each step. Or with each step not taken.* She sat in her chair until everyone else had left the lecture hall. Then she got up slowly, her back and her knees giving her pain, and she took a step. She pictured myriad mirror-Jehans taking that step along with her, and a myriad that didn't. And in all the worlds across time, it was another step into the future.

*   *   *

At last there was no doubt about it: It was dawn. Jehan fingered her father's dagger and felt a thrill of excitement. Strange words flickered in her mind. "The Heisenty uncertainberg principle," she murmured, already hurrying toward the mouth of the alley. She felt no fear.

HOWARD WALDROP

Do Ya, Do Ya, Wanna Dance?

Howard Waldrop is widely considered to be one of the best short-story writers in the business, and his famous story "The Ugly Chickens" won both the Nebula and the World Fantasy Awards in 1981. His work has been gathered in two collections: *Howard Who?* and *All About Strange Monsters of the Recent Past: Neat Stories by Howard Waldrop*, and more collections are in the works. Waldrop is also the author of the novel *Them Bones*, and, in collaboration with Jake Saunders, *The Texas-Israeli War: 1999*. Another solo novel is coming up. He lives in Austin, Texas.

Here he gives us a hilarious, high-energy look back at the '60s, a look as funny, poignant, and quirky as one would expect from Waldrop, who has been called "the resident Weird Mind of his generation."

DO YA, DO YA, WANNA DANCE?

Howard Waldrop

The light was so bad in the bar that everyone there looked like they had been painted by Thomas Hart Benton, or carved from dirty bars of soap with rusty spoons.

"Frank! Frank!" the patrons yelled, like for Norm on *Cheers* before they canceled it.

"No need to stand," I said. I went to the table where Barb, Bob, and Penny sat. Carole the waitress brought over a Ballantine Ale in a can, no glass.

"How y'all?" I asked my three friends. I seemed *not* to have interrupted a conversation.

"I feel like six pounds of monkey shit," said Bob, who had once been tall and thin and was now tall and fat.

"My mother's at it again," said Penny. Her nails looked like they had been done by Mungo of Hollywood, her eyes were like pissholes in a snowbank.

"Jim went back to Angela," said Barb.

I stared down at the table with them for five or six minutes. The music over the speakers was "Wonderful World, Beautiful People" by Johnny Nash. We usually came to this bar because it had a good jukebox that livelied us up.

"So," said Barb, looking up at me, "I hear you're going to be a tour guide for the reunion."

There are terrible disasters in history, and there are always great catastrophes just waiting to happen.

But the greatest one of all, the thing time's been holding its breath for, the *capo de tutti capi* of impending disasters, was going to happen this coming weekend.

Like the *Titanic* steaming for its chunk of polar ice, like the *Hindenberg* looking for its Lakehurst, like the guy at Chernobyl wondering what *that* switch would do, it was inevitable, inexorable, a psychic juggernaut.

The Class of '69 was having its twentieth high school reunion.

And what they were coming back to was no longer even a high school—it had been phased out in a magnet school program in '74. The building had been taken over by the community college.

The most radical graduating class in the history of American secondary education, had, like all the ideals it once held, no real place to go.

Things were to start Saturday morning with a tour of the old building, then a picnic in the afternoon in the city park where everyone used to get stoned and lie around all weekend, then a dance that night in what used to be the fanciest downtown hotel a few blocks from the state capitol.

That was the reunion Barb was talking about.

"I found the concept of the high school no longer being there so existential that I offered to help out," I said. "Olin Sweetwater called me a couple of months ago—"

"Olin Sweetwater? Olin *Sweetwater*!" said Penny. "Geez! I haven't heard that name in the whole damn twenty years." She held onto the table with both hands. "I think I'm having a drug flashback!"

"Yeah, Olin. Lives in Dallas now. Runs an insurance agency. He got my name from somebody I built some bookcases for a couple of years ago. Anyway, asked if I'd be one of the guides on the tour Saturday morning—you know, point out stuff to husbands and wives and kids, people who weren't there."

I didn't know if I should go on.

Bob was looking at me, waiting.

"Well, Olin got me in touch with Jamie Lee Johnson—Jamie Lee Something hyphen Something now, none of them Johnson. She's the entertainment chairman, in charge of the dance. I made a couple of tapes for her."

I don't have much, but I do have a huge bunch of Original Oldies, Greatest Hits albums and other garage sale wonders. Lots of people know it and call me once or twice a year to make dance tapes for their parties.

"Oh, you'll like this," I said, waving to Carole to bring me another Ballantine Ale. "She said 'Spring for some Maxell tapes, not the usual four for eighty-nine cents kind I hear you buy at Revco.' Where you think she could have heard about that?"

"From me," said Barb. "She called me a month ago, too." She smiled a little.

"Come on, Barb." I said. "Spill it."

"Well, I wanted to—"

"I'm not going," said Penny.

We all looked at her.

"Okay. Your protest has been noted and filed. Now start looking for your granny dress and your walnut shell beads." I said.

"Why should I go back?" said Penny. "High school was shit. None of *us* had any fun there, we were all toads. Sure, things got a little exciting, but you could have been on top of Mount Baldy in Colorado in the late '60s and it would have been exciting. Why should I go see a bunch of jerks making fools of themselves trying to recapture some, some *image* of themselves another whole time and place?''

"Oh," said Bob, readjusting his gimme hat, "You really should hang around jerks more often."

"And why's that, Bob?" asked Penny, peeling the label from her Lone Star.

" 'Cause if you watch them long enough," said Bob, "you'll realize that jerks are capable of *anything*."

Bob's the kind of guy who holds people's destinies in his hands and they never realize it. When someone does something especially stupid and life-threatening in traffic, Bob doesn't honk his horn or scream or shake his fist.

He follows them. Either to where they're going, or the city limits, whichever comes first. If they go to work, or shopping, he makes his move then. If they go to a residence, he jots down the make, model and license plate of the car on a notepad he keeps on his dashboard, and comes back later that night.

Bob has two stacks of bumper stickers in the glove compartment of his truck. He takes one from each.

He goes to the vehicle of the person who has put his life personally in jeopardy, and he slaps one of the stickers on the left front bumper and one on the right rear.

The one on the back says SPICS AND NIGGERS OUT OF THE U.S.!

The one he puts on the front reads KILL A COP TODAY!

He goes through about fifty pairs of stickers a year. He's self-employed, so he writes the printing costs off on his Schedule A as "Depreciation."

Penny looked at Bob a little longer. "Okay. You've convinced me," she said. "Are you happy?"

"No," said Bob, turning in his chair. "Tell us whatever it is that'll make us happy, Barb."

"The guys are going to play."

Just *the guys*. No names. No *what guys*? We all knew. I had never before in my life seen Bob's jaw drop. Now I have.

The guys.

Craig Beausoliel. Morey Morkheim. Abram Cassuth. Andru Esposito. Or, taking them in order of their various band names from junior high on: Four Guys in a Dodge. Two Jews, A Wop, and A Frog. The Hurtz Bros. (Pervo, Devo, Sado, and Twisto). The Bug-Eyed Weasels. Those were when they were local, when they played Yud's, the Vulcan Gas Company, Tod's Hi-Spot. Then they got a record label and went national just after high school.

You knew them as *Distressed Flag Sale*.

That was the title of their first album (subtitled *For Sale Cheap One Country Inquire 1600 Pennsylvania Avenue*). You probably knew it as the "blue-cake-with-the-white-stars-on-the-table-with-the-red-stripes-formed-on-the-white-floor-by-the-blood-running-in-seven-rivulets-from-the-dead-G.I." album.

Their second and last was *NEXT*! with the famous photo of the Saigon police chief blowing the brains out of the suspected VC in the checked shirt during the Tet Offensive of 1968, only over the general's face they'd substituted Nixon's, and over the VC's, Howdy Doody's.

Then of course came the seclusion for six months, then the famous concert/riot/bust in Miami in 1970 that put an end to the band pretty much as a functioning human organization.

Morey Morkheim tried a comeback after his time in the *jusgado*, in the mid-70s, as Moe in Moe and the Meanies' *Suck My Buttons*, but it wasn't a very good album and the times were *already* wrong.

"I can't believe it," said Penny. "None of them have played in what, fifteen years? They probably'll sound like shit."

"Well, I'll tell you what I know," said Barb. "Jamie Lee—Younts-Fulton is the name, Frank—said after his jail term and the try at the comeback, Morey threw it all over and moved down to Corpus where his aunt was in the hotel business or something, and he opened a souvenir shop, a whole bunch of 'em eventually, called Morey's Mementoes. Got pretty rich at it supposedly, though you can never tell, especially from Jamie Lee—I mean, anyone, *anyone* who'd take as part of her second married name a hyphenated name from her *first* husband that was later convicted of mail fraud just because Younts is more sophisticated than Johnson—Johnson Fulton sounds like an 1830 politician from Tennessee, know what I mean?—you just can't trust about things like who's rich and who's not. Anyway, Morey was at some convention for seashell brokers or something —Jamie says about half the shells and junk sold in Corpus come from Japan and Taiwan—he ran into Andru, of all people, who was in the freight business! Like, Morey had been getting shells from this shipping company for ten years and it turns out to belong to Andru's uncle or brother-in-law or something! So they start writing to each other, then somehow (maybe it was from Bridget, you remember Bridget? from UT? Yeah.) she knew where Abram was, and about that time the people putting all this reunion together got a hold of Andru. So the only thing left to do was find Craig."

She looked around. It was the longest I'd ever heard Barb talk in my life.

"You know where he was?"

"No. Where?" we all three said.

"Ever eat any Dr. Healthy's Nut-Crunch Bread?"

"A loaf a day," said Bob, patting his stomach.

"Craig is Dr. Healthy."

"Shit!" said Bob. "Isn't that stuff baked in Georgetown?"

"Yeah. He's been like thirty miles away for fifteen years, baking bread and sweet rolls. Jamie said, like some modern-day Cactus Jack Garner, he vowed never to go south of the San Gabriel River again."

"But now he is?"

"Yep. Supposedly, Andru's gonna fly down to Morey's in Corpus this week and they're going to practice before they come up here. Abram always was the quickest study and the only real musical genius, so he'll be okay."

"That only leaves one question," said Penny, speaking for us all. "Can Craig still sing? Can Craig still *play*? I mean, look what happened after the Miami thing."

"Good question," said Bob. "I suppose we'll all find out in a big hurry Saturday night. Besides," he said, looking over at me, "we always got your tapes."

The name's Frank Bledsoe. I'm pushing forty, which is exercise enough.

I do lots of odd stuff for a living—a little woodwork and carpentry, mostly speakers and bookcases. I help people move a lot. In Austin, if you have a pickup, you have friends for life.

What I mostly do is build flyrods. I make two kinds—a 7' one for a #5 line and an 8'2" one for a #6 line. I get the fiberglass blanks from a place in Ohio, and the components like cork grips, reel seats, guides, tips and ferrules, from whoever's having a sale around the country.

I sell a few to a fishing tackle store downtown. The seven-footer retails for $22, the other for $27.50. Each rod takes about three hours of work, a day for the drying time on the varnish on the wraps. So you can see my hourly rate isn't too swell.

I live in a place about the size of your average bathroom in a real person's house. But it's quiet, it's on a cul-de-sac, and there's a converted horse stable out back I use for my workshop.

What keeps me in business is that people around the country order a few custom-made rods each year, for which I charge a little more.

Here's a dichotomy: as flyfishing becomes more popular, my business falls off.

That's because, like everything else in these post-modernist times, the Yups ruined it. As with every other recreation, they confuse the sport with the equipment.

Flyfishing is growing with them because it's a very status thing. When the Yups found it, all they wanted to do was be seen on the rivers and lakes with a six hundred-dollar split-bamboo rod, a pair of two hundred-dollar waders, a hundred-dollar vest, shirts with a million zippers on them, a seventy-five-dollar tweed hat, and a patch from a flyfishing school that showed they'd paid one thousand dollars to learn how to put out enough fly line to reach across the average K-Mart parking lot.

What I make is cheap fiberglass rods, not even boron or graphite. No glamor. And the real fact is that in flyfishing, most fish are caught within twenty feet of your boots. No glory there, either.

So the sport grows, and money comes in more and more slowly.

All this talk about the reunion has made me positively reflective. So let me put 1969 in perspective for you.

Richard Milhous Nixon was in his first year in office. He'd inherited all the good things from Lyndon Johnson—the social programs—and was dismantling them, and going ahead with all the bad ones, like the War in Nam. The Viet Cong and NVA were killing one hundred Americans a week, and according to the Pentagon, we were killing two thousand of them, regular as clockwork, as announced at the five P.M. press briefing in Saigon every Friday. The draft call was fifty thousand a month.

The Beatles released *Abbey Road* late in the year. At the end of the summer we graduated there was something called the Woodstock Festival of Peace and Music; in December there would be the disaster at the Altamont racetrack (in which, if you saw the movie that came out the next year, you could see a Hell's Angel with a knife kill a black man with a gun on camera while all around people were freaking out on bad acid and Mick Jagger, up there trying to sing, was saying "Brothers and sisters, why are we fighting each other?"). On the nights of August 8 and 9 were the Tate-LaBianca murders in L.A. (Charles Manson had said to his people "Kill everybody at Terry Melcher's house," not knowing Terry had moved. Terry Melcher was Doris Day's son. Chuck thought Terry owed him some money or had reneged on a recording deal or something. When he realized what he'd done, he had them go out and kill some total strangers to make the murders at the Tate household look like the work of a kill-the-rich cult.) On December 17, Tiny Tim married Miss Vickie on the *Tonight Show*, with Johnny Carson as best man.

The Weathermen, the Black Panthers and, according to agent's reports, "frizzy-haired women of a radical organization called NOW," were disturbing the increasingly senile sleep of J. Edgar Hoover of the FBI. He longed for the days when you could shoot criminals down in the streets like dogs and have them buried in handcuffs, when all the issues were clear-cut. Spirotis T. Agnew, the vice-president, was gearing up to make his "nattering nabobs of negativism" speech, and to coin the term Silent Majority. This was four years before he made the most moving and eloquent speech in his, life, which went: "*Nolo contendere.*"

We were reading Vonnegut's *Slaughterhouse-Five*, or rereading *The Hobbit* for the zillionth time, or Brautigan's *In Watermelon Sugar*. And on everybody's lips were the words of Nietzsche's Zarathustra: That which does not kill us makes us stronger. (Nixon was working on that, too.)

There were weeks when you thought nothing was ever going to change, there was no wonderment anymore, just new horrors about the War, government repression, drugs. (They were handing out life sentences for the possession of a single joint in some places that year.)

Then, in three days, from three total strangers, you'd hear the Alaska vacation—flannel shirt—last man killed by an active volcano story, all the people *swearing* they'd heard the story from the kid in the flannel shirt himself, and you'd say, yeah, the world is *still* magic . . .

I'll really put 1969 in a nutshell for you. There are six of you sharing a three-bedroom house that fall, and you're splitting rent you think is exorbitant, $89.75 a month. Minimum wage was $1.35 an hour, and none of you even has any of *that*.

Somebody gets some money from somewhere, God knows, and you're all going to pile into the VW Microbus which is painted green, orange, and fuchsia, and going to the H.E.B. to score some food. But first, since there are usually hassles, you all decide to smoke all the grass in the house, about three lids' worth.

When you get to the store you split up to get food, and are to meet at checkout lane Number Three in twenty minutes. An hour later you pool the five shopping carts and here's what you have:

Seven two-pound bags of lemon drops. Three bags of orange marshmallow goobers. A Hostess Ding-Dong assortment pack. A twelve-pound bag of Kokuho Rose New Variety Rice. A two-pound can of Beer-Nuts. A fifty-foot length of black shoestring licorice. Three six-packs of Barq's Root Beer. Two quarts of fresh strawberries and a pint of Half and Half. A Kellog's Snak-Pak (heavy on the Frosted Flakes). A five-pound bag of turbinado sugar. Two one-pound bags of Bazooka Joe bubble gum (with double comics). A blue 75-watt light bulb.

It fills up three dubl/bags and the bill comes to $8.39, the last seventy-four cents of which you pay the clerk in pennies.

Later, when somebody finally cooks, everybody yells, "Shit! Rice again? Didn't we just go to the grocery store?"

PS: On July 20 that year we landed on the Moon.

Now I'll tell you about this year, 1989.

The Republicans are in the tenth month of their new Presidency, naturally. After Cuomo and Iacocca refused to run, the Democrats, like always, ran two old warhorses who quit thinking along about 1962. ("If nominated, I refuse to run," said Iacocca, "if elected, I refuse to serve. And that's a promise.")

We have six thousand military advisors in Honduras and Costa Rica. All those guys who went down to the post office and signed their Selective Service postcards are beginning to look a little grey around the gills.

There are 1,800,000 cases of AIDS in America, and 120,000 have died of it.

On Wall Street the Dow Jones just passed the 3000 mark after its near-suicide in '87. "Things are looking just great!" says the new president.

Congress is voting on the new two trillion dollar debt ceiling limit.

Things are much like they have been forever. The rich are richer, the poor poorer, the middle class has no choices. The cities are taxing them to death, the suburbs can't hold them. Every state but those in the Bible-belt South has horse *and* dog racing, a lottery, legalized pari-mutuel Bingo *and* a state income tax, and they're still going broke.

Everything is wrong everywhere. The only good thing I've noticed is that MTV is off the air.

You go to the grocery store and get a pound of bananas, a six foot electric extension cord, a can of powder scent air freshener, a tube of store-brand toothpaste and a loaf of bread. It fits in the smallest plastic sack they have and costs $7.82.

Let me put 1989 in another nutshell for you:

A friend of mine keeps his record albums (his CDs are elsewhere) in what looks like a haphazard stack of orange crates in one corner of his living room.

They're not orange crates. What he did was get a sculptor friend of his to make them. He got some lengths of stainless steel, welded and shaped them to look like a haphazard stack of crates. Then with punches and chisels and embossing tools the sculptor made the metal look like grained unseasoned wood, and then painted them, labels and all, to look like crates.

You can't tell them from the real things, and my friend only paid three thousand dollars for them.

Or to put it another way: And Zarathustra came down from the hills unto the cities of men. And Zarathustra spake unto them, and what he said to them was: "Yo!"

PS: Nobody's been to the Moon in sixteen years.

MY TRIP TO THE POST OFFICE by FRANK BLEDSOE AGE 38

I'd finished three rods for a guy in Colorado the day before. I put the clothes back on I'd worn working on them, all dotted with varnish. I was building a bookcase, too, so I hit it a few licks with a block plane to get my blood going in the early morning.

It was a nice crisp fall day, so I decided to ride my bike to the post office substation to mail the rods. I was probably so covered with wood shavings I looked like a Cabbage Patch Kid that had been hit with a slug from a .45.

I brushed myself off, put the rods in their cloth bags, put the bags in the tubes with the packing paper, and put the tubes in the carrier I have on the bike. Then I rode off to the branch post office.

I'm coming out of the substation with the postage and insurance receipts in my hand when I hear a lot of brakes squealing and horns honking.

A lady in a white Volvo has managed to get past two One Way Do Not Enter signs at the exit to the parking lot and is coming in against the traffic, and all the angles of the diagonal parking places. She has a look of calm imperturbability on her face.

Nobody's looking for a car from her direction. As they back out, suddenly there she is in the rear-view mirror. They slam on their brakes and honk and yell.

"Asshole!" yells a guy who's killed his engine in a panic stop. She gets to the entrance of the lot, does a 290 degree turn, and pulls into the Reserved Handicapped spot at the front door, acing out the one-armed guy with Disabled American Vets license plates who was waiting for the guy who was illegally parked against the yellow curbing in the entrance to move so he could get in.

She gets out of the car. She's wearing a silk blouse, a set of June Cleaver double-strand pearls and matching earrings, and a pair of those shorts that make the wearer look like they have a refrigerator stuffed down the back of them.

"Are you handicapped?" I ask.

She looks right through me. She's taking a yellow Attempt to Deliver slip out of her sharkskin purse. She has on shades.

"I said, are you handicapped? I don't see a sticker on your car."

"What business is it of yours?" she asks. "Besides, I'm only going to be in there a minute."

That's what you think. She goes inside. I shrug at the one-armed guy. With some people it was their own fault they went to Korea or Viet Nam and got their legs and stuff blown off, with others it wasn't.

He drives off down the packed lot. He probably won't find a space for a block.

I take my bike tools out of my pocket. I go to the Volvo. In deference to Bob, I undo the valve cores on the left front and right rear tires.

Then I get on my bike and ride down to the pay phone at the bakery three blocks away, call the non-emergency police number, and tell them there's a lady without a handicap sticker blocking the reserved spot at the post office substation.

After mailing the rods and using the quarter for the phone, I have eighty-two cents left—just enough for coffee at the bakery. It's a chi-chi place I usually never go to, but I haven't had any coffee this morning and I know they make a cup of Brazilian stuff that would bring Dwight D. Eisenhower back to life.

I go in. They've got one of those European doorchimes that sets poor people's nerves on edge and lets those with a heavy wallet know they're in a place where they can really drop a chunk of money.

The clerk is Indian or Paki; he's on the phone talking to someone. I start tapping my change on the counter looking around. Maybe ten people in the place. He hangs up and starts toward me.

"Large cuppa—" I start to say.

The chime jingles and the smell hits me at the same time as their voices; a mixture of Jovan Musk for Men and Sassoon styling mousse.

"—game." says a voice. "How many croissants you still got?" says the voice over my shoulder to the clerk.

The counterman has one hand on the coffee spigot and a sixteen ounce styrofoam cup in the other.

"Oh, very many, I think," he says to the voice behind me.

"Give us about—oh, what, John?—say, twenty-five assorted fruit-filled, no lemon, okay?"

The clerk starts to put down the styrofoam cup. In ambiguous situations, people always move toward the voice that sounds most like money.

"My coffee?" I say.

The clerk looks back and forth like he's just been dropped on the planet.

"Could you sort of hurry?" says the voice behind me. "We're double-parked."

I turn around then. There are three of them in warmup outfits—gold and green, blue and orange, blue and silver. They look maybe twenty-five. Sure enough, there's a blue Renault blocking three cars parked at the laundromat next door. The handles of squash racquets stick up out of the blue and orange, blue and silver, gold and green duffles in the back seat.

"No lemon," says the blond-haired guy on the left. "Make sure there's no lemon, huh?"

"You gonna fill our order?" asks the first guy, who looks like he was raised in a meatloaf mold.

"No," I say. "First he's going to get my coffee, then he'll get your order."

They notice me for the first time then, suspicion dawning on them this wasn't covered in their Executive Assertiveness Training program.

The clerk is turning his head back and forth like a radar antenna.

"I thought they gave *free* coffee at the Salvation Army," says the blond guy, looking me up and down.

"Tres, tres amusant." I said.

"Are you going to fill our $35 order, or are you going to give him his big fifty cent cup of coffee?" asked the first guy.

The ten other people in the place were all frozen in whatever attitude they had been in when all this started. One woman actually had a donut halfway to her mouth and was watching, her eyes growing wider.

"My big seventy-five cent order," I said, letting the change clink on the glass countertop. "Any time you come in *any* place," I went on, "you should look around the room and you should ask yourself, who's the only, *only* possible one here who could have taken Taiwanese mercenaries into Laos in 1968? And you should act accordingly."

"Who the fuck do you think *you* are?" asked the middle one, who hadn't spoken before and looked like he'd taken tai-kwon-do since he was four.

"Practically nobody," I said. "But if any of you say *one more word* before I get my coffee, I'm going out to the saddlebag on my bike, and I'm going to take out a product backed by 132 years of Connecticut Yankee know-how and fine American craftsmanship and I'm coming back in here and showing you *exactly* how the rat chews the cheese."

Then I gave them the Thousand Yard Stare, focusing on something about a half mile past the left shoulder of the guy in the middle.

They backed up, jangling the doorbell, out onto the sidewalk, bumping into a lady coming out with a load of wash.

"Crazy fuck," I heard one of them say as he climbed into the car. The tai-kwon-do guy kept looking at me as the driver cranked the car up. He said something to him, jumped around the car and started kicking the shit out of the back tire of the twelve-speed white Concord leaning against the telephone pole out front.

I heard people sucking in their breaths in the bakery.

The guy kicked the bike three times, watching me, breaking out the spokes in a half moon, laughing.

"My bike!" yelled a woman on one of the stools. "That's my bike! You assholes! Get their license number!" She ran outside.

I turned to the clerk, who had my cup of coffee ready. I plunked down eighty cents in nickels, dimes and pennies, and put two cents in the TIPS cup. Then I put saccharine and cream in the coffee.

Out on the sidewalk, the woman was screaming at the tai-kwon-do-looking guy, and she was crying. His two friends were talking to him in low voices and reaching for their billfolds. He looked like a little kid who'd broken a window in a sandlot ball game. People had come out of the grocery store across the street and were watching.

I got on my bike and rode to the corner unnoticed.

A cop car, lights flashing but with the siren off, turned toward the bakery as I turned out onto the street.

It was only 9:15 A.M. It was looking to be a nice day.

I got two-and-three-fourths stars in the 1977 *Career Woman's Guide to Austin Men*. Here's the entry: Working-class bozo, well-read. Great for a rainy Tuesday night when your regular feller is out of town. PS: You'll have to pick up all the tabs.

I'm still friends with about two-thirds of the women I've ever gone with, which I'm as proud of as anything else in my life, I guess. I care a lot, I'm fairly intelligent, and I have a sense of humor. You know, the doormat personality.

At one time, in those days before herpes and AIDS, when everybody was trying to figure out just who and what they were, I was sort of a Last Station of the Way for women who, in Bob's words, "were trying to decide whether to go nelly or not." They usually did anyway, more often than not with another old girlfriend of mine.

(It all started when I was dating the ex-wife of the guy who was then living with my ex-girlfriend. The lady who was then the ex-wife now lives with a nice lady who used to be married to another friend of mine. They each have tattoos on their left shoulders. One of them has a portrait of Karl Marx and under it the words *Hot to Trotsky*.

The other has the Harley-Davidson symbol but instead of the usual legend it says *Born to Read Hegel*.)

No one set out an agenda or anything for me to be their Last Guy on Earth. It just happened, and expanded outward like ripples in a pond.

About two months ago at a party some young kid was listening to a bunch of us old farts talk, and he asked me, "If the Sixties were so great, and the Eighties suck so bad, then what happened in the Seventies?"

"Well," I said. "Richard Nixon resigned, and then, and then . . . gee, I don't know."

Another woman I dated for a while had only one goal in life: to plant the red flag on the rubble of several prominent landmarks between Virginia and Maryland.

We used to be coming home from the dollar midnight flicks on campus (*Our Daily Bread, Sweet Movie, China Is Near*) and we would pass this neat old four-story hundred-year-old house, and every time, she would look up at it and say "That's where I'm going to live after the Revolution."

I'm talking 1976 here, folks.

We'd gone out together five or six times, and we went back to her place and were going to bed together for the first time. We were necking, and she got up to go to the bathroom. "Get undressed," she said.

When she came back in, taking her sweater off over her head, I was naked in the bed with the sheets pulled up to my neck. I was wearing a Mao Tse Tung mask.

It was *wonderful*.

Friday. Reunion Eve.

It was one of those days when everything is wrong. All the work I started I messed up in some particularly stupid way. I started everything over twice. I gave up at three P.M.

Things didn't get any better. I tried TV. A blur of talking heads. Nothing interested me for more than thirty seconds.

Outside the sun was setting past Mt. Bonnell and Lake Austin. Over on Cat

Mountain the red winks of the lights on the TV towers came on. A Continental 737 went over, heading towards California's golden climes.

I put on a music tape I'd made and tried to read a book. I got up and turned the noise off. It was too Sixties. I'd hear enough of that tomorrow night. No use setting myself up for a wallow in the good times and peaking too early. I drank a beer that tasted like kerosene. It was going to be a cool clear October night. I closed the windows and watched the moon come up over Manor, Texas.

The book was Leslie Fiedler's *Love and Death in the American Novel*. I tried to read it some more and it began to go *yammer yammer yibble yibble* Twain, *yammer yibble* Hemingway. Enough.

I turned the music back on, put on the headphones and lay down on the only rug in the house, looking up at the cracks in the plaster and listening to the Moody Blues. What a loss of a day, but I was tired anyway. I went to bed at nine P.M.

It was one of those nights when every change in the wind brings an erection, when every time you close your eyes you see penises and vulvas, a lot of them ones you haven't seen before. After staring up at the ceiling for an hour, I got up, got another beer, went into the living room and sat naked in the dark.

I had one of those feelings like I hadn't had in years. The kind your aunt told you she'd had the day your grandfather died, before anybody knew it yet. She told you at the funeral that three days before she'd felt wrong and irritable all day and didn't know why, until the phone rang with the news. The kind of feeling Phil Collins gets on "In the Air Tonight," a mood that builds and builds with no discernible cause.

It was a feeling like in a Raymond Chandler novel, the kind he blames on the Santa Ana winds, when all the dogs bark, when people get pissed off for no reason, when yelling at someone you love is easier than going on silently with the mood you have inside.

Only there were no howling dogs, no sound of fights from next door. Maybe it was just me. Maybe this reunion thing was getting to me more than I wanted it to.

Maybe it was just horniness. I went to the VCR, an old Beta II, second one they ever made, no scan, no timer, all metal, weighs 150 pounds, bought at Big State Pawn for fifty bucks, sometimes works and sometimes doesn't. I put in *Cum Shot Revue #1* and settled back in my favorite easy chair.

The TV going *kskksssssssss* woke me up at 4:32 A.M. I turned everything off. So this is what me and my whole generation come down to, people sleeping naked in front of their TVs with empty beer cans in their laps. It was too depressing to think about.

I made my way to bed, lay down, and had dreams. I don't remember anything about them, except that I didn't like them.

*   *   *

I've known three women the latter part of the twentieth century has driven slapdab crazy.

For one, it was through no fault of her own. Certain chemicals were missing in her body. She broke up with me quietly after six months and checked herself into the MHMR. That was the last time I saw her.

She evidently came back through town about three years ago, *after* she quit taking her lithium. I got strange phone calls from old friends who had seen her. Her vision, and that of the one we call reality, no longer intersected. Having destroyed her present, she had begun to work on the past and the future also.

Last I heard she had run off with a cook she met at a Halfway House; they were rumored to be working Exxon barges together on the Mississippi River.

The second, after affairs with five real jerks in a row in six months, began to lose weight. She'd only been 111 pounds to begin with. People whispered about leukemia, cancer, some wasting disease. Of course it wasn't—in the rest of the world, dying by not getting enough to eat is a right, in America, it's a privilege. She began to look like sticks held together with a pair of kid's blue-jeans and a shirt, with only two brightly-glowing eyes watching you from the head to show she was still alive. She was fainting a lot by then.

One day Bob, who had been her lover six years before, went over to her house. (By then she was forgetting to do things like close and lock the doors, or turn on the lights at night.)

Bob picked her up by her shirt collar (it was easy, she only weighed eighty-three pounds by then) and slapped her, like in the movies, five times as hard as he could.

It was only on the fifth slap that her eyes came to life and filled with fear.

"Stop it, Gabriella," said Bob. "You're killing yourself." Then he kissed her on her bloody, swelling lips, set her down blinking, and walked out her door and her life, and hasn't seen her since.

He saved her. She met another nice woman at the eating disorder clinic. They now live in Westlake Hills, raising the other woman's two boys by her first marriage.

The third one's cat ran away one morning. She went back upstairs, wrote a long apologetic note to her mother, dialed 911 and told them where she was, hung up and drank most of an eleven-ounce can of Crystal Drano.

She lived on for six days in the hospital in a coma with no insides and a raging 107° fever.

Her friends kept checking, but the cat never came back.

*   *   *

"Yo!" said Olin Sweetwater. He and two or three others were standing outside the community college on the cool Saturday morning. He had on a sweatshirt, done up in the old school colors, that said Bull Goose Tour Guide. We shook hands (thumbs locked, sawing our arms back and forth). He was balding; what hair he had left had a white plume across the left side.

The two women, Angela Pardo and Rita Jones when I'd known them, were nervous. Olin handed us sweatshirts that said Tour Guide. We thanked him.

I looked at the brick facade. The school had been an ugly dump in 1969; it was still a dump, but with a charm all its own.

(One of the reasons Olin asked me to help with the tour is that I'd lived with a lady artist for a year who had worked part-time as a clerk in the admissions office of the community college. I guess he thought that qualified me as an Expert.)

The tours were supposed to start at ten A.M. Sleepy college students who had Saturday labs were wandering in and out of the two-and-a-half story building or some of the other outbuildings the college leased. Olin had pulled lots of strings to let us guide people without any interference, or so he kept telling us.

Around 9:45 people started wandering up, trailing kids, shy husbands, wives, lovers. God, I thought recognizing a few here and there. We're so fucking normal looking. We look like our mothers and fathers did in 1969.

(Remember in 1973 when you saw *American Graffiti* for the first time and everybody laughed at the short haircuts and long skirts, then when you went back to see it in 1981 those parts didn't seem so strange anymore?)

I was talking to one of the few women who'd been nice to me in high school, a quiet girl named Sharon, whose front teeth then had reminded me, sweetly and not at all unpleasantly, of Rocket J. Squirrel's. She was now, I learned, on her second divorce. She introduced me to her kids—Seth and Jason—who looked like they'd rather be on Mars than here.

Sharon stopped talking and stared behind me. I saw other people turning and followed their gaze toward the street. "Jesus," I said. A pink flowered VW Beetle pulled up to the curb as a student drove away. Out of it came something from Mr. Natural—the guy had hair down to his butthole (a wig, it turned out), headband, walnut shell beads, elephant bell pants with neon green flash panels, a khaki shirt and wool vest, Ben Franklin specs tinted Vick's Salve blue. There was a B-52 peace symbol button big as a dinner plate on his left abdomen, and the vest had a leather stash pocket at the bottom snaps.

Something in the way he moves . . .

Seth and Jason were pointing and laughing, other people were looking embarrassed.

"Peace, Love, and Brotherhood," he said, flashing us the peace sign.

The voice. I knew it after twenty years. Hoyt Lawton.

Hoyt Lawton had been president of the fucking Key Club in 1969! He'd worn three-piece suits to school even on the days when he didn't *have* to go eat with the Rotarians! His hair was never more than three-eighths of an inch off his skull—we said he never got it cut, it just never grew. He won a bunch of money from something like the DAR for a speech he made at a Young Republicans convention on how all hippies needed was a good stiff tour of duty in Vietnam that would show them what America was all about. Hoyt Lawton, what an asshole!

And yet, there he was, the only one with enough *chutzpah* to show up like we were all supposed to feel. Okay, I'm older and more tolerant now. Hoyt, you're still an asshole, but with a little style.

By about 10:10 there were a hundred people there. Excluding husbands, wives, Significant Others and kids, maybe sixty of the Class of '69 had taken the trouble to show up.

Olin divided us up so we wouldn't run into each other. I started my group of twenty or so (Hoyt was in Olin's group thank god) on the second floor. We climbed the stairs.

"You'll notice they have air conditioning now?" I said. There were laughs. Austin hits ninety-five by April 20 most years. We'd sweltered through Septembers and died in Mays here, to the hum of ineffectual floor fans. The ceilings were twenty feet high and the ceiling fans might as well have been heat pumps.

"How many of you spent most of the last semester here?" I said, pointing. Two or three held up their hands. "This used to be the principal's office; now it's the copy center. Over there was Mr. Dix's office itself." Lots of people laughed then, probably hadn't thought of the carrot-headed principal since graduation day. He'd had it bad enough before someone heard him referred to as "Red" by the Superintendent of Schools one day.

"That used to be the only office that was air-conditioned, remember? At least you could get cool while waiting to be yelled at." I pointed to the air-conditioning vents.

That there air duct I didn't say *is the one that Morey Morkheim got into and took a big dump in one night after they'd expelled him one of those times.* Only in America is the penalty for skipping school expulsion for three days.

Mr. Dix had yelled at him after the absence, "What are you going to do with your life? You'll never amount to anything without an education!"

In seven months Morey was pulling in more money in a weekend than Dix would make in ten years—legally, too.

We moved through the halls, getting curious stares from students in classrooms with closed glass doors.

"Down here was where the student newspaper office was. Over there was the library, which the community college is using as a library." We went down to the first floor.

"Ah, the cafeteria!" It was now the study room, full of chairs and tables and vending machines. "Remember tomato surprise! Remember macaroni and cheese!" "Fish lumps on Friday!" said someone.

Half the student body in those days had come from the parochial junior highs around town. In 1969, parochial was the way you spelled Catholic. Nobody in the school administration ever read a paper, evidently, so they hadn't learned that the Pope had done away with "going to hell on a meat rap" back in 1964. So you still had fish lumps on Friday when we were there. The only good thing about having all those Catholic kids there was that we got to hear their jokes for the first time, like what's God's phone number? ETcumspiri 220!

"Down there, way off to the left," I said "was the band hall. You remember Mr. Stoat?" There were groans. "I thought so. Only musician I ever met who had *absolutely* no sense of rhythm."

Ah, the band hall. Where one morning a bunch of guys locked themselves in just before graduation, wired the intercom up to broadcast all over school, and played "Louie, Louie" on tubas, instead of the National Anthem, during home room period. It was too close to the end of school to expel them, so they didn't let them come to the commencement exercise. In protest of which, when they played "Pomp and Circumstance," about three hundred of us Did the Freddy down the aisles of the municipal auditorium in our graduation gowns.

We passed a door leading to the boiler room, where all the teachers popped in for a smoke between classes, it being forbidden for them to take a puff anywhere on school grounds but in the Teachers' Lounge during their off-hour.

I stopped and opened it—sure enough, it was there, dimmed by twenty years and several attempts to paint over it, but in the remains of smudged-over day-glo orange paint on the top inside of the door it still said: *Ginny and Ray's Motel.*

Ginny Balducci and Ray Petro had come to school one morning ripped on acid and had wandered down to the boiler room and had taken their clothes off. My theory is that it was warm and nice and they wanted to feel the totality of the sensuous space. The school's theory, after they were interrupted by Coach Smetters, was that they had been Fornicating During Home Room Period, and without hall passes, too!

After Ginny came down, and while her father was screaming at Ray's parents across Dix's desk, she said to her father, "Leave them alone. They didn't have *their* clothes off!"

"Young lady," said Dix. "You don't seem to realize what serious trouble you're in."

"What are you going to do?" asked Ginny, looking the principal square in the eye, "Castrate me?"

I answered some questions about the fire escape that used to be on the south side of the building. "They fell on a community college student one day four years ago,'' I said. "Good thing we never *had* to use them." We were outside again.

"Over there was the gym. World's worst dance floor, second worst basketball court. Enough sweat was spilled there over the years to float the *Big Mo*. We can't go in, though, they now use it to store visual aids for the Parks and Rec department."

There was the morning when Dix had us all go to the gym for Assembly. His purpose, it went on to appear after he had talked for ten minutes, was to try to explain why the Armed Forces recruiters would be there on Career Day, along with the realtors and college reps and Rotarians who would come to tell you about the wonders of their profession in the Great Big World Out There. (Some nasty posters had appeared on every bare inch of wall in the building that morning questioning not only their presence on Career Day but also their continuing existence on the third rock from the sun.)

He was going on about how they had been there, draft or no draft, war or no war, every Career Day when a small sound started at the back of the ranked bleachers. The sound of two stiffened index fingers drumming slowly but very deliberately dum-dum-thump dum-dum-thump. Then a few other sets of fingers joined in *dum-dum-thumb dum-dum-thump*, at first background, then rising, louder and more insistent, then feet took it up, and it spread from section to section, while the teachers looked around wildly Dum-Dum-Thump Dum-Dum-Thump.

Dix stopped in mid-sentence, mouth open, while the sound grew. He saw half the student body—the other half was silent, or like the jocks led by Hoyt Lawton, beginning to boo and hiss—rise to its feet clapping its hands and stamping its feet in time—

DUM DUM THUMP DUM DUM THUMP

He yelled at people and pointed, then he quit and his shoulders sagged. And on a hidden passed signal, everybody quit on the same beat and it was deathly silent in the gym. Then everybody sat back down.

I think Dix had seen the future that morning—Kent State, the Cambodian incursion, the cease fire, the end of Nixon, the fall of Saigon.

He dismissed us. The recruiters were there on Career Day anyway.

I'd almost finished my tour. "One more place, not on the official stops," I said. I took them across the side street and down half a block.

"Ow wow!" said someone halfway there. "The Grindstone!"

We got there. It was a one-story place with real glass bricks across the whole front that would cost $80 a pop these days. The place was full of tools and cars.

"Oh, gee," said the people.

"It's now the Skill Shop," I said. "Went out of business in 1974, bought up by the city, leased by the community college."

Ah, the Grindstone! A real old-fashioned cafe/soda fountain. You were forbidden on pain of death to leave the school grounds except at lunch, so three thousand people tried to get in every day between 11:30 and 12:30.

One noon the place was packed. There was the usual riot going on over at UT ten blocks away. All morning you could hear sirens and dull *whoomps* as the increasingly senile police commissioner, who had been in office for thirty-four years, tried dealing with the increasingly complex late twentieth century. *Why, the children have gone mad* he once said in a TV interview.

Anyway, we were all stuffing our faces in the Grindstone when this guy comes running in the front door and out the back at two-hundred miles an hour. Somebody made the obvious stoned joke—"Man, I thought he'd *never* leave!"—and then a patrol car slammed up to the curb, and a cop jumped out. You could see his mind work.

A. Rioter runs into the Grindstone. B. Grindstone is full of people. Therefore: C. Grindstone is full of rioters.

He opened the door, fired a tear-gas grenade right at the lunch counter, turned, got in his car and drove away.

People were barfing and gagging all over the place. There were screams, tears, rage. The Grindstone was closed for a week so they could rent some industrial fans and air it out. The city refused to pick up the tab. "The officer was in hot pursuit," said the police commissioner, "and acted within the confines of departmental guidelines." Case closed.

"Ah, the Grindstone," I said to the tour group. "What a *nice* place." A wave of nostalgia swept over me. "Today, shakes and fries. Tomorrow, a lube job and tune-up."

I was so filled with *mono no aware* that I skipped the picnic that afternoon.

The Wolfskill Hotel! Scene of a thousand-and-one nights' entertainments and more senior proms than there are fire ants in all the fields in Texas.

A friend of mine named Karen once said people were divided into two classes: those who went to their senior proms and went on to live fairly normal lives, and those who didn't, who became perverts, mass murderers or romance novelists.

If you were a guy you got maybe your first blow job after the prom, or if a girl a quick boff in the back seat of some immemorial Dodge convertible out at Lake Travis. The hotel meant excitement, adventure, magic.

I hadn't gone to my senior prom. A lot of us hadn't, looking on it as one more corrupt way to suck money from the working classes so that orchids could die all over the vast American night.

There were some street singers outside the hotel, playing jug band music without a jug—two guitars, a flute, tambourine and harmonica. They were fairly quiet. The cops wouldn't hassle them until after eleven P.M. They were pretty good. I dropped a quarter into their cigar box.

You could hear the strains of the Byrds' "Turn! Turn! Turn!" before you got through the lobby. The entertainment committee must have dropped a ton o'bucks on this—they had a bulletin board out front just past the registration table with everybody's pictures from the yearbook blown up, six to a sheet.

It was weird seeing all those people's names and faces—the beginnings of mustaches and beards on the guys, we'd fought tooth and nail for facial hair— long straight hair on the women—names that hadn't been used, or gone back to three or four times, in the last twenty years.

I paid my $10.00 fee (like in the old days. Dance Tonight! Guys fifty cents Girls Free!).

Inside the ballroom people were already dancing, maybe a hundred, with that many more standing around talking and laughing in knots and clumps, being polite to each other, sizing up what Time's Heedless Claws had done to each other's bodies and outlooks.

Bob and Penny were already there. He was in a bluejean jacket and pants and wore a clear plastic tie. Penny was stunning, in a green velour thing, beautiful as she always is early in the evenings, before alcohol turns her into a person I don't know.

I was real spiffed out, for me: a nice sport coat, black slacks, a red silk tie with painted roses wide as the racing stripe on a Corvette.

There were people there in $500 gowns, $300 suits, tuxes, jeans, coveralls. Several were in period costumes; Hoyt had on another, much better than this morning's nightmare, but still what I describe as Early Neil Young. He was, of course, with a slim blonde who had once been a Houston cheerleader, I'm sure.

I saw some faculty members there. They had all been invited, of course. Ten or so, with their husbands or wives, had come. Even Mr. Stoat was there. It hit me as I looked at them that most of them had been in their twenties and thirties when they were trying to deal with us on a daily basis, much younger than we were now. God, what a thankless job they must have had—going off every day like going back up to the Front in WWI, trying to teach kids who viewed you as The Enemy, following along behind everything you did with the efficient erasers in their minds! Maybe I'm getting too mellow—they had it easier with us than teachers do now—at least most of us *could* read, and music was more important than TV to us. Later, I told myself, I'll go over and talk to Ms. Nugent who was always my favorite and who had been a good teacher in spite of the chaos around her.

There were two guys working the tapes and CDs up on the raised stage. I didn't recognize the order of the songs so knew they weren't playing one of my tapes. On the front part of the stage were a guitar and bass, a drum set and keyboards.

So it was true, and seemed the main topic of conversation, although as I passed one bunch of people I heard someone say "Those assholes? Them?"

Barb showed up, without a date, of course. She took my hand and led me toward the dance floor. "Let's dance until our shoulders bleed," she said.

"Yes, ma'am!" I said.

I don't know about you, but I've been hypnotized on dance floors before. Sometimes it seems as if the tune stretches out to accommodate how long and hard you want to dance, or think you can. The guys working the decks were switching back and forth between two cassette players and the music never stopped—occasionally songs *only* I could have recorded showed up. I didn't care. I was dancing.

(I've seen some strange things on dance floors in my life—the strangest was people forming a conga line to a song by the band Reptilikus called "After Today, You Got One Less Day To Live.")

"Ginny's here," I said to Barb. Barb looked over toward the door where Ginny Balducci's wheelchair had rolled in. One weekend in 1973 Ginny had gone off for a ski weekend with an intern, and had come back out of the hospital six months later with a whole different life. "I'll say hi in a minute." said Barb.

We danced to the only Dylan song you can dance to, "I Want You," "Back in the U.S.S.R.," Buffalo Springfield, Blue Cheer, Sam and Dave, slow tunes by Jackie Wilson and Sam Cooke, then Barb went over to talk to Ginny. I was a sweating wreck by then, and the ugly feeling from the night before was all gone.

I started for the *whizzoir*.

"You won't like it," said a guy coming out of the men's room.

The smell hit me like a hammer. Someone had yelled New York into one of the five washbasins. It was half full. It appeared the person had lived exclusively for the last week on Dinty Moore Beef Stew and Fighting Cock Bourbon.

A janitor came in cursing as I was washing my hands.

I went back out to the ballroom. Mouse and the Trapps "Public Execution" was playing—someone who doesn't *dance* recorded that. Then came Jackie Wilson's "Higher and Higher."

"Dance with me?" asked someone behind me. I turned. It was Sharon. She must have Gone Borneo that afternoon. She'd been somewhere where they do things to you, wonderful things. She had on a blue dress and seamed silk stockings, and now she had an Aunt Peg haircut.

"You bet your ass!" I said.

About halfway through the next dance, I suffered a real sense of loss. I missed my butthole-length hair for the first time in ten years. The song, of course, was "Hair" off the original Broadway cast recording, Diane Keaton and all, and Joe Morton's wife Patricia, who had never cut hers, it grew within inches of the floor, suddenly grabbed it near her skull with one hand and whipped it around and around her head, the ends fanning out like a giant hand across the colored lights above the stage. Joe continued his Avalon-ballroom-no-sweat dancing, oblivious to the applause his wife was getting.

Then they played the Fish Cheer and we all sang and danced along with "I-Feel-Like-I'm-Fixin'-To-Die-Rag."

Then the lights came up and the entertainment director, Jamie Younts-Fulton, came to the mike and treated us to twenty minutes of nostalgic boredom and forced yoks. The tension was building.

"Now," she said, "for those of you who don't know, we've got them together again for the first time in nineteen years, here they are, Craig Beausoliel, Morey Morkheim, Abram Cassuth, and Andru Esposito, or, as you know them, *Distressed Flag Sale!*"

It was about what you'd expect—four guys in their late thirties in various pieces of clothing stretching across twenty years of fashion changes.

Morey'd put on weight and lost teeth, Andru had taken weight off. Abram, who'd been the only one without facial hair in our day, now had a full Jerry Garcia beard. Craig, who came out last, like always, and plugged in while we applauded—all four or five hundred people in the ballroom now—didn't look like the same guy at all. He looked like a businessman dressed up at Halloween to look like a rock singer.

He was a little unsteady on his feet. He was a little drunk.

"Enough of this Sixties crap!" he said. People applauded again. "Tonight, this first and last performance, we're calling ourselves *Lizard Level!*"

Then Abram hit the keyboard in the opening trill of "In-a-Gadda-da-Vida" for emphasis, then they slammed into "Proud Mary," Creedence's version, and the place became a blur of flying bodies, drumming feet, swirling clothes. The band started a little raggedy, then got it slowly together.

They launched into the Chambers Bros.' "Time Has Come Today," always a show stopper, a hard song for everybody *including* the Chambers Bros., if you ever saw them, and the place went really crazy, especially in the slow-motion parts. Then they did one of their own tunes, "The Moon's Your Harsh Mistress, Buddy, Not Mine," which I'd heard exactly once in two decades.

We were dancing, all kinds, pogo, no-sweat, skank, it didn't matter. I saw a few of the hotel staff standing in the doorways tapping their feet. Andru hit that screaming wail in the bass that was the band's trademark, sort of like a whale dying in your bathtub. People yelled, shook their arms over their heads.

Then they started to do "Soul Kitchen." Halfway through the opening, Craig raised his hand, shook it, stopped them.

"Awwwww," we said, like when a film breaks in a theater.

Craig leaned toward the others. He was shaking his head. Morey pointed down at his playlist. They put their heads together. Craig and Abram were giving the other two chord changes or something.

"Hey! Make music!" yelled some jerk from the doorway.

Craig looked up, grabbed the mike. "Hold it right there, asshole," he said, becoming the Craig we had known twenty years ago for a second. He leaned against the mike stand in a Jim Morrison vamp pose. "You stay right here, you're going to hear the god-damnedest music you ever heard!"

They talked together for a minute more. Andru shrugged his shoulders, looked worried. Then they all nodded their heads.

Craig Beausoliel came back up front. "What we're gonna do now, what we're gonna do now, gonna do," he said in a Van Morrison post-Them chant, "is we're gonna do, gonna do, the song we were gonna do that night in Miami . . ."

"Oh, geez," said Bob, who was on the dance floor near Sharon and me.

Distressed Flag Sale had gone into seclusion early in 1970, holing up like The Band did in the *Basement Tapes* days with Dylan, or like Brian Wilson and the Beach Boys while they were working on the never-finished *Smile* album. They were supposedly working on an album (we heard through the grapevine) called either *New Music for the AfterPeople* or *A Song to Change the World*, and there were supposedly heavy scenes there, lots of drugs, paranoia, jealousy, and revenge, but also great music. We never knew, because they came out of hiding to do the Miami concert to raise money for the family of a janitor blown up by mistake when somebody drove a car-bomb into an AFEES building one four A.M.

"It was a great song, man, a great song," said Craig, "It was going to change the world we thought." We realized for the first time how drunk Craig really was about then. "We were gonna play it that night, and the world was gonna change, but instead they got us, they *got us*, man, and we were the ones that got changed, not them. Tonight we're not Distressed Flag Sale, we're Lizard Level, and just once anyway, so you'll all know, tonight we're gonna do 'Life Is Like That.' "

(What changed in Miami was the next five years of their lives. The Miami cops had been holding the crowd back for three hours and looking for an excuse, anyway, and they got it, just after Distressed Flag Sale made its reeling way onstage. The crowd was already frenzied, and got up to dance when the guys started playing "Life Is Like That" and Andru took out his dong on the opening notes and started playing slide bass with it. The cops went crazy and jumped them, beat them up, planted heroin and amphetamines in their luggage in the dressing rooms, carted them off to jail and turned firehoses on the rioting fans.

Everybody knew the bust was rigged, because they charged Morey with possession of heroin, and everybody *knew* he was the speed freak.

And that was the end of Distressed Flag Sale.

It was almost literally the end of Andru, too. What the papers didn't tell you was that, as he was uncircumcised, he'd torn his frenum on the strings of the bass, and he almost lost, first, his dong, and then his life before the cops let a doctor in to see him.)

That's the history of the song we were going to hear.

Notes started from the keyboard, like it was going to be another Doors-type song, building. Then Craig moved his fingers a few times on the guitar strings, tinkling things rang up high, like birds were in the air over the stage, sort of like the opening of "Touch of Grey" by the Dead, but not like that either. Then Andru came in, and Morey, then it began to take on a shape and move on its own, like nothing else at all.

It moved. And it moved me, too. First I was swaying, then stomping my right foot. Sharon was pulling me toward the dance floor. I'd never heard anything like it. *This* was dance music. Sharon moved in large sways and swings; so did I.

The floor filled up fast. *Everybody* moved toward the music. Out of the corner of my eye I saw old Mr. Stoat asking someone to dance. Other teachers moved towards the sound.

Then I was too busy moving to notice much of anything. I was dancing, dancing not with myself but with Sharon, with Bob and Penny, with *everyone*.

All five hundred people danced. Ginny Balducci was at the corner of the floor, making her chair move in small tight graceful circles. I smiled. We all smiled.

The music got louder; not faster, but more insistent. The playing was superb, immaculate. *Lizard Level's* hands moved like they were a bar band that had been playing together every night for twenty years. They seemed oblivious to everything, too, eyes closed, feet shuffling.

Something was happening on the floor, people were moving in little groups and circles, couples breaking off and shimmying down between the lines of the others, in little waggling dance steps. It was happening all over the place. Then *I* was doing it—like Sharon and I had choreographed every move. People were clapping their hands in time to the music. It sounded like steamrollers were being thrown around in the ballroom.

Above it the music kept building and building in an impossible spiral.

Now the hotel staff joined in, busboys clapping hands, maids and waitresses turning in circles.

Then the pattern of the dance changed, magically, instantly, it split the room right down the middle, and we were in two long interlocking linked chains of people, crossing through each other, one line moving up the room, the other down it, like it was choreographed.

And the guys kept playing, and more people were coming into the ballroom. People in pajamas or naked from their rooms, the night manager and the bellboys. And as they joined in and the lines got more unwieldy, the two lines of people broke into four, and we began to move toward the doors of the ballroom, clapping our hands, stomping, dancing, making our own music, the same music, more people and more people.

At some point they walked away from the stage, joining us, left their amps, acoustic now. Morey had a single drum and was beating it, you could hear Andru and Craig on bass and guitar, Cassuth was still playing the keyboard on the batteries, his speaker held under one arm.

The street musicians had come into the hotel and joined in, people were picking up trash cans from the lobby, garbage cans from the streets, honking the horns of their stopped cars in time to the beat of the music.

We were on the streets now. Windows in buildings opened, people climbed down from second stories to join in. The whole city jumped in time to the song, like in an old Fleischer cartoon; Betty Boop, Koko, Bimbo, the buses, the buildings, the moon all swaying, the stars spinning on their centers like pinwheels.

Chains of bodies formed on every street, each block. At a certain beat they all broke and reformed into smaller ones that grew larger, interlocking helical ropes of dancers.

I was happy, happier than ever. We moved down one jumping chain of people. I saw mammoths, saber-toothed tigers, dinosaurs, salamanders, fish, insects, jellies in loops and swirls. Then came the beat and we were in the other chain, moving up the street, lost in the music, up the line of dancing people, beautiful fields, comets, nebulae, rockets and galaxies of calm light.

I smiled into Sharon's face, she smiled into mine.

Louder now the music, stronger, pulling at us like a wind. The cops joined in the dance.

Up Congress Avenue the legislators and government workers in special session came streaming out of their building like beautiful ants from a shining mound.

Louder now and happier, stronger, dancing, clapping, singing.

We will find our children or they will find us, before the dance is over, we can feel it. Or afterwards we will responsibly make more.

The chain broke again, and up the jumping streets we go, joyous now, joy all over the place, twenty, thirty thousand people, more every second.

As we swirled and grew, we would sometimes pass someone who was staring, not dancing, feet not moving; they would be crying in uncontrollable sobs and shakes, and occasionally committing suicide.

BRIAN STABLEFORD

The Growth of the House of Usher

Here's an unsettling examination of a bizarre Dream House of a future age, and the cost one pays for living there, by Brian Stableford, whose "The Man Who Loved the Vampire Lady" appears elsewhere in this anthology.

THE GROWTH OF THE HOUSE OF USHER

Brian Stableford

It was a dull, dark and soundless day on which I approached by motor-boat the house which my friend Rowland Usher had built in the loneliest spot he could find, in the southern region of the Orinoco delta. There are plenty of lonely spots to be found there nowadays, after a century and a half of changing sea levels due to the greenhouse effect.

The edifice which Rowland was raising from the silt of that great stagnant swamp was like nothing I had ever seen before, and I am morally certain that it was the strangest dwelling ever planned in the imagination of man. It loomed out of the swamp like a black mountain, without an angle anywhere, and with no windows (though that is the fashion in modern times). Near its crown there were soft crenellations, mere suggestions of battlements, and a number of projections that might have been balconies, but the whole seemed to me languidly shapeless.

Exactly to what extent he had been inspired by the coincidence of nomenclature that linked him with the famous story by Edgar Allan Poe I do not know, but there is surely some sense in which *one* of the true architects of that remarkable tower was a long-dead nineteenth-century fantasist, even though the other was a twenty-second century civil engineer. Rowland had always wanted to erect a House of Usher that could not and would not fall into ruin.

I was not sure, either, of the extent to which the letter summoning me here— which gave every evidence of nervous agitation and spoke of "mental disorder"—might be construed as a kind of satire on Poe. I had never thought of Rowland as a joker, but I could not entirely believe that his protestations were serious. I obeyed his summons, of course, but I was uncertain what to expect.

I had first met Rowland Usher at college, where we studied civil engineering together. We were partners in practical classes, and we became adept together in the deployment of the Gantz bacteria which are used in modern cementation processes. These engineered bacteria, which can be adapted to almost any kind of raw materials, had already wrought their first revolution, and were helping to transform whole vast areas of land where it had been impossible to build in the past: deserts, steppes and bare mountains alike. While the ecological engineers were transforming the world's environments, Gantz-inspired structural engineers were building entire new cities for people whose ancestors had never known adequate shelter; thanks to Leon Gantz, there need be no more mud huts—great palaces could be raised from any kind of dirt, whether mud, or sand, or shale.

Rowland and I had been fired with a similar sense of mission, determined to use the tools which our education provided to their very best purpose, to play our part in a Utopian remaking of the world, which would save it from its multiple crisis. We had shared a sense of vision and an ambition which many of our fellows lacked, and this brought us closer together. We both became increasingly interested in the techniques of genetic engineering involved in the manufacture of Gantz bacteria, and dreamed of imparting new powers to these living instruments, which would equip them to perform more astounding miracles.

Pioneers in our field were even then experimenting with living systems integrated into the walls of Gantzed structures, so that houses could put down tap roots into the ground on which they stood, to secure their own water-supplies. Living systems for the disposal of human wastes had been in use for some time, and ingenious engineers were trying to adapt these systems to the production of useful materials. These were the kinds of projects which had seized our imaginations, and we often collaborated on the design of imaginary living dwellings which would serve every human purpose.

As I approached the remarkable house which Rowland had built for himself, I could not help but recall these flights of fancy, and I wondered how much progress his genius had made. The castles in the air which *I* had built had been without exception edifices of considerable beauty and profound charm. No one could say that about the thing which Rowland had elevated from the silt of this great swamp, which retained the blackness of that silt and possessed an outward form that reminded me of nothing so much as one of the great termite mounds I had seen in southern Africa, where I had been working in recent years. The walls seemed slightly less than solid, as though capable of a certain sluggish protoplasmic flow, and this appearance gave me an uneasy feeling as I came to the threshold, recalling to my mind the story of Jonah who was swallowed by a whale.

Rowland met me at the open door and greeted me with enthusiasm. He conducted me through black, smooth-walled corridors which curved eccentrically into the bowels of the house, to a study where he obviously spent much of his time —there were three telescreens, a well-stocked disc library of miscellaneous publications, an integrated sound system and two well-worn sofas. The chamber was lighted by artificial bioluminescence, which was oddly ruddy and subdued.

A pot of China tea was waiting for me, timed to perfection, and we sat together drinking from small cups, exchanging platitudes. I had not seen Rowland for more than seven years, thanks to the reclusive habits which kept him apart from human society. I had expected to find him changed, but in spite of his letter I was surprised by the difference in him. He was very thin and pale, and his hair was quite white. His voice was uncertain, sometimes stumbling over simple sentences, and he gave the impression of slight intoxication, though there was no wine to be seen in the room.

I asked him if he was ill, and he confirmed that he was. Even the most modern diagnostic computers had failed to identify the biochemistry of its cause, despite the most comprehensive sampling and analysis of his bodily fluids. He was continually in touch, electronically, with the medical research foundation at Harvard.

"You need have no fear for yourself," he assured me. "This is no virus, or other infection; the fault is integral. This is the same malady which destroyed my father, and my sister Magdalen; somehow, it is in our genes. It seems strange that in this age when we have won such command over the formative powers of DNA, that the cunning double helix should still harbour mysteries, but it does. We have not entirely conquered those inner blights and pestilences which rot the very core of our being."

I inferred from this rather florid speech that Rowland was suffering from some exotic form of cancer, associated with a heritable chromosomal abnormality.

"Your sister died of this same illness?" I remarked.

He favoured me, as he answered, with a peculiar smile. "Oh yes," he said. "Many years ago, before I knew you at college. She was seventeen years old— she was born a year before me. The disease afflicts females more severely than males; my father lived to be forty, and I am now forty-seven. My grandfather's sister—the last female sufferer I have been able to identify—died at nineteen. You will readily understand why the disease is inherited through the male line. It is an Usher complaint, like the one which afflicted my famous namesake. Did I not know he were a fiction, I would suspect a line of actual descent."

I think I might have been alarmed if Rowland had told me that his sister were still alive, and had I seen her flitting ethereally through the apartment just then. This would have been one parallel too many for my tired mind to bear. As it was, though, I laughed politely.

"With Harvard on your side," I said, "there must be hope of a cure."

"No," he replied. "I do not hope for a cure, but merely an understanding. Modern medicine has helped me to ameliorate the symptoms of my condition, but having failed precisely to identify its biochemical nature, there is no hope of permanent remission. Its origin is in the brain, which is the least understood of all the organs—perhaps the last great mystery, in this our new Age of Enlightenment. You will have noticed that my speech is affected, and my sight too— which is why, I fear, the lighting here will seem a little eerie to your eyes. The mental disorder of which I spoke in my letter is increasingly perceptible, and I know that my working days are almost over. That is why I asked you to come to me—I want to explain to you what it is that I have been doing all these years, in my solitude, while you have been helping the poor in Africa.

"I want you to get to know my house, to understand what I have achieved here. I want you, in brief, to be the executor of my will. My personal possessions are worthless, but my additions to the sum of human knowledge and creativity are not. I leave everything to mankind in general, for the joy and benefit of all future generations—and you, my old friend, must convey my legacy to those heirs. There are full records of my data here, of course, but you know as well as I that the world is laden down beyond endurance with stored data, and that knowledge needs human champions if it is to be properly disseminated and developed."

I told him that I understood (though in truth I was not entirely sure that I did) and gave him my most earnest promise that I would try to do as he wished. He was delighted by this response, but his enthusiasm seemed suddenly to weaken him, and when we dined he ate almost nothing. Soon afterwards he begged leave to desert me, and after showing me to my bedroom he left me alone, begging me to make full use of the facilities of the house and apologizing profusely for not being able to give me a more thorough introduction to them.

Because the room had no window I could not ascertain whether the threatened storm had begun, but when I lay silently in my bed I thought that I could perceive a vibration in the dull, warm walls that might have been an echo of lashing rain and howling wind—or which might, instead, have been some mysterious internal process at work within the living fabric of the fabulous structure. After a time I found it strangely comforting, as if it were a subliminal lullaby, and I was carried off by it into peaceful sleep.

When I awoke the next day Rowland seemed better, and we breakfasted together. He told me, though, that he did not feel well enough to guide me about the house. He promised that he would show me its wonders at a later date, and offered instead to tell me something of the researches which had led to its construction, and which formed the substance of his intellectual legacy.

"You may recall from discussions we had nearly a quarter of a century ago," he said, "that I was always impatient with the traditional Gantz techniques which were in common use in our youth, and which we were expected to learn in a more-or-less slavish fashion in the course of our education in civil engineering.

"One of my chief interests—which we shared, I think—was the possibility of integrating better artificial living systems into the structure of buildings. It will not be long now, I am sure, before biotechnologists develop methods of artificial photosynthesis, and truly sophisticated living dwellings will not come into being until then. Houses will one day be living machines harvesting the energy of the sun as plants do. My house simulates, by necessity, a more primitive kind of organism: a lowly scavenger which draws its energy from the organic detritus of the silt out of which it is constructed. It is no more sophisticated than many sedentary creatures which live in shallow seas, filtering food from the murky waters which overflow them. Its closest analogues, if you wish to think in such terms, are coral polyps, barnacles and tubeworms. Nevertheless, however primitive it is, it lives and it grows. The Orinoco feeds it with all manner of decayed vegetable matter *via* the network of filters which extend from the foundations.

"You will probably remember another of my fascinations, which is similarly embodied in this house. Ordinary Gantz processes involve the use of inert moulds—the cementing organisms simply bind the material brought to them, and the architect controls the shape of what they produce by crude mechanical means. I was always impressed, though, by the way that living organisms adapt *themselves* to the construction of complicated edifices: the nests of wasps and termites, of bower-birds and ovenbirds; the supporting structures of corals; the astonishing forms of flowering plants and trees. I designed this house, therefore, by programming into the genes of its microorganic creators the kind of structure it should be.

"Its main structure is, of course, built primarily from non-living tissue, like the xylem of a tree or the shell of a mollusc, but that structure retains its connections with living cells, and is formed more-or-less precisely by the pattern of their activity."

"The house, then, is really a gargantuan living organism," I observed.

"Not strictly speaking," he corrected me. "It's builders are micro-organisms, which associate and collaborate like the members of a beehive or the individual cells in a slime-mould. If it is to be seen as a single entity, then it is a colony— a colony of trillions of quasi-bacterial cells. In adapting it for habitation, though, I do have cause to use other engineered organisms, which might be regarded as symbiotes of the elementary cells. The structure is naturally honeycombed by tunnels and chambers, but the precise design of the corridors and the rooms— not to mention the various connecting conduits which carry water, electricity and optical fibres—requires supplementary work."

Such work in ordinary Gantzed structures tends to be carried out by de-cementing bacteria whose work is precisely the opposite of the cementers, but from Rowland's reference to "other engineered organisms" I inferred that he was using "worms" more akin to the artificial organisms used to pulverize rocks like granite and basalt. Most such organisms are, though vermiform, not really worms—most are the larvae of insects, akin to "woodworm", these frequently being equipped with jaws and rasps powerful enough to cope with stone and metal.

"I have always been interested in insect larvae," he explained, when I asked him to elaborate. "They have in them so much *potential*—the phenomenon of metamorphosis has always fascinated me."

This was an interesting sideline to the discussion, and I pursued it. "None of the larvae which are conventionally used to tunnel through rock are capable of metamorphosis,'' I said. ''They are of such a size that the insects which would emerge from their pupae would be inviable giants—incapable of breathing or of locomotion.''

''That is because Gantzian engineers have not been interested in the genes which the larvae will only switch on during and after metamorphosis,'' Rowland told me. ''They have made only feeble efforts to modify such genes, and the giant insects they have managed to produce are mere grotesques. No one has tried to explore fully the real metamorphic potential of these larvae. Crudely utilitarian research into rock-breaking organisms can do no more than scratch the surface.''

''But you have gone further?''

''I have . . . taken an interest. The humble servants which help to hollow out my rooms have been my only companions for many years, and I have used them in certain unorthodox experiments quite unconnected with their more obvious purpose.''

I could see that this was a point upon which Rowland was, as yet, unwilling to elaborate. He seemed very tired and strained.

''Would it not be a good idea,'' I asked, ''if we were to return together, however briefly, to the United States? I know you are in touch with medical researchers there, and can transmit information gleaned from analysis of your blood and other fluids, but if you are suffering from a tumour in the brain, you surely need a sophisticated scan, which must be beyond the capacity of your own facilities.''

''Although my illness has its origins in the brain,'' he told me, ''it is not a localized tumour. It is some kind of genetic defect which is capable of affecting *all* the cells, and will eventually affect enough of them to kill me, as it killed my sister. The researchers at Harvard have quite enough samples of my cells—and, for that matter, my sister's cells—in their freezers to allow them to continue examining the chromosomes for many years. Eventually, I feel sure, they will map and identify the anomaly, though by then the knowledge may be redundant as the last known sufferer will be dead—I shall leave no children of my own.

''I hope that the work done on my cells after I am dead will serve to pave the way for their successful treatment and cure. I have been doing my own research, too, using the apparatus that permits me to engineer my bacteria and my worms, to do what I can to study my own chromosomes. I have my own cryonic chambers, and my own tissue-cultures—my father made the first contribution to my stocks before he died.''

''I wonder that you have not devoted your life to that research,'' I said, ''instead of spending so much time on your other project.''

''Ah!'' he said. ''My *other* project will assure me something worth far more than an extended lifespan—it will provide a kind of immortality. Even had I succeeded in curing myself I would have died after seventy or eighty years, but this house will live for centuries, perhaps for millennia. The Usher family will die out with me, but the House of Usher will continue to grow for many generations, and will be one of the wonders of this world when *your* descendants have built new worlds around distant stars. You see, my friend, that I have lost none of that Romantic imagination which drew you to me all those years ago!''

Indeed he had not, and as we talked further he waxed rhapsodic on the subject of the futures that were already nascent in the genetic technologies of the present day, his inventiveness vaulting across the centuries with talk of the miracles that godlike genetic engineers of the far future would work.

"It is not for you and I to see such things," he told me, after some while, "but your grandchildren will come into a world that will discover how to offer them immortality, and they will see the world transformed in ways we can hardly imagine. I will have my monument then, as Khufu has his—one of the last and greatest achievements of mortal mankind. We are members of one of the last generations to need tombs, my friend, and I intend that my sister and I shall have one of the very finest!''

His speech was becoming slurred and his tone was feverishly excited. I knew that his illness was taking hold of him, and I made every effort to calm him. In the afternoon, though, he had to leave me again, and I dined that evening alone.

The hours before I retired to my bed I spent in reading, but I was not tempted to begin the work of making my way through the discs which contained the long record of Rowland Usher's experiments. Instead, I sought solace in more familiar works—in the poetry of Blake and Byron, and (how could I avoid it?) Edgar Allan Poe. I say solace, but I really mean distraction, because the more time I spent in my tiny apartment deep in the heart of that utterly strange house, the more uneasy I began to feel about my virtual captivity. I did not like to be so cut off from the world outside and the sound of the everpresent murmur in the smooth, warm walls that surrounded me no longer seemed quite so comforting.

When I finally went to my bed I had a turbulent night, full of vague nightmares in which the imagery of Poe's poems mingled with the dreams and achievements of Rowland Usher. Conqueror worms continually triumphed in an uncertain tragedy, from whose toils I could not escape until I woke in a cold sweat, many hours before morning.

My nightmare had had such a profound effect on me that I did not like to close my eyes again for fear of its return. I reached out to activate the bioluminescent strips that would light my room, threw back the quilt and rose unsteadily to my feet. I went to the sink on the far side of the chamber, and obtained a cup of water.

No sooner had I taken a sip than my attention was caught by a sound in the corridor outside. Though there was nothing sinister in the sound itself, I had not yet escaped the effects of my evil dream, and it drew from me a gasp of pure terror.

I knew, at the level of reason, that I ought not to be afraid, and I forced myself to go to the door and open it. Such was my state of mind, though, that it was only by the merest crack that I pulled it ajar, and as I peeped out into the corridor my heart was pounding in my breast.

The corridor was not quite dark, though its bioluminescence was considerably toned down, so that what remained was a faint bluish radiance. Because the corridor curved I could see only a few metres in either direction, and could see only one other door—that of Rowland Usher's bedroom.

That door too seemed to be ajar, but there was darkness within. Moving away from the door, though—just disappearing from sight around the gentle angle of the tunnel—was a human figure. I caught no more of the merest glimpse of it, but I had the distinct impression that it was a young female, perhaps fourteen or fifteen years of age. She was quite naked.

The idea that this was Rowland's sister Magdalen, somehow risen from the dead, sprang into my mind, provoked by my dream even though I knew full well that it could not be. The power of the thought, even as I fought to dispel it, was sufficient to make me close my door again, and I found to my disgust that I was actually trembling. I—a scientist of the twenty-second century—was infected by the morbidity of the Gothic Imagination! I cursed Rowland Usher and his absurd termitary of a house, and resolved to demand an explanation in the morning.

When morning came, though, the matter seemed far less urgent to me. I had slept again, more restfully, and when I awoke at the proper time my experience in the corridor seemed rather to belong to the realm of my nightmare than to the realm of reality. I honestly could not tell whether or not it had been part of my dream, and even though the cup from which I drank was still on the side of the sink, I could not take seriously what I thought I had seen. Perhaps I simply did not want to.

In any case, I asked no questions of Rowland over breakfast regarding the possibility of his being haunted by the ghost of his sister.

That day, Rowland felt well enough to conduct me on a tour of his abode, and so we set forth into its amazing winding corridors. He showed me several other guest-rooms—none of which showed the slightest sign of ever having been inhabited—and several storerooms, some of them crammed with collections of objects which he had obviously inherited from past generations, as well as hoards of his own.

There were many antique books, some with acid-rotten pages that should have decayed a century ago, some even dating back to the nineteenth century. There was a collection of minerals, one of medical specimens, one of ancient navigational instruments, and a particularly quaint assembly of display screens and keyboards from the early days of information technology. I asked if these devices were in working order, but Rowland simply shrugged his shoulders; he did not know.

When we descended into the lower strata of the house I found things much more coherently organized, and there were clearly many rooms in active use. First he showed me the laboratories where he conducted his experiments in genetic analysis and his transformations of Gantzing bacteria. His equipment was reasonably modern, though no private individual, however rich, can possibly keep up with the larger research institutions.

His fermenters, where his bacterial cultures grew, were built into the fabric of the house, and it was not until he told me their cubic capacity that I realized how much of the house was hidden, circled by the spiralling corridors. Clearly, that space was not wasted.

I marvelled that any one man could possibly make use of the extensive laboratory facilities, but he assured me that the high level of automation made it reasonably easy. He had relatively few household robots, regarding the motile varieties as inherently unreliable examples of the mechanician's art, but some routine activities were contracted out to service personnel who operated machines by remote control.

At a lower level still, he showed me other holding tanks, where he kept his many species of burrowing worms. Most species needed special containers of some substance which they could not break up or digest. There were observation-windows which let us look in upon the creatures, though sometimes we could see little enough within because of the difficulties of providing lighting systems immune from their ravages.

Rowland allowed a few species of these worms to live free in the structure of the house, almost as parasites, because they could not damage its structure and performed useful waste-disposal functions as they foraged for food. At first it was disconcerting to come across these creatures at irregular intervals, but I soon got used to it.

"How do you direct the burrowing of the more voracious species?" I asked him. "Surely, any kind of escape would be desperately dangerous—the worms could devour the entire fabric of the house."

"Elementary cyborgization," he told me. "These creatures have little or no brain, and are guided through life by simple behavioural drives. It is a relatively easy matter to fit them with electronic devices which deliver the appropriate commands by electrical or biochemical stimulation. I handle them with great care. They cannot live, of course, on the materials they are designed to tunnel through, and their diets are deliberately exotic. I feed them what they need in order to execute a particular task, and no more. They cannot escape, and could not live wild if they did."

Watching these curious creatures, roaming loose or in their tanks, made me slightly nauseous, though I had often seen their like before. Most were like blowfly maggots—big and soft and white, their body walls so transparent that one could see the organs inside them. Rowland's were the biggest I had ever encountered, a metre and a half in length and at least eighty centimetres in girth. Their internal organs were not themselves coloured, but were enwrapped in a webwork of blue and pink. I asked Rowland to explain this, and he told me that he had equipped their circulatory systems with haemoglobin in order to serve the oxygen-needs of their organs; like us these creatures had deoxygenated blue blood in their veins and oxygenated red blood in their arteries.

Some others looked more like elongated centipedes than maggots, being bright yellow in colour and equipped with hundreds of pairs of limbs along the length of their plated bodies. These too were the largest of their kind I had ever encountered, being at least four metres long, though only as thick as a man's wrist. A few of these living machines were, on the other hand, surprisingly small: there were black, hard-skinned creatures that were only a few centimetres from head to tail, though they had vast heads that were almost all jaw. Rowland informed me that these were very difficult to rear because of the enormous amounts of food they had to consume in order to work those massive jaws. In their holding tank, they were virtually submerged in high-protein fluid.

These marvels impressed me tremendously, and we spent many hours in these lower regions. He showed me something of the "roots" which the house extended into the substrate of the swamp, and the apparatus for gathering in organic materials from the silt. He also showed me the biological batteries which produced the houses's electricity—which had a potential output, Rowland boasted, equivalent to thirty billion electric eels. Most of this, however, remained inevitably hidden; what could be seen of the house's systems was far less, in metaphorical terms, than the tip of an iceberg. Rowland assured me that there was much more to be seen than could be taken in during a single day. He reeled off statistics in an impressively casual manner, telling me that the biomass of the house was greater than ten thousand elephants, and that if it *had* been a single organism then it would have been the vastest that had ever existed on Earth.

By the time afternoon came, though, he was becoming increasingly tired, and his graphic descriptions began again to diversify into flights of fantasy, in which houses such as this one would gradually replace the plants and animals making up the world's ecosystems, so that in a thousand years the entire ecosphere might consist of nothing but organic artifacts—not merely houses but entire cities—all locked into a carefully symbiotic relationship controlled by men.

In such a world, he hypothesized, sexual reproduction would be the sole prerogative of mankind, everything else in the organic realm being capable only of vegetative growth or of being cloned and transformed by human genetic engineers.

I confess that I did not find this a wholly attractive prophecy (or speculation, for Rowland was talking of opportunity rather than destiny), but there was something very attractive in the sheer grandiosity of Rowland's ecstatic voyages of the imagination, and the magic of his ideas took a firm grip on me, encouraging my own mind to the contemplation of vistas of future history extending toward infinite horizons.

I joined in, for a while, with his game, and became so carried away that I did not notice for some time that Rowland's condition was becoming desperate, and that he was on the brink of losing his powers of motor co-ordination. He demanded that he should be allowed to show me the upper parts of the house, above our apartments, and uttered dark hints about there being more in the basements than I was yet prepared to imagine, but I had to forbid any further wandering, and in the end I had to support him as we made our way back up to the dining room.

For once, though, dinner seemed to revive Rowland's spirits, and he ate a good meal. After he had rested for a while he was restored sufficiently to conduct a longer conversation than had been possible on the evenings of my first two days as his guest.

He set out to tell me more about the history of his researches, but soon went on to personal matters, including secrets which he had hesitated to share with me when we were intimates in our younger days. In particular, he spoke of Magdalen, and I listened in fascination as he gradually peeled away the layers of inhibition which had hitherto concealed the inner mainsprings of his motivation. He granted me then such an insight into his character as he would surely never have conceded if he had not been certain that he was very close to death.

Alas, he was closer than he knew!

"Magdalen lived always under the shadowy threat of death," said Rowland, his voice weakening almost to a whisper as the process of recall carried him into a trance-like reverie. "My parents treated her with extraordinary indulgence; she was never sent to school because there seemed little point in trying to secure the kind of education that would be useful only as preparation for a later life which would not be her privilege. Instead, my father educated her himself, after his own theory, trying to equip her to obtain the greatest enjoyment from the years she actually would have. She was a beautiful child, who won the admiration of everyone, and of my father's eccentric tutelage I can say only that it seemed to work magnificently, for she was the happiest being I have ever met.

"Although I was allowed a more conventional schooling, I was also much involved in her life. My father sought to provide her with what he considered to be an ideal companionship; I too was a part of his scheme, though at first I did not know it. As he sought to mould her, so he sought to mould me, to build between the two of us such a bond of affection and community as to make us the lights of one another's lives. Such a uniquely close companionship he considered to be the greatest treasure which any human life is capable of discovering. I have not had cause to disagree with him in the decades through which I have lived since I lost that perfect relationship.

"I am a little sceptical now of my father's motivations. I wonder why, knowing that he was the victim of a heritable disease, he chose to have children at all. At the time, I thought the way that he took such careful and absolute control over our nurture was a measure of his heroic desperation in trying to save us from a misfortune of fate. Now I suspect that he had children precisely in order to carry out this remarkable experiment, and that we were his guinea-pigs. Nevertheless, I do know that he loved us very dearly indeed, and that the grief which he felt when Magdalen died robbed his life, as it robbed mine, of almost all meaning.

"You see around you the extraordinary lengths to which I have been driven in my attempts to find a meaningful project in which to absorb myself. He never did find another; he lived and died a sad man, save for those years when Magdalen gave him a reason to exercise his unusual powers of creativity. You and I work with the elements of physical heredity, and cannot fully understand the difficulties which attended his work in delicately manipulating the psyche and the environment, but I think you can appreciate what a triumph was his when I say that I wholeheartedly believe that Magdalen's was the most joyful, the most compassionate, the most *complete* life that I think a human being might live, in spite of—or perhaps because of—its brevity.

"He taught her only those things that might stimulate her sense of beauty and her sense of wonder, to give her the fullest measure of delight in the world where her mayfly existence was to be lived. He controlled all that she saw, and heard, and felt. When I became old enough to understand what was happening, he made me his collaborator instead of his instrument, and toward the end I conspired with him in planning her last few months. We were determined that there should be no joyful aspect of human experience denied to her and we discussed carefully the question of whether it should be he or I that would introduce her to sexual love. Despite the value of his experience in such matters, the responsibility was given to me—old taboos against father/daughter incest still have some power, while brother/sister intercourse is widely accepted, and we were scrupulously respectful of prevailing social attitudes even though we had established for Magdalen a private society in which the world at large could not interfere.

"There is a sense, I think, in which the climax of my life had already passed when you first met me. You found in me a man who felt that he had already finished one life, attempting the impossible in trying to make another. All I can say is that I have done my best, and that I am proud of what I have achieved. I do not regret having become a recluse, separating myself as far as it has been practicable from the society of other men. My memories of Magdalen are far more precious to me than any other relationship with a woman or a man could ever have been.

"I realize that you are bound to think this unusual, but if you are to be the interpreter of my achievement, who must explain to the world the measure of my genius and its productions, then you must try to understand."

Indeed, I did try to understand. He was correct in saying that in our enlightened times we are no longer so fearful of the taboos which preyed upon the consciences of our ancestors. We are no longer horrified by the idea of incest, so I was not particularly shocked to find out that Rowland had been his sister's lover. Nevertheless, the tale he told was so singular that I did have to struggle imaginatively to accommodate it. How odd and unparalleled the life of Magdalen Usher must have been!

Frankly, I doubted Rowland's assurances about the perfection of his sister's existence. I could not believe that this experiment in eupsychian engineering could possibly have been as successful as he claimed. No human being can be kept so utterly insulated from the darker side of life—from the ominous aspects of her own inner nature—as to be held inviolate from all dread, all sorrow, all splenetic impulse. Nevertheless, I did not doubt that *he* believed it, and that in his mind his sister's image must have a significance of purity greater than that of any saint or other idol.

I remembered the apparition of the previous night, of which I still feared to speak. I could not help but touch upon the subject, but felt compelled to do so *elliptically*, without directly saying what I had seen.

"She must be very much in your thoughts now," I said. "You must feel her nearness very acutely."

"I do," he said, dreamily. He seemed now to have been overcome by a tremendous tiredness, which carried him off into a kind of euphoric altered consciousness. Despite the fact that he had resolved to tell me his secrets, I do not believe that he would have told me any more at that time had he been in full possession of his faculties. He had surely planned a more gradual process of revelation. He was in the grip of his disease, though, and in a state of mind that few humans can ever have attained.

"At first," he said, "I dreamed of re-creating her. So many of her cells, including oöcytes from her womb, were taken from her even before death, to make the tissue-cultures that would be used for the study of our freakish disease. I wanted to clone her, to bring her back from the dead, to make her anew. I soon realized, though, that it would be a dreadful thing to do. All the best efforts of my father and myself had gone into giving her a perfect existence within its prescribed limits. To create another of her would be to spoil our design, as if we were to take a great painting and daub over it an inferior copy. She could *never* be re-created, and to make another individual out of her genes would be an appalling travesty of all that my father and I had done.

"When I went to college, therefore, I deliberately elected to stay away from medicine, from human engineering. I went into the kind of work that would help me to transform the human *environment* rather than the human body. I wanted to build houses, not people—places for people to live, where they could live *well*, in privacy. I soon realized that it would not be enough to build the kind of houses that are now being built—I wanted to create something much more ambitious. But I could not entirely forget Magdalen, and there remained a sense in which my house . . . my private world . . . must in some way contain her. That was when I conceived the notion of working with larvae.

"We are so proud these days of our own biotechnic miracles that we tend to forget nature's, and we tend to forget what a colossal bounty was made available to our early genetic engineers, in terms of the raw materials with which they began to work. I have always been fascinated by metamorphosis, by the fact that a maggot or a caterpillar can carry within it genes which code for an entirely different creature, so that when the time comes it builds itself a temporary tomb from which it will one day emerge anew.

"It struck me as a terrible waste that structural engineers should breed hundreds or thousands of new kinds of larvae to work for us, without sparing a thought for the fact that their eventual pupation would now be the end of their story. No one cared, it seemed, about the fact that these modified larvae could no longer advance to a final stage in their development, because the imagos programmed into their altered genes were hopelessly inviable.

"Thus, when I began engineering larvae for work within my house, I also began engineering them so that they *would* be able to pupate and metamorphose successfully. I knew that they could not produce giant insects, with wings and exoskeletons, so I set about reprogramming them to produce creatures that *are* viable at that size. The creatures which I showed you today, which resemble blowfly maggots, have approximately the same biomass as a human being; they lose much of that in pupation, but can still produce something the size of a young adolescent. Mindless creatures, of course, but beautiful, in their way. They do not live long, at present, but I have laid the foundations for work which has limitless scope. In time, the engineers of the future might produce another human race.

"I have tried hard to gain sufficiently refined control over the features of these individuals, and I regret to say that I have not succeeded in producing one which bears more than a passing resemblance to my beloved Magdalen, despite using her own genetic material, but my quest has always been a hopeful one and I have derived much comfort from it. I needed *something* of her, you understand, to sustain me in my solitude . . . and they have given me that. *Something*, albeit so little . . ."

Rowland began suddenly to cough, and the cough developed into a kind of seizure.

Anxiously, I went to his side, and tried to calm him, but blood spattered my hand, and I suddenly realized that his condition was critical. His face had a ghastly pallor, and he struggled to whisper.

"So soon . . . *Magdalen*!"

It was as though the words themselves choked him. I tried to clear the blockage from his throat, to administer artificial respiration, but I could not start his heart beating again.

Within minutes, he was dead.

I checked Rowland's body for signs of life, and finding none I called Harvard, and asked to be put in touch with someone familiar with the details of his case. Then I went to another screen, and began to interrogate the data stores within the integral system. Within minutes I had a series of printed schematics which would serve as a map of the house. I located a wheeled stretcher in a nearby storeroom, and took him down to the room which housed his diagnostic computer and its ancillary apparatus. There I took the return call from Harvard. When I had manoeuvred the body into the cradle of the apparatus, the surgeon took over the remote controls, and began to check again for signs of life before continuing with the post-mortem.

This I could not bear to watch, and so I made my way back to the study where Rowland had told me his remarkable story. There, obsessed with the necessity of being reasonable, I set about the task which he had set for me. I began to inspect the discs on which he had carefully kept the records of all his experiments and all his projects.

In time, I could carry all the information away to more congenial surroundings, but I knew that if I were to do the job properly, then I would have to work in the house for at least a fortnight, in order to know exactly what ought to be taken away or transmitted electronically to my own home.

I took three further calls from Harvard, but I was not required to do anything further—the doctors there, working in association with the house's automatic systems, completed their examination, took their samples, issued a death certificate and wrapped the body in preparation for interment. By this time I had located Rowland's actual last will and testament, and I set in motion the legal machinery needed to put it through probate. The will provided for the burial of the body beneath the house, and I knew that this was a task that I would have to carry out myself, but it was one that could safely be left for another day.

It was late when I finally dimmed the lights and returned to my own room. Midnight had long gone, but insulated as I was from any knowledge of the setting and rising of the sun my sense of time was confused, and I did not feel tired until I actually took the decision to stop and rest. Then, fatigue suddenly swept over me like a wave.

With darkness and fatigue, though, came an inevitable relaxation of reason, and when I slept, my self-control—so carefully maintained by the iron grip of consciousness—was banished. I dreamt more nightmarishly than I had done the previous night, and my dreams were pure Poe.

I dreamt that I buried Rowland not in his own house but in that other—that haunted purgatory of fantasy. Our journey to the grave was through rotting passages weeping with cold slime, lit only by smoky torches whose flames were angry red. I dragged the coffin behind me, supporting only one end, and I think that Rowland somehow spoke to me from dead lips as we went, mocking my slowness.

This was bad enough, but after I had immured him in a vault behind a great metal door I remained anchored to the spot, listening for an eternity, waiting for the sound that I knew would come—the sound of the body risen from its rest, its fingers tapping and scratching at the door.

Inevitably (probably there was no *real* lapse of time, but simply an aching false consciousness of time passed) the sound began, and taunted my soul with echoes of dread and anguish which reverberated in my being until I felt myself literally driven insane, and howled at myself in the fury of my hallucination: *"Madman! Madman! Madman!"*

Then I woke in a cold sweat, thirsting.

And I heard, outside the door of my chamber, a faint tapping and scratching.

For a moment, I convinced myself that I was still asleep, and struggled manfully to wake. Then I could deny my senses no longer, and knew that the sound was real.

I dragged myself from my bed, feeling very heavy, my body requiring an agony of effort to move at all. I stumbled to the door, and opened it, at first by the merest crack and then—in consequence of what I saw—much wider.

There in the faintly-lit corridor, prostrate at my feet, one hand still groping for the door, was what seemed to be a teenage girl.

I knew, of course, that it was not. How many human genes were in it— Magdalen Usher's genes—I could not guess, but I knew that it was but a sham, a phantasm, no more human than the maggots which would soon consume Rowland Usher's body—and one day, no doubt, my own. But still, it was a pitiful creature, and in such a form it could not help but attract my sympathies. I remembered what Rowland had said about their not living long.

Some insect "adults" are born without digestive systems, unable to feed; they exist only to exchange genes in the physiological ritual of sexual intercourse. These creatures of Rowland's had not even reproductive organs inside them. They existed neither to eat nor to breed, being equipped only with the very minimum of a behavioural repertoire in order to serve their maker's purpose.

They existed to cling and caress, to soothe and be soothed, and that was the entirety of their existence. Like mayflies they were born and they died, innocent and ignorant of time, space and the world at large. Their universe was the House of Usher, and one can only hope that they passed their brief existence in a kind of bliss.

I was awake again now, and though startled and a little appalled, I found no alternative but to pick up the poor creature and carry her to my bed, where I stroked her gently and calmed her (I could no longer think in terms of "it" once I had touched her).

She died before morning.

Later, I visited the caverns deep underground (but still within the living walls of the growing manse) where the free-living maggots pupated, and saw rank upon rank of grey pupae, shaped like the sarcophagi in which the Egyptians entombed their mummified dead. I watched the hatching of the humanoid ephemerae, and studied them through their brief life-cycle—a mere handful of days. They did not, left to themselves, find their way into the upper parts of the house, though when I led one of them—as Rowland Usher often must have done—to my own bedroom, she knew both the way back to the deepest cellars and the way to return to the room, unescorted.

They did not really need me, I found, for it was rare that they hatched out alone. Usually, there were half a dozen alive at any one time, and they could obey their inner drives in fondling one another, achieving their fulfilment easily, comfortably, and by their own standards *naturally*.

When the time eventually came for me to leave Rowland's house, to convey his legacy to the greater world so that his methods and techniques might be employed for the betterment of mankind, I was sorry to leave these ephemerae, because I had grown fond of them, in my fashion. It was in their chamber that I buried Rowland Usher, for it was there that I found the grave of his beloved Magdalen, and I knew that brother and sister would have wished to rest side by side. I left him lightly coffined, as I knew that he would have left her, so that in time his decaying flesh might be absorbed, with hers, by the scavenging cells of the house, to become a part of its extending body, dissipated within it, united in substance if not in spirit.

When I finally did come out of the house again, and found myself in the full glare of the tropic sun, I had to wrinkle my nose against the stench of the swamp, for I had become used to breathing clean and sterile air. The sky seemed very blue, its light wild and abandoned, and my eyes ached for the gentle roseate light of bioluminescence.

As the motor-boat sped away toward the main stream of the Orinoco I looked back at the astonishing edifice, and saw that in this light its ebon walls gleamed and sparkled like jet, and that its softened shape resembled a Daliesque hand reaching up as though to touch the sun with molten fingers.

It was not ugly at all, but perfectly lovely.

The first House of Usher—that shameful allegory of the disturbed psyche—was burst asunder and swallowed by dark waters. In stark contrast, Rowland's house still stands, soaring proudly above the tattered canopy of the twisted trees.

It is still growing, and though it stands today in a noisome swamp there will come a time, I know, when it has purified the lakes and the islands, absorbing their stagnancy into its own vitality.

I was afraid, for a time, that the mysterious canker which was implicit in Rowland Usher's being might in some curious fashion be replicated in his house—perhaps by infection as the house absorbed his mortal remains. I am glad to say, though, that in the ten years since I quit that house it has shown no outward sign of any malady, and I become more confident with every year that passes that it will truly stand the test of time.

In one of the notes which he appended to his data discs Rowland contrasts his own house with Poe's imaginary one, damning the fictitious original as a typical product of the nineteenth century imagination and its myriad demonic afflictions. His own house, he claims, belongs not just to the twenty-second century but to the *third millennium*, and hazards the speculation that its life might not even be confined by a thousand years, but might go on forever, into that far-off Golden Age when the entire ecosphere of this planet (and who knows how many more) will be subject to the dominion of the mind of man.

We can only hope that his faith will be justified.

KIM STANLEY ROBINSON

Glacier

Here's a thoughtful and intensely rendered study of a boy's difficult coming-of-age in a future Boston caught in a deadly grip of ice . . .

Kim Stanley Robinson sold his first story in 1976, and quickly established himself as one of the most respected and critically acclaimed writers of his generation. He is a frequent contributor to such markets as *Isaac Asimov's Science Fiction Magazine, The Magazine of Fantasy and Science Fiction, Universe*, and *Omni*. His brilliant story "Black Air" was both a Nebula and Hugo finalist in 1984, and went on to win the World Fantasy Award that year. "Black Air" was in our First Annual Collection. His excellent novel *The Wild Shore* was published in 1984 as the first title in the resurrected Ace Special line, and was one of the most critically acclaimed novels of the year. Other Robinson books include the novels *Icehenge* and *The Memory of Whiteness*, and the critical book *The Novels of Philip K. Dick*. His most recent books are *The Planet on the Table*, a collection, and a new novel, *The Gold Coast*. His story "The Lucky Strike" was in our Second Annual Collection, "Green Mars" was in our Third Annual Collection, "Down and Out in the Year 2000" was in our Fourth Annual Collection, and his "Mother Goddess to the World" was in our Fifth Annual Collection. Robinson and his wife Lisa, are back in the United States again after several years in Switzerland.

GLACIER

Kim Stanley Robinson

"This is Stella," Mrs. Goldberg said. She opened the cardboard box and a gray cat leaped out and streaked under the corner table.

"That's where we'll put her blanket," Alex's mother said.

Alex got down on hands and knees to look. Stella was a skinny old cat; her fur was an odd mix of silver, black, and pinkish tan. Yellow eyes. Part tortoise-shell, Mom had said. The color of the fur over her eyes made it appear her brow was permanently furrowed. Her ears were laid flat.

"Remember she's kind of scared of boys," Mrs. Goldberg said.

"I know." Alex sat back on his heels. Stella hissed. "I was just looking." He knew the cat's whole story. She had been a stray that began visiting the Goldbergs' balcony to eat their dog's food, then—as far as anyone could tell— to hang out with the dog. Remus, a stiff-legged ancient thing, seemed happy to have the company, and after a while the two animals were inseparable. The cat had learned how to behave by watching Remus, and so it would go for a walk, come when you called it, shake hands and so on. Then Remus died, and now the Goldbergs had to move. Mom had offered to take Stella in, and though Father sighed heavily when she told him about it, he hadn't refused.

Mrs. Goldberg sat on the worn carpet beside Alex, and leaned forward so she could see under the table. Her face was puffy. "It's okay, Stell-bell," she said. "It's okay."

The cat stared at Mrs. Goldberg with an expression that said *You've got to be kidding*. Alex grinned to see such skepticism.

Mrs. Goldberg reached under the table; the cat squeaked in protest as it was pulled out, then lay in Mrs. Goldberg's lap quivering like a rabbit. The two women talked about other things. Then Mrs. Goldberg put Stella in Alex's mother's lap. There were scars on its ears and head. It breathed fast. Finally it calmed under Mom's hands. "Maybe we should feed her something," Mom said. She knew how distressed animals could get in this situation: they themselves had left behind their dog Pongo, when they moved from Toronto to Boston. Alex and she had been the ones to take Pongo to the Wallaces; the dog had howled as they left, and walking away Mom had cried. Now she told Alex to get some chicken out of the fridge and put it in a bowl for Stella. He put the bowl on the couch next to the cat, who sniffed at it disdainfully and refused to look at it. Only after much calming would it nibble at the meat, nose drawn high over one sharp eyetooth. Mom talked to Mrs. Goldberg, who watched Stella eat. When the cat was done it hopped off Mom's lap and walked up and down the couch. But it wouldn't let Alex near; it crouched as he approached, and with a desperate look dashed back under the table. "Oh Stella!" Mrs. Goldberg laughed. "It'll take her a while to get used to you," she said to Alex, and sniffed. Alex shrugged.

Outside the wind ripped at the treetops sticking above the buildings. Alex walked up Chester Street to Brighton Avenue and turned left, hurrying to counteract the cold. Soon he reached the river and could walk the path on top of the embankment. Down in its trough the river's edges were crusted with ice, but midstream was still free, the silty gray water riffled by white. He passed the construction site for the dam and came to the moraine, a long mound of dirt, rocks, lumber, and junk. He climbed it with big steps, and stood looking at the glacier.

The glacier was immense, like a range of white hills rolling in from the west and north. The Charles poured from the bottom of it and roiled through a cut in the terminal moraine; the glacier's snout loomed so large that the river looked small, like a gutter after a storm. Bright white iceberg chunks had toppled off the face of the snout, leaving fresh blue scars and clogging the river below.

Alex walked the edge of the moraine until he was above the glacier's side. To his left was the razed zone, torn streets and fresh dirt and cellars open to the sky; beyond it Allston and Brighton, still bustling with city life. Under him, the sharp-edged mound of dirt and debris. To his right, the wilderness of ice and rock. Looking straight ahead it was hard to believe that the two halves of the view came from the same world. Neat. He descended the moraine's steep loose inside slope carefully, following a path of his own.

The meeting of glacier and moraine was a curious juncture. In some places the moraine had been undercut and had spilled across the ice in wide fans; you couldn't be sure if the dirt was solid or if it concealed crevasses. In other places melting had created a gap, so that a thick cake of ice stood over empty air, and dripped into gray pools below. Once Alex had seen a car in one of these low wet caves, stripped of its paint and squashed flat.

In still other places, however, the ice sloped down and overlaid the moraine's gravel in a perfect ramp, as if fitted by carpenters. Alex walked the trough between dirt and ice until he reached one of these areas, then took a big step onto the curved white surface. He felt the usual quiver of excitement: he was on the glacier.

It was steep on the rounded side slope, but the ice was embedded with thousands of chunks of gravel. Each pebble, heated by the sun, had sunk into a little pocket of its own, and was then frozen into position in the night; this process had been repeated until most chunks were about three-quarters buried. Thus the glacier had a peculiarly pocked, rocky surface, which gripped the torn soles of Alex's shoes. A non-slip surface. No slope on the glacier was too steep for him. Crunch, crunch, crunch: tiny arabesques of ice collapsed under his feet with every step. He could change the glacier, he was part of its action. Part of it.

Where the side slope leveled out the first big crevasses appeared. These deep blue fissures were dangerous, and Alex stepped between two of them and up a narrow ramp very carefully. He picked up a fist-sized rock, tossed it in the bigger crack. *Clunk clunk . . . splash.* He shivered and walked on, ritual satisfied. He knew from these throws that at the bottom of the glacier there were pockets of air, pools of water, streams running down to form the Charles . . . a deadly subglacial world. No one who fell into it would ever escape. It made the surface ice glow with a magical danger, an internal light.

Up on the glacier proper he could walk more easily. Crunch crunch crunch, over an undulating broken debris-covered plain. Ice for miles on miles. Looking back toward the city he saw the Hancock and Prudential towers to the right, the lower MIT towers to the left, poking up at low scudding clouds. The wind was strong here and he pulled his jacket hood's drawstring tighter. Muffled hoot of wind, a million tricklings. There were little creeks running in channels cut into the ice: it was almost like an ordinary landscape, streams running in ravines over a broad rocky meadow. And yet everything was different. The streams ran into crevasses or potholes and instantly disappeared, for instance. It was wonderfully strange to look down such a rounded hole: the ice was very blue and you could see the air bubbles in it, air from some year long ago.

Broken seracs exposed fresh ice to the sun. Scores of big erratic boulders dotted the glacier, some the size of houses. He made his way from one to the next, using them as cover. There were gangs of boys from Cambridge who occasionally came up here, and they were dangerous. It was important to see them before he was seen.

A mile or more onto the glacier, ice had flowed around one big boulder, leaving a curving wall some ten feet high—another example of the glacier's whimsy, one of hundreds of strange surface formations. Alex had wedged some stray boards into the gap between rock and ice, making a seat that was tucked out of the west wind. Flat rocks made a fine floor, and in the corner he had even made a little fireplace. Every fire he lit sank the hearth of flat stones a bit deeper into the otherwise impervious ice.

This time he didn't have enough kindling, though, so he sat on his bench, hands deep in pockets, and looked back at the city. He could see for miles. Wind whistled over the boulder. Scattered shafts of sunlight broke against ice. Mostly shadowed, the jumbled expanse was faintly pink. This was because of an algae that lived on nothing but ice and dust. Pink; the blue of the seracs; gray ice;

patches of white, marking snow or sunlight. In the distance dark clouds scraped the top of the blue Hancock building, making it look like a distant serac. Alex leaned back against his plank wall, whistling one of the songs of the Pirate King.

Everyone agreed the cat was crazy. Her veneer of civilization was thin, and at any loud noise—the phone's ring, the door slamming—she would jump as if shot, then stop in mid-flight as she recalled that this particular noise entailed no danger; then lick down her fur, pretending she had never jumped in the first place. A flayed sensibility.

She was also very wary about proximity to people; this despite the fact that she had learned to love being petted. So she would often get in moods where she would approach one of them and give an exploratory, half-purring mew; then, if you responded to the invitation and crouched to pet her, she would sidle just out of arm's reach, repeating the invitation but retreating with each shift you made, until she either let you get within petting distance—just—or decided it wasn't worth the risk, and scampered away. Father laughed at this intense ambivalence. "Stella, you're too stupid to live, aren't you," he said in a teasing voice.

"Charles," Mom said.

"It's the best example of approach avoidance behavior I've ever seen," Father said. Intrigued by the challenge, he would sit on the floor, back against the couch and legs stretched ahead of him, and put Stella on his thighs. She would either endure his stroking until it ended, when she could jump away without impediment—or relax, and purr. She had a rasping loud purr, it reminded Alex of a chainsaw heard across the glacier. "Bug brain," Father would say to her. "Button head."

After a few weeks, as August turned to September and the leaves began to wither and fall, Stella started to lap sit voluntarily—but always in Mom's lap. "She likes the warmth," Mom said.

"It's cold on the floor," Father agreed, and played with the cat's scarred ears. "But why do you always sit on Helen's lap, huhn, Stell? I'm the one who started you on that." Eventually the cat would step onto his lap as well, and stretch out as if it was something she had always done. Father laughed at her.

Stella never rested on Alex's lap voluntarily, but would sometimes stay if he put her there and stroked her slowly for a long time. On the other hand she was just as likely to look back at him, go cross-eyed with horror and leap desperately away, leaving claw marks in his thighs. "She's so weird," he complained to Mom after one of these abrupt departures.

"It's true," Mom said with her low laugh. "But you have to remember that Stella was probably an abused kitty."

"How can you abuse a stray?"

"I'm sure there are ways. And maybe she was abused at home, and ran away."

"Who would do that?"

"Some people would."

Alex recalled the gangs on the glacier, and knew it was true. He tried to imagine what it would be like to be at their mercy, all the time. After that he thought he understood her permanent frown of deep concentration and distrust, as she sat staring at him. "It's just me, Stell-bells."

Thus when the cat followed him up onto the roof, and seemed to enjoy hanging out there with him, he was pleased. Their apartment was on the top floor, and they could take the pantry stairs and use the roof as a porch. It was a flat expanse of graveled tarpaper, a terrible imitation of the glacier's non-slip surface, but it was nice on dry days to go up there and look around, toss pebbles onto other roofs, see if the glacier was visible, and so on. Once Stella pounced at a piece of string trailing from his pants, and next time he brought up a length of Father's yarn. He was astonished and delighted when Stella responded by attacking the windblown yarn enthusiastically, biting it, clawing it, wrestling it from her back when Alex twirled it around her, and generally behaving in a very kittenish way. Perhaps she had never played as a kitten, Alex thought, so that it was all coming out now that she felt safe. But the play always ended abruptly; she would come to herself in mid-bite or bat, straighten up, and look around with a forbidding expression, as if to say *What is this yarn doing draped over me?*—then lick her fur and pretend the preceding minutes hadn't happened. It made Alex laugh.

Although the glacier had overrun many towns to the west and north, Watertown and Newton most recently, there was surprisingly little evidence of that in the moraines, or in the ice. It was almost all natural: rock and dirt and wood. Perhaps the wood had come from houses, perhaps some of the gravel had once been concrete, but you couldn't tell that now. Just dirt and rock and splinters, with an occasional chunk of plastic or metal thrown in. Apparently the overrun towns had been plowed under on the spot, or moved. Mostly it looked like the glacier had just left the White Mountains.

Father and Gary Jung had once talked about the latest plan from MIT. The enormous dam they were building downstream, between Allston and Cambridge, was to hold the glacier back. They were going to heat the concrete of the inner surface of the dam, and melt the ice as it advanced. It would become a kind of frozen reservoir. The melt water would pour through a set of turbines before becoming the Charles, and the electricity generated by these turbines would help to heat the dam. Very neat.

The ice of the glacier, when you got right down to look at it, was clear for an inch or less, cracked and bubble-filled; then it turned a milky white. You could see the transition. Where the ice had been sheared vertically, however—on the side of a serac, or down in a crevasse—the clear part extended in many inches.

You could see air bubbles deep inside, as if it were badly made glass. And this ice was distinctly blue. Alex didn't understand why there should be that difference, between the white ice laying flat and the blue ice cut vertically. But there it was.

Up in New Hampshire they had tried slowing the glacier—or at least stopping the abrupt "Alaskan slides"—by setting steel rods vertically in concrete, and laying the concrete in the glacier's path. Later they had hacked out one of these installations, and found the rods bent in perfect ninety degree angles, pressed into the scored concrete.

The ice would flow right over the dam.

One day Alex was walking by Father's study when Father called out. "Alexander! Take a look at this."

Alex entered the dark book-lined room. Its window overlooked the weed-filled space between buildings, and green light slanted onto Father's desk. "Here, stand beside me and look in my coffee cup. You can see the reflection of the Morgelis' window flowers on the coffee."

"Oh yeah! Neat."

"It gave me a shock! I looked down and there were these white and pink flowers in my cup, bobbing against a wall in a breeze, all of it tinted sepia as if it were an old-fashioned photo. It took me a while to see where it was coming from, what was being reflected." He laughed. "Through a looking glass."

Alex's father had light brown eyes, and fair wispy hair brushed back from a receding hairline. Mom called him handsome, and Alex agreed: tall, thin, graceful, delicate, distinguished. His father was a great man. Now he smiled in a way Alex didn't understand, looking into his coffee cup.

Mom had friends at the street market on Memorial Drive, and she had arranged work for Alex there. Three afternoons a week he walked over the Charles to the riverside street and helped the fishmongers gut fish, the vegetable sellers strip and clean the vegetables. He also helped set up stalls and take them down, and he swept and hosed the street afterwards. He was popular because of his energy and his willingness to get his hands wet in raw weather. The sleeves of his down jacket were permanently discolored from the frequent soakings—the dark blue almost a brown—a fact that distressed his mom. But he could handle the cold better than the adults; his hands would get a splotchy bluish white and he would put them to the red cheeks of the women and they would jump and say *My God*, Alex, how can you stand it?

This afternoon was blustery and dark but without rain, and it was enlivened by an attempted theft in the pasta stands, and by the appearance of a very mangy, very fast stray dog. This dog pounced on the pile of fishheads and entrails and disappeared with his mouth stuffed, trailing slick white-and-red guts. Everyone who saw it laughed. There weren't many stray dogs left these days, it was a pleasure to see one.

An hour past sunset he was done cleaning up and on his way home, hands in his pockets, stomach full, a five dollar bill clutched in one hand. He showed his pass to the National Guardsman and walked out onto Weeks Bridge. In the middle he stopped and leaned over the railing, into the wind. Below the water churned, milky with glacial silt. The sky still held a lot of light. Low curving bands of black cloud swept in from the northwest, like great ribs of slate. Above these bands the white sky was leached away by dusk. Raw wind whistled over his hood. Light water rushing below, dark clouds rushing above . . . he breathed the wind deep into him, felt himself expand until he filled everything he could see.

That night his parents' friends were gathering at their apartment for their bi-weekly party. Some of them would read stories and poems and essays and broadsides they had written, and then they would argue about them; and after that they would drink and eat whatever they had brought, and argue some more. Alex enjoyed it. But tonight when he got home Mom was rushing between computer and kitchen and muttering curses as she hit command keys or the hot water faucet, and the moment she saw him she said, "Oh Alex I'm glad you're here, could you please run down to the laundry and do just one load for me? The Talbots are staying over tonight and there aren't any clean sheets and I don't have anything to wear tomorrow either—thanks, you're a dear." And he was back out the door with a full laundry bag hung over his shoulder and the box of soap in the other hand, stomping grumpily past a little man in a black coat, reading a newspaper on the stoop of 19 Chester.

Down to Brighton, take a right, downstairs into the brightly lit basement laundromat. He threw laundry and soap and quarters into their places, turned the machine on and sat on top of it. Glumly he watched the other people in there, sitting on the washers and dryers. The vibrations put a lot of them to sleep. Others stared dully at the wall. Back in his apartment the guests would be arriving, taking off their overcoats, slapping arms over chests and talking as fast as they could. David and Sara and John from next door, Ira and Gary and Ilene from across the street, the Talbots, Kathryn Grimm, and Michael Wu from Father's university, Ron from the hospital. They would settle down in the living room, on couches and chairs and floor, and talk and talk. Alex liked Kathryn especially, she could talk twice as fast as anyone else, and she called everyone darling and laughed and chattered so fast that everyone was caught up in the rhythm of it. Or David with his jokes, or Jay Talbot and his friendly questions. Or Gary Jung, the way he would sit in his corner like a bear, drinking beer and challenging everything that everyone read. "Why abstraction, why this distortion from the real? How does it help us, how does it speak to us? We should forget the abstract!'' Father and Ira called him a vulgar Marxist, but he didn't mind. ''You might as well be Plekhanov, Gary!'' ''Thank you very much!'' he would say with a sharp grin, rubbing his unshaven jowls. And someone else would read. Mary Talbot once read a fairy tale about the Thing under the glacier; Alex had *loved* it. Once they even got Michael Wu to bring his violin along, and he hmm'd and hawed and pulled at the skin of his neck and refused and said he wasn't good enough, and then shaking like a leaf he played a melody that stilled them all. And Stella! She hated these parties, she spent them crouched deep in her refuge, ready for any kind of atrocity.

And here he was sitting on a washer in the laundromat.

When the laundry was dry he bundled it into the bag, then hurried around the corner and down Chester Street. Inside the glass door of Number 21 he glanced back out, and noticed that the man who had been reading the paper on the stoop next door was still sitting there. Odd. It was cold to be sitting outdoors.

Upstairs the readings had ended and the group was scattered through the apartment, most of them in the kitchen, as Mom had lit the stovetop burners and turned the gas up high. The blue flames roared airily under their chatter, making the kitchen bright and warm. ''Wonderful the way white gas burns so clean.'' ''And then they found the poor thing's head and intestines in the alley—it had been butchered right on the spot.''

''Alex, you're back! Thanks for doing that. Here, get something to eat.''

Everyone greeted him and went back to their conversations. ''Gary you are so *conservative*,'' Kathryn cried, hands held out over the stove. ''It's not conservative at all,'' Gary replied. ''It's a radical goal and I guess it's so radical that I have to keep reminding you it exists. Art should be used to *change* things.''

''Isn't that a distortion from the real?''

Alex wandered down the narrow hall to his parents' room, which overlooked Chester Street. Father was there, saying to Ilene, ''It's one of the only streets left with trees. It really seems residential, and here we are three blocks from Comm Ave. Hi, Alex.''

''Hi, Alex. It's like a little bit of Brookline made it over to Allston.''

''Exactly.''

Alex stood in the bay window and looked down, licking the last of the carrot cake off his fingers. The man was still down there.

''Let's close off these rooms and save the heat. Alex, you coming?''

He sat on the floor in the living room. Father and Gary and David were starting a game of hearts, and they invited him to be the fourth. He nodded happily. Looking under the corner table he saw yellow eyes, blinking back at him; Stella, a frown of the deepest disapproval on her flat face. Alex laughed. ''I knew you'd be there! It's okay, Stella. It's okay.''

*   *   *

They left in a group, as usual, stamping their boots and diving deep into coats and scarves and gloves and exclaiming at the cold of the stairwell. Gary gave Mom a brief hug. "Only warm spot left in Boston," he said, and opened the glass door. The rest followed him out, and Alex joined them. The man in the black coat was just turning right onto Brighton Avenue, toward the university and downtown.

Sometimes clouds took on just the mottled gray of the glacier, low dark points stippling a lighter gray surface as cold showers draped down. At these times he felt he stood between two planes of some larger structure, two halves: icy tongue, icy roof of mouth. . . .

He stood under such a sky, throwing stones. His target was an erratic some forty yards away. He hit the boulder with most of his throws. A rock that big was an easy target. A bottle was better. He had brought one with him, and he set it up behind the erratic, on a waist-high rock. He walked back to a point where the bottle was hidden by the erratic. Using flat rocks he sent spinners out in a trajectory that brought them curving in from the side, so that it was possible to hit the concealed target. This was very important for the rock fights that he occasionally got involved in; usually he was outnumbered, and to hold his own he relied on his curves and his accuracy in general, and on a large number of ammunition caches hidden here and there. In one area crowded with boulders and crevasses he could sometimes create the impression of two throwers.

Absorbed in the exercise of bringing curves around the right side of the boulder—the hard side for him—he relaxed his vigilance, and when he heard a shout he jumped around to look. A rock whizzed by his left ear.

He dropped to the ice and crawled behind a boulder. Ambushed! He ran back into his knot of boulders and dashed a layer of snow away from one of his big caches, then with hands and pockets full looked carefully over a knobby chunk of cement, in the direction the stone had come from.

No movement. He recalled the stone whizzing by, the brief sight of it and the *zip* it made in passing. That had been close! If that had hit him! He shivered to think of it, it made his stomach shrink.

A bit of almost frozen rain pattered down. Not a shadow anywhere. On overcast days like this one it seemed things were lit from below, by the white bulk of the glacier. Like plastic over a weak neon light. Brittle huge blob of plastic, shifting and groaning and once in a while cracking like a gunshot, or grumbling like distant thunder. Alive. And Alex was its ally, its representative among men. He shifted from rock to rock, saw movement and froze. Two boys in green down jackets, laughing as they ran off the ice and over the lateral moraine, into what was left of Watertown. Just a potshot, then. Alex cursed them, relaxed.

He went back to throwing at the hidden bottle. Occasionally he recalled the stone flying by his head, and threw a little harder. Elegant curves of flight as the flat rocks bit the air and cut down and in. Finally one rock spun out into space and turned down sharply. Perfect slider. Its disappearance behind the erratic was followed by a tinkling crash. "Yeah!" Alex exclaimed, and ran to look. Icy glass on glassy ice.

Then, as he was leaving the glacier, boys jumped over the moraine shouting "Canadian!" and "There he is!" and "Get him!" This was more a chase than a serious ambush, but there were a lot of them and after emptying hands and pockets Alex was off running. He flew over the crunchy irregular surface, splashing meltwater, jumping narrow crevasses and surface rills. Then a wide crevasse blocked his way, and to start his jump he leaped onto a big flat rock; the rock gave under his foot and lurched down the ice into the crevasse.

Alex turned in and fell, bringing shoe-tips, knees, elbows and hands onto the rough surface. This arrested his fall, though it hurt. The crevasse was just under his feet. He scrambled up, ran panting along the crevasse until it narrowed, leaped over it. Then up the moraine and down into the narrow abandoned streets of west Allston.

Striding home, still breathing hard, he looked at his hands and saw that the last two fingernails on his right hand had been ripped away from the flesh; both were still there, but blood seeped from under them. He hissed and sucked on them, which hurt. The blood tasted like blood.

If he had fallen into the crevasse, following the loose rock down . . . if that stone had hit him in the face . . . he could feel his heart, thumping against his sternum. Alive.

Turning onto Chester Street he saw the man in the black coat, leaning against the florid maple across the street from their building. Watching them still! Though the man didn't appear to notice Alex, he did heft a bag and start walking in the other direction. Quickly Alex picked a rock out of the gutter and threw it at the man as hard as he could, spraying drops of blood onto the sidewalk. The rock flew over the man's head like a bullet, just missing him. The man ducked and scurried around the corner onto Comm Ave.

Father was upset about something. "They did the same thing to Gary and Michael and Kathryn, and their classes are even smaller than mine! I don't know what they're going to do. I don't know what *we're* going to do."

"We might be able to attract larger classes next semester," Mom said. She was upset too. Alex stood in the hall, slowly hanging up his jacket.

"But what about now? And what about later?" Father's voice was strained, almost cracking.

"We're making enough for now, that's the important thing. As for later— well, at least we know now rather than five years down the road."

Father was silent at the implications of this. "First Vancouver, then Toronto, now here—"

"Don't worry about all of it at once, Charles."

"How can I help it!" Father strode into his study and closed the door, not noticing Alex around the corner. Alex sucked his fingers. Stella poked her head cautiously out of his bedroom.

"Hi Stell-bell," he said quietly. From the living room came the plastic clatter of Mom's typing. He walked down the long hallway, past the silent study to the living room. She was hitting the keys hard, staring at the screen, mouth tight.

"What happened?" Alex said.

She looked up. "Hi, Alex. Well—your father got bad news from the university."

"Did he not get tenure again?"

"No, no, it's not a question of that."

"But now he doesn't even have the chance?"

She glanced at him sharply, then back at the screen, where her work was blinking. "I suppose that's right. The department has shifted all the new faculty over to extension, so they're hired by the semester, and paid by the class. It means you need a lot of students. . . ."

"Will we move again?"

"I don't know," she said curtly, exasperated with him for bringing it up. She punched the command key. "But we'll really have to save money, now. Everything you make at the market is important."

Alex nodded. He didn't mention the little man in the black coat, feeling obscurely afraid. Mentioning the man would somehow make him significant—Mom and Father would get angry, or frightened—something like that. By not telling them he could protect them from it, handle it on his own, so they could concentrate on other problems. Besides the two matters couldn't be connected, could they? Being watched; losing jobs. Perhaps they could. In which case there was nothing his parents could do about it anyway. Better to save them that anger, that fear.

He would make sure his throws hit the man next time.

Storms rolled in and the red and yellow leaves were ripped off the trees. Alex kicked through piles of them stacked on the sidewalks. He never saw the little man. He put up flyers for his father, who became even more distracted and remote. He brought home vegetables from work, tucked under his down jacket, and Mom cooked them without asking if he had bought them. She did the wash in the kitchen sink and dried it on lines in the back space between buildings, standing knee deep in leaves and weeds. Sometimes it took three days for clothes to dry back there; often they froze on the line.

While hanging clothes or taking them down she would let Stella join her. The cat regarded each shifting leaf with dire suspicion, then after a few exploratory leaps and bats would do battle with all of them, rolling about in a frenzy.

One time Mom was carrying a basket of dry laundry up the pantry stairs when a stray dog rounded the corner and made a dash for Stella, who was still outside. Mom ran back down shouting, and the dog fled; but Stella had disappeared. Mom called Alex down from his studies in a distraught voice, and they searched the back of the building and all the adjacent backyards for nearly an hour, but the cat was nowhere to be found. Mom was really upset. It was only after they had quit and returned upstairs that they heard her, miaowing far above them. She had climbed the big oak tree. "Oh *smart*, Stella," Mom cried, a wild note in her voice. They called her name out the kitchen window, and the desperate miaows redoubled.

Up on the roof they could just see her, perched high in the almost bare branches of the big tree. "I'll get her," Alex said. "Cats can't climb down." He started climbing. It was difficult: the branches were close-knit, and they swayed in the wind. And as he got closer the cat climbed higher. "No, Stella, don't do that! Come here!" Stella stared at him, clamped to her branch of the moment, cross-eyed with fear. Below them Mom said over and over, "Stella, it's okay—it's okay, Stella." Stella didn't believe her.

Finally Alex reached her, near the tree's top. Now here was a problem: he needed his hands to climb down, but it seemed likely he would also need them to hold the terrified cat. "Come here, Stella." He put a hand on her flank; she flinched. Her side pulsed with her rapid breathing. She hissed faintly. He had to maneuver up a step, onto a very questionable branch; his face was inches from her. She stared at him without a trace of recognition. He pried her off her branch, lifted her. If she cared to claw him now she could really tear him up. Instead she clung to his shoulder and chest, all her claws dug through his clothes, quivering under his left arm and hand.

Laboriously he descended, using only the one hand. Stella began miaowing fiercely, and struggling a bit. Finally he met Mom, who had climbed the tree quite a ways. Stella was getting more upset. "Hand her to me." Alex detached her from his chest paw by paw, balanced, held the cat down with both hands. Again it was a tricky moment; if Stella went berserk they would all be in trouble. But she fell onto Mom's chest and collapsed, a catatonic ball of fur.

Back in the apartment she dashed for her blanket under the table. Mom enticed her out with food, but she was very jumpy and she wouldn't allow Alex anywhere near her; she ran away if he even entered the room. "Back to square one, I see," Mom commented.

"It's not fair! I'm the one that saved her!"

"She'll get over it." Mom laughed, clearly relieved. "Maybe it'll take some time, but she will. Ha! This is clear proof that cats are smart enough to be crazy."

Irrational, neurotic—just like a person." They laughed, and Stella glared at them balefully. "Yes you are, aren't you! You'll come around again."

Often when Alex got home in the early evenings his father was striding back and forth in the kitchen talking loudly, angrily, fearfully, while Mom tried to reassure him. "They're doing the same thing to us they did to Rick Stone! But why!" When Alex closed the front door the conversation would stop. Once when he walked tentatively down the quiet hallway to the kitchen he found them standing there, arms around each other, Father's head in Mom's short hair.

Father raised his head, disengaged, went to his study. On his way he said, "Alex, I need your help."

"Sure."

Alex stood in the study and watched without understanding as his father took books from his shelves and put them in the big laundry bag. He threw the first few in like dirty clothes, then sighed and thumped in the rest in a businesslike fashion, not looking at them.

"There's a used book store in Cambridge, on Mass Ave. Antonio's."

"Sure, I know the one." They had been there together a few times.

"I want you to take these over there and sell them to Tony for me," Father said, looking at the empty shelves. "Will you do that for me?"

"Sure." Alex picked up the bag, shocked that it had come to this. Father's books! He couldn't meet his father's eye. "I'll do that right now," he said uncertainly, and hefted the bag over one shoulder. In the hallway Mom approached and put a hand on his shoulder—her silent thanks—then went into the study.

Alex hiked east toward the university, crossed the Charles River on the great iron bridge. The wind howled in the superstructure. On the Cambridge side, after showing his pass, he put the heavy bag on the ground and inspected its contents. Ever since the infamous incident of the spilled hot chocolate, Father's books had been off-limits to him; now a good twenty of them were there in the bag to be touched, opened, riffled through. Many in this bunch were in foreign languages, especially Greek and Russian, with their alien alphabets. Could people really read such marks? Well, Father did. It must be possible.

When he had inspected all the books he chose two in English—*The Odyssey* and *The Colossus of Maroussi*—and put those in his down jacket pockets. He could take them to the glacier and read them, then sell them later to Antonio's—perhaps in the next bag of books. There were many more bagfuls in Father's study.

A little snow stuck to the glacier now, filling the pocks and making bright patches on the north side of every boulder, every serac. Some of the narrower crevasses were filled with it—bright white lines on the jumbled gray. When the whole surface was white the crevasses would be invisible, and the glacier too dangerous to walk on. Now the only danger was leaving obvious footprints for trackers. Walking up the rubble lines would solve that. These lines of rubble fascinated Alex. It looked just as if bulldozers had clanked up here and shoved the majority of the stones and junk into straight lines down the big central tongue of the glacier. But in fact they were natural features. Father had attempted to explain on one of the walks they had taken up here. "The ice is moving, and it moves faster in the middle than on the outer edges, just like a stream. So rocks on the surface tend to slide over time, down into lines in the middle."

"Why are there two lines, then?"

Father shrugged, looking into the blue-green depths of a crevasse. "We really shouldn't be up here, you know that?"

Now Alex stopped to inspect a tire caught in the rubble line. Truck tire, tread worn right to the steel belting. It would burn, but with too much smoke. There were several interesting objects in this neat row of rock and sand: plastic jugs, a doll, a lampbase, a telephone.

His shelter was undisturbed. He pulled the two books from his pockets and set them on the bench, propping them with rock bookends.

He circled the boulder, had a look around. The sky today was a low smooth pearl gray sheet, ruffled by a set of delicate waves pasted to it. The indirect light brought out all the colors: the pink of the remarkable snow algae, the blue of the seracs, the various shades of rock, the occasional bright spot of junk, the many white patches of snow. A million dots of color under the pewter sheet of cloud.

Three creaks, a crack, a long shuddering rumble. Sleepy, muscular, the great beast had moved. Alex walked across its back to his bench, sat. On the far lateral moraine some gravel slid down. Puffs of brown dust in the air.

He read his books. *The Odyssey* was strange but interesting. Father had told him some of the story before. *The Colossus of Maroussi* was long-winded but funny—it reminded Alex of his uncle, who could turn the smallest incident into an hour's comic monologue. What he could have made of Stella's flight up the tree! Alex laughed to think of it. But his uncle was in jail.

He sat on his bench and read, stopped occasionally to look around. When the hand holding the book got cold, he changed hands and put the cold one in a pocket of his down jacket. When both hands were blue he hid the books in rocks under his bench and went home.

There were more bags of books to be sold at Antonio's and other shops in Cambridge. Each time Alex rotated out a few that looked interesting, and replaced them with the ones on the glacier. He daydreamed of saving all the books and earning the money some other way—then presenting his father with the lost library, at some future undefined but appropriate moment.

Eventually Stella forgave him for rescuing her. She came to enjoy chasing a piece of yarn up and down their long narrow hallway, skidding around the corner by the study. It reminded them of a game they had played with Pongo, who would chase anything, and they laughed at her, especially when she jerked to a halt and licked her fur fastidiously, as if she had never been carousing. "You can't fool us, Stell! We *remember*!"

Mom sold most of her music collection, except for her favorites. Once Alex went out to the glacier with the *Concerto de Aranjuez* coursing through him— Mom had had it on in the apartment while she worked. He hummed the big theme of the second movement as he crunched over the ice: clearly it was the theme of the glacier, the glacier's song. How had a blind composer managed to capture the windy sweep of it, the spaciousness? Perhaps such things could be heard as well as seen. The wind said it, whistling over the ice. It was a terrifically dark day, windy, snowing in gusts. He could walk right up the middle of the great tongue, between the rubble lines; no one else would be up there today. Da-da-da . . . da da da da da da, da-da-da. . . . Hands in pockets, chin on chest, he trudged into the wind humming, feeling like the whole world was right there around him. It was too cold to stay in his shelter for more than a minute.

Father went off on trips, exploring possibilities. One morning Alex woke to the sound of *The Pirates of Penzance*. This was one of their favorites, Mom played it all the time while working and on Saturday mornings, so that they knew all the lyrics by heart and often sang along. Alex especially loved the Pirate King, and could mimic all his intonations.

He dressed and walked down to the kitchen. Mom stood by the stove with her back to him, singing along. It was a sunny morning and their big kitchen windows faced east; the light poured in on the sink and the dishes and the white stove and the linoleum and the plants in the window and Stella, sitting contentedly on the window sill listening.

His mom was tall and broad-shouldered. Every year she cut her hair shorter; now it was just a cap of tight brown curls, with a somewhat longer patch down the nape of her neck. That would go soon, Alex thought, and then her hair would be as short as it could be. She was lost in the song, one slim hand on the white stove top, looking out the window. She had a low, rich, thrilling voice, like a real singer's only prettier. She was singing along with the song that Mabel sings after she finds out that Frederick won't be able to leave the pirates until 1940.

When it was over Alex entered the kitchen, went to the pantry. "That's a short one," he said.

"Yes, they had to make it short," Mom said. "There's nothing funny about that one."

One night while Father was gone on one of his trips, Mom had to go over to Ilene and Ira and Gary's apartment: Gary had been arrested, and Ilene and Ira needed help. Alex and Stella were left alone.

Stella wandered the silent apartment miaowing. "I *know*, Stella," Alex said in exasperation. "They're *gone*. They'll be back tomorrow." The cat paid no attention to him.

He went into Father's study. Tonight he'd be able to read something in relative warmth. It would only be necessary to be *very careful*.

The bookshelves were empty. Alex stood before them, mouth open. He had no idea they had sold that many of them. There were a couple left on Father's desk, but he didn't want to move them. They appeared to be dictionaries anyway. "It's all Greek to me."

He went back to the living room and got out the yarn bag, tried to interest Stella in a game. She wouldn't play. She wouldn't sit on his lap. She wouldn't stop miaowing. "Stella, shut up!" She scampered away and kept crying. Vexed, he got out the jar of catnip and spread some on the linoleum in the kitchen. Stella came running to sniff at it, then roll in it. Afterwards she played with the yarn wildly, until it caught around her tail and she froze, staring at him in a drugged paranoia. Then she dashed to her refuge and refused to come out. Finally Alex put on *The Pirates of Penzance* and listened to it for a while. After that he was sleepy.

They got a good lawyer for Gary, Mom said. Everyone was hopeful. Then a couple of weeks later Father got a new job; he called them from work to tell them about it.

"Where is it?" Alex asked Mom when she was off the phone.

"In Kansas."

"So we will be moving."

"Yes," Mom said. "Another move."

"Will there be glaciers there too?"

"I think so. In the hills. Not as big as ours here, maybe. But there are glaciers everywhere."

He walked onto the ice one last time. There was a thin crust of snow on the tops of everything. A fantastically jumbled field of snow. It was a clear day, the sky a very pale blue, the white expanse of the glacier painfully bright. A few cirrus clouds made sickles high in the west. The snow was melting a bit and there were water droplets all over, with little sparks of colored light in each drip. The sounds of water melting were everywhere, drips, gurgles, splashes. The intensity of light was stunning, like a blow to the brain, right through the eyes. It pulsed.

The crevasse in front of his shelter had widened, and the boards of his bench had fallen. The wall of ice turning around the boulder was splintered, and shards of bright ice lay over the planks.

The glacier was moving. The glacier was alive. No heated dam would stop it. He felt its presence, huge and supple under him, seeping into him like the cold through his wet shoes, filling him up. He blinked, nearly blinded by the light breaking everywhere on it, a surgical glare that made every snow-capped rock stand out like the color red on a slide transparency. The white light. In the distance the ice cracked hollowly, moving somewhere. Everything moved: the ice, the wind, the clouds, the sun, the planet. All of it rolling around.

As they packed up their possessions Alex could hear them in the next room. "We can't," Father said. "You know we can't. They won't let us."

When they were done the apartment looked odd. Bare walls, bare wood floors. It looked smaller. Alex walked the length of it: his parents' room overlooking Chester Street; his room; his father's study; the living room; the kitchen with its fine morning light. The pantry. Stella wandered the place miaowing. Her blanket was still in its corner, but without the table it looked moth-eaten, fur-coated, ineffectual. Alex picked her up and went through the pantry, up the back stairs to the roof.

Snow had drifted into the corners. Alex walked in circles, looking at the city. Stella sat on her paws by the stairwell shed, watching him, her fur ruffled by the wind.

Around the shed snow had melted, then froze again. Little puddles of ice ran in flat curves across the pebbled tar paper. Alex crouched to inspect them, tapping one speculatively with a fingernail. He stood up and looked west, but buildings and bare treetops obscured the view.

Stella fought to stay out of the box, and once in it she cried miserably.

Father was already in Kansas, starting the new job. Alex and Mom and Stella had been staying in the living room of Michael Wu's place while Mom finished her work; now she was done, it was moving day, they were off to the train. But first they had to take Stella to the Talbots'.

Alex carried the box and followed Mom as they walked across the Commons and down Comm Ave. He could feel the cat shifting over her blanket, scrabbling at the cardboard against his chest. Mom walked fast, a bit ahead of him. At Kenmore they turned south.

When they got to the Talbots', Mom took the box. She looked at him. "Why don't you stay down here," she said.

"Okay."

She rang the bell and went in with the buzzer, holding the box under one arm.

Alex sat on the steps of the walk-up. There were little ones in the corner: flat fingers of ice, spilling away from the cracks.

Mom came out the door. Her face was pale, she was biting her lip. They took off walking at a fast pace. Suddenly Mom said, "Oh, Alex, she was so *scared*," and sat down on another stoop and put her head on her knees.

Alex sat beside her, his shoulders touching hers. Don't say anything, don't put arm around shoulders or anything. He had learned this from Father. Just sit there, be there. Alex sat there like the glacier, shifting a little. Alive. The white light.

After a while she stood. "Let's go," she said.

They walked up Comm Ave. toward the train station. "She'll be all right with the Talbots," Alex said. "She already likes Jay."

"I know." Mom sniffed, tossed her head in the wind. "She's getting to be a pretty adaptable cat." They walked on in silence. She put an arm over his shoulders. "I wonder how Pongo is doing." She took a deep breath. Overhead clouds tumbled like chunks of broken ice.

JAMES LAWSON

Sanctuary

Here's a hard-edged look into a bristling, grimy, overpopulated future, vigorous and multifaceted and gritty, where we'll encounter a complex, baffling high-tech mystery . . . whose resolution ultimately depends on an old-fashioned understanding of the human heart.

The mysterious James Lawson grew up in California and has a College Teaching Certificate in Communications Arts and Printing. After traveling extensively on work for the U.S. Army, he left the military and is currently a government consultant. He and his wife have dedicated themselves to raising six orphans of multiple ancestry, although just *where*, no one will say.

SANCTUARY

James Lawson

"Hey, Cardenas, don't you retire today, man?"

"Chief's got it in for you sure today."

"Naw, he's gonna fire Cardenas and promote the dog!"

He smiled as he walked past their desks, the laughter lapping against him in friendly, cool waves before falling away behind him. Occasionally he replied, brief verbal jousts with those he knew well that left no one injured. He always gave as good as he got. When you were the oldest sergeant on the force, not to mention the smallest, you had to expect a certain amount of ribbing.

"Don't sweat it, Charliebo," he told his companion. "Good boy."

At the mention of his name the German shepherd's ears cocked forward, and he looked up curiously. Same old Charliebo. The laughter didn't bother him. Nothing bothered him. That's how he'd been trained, and the years hadn't changed him.

We're both getting old, Cardenas thought. Jokes now, but in another year or two they'll make me hang it up no matter what. Then we double the time in front of the video, hoh. Just you and me and the ol' TV, dog. Maybe that's not such a bad idea. We could both use some rest. Though he had a hunch the chief hadn't called him in to talk about rest.

A visitor might've found the big dog's presence in the ready room unusual, but not the Nogales cops. The dog had been Sergeant Cardenas's shadow for twelve years. For the first six, he'd also been his eyes. Eyes which had been taken from him by a frightened nineteen-year-old ninloco Cardenas had surprised in the process of rotoing an autofill outside a Tucson hydro station. Pocket change. Pill credit.

Cardenas and his partner had slipped up on the kid without expecting anything more lethal than some angry words. The ninloco had grabbed his pants and extracted an Ithaca spitter. The high-pocket twenty-gauge shattered Cardenas's partner and made jelly of the sergeant's face. Backup told him that the ninloco had gone down giggling when they'd finally expiated him. His blood analysis showed .12 spacebase and an endorphin-based expander. He was so high he should have flown away. Now he was a memory.

The surgeons plastered Cardenas's face back together. The drooping mustache regrew in sections. When he was recovered enough to comprehend what had happened to him, they gave him Charliebo, a one-year-old intense-trained shepherd, the best guide dog the school had. For six years Charliebo had been Cardenas's eyes.

Then the biosurges figured out a way to transplant optic nerves as well as just the eyeballs, and they'd coaxed him back into the hospital. When he was discharged four months later, he was seeing through the bright perfect blue eyes of a dead teenager named Anise Dorleac whose boyfriend had turned him and her both to ground chuck while drag racing a Lotusette at a hundred and ninety on Interstate Forty up near Flag. Not much salvageable out of either of them except her eyes. They'd given them to Cardenas.

After that, Charliebo didn't have to be his eyes anymore. Six years, though, an animal becomes something more than a pet and less than a person. Despite the entreaties of the guide-dog school, Cardenas wouldn't give him up. Couldn't. He'd never married, no kids, and Charliebo was all the family he'd ever had. You didn't give up family.

The police association stood by him. The school directors grumbled but didn't press the matter. Besides, it was pretty funny, wasn't it? What could be more outré than a short, aging, blue-eyed Tex-Mex cop who worked his terminal with a dog guarding his wastepaper basket? So they left him alone. More importantly, they left him Charliebo.

He didn't pause outside the one-way plastic door. Pangborn had told him to come right in. He thumbed a contact switch and stepped through as the plastic slid aside.

The chief didn't even glance at Charliebo. The shepherd was an appendage of the sergeant, a canine extrusion of Cardenas's personality. Cardenas wouldn't have looked right without the dog to balance him. Without having to be told, the shepherd lay down silently at the foot of Cardenas's chair, resting his angular gray head on his forepaws.

"Cómo se happening, Nick?"

The chief smiled thinly. "De nada, Angel. You?"

"Same old this and that. I think we wormed a line on the chopshop down in Nayarit."

"Forget it. I'm taking you off that."

Cardenas's hand fell to stroke Charliebo's neck. The dog didn't move, but his eyes closed in pleasure. "I got eighteen months before mandatory retirement. You pasturing me early?"

"Not a chance." Pangborn understood. The chief had five years left before they'd kick him out. "Got some funny stuff going on over in Agua Pri. Lieutenant there, Danny Mendez, is an old friend of mine. They're oiled and it's getting uncomfortable. Some real specific gravity on their backs. So he called for help. I told him I'd loan over the best intuit in the Southwest. We both know who that is.''

Cardenas turned and made an exaggerated search of the duty room outside. Pangborn smiled.

"Why not send one of the young hotshots? Why me?''

"Because you're still the best, you old fart. You know why.''

Sure, he knew why. Because he'd gone six years without eyes and in that time he'd developed the use of his other senses to the opto. Involuntary training, but unsurpassingly effective. Then they'd given him back his sight. Of course, he was the best. But he still liked to hear it. At his age compliments of any kind were few and far between, scattered widely among the ocean of jokes.

Under his caressing fingers Charliebo stretched delightedly. "So what's skewed in Agua Pri?''

"Two designers. Wallace Crescent and a Vladimir Noschek. First one they called Wondrous Wallace. I dunno what they called the other guy, except irreplaceable. Crescent was the number one mainline man for GenDyne. Noschek worked for Parabas S.A.''

"Also mainline design?'' Pangborn nodded. "Qué about them?''

"Crescent two weeks ago. Noschek right afterward. Each of them wiped clean as a kid's Etch-a-Sketch. Hollow, vacuumed right back through childhood. Both of them lying on an office couch, relaxed—Crescent with a drink half-finished, Noschek working on a bowl of pistachios. Like they'd been working easy, normal, then suddenly they ain't at home anymore. That was weird enough.''

"Something was weirder?''

Pangborn looked uneasy. That was unusual. It took a lot of specific gravity to upset the chief. He'd been a sparkler buster down Guyamas way. Everybody knew about the Tampolobampo massacre. Late night and the runners had buffooned into an ambush laid by local spitters trying to pull a rip-off. By the time the cops arrived from halfway across Sonora and Sinaloa, the beach was covered with guts the waves washed in and out like spawning grunion. Through it all Pangborn hadn't blinked, not even when older cops were heaving their insides all over the Golfo California. He'd just gone along the waterline, kicking pieces of bodies aside, looking for evidence to implicate the few survivors. It was an old story that never got old. Decaders liked to lay it on rookies to see how green they'd get.

But there was no record of Pangborn looking uneasy.

"Nobody can figure out how they died, Angel. Parabas flew their own specialists up from São Paulo. Elpaso Juarez coroner's office still won't acknowledge the certification because they can't list ceeohdee. Both bodies were clean as the inside of both brains. No juice, no soft intrusions, no toxins, nothing. Bare as

Old Mother Hubbard's cupboard. Inviolate, the reports said. Hell, how do you kill somebody without intruding? Even ultrasound leaves a signature. But according to Mendez, there wasn't a damn thing wrong with either man except nobody was home.''

"Motives?''

Pangborn grunted. "Tired of small talk? Working already?''

"Aren't I?''

The chief scrolled crunch on his desk screen, muting the audio. "Money, shematics, razzmatazz, who knows? Parabas and GenDyne Internal Security immediately went over homes, friends, and work stations with good suction. Nothing missing, everything in place. Both men were straight right up and down the lifeline. No Alley-Oops. GenDyne's frizzing the whole Southwest Enforcement Region. They want to know how as much as why. They also want to know if anybody's going to be next. Bad for morale, bad for business.'' He scratched at his prosthetic left ear. The real one had been chewed off by a ninloco ten years ago, and the replacement never seemed to quite fit.

Cardenas was quiet for a long moment. "What do you think?''

Pangborn shrugged. "Somebody vacuums two mainline designers after penetrating state-of-the-art corporate security but doesn't steal anything insofar as anybody can tell. Both work files were checked. Both are regularly monitored, and everything was solid. So nobody did it to steal crunch. Just a whim, but I think maybe it was somehow personal. Not corporate at all. You can't tell that to GenDyne or Parabas. They don't like to hear that kind of stuff.''

"You'd expect them to go paranoid. Any connections between the two men?''

"Not that Mendez and his people have been able to find. Didn't eat at the same restaurants, moved in different circles entirely. Crescent was married, one wife, family. Noschek was younger, a loner. Separate orbits, separate obits. Me, I think maybe they were flooded with a new kind of juice. Maybe involuntarily.''

"No evidence for that, and it still doesn't give us a motive.''

Pangborn stared at him. "Find one.''

Cardenas was at home in the Strip, a solid string of high tech that ran all the way from LaLa to East Elpaso Juarez. It followed the old and frayed USA-Mehico border with less regard for actual national boundaries than the Rio Grande. Every multinational that wanted a piece of the Namerica market had plants there, and most had several. In between were kilometers of upstarts, some true independents, others intrapreneurs spun off by the electronic gargantuas. Down amidst the frenzy of innovation, where bright new developments could be outdated before they could be brought to market, fortunes were risked and lost. If you were a machinist, a mask sculptor, or a programmer, you could make six figures a year. If you were a peon from Zacatecas or Tamulipas, a dirt farmer made extinct by new tech, or a refugee from the infinite slums of Mexico City, you could always find work on the assembly lines. Someday if you worked hard and didn't lose your eyesight to overstrain, they might give you a white lab coat and hat and promote you to a clean room. Kids, women, anybody who could control their fingers and their eyes could make hard currency in the Montezuma Strip, where First World technology locked hands with Third World cheap labor.

Spin-offs from the Strip extended north to Phoenix, south to Guyamas. Money brought in subcultures, undercultures, anticultures. Some of the sociologists who delved into the underpinnings of the Strip didn't come out. The engineers and technocrats forced to live in proximity to their labor and produce lived in fortified suburbs and traveled to work in armored transports. Cops in transit didn't rate private vehicles.

Cardenas squeezed into a crowded induction shuttle bound for Agua Prieta. The plastic car stank of sweat, disinfectant, Tex-Mex fast food. Other passengers grudgingly made way for Charliebo, but not for his owner. The dog wouldn't take up a seat.

Cardenas found one anyway, settled in for the hour-long rock-and-ride. Advertising bubbled from the overhead speakers, behind spider steel grates. A ninloco tried to usurp Cardenas's seat. He wore his hair long and slick. The Aztec snake tattooed on his right cheek twitched its coils when he grinned. Cardenas saw him coming but didn't meet his eyes, hoping he'd just bounce on past. The other commuters gave the crazyboy plenty of room. He came straight up to Cardenas.

"No spitting, Tío. Just evaporate, bien?"

Cardenas glanced up at him. "Waft, child."

The ninloco's gaze narrowed. When Cardenas tensed, Charliebo came up off the floor and growled. He was an old dog and he had big teeth. The ninloco backed up a step and reached toward a pocket.

"Leave it, leave you." Cardenas shook his head warningly, holding up his right arm so the sleeve slid back. The ninloco's eyes flicked over the bright blue bracelet with its gleaming LEDs.

"Federale. Hey, I didn't know, compadre. I'll jojobar."

"You do that." Cardenas lowered his hand. The crazyboy vanished back into the crowd. Charliebo grunted and settled back on his haunches.

Surprised at the tightness in his gut, Cardenas leaned back against the curved plastic and went through a series of relaxation breathing exercises. This ninloco wasn't the one who'd flayed him years ago. He was a newer, younger clone, no better and no worse. A member of the hundreds of gangs that broke apart and coalesced as they drifted through the length of the Strip like sargassum weed in the mid-Atlantic. The ninlocos hated citizens, but they despised each other.

Across the aisle two teenage girls, one Anglo and the other Spanglo, continued to stare at him. Only they weren't seeing him, he knew, but rather the vits playing across the interior lenses of the oversized glasses they wore. The arms of each set of lenses curved down behind their ears to drive the music home by direct transduction, straight to the inner ear. Cardenas didn't mind the music, but the vibrations were something else.

By the time the induction car pulled into Agua Pri station, he'd completely forgotten the confrontation with the ninloco.

The flashman at GenDyne would've taken him through the whole damn plant if Cardenas hadn't finally insisted on being shown Crescent's office. It wasn't his escort's fault. A flashman just naturally tried to promote and showoff his company at every opportunity. Wasn't that what sales-pr was all about? Even the police departments engaged flashmen. If you didn't have a professional to intercede for you with the media, they'd eat you alive.

That didn't mean you had to like them, and most people didn't. Cardenas thought they were one with the lizards that still scuttled across the rocks north and south of the Strip.

The GenDyne think tank was built like a fortress. In point of fact, it was a fortress, the architecture inspired by Assyrian fortifications unearthed in Meso-potamia. Only instead of stone, it rose from the desert whose sand it crowded onto on foundations of reinforced concrete. Its walls were bronze glass set in casements of white high-construct plastic. It was built on the southern edge of this part of the Strip, so the south-facing alcoves and offices all had views of once-hostile terrain. Expensive real estate. This was a place for a multinational's pets, its most privileged people. Designers and engineers, who conjured money out of nothing.

Crescent had been important enough to rate a top-floor work station, right up there with the modem mongers who swapped info and crunch with the home office in LaLa. Through the window that dominated one wall could be seen the smog-shrouded heights of the Sierra de la Madera. Like a python dressed for Christmas, the arc of the Strip curved around toward Laguna de Guzman and the new ar-complex of Ciudad Pershing-Villa.

The office itself had been furnished professionally. Thick, comfortable chairs, a cabinet containing ice maker and drink dispenser, indirect lighting, everything designed to produce a work environment conducive to the sort of brainstorms that added fractions to a multinat's listing on the International Exchange. An expensive colorcrawl by an artist Cardenas didn't recognize lit the wall behind the couch, two square meters of half-sentient neon gone berserk. The pale orange and brown earth-tone carpet underfoot was thicker than the upholstery on his furniture back in Nogales. It smelled of new-mown hay and damp sandstone, having been sense-recharged not more than a week ago. To cover the smell of death? But Crescent's passing had been neat. As the flashman spieled on, Cardenas studied the couch where the body had been found, calm and unstressed.

The desk was a sweep of replicant mesquite, complete to the detailed grain. The east wall was, of course, all screen. It was just a flat beige surface now, powered down.

"It's been scanned, scraped, and probed, but nothing except the, uh, body's been moved." The flashman finally saw him staring at the couch. The death frame. He wore a metallic green suit with short sleeves. The set of red lenses swathed his eyes. The other two primaries were pushed back atop his head, bracketed by the high blond crewcut. A hearsee stuck out of his right ear like a burrowing beetle. His green shoes were soled in teflink, and he slid noiselessly across the carpet without slipping. Lizard, Cardenas thought.

Ignoring the mute workscreen, Cardenas strolled behind the desk. A couple of holos drifted a centimeter above the replicant wood, off to the left. He'd only been able to see them from the back. They were set to rotate every half-hour. They showed a pretty young woman, two kids. The boy and girl were also pretty. Everyone smiled warmly. Crescent was in one of the holos. Images of a happy, content family on its way up. Soaring, if Crescent was half as brilliant as GenDyne's files had led him to believe.

In his mind's eye he conjured up the coroner's vit of the victim, the designer sitting placidly on the couch, his body undamaged, heart pumping steadily. The eyes staring but not seeing because everything behind them that had been Wallace Crescent had been removed. This space for rent.

Who would do that to a man who, according to every record, had no enemies, had never bothered a soul, wanted nothing but to succeed at his job and take care of his handsome family? Cardenas felt sick. Nearby, Charliebo whined, gazing up at his two-legged friend out of brown, limpid eyes.

The flashman's lenses dropped. "Something new? I know they used to train them to sniff juice, but that was a long time ago."

"Just a friend." Cardenas spoke absently, still inspecting the couch. "That's where they found him?"

The flashman flipped up his reds. His eyes were pale, weak. Spent too much time relying on the lenses, Cardenas thought. No wonder he needed triples.

"Right there, on the middle cushion. Could've been sleeping except that his eyes were wide open."

Cardenas nodded and walked over to run his fingers over the upholstery. No blood, no signs of any kind. So sayeth the Official Inquiry. If it had been otherwise, they wouldn't have called for help. He straightened and strolled back to sit behind the desk. Hydraulics cushioned his weight, all but silent. Crescent's body was being kept alive in a Douglas hospital. The family insisted on it, hoping against hope he'd return some day from wherever he'd gone. They hadn't listened to the police. Crescent hadn't *gone*. He'd been moved out forcibly. There was nothing to come back. But the family wouldn't listen. Gradually, the police stopped bothering them.

What had happened to this stable, incisive, innovative mind?

He let his fingers slide along the top of the desk until he found what he was searching for. A center drawer snapped open. He ignored the printouts, storage cubes, miscellanea, and picked up the vorec. Small, the very latest model, a Gevic Puretone-20. It was slim and smooth, the size of a small hot dog, no bun. Twiddling it between thumb and fingers, he slowly turned in the chair until he was facing the workscreen wall. He flicked a tiny button set in the polished metal surface. The east wall lit with a soft light. A barely perceptible hum filled the office.

The flashman took a nervous step toward the desk. "You can't do that."

Cardenas spared him a sideways glance. "I have to. I have to know what he was working on when he was vacuumed."

"I'll need to get you clearance. You can't open the Box without clearance."

Cardenas grinned at him. "Want to bet?"

"Wait." The flashman was backing toward the door. "Please, just wait a moment." He hurried out.

The sergeant hesitated, continued to play with the vorec mike. Charliebo stared eagerly at the wall. He knew what was coming. This was something Cardenas did frequently. So far as he knew, the dog enjoyed it as much as he did. Whether he was rummaging through a personal Box or a much larger one holding company records, it was always interesting to examine the contents. The mike in his hand was cool to the touch, uncontaminated.

The flashman came back with someone in tow. She didn't look pleased.

"Company policy. We need someone equally capable of interpreting data present when you go in." So we're sure you don't pocket anything on the side, was the unspoken corollary. "Senior Designer Hypatia Spango, this is Sergeant Angel Cardenas. He's over from Nogales to work on—"

"I know what he's here to work on. Why else would anyone be in Wally's office?" She stared evenly at him.

Straight on, Cardenas noted. No flinching, no deference, certainly no worry. She was at least fifteen years younger than he. Handsome, not pretty. Black hair permed in tight ringlets that fell to her shoulders. Black eyes too, but oddly pale skin. Body voluptuous beneath the white corporate jumpsuit. Mature. He wondered how much of her was held up by polymers and how much by herself. She was taller than he, but it would've been unusual if she wasn't. Everybody was taller than he was. She wore a reducer cap over her right eye. When she saw him looking at it, she removed it and dropped it into a pocket. Three chevrons on each sleeve of the jumpsuit. The woman carried some weight, and not just in her pants.

Well, they wouldn't set a post-grad scanner to keep watch on him.

Reluctantly, she advanced until she was standing on the other side of the desk. Then she noticed the gray-black lump near his feet. "Nice dog."

"That's Charliebo. He's nicer than most people."

"Look, I didn't want to do this, but they insisted Optop. I don't want to like you either, but you've got a dog, so I guess I'm stuck there, too.'' She extended a hand across the desk top. Her grip was firm and full, not the half-dance tentativeness favored by most women. Her nails were cut short and clean, no polish, none of the rainbow insets currently in fashion. Soft but efficient. Working hands.

"You from around here?'' He meant the Strip.

She shook her head tersely. The ringlets jangled silently. If they'd been made of metal, there would have been music. "Iowa. Des Moines. It's a long story.''

"Aren't they all, verdad?'' He sat up straight and looked past her. "You can go now.''

The flashman licked his lips as he fiddled with his lenses. They dehumanized him, if it was possible to dehumanize a flashman further. "I should stay.''

Spango turned. "Waft.''

He did.

She sat down without being asked, pulling one of the chairs up to the other side of the desk.

"How long have you been with GenDyne?'' he asked her.

"Is this being recorded?''

He tapped his breast pocket. "*Everything's* being recorded.''

She sighed. "All my life. Univ in Des Moines, then three years graduate work. Vegas School of Design. Then GenDyne. Five promotions and two husbands along the way. Kept the promotions, lost the husbands.'' A shrug. "That's life. All of mine, anyway.''

"And how long's that?''

A slightly wicked smile. "I'm not sure that information's pertinent to your investigation here, Federale.''

It was his turn to grin. "All right. Pax. How long did you know Crescent?''

"Ten years. All of it off and on. You know designers. We spend most of our time inside the Box. Wally was friendly enough, knew everybody, and they knew him. Except I don't guess anybody really *knew* him. His wife, Karen, a real quiet, sweet gal. They made all the company picnics, reward trips; for all the expected functions, they were both there. Wally played high goal on the division socball team.''

"Ever notice anything that would make you think he was an abuser?''

She shook her head. "As far as I knew, he was clean as the Box Room. Of course, you never know what anybody does in private.''

"No, you don't. How good was he?''

"As a designer? The best. Wally knew how to use imagination *and* logic. He had a flair most of us don't, no matter how long we work at it. Talent, you know? I don't know what else to call it. He knew the inside of the Box the way most of us know our own bodies.

"GenDyne knew it, too. The rest of us had to beg for a raise or an extra day off. All Crescent had to do was sneeze, and he'd have the whole marketing department cleaning his shoes with their tongues. Are you familiar with the GS Capacitate?'' Cardenas nodded. ''That was Crescent's baby. Sensitized microbio circuit. Plug one into your screen, feed it, and it automatically replicates existing storage until you turn off the power. Gallium arsenide proteins are a lot cheaper in bulk than predesigned slabs. Revolutionized peripheral information storage.''

Cardenas was impressed. ''Crescent came up with that?'' She nodded. ''So obviously money wasn't a problem for him.''

Spango leaned back in her chair. For a big woman she had small feet, he mused. ''He wasn't independently wealthy, but he made more than you or I'll ever see.''

''Maybe he was on to something new. Something potentially as big as the GS.''

''If so, he was keeping it to himself. We couldn't find anything revolutionary in his section of the Box. Of course, Crescent was a genius. The rest of us are just plodders. It could still be in there, tucked away where nobody but Wally himself could find it.''

''Isn't that kind of unusual?''

''I see what you're thinking. Not only isn't it unusual, it's standard policy. The company understands and accepts it. I do it myself. Hey, if you don't protect your ideas from your good compadre next door, next thing you know he's accessed your storage and is presenting your hard-won innovation to the Board. How do you prove you thought of it first? It's tough to ident an idea.''

''So there's serious competition even within a division. You sure he wasn't planning to sell to somebody else?''

''Outside GenDyne? How the hell would I know that? How would anybody? Is that what you think?''

''Right now I'm thinking of everything. You say he had plenty of money. But he wasn't independent. Maybe some other outfit was willing to set him up for life. Maybe he wanted something GenDyne couldn't or wouldn't get for him. Something nobody else knew about. Got nervous, changed his mind, I don't know. The people he was dealing with got angry. They argued, they sent someone in after him, they vacuumed him to get what they wanted. No such thing as selective vacuuming, of course. Not yet. Not that the type of person another corporation would send to do something like that would care. Why leave a witnessing consciousness around to make noise afterward?''

''You make a good case, but I think it's all idletime. You didn't know Wally Crescent. Subside dealings weren't his style.''

''People are full of surprises.'' He twirled the vorec. ''Time to start digging.''

She turned to face the wallscreen. ''GenDyne Security's already combed his storage. Nothing but what you'd expect. You won't find anything either.''

''Maybe not, but I've got to start someplace. You want to give me the access, or you want to make me work?''

Those deep black eyes studied him. "Maybe I'll get you to work some other time. You've already got the access."

He smiled. "What makes you think that?"

"Security wouldn't have asked you to look around without giving it to you. Without access, there wouldn't be anything for you to look at. And if I knew it, then I'd be a suspect, wouldn't I?"

"You're a suspect already. Everyone in this building's a suspect."

She sniffed. "Can I stay and watch?"

He shrugged. "This kind of examination can get pretty dull. Looking for useful concepts to swipe?"

"If there was anything readily extractable in there worth stealing, Security's done it already."

He nodded and turned to face the blank wall, raising his voice recognition mike to his lips. "Coordinate Hapsburg Hohenzollern Mermaid."

The wall seemed to disappear. He was looking across the carpet down an infinite rectangular tunnel. Within the tunnel, tiny flecks of light and color swarmed like protozoa in pond water. As he stared, the flecks began to coalesce to form a simple holographic square, neatly lettered on all six sides. A musical female voice, the synthesized duplicate of a reconstructed nineteenth-century singer known as the Swedish Nightingale, spoke from concealed speakers.

"Welcome to the GenDyne Box, Mermaid storage and files. You are not Wallace Crescent."

"Federales Security Special Forces Bomo Bomo Six." Cardenas withdrew a plastic card from a shirt pocket and slipped it into a receptacle in the side of the desk.

"Welcome Sergeant Cardenas. Security clearance processed. Mermaid awaits."

Cardenas frowned. "That was too easy."

"Not if Crescent had nothing to hide. I told you company security's already run this. Mermaid let them go anywhere they wanted to. If Wally'd been hiding something, they would've found a block."

"Maybe not, if this guy was as clever as you say. What better way to hide something than to let everybody look around for it?"

"You mean like hide it in plain sight? You can't do that in a Box. If Crescent had tucked something into a seam, Security would've smelled it out even if they couldn't crack it. Besides, Crescent didn't design for Security. He was strictly heavy-duty industrial."

"How do you know what Crescent was and wasn't into?"

She had no reply for that.

He started in. He was methodical, efficient, experienced, able to skip whole blocks of information without so much as a surface scan. He pumped the vorec up to three times normal speed. It impressed Spango, though that wasn't his intention. That was just the way he worked. Within GenDyne itself, nobody except the vorec designers worked even double speed.

Sometimes he switched to printout when he wanted to be sure of something, reading the words as they formed in the void created by the screen, but most of the time he stuck with the faster vorec. Much of the time he kept his eyes closed as the Mermaid storage spoke to him. He did it because it helped his concentration. He was used to analyzing without being able to see. What he couldn't detect with his eyes shut was Hypatia watching him.

Not so very long ago, people had wasted time tapping out their commands on keyboards. Nobody used keyboards anymore except hobbyists. With the perfection of voice recognition circuitry, you just talked to your Box and it replied in a voice of your choice. A whole industry had been created just to supply custom voices. Your Box could reply in the measured tones of Winston Churchill, Shiela Armstrong, or even Adolph Hitler. Or your dead father. Or your favorite seamyvit star.

He probed and dug and inquired without wondering who might be listening in. He took it for granted this room was smothered. GenDyne Security would've seen to that.

Mermaid was stuffed with notions, ideas incomplete, concepts partly rounded, files that dead-ended, rotating neural highways, and biochem cylinders. Most of it was far above a cop's venue, but so far he hadn't encountered anything he couldn't recognize as incomplete. Even so, he found himself glad they'd pushed Hypatia on him. If anything slipped past his notice, she'd pin it for him. He didn't have to ask. Having been allowed to see another designer's private sanctum, she was studying eagerly. But so far she gave no indication they'd stumbled into anything unusual or out of the ordinary.

Nothing worth vacuuming a man for.

"Hey?"

"Hmmm?"

"C'mon, Cardenas. Give it a rest. You're starting to put down roots."

He blinked. He hadn't been asleep, not really. Just dozing, his mind lazy and open to the steady flow of verbosity from the wall. He sat up and saw Charliebo resting his head in her lap. A glance the other way showed it was dark outside. He checked his bracelet. Tiny lights flashed accusingly at him. It was after nine. He'd been sponging for eight straight hours.

"I'm not tired."

"The hell you're not."

Slowly, he eased out of the chair. His muscles protested. His bladder was tight as a slipknot.

"Where's the—?"

"Down the hall." She stood, grinning at him. "Come on, I'll show you."

"Show me what?"

"Just the door, man. Just the door."

She took him to a French restaurant. Cardenas had never been to a French restaurant in his life. Spanglish was near enough to French to enable him to read half the menu, and Hypatia translated the other half. Ten minutes later, he gazed helplessly across the table.

"Isn't there *anything* in this place that doesn't have some kind of sauce on it?"

"I'll take care of it." She ordered for both of them. The place was fancy enough to afford live waiters. Cardenas waited until the man left.

"What am I getting?"

"Poulet. Pollo. Plain. Don't worry, I wouldn't poison you with Bernaise or worse."

He pushed the menu aside. "The only thing I'm worried about is the bill."

"Don't. This was my invite, so I'm paying." He went through the motions of protesting. "Look, my salary's five times yours. Don't go ancien-macho on me."

"Not a chance. Why the largess?"

"Suspicious little northie, aren't you?"

"Consider my profession."

"I'm doing it because you didn't ask me. Because even though you didn't want me around back in Crescent's office, you still talked to me. Civil. Because you didn't make a pass at me. Because I like your dog. Enough reasons?"

"I'm too old to make passes at girls."

"That may be, but then I'm no girl. I haven't been a girl for a long time. Also, you spoke to my face instead of my chest."

"I wanted answers from you."

She giggled. It was an extraordinary and utterly unexpected sound, fluting up from the depths of that mature shape, as though for a few seconds it was suddenly home to a wandering seventeen-year-old.

"That's not what most men want."

Not knowing what to say next, he found himself looking toward the entrance. The curving plastic tunnel led up and out to the street above. They were down in fancy undersand, where corporate execs came to do business, where the flashmen sat, selling and stealing, and sylphs sold themselves to worms from Asia and Europa. Occasionally, the patrons ate.

"Worried about your dog?"

He looked back to her. "I could have brought him in with us. Claimed impaired vision. That's what Charliebo's trained for. Sometimes I do it."

"Unnecessary. He's fine in the checkroom. I told the girl there to filch him some kitchen scraps. She said she'd be glad to. Charliebo's a lover. He'll probably enjoy this dinner more than you will.''

His eyebrows rose. "I didn't hear you say anything about scraps. Thanks.''

Her eyes dropped. Beneath her forearms the thermosensitive lexan tabletop changed color as the plastic responded to the subtle shifts in her body temperature.

"I like Charliebo. I've always preferred animals to people. Maybe because I haven't had much luck in my relationships with people.'' She looked back up at him. "Aren't you going to ask me about my wonderful marriages?''

"Hadn't planned on it.''

"For a man, you're pretty understanding. Maybe I should've kept away from the pretty boys. The first one was a designer. Good, though not as good as me, not anywhere near Crescent's class. But he was slick. Did furniture. Did me, too. Designed me right out of his life. The second one lasted four years. I guess I went to the other extreme. Max had a body like a truck and a brain to match. After a while that got old. It was my turn to move on.'' She palmed a handful of shrimp crackers from a bowl. "That was ten years ago.''

"Maybe you should have stuck with it awhile longer.''

"You're one to talk.'' She looked around wildly. "God, I wish I had a cigarette.''

"I saw a den up the block as we were coming down here.'' He did not offer the expected criticism.

"Can't anyway. Company doctors tell me I've got 'thin lungs,' whatever the hell those are.''

"Sorry. You get anything from what we saw and heard today?''

She shook her head sadly. "Typical cop. Can't you leave business outside for a while?''

"I've done pretty good so far.''

"I didn't sponge a thing. Nothing in Mermaid lively enough to prick a neuron. Oh, lots of fascinating design work, enough to awe just about anybody except Wally himself, but nothing worth killing for.''

He found himself nodding agreement. "That's what I thought. I spent most of my time looking for what wasn't there. Blocks, wells, verbal codes, Janus gates. Didn't find any, though.''

"I warned you. How can you sponge a code? Don't they sound the same as everything else?''

"To most people.''

"What do you mean, 'to most people'?''

He met her eyes once more. "Hypatia, why do you think they put me on this case? Why do you think Agua Prieta had to bring somebody all the way over from Nogales?''

"Because you're good?''

"I'm more than that. Hypatia, I'm an intuit."

"Oh. Well."

Her expression stayed carefully neutral. She didn't look at him like he was some kind of freak. Which, of course, he wasn't. He was just infinitely more sensitive to sounds and verbal programming than practically everyone else. But the sensationalist media delighted in putting their spotlights on anything that hinted of the abnormal. Intuits were a favorite subject.

Cardenas could hear things in speech nobody except another intuit would notice. Previously that was something useful only to actors, lawyers, and judges. With the advent of verbal programming, it was recognized as more than a talent. It became a science.

In the late twentieth century, primitive machines had been devised which were crude mimics of natural intuits. When the majority of information programming and storage switched from physical to verbal input, the special abilities of those people identified as intuits were suddenly much in demand, since people could hide information with delicate phraseology and enunciation. They could also steal. The impetus came from the Japanese, who, after decades of trying to solve the difficulty of how to program in characters, leapfrogged the entire problem by helping to develop verbal programming.

Not all intuits went into police work. Cardenas knew of one who did nothing but interview for major corporations, checking on potential employees. As living lie detectors, their findings were not admissible in court, but that didn't prevent others from making use of their talents.

Six years of blindness had only sharpened Cardenas's talents.

He'd attended a few intuit conferences, where the talk was all about new vorec circuits and semantics. Little was said. Little had to be, since there were no misunderstandings between speakers. Among the attendees had been other cops, translators for multinats and governments, and entertainers. He remembered with special pleasure his conversation with the famous Eskimo Billy Oomigmak, a lieutenant with the Northwest Territories Federales. An Innuit intuit would be an obvious candidate for celebrity status and Billy Oo had taken full advantage of it. Cardenas had no desire to trade places with him.

"Can you read my thoughts?"

"No, no. That's a common misconception. All I can do is sense the real meaning of a statement, detect if what's being said is what's being meant. If somebody utilizes phraseology to conceal something either in person or through an artvoc, I can often spot it. That's why there are so many intuit judges. Why do you think . . . ?"

He stopped. Hypatia had a hand over her mouth, stifling a laugh. Obviously, she knew intuits weren't mind readers. She'd been teasing him. He pouted without realizing how silly it made him look.

"Why'd you take me out, anyway? Charliebo aside."

Her hand dropped. She wasn't smiling now, he saw. "Because it's been a long time since I was out with a real grown-up, Angel. I like children, but not as dates."

He eyed her sharply. "Is that what this is? A date?"

"Fooled you, didn't I? All this time you thought it was a continuation of business. Tell me: how'd they let somebody as small as you on the force?"

He almost snapped at her, until he realized she was still teasing him. Well, he could tease, too. But all he could think of to say was "Because there's nobody better at breaking into a Box."

"Is that so? You haven't proven that to my satisfaction. Listening and probing at triple verbal's impressive, but you still didn't find anything."

"We don't know yet that there's anything to find."

"If there isn't?"

He shrugged. "I go back to Nogales where I can't hear GenDyne scream."

"Dinner," she said as their main course arrived. Cardenas's chicken was simply and elegantly presented. He hadn't realized how hungry he was. Eight hours of sponging had left him drained. He hardly heard her as he reached for his silverware.

"Maybe later we'll see how efficient a prober you really are."

He intuited that easily, but didn't let on that he had. Steam hissed from the chicken as he sliced into it.

Each day he went into the GenDyne Box, and each evening he left the corporate offices, feeling more baffled and disturbed than when he'd gone in. Not that Mermaid wasn't full of accessible, fascinating information: it was. It was just that none of it was of the slightest use.

Hypatia was of inestimable help, explaining where he didn't understand, patiently elaborating on concepts he thought he understood but actually did not. GenDyne assigned her to him for the duration of his investigation. It pleased him. He thought it might have pleased her. After a week, even she couldn't keep his spirits up. He could be patient, he was methodical, but he was used to progressing, even at a creep. They weren't learning anything. It was worse than going nowhere; he felt as if they were going backward. Nor could he escape the feeling that somebody somewhere was laughing at him. He didn't like it. Cardenas had a wry, subtle sense of humor, but not where his work was concerned.

Anything that smelled of potential he recorded for playback at half-speed, then quarter-speed. His senses were taut as the high string on a viola. He listened for the slightest off-pronunciation, the one quirky vowel that might suggest an amorphous anomaly in the data. He found nothing. Mermaid was clean, neat, tidy, and innocuous as baby powder.

On the eight day he gave up. The solution to Crescent's murder wasn't going to be found in his files.

It was time to look for parallels. He'd spent too much time at GenDyne, but he was used to finding hints, clues, leads wherever he searched, and this utter failure rankled. Perhaps the Parabas Box would be more revealing. It was time to access Noschek's work.

Half on a whim, he requested Hypatia's assistance. It was a measure of the importance GenDyne attached to his work that they agreed immediately. As for Spango, she was delighted, though she concealed her pleasure from the dour company official who pulled her off her current project to give her the news. It was like a paid vacation from designing.

When the people at Parabas were told, they went spatial. They'd sooner shut down than let a GenDyne designer into their Box. Important people in LaLa talked reassuringly to their counterparts in São Paulo. It was agreed that finding out what had happened to the two designers was paramount. There were certain safeguards that could be instituted to ensure that Parabas's visitor saw only the contents of Noschek's files. Parabas consented. Agua Pri was overruled. Hypatia would be allowed in. But nobody smiled when Cardenas and his GenDyne "spy" were admitted to the dead designer's office.

It was larger than Crescent's, and emptier. No charming domestic scenes floating above this desk. No expensive colorcrawl on the walls. Noschek had been a bachelor. Barely out of design school, top of his class, brilliant in ways his employers hadn't figured out how to exploit before his death, he'd been the object of serious executive headhunting by at least two European and one Soviet multinat in the three years he'd been at Parabas.

Hypatia'd read his history, too. As she looked around the spartan office, her voice was muted. "Nobody becomes a senior designer before thirty. Let alone twenty-five."

Cardenas called up the pictures they'd been shown of the vacuumed designer. Noschek was tall and slim, still looked like a teenager, a beautiful Slav with delicate features and the soulful dark eyes of some Kafkaesque antihero. Something in all the holos struck Cardenas the instant he saw them, but he couldn't stick a label on it.

The Parabas Box was approximately the same size as GenDyne's. Noschek's key was Delphi Alexander Philip. The voice of the wallscreen was deep and resonant, instantly responsive to his sponging, as he scanned the meteoric career of the young designer. Parabas's security team had been at work 'round the clock. Some of the information would reveal itself only when Hypatia was out of the room. The South Americans might be cooperative, but they weren't stupid.

Each time Hypatia left, she took Charliebo with her for company. She liked playing with the dog, and the hair she scratched out of him gave Parabas's cleanteam fits. Each day brought them closer together. Her and Charliebo, that is. Cardenas still wasn't sure about her and himself.

It didn't matter whether she was present or not. Three days of hard sponging saw him no nearer any answers than when he'd stepped off the induction shuttle from Nogales.

On the fourth day the screen went hostile and nearly took him with it.

He was sponging off a hard-to-penetrate corner of Philip, down in the lower right corner of the Box. Hypatia had gone outside with Charliebo. Biocircuits spawned the same steady, sonorous flow of information he'd been listening to for hours, revealing themselves via concomitant word streams and images on the wallscreen. If he'd been watching intently, he might have had time to see a flicker before it declared itself, but as usual, he was most attuned to aural playout. Maybe that saved him. He never knew.

Wind erupted into the office, blasting his thinning hair back across his head. On the screen the visual had gone berserk, running at ten speed through emptiness, reason gone, bereft of logic and organization. A dull roaring pounded in his ears. Dimly, he thought he could hear Charliebo frantically howling outside the door. There was a hammering, though whether outside the screen-secured door or inside his brain he couldn't tell. He pressed his palms over his ears, letting the vorec spill to the floor.

Something was coming out of the wall.

A full-sense holo, a monstrous alien shape thick with slime and smelling of ancient foulness, an oozing shifting mass of raw biocircuitry-generated false collagen that pulsed slowly and massively, booming with each heave. Reflective pustules lining its epidermis bristled with raw neural connectors that reached for him. The hammering on the door was relentless now, and he thought he could hear people shouting. They'd have to be shouting very loudly indeed to make their presence known through the sound-dampened barrier.

He tried to block out sight and sound of the ballooning apparition. The door was security-sealed to prevent unauthorized access. Where was the override? It was manual, he remembered. He fought the sensorial assault, tears streaming from his eyes, as he struggled to locate the switch.

Bits and pieces of the false collagen were sloughing away from the nightmare's flanks as it drifted toward him. The amount of crunch required to construct a projection of such complexity and reality had to be astronomical, Cardenas knew. He wondered how much of Parabas's considerable power had suddenly gone dead as it was funneled into this single gate.

As it drew near, it became mostly mouth, a dark, bottomless psychic pit that extended back into the wall, lined with teeth that were twitching, mindless biogrowths.

He stumbled backward, keeping the desk between the projection and himself. Near the center of the desk a line of contact strips was glowing brightly as a child's toy. The expanding mouth was ready to swallow him, the steady roar from its nonexistent throat like the approach of a train inside a tunnel.

Hit the release. The voice that screamed at him was a tiny, fading squeak. His own. *The yellow strip.* He extended a shaky hand. He thought he touched the right strip. Or maybe he fell on it.

When he regained consciousness, he was lying on the floor, staring at the ceiling of Vladimir Noschek's office. Someone said two words he would never forget.

"He's alive."

Then hands, lifting him. The view changing as he was raised. He broke free, staggering away from his saviors, and they waited silently while he heaved into a wastebasket. When someone pressed a mild sting against his right arm, he looked around sharply.

There must have been something in his expression that made the man retreat. His expression, however, was reassuring. "No combinants. Just a pick-me-up. To kill the nausea and dizziness."

He managed to nod. The Brazilian turned to whisper to his companion. Like images drawn on transparent gels, Cardenas saw collagen teeth bursting before his retinas as the afterimage of the monster continued to fade from his memory.

"You scared the shit out of us." Hypatia was watching him carefully. She looked worried.

Something heavy and warm pressed against his legs. He glanced down, automatically stroked Charliebo's spine. The shepherd whined and tried to press closer.

"What happened?" one of the medicos asked as he closed his service case.

Somehow Cardenas managed to keep down the anger that was building inside him. "It was a psychomorph. Full visual, audio, collagenic presence. The works. Sensorium max. *Why the hell didn't somebody tell me this was a tactile screen?*"

"Tac . . .?" Both medicos turned dumbfounded stares on the east wall. It was Hypatia who finally spoke.

"Can't be, Angel. Designers aren't given access to tactile. Nobody is. Uses too much crunch. Besides, that's strictly military stuff. Even somebody as valued as Noscheck wouldn't be allowed near it."

The chief medico looked back at him. "No tactiles in Parabas S.A. I'd know, my staff would know. You sure it was a psychomorph?" Cardenas just stared at him until the man nodded. "Okay, so it was a psychomorph. I don't know how, but I'm not in a position to argue with you. I wasn't here."

"That's right, compadre," Cardenas told him softly. "You weren't here."

"You gonna be all right?" The same stare. The medico shrugged, spoke to his assistant. "So okay. So we'll sort it out later. Come on." They left, though not without a last disbelieving glance in the direction of the now-silent wallscreen.

As soon as the door shut behind them and sealed, Hypatia turned on him.

"What's going on here? That couldn't have been a psychomorph that hit you. There isn't enough crunch in the whole Parabas Box to structure one!"

"That's exactly what I've been thinking," he told her quietly. "But it was a psychomorph. The most detailed one I've ever seen. I do not want to see it again. It was a trap, a guard, something to wipe out the nosy. It almost wiped me."

She was watching him closely. "If it was as bad as you claim, how come you're standing there talking to me instead of lying on the floor babbling like a spastic infant?"

"I—felt it coming. Intuition. Just in time to start closing down my perception. I can do that, some. When you're blind for six years, you get practice in all sorts of arcane exercises. I sidestepped it right before it could get a psychic fix on me, and managed to cue the door. It must have cycled when you all came in. They can't fix on more than one person at a time. Takes too much crunch."

"I thought that kind of advanced tech was beyond you."

He met her gaze. "Did I ever say that?"

"No. No, you didn't. I just assumed, you being a duty cop and all—people do a lot of assuming about you, don't they?"

He nodded tersely. "It helps. People like to think of cops as dumber than they are. Some of us are. Some of us aren't. I don't discourage it."

"How old are you, anyway?"

"Fifty-three in two months."

"Shit. I thought you were my age. I'm forty-one."

"Part of it's being small. You always look younger."

"What kind of cop are you, anyway, Cardenas?"

He was searching beneath the desk, straightened when he found the vorec mike. "A good one."

You just didn't brew a full-scale sensorium-max hostile psychomorph out of a standard industrial Box, no matter how big the company. Hypatia knew that. Not unless Parabas was into illegal military design, and under questioning the company reps did all but cut their wrists to prove their innocence. Cardenas believed them. They had more to lose by lying than by telling the truth.

He was beginning to think brilliant was too feeble a word to use to describe the talents of the late Vladimir Noscheck.

But Noscheck had made a mistake. By slipping something as powerful as the psychomorph into Philip storage, he'd as much as confessed to having something to hide, something to protect. Ordinarily, that wouldn't have mattered because the sponger discovering it would have been turned to mental jelly. Only Cardenas's training and experience had saved him. With Hypatia at his side he continued to probe.

They solved the secret of the commercial wallscreen quickly enough. It was numb as a sheet of plywood—until you went someplace you weren't wanted.

Then you tripped the alert and the screen went tactile. It was one hell of a modification, worth plenty. Cardenas could have cared less. He wasn't interested in how it was done as much as he was *why*. The camouflage was perfect.

A tactile screen could spit back at you. One that looked normal and then suddenly became tactile was unheard of. The Parabas executives went silly when the medicos made their report. They wanted to take the screen apart immediately, resorting to furious threats when Cardenas refused. Gradually, they gave up and left him alone again. They'd get their hands on Noschek's last innovation soon enough.

If it was Vladimir Noschek's last innovation, Cardenas thought.

There was also the possibility that the dual tactile-numb screen wasn't the work of Noschek at all, that it had been set up by whoever had vacuumed him. The psychomorph could have been inserted specifically to deal with trackers like Angel Cardenas. Or it could be a false lead, spectacular enough to divert any probers from the real answers.

Answers hell. He wasn't sure he knew the right questions yet.

They'd find them.

First, he needed to know how a max psychomorph had been inserted into a conventional industrial Box. Hypatia confirmed his suspicions about the requisite parameters.

"If you saw what you say you saw, then Noschek or whoever built the insert needed a lot more crunch than Parabas employs here in Agua Pri."

"How do you know how much crunch Parabas has here?"

"It gets around. No reason to keep it a deep dark secret."

"Assuming for the sake of discussion that it's Noschek's toy we're dealing with, could he have drawn on crunch from the home office?"

"Possible, but considering the distance, it would've been mighty risky. Would make more sense to steal locally."

"How much would he have had to steal?"

"Based on what you describe, I'd say he would've needed access to at least one Cray-IBM."

"GenDyne?"

She laughed. "That's more crunch than our whole installation would use in a year. No way. Though I'd love to have the chance to play with one."

"So who on the Strip uses a Cribm?"

"Beats the hell out of me, Angel. You're the cop. You find out."

He did. Fast, using Parabas's circuits to access the major utility files for the whole Southwest Region in Elpaso Juarez. His opto police security clearance let him cut through normal layers of bureaucratic infrastructure like a scalpel through collagen.

"Sony-Digital," he finally told her as the records flashed on screen. The wall's audio checked his pronunciation. "Telefunken. Fordmatsu. That's everybody."

She stared at the holoed info. "What now?"

"We find out who's been losing crunch—if we can."

They could. Word of what had happened at GenDyne and Parabas had made the corporate rounds. As soon as Cardenas identified himself and the case he was working on, they had plenty of cooperation.

It was Fordmatsu. Their own security was unaware of the theft, much less its extent, so cleverly had it been carried out. Cardenas sourced it, though. He didn't bother to inform them. He was no accountant, and he didn't want anybody sponging around until he'd finished what he'd come to Agua Pri for. Though no expert, he knew enough to admire the skill that had been at work in Fordmatsu's Box. Everything had been done during off-hours and painstakingly compensated for throughout the crunchlines. Neat.

"How much?" Hypatia asked him.

"Can't tell for sure. Hard to total, the way its tucked in here and there. Weeks' worth. Maybe months'."

She stared at him. "A Cribm can crunch trillions of bytes a second. I can't think of a problem it couldn't solve inside an hour. There isn't anything that needs days of that kind of crunch, let alone months."

"Somebody needed it." He rose from behind the desk. "Come on."

"Where are we going?"

"Back to GenDyne. There are some sequences I ran here I want to rerun on Crescent's wall."

"What about the psychomorph?"

He put an arm around her shoulders. She didn't shrug it off. "I'm going to endrun that sucker so slick it won't have time to squeal."

It was all there in Crescent's Mermaid. If he hadn't tripped the psychomorph in Noschek's storage, they never would have found it. He leaned back in the dead man's chair and rubbed his eyes.

"Fordmatsu is out millions, and they don't even know it. Somebody was running one gigabox of a sequence."

"Noschek?"

"Not just Noschek. Maybe he designed the sponge schematic, but they were both into it."

"Damn," she muttered. "What for?"

"Aye, there's the rub. That we don't know yet."

"But it doesn't make any sense. Why would a GenDyne designer co-opt with somebody out of Parabas? You think maybe they were going to fracture and set up their own firm?"

"I don't think so. If that was their intent, they could have done it by intrapreneuring. Easier and cheaper." He leaned back in the chair and ran a hand down Charliebo's neck. "Besides, it doesn't fit their profiles. Crescent was pure company man, GenDyne do or die. Noschek was too unstable to survive outside the corporate womb."

"Then why?"

"I thought they might've been doing some work for somebody else, but there's no indication of that anywhere. They did a hell of a job of hiding what they were up to, but no way could they hide all that crunch. You know what I think?" He gave Charliebo a pat and swiveled around to face her. "I think there's a Box in here that doesn't belong to GenDyne."

"And Noschek?"

"Maybe there's one in Parabas, too. Or maybe the same Box floating between both locations. With that much crunch you could do just about anything. Quién sabe what they were in to?"

"So you're thinking maybe whoever they were working for vacuumed them for the crunch?"

"Not the crunch, no. Whatever our boys were using it for. Haven't got a clue to that yet." He found himself rubbing his eyes again.

She rose and walked over to stand behind his chair. Her hands dug into his shoulders, kneading, releasing the accumulated tension. "Let's get out of here for a while. You're spending too much time sponging. You try doing that and playing the analytical cop simultaneously, you're going to turn your brain to mush."

He hardly heard her. "I've got to figure the why before we can figure the how."

"Later. No more figuring for today." She leaned forward. He was enveloped by the folds of her jumpsuit and the heavy, warm curves it enclosed. "Even a sponge needs to rest."

It came to him when he wasn't thinking about it, which is often the path taken by revelation. He was lying prone on the oversized hybred, feeling the preprogrammed wave motion stroking his back like extruded lanolin. Hypatia lay nearby, her body pale arcs and valleys like sand dunes lit by moonlight. The ceaseless murmur of the Strip seeped through the downpolarized windows, a susurration speaking of people and electronics, industry and brief flaring sparks of pleasure.

He ran a hand along her side, starting at her shoulder and accelerating down her ribs, slowing as it ascended the curve of her hip. Her skin was cool, unwrinkled. Her mind wasn't the only thing that had been well taken care of. She rolled over to face him. Next to the bed Charliebo stirred in his sleep, chasing ghost rabbits which stayed always just ahead of his teeth.

"What is it?" She blinked sleepily at him, then made a face. "God, don't you *ever* sleep? I thought I wore you out enough for that, anyway."

He smiled absently. "You did. I just woke up. Funny. You spend all your waking hours working a problem, and all you get for your efforts is garbage. Then when you're not concentrating on it—there it is. Set out like cake at a wedding. I just sorted it out."

She sat up on the hybred. Not all the lingering motion was in the mattress. He luxuriated in the sight of her.

"Sorted what out?"

"What Crescent and Noschek were doing together. It wasn't in the Boxes, and it wasn't in their files. No wonder corporate security couldn't find anything. They never would have. The answer wasn't in their work. It was in them. In their voices, their attitudes, what they had in common and what they didn't. In what they didn't commit to storage. They shared their work, but they kept themselves to themselves."

"A cop shouldn't be full of riddles."

"Have you got a terminal here?"

"Does a cow have udders?" She slid off the bed, jounced across the room, and touched a switch. A portion of the wall slid upward to reveal a small screen, while the vorec popped out of a slot nearby, an obedient metal eel. He walked over and plucked it from its holder, studied the screen. They were both naked, both comfortable with it and each other.

"Pretty fancy setup for a household."

"Think. I have to work at home sometimes. I need more than a toy." She leaned against him.

"Look, let me concentrate for a minute, will you?"

She straightened. He saw her teeth flash in the dim light. "Okay. But only for a minute."

He activated the screen, filled the vorec with a steady stream of instructions. It was slower than the designer units he'd sponged at Parabas and GenDyne but far faster than any normal home unit. Soon he was running the files he needed from both companies. Then he surprised Hypatia by accessing Nogales. The problem he set up was for the Sociopsycultural Department at the U of A. It didn't take the university Box long to render its determination.

"There it is."

She stared at the screen, then back at him. "There *what* is?"

"Answers, maybe." He slipped the vorec back into its slot. The screen went dark. "Let's ambulate."

"What, now?" She ran fingers through her unkempt hair. "Don't you ever give a lady a chance to catch up?"

"You can catch up next week, next month." He found his pants and was stepping into them. "I think I know what happened. Most of it, anyway. The data make sense. It's what our two boys did that doesn't make sense, but I think they went and did it, anyway."

She thumbed a closet open and began rummaging through her clothes. "You mean you know who vacuumed them?"

He fastened the velcrite of his waistband. The blue Federales bracelet bounced on his wrist. "Nobody vacuumed them. They vacuumed themselves."

She paused with the velcrite catch of her bra. "Another riddle? I'm getting tired of your riddles, Angel."

"No riddle. They vacuumed themselves. Simultaneously, via program. I think it was a double suicide. And by the way, I'm no Angel. It's 'Ahn-hell,' for crissakes."

"That's Tex-Mex. I only speak Anglo."

"Screw you."

She struck a pose. "I thought you were in a hurry to leave?"

Security let them back into GenDyne, but they weren't happy about it. There was something wrong about cops going to work at three A.M. The guard in the hall took his time. His helmet flared as the scanner roved over both nocturnal visitors. Just doing his job. Eventually, he signed them through.

They went straight to Crescent's office. It was the same as they'd left it, nothing moved, unexpectedly sterile-looking under the concealed incandescents. Cardenas found his gaze returning unwillingly to the bright family portraits that hovered above the desk.

He flicked the vorec and brought the wallscreen online. He warmed up with some simple mnemonics before getting serious with the tactical verbals he'd decided to use. Hypatia caught her breath as the wall flared, but no psychomorph coalesced to threaten them. Cardenas was being careful, additionally so with Hypatia in the room. Charliebo cocked his head sideways as he stared at the screen.

Five minutes later Cardenas had the answer to the first of his questions.

"It's tactile. Same kind of concealed setup Noschek had in his place."

"Jesus! You could warn a body."

"There's no danger. I'm not sponging deep yet. All surface. There are ways. I was pretty sure I wasn't going to trigger anything."

"Thanks," she said dryly.

He dove in, the words flowing in a steady stream into the vorec as he keyed different levels within the main GenDyne Box. This time he went in fast and easy. He went wherever he wanted to without any problem—and that was the problem. After what seemed like fifteen minutes, he paused to check his bracelet. Two hours gone. Soon it would be light outside.

Hypatia had settled herself on the edge of the desk. She was watching him intently. "Anything?"

"Not what I came for. Plenty Parabas would pay to get their hands on. I'm sure the reverse would be true if I was sponging their Box like this." He shook his head as he regarded the screen. "There's got to be another Box in there, somewhere. Or a section that's reading out dead."

"Impossible. You need full cryo to keep the Box wet and accessible. You can't just set something like that up in the middle of an outfit like GenDyne without tripping half a dozen alarms.''

''Alarms are usually set to warn of withdrawal, not entry.''

''Any kind of solid insertion like that would have people asking questions.''

''You can avoid questions if you can avoid notice. These guys were wizards at avoiding notice.''

She crossed her arms. ''I still say its impossible.''

He turned back to the wall. ''We'll see.''

He found it only because he had some idea what he was looking for. No one else would have glanced at it. There was no separate Box. Hypatia was right about that. Instead, it was buried deep within the basic GenDyne Box itself, disguised as a dormant file for a biolight conveyor. When he sponged it, Hypatia caught her breath.

''My God. A subox tunnel.''

''I've heard about them,'' Cardenas murmured tightly, ''but I've never actually seen one before.''

''That's as close to being invisible as you can get and still be inside a Box.'' She was standing close to the wall now, examining the holo intensely. ''Whoever made this was half-designer and half-magician.''

Cardenas found himself nodding. ''That's our boys.'' He studied the slowly rotating cylindrical schematic. ''The key question is, where does it go?'' He was set to start in when Hypatia stopped him, walking over to put a hand on his arm and block his view of the screen.

''Maybe we better get some help. This is way over my head.''

''And therefore mine, too?'' He smiled. ''You don't have to know how to build a plane to know how to fly one. I can handle it.''

''More psychomorphs? And who knows what else.''

''I'm ready for it this time. Hypatia, I can intuit *fast*. Anything starts coming out of that tube, I'll just dry out.''

''Man, I hope you know what you're doing.'' She stepped aside. Together they stared as he spoke into the vorec and started down the tube.

They encountered no traps, no guards. Smart. Oh so smart, he thought to himself. Make it look like an ordinary part of the Box. Make it look like it belongs. Normalcy was the best disguise.

They wouldn't put him off the track with that. Because even though he didn't understand the how yet, he knew the why.

Hypatia asked him about it again. ''I still don't get this double-suicide business.''

''It's what they were.'' He spoke between commands to the vorec, waiting while the wall complied with each sequence of instructions. He was tense but in control. It was one lon-n-n-ng tube.

"Noschek particularly. He was the key. You see, part of the tragedy was that they could never meet in person. Security would have found out right away, and that would have finished both of them. It meant they could only communicate through the joint Fordmatsu link they established. Like in the old times when people sent information by personal messenger. It was too complex, too involved, too *intense* for it to just be business. There had to be more to it than that. And then when I couldn't find any business at all, that clinched it.''

"Clinched what?''

"The fact that they had to be lovers. Via the Fordmatsu link. Crescent and Noschek were homosexual, Hypatia.''

She went dead quiet for several minutes before replying. "Oh come on, Angel! Crescent had a family. Two kids.''

"He was latent. Probably all his life. That's why I had to run double profiles together with what I suspected through the Sociopsycultural Box up at U of A. It confirmed. I'm sure if we had time to go over their lives in more detail, we'd find plenty of other clues.

"You told me Crescent was a trueglue GenDyne man. I'm sure he was. GenDyne's about as liberal as its multinat counterparts. Which is to say, not at all. Two Fundamentalists on its Board. Crescent knew if he strayed once, it would put an end to his career. So he stayed in the closet. Covered himself thoroughly for the sake of his future. I've no doubt he loved his wife. Meanwhile, everything proceeded the way he'd probably dreamed it might. Gradually, his tendencies faded as he buried himself in his family and work.

"Then Noschek came along, probably through a casual social hookup. A brilliant, wild young talent. Pretty to boot. And they got to know each other. Most relationships develop. This one exploded.''

"So they 'related' through Box links?''

He nodded. "Try to imagine what they must have gone through. It's all there in their voices, in the stuff I was able to sponge from the months before they vacuumed. They knew they couldn't meet. Crescent knew it would ruin him. I don't know if that bothered Noschek—he didn't seem to give a damn for social conventions. But he cared about Crescent. So they built this Fordmatsu link out of stolen crunch.''

"They wouldn't need all that crunch just to maintain a private communication.''

"Exactly. So they started discussing their problem, fooling around with all that excess crunch they had access to. Meanwhile, their relationship just kept getting tighter and tighter at the same time as they were becoming increasingly frustrated with their situation.

"Eventually, they found something. Noschek was the innovator, Crescent the experienced constructor. They discovered a way to be together. Always.''

"Through mutual suicide?'' She shook her head. "That doesn't bring people together. It doesn't profile either. Noschek sure, but Crescent was too stable to go for that."

"How stable do you think he would have been if his wife had ever found out? Or his kids? The only way to spare them the disgrace was to make it look like a murder. That way our boys would be able to slip away untarnished and untroubled."

"So they figured out a way to vacuum themselves? Papier-mâché wings and brass harps and the whole metaphysical ensemble?"

"No. They're vacuumed all right, but they're not gone. They're together, like they wanted to be. Together in a sense no one else can understand. I wonder if they fully understood it themselves. But they were willing to take the risk."

"That doesn't make any sense."

He took a deep breath. "Consider all the crunch they'd been siphoning from Fordmatsu. Then consider Noschek's hobbies. One of them is real interesting. You ever hear of MR?"

"Like in 'mister'?"

"No. Like in morphological resonance."

She made another face. "Gimme a break, Angel. I'm just a lousy designer. What the hell is morphological resonance?"

"The concept's been around for decades. Not many people take it seriously. The scientific establishment has too much invested in existing theories. That doesn't put off those folks who are more interested in the truth than intellectual comfort. People like Noschek. When I found out he was into it, I did some reading.

"A long time ago somebody ran a bunch of rats through a series of mazes in Scotland. The same mazes, over and over, for much longer than anyone would think necessary to prove a point. Each time the rats ran a maze, they managed it a little faster."

"That's a revelation?"

"Consider this, then." He leaned forward. "Some folks in Australia decided to run the same maze. Identical as to size, distance, configuration, reward at the end, everything. The first time they tried it, the rats ran the distance just a hair faster than the first time their Scottish cousins ran it. Then they repeated the experiment in India. Same thing. The Indian rats got off to a quicker start than did the Australians. What do you get from that?"

She looked bemused. "That Indian rats are smarter than Scottish or Australian rats?"

He shook his head impatiently. "It wasn't just done with rats and mazes. Other similar experiments were run, with identical results. For the scientific establishment, that hasn't been conclusive enough. But it hasn't stopped theorists from making proposals."

"It never does."

"It was suggested that each time an intelligent creature repeats something exactly as previously done, it sets up a resonance. Not in the air. In—spacetime, the ether, I don't know. But it's there, and the more it's repeated, the stronger and more permanent the resonance becomes, until it spreads far enough to affect the identical pattern no matter where it's repeated. That's where the rats come in. The theory holds that the rats in Australia were picking up on the resonance set up by the maze runners in Scotland. Then again in India. Which is why they ran the maze slightly faster at the start and progressively thereafter for the duration of the experiment. The resonance gave them a head start.

"MR's been used to explain a lot of things since it was first formulated, up to and including mankind's exponential progress in science and technology. According to the theory, we're working on one hell of an expanding resonance. Each time we come up with something new, it's because we're building on thought patterns or experimental methodologies that've been repeated in the past."

"What's all this got to do with our departed designers?"

"You told me what a supercooled Cribm can do. Trillions of crunch a second. Unthinkable quantity in an hour. Incalculable content in a day. Cribm's are used to crunch whole bushels of problems. Suppose you set it to process just one problem, instead of hundreds. Set it to run the sequence over and over, trillions upon trillions of times. Think of the resonance you could set up. Enough to last a long time without fading. Maybe even enough to become permanent." He nodded toward the flickering, flaring wallscreen.

"You could set it up in there."

She followed his gaze, found herself whispering. "Crescent and Noschek?"

"Safe, together. As a dual resonance. Patterns of memory, electrical impulses: what we call memory. Reduced to streams of electrons and run over and over and over until brought separately into being as a floating resonance inside a Box. Not in formal storage, exactly. Different. Independent of the Box systems and yet localized by them. So they'd hang together even better. They reduced themselves to a program the Cribm could process and set it to repeating the designated patterns, using all that stolen crunch. They're in there, Hypatia. In a Box built for two."

"That's crazy." Her mouth was suddenly dry. For the first time she felt uncomfortable in the cool office. The door, the unbreakable window was keeping them in instead of others out. "You can't *Box* a person."

"Resonance, Hypatia. Not a program as we conceive of one. Repetition creates the pattern, brings it into existence. You vacuum yourself into the Cribm, and it repeats you back into existence. As to whether that includes anything we'd recognize as consciousness, I don't know."

"If it's a pattern the Cribm can repeat, maybe it could be—accessed?"

His expression was somber. "I don't know. I don't know how they're in there, if they're just frozen or if they have some flexibility. If they're anything more than just a twitch in space-time, Hypatia, they've found immortality. Even if the power to the Box fails, the resonance should remain. It may be restricted in range, but it's independent of outside energy. The resonance maintains itself. Don't get me started on thermodynamics. The whole thing's cockeyed. But it's not new. People have been discussing it for decades.''

"Easier when they're talking about rats," she murmured. "You say they're restricted by the confines of the Box. Can they move around inside it?''

"You've got the questions, I haven't got the answers. We're dealing with something halfway between physics and metaphysics. I don't know if I should consult a cyberneticist or a medium.'' He indicated the tunnel on the screen. "Maybe when we get to the end of that, we'll find something besides a dead end.''

She joined him in monitoring their progress. The tunnel seemed endless. By now it should have pushed beyond the confines of the GenDyne Box, yet it showed no signs of weakening.

"They took a terrible chance. They worked awfully hard to hide themselves.''

Cardenas stroked Charliebo. "Maybe all to no end. The theories I've enumerated might be just that. It's more than likely they're as dead as their physical selves.''

"Yeah. But if there's anything to it—if there's anything *in there*—they might not like being disturbed. Remember the psychomorph.''

"I'm pretty sure I can handle the screen if it goes tactile again, now that I've got an idea what to expect. I can always cut the power.''

"Can you? You said this resonance, if it exists, would remain whether the power was on or not.''

"Their resonance, yes, but cutting the power would deprive them of access to the system—assuming they're able to interface with it at all. They could have inserted traps like the psychomorph before they vacuumed themselves.''

"And you think you can access this resonance?''

"If it exists, and only if it's somehow interfaced with the GenDyne Box.''

Two hours later the rising sun found them no nearer the end of the tunnel than when they'd begun. Thirty years earlier Cardenas could have hung on throughout the day. Not anymore. There were times when mandatory retirement no longer seemed a destination to be avoided. This was one of them.

He let Hypatia drive him back to her place and put him to bed. He fell asleep fast, but he didn't sleep well.

A psychomorph was chasing him: a gruesome, gory nightmare dredged up from the depths of someone else's disturbed subconscious. Frantically, he tried to find a kill strip to shut down the power, but someone had removed them all from the control panel in front of him. And there were screens all around him now, and on the ceiling, and beneath his feet, each one belching forth a new and more horrible monstrosity. He curled into a fetal ball, whimpering as they touched him with their filthy tendrils, hunting for his psychic core so they could enter and drive him insane. One used a keyword to open the top of his skull like a can opener.

He sat up in bed, sweating. Beneath his buttocks the sheet was soaked. A glance at the holo numerals that clung like red spiders to the wall behind the bed showed 0934. But it was still dark outside. Then he noticed the tiny P.M. to the right of the last numeral. He'd slept the whole day. His mouth confirmed it, his tongue conveying the taste of old leather.

"Hypatia?" Naked, he slid slowly off the hybred and stumbled toward the bathroom, running both hands through his hair. Water on his face helped. More down his throat helped to jump-start the rest of his body. He used one of her lilac towels to dry himself, turned back to the bedroom.

"Hypatia? Charliebo?"

She wasn't in the kitchen, nor the greeting room. Neither was the shepherd. Both gone out. Maybe she'd taken him for a walk. Charliebo was well-trained, but his insides were no different from any other dog's. He'd go with her. Dog and designer had grown close to each other this past week.

He knew she was worried about him. While he would have preferred to have spared her the concern, he was pleased. Been a long time since anyone besides Charliebo had really cared about Angel Cardenas, and Hypatia had better legs than the shepherd. Sure, he was stressing himself, but he could take it. All part of the job. Experience compensated for the lack of youthful resilience. He could handle any traps Crescent and Noschek had left behind, even if she didn't think he could.

He stopped in the middle of the room. Concerned about him, yeah. About his ability to deal with another psychomorph or worse. Under those circumstances what would a caring, compassionate woman do? What could she do, to spare him another dangerous, possibly lethal confrontation? Couldn't an experienced, younger designer follow the path he'd already found and thus keep him from possible danger?

Shit.

He was wide awake now; alert, attuned, and worried. He didn't remember getting dressed, didn't recall the short elevator ride to the subterranean garage. Sure enough, her little three-wheeler was gone. She wasn't out for an evening stroll with Charliebo, then. His lungs heaved as he raced for the nearest induction station. It would be faster than trying to call for police backup.

Besides, he might be getting himself all upset over nothing. If he was wrong, he'd end up looking the prize fool. If he was right, well, Hypatia was highly competent. But he'd much rather play the fool.

The only thing that saved him was three decades on the force. Thirty years' experience means you don't go barging into a room. Thirty years' handling ninlocos and juice dealers and assorted flakes and whackos says you go in quietly. Go in fast and loud, and you might upset somebody, and he might react before you had time to size things up.

Thirty years' experience told him Hypatia would have security-sealed the door to the office. When he discovered it wasn't, he opened it as slowly as possible.

The lights were on low. The wallscreen was alive with flaring symbols and muted verbal responses. In the center was the tunnel, twisting and glowing like an electrified python. He picked out the desk, the muted holo portraits of Wallace Crescent's abandoned, innocent family.

Hypatia was on the floor. There was enough light to illuminate the figure bent over her. Enough light to show the still, motionless lump of Charliebo lying not far away.

Quiet as he'd been, the figure still sensed his presence. It turned to face him. The blend suit melted into the background, but he recognized the triple lenses that formed a multicolored swath across the face instantly. All three primaries were down and functioning now.

Cardenas saw that Hypatia's jumpsuit was unzipped all the way down to her thighs. A handful of secrylic had been slapped across her mouth, muffling her as it hardened. More of the so-called police putty bound her ankles and wrists. She tried to roll toward him but found it hard to move because the figure had one knee resting on her hip.

His gaze flicked to Charliebo. The shepherd's chest was still, the eyes vacant. Cardenas's vision blurred slightly, and his teeth moved against each other.

"Don't," said the flashman. He didn't sound uncertain tonight. He glanced down at Hypatia, then smiled up at the Federale. "Worried about baby? No need to. Maybe. Come in, close the door behind you. If I'd sealed it, you would've gone for help. This way I only have to deal with you, right?" He leaned slightly to his left as if to see behind Cardenas.

"Right." Cardenas kept his hands in view, his movements slow and unambiguous. Hypatia stared at him imploringly. He saw that she'd been crying. Easy, he told himself. Keep it easy.

But it wasn't easy, it wasn't easy at all.

"You so much as twitch the wrong way, Federale, and she'll be sorry." The flashman was grinning at something only he found amusing. "You should've stayed in bed, man."

No hurry. No emergency. Not yet. He moved off to his right. "Why'd you have to kill my dog?"

He didn't get the response he expected. The flashman let out a short, sharp laugh. "Hey, that's funny! You don't know why it's funny, do you? I'll tell you later, after I'm through here. Or maybe I'll let her tell you." He glanced quickly at the screen, not giving Cardenas any time. "Got to be an end to this damn tunnel soon."

"All I have to do," Cardenas said softly, "is shout, and Security'll be down on you like bad news."

Again the unhealthy, relaxed laugh, a corrugated giggle. "Sure they would, but you won't shout." He held something up so Cardenas could see it.

A scrambler. Military model, banned from private use. Of course, banning was only a legal term. It didn't keep things from falling into the hands of people who wanted to have them. When everything else failed, the police used less powerful versions of the same device to subdue juice addicts who outgrabed. It put them down fast, but it didn't do permanent damage. Fourth World military types used powered-up models for less reputable purposes. The flashlight-shaped device scrambled nerve endings. The Federale issue paralyzed. The military model could break down neurons beyond hope of surgical repair. In hand-to-hand combat it was much more efficient than knife or bayonet and a lot easier to use. You didn't have to penetrate. All you had to do was make contact.

"Go ahead and shout, if you want to." The flashman calmly touched the scrambler to Hypatia's exposed left breast.

She thrashed. Hard, but not hard enough to break the secrylic. She whined loud enough to penetrate the slightly porous gag. The flashman showed the scrambler to Cardenas again, ignoring the heavy, gasping form behind him.

"See here? No safety. A simple modification." Cardenas bit down on his lower lip hard enough to draw blood, but he kept his hands at his sides, his feet motionless. "You shout, you move funny, and I'll shove this between her legs. Maybe it won't kill her, but she won't care."

"I won't shout." Only practice enabled him to reply calmly, quietly. His fingers were bunched into fists, the nails digging into the flesh of his palms.

"That's a good little sponger."

"How long?"

Again the grin. "Since Crescent vacuumed himself. Since the investigation started." He looked ceilingward, toward the low-key incandescents. "One bulb up there's got an extra filament. Records and holds. Can't broadcast each pickup. Security would track it. Just a five-second high-speed burst when a receive-only passes outside the door. Me. Just enough range to clear the room. Not real noticeable, if you know what I mean. I walk by once a day, stop long enough to sneeze, move on. Hardly suspicious. Then playback at normal speed when I'm home. Nothing very entertaining until you showed up."

"You've been monitoring her place, too."

The flashman chuckled. "Sure now. You think I knew she'd be coming here tonight via esp? Expected you to snore on. Been getting some custom design work of your own?"

He took a step forward. The flashman lowered the scrambler slightly. Cardenas saw Hypatia's eyes widen, her body tense.

"Ah-ah. Don't want to make me nervous, Federale." Cardenas took back the step, his expression bland, screaming inside. "Glad you started pushing your hypothesis here, man. I would've been in a world of hurt if you'd started down this tunnel over at Parabas. Guess I'm just lucky."

"What do you want?"

"Don't game me. I want whatever's at the end of this tunnel. A subox, resonance, miracle crunch. Access. Same thing you've been after. 'Morphological resonance.' That's wild, man. Immortality? Wilder still. Relax. You'll cramp your head."

"And if you find it?"

The flashman nodded toward the side of the desk. Cardenas saw the metal and plastic plug-in lying there. He couldn't see the cable link but knew it must be there, running to jacks beneath the desk.

"One sequence. I finalize, then do a quick store-and-transfer. Anything valuable, and there ought to be plenty." He licked his lips. "Never seen a tunnel like this. Nobody has. Construction crunch alone's worth all the trouble this has taken."

"But you want more."

The flashman smiled broadly. "Man, I want it *all*."

"You'll take it and leave?"

The man nodded. "I'm a thief. Not a vacuumer. Not unless you make me. I get what I've been after for months, and I waft." He gestured with the scrambler. Hypatia flinched. "I'll even leave you this. Memories can be so much fun."

"Assuming there's even anything in there to steal, what makes you think you can transfer a resonance?"

"Don't know unless you try, right? If you can get something in, you ought to be able to get it out. It's only crunch. Key the Box, key the transfer, and it's off to friends in the Mideast."

"Immortality for the petrochem moguls?" Cardenas's tone was thick with contempt.

"That's up to them to figure out. Not my department. I just borrow things. But they'll have the subox, if there is one. Our farseeing pinkboys are going on another trip. Suppose they can slip in and out of any Box they are introduced to? My employers could send them on lots of vacations. A little crunch out of First EEC Bank, some extra out of Soventern. With that kind of access, petrochem will seem like petty-cash stuff."

Cardenas shook his head. "You *are* crazy. Even if they're in there in any kind of accessible shape, what makes you think you can force Noschek and Crescent to do what you want?"

"Also not my job. I'm just assured it can be done, theoretically anyway. But then this is all theory we're jawing, isn't it? Unless I find something to transfer."

He turned to the screen. "Starting to narrow. I think maybe we're getting near tunnel-end. Stay put." He rose, straddling Hypatia. He wasn't worried about her moving. The scrambler assured that.

The petit-point pusher in Cardenas's shirt pocket felt big as a tractor against his chest. The little gun would make a nice, neat hole in the flashman's head, but he couldn't chance it. If he missed, if he was a second too slow, the man could make spaghetti of half of Hypatia's nervous system. Thirty years teach a man patience. He restrained himself.

But he'd have to do something soon. If there was a subox holding a resonance named Crescent and Noschek, he couldn't let this bastard have it.

The flashman removed a vorec, still clutching the scrambler tight in his other hand. He was trying to watch Cardenas and the wallscreen simultaneously. Hypatia he wasn't worried about. As Cardenas looked on helplessly, the man spoke softly into the vorec. Patterns shifted on the wall. The steady thrum of the aural playback became a whispery moan, an electronic wind. The tunnel continued to narrow. They were very near the end now and whatever lay there, concealed and waiting. The flashman smiled expectantly.

Teeth began to come out of the wall.

The flashman retreated until he was leaning against the side of the desk, but it was an instinctive reaction, not a panicky one. Clearly, he knew what he was doing. Now he would use the key Cardenas had concocted following his own previous confrontation, use it to dry up the power to the psychomorph. Then he could continue on to the end of the tunnel, having bypassed the psychic trap. Cardenas watched as he spoke into the vorec.

The teeth were set in impossibly wide jaws. Above the jaws were pupilless crimson eyes.

The flashman spoke again, louder this time. A third time. The psychomorph swelled out of the wall, looming over Hypatia. She lay on her back, staring up at it. It ignored her as it concentrated on the flashman.

"No. That was the key." He turned toward the Federale, and Cardenas saw stark terror in the man's eyes. "I took it off the filament. THAT WAS THE KEY!" He screamed the words into the vorec. They were the right words, the proper inflection. Then he threw the scrambler at the opaque shape and turned to run.

The psychomorph bit off his head.

As a psychic convergence, it was the most realistic Cardenas had ever seen. The decapitated body stood swaying. Blood appeared to fountain from the severed neck. Then the corpse toppled forward onto the floor.

He stood without moving, uncertain whether to run, shout for Security, or reach for the petit point. The psychomorph turned slowly to face him. It was a thousand times more real, more solid than any convergence he'd ever seen. He thought it stared at him for a moment. Since it had no pupils, it was hard to tell. Then it whooshed back into the wall, sucked into the holodepths that had given it birth. As it vanished, the tunnel collapsed on top of it.

It was quiet in the office again. The wallscreen was full of harmless, flickering symbology. The speakers whispered of mystery and nonsense. On the floor behind the desk, the flashman lay in a pool of his own blood, the expression on his face contorted, his eyes bulged halfway out of their sockets. His ragged nails showed where he'd torn out his own throat. Cardenas searched through blood-stained pockets until he found the applicator he needed. Then he turned away, sickened.

The applicator contained debonder for the secrylic. First, he dissolved the gag, then went to work on Hypatia's wrists. She spat out tasteless chunks of the pale green putty. She was crying, brokenly but not broken. "Jesus, Angel, Jesus, God, I thought he was going to kill me!"

"He was. Would have." He ripped away sagging lumps of putty and carefully began applying debonder to her bound ankles. "After he'd finished his transferring. Nothing you or I could have said would have mattered. He couldn't leave any witnesses. He knew that." He glanced up at the innocuous wallscreen. "You saw it?"

"Saw it?" She sat up and rubbed her wrists, then her chest where the scrambler had been applied. There was a painful red welt there, but no permanent damage. She was breathing in long steady gasps. "It was right on top of me."

"What did it look like?"

"It was a psychomorph, Angel. The worst one I ever saw. The worst one anyone ever saw." She was looking past him, at the torn body of the flashman. "Talk about tactile. It really got inside him."

He finished with her ankles. "Don't try to stand yet."

"Don't worry. Jesus." She moved her legs tentatively, loosening the cramped muscles. Behind her was harmless holospace. If you put out your hand, you'd touch solid wall. Or would you? Could they be sure of anything anymore? Could anyone?

"Another trap." Cardenas too was studying the wall. "The last trap. Why'd he kill Charliebo? He said he didn't." He found he couldn't look at the pitiful gray shape that lay crumpled alongside the desk.

Hypatia inhaled, coughed raggedly. "He didn't."

That made him look down at her. "What?"

"He was telling the truth. He didn't kill Charliebo. The tunnel did. Or the subox working up the tunnel. I don't know." She rubbed her forehead. "The psychomorph was the last trap, but there was one inserted in front of it. It—it was my fault, Angel. I thought I knew how to protect myself. I thought I was being careful, and I was. But there's never been a tunnel like that one. Part of the tunnel, before the psychomorph.

"I was worried about you, Angel. I thought maybe you were working too hard, too long. You don't see yourself, sitting there, reciting in that unbroken monotone into that damn vorec. It's like it becomes an extension of your own mouth."

"It does," he told her softly.

"So I thought I'd do some tunneling myself. Before the psychomorph there's—I don't know what you'd call it. Not a psychomorph. Subtler. Like a reciprocal program. It vacuumed the first thing it focused on." Maybe he couldn't look at the shepherd's corpse, but she could. "If Charliebo hadn't been where he was, it'd be me lying there instead of him. The tunnel, the program—it vacuumed him, Angel. Sucked him right out. It was quick. He just whimpered once and fell over on his side. The look in his eyes—I've seen that look on people who've been vacuumed. But I didn't know you could do it to an animal."

"The crunch consumption figures went stratospheric. Maybe it was the same program Crescent and Noschek used to vacuum themselves. I guess they figured that'd be one way to make sure anybody who got this close to them wouldn't bother them."

"Charliebo wasn't an animal."

"No. Sure he wasn't, Angel." It was quiet for a long time. Later: "I cut power and figured out a key to get around the trap. I thought it was the last one. That's when he came in." She indicated the flashman. "But it wasn't the last one. The psychomorph was. There were no warnings, no hints. I never would've seen it coming. Neither did he."

"Not surprising, really. I wonder if it would've made a difference if you or I had tripped it first. Because it wasn't a psychomorph."

She gaped at him.

"It wasn't a psychomorph," he said again. "It was a—let's call it a manifesting resonance. A full-field projection. I asked you if you saw it. I asked you what it looked like. You had a ventral view. I saw it face on." Now he found he was able to turn and look at the shepherd's corpse.

"It wasn't a psychomorph. It was Charliebo."

She said nothing this time, waiting for him to continue, wondering if she'd be able to follow him. She could. It wasn't that difficult to understand. Just slightly impossible. But she couldn't find the argument that would contradict him.

"Their last defense," he was saying. "If you can't lick 'em, make 'em join you. You were right when you called it a reciprocal program. Vacuum the first intruder and use him to keep out anybody thereafter. That way you don't expose yourself. Co-opt the first one clever enough to make it that far down the tunnel. It could've been you. It could've been me. They were luckier than they could've dreamed. They got Charliebo.

"Noschek and Cresent. Couple of clever boys. Too clever by half. I won't be surprised if they've learned how to manipulate their new environment. If so, they'll know their reciprocal's been triggered. Maybe they'll try to move. Somewhere more private. Maybe they can cut the tunnel. We're dealing with entirely new perceptions, new notions of what is and what isn't reality, existence. I don't think they'd take kindly to uninvited visitors, but now Charliebo's in there somewhere with them, wherever 'there' is. Maybe they'll be easier on him. I don't think he'll be perceived as much of a threat.''

She chose her words slowly. ''I think I understand. The first key triggered the reciprocal program and Charliebo got vacuumed. When that bastard tried to go around it—''

''He got Charliebo's resonance instead of Crescent's or Noschek's. I hope they enjoy having him around. I always did.'' He helped her stand on shaky legs.

''What now?''

As he held on to her, he began to wonder who was supporting whom. ''I could go back to Nogales, close the file, report it officially as unsolvable. Leave Noschek and Crescent to their otherwhere privacy. Or—we could dig in and try going back.''

She whistled softly. ''I'm not sure I can take anymore of their surprises. What if next time they come out for us instead of Charliebo? Or if they send something else, something new they've found floating around down in the guts of otherwhere?''

''We'll go slow. Put up our own defenses.'' He jerked his head in the flashman's direction. ''He seemed to think his people would know how to do it. Maybe with a little help from GenDyne's Box we can, too.''

''Then what?''

''Then we'll see.''

It took almost a month for them to learn how to recognize and thereby avoid the remaining tunnel guards. Crescent and Noschek failed to manifest themselves when the end of the tunnel was finally reached. There was a subox there, all right, but it proved empty. The designers' resonances had gone elsewhere. There were hints, clues, but nothing they could be certain of. Tiny tracks leading off into a vast emptiness that might not be as empty as everyone had once suspected. Suggestions of a new reality, a different otherwhere.

They didn't push. There was plenty of time, and Cardenas had no intention of crowding whatever the two men had become. It/They was dangerous.

But there was another way, clumsy at first. It would take patience to use it. What was wonderfully ironic was that in their attempt to defend themselves, to seal their passage, Crescent and Noschek had unwittingly provided those who came after a means for following.

First, it was necessary to have Hypatia jumped several grades. GenDyne balked but finally gave in. Anything to aid the investigation, to speed it along its way. What the company didn't know, couldn't imagine, was what way that investigation was taking. And Senior Designer Spango and Sergeant Cardenas weren't about to tell them. Not yet. Not until they could be sure.

Besides, the additional salary would be useful to a newly married couple.

There was uncertainty on both sides at first. Gradually, hesitation gave way to recognition, then to understanding. After that, there was exchange of information, most but not all of it one-way. Once this had been established, not only GenDyne's Box was open to inspection but also that of Parabas S.A., and through the power of the Fordmatsu link, so was everything one would ever want to access. Including an entirely new state of reality that had yet to be named.

Cardenas and Spango played with it for a while, kids enjoying the biggest toy that had ever been developed. Then it was time to put aside childish things and take the plunge into that otherwhere Crescent and Noschek had discovered, where existence meant something new and exciting and a whole universe of new concepts and physical states of matter and energy danced a dance that would need careful exploration and interpretation.

But they had an advantage that could not have been planned for, one even Noschek and Crescent hadn't had.

They wouldn't be jumping in blind because they wouldn't be alone.

Hypatia had pulled her chair up next to his. It was quiet in the office. The climate conditioning whispered softly. The walls and door were security-sealed. Cardenas had checked every light bulb by hand.

In front of them, Crescent's wallscreen glowed with symbols and figures and words, with rotating holo shapes and lines. The tunnel stretched out before them, narrowing now to a point. Only it wasn't a point; it was an end, and a beginning. The jumping-off place. The ledge overlooking the abyss of promise.

They knew what they wanted, had worked it out in the previous weeks. They knew where they wanted to go and how to get there.

Cardenas took Hypatia's hand in his, squeezed tightly. Not to worry now. Not anymore. Because they weren't doing this alone. He raised the vorec to his lips.

"Fetch," he said.

MICHAEL SWANWICK

The Dragon Line

One of the most popular and respected of all the decade's new writers, Michael Swanwick made his debut in 1980 with two strong and compelling stories, "The Feast of St. Janis" and "Ginungagap," both of which were Nebula Award finalists that year. Since then, he has gone on to become a frequent contributor to *Omni, Isaac Asimov's Science Fiction Magazine,* and *Amazing*; his stories have also appeared in *Penthouse, Universe, High Times, Triquarterly,* and *New Dimensions,* among other places. His powerful story "Mummer Kiss" was a Nebula Award finalist in 1981, and his story "The Man Who Met Picasso" was a finalist for the 1982 World Fantasy Award. He has also been a finalist for the John W. Campbell Award. His fast-paced and evocative first novel, *In the Drift,* was published in 1985 as part of the resurrected Ace Specials line. His most recent book is the popular novel *Vacuum Flowers,* and he is currently at work on a third novel. His story "Trojan Horse" was in our Second Annual Collection; his story "Dogfight," written with William Gibson, was in our Third Annual Collection; his story "Covenent of Souls" was in our Fourth Annual Collection. Swanwick lives in Philadelphia with his wife Marianne Porter and their young son Sean.

In the hard-edged and evocative story that follows, he takes us down some Mean Streets in modern-day Philadelphia, for an encounter among the oil refineries and tank farms with some very ancient magic.

THE DRAGON LINE

Michael Swanwick

Driving by the mall in King of Prussia that night, I noticed that between the sky and earth where the horizon used to be is now a jagged-edged region, spangled with bright industrial lights. For a long yearning instant, before the car topped the rise and I had to switch lanes or else be shunted onto the expressway, I wished I could enter that dark zone, dissolve into its airless mystery and cold ethereal beauty. But of course that was impossible: Faerie is no more. It can be glimpsed, but no longer grasped.

At the light, Shikra shoved the mirror up under my nose, and held the cut-down fraction of a McDonald's straw while I did up a line. A winter flurry of tinkling white powder stung through my head to freeze up at the base of the skull, and the light changed, and off we went. "Burn that rubber, Boss-man," Shikra laughed. She drew up her knees, balancing the mirror before her chin, and snorted the rest for herself.

There was an opening to the left, and I switched lanes, injecting the Jaguar like a virus into the stream of traffic, looped around and was headed back toward German-town. A swirling white pattern of flat crystals grew in my left eye, until it filled my vision. I was only seeing out of the right now. I closed the left and rubbed it, bringing tears, but still the hallucination hovered, floating within the orb of vision. I sniffed, bringing up my mouth to one side. Beside me, Shikra had her butterfly knife out and was chopping more coke.

"Hey, enough of that, okay? We've got work to do."

Shikra turned an angry face my way. Then she hit the window controls and threw the mirror, powder and all, into the wind. Three grams of purest Peruvian offered to the Goddess.

"Happy now, shithead?" Her eyes and teeth flashed, all sinister smile in mulatto skin, and for a second she was beautiful, this petite teenaged monstrosity, in the same way that a copperhead can be beautiful, or a wasp, even as it injects the poison under your skin. I felt a flash of desire and of tender, paternal love, and then we were at the Chemical Road turnoff, and I drifted the Jag through three lanes of traffic to make the turn. Shikra was laughing and excited, and I was too.

It was going to be a dangerous night.

Applied Standard Technologies stood away from the road, a compound of low, sprawling buildings afloat on oceanic lawns. The guard waved us through and I drove up to the Lab B lot. There were few cars there; one had British plates. I looked at that one for a long moment, then stepped out onto the tarmac desert. The sky was close, stained a dull red by reflected halogen lights. Suspended between vastnesses, I was touched by a cool breeze, and shivered. How fine, I thought, to be alive.

I followed Shikra in. She was dressed all in denim, jeans faded to white in little crescents at the creases of her buttocks, trade beads clicking softly in her cornrowed hair. The guards at the desk rose in alarm at the sight of her, eased back down as they saw she was mine.

Miss Lytton was waiting. She stubbed out a half-smoked cigarette, strode briskly forward. "He speaks modern English?" I asked as she handed us our visitor's badges. "You've brought him completely up to date on our history and technology?" I didn't want to have to deal with culture shock. I'd been present when my people had dug him, groggy and corpse-blue, sticky with white chrysalid fluids, from his cave almost a year ago. Since then, I'd been traveling, hoping I could somehow pull it all together without him.

"You'll be pleased." Miss Lytton was a lean, nervous woman, all tweed and elbows. She glanced curiously at Shikra, but was too disciplined to ask questions. "He was a quick study—especially keen on the sciences." She led us down a long corridor to an unmanned security station, slid a plastic card into the lockslot.

"You showed him around Britain? The slums, the mines, the factories?"

"Yes." Anticipating me, she said, "He didn't seem at all perturbed. He asked quite intelligent questions."

I nodded, not listening. The first set of doors sighed open, and we stepped forward. Surveillance cameras telemetered our images to the front desk for reconfirmation. The doors behind us closed, and those before us began to cycle open. "Well, let's go see."

The airlock opened into the secure lab, a vast, overlit room filled with white enameled fermentation tanks, incubators, autoclaves, refrigerators, workbenches, and enough glass plumbing for any four dairies. An ultrafuge whined softly. I had no clear idea what they did here. To me AST was just another blind cell in the maze of interlocking directorships that sheltered me from public view. The corporate labyrinth was my home now, a secure medium in which to change documentation, shift money, and create new cover personalities on need. Perhaps other ancient survivals lurked within the catacombs, mermen and skinchangers, prodigies of all sorts, old Grendel himself; there was no way of telling.

"Wait here," I told Shikra. The lab manager's office was set halfway up the far wall, with wide glass windows overlooking the floor. Miss Lytton and I climbed the concrete and metal stairs. I opened the door.

He sat, flanked by two very expensive private security operatives, in a chrome swivel chair, and the air itself felt warped out of shape by the force of his presence. The trim white beard and charcoal-grey Saville Row pinstripe were petty distractions from a face as wide and solemn and cruel as the moon. I shut my eyes and still it floated before me, wise with corruption. There was a metallic taste on my tongue.

"Get out," I said to Miss Lytton, the guards.

"Sir, I—"

I shot her a look, and she backed away. Then the old man spoke, and once again I heard that wonderful voice of his, like a subway train rumbling underfoot. "Yes, Amy, allow us to talk in privacy, please."

When we were alone, the old man and I looked at each other for a long time, unblinking. Finally, I rocked back on my heels. "Well," I said. After all these centuries, I was at a loss for words. "Well, well, well."

He said nothing.

"Merlin," I said, putting a name to it.

"Mordred," he replied, and the silence closed around us again.

The silence could have gone on forever for all of me; I wanted to see how the old wizard would handle it. Eventually he realized this, and slowly stood, like a thunderhead rising up in the western sky. Bushy, expressive eyebrows clashed together. "Arthur dead, and you alive! Alas, who can trust this world?"

"Yeah, yeah, I've read Malory too."

Suddenly his left hand gripped my wrist and squeezed. Merlin leaned forward, and his face loomed up in my sight, ruthless grey eyes growing enormous as the pain washed up my arm. He seemed a natural force then, like the sun or wind, and I tumbled away before it.

I was on a nightswept field, leaning on my sword, surrounded by my dead. The veins in my forehead hammered. My ears ached with the confusion of noises, of dying horses and men. It had been butchery, a battle in the modern style in which both sides had fought until all were dead. This was the end of all causes: I stood empty on Salisbury Plain, too disheartened even to weep.

Then I saw Arthur mounted on a black horse. His face all horror and madness, he lowered his spear and charged. I raised my sword and ran to meet him.

He caught me below the shield and drove his spear through my body. The world tilted and I was thrown up into a sky black as wellwater. Choking, I fell deep between the stars where the shadows were aswim with all manner of serpents, dragons, and wild beasts. The creatures struggled forward to seize my limbs in their talons and claws. In wonder I realized I was about to die.

Then the wheel turned and set me down again. I forced myself up the spear, unmindful of pain. Two-handed, I swung my sword through the side of Arthur's helmet and felt it bite through bone into the brain beneath.

My sword fell from nerveless fingers, and Arthur dropped his spear. His horse reared and we fell apart. In that last instant our eyes met and in his wondering hurt and innocence I saw, as if staring into an obsidian mirror, the perfect image of myself.

"So," Merlin said, and released my hand. "He is truly dead, then. Even Arthur could not have survived the breaching of his skull."

I was horrified and elated: He could still wield power, even in this dim and disenchanted age. The danger he might have killed me out of hand was small price to pay for such knowledge. But I masked my feelings.

"That's just about fucking enough!" I cried. "You forget yourself, old man. I am still the Pen-dragon, *Dux Bellorum Britanniarum* and King of all Britain and Amorica and as such your liege lord!"

That got to him. These medieval types were all heavy on rightful authority. He lowered his head on those bullish shoulders and grumbled, "I had no right, perhaps. And yet how was I to know that? The histories all said Arthur might yet live. Were it so, my duty lay with him, and the restoration of Camelot." There was still a look, a humor, in his eye I did not trust, as if he found our confrontation essentially comic.

"You and your fucking Camelot! Your bloody holy and ideal court!" The memories were unexpectedly fresh, and they hurt as only betrayed love can. For I really had loved Camelot when I first came to court, and adolescent true believer in the new myth of the Round Table, of Christian chivalry and glorious quests. Arthur could have sent me after the Grail itself, I was that innocent.

But a castle is too narrow and strait a space for illusions. It holds no secrets. The queen, praised for her virtue by one and all, was a harlot. The king's best friend, a public paragon of chastity, was betraying him. And everyone knew! There was the heart and exemplar of it all. Those same poetasters who wrote sonnets to the purity of Lodegreaunce's daughter smirked and gossiped behind their hands. It was Hypocrisy Hall, ruled over by the smiling and genial Good King Cuckold. He knew all, but so long as no one dared speak it aloud, he did not care. And those few who were neither fools nor lackeys, those who spoke openly of what all knew, were exiled or killed. For telling the truth! That was Merlin's holy and Christian court of Camelot.

Down below, Shikra prowled the crooked aisles dividing the workbenches, prying open a fermenter to take a peek, rifling through desk drawers, elaborately bored. She had that kind of rough, destructive energy that demands she be doing something at all times.

The king's bastard is like his jester, powerless but immune from criticism. I trafficked with the high and low of the land, tinsmiths and river-gods alike, and I knew their minds. Arthur was hated by his own people. He kept the land in ruin with his constant wars. Taxes went to support the extravagant adventures of his knights. He was expanding his rule, croft by shire, a kingdom here, a chunk of Normandy there, questing after Merlin's dream of a Paneuropean Empire. All built on the blood of the peasantry; they were just war fodder to him.

I was all but screaming in Merlin's face. Below, Shikra drifted closer, straining to hear. "That's why I seized the throne while he was off warring in France— to give the land a taste of peace; as a novelty, if nothing else. To clear away the hypocrisy and cant, to open the windows and let a little fresh air in. The people had prayed for release. When Arthur returned, it was my banner they rallied around. And do you know what the real beauty of it was? It was over a year before he learned he'd been overthrown."

Merlin shook his head. "You are so like your father! He too was an idealist —I know you find that hard to appreciate—a man who burned for the Right. We should have acknowledged your claim to succession."

"You haven't been listening!"

"You have a complaint against us. No one denies that. But, Mordred, you must understand that we didn't know you were the king's son. Arthur was . . . not very fertile. He had slept with your mother only once. We thought she was trying to blackmail him." He sighed piously. "Had we only known, it all could have been different."

I was suddenly embarrassed for him. What he called my complaint was the old and ugly story of my birth. Fearing the proof of his adultery—Morgawse was nominally his sister, and incest had both religious and dynastic consequences— Arthur had ordered all noble babies born that feast of Beltaine brought to court, and then had them placed in an unmanned boat and set adrift. Days later, a peasant had found the boat run aground with six small corpses. Only I, with my unhuman vigor, survived. But, typical of him, Merlin missed the horror of the story—that six innocents were sacrificed to hide the nature of Arthur's crime—and saw it only as a denial of my rights of kinship. The sense of futility and resignation that is my curse descended once again. Without understanding between us, we could never make common cause.

"Forget it," I said. "Let's go get a drink."

I picked up 476 to the Schuylkill. Shikra hung over the back seat, fascinated, confused and aroused by the near-subliminal scent of murder and magic that clung to us both. "You haven't introduced me to your young friend." Merlin turned and offered his hand. She didn't take it.

"Shikra, this is Merlin of the Order of Ambrose, enchanter and master politician." I found an opening to the right, went up on the shoulder to take advantage

of it, and slammed back all the way left, leaving half a dozen citizens leaning on
their horns. "I want you to be ready to kill him at an instant's notice. If I act
strange—dazed or in any way unlike myself—slit his throat immediately. He's
capable of seizing control of my mind, and yours too if you hesitate."

"How 'bout that," Shikra said.

Merlin scoffed genially. "What lies are you telling this child?"

"The first time I met her, I asked Shikra to cut off one of my fingers." I held
up my little finger for him to see, fresh and pink, not quite grown to full size.
"She knows there are strange things astir, and they don't impress her."

"Hum." Merlin stared out at the car lights whipping toward us. We were on
the expressway now, concrete crashguards close enough to brush fingertips against.
He tried again. "In my first life, I greatly wished to speak with an African, but
I had duties that kept me from traveling. It was one of the delights of the modern
world to find I could meet your people everywhere, and learn from them." Shikra
made that bug-eyed face the young make when the old condescend; I saw it in
the rearview mirror.

"I don't have to ask what you've been doing while I was . . . asleep," Merlin
said after a while. That wild undercurrent of humor was back in his voice. "You've
been fighting the same old battles, eh?"

My mind wasn't wholly on our conversation. I was thinking of the *bon hommes*
of Languedoc, the gentle people today remembered (by those few who do remember) as the Albigensians. In the heart of the thirteenth century, they had
reinvented Christianity, leading lives of poverty and chastity. They offered me
hope, at a time when I had none. We told no lies, held no wealth, hurt neither
man nor animal—we did not even eat cheese. We did not resist our enemies, nor
obey them either, we had no leaders and we thought ourselves safe in our poverty.
But Innocent III sent his dogs to level our cities, and on their ashes raised the
Inquisition. My sweet, harmless comrades were tortured, mutilated, burnt alive.
History is a laboratory in which we learn that nothing works, or even can. "Yes."

"Why?" Merlin asked. And chuckled to himself when I did not answer.

The Top of Centre Square was your typical bar with a view, a narrow box of
a room with mirrored walls and gold foil insets in the ceiling to illusion it larger,
and flaccid jazz oozing from hidden speakers. "The stools in the center, by the
window," I told the hostess, and tipped her accordingly. She cleared some businessmen out of our seats and dispatched a waitress to take our orders.

"Boodles martini, very dry, straight up with a twist," I said.

"Single malt Scotch. Warm."

"I'd like a Shirley Temple, please." Shikra smiled so sweetly that the waitress
frowned, then raised one cheek from her stool and scratched. If the woman hadn't
fled it might have gotten ugly.

Our drinks arrived. "Here's to progress," Merlin said, toasting the urban landscape. Silent traffic clogged the far-below streets with red and white beads of light. Over City Hall the buildings sprawled electric-bright from Queen Village up to the Northern Liberties. Tugs and barges crawled slowly upriver. Beyond, Camden crowded light upon light. Floating above the terrestrial galaxy, I felt the old urge to throw myself down. If only there were angels to bear me up.

"I had a hand in the founding of this city."

"Did you?"

"Yes, the City of Brotherly Love. Will Penn was a Quaker, see, and they believed religious toleration would lead to secular harmony. Very radical for the times. I forget how many times he was thrown in jail for such beliefs before he came into money and had the chance to put them into practice. The Society of Friends not only brought their own people in from England and Wales, but also Episcopalians, Baptists, Scotch-Irish Presbyterians, all kinds of crazy German sects—the city became a haven for the outcasts of all the other religious colonies." How had I gotten started on this? I was suddenly cold with dread. "The Friends formed the social elite. Their idea was that by example and by civil works, they could create a pacifistic society, one in which all men followed their best impulses. All their grand ideals were grounded in a pragmatic set of laws, too; they didn't rely on goodwill alone. And you know, for a Utopian scheme it was pretty successful. Most of them don't last a decade. But . . ." I was rambling, wandering further and further away from the point. I felt helpless. How could I make him understand how thoroughly the facts had betrayed the dream? "Shikra was born here."

"Ahhh." He smiled knowingly.

Then all the centuries of futility and failure, of striving for first a victory and then a peace I knew was not there to be found, collapsed down upon me like a massive barbiturate crash, and I felt the darkness descend to sink its claws in my shoulders. "Merlin, the world is dying."

He didn't look concerned. "Oh?"

"Listen, did my people teach you anything about cybernetics? Feedback mechanisms? Well, never mind. The Earth"—I gestured as if holding it cupped in my palm—"is like a living creature. Some say that it is a living creature, the only one, and all life, ourselves included, only component parts. Forget I said that. The important thing is that the Earth creates and maintains a delicate balance of gases, temperatures, and pressures that all life relies on for survival. If this balance were not maintained, the whole system would cycle out of control and . . . well, die. Us along with it." His eyes were unreadable, dark with fossil prejudices. I needed another drink. "I'm not explaining this very well."

"I follow you better than you think."

"Good. Now, you know about pollution? Okay, well now it seems that there's some that may not be reversible. You see what that means? A delicate little wisp of the atmosphere is being eaten away, and not replaced. Radiation intake increases. Meanwhile, atmospheric pollutants prevent reradiation of greater and greater amounts of infrared; total heat absorption goes up. The forests begin to die. Each bit of damage influences the whole, and leads to more damage. Earth is not balancing the new influences. Everything is cycling out of control, like a cancer.

"Merlin, I'm on the ropes. I've tried everything I can think of, and I've failed. The political obstacles to getting anything done are beyond belief. The world is dying, and I can't save it."

He looked at me as if I were crazy.

I drained my drink. " 'Scuse me," I said. "Got to hit up the men's room."

In the john I got out the snuffbox and fed myself some sense of wonder. I heard a thrill of distant flutes as it iced my head with artificial calm, and I straightened slightly as the vultures on my shoulders stirred and then flapped away. They would be back, I knew. They always were.

I returned, furious with buzzing energy. Merlin was talking quietly to Shikra, a hand on her knee. "Let's go," I said. "This place is getting old."

We took Passayunk Avenue west, deep into the refineries, heading for no place in particular. A kid in an old Trans Am, painted flat black inside and out, rebel flag flying from the antenna, tried to pass me on the right. I floored the accelerator, held my nose ahead of his, and forced him into the exit lane. Brakes screaming, he drifted away. Asshole. We were surrounded by the great tanks and cracking towers now. To one side, I could make out six smoky flames, waste gases being burnt off in gouts a dozen feet long.

"Pull in there!" Merlin said abruptly, gripping my shoulder and pointing. "Up ahead, where the gate is."

"Getty Gas isn't going to let us wander around in their refinery farm."

"Let me take care of that." The wizard put his forefingers together, twisted his mouth, and bit through his tongue; I heard his teeth snap together. He drew his fingertips apart—it seemed to take all his strength—and the air grew tense. Carefully, he folded open his hands, and then spat blood into the palms. The blood glowed of its own light, and began to bubble and boil. Shikra leaned almost into its steam, grimacing with excitement. When the blood was gone, Merlin closed his hands again and said, "It is done."

The car was suddenly very silent. The traffic about us made no noise; the wheels spun soundlessly on the pavement. The light shifted to a melange of purples and reds, color dopplering away from the center of the spectrum. I felt a pervasive queasiness, as if we were moving at enormous speeds in an unperceived direction. My inner ear spun when I turned my head. "This is the wizard's world," Merlin said. "It is from here that we draw our power. There's our turn."

I had to lock brakes and spin the car about to keep from overshooting the gate.

But the guards in their little hut, though they were looking straight at us, didn't notice. We drove by them, into a busy tangle of streets and accessways servicing the refineries and storage tanks. There was a nineteenth-century factory town hidden at the foot of the structures, brick warehouses and utility buildings ensnarled in metal, as if caught midway in a transformation from City to Machine. Pipes big enough to stand in looped over the road in sets of three or eight, nightmare vines that detoured over and around the worn brick buildings. A fat indigo moon shone through the clouds.

"Left." We passed an old meter house with gables, arched windows, and brickwork ornate enough for a Balkan railroad station. Workmen were unloading reels of electric cable on the loading dock, forklifting them inside. "Right." Down a narrow granite block road we drove by a gothic-looking storage tank as large as a cathedral and buttressed by exterior struts with diamond-shaped cutouts. These were among the oldest structures in Point Breeze, left over from the early days of massive construction, when the industrialists weren't quite sure what they had hold of, but suspected it might be God. "Stop," Merlin commanded, and I pulled over by the earth-and-cinder containment dike. We got out of the car, doors slamming silently behind us. The road was gritty underfoot. The rich smell of hydrocarbons saturated the air. Nothing grew here, not so much as a weed. I nudged a dead pigeon with the toe of my shoe.

"Hey, what's this shit?" Shikra pointed at a glimmering grey line running down the middle of the road, cool as ice in its feverish surround. I looked at Merlin's face. The skin was flushed and I could see through it to a manically detailed lacework of tiny veins. When he blinked, his eyes peered madly through translucent flesh.

"It's the track of the groundstar," Merlin said. "In China, or so your paperbacks tell me, such lines are called *lung mei*, the path of the dragon."

The name he gave the track of slugsilver light reminded me that all of Merlin's order called themselves Children of the Sky. When I was a child an Ambrosian had told me that such lines interlaced all lands, and that an ancient race had raised stones and cairns on their interstices, each one dedicated to a specific star (and held to stand directly beneath that star) and positioned in perfect scale to one another, so that all of Europe formed a continent-wide map of the sky in reverse.

"Son of lies," Merlin said. "The time has come for there to be truth between us. We are not natural allies, and your cause is not mine." He gestured up at the tank to one side, the clusters of cracking towers, bright and phallic to the other. "Here is the triumph of my Collegium. Are you blind to the beauty of such artifice? This is the living and true symbol of Mankind victorious, and Nature lying helpless and broken at his feet—would you give it up? Would you have us again at the mercy of wolves and tempests, slaves to fear and that which walks the night?"

"For the love of pity, Merlin. If the Earth dies, then mankind dies too!"

"I am not afraid of death," Merlin said. "And if I do not fear mine, why should I dread that of others?" I said nothing. "But do you really think there will be no survivors? I believe the race will continue beyond the death of lands and oceans, in closed and perfect cities or on worlds built by art alone. It has taken the wit and skill of billions to create the technologies that can free us from dependence on Earth. Let us then thank the billions, not throw away their good work."

"Very few of those billions would survive," I said miserably, knowing that this would not move him. "A very small elite, at best."

The old devil laughed. "So. We understand each other better now. I had dreams too, before you conspired to have me sealed in a cave. But our aims are not incompatible; my ascendancy does not require that the world die. I will save it, if that is what you wish." He shrugged as he said it as if promising an inconsequential, a trifle.

"And in return?"

His brows met like thunderstorms coming together; his eyes were glints of frozen lightning beneath. The man was pure theatre. "Mordred, the time has come for you to serve. Arthur served me for the love of righteousness; but you are a patricide and cannot be trusted. You must be bound to me, my will your will, my desires yours, your very thoughts owned and controlled. You must become my familiar."

I closed my eyes, lowered my head. "Done."

He owned me now.

We walked the granite block roadway toward the line of cool silver. Under a triple arch of sullen crimson pipes, Merlin abruptly turned to Shikra and asked, "Are you bleeding?"

"Say what?"

"Setting an egg," I explained. She looked blank. What the hell did the kids say nowadays? "On the rag. That time of month."

She snorted. "No." And, "You afraid to say the word menstruation? Carl Jung would've had fun with you."

"Come." Merlin stepped on the dragon track, and I followed, Shikra after me. The instant my feet touched the silver path, I felt a compulsion to walk, as the track were moving my legs beneath me. "We must stand in the heart of the groundstar to empower the binding ceremony." Far, far ahead, I could see a second line cross ours; they met not in a cross but in a circle. "There are requirements: We must approach the place of power on foot, and speaking only the truth. For this reason I ask that you and your bodyguard say as little as possible. Follow, and I will speak of the genesis of kings.

"I remember—listen carefully, for this is important—a stormy night long ago, when a son was born to Uther, then King and bearer of the dragon pennant. The mother was Igraine, wife to the Duke of Tintagel, Uther's chief rival and a man who, if the truth be told, had a better claim to the crown than Uther himself. Uther begot the child on Igraine while the duke was yet alive, then killed the duke, married the mother, and named that son Arthur. It was a clever piece of statecraft, for Arthur thus had a twofold claim to the throne, that of his true and also his nominal father. He was a good politician, Uther, and no mistake.

"Those were rough and unsteady times, and I convinced the king his son would be safest raised anonymously in a holding distant from the strife of civil war. We agreed he should be raised by Ector, a minor knight and very distant relation. Letters passed back and forth. Oaths were sworn. And on a night, the babe was wrapped in cloth of gold and taken by two lords and two ladies outside of the castle, where I waited disguised as a beggar. I accepted the child, turned and walked into the woods.

"And once out of sight of the castle, I strangled the brat."

I cried aloud in horror.

"I buried him in the loam, and that was the end of Uther's line. Some way farther in was a woodcutter's hut, and there were horses waiting there, and the wet-nurse I had hired for my own child."

"What was the kid's name?" Shikra asked.

"I called him Arthur," Merlin said. "It seemed expedient. I took him to a priest who baptised him, and thence to Sir Ector, whose wife suckled him. And in time my son became king, and had a child whose name was Mordred, and in time this child killed his own father. I have told this story to no man or woman before this night. You are my grandson, Mordred, and this is the only reason I have not killed you outright."

We had arrived. One by one we entered the circle of light.

It was like stepping into a blast furnace. Enormous energies shot up through my body, and filled my lungs with cool, painless flame. My eyes overflowed with light: I looked down and the ground was a devious tangle of silver lines, like a printed circuit multiplied by a kaleidoscope. Shikra and the wizard stood at the other two corners of an equilateral triangle, burning bright as gods. Outside our closed circle, the purples and crimsons had dissolved into a blackness so deep it stirred uneasily, as if great shapes were acrawl in it.

Merlin raised his arms. Was he to my right or left? I could not tell, for his figure shimmered, shifting sometimes into Shikra's, sometimes into my own, leaving me staring at her breasts, my eyes. He made an extraordinary noise, a groan that rose and fell in strong but unmetered cadence. It wasn't until he came to the antiphon that I realized he was chanting plainsong. It was a crude form of music—the Gregorian was codified slightly after his day—but one that brought back a rush of memories, of ceremonies performed to the beat of wolfskin drums, and of the last night of boyhood before my mother initiated me into the adult mysteries.

He stopped. "In this ritual, we must each give up a portion of our identities. Are you prepared for that?" He was matter-of-fact, not at all disturbed by our unnatural environment, the consummate technocrat of the occult.

"Yes," I said.

"Once the bargain is sealed, you will not be able to go against its terms. Your hands will not obey you if you try, your eyes will not see that which offends me, your ears will not hear the words of others, your body will rebel against you. Do you understand?"

"Yes." Shikra was swaying slightly in the uprushing power, humming to herself. It would be easy to lose oneself in that psychic blast of force.

"You will be more tightly bound than slave ever was. There will be no hope of freedom from your obligation, not ever. Only death will release you. Do you understand?"

"Yes."

The old man resumed his chant. I felt as if the back of my skull were melting and my brain softening and yeasting out into the filthy air. Merlin's words sounded louder now, booming within my bones. I licked my lips, and smelled the rotting flesh of his cynicism permeating my hindbrain. Sweat stung down my sides on millipede feet. He stopped.

"I will need blood," said Merlin. "Hand me your knife, child." Shikra looked my way, and I nodded. her eyes were vague, half-mesmerized. One hand rose. The knife materialized in it. She waved it before her, fascinated by the colored trails it left behind, the way it pricked sparks from the air, crackling transient energies that rolled along the blade and leapt away to die, then held it out to Merlin.

Numbed by the strength of the man's will, I was too late realizing what he intended. Merlin stepped forward to accept the knife. Then he took her chin in hand and pushed it back, exposing her long, smooth neck.

"Hey!" I lunged forward, and the light rose up blindingly. Merlin chopped the knife high, swung it down in a flattening curve. Sparks stung through ionized air. The knife giggled and sang.

I was too late. The groundstar fought me, warping up underfoot in a narrowing cone that asymptotically fined down to a slim line yearning infinitely outward toward its unseen patron star. I flung out an arm and saw it foreshorten before me, my body flattening, ribs splaying out in extended fans to either side, stretching tautly vectored membranes made of less than nothing. Lofted up, hesitating, I hung timeless a nanosecond above the conflict and knew it was hopeless, that I could never cross that unreachable center. Beyond our faint circle of warmth and life, the outer darkness was in motion, mouths opening in the void.

But before the knife could taste Shikra's throat, she intercepted it with an outthrust hand. The blade transfixed her palm, and she yanked down, jerking it free of Merlin's grip. Faster than eye could follow, she had the knife in her good hand and—the keen thrill of her smile!—stabbed low into his groin.

The wizard roared in an ecstasy of rage. I felt the skirling agony of the knife as it pierced him. He tried to seize the girl, but she danced back from him. Blood rose like serpents from their wounds, twisting upward and swept away by unseen currents of power. The darkness stooped and banked, air bulging inward, and for an instant I held all the cold formless shapes in my mind and I screamed in terror. Merlin looked up and stumbled backward, breaking the circle.

And all was normal.

We stood in the shadow of an oil tank, under normal evening light, the sound of traffic on Passayunk a gentle background surf. The groundstar had disappeared, and the dragon lines with it. Merlin was clutching his manhood, blood oozing between his fingers. When he straightened, he did so slowly, painfully.

Warily, Shikra eased up from her fighter's crouch. By degrees she relaxed, then hid away her weapon. I took out my handkerchief and bound up her hand. It wasn't a serious wound; already the flesh was closing.

For a miracle, the snuffbox was intact. I crushed a crumb on the back of a thumbnail, did it up. A muscle in my lower back was trembling. I'd been up days too long. Shikra shook her head when I offered her some, but Merlin extended a hand and I gave him the box. He took a healthy snort and shuddered.

"I wish you'd told me what you intended," I said. "We could have worked something out. Something else out."

"I am unmade," Merlin groaned. "Your hireling has destroyed me as a wizard."

It was as a politician that he was needed, but I didn't point that out. "Oh come on, a little wound like that. It's already stopped bleeding."

"No," Shikra said. "You told me that a magician's power is grounded in his mental somatype, remember? So a wound to his generative organs renders him impotent on symbolic and magical levels as well. That's why I tried to lop his balls off." She winced and stuck her injured hand under its opposite arm. "Shit, this sucker stings!"

Merlin stared. He'd caught me out in an evil he'd not thought me capable of. "You've taught this . . . chit the inner mysteries of my tradition? In the name of all that the amber rose represents, why?"

"Because she's my daughter, you dumb fuck!"

Shocked, Merlin said, "When—?"

Shikra put an arm around my waist, laid her head on my shoulder, smiled. "She's seventeen," I said. "But I only found out a year ago."

We drove unchallenged through the main gate, and headed back into town. Then I remembered there was nothing there for me anymore, cut across the median strip and headed out for the airport. Time to go somewhere. I snapped on the radio, tuned it to 'XPN and turned up the volume. Wagner's valkyries soared and swooped low over my soul, dead meat cast down for their judgment.

Merlin was just charming the pants off his greatgranddaughter. It shamed reason how he made her blush, so soon after trying to slice her open. "—make you Empress," he was saying.

"Shit, I'm not political. I'm some kind of anarchist, if anything."

"You'll outgrow that," he said. "Tell me, sweet child, this dream of your father's—do you share it?"

"Well, I ain't here for the food."

"Then we'll save your world for you." He laughed that enormously confident laugh of his that says that nothing is impossible, not if you have the skills and the cunning and the will to use them. "The three of us together."

Listening to their cherry prattle, I felt so vile and corrupt. The world is sick beyond salvation; I've seen the projections. People aren't going to give up their cars and factories, their VCRs and styrofoam-packaged hamburgers. No one, not Merlin himself, can pull off that kind of miracle. But I said nothing. When I die and am called to account, I will not be found wanting. "Mordred did his devoir"—even Malory gave me that. I did everything but dig up Merlin, and then I did that too. Because even if the world can't be saved, we have to try. We have to try.

I floored the accelerator.

For the sake of the children, we must act as if there is hope, though we know there is not. We are under an obligation to do our mortal best, and will not be freed from that obligation while we yet live. We will never be freed until that day when Heaven, like some vast and unimaginable mall, opens her legs to receive us all.

The author acknowledges his debt to the unpublished "Mordred" manuscript of the late Anna Quindsland.

JOHN KESSEL

Mrs. Shummel Exits a Winner

Here's an icy little tale that suggests that how high you bet should depend on how much you're willing to lose . . .

Born in Buffalo, New York, John Kessel now lives with his wife, Sue Hall, in Raleigh, North Carolina, where he is a professor of American literature and creative writing at North Carolina State University. Kessel made his first sale in 1975, and has since also become a frequent contributor to *The Magazine of Fantasy and Science Fiction* and *Isaac Asimov's Science Fiction Magazine*; his stories have also appeared in *Galileo, New Dimensions, The Twilight Zone Magazine, The Berkley Showcase*, and elsewhere. In 1983, Kessel won a Nebula Award for his brilliant novella "Another Orphan," which was also a Hugo finalist that year. His most recent books are the novel *Freedom Beach*, written in collaboration with James Patrick Kelly, and the Tor Double *Another Orphan*. He has just completed his first solo novel, *Good News from Outer Space*. Kessel's story "Hearts Do Not in Eyes Shine" was in our First Annual Collection; his story "Friend," written with James Patrick Kelly, was in our Second Annual Collection; his story "The Pure Product" was in our Fourth Annual Collection.

MRS. SHUMMEL EXITS A WINNER

John Kessel

The bingo hall at the Colonel S.L.A. Marshall VFW Post was filling when Martha Shummel and her friend Betty Alcyk arrived. To the right of the platform where the machine sat waiting, in the gloom that would be dispelled once the caller stepped up to begin the game, hung the flag of Florida. To the left hung the tattered flag of the United States that Pete Cullum had brought back from Saigon. They said that the brown stain that ran up the right edge was from the mortal wound of one of the heroes who died in the Tet offensive, but although Martha did not question the story she always wondered how that could have happened unless he had wrapped himself in it. The rows of wooden tables with "Col. Marshall" stenciled on their centers were already half covered with mosaics of bingo boards; people leaned back in the folding chairs and filled the hall with cigarette smoke and the buzz of conversation.

Martha did not like getting there so late. She liked to be early enough to get her favorite seat, set her boards neatly in order, and sit back and watch the people come in. She would chat with her neighbors about children and politics and the weather while the feeling of excitement grew. Once a month or so she worked in the kitchen and sometimes on the other nights she brought in her special pineapple cake. It was like being in a club. You got together as friends, forgot how bad your digestion was or how hard it was to pay the bills or how long it had been since your kids had called. You took a little chance. Maybe when you left you still had to go back through streets where punks sold drugs on street corners, to a stuffy room in a retirement home, but for a couple of hours you could put that away and have some fun.

But Betty had not been ready when Martha came by. So instead of getting there early they got stuck in line behind Sarah Kinsella, the human cable news network. With Sarah you could hardly get a word in edgewise, despite the fact that she had emphysema and her voice sounded like it was coming at you through an aqualung. She told them about the UFO landing port beneath Apalachee Bay, about the Cuban spies pawing through her trash cans, and about how well her grandson Hugh was doing at the University of Florida—starting quarterback on the football team, treasurer of his fraternity, and he was making straight A's. Martha and Betty listened patiently even though they had heard it all before. Finally they got to the front of the line. Sarah bought five boards and headed past the table, down an aisle. The two women sighed in relief.

"He makes straight A's," Betty muttered.

"Yes," said Martha. "But his B's are a little crooked." They both laughed until their eyes were damp.

Ed Kelly, who sold the boards, smiled at them. "Come on, girls. Settle down. You're gonna wet those cute pants."

"Don't be fresh," Martha said. "Six." She handed over twelve dollars.

Betty bought three boards and they went their separate ways. Betty's eyesight was failing, so she insisted on sitting close to the front where she could peer up at the number board. But Martha's eyes were fine—she could handle the twelve game panels on her six boards without trouble—and the people who sat in front were too eager for her. They made her mad when they shouted "Bingo!" so loud, as if someone was trying to cheat them. Her own spot was over against the windows on the side, with her back to one of the mock Greek pillars. When she got to her place a young man was already sitting there. Martha began to put down her purse and boards. She started to say, "Son, this is my spot—" but then the boy looked up at her.

His tousled hair, in dazzling contrast to the narrow face beneath it, shone downy white. He had the darkest of brown eyes. His expression was one of dazed accusation, as if he had just awoken from being beaten senseless to find Martha gazing at him. His bruised eyes reminded her of David's. She stood there, holding the straps of her purse, neither setting it down nor picking it up.

Finally she managed to speak. "This is my spot," she said. "Please go someplace else."

The boy sighed. Instead of getting up he pulled a card and a stylus from the gym bag beside him. It was a magic slate, a film of plastic laid over a black background. Martha's children had played with such slates. On the slate, before he pulled up the plastic sheet to erase them, she read the words, CHARITY NEVER FAILETH. The boy cleared the old message and wrote, then held the slate up for Martha to see: FUCK OFF BITCH.

Martha felt her heart skip a beat, then race. Were people watching? Just when she decided to call one of the men, the boy pulled up the plastic sheet and the neatly printed block letters vanished.

He looked at her, then silently slid his slate and his single bingo board to the opposite side of the table. He walked around and sat, facing her, with his back to the front of the room and the bingo machine. He straightened his board in front of himself. Martha hesitated, then sat down. She spread out her boards, got the plastic box of chips and magnetic wand from her purse. She covered the free square of each panel with one of the metal-rimmed red chips. When she looked up again the boy was staring at her.

Martha wondered if she had seen him in the neighborhood. He was probably one of those boys who could get your prescriptions filled cheap. The intensity of his stare made her nervous and for a moment she wished she'd sat someplace else. But she'd be damned if she'd let some punk push her around, let alone a mute, retarded one. If you did that then pretty soon you were at their mercy. She'd seen it happen.

The boy sat back in the wooden folding chair, somehow managing to look innocent and alert at the same time. Martha had at first thought his hair was bleached, but now she decided it was naturally white. His face was cool as the moon on a hot night. Watching him, Martha felt her heart still sprinting, and she could not draw her breath. She did her best not to let on. It was like the beginning of one of her dizzy spells.

Trying hard not to be aware of the boy, she looked around the hall. From the kitchen at the back came the smells of pizza and hot dogs. Men and women returned from the bar carrying beer in plastic cups and slices of pizza on paper plates with the grease already soaking through. The light was dying outside the rows of windows, and the gabble of voices competed with the whir of the ceiling fans.

Martha could spot dozens of people she knew from the Paradise Beach condos, and those she did not know by name she recognized as regulars at the Colonel Marshall. They were of every color, Italians, Germans, Poles, Blacks, Cubans, Vietnamese, and Anglos, ex-New Yorkers and ex-Chicagoans and native Southerners, the physically fit and the terminally ill, Republicans, Democrats, Libertarians, and even Hyman Spivek who preached a loudmouthed brand of Communism, men turned milk white by leukemia and women turned to brown leather by the sun, Baptists, Jews, Episcopalians, Catholics, and Seventh-Day Adventists, some with money to burn and others without two dimes to rub together, tolerable people like Betty, and fools like Sarah. Most were senior citizens managing to scrape along on pensions and savings, talking trash and hoping to win the $250 coverall so they could enjoy themselves a little more before the last trip to the hospital. As decent a crowd of people, Martha supposed, as you could scrape together in all the panhandle of Florida.

All of which made the sudden appearance of this mute boy even more puzzling: he couldn't be any more than fifteen and he acted more like he'd grown up on Mars than in America. He was a total stranger.

Her heartbeat seemed to be slowing. It was almost time to begin. Tony Schuster passed by them up the aisle, joking with the women on his way to the platform. He fired up the bingo machine: the board lit up, the numbered balls rattled into the transparent box and began to dance around like popcorn on the jet of air. "First game," he announced through the P.A., "regular bingo on your cards, inside corners, outside corners, horizontal, vertical, diagonal rows. Ready for your first number?'' The machine made a noise like a man with his larynx cut out taking a breath, and sucked up a ball. ''I-18,'' Schuster called.

Martha covered the number on two of her boards. One of them was an inside corner. ''G-52.'' She had two of those, too, but they were on different panels from the first number. ''G-47.'' Nothing. ''I-29.'' Three covers. She looked up. Ed Kelly, now patrolling the aisles, was looking over the boy's shoulder: on his top panel the boy had covered the four inside corners. He seemed oblivious. ''Bingo!'' Kelly called out, just as Schuster was about to announce the next number. The crowd groaned; Martha sighed.

''I-18, I-29, G-52, G-47,'' Kelly read aloud.

''We have a bingo,'' Schuster called. The room was filled with the clicking of chips being wiped from several hundred boards, a field full of locusts singing. Martha ran her wand over her boards and pulled up her own chips while Kelly counted twenty dollars out to the silent boy. ''Speak up next time, kid,'' Kelly said good-naturedly.

''He's deaf and dumb,'' Martha said.

''Can't be deaf, Martha—he's got his back to the machine. Whyn't you help him out?''

Martha just stared at Kelly, and he went away. Schuster began the second game, a series beginning with a fifteen-dollar regular bingo and ending in an $80 coverall. Martha tried to ignore the boy and the injustice of his playing only one board yet winning. She managed to get four in the ''O'' column before someone across the room yelled ''Bingo!'' She sighed again. In the follow-up, the inner square, she had gotten nowhere when a black woman in the front bingoed. While the attendant called out the numbers for Schuster to check, Martha glanced over at the boy's card. The inner square on one panel was completely covered.

Martha thought about pointing it out to him, but held back. He turned his face up to her. He smiled. She ducked her head to look at her own boards.

The kid was lucky but didn't even know it. Luck was like that. Who could say how the numbers would come: Martha only knew that they did not come for her often enough to make up for her losses. Only the night before she had blown twenty dollars when the Red Sox lost the series to the Mets. She had never seen as clear a case of bad luck as had cost the Sox the series. Martha had been a Red Sox fan since she was a girl. She had met her husband Sam at Fenway Park on June 18, 1938, Sox over the Yankees 6-2.

Sam was lucky about the Sox—he had won more than his share of bets on them over the years, which was no easy job—but not so lucky when the cancer ate him up at fifty-five. He had collected baseball cards. For fifteen years after his death Martha kept them, even though they didn't mean anything to her. Sometimes she would take the cards out of their plastic envelopes and look at them, remember how Sam would worry over them and rearrange their vacations so they could go to swap meets where he might pick up a 1950 Vern Stephens or Walt Dropo. He had cared for those cards more than for her. She would sigh in resignation. Staring at some corny action photo or head-and-shoulders shot of a bullet-headed ballplayer wearing an old-fashioned uniform, it would become all she could do to keep from crying. She would slide the card back into its envelope, stick the envelope in among the others, shove the collection back on its shelf in the closet. She would poke at her eyes with the wrist of her sweater and make a cup of coffee. It would almost be time for "The Young and the Restless."

Of their three kids, Robert, the eldest, was a CPA in Portland, and Gloria bought clothes for Macy's in New York. Their youngest, David, her favorite, a beautiful boy—in some ways as beautiful a boy as this punk who insulted her in the Colonel Marshall—had died at the age of fifteen, in 1961. David had snuck off to Cape Cod one weekend with his friends. He did not have her permission, would never have gotten it if he had asked. Despite the fact that he had been a very good swimmer, he had drowned off the beach at Hyannis.

After that her life started to go to pieces. Sam and she had moved to Florida in 1970, and a year later he was dead, too. His pension had seemed to shrink as time went by. Last year she had sold the baseball cards to raise some cash.

"B-9." She placed her chips, glanced up from her board and saw the boy covering the number on his own, completing the outer square, covering the complete panel as well. He made no attempt to draw the attention of one of the men. Schuster called three more numbers. The kid had all of those numbers too, on the lower panel of his board. With the fourth number came simultaneous shouts of "Bingo!" from three spots around the hall. The crowd groaned. The boy just sat there. He didn't yell, he didn't sigh, he didn't even seem to realize that he had won, did not seem even to hear the babble of disappointed voices filling the room.

Martha felt herself getting mad. They ought not to allow such a fool into the place. She supposed she could call out for him, but that would only tie her to him, and he had insulted her. If he won, she couldn't. The men finished checking the winners' boards and divided up the money.

"Now, for the $80 coverall," Schuster announced. "I-22." Martha was so distracted staring at the boy's board, completely covered with red chips, that she forgot to check her own boards. "O-74."

"Bingo!" a man shouted.

The boy tilted his board and all the chips slid off onto the table.

The kid was trying to get to her. He had to have been cheating. That was why he had not called out—he knew that when the attendant came to check his board, they would find that he had not really won. She decided to keep an eye on him through the next game.

Schuster called five numbers. The boy had four of them, a clear winning diagonal that shot across the board like an arrow into Martha's heart. He remained mute as a snake, and somebody else won two numbers later. He had both of those numbers, too.

She sat there and, with an anxiety that grew like a tumor, watched him win the next five games in a row, none of which he called out. The room faded into the background until all there was was the boy's bingo board. Schuster would call a number, and it was as if he were reading them off the kid's battered pasteboard. Still the boy said nothing. He let other people take $150 that could have been his.

Martha had trouble breathing. She needed some air. But more than air, more than life itself, she needed that board.

By the time of the break after the tenth game, Martha's anxiety had been transformed from anger to fear. The boy had won every game and called out none. There was no way one card could win game after game unless the numbers on it changed from moment to moment, but as close as she watched Martha could not see them change. At the end of the last coverall, when two women, one of them Betty Alcyk, shouted bingo simultaneously, the boy looked up at Martha. Placidly, he pointed to the cards in front of her. She had not covered half of her own numbers. The boy wrote on his slate: DON'T YOU WANT TO WIN?

"Shut up!" she said, loud enough so that the people at the next table looked over at them.

He ripped off the old words and printed something new. He held up the slate and the bingo board simultaneously, scattering colored chips across the table. One of them rolled off into her lap. YOU WANT IT?

Martha bit her lip. She feared a trick. She nodded furtively.

He wrote: COME OUTSIDE.

The boy got up quickly and went out the double doors at the side of the auditorium without looking back at her. After a minute Martha followed. She tried to look as if she was simply going outside for a breath of air, and in truth the weight of the evening and her losses seemed to have lodged in her chest like a stone.

Outside, in the parking lot, a few men and women were talking and smoking. Paula Lorenzetti waved to her as she came out, but Martha acted as if she did not see her. She spotted the boy standing by the street under one of the lights. At first that reassured her, but then she realized it was only because he needed the light to use his slate.

When she got to him he held the bingo board out toward her. She took it, examined it. It seemed perfectly normal. A Capitol: dog-eared pasteboard, two game grids printed green and black on white, a little picture of the dome of the Congress in each of the free squares. In the corner someone had written, in childish handwriting, "Passions Rule!"

"How much?" she asked.

He wrote on the slate: YOUR VOICE.

"What?"

YOU WILL GIVE UP YOUR VOICE.

Martha felt flushed. She could see everything so clearly it almost hurt. Her senses seemed as sharp as if she were twenty again; her eyes picked out every hair on the boy's arm, she smelled the aroma of food from the hall and garbage from the alley. Across the city somewhere a truck was climbing up the gears away from a stoplight.

"You're kidding."

NO.

"How will you take my voice?"

I DON'T TAKE—YOU GIVE.

"How can I give you my voice?"

SAY YES.

What did she have to lose? There was no way he could steal a person's voice. Besides, you had to take a chance in your life. "All right," she said.

The boy nodded. "Good-bye," he said: softly, almost a whisper.

He lifted his chin and turned. Something in the way he did this so reminded her of the insolence with which David had defied her more than once, that she felt it like a blow—it *was* David, or some ghost come to torment her with his silence and insult—and she almost cried out for him to wait, to please, please speak to her. She hesitated, and in a moment he was down an alley and around the corner. She held the board in her damp hand. She moved, sweating, back toward the hall. She felt light, as if at any moment her step might push her away from the earth and she would float into the night.

She remembered making the long drive with Sam down to the hospital, fighting the traffic on the Sagamore Bridge. Sam had urged her not to go; it was no thing for a woman to have to do, but she had insisted in a voice that even Sam could hear that she was going. The emergency room was hot and smelled of Lysol. The staff had wheeled David from a bay in emergency to a side corridor, left him on the gurney against the wall with a sheet over him like a used tray from room service. For the first time in her life she had the feeling that the world was unreal, that her body was not her: she was merely living in it, peering out through the eyes, running her arms and legs like a man running a backhoe. There was David, pale, calm. His hair, long on the sides and in back so he could comb it into the silly D.A. that they had fought over, was still damp but not wet, beginning to stand away from his head. She touched his face and it was cool as a satin sofa pillow. Sam had had to pull her away, trying to talk to her. It was a day before she spoke to him and then it was only to tell him to be quiet.

"Martha!"

It was Paula, come across the lot to speak to her. "What are you doing? Who was that boy?" She looked at the card in Martha's hand, looked away.

It took a moment for Martha to come back to reality. This would be the test. "Some punk kid," she said. "Hot night."

"It's that ozone layer. Messing up the air."

"It's always hot in October." Her voice flowed as easily as water.

"Not like this," said Paula.

"I like your blouse."

"This? It's cheap. If you don't like the pattern, all you got to do is wash it."

Martha laughed. They went back into the hall. Most of the people were already seated. Martha hurried to her place. She put her other boards aside and set the new one directly in front of her. Magenta chips for the center squares. Mel Shiffman, balding, athletic, wearing his teasing grin, took over the platform to announce the rest of the games.

"Settle down, settle down," he said, like a homeroom teacher coming into class just after the bell. "Eleventh game, on your reg'lar boards, straight bingo. First number: Under the O, 65."

The room was dead silent. Martha had that number, on the lower playing card—bottom right corner.

"B-14." Upper left corner.

"N-33." Middle top.

"N-42." No cover. Martha began to worry.

"O-72." Upper right. One more for the outer corners: B-1. B-1, she thought. "B-1."

It was a flood of light, a joy that filled her, as if the number machine, the voice of Mel Shiffman, the world itself were under her control. "Bingo!" she shouted. The buzz of the people roared in her ears. Ed Kelly came by and checked off her numbers. "We have a bingo," Mel announced.

Kelly paid out twenty dollars to her. The bills were crisp and dry as dead leaves. "Inner or outer square," Shiffman called. The people settled down. "Next number: I-25." Both panels on Martha's board had that number. Shiffman called three more. Each number found its counterpart on her board. All her senses were heightened: the board before her, the grain of the wooden table it rested on, stood out with the three dimensionality of a child's Viewmaster picture; their colors were distinct and pure. In the air she could pick out the mingled smells of pizza and cigarette smoke and a wisp of bus exhaust that trailed through the window. She heard the gasps and mutterings of the restless crowd, could almost identify the individual voices of her friends as they hovered above their bingo boards, wishing, hoping, to win. Except Martha knew that they wouldn't: *she* would. As if ordered by God, the numbers fell to her, one by one, and the inner square was covered. "Bingo!" she shouted again.

She heard the groan of the crowd more clearly, an explosive sigh heavy with frustration, and immediately after, the voices: "Twice in a row." "She's lucky tonight." "I never win." "N-32; that's all I needed!" "She always wins." The last was the voice of Betty, from twenty feet away as clear as if she were whispering in Martha's ear.

Kelly came by and paid out the forty dollars. Forty dollars would keep her for a week. She could buy a new dress, get the toilet fixed, buy a pound of sirloin. "Looks like your night," Kelly said. "Or maybe it's just this table."

"I never won like this before," she said.

"Don't act too guilty," Kelly said, and winked at her.

She started to protest, but he was gone. There was something wrong with her hearing. She heard the people around her in too much detail, could pick out individual voices. The next game began. Martha tried to concentrate. She could feel the tension, and every sigh she heard as a number was called that was on her board and not on that of the sigher was like a needle in her chest. When the last number came, the one that both completed the outer square on her upper game panel and covered the entire panel, it was a moment before she could muster the breath to shout, "Bingo!"

The groan that came was full of barely repressed jealousy. Despair. Even hatred. It boomed hollowly in Martha's altered hearing. She looked up and saw envious faces turned to her. From across the room she saw Betty's peevish squint. The crowd buzzed. Kelly read the numbers off her board. Someone shushed someone else. Shiffman announced that this was indeed, miraculously, a valid bingo. Someone laughed. Kelly paid out the combined prize of $120, an amount that would see some of these people through a month. She smiled sickly up at him. He counted out the bills without comment.

It was all she could do to cover the free squares for the next game. Shiffman, so nervous now that his smile had faded for the first time in Martha's memory, began. The first four numbers he called, like a dream turning into a nightmare, ran a diagonal winner across Martha's board. When she stammered out "bingo," it was with half the force that she had managed before.

The cries of dismay were crushing. The hall seemed filled with envious voices. A worm of pain moved in her chest. She tried not to take the money, but Kelly insisted. Each bill as it was counted out was like a blow, and when he was at last done she could not find breath to thank him.

When, in the next game, she saw that she had won again, she realized that she could not stand it. She didn't even put chips on the squares, until at last another woman in the room shouted "Bingo!" The woman's triumphant screech was greeted by cheers.

Martha tried to leave, but her legs were too weak. She sat through the last games, watching her card, silent, as the pain climbed from her chest to her throat. Had she been able to face the rest, she could have taken every dollar. At last it was over. She gathered up her chips and markers and stumbled toward the door. Friends tried to talk to her. Betty Alcyk called her name. But the memory of Betty's voice among the others silenced her. She couldn't talk to Betty. Their friendship had been only a pact of losers, unable to stand the strain of one of them winning. But there was worse. If someone else had had the magic card, even if that person was the dearest one in the world to Martha—Betty—Sam, her lost husband—even her beautiful, lost son, David—would her own voice have held that same hatred?

The people filed out. Their voices rang in her head. She had nothing to say to them.

She wondered if she ever would.

STEPHEN KRAUS

Emissary

Here new writer Stephen Kraus, a frequent contributor to *Analog*, gives us an entertaining and provocative look at a Close Encounter of a very odd kind . . . Stephen Kraus lives in Menlo Park, California.

EMISSARY

Stephen Kraus

Roger shed his backpack and collapsed into one of my dining room chairs. He looked dilapidated—long hair tangled, face sunken and colorless. But he was alive, anyway. After months without a word from him I had begun to think otherwise.

He dug through his backpack and produced a worn, leather-bound book.

"What do you make of this?" he asked.

A brief phone call from the airport excepted, those were his first words to me in three months.

Roger was like that.

I played along. I opened the book to the flyleaf, which was inscribed "Capn Jn Knowles," in an assertive hand. The surname was the same as Roger's.

"A relative of yours?"

He nodded. "My three-times-great-grandfather."

The text was written in a faint, crabbed hand clearly not that of its owner. The legend was self-explanatory:

Memoryes of the Parish of Birwood
Written by: Dnl. Meese, Rector
Anno scriv. 1781

"A parish history?"

Roger nodded again.

The writing was old-fashioned—quaint abbreviations, misspellings, curly f's where s's ought to be. Heavy going. I picked my way through the introduction:

Birwood stands at the crossing of the Peirce Highwaye and the Marle Brooke in the Countye of Salop. Marle Brooke, which hath its rise head near Marton, forms the boundrye of our Parish with Onslow, and there a stone bridge passes across this brooke at whose foote our Church stands. The bridge is now sorely ruinous, but repairs cannot be made because the parishioniers of Onslow saye the bridge is on our lande and we saye it is on theirs.

There was quite a bit more in that vein, alternately pedantic and catty.

"Where did you get this?" I asked. "It looks valuable."

"From my uncle Claude. He died, I ended up with it. I found it in a cookie tin, along with a bunch of papers and photographs—genealogical stuff. The photographs were all of these somber, dark-suited fellows with identical beaked noses." Roger felt his own nose. "Quite a lot like mine, actually.

"The papers were certificates, clippings—that sort of thing. They traced my family back ten generations to a tiny village in the English midlands."

"Birwood?" I guessed.

"Right. That's where I've been." He brushed his hair back nervously. "Thanks for putting me up on such short notice, by the way." He hesitated. "I really need to talk to you."

"No problem."

He looked past me to the window and the quiet street that ran past my house. "This could take a while."

"I'm not in a hurry."

Roger gave me a tired smile. When he started speaking again his voice was low and measured, as if he were afraid of running out of words too soon.

"I got a letter from the National Science Foundation last August," he began, "pulling my grant. I suppose you heard about that—everyone else in the department seemed to know within hours. I couldn't believe it. One sheet of cheap government stationery and all my soft money was gone." He snapped his fingers. "Just like that.

"I sat in my office all afternoon, staring at the letter. That project was my life." He stopped for a moment and shook his head. "That must sound really stupid, but it's true.

"I went home after a while, passed out on my couch. When I woke up the next morning I found three suitcases waiting on my front step. There was a note from an attorney taped to one explaining that my uncle had died and naming me as his next of kin.

"I started going through his stuff. I was pretty clinical about it—I hadn't seen Uncle Claude in ten years. I ended up giving almost everything to Goodwill. None of it had any personal flavor. It was just stuff. Useful to him, I suppose, useless to me.

"Then I found the cookie tin with the book and the photographs. Beneath that were a locket, some pressed flowers, and an odd sort of plastic part—black, with a disk at one end and four hollow tubes at the other. Heirlooms, I guessed, though the plastic part certainly didn't fit.

"I ended up reading the Birwood manuscript all the way through that night.

I'd never been much interested in history, but that old Reverend Meese had a nasty streak in him that kept me turning those brittle pages.

"He had it in for my family in particular. There's a chapter devoted to us near the end—see if you can find it."

I did, after a few minutes of squinting at the gnarled script. The section began:

> The Familye of Wm. Knowles of the Mill Farme.
> Wm. Knowles was the first of his lineage to dwell at Birwood, living verie poorly at the outset in the ruines of Blanthorne Castel.
> While still a younge man, Wm. Knowles left the countrye to fight with the Duke of Marlborough and did not return to the Parish until some yeares later. He then built a mill by the Marle Brooke and a goode house with monies he had got somewhere.

Then followed a long account of a lawsuit between William Knowles and a Mr. Oakely. They were fighting about the right to sit in a particular church "piew," of all things. Roger's ancestor won. Then events became more dramatic:

> Wm. Knowles begat manye other disputes, but his last was with a Thomas Norris, who was an alehouse companion. They finallye brawled (over a woman, witnesses saye) and Mr. Norris was cut on the arme, which he lost the use of, but Mr. Knowles was stabbed to the harte.

Roger grinned. The effect was a bit cadaverous. "I never would have believed my family started out that way. I mean, look at us now—we're all accountants or chemists or whatever. Keep going, it gets better."

The next section read:

> W. Knowles had isshue by Anne Newcombe, a son Martin, who inherited the Mill Farme. Martin Knowles styled himself a gentleman and went down to Cambridge to reade the classicks, but he returned on his father's death with two fingers missynge on his right hand from some mischiefe he had played.
> A short time later Martin Knowles found a vein of a goode ore of leade (called Galena) at the bottom of a marle pit on his propertye. This was accompted strange (if fortunate) for leade is otherwise only known in Wales and manye leagues distant. Mr. Knowles hired men from Birwood and elsewhere to work the myne and proffited greatlye.
> But in the ende the myne led to a dispute with one Jn. Bender, who worked it on Martin Knowles's behalf. Mr. Bender, who is a stout and able man even today, broke a picke of Mr. Knowles's. Mr. Bender saide he would not paye for the toole, maintaining that it broke because it was not adequate to the taske rather than through any fault of his owne (he still says that there was something in the ore too harde for the toole).

The two men fell to fighting over this difference, with the result that Mr. Bender cracked his hip and now walks onlye with a sticke. He later tooke up the trade of wheelwright, and so is more fortunate than manye of his fellowes who lost their livelihoods when Martin Knowles closed down the mynes soon after.

That incident seemed to end Martin Knowles's career. I found only one more reference to him:

Martin Knowles is now little seen in publick, nor at the alehouses he used to frequent. Those who visit the Mill Farme says he sits by a window with a small object in his ruined hand and tosses it repeatedly into the aire. I have seen him do this myself and asked him where he got the thing (which is the color of coale and has four small projections on it) and he will onlye saye he got it in the mynes.

I looked up, startled.

Roger nodded. "The same thing occurred to me when I read that section. I dug through the cookie tin until I found that plastic part. Black, four projections—there was no mistaking it. My class ring had a small diamond set in it. I dragged the ring across the part's surface, and the diamond ground itself into dust."

Roger leaned across the table and looked straight into my eyes.

"I put the part in my pocket and drove down to my lab. I tried to grind off a bit to analyze. No luck. Finally I was able to boil away a few molecules with a dye laser and blow them through my mass spectrometer.

"The material turned out to be a boron ceramic with some molybdenum and a few rare earths mixed in. Somehow that added up to a substance so hard I had no way of measuring just *how* hard.

"I looked up the Welsh lead deposits the manuscript referred to. They were Cretaceous in age; presumably the Birwood deposits were similar. If Martin Knowles really found the artifact in his mine, the material had to be tough enough to survive beneath the earth for a hundred million years.

"I wasn't quite ready to believe *that*, but I kept running the facts back and forth in my head. I could safely assume that Martin Knowles found the thing— he couldn't have *made* it, the technology to make it doesn't exist *now*. I could further assume that it was part of something larger, something an unfortunate miner named John Bender broke one of his employer's picks on.

"Then, a short time later, Martin Knowles shut down a profitable mine, throwing half the town out of work, and for the rest of his life he stayed scrupulously clear of his beloved alehouses. Why? To assure his own silence? Or was it just superstition?

"I did some more checking. I found Birwood on a contemporary map, and I talked to the local tourist bureau, one Irene Adams. She was only too glad to tell me about the town, but she had never heard about any old lead mines—seemed horrified at the idea, actually.

"Right about then the chairman called into his office. He told me that I'd have to leave the department at the end of the summer. I'd been expecting that; I didn't say anything. We discussed what would happen to my equipment, and so on. Then he asked about my immediate plans.

"I told him that I was about to take a short trip to England to complete a side project. The idea just sort of popped into my head as I answered.

"I wasn't planning to be gone long, maybe two or three weeks. But I took the precaution of putting all my stuff in storage and giving notice on my apartment. I really should have told you where I was going—I almost called you three or four times. But I wouldn't have known what to say if you'd asked why.

"I left the next day. I only spent one night in London before heading north by train. I didn't want to stop moving. I bought an old bicycle in Shrewsbury, and pedaled the rest of the way. Very pleasant, really. Lovely countryside: thatched cottages, rolling green hills with hedgerows and sheep.

"I reached Birwood in a couple of hours, and Irene found me a bed and breakfast in the middle of town. I told my landlady that I was a naturalist.

"I had this curious sense of *déjà vu* about the town. Besides the single paved road and a few row houses, I don't think anything has changed there since 1781. The church is still standing by the Marle Brook, and the stone bridge still hasn't been repaired.

"I looked up some records of my family at the church and the town hall. The minister was very helpful once he found out who I was: tenth generation descendent of Birwood stock and all that.

"William Knowles—the first Knowles mentioned in the manuscript—died in 1734. I never found any record of his birth. Martin Knowles lived from 1713 to 1788. And Captain John—the owner of the book—was his great-great-grandson. Everything checked, right down to the pew William Knowles and Mr. Oakley fought over. I sat there during a Sunday service at the minister's insistence.

"Locating the Knowles property was more of a problem. I had to dig a century deep into the town records. I finally found the surveyor's boundaries of the Mill Farm on an old tract chart: 'In longitude from the Meridian of the Isles of the Azores (or Fortunate Islands) 21 deg. 37 min. 12 sec. and in latitude 52 deg. 53 min. 14 sec. northwards from the world's equator.'

"The area is completely wild now; even sheep don't graze there. But I recognized the remnants of the farm easily enough. The mill used to straddle the brook—the stone tower on the Birwood side is still standing. And behind the charred foundations of one of the outbuilding I found a small plot with half a dozen tilted headstones. One of them belonged to Martin Knowles, died in 1788, aged seventy-five years.

"I spent the rest of the afternoon down by the brook, knee deep in marle. I looked up the word in my landlady's dictionary afterwards: it's a crumbly soil with a high carbonate content, used for fertilizer and bricks. Good stuff to have on a farm, I suppose. Dreadful to walk through. After an hour I felt as if someone had poured concrete on my boots. But the manuscript said that Martin Knowles had found his vein of lead at the bottom of a marle pit, so I kept looking.

"I located the mine on the third day. Nothing dramatic. I slogged across another marsh and through another patch of thistles, and suddenly, right in front of me, was a pit with an obvious tailing pile on the side nearest the brook.

"Rusted equipment was piled in front, but the entrance was unguarded. What stopped me was the darkness. Light just wouldn't penetrate more than a foot or two past the timbers that bracketed the opening. There were no signs of recent exploration, no bottles or empty beer cans. The place just seemed to have been forgotten.

"I took a train to Birmingham that afternoon and spent a small fortune on rock-climbing gear. I was back at the mine the next morning, hammering in expansion bolts for anchors and rigging carabiners and abrasion pads. I hadn't used stuff like that in years, but the skills came back quickly.

"The rappel was easy enough—maybe fifty feet of descent through cobwebs and bat droppings before the shaft flattened out. After that I could walk, sort of, bent in half at the waist.

"The books tell you not to fool around in old mine shafts, but this one seemed solid enough. I checked the roof and supporting pillars frequently, but I never found anything to worry about.

"I moved as quickly as I could at first—whatever John Bender found, I figured it would be near the end of the shaft. But my back began to ache after a few hundred yards, and I kept hitting my head against the low ceiling. Half an hour later I had to drop to my hands and knees.

"I crawled along, listening to my ragged breathing reflecting back from infinity, until I found my hands trying to rest on empty air. I scrambled backwards, then aimed my headlamp straight down into a vertical pit ten feet deep. I had to wait until I stopped shaking before I could rig for the descent.

"I took the next section very slowly; the passage was terribly narrow. After a short distance it turned a sharp corner and ended at a rectangular cross-section of glossy grey ore. There was no sign of an artifact.

"I remember sitting perfectly still, swallowing sour air. What had I been thinking? Did I really believe that some forgotten manuscript was going to prevent the extinction of my career? Was I that desperate?

"I wasn't sure I wanted to know. But too much fitted together. The black part was real enough, certainly. There *had* to be something down there.

"I began to crawl back towards the surface. Every step sent a jolt of pain through my knees and my arms. After I reached the base of the pit I'd nearly fallen into on the way down, I had to stop to rest.

"The air circulation in the shaft was especially strong there. The mine seemed to be taking long, slow breaths. Dampness dripped down the stone faces. And I found myself looking into a side passage I hadn't noticed on the way in.

"The timbers framing the entrance had collapsed; rubble blocked it almost entirely. I wondered why the supports had fallen—hundreds of others stood firmly in place along a mile or more of mine shaft. I could only imagine that someone had pulled them down to discourage access to the passage.

"I began rolling rocks to one side. I tied a rope around one of the timbers and yanked until it was out of the way. I wiped sweat out of my eyes and kept at it until I had cleared a hole just the width of my shoulders.

"I waited for the dust to settle, then I swept my light along the passage. It extended back only a few yards. At the end, still embedded in a slanting vein of ore, was a black, refrigerator-sized mass. It had rounded corners and smooth flanks that were opalescent in the harsh white glare of my lamp."

"The black radiance reminded me of the part I'd found in my uncle's trunk, and the object seemed completely intact except for some deep scratches in the top surface.

"As I inched closer through the rubble, I noticed that the scratches on the top were very regular; closer still I decided that they were markings of some kind, repeated in a hexagonal array. I braced myself against the back wall of the passage and tried to catch my breath. From there I could just touch one of the artifact's sides. The surface felt as smooth as glass. I moved close enough to brush the dust out of the figures on the top. They seemed to form a diagram, but it was like a puzzle, meaningless, lines in interlocking hexagonal patterns. . . .

"I stared until my head hurt. Then I closed my eyes for a moment. When I opened them again, the meaning leaped right off the surface. The diagram was telling me—in the clearest possible way—how to open the top of the artifact.

"Eight fasteners were indicated: threaded cylinders that fitted flush and screwed in at a slight angle. Each had six depressions that were slightly smaller than the ends of my fingers.

"I tore several fingernails before I had the idea of making a wrench out of bolts pounded through a piece of wood. Once I realized that the threads were left-handed, the cylinders turned easily. That astonished me more than anything else. Any mechanism trapped in a vein of Cretaceous ore should have welded solid millions of years ago.

"I was ready to pry off the top within five minutes. As the lid started to come up, I suddenly realized how much the artifact resembled a sarcophagus. I hesitated before looking inside, half afraid that I'd see the remains of . . . I don't know what. A time traveler? A squat alien creature with six tiny fingers?

"I aimed my lamp inside and took a deep breath. No bones or rotted clothing. Just diagrams and hundreds and hundreds of marvelously precise interlocking parts.

"I studied the diagrams first. I had the knack of interpreting them quickly by then. Everything had a deeply rooted six-sided symmetry. The figures and their groupings all formed partial or complete hexagons. But it wasn't so much the patterns that were organized that way, I realized, as the brain of whoever had made them.

"There was one diagram all the others branched from, a sort of table with diverging columns. In the center was a single hexagon, then a space, then two hexagons, then three. Each group of hexagons was paired with a symbol—a number system.

"Then I found a periodic table. The six inert gases formed a hexagon at the center; the elements with partially filled shells swirled outwards. A table of molecules surrounded that. Each item was assigned its own symbol, modified by other symbols that indicated isomers or ionic states.

"I followed one of the branches of the interior diagram, loosening cylinder screws as I went. I found that an assembly about a foot square and a couple of inches thick swung up and to one side. Below it were more instructions, more assemblies.

"I was bent over in an impossibly awkward position working by entirely inadequate light. But I couldn't leave. I kept disassembling and cataloguing, copying, drawing, reassembling.

"The primary elements were tiny chambers—sometimes just widenings in pinhole channels—each attached to a sort of valve. Hexagonal tubes the thickness of a hair were fused to all the surfaces, constantly branching and joining. I thought at first they were electrical connections, then I decided they were optical. Later, very deep in the clockwork, I found a nest of icosahedral crystals that fit flush against the polished faces of thousands of those hexagonal tubes.

"I didn't return to the surface until my backup lamp began to dim. I stood at the mine entrance and stared at the daylight until my retinas burned. I had almost forgotten what it looked like.

"I was too tired to invent excuses concerning my torn clothes or eccentric hours. Fortunately, my landlady was polite enough not to inquire. She made me scones and orange marmalade while I tried to make up my mind.

"Who should I tell? The police? The newspapers? I decided that I'd feel more comfortable contacting somebody at a university. But I was still uneasy. If only I had a better idea of what the artifact was *for*.

"Eventually, I decided on sleep and another visit.

"The second descent went quickly—my climbing gear was still in place, and I knew what to expect. But I was more daunted than ever by the artifact's complexity. I tried to copy down some of the simpler diagrams to study later, but I realized right away that I'd be drawing for days. Then I had the idea of making rubbings, like people do with gravestones. That worked beautifully, even for the smallest figures. I returned with a notebook full of them."

Roger reached into his pack and produced a sheaf of papers. He tore one out and handed it to me. Spidery white lines stood out in relief against thick black pencil marks. The markings were incomprehensible. All I could discern was a six-sided symmetry.

"Can I keep this?" I asked.

Roger waved as if it were a matter of the least possible importance.

"The figures were mostly warnings," he said. "It could all operate as long as water was a liquid—indicated by pictures of water in different states. The proper environment was nitrogen and oxygen with traces of water vapor and some other components. As far as I could remember, Earth's atmosphere qualified with no trouble.

"Starting the thing up involved filling several chambers with chemicals— simple organics mostly: amino acids, lipids, monosaccharides, plus some trace metals, water, sodium hydroxide. The power requirements were marvelously simple: just plenty of light.

"Ultimately, the instructions told me everything except what the artifact *did*. I spent quite a bit of time thinking about that. My best guess was a piece of survival equipment from an alien colony—a safe food source, say, for use in a strange ecosystem. But then why didn't I find other artifacts in the vicinity? And why build an auto-kitchen to last for a hundred million years?

"After four trips I'd examined a dozen assemblies. I expected them to get simpler as I reached deeper into the artifact, with bigger chambers to accommodate steaming slabs of alien rump roast, or whatever. Nothing of the sort. The components became smaller and more intricate. I couldn't even make out most of them.

"For a while I tried to follow the pathways, guess at the reactions. Two or three levels deep I had to give up. About all I could do was estimate the number of connections. I came up with 200,000 reaction products, give or take a factor or two. That's when I knew my auto-kitchen hypothesis wouldn't hold up. It was much too complicated.

"The diagrams terminated at the right front corner of the box. The directions there had me remove and inspect a long conical assembly that ran almost to the bottom of the artifact. It ended in a hollow needle and a very fine screen connected to the main body by a dozen tubes.

"I pointed my lamp into the cavity left by the assembly's absence. The chamber was spherical, a few inches across, right up against the front. On one side was a smaller cavity with a very familiar shape. I reached into my pack and took out the part that Martin Knowles had passed down to me. Then I slid it back into place for the first time in two hundred years.

"I remember sitting quietly on a broken timber after that, wondering what kind of man my seven-times-great-grandfather was. Of course it might have been someone else who first dismantled the artifact. But I doubted it. Who else would have dared touch the thing? The blackness, the depth below the earth—it must have seemed the devil's handiwork to the miners who found it.

"For a moment I could feel Martin Knowles in the shaft beside me, looking over my shoulder at the diagrams, shivering in his frock coat and buckle shoes. He was an educated man. He could read the instructions as well as I. But he was born a century too early to make sense out of the chemistry.

"Can you imagine his frustration? I could see him pulling down the timbers himself—he had his family's violent temper. Something was trying to speak to him across an unimaginable gulf of time and space, but he couldn't quite understand, couldn't quite answer.

"I wonder if he guessed at the artifact's purpose. I knew for certain by then. It was a machine for manufacturing aliens. All those thousands of reactions just sufficed to synthesize a fertilized ovum and implant it in that spherical black womb."

Roger closed his eyes. He looked very tired.

"I couldn't tell anyone. Can you see that? If I did, the British government would almost certainly seal off the mine as a matter of national security.

"I couldn't risk it. I needed to publish. I needed that very badly.

"I heard somewhere that the chemicals in a man are only worth thirty dollars or so. I can vouch for the fact that alien chemistry is a *lot* more expensive. Between the reagents and the laser I needed as a light source, the project started to push the limits of my credit cards.

"My biggest problem was the generator—it weighed nearly a hundred pounds. I ended up disassembling it and hauling it down in sections. But everything else was simple enough. I was ready to go in a few days. Starting the mechanism up was just a matter of moving a few cylinder screws. The operation was automatic after that—and completely silent. I had a hard time believing that anything was happening at all.

"The indicated gestation period, or whatever, was five weeks—it seemed like five years. Mornings I hauled gasoline for the generator into the mine: my hands smelled perpetually of the stuff. Otherwise I walked around the village, read, ate. There were two pubs in town that dated back to the days of my ancestors. I stayed well clear of both.

"I spent the last night in the mine, sitting with my arms around my shins, facing the box. My landlady had baked some extra scones for me, and I swallowed one mechanically every hour or so. At some point I must have fallen asleep.

"I woke to the sensation of something nuzzling my foot. It felt slick and warm, not quite wet. My eyes snapped open. A stray bit of light reflected off a shape about a foot long and six inches high, a smooth, continuous curve.

"I jumped up and scrambled backwards into a corner. I heard a snuffling noise and smelled a faint, sweet odor overlaying the usual mildew.

"The smooth shape waddled towards me. It was more or less ellipsoidal, no feet. Its skin was jet black, and slightly corrugated. The only distinctive feature was an inquisitive, tapering protrusion in front.

"I edged around to the artifact. A door had slid open near the bottom, exposing the spherical chamber I had seen earlier from above. The chamber was empty except for a pool of moisture at the bottom.

"I looked at the creature again. It was feeling aimlessly at the ground with its snout-like protrusion. Helpless. And hungry. It just *radiated* hunger.

"I didn't know what to do. All I had were the scones. I dug one out of my pack and rolled it towards the creature. The snout found it after a while. The creature snuffled again—the noise seemed to be caused by the contraction of its body when it moved. Eventually it climbed on top of the scone. After a few minutes and considerable snuffling it got off again. There was a damp spot where the scone had been.

"My knowledge of zoology is practically nil, but I was quite sure that nothing native to Earth ate that way.

"I sat down on a rock and stared at the thing. After a while I scooped it up and dropped it into my backpack.

"I got to think of the creature as a him, despite the absence of any distinguishing sexual features—any features at all, really, except for the snout. Sort of a minimalist's animal. I named him Martin, after Martin Knowles.

"He needed lots of water, I discovered—he absorbed it through his skin. And he was quite sensitive to light. Otherwise he was easy enough to take care of. He ate everything, even the kippers I pocketed at breakfast so as not to hurt my landlady's feelings. He liked being scratched just behind his snout.

"I watched Martin all that first day and night. He sensed my presence somehow, and he tried to follow wherever I went. He could move surprisingly quickly when he wanted to.

"I finally fell asleep late during the second day. I dreamt in bright colors and woke to find Martin patiently unraveling the hooked rug with his snout. I dissuaded him gently, then spent the rest of the morning wondering what to do with him.

"The situation had clearly changed. A hulking black artifact of unknown function was one thing, but Martin . . . well, who could possibly see him as a threat to national security? He fit more naturally into the soft toy category. I wondered idly if I could claim the residual rights.

"But I still wanted to contact someone at a university first. I flipped through the journals I'd brought until I happened on a reference to Richard Burns, a Cambridge physical chemist I remembered from a conference. He seemed like the political sort; he probably knew his way around the infrastructure. I called his office and made an appointment for the following week.

"The clock had started ticking. In a few days, I told myself, the world would become a very different place. And NSF would no doubt treat my next proposal with new-found respect. . . .

"I moved around my room in a sort of delirium. Then I'd look at Martin and come right back to my senses. The truth was that I didn't know any more than on the day Uncle Claude's trunk arrived at my apartment. What *was* Martin, anyway? Could my cosmic kitchen hypothesis have been right all along? Martin might be an alien cow-equivalent, a protein source. He seemed smarter than a cow, but that didn't prove anything. The aliens who ate him were probably smarter than us, too.

"The problem was that his species couldn't possibly have built the artifact. The dolphin's fate: no hands. Of course, he might be an early stage in some complex alien life cycle, or telekinetic, or something.

"None of that really mattered, of course. Martin's existence was the most important fact. We could study his metabolism, cell structure, molecular biology. I told myself that, but I didn't believe it. I wanted to make *contact*.

"The next day was a quiet one; inclement weather kept us indoors. I taught Martin how to play baseball. I tossed a wadded-up piece of paper towards him, and he batted it back with his snout. Silly, but we played for a couple of hours.

"In the afternoon I sat in the shabby armchair in my room and watched the rain. The irony of my situation impressed me mightily. I would soon be the most famous person on Earth—after so long being one of its most obscure. I wondered about my clothes. Did I own anything suitable for meeting presidents in? No doubt some picture of me in my torn jeans and flannel shirt would show up in elementary school texts for the rest of eternity. I thought about book contracts, TV appearances, interviews. What would I talk about? All I knew was chemistry.

"At some point I fell asleep in the chair, and I had the most extraordinary dream.

"I didn't have the fuzzy, unworldly sensation I usually associate with dreams. Everything was clear and hard and definite, as if I'd simply woken up in a different place. The time was dawn or twilight, and I was surrounded by a sort of ingeniously organized junkyard that stretched out of sight in every direction. And it all seemed to be moving.

"A sliver of red sun poked above the horizon, drowning the brilliant night sky and throwing long, leaping shadows. As my eyes adjusted, I could tell that I was standing on an gigantic brass gear that kept trying to slide out from beneath my feet. It moved irregularly, in jumps, with a ghastly screeching. The air smelled of burning oil.

"I started moving carefully—almost shuffling—towards a high, distant point that looked stationary. I hopped from the gear to a pinion that was impaled on a shaft the diameter of a tree trunk. Its end was sunk in an elegantly faceted jewel.

"The pinion swung me around to the edge of a shelf. I grabbed it and pulled myself up. The shelf was toothed along its other edge. A hundred yards away in the dim red light I could see a huge, fitfully spinning worm gear that meshed with the rack I was clinging to. The sun remained fixed on the horizon.

"I crawled along until I was directly across from the stable spot I had seen from below. I took a running start, jumped over three meters of black space and rolled to a stop.

"I was on a sort of stainless steel mesa, the highest point in the landscape of sprockets and armatures and escapements—all clanking and tearing and grinding against each other. Something was terribly wrong.

"After a while the logic of mechanism became clearer to me. There were groups of components, and groups of groups, and so on to the fifth or sixth order. At a great distance, among the less immediately related groups, the gears seemed to be spinning more regularly. The disorder grew with proximity to my position. The focal point seemed to be somewhere in the shadows directly beneath my feet. I studied the situation for a few more minutes, then I lowered myself from the ledge into the chaos below.

"I worked my way around a spring and a halted flywheel to a point where black smoke was rising and the screeching sounded continuously. I could just make out a machine head screw the size of a oil drum jammed between two gears.

"I don't remember the next few minutes very well—just the sounds of machinery tearing itself apart, and shifting shadows and plumes of sparks that flew each time the gears ground against the screw. I crawled down into the mechanism—I don't know why exactly, but it seemed very important that I do so. I braced myself against something and pushed at the screw until it jumped free and went skittering across a field of polished chrome.

"I stood up, breathing deeply. The clamor softened, became more rhythmic and tonal. After a few minutes I could distinguish notes, then melodies, then antiphonal responses from more distant parts of the mechanism. As I climbed back onto the mesa, the music synchronized and resonated and interwove until it became something I could almost feel and taste.

"I stood on a ledge, head thrown back, consumed by the music, while, haltingly at first, then more surely, the sun began to rise.

"I closed my eyes, and when I opened them again I was back in my room. I saw Martin sitting near me with his snout extended. Something in his posture exuded pride and pleasure."

*   *   *

"The rain stopped just after dark, and Martin and I went for a walk on a back lane bordered by dripping trees. Grouse rushed through the heather from time to time as we passed. Otherwise, the world was perfectly still. Martin moved quickly. I puffed a bit trying to keep up.

"After an hour or so, the fields on either side of us began to turn translucent. The effect seemed perfectly natural to me—I took only the most casual notice of it. I had the sensation of stars rushing by overhead.

"We crested a hill, and Martin grew more excited. At the top I could just make out the dark silhouette of a large, angular house.

"A cobbled pathway led up to the entrance. Martin shuffled forward expectantly. I stopped short of the front door—I didn't want to alarm the residents. Each of the cobbles, I noticed, had a figure inscribed into it. I had my notebook in my back pocket; I knelt over and made a quick rubbing. When I looked up, Martin was knocking on the front door with his snout.

"The wind off the plowed fields began to bite. I observed peripherally that the stars had slowed and stopped in unfamiliar patterns. I shifted my weight from one foot to the other. Martin seemed very sure of himself. He knocked again.

"At the second knock the door swung heavily inwards. The entryway was very dark, very empty—just a long expanse of bare wall and odd, twisted floorboard. What held my attention was the figure at the door. It was a squat shape about three feet high, enveloped in a loose black cloak. The cloak hid all its features, but I could distinguish a rounded projection at floor level, like the head of a beetle. The shape rose up slowly, and the cloak fell back.

"The night was very dark. Even the starlight was dim, almost red, as if the stars themselves had grown terribly old. But I could see the creature's face well enough. It was a circle of six lidless, compound eyes surrounding a mass of waving tentacles with a black, glistening hole in the center.

"I stood frozen in the doorway for a moment. Then . . . I turned and walked away. I remember the night being terribly quiet. The only sounds were my footsteps striking the incised cobbles in front of the house and the splashing of huge wet drops falling from the trees. After a few yards I tripped over a root and fell heavily. I scrambled to my feet and ran.

"I didn't slow down until I could see the lights of the village. I leaned against a tree and gulped air until my chest stopped burning. I finally remembered to look around for Martin. He was at my feet, shivering."

"I didn't sleep that night. I paced around my room, replaying the scene at the door. I tried to recall more details. I couldn't be sure—the house was so dark, and I was so startled by that alien figure—but I thought I remembered more of the black creatures huddled at the end of the corridor.

"The next morning—as soon as the sun was up—I dropped Martin in my pack and went looking for the house. The roads looked different in the daylight, and I wasn't entirely sure of the route I'd taken. I must have crisscrossed the countryside a dozen times. I went again the next night, letting Martin walk alongside me, then again the night after that.

"I never found it.

"Very early one morning—we'd been out all night—we had to walk back through the village green on the way home. I let Martin play on the lawn for a while. He seemed to enjoy that. He rolled in the grass, poked at it with his snout, ate some. I could tell where he'd been from the faint hexagonal patterns he left behind.

"He was nosing around a sign post when an elderly gentleman with a splendid mustache popped out of the shadows right in front of us.

"I smiled weakly and said good evening—I didn't know what else to do.

"The old fellow came gradually to a stop and looked us over. His eyesight, I suspected, wasn't what it had once been.

" 'That's a fine looking animal you have there,' he said. He tended to shout a bit.

"I thanked him.

" 'Ah, what is it exactly?'

"I thought for a while. 'A jabberwock?' I meant it as a lame sort of joke.

" 'A sort of terrier then?'

" 'Exactly.'

"He nodded in a knowledgeable way. 'American breed?'

" 'Right.'

" 'A fine specimen. Well, see that you curb him, sir.' With that he pushed on.

"I nearly expired on the spot."

"That was enough. The next day I said goodbye to my landlady and caught the train to London. I took the first plane home, called you from the airport." He shrugged. "And here I am."

Roger's voice had faded almost to extinction. He seemed desperately tired. But I couldn't let him stop.

"Go on," I said.

"That's all."

I shook my head. "What happened to Martin?"

"Martin's in my backpack."

I tried to say something, failed. I looked at his pack. "He's *here*?"

"Of course. Did you think I'd left him behind? I was a little concerned about customs, but they didn't inspect my bag, so there wasn't a problem. Would you like to see him?"

A truck drove by, rumbling through half a dozen gears as it rounded a corner.
"Now?" I asked.

"It's a little bright in here . . ."

Roger waited while I turned out the lights, then he unzipped the bottom compartment of his pack and reached inside. I noticed a tart smell, rather pleasant, with strains of cinnamon and an earthier tone I couldn't identify.

He took out something elongated and blackly iridescent and put it on the floor. It moved towards me with a sound like rustling silk.

I took an involuntary step backwards.

"Jesus, Roger . . . what *is* it?"

"It's an instrument, like the thing my ancestor found. Only this one is organic. The artifact in the mine had to last for millions of years, so it was built out of a material that served that purpose. But ceramic couldn't do Martin's job."

The creature—there was no doubting that it was alive—moved closer. As my eyes adjusted to the dark, I could see the tapering projection that Roger referred to as its snout. It uncoiled to a length of eight inches or more and sought one of my shoes. I nearly fell over getting out of the way. Roger steadied me.

"Really, there's nothing to be afraid of."

I took a deep breath. "All right. But what *is* it? Something like . . . that can't be space-faring."

"No, of course not. Martin isn't a sentient alien. He's a machine. Very specialized. His function is to help me contact his people."

I held out my hand tentatively and let the creature probe it with its snout. The touch was slightly electric.

"The information was stored in his genetic material somehow. And he was able to pass it directly into my brain, like copying a computer file. His job amounted to establishing a communications protocol, then performing a tricky format conversion—translating his data into our neural idioms. I wish I understood how he did it."

I rubbed my forehead. "Roger, stop. What are you talking about?"

"The dark house, that's what this is all about. I think it was Martin's idiom for his home planet. He took me there somehow—I don't know if we moved physically or what. But I'm sure the house only existed within Birwood city limits on that one night."

I shook my head. "I still don't understand. It sounds so complicated. Why not just leave . . . I don't know, a transmitter or a spaceship or something?"

Roger picked Martin up, scratched him gently behind the snout. "I thought about that. Too risky. You don't want just anyone knowing where you are. One of Martin's jobs must have been to test us, me—that's what the clockwork dream was for. Were we smart enough? Harmless enough? I suppose we were. He tried to take me home.

"But I only got the one chance. We never went back, and I haven't had any more dreams."

His voice was like broken glass.

"It all sounds so . . . ephemeral," I said. "Are you sure the house was real?"

Roger reached into a pocket and took out a sheet of paper covered with pencil rubbings. He unfolded it carefully.

"I found this in my notebook the morning after I visited the house—the inscription on the cobble."

The revealed figure showed a striking, stylized design: a ring of six small circles surrounding a radiating swirl of short, wavy lines. A face.

My hands trembled a bit. "What are you going to do? Call a press conference?"

Roger shook his head. "Would you mind if I went to sleep first? You can't begin to imagine how tired I am."

The smell of fresh coffee mixed with the faintest of cinnamon scents early the next morning. I called to Roger. No answer. With the curtains drawn, the living room was quite dark. Even so, I knew immediately that he was gone.

There was a familiar leather-bound book on the coffee table with a note tucked inside its front cover. I picked up the note; I had to push the curtains apart before I could make it out. I was struck by how similar the handwriting was to Captain John Knowles's inscription on the flyleaf. The voice, though, was very much Roger's:

I'm sorry I evaded your question last night. No, I won't be giving a press conference. *You* will. I've left you with enough evidence, I think, to convince anyone. You'll be able to handle the reporters much better than I could.

I'm not really much of a hero.

That's a subject I've had occasion to think considerably on during the last few days. Mostly I've been trying to understand why I walked away from that dark house at the top of the hill. I was terrified, of course; but I could control that. I also felt, rationally or otherwise, that if I walked through the door, I wouldn't be coming back. I can honestly say that frightened me even less.

But I'd been so secretive. I hadn't told *anyone*. I had reasons at the time. Still, if I'd accepted the creature's invitation, the artifact and Martin and everything else would have vanished along with me. I really couldn't let that happen—even an unemployed scientist has some professional responsibilities. And, to be honest, there was more to it than that. I wanted people to know who I was, what I'd done.

You'll tell them won't you?

And I'll ask one more favor. I need two months. That's why I came back instead of keeping my appointment in Cambridge. I needed someone I could trust.

As you read this I'm on my way to England. I've already bought the chemicals. The artifact is intact; I can make another Martin, find that house again.

I won't run this time.

Roger's glyph was scrawled at the bottom. I put the note down and drew the curtain shut. Martin's snout curled towards me inquisitively from beneath the table. He looked *very* hungry.

PAT CADIGAN

It Was the Heat

Pat Cadigan was born in Schenectady, New York, and now lives in Overland Park, Kansas. One of the best new writers in SF, Cadigan made her first professional sale in 1980 to *New Dimensions*, and soon became a frequent contributor to *Omni, The Magazine of Fantasy and Science Fiction*, and *Shadows*, among other markets. She was the co-editor, along with husband Arnie Fenner, of *Shayol*, perhaps the best of the semiprozines; it was honored with a World Fantasy Award in the "Special Achievement, Nonprofessional" category in 1981. She has also served on the Nebula Award Jury and as a World Fantasy Award Judge. Her first novel, *Mindplayers*, was released in 1987 to excellent critical response, and she has just completed her second novel. Her story "Angel" was in our Fifth Annual Collection; "Pretty Boy Crossover" was in our Fourth Annual Collection; "Roadside Rescue" was in our Third Annual Collection; "Rock On" was in our Second Annual Collection; and "Nearly Departed" was in our First Annual Collection.

Here she takes us to the French Quarter in old New Orleans for a scary and deliciously erotic look at how easy it is to lose yourself, once you let go just a *little*. . . .

IT WAS THE HEAT

Pat Cadigan

It was the heat, the incredible heat that never lets up, never eases, never once gives you a break. Sweat till you die; bake till you drop; fry, broil, burn, baby, burn. How'd you like to live in a fever and never feel cool, never, never, never?

Women think they want men like that. They think they want someone to put the devil in their Miss Jones. Some of them even lie awake at night, alone, or next to a silent lump of husband or boyfriend, or friendly stranger, thinking, *Let me be completely consumed with fire. In the name of love.*

Sure.

Right feeling, wrong name. Try again. And the thing is, they do. They try and try and try, and if they're very, very unlucky, they find one of them.

I thought I had him right where I wanted him—between my legs. Listen, I didn't always talk this way. That wasn't me you saw storming the battlements during the Sexual Revolution. My ambition was liberated but I didn't lose my head, or give it. It wasn't me saying, *Let them eat pie.* Once I had a sense of propriety but I lost it with my inhibitions.

You think these things happen only in soap operas—the respectable, thirty-five-year-old wife and working mother goes away on a business trip with a suitcase full of navy blue suits and classy blouses with the bow at the neck and a briefcase crammed with paperwork. Product management is not a pretty sight. Sensible black pumps are a must for the run on the fast track and if your ambition is sufficiently liberated, black pumps can keep pace with perforated wing tips, even outrun them.

But men know the secret. Especially businessmen. This is why management conferences are sometimes held in a place like New Orleans instead of the professional canyons of New York City or Chicago. Men know the secret and now I do, too. But I didn't then, when I arrived in New Orleans with my luggage and my paperwork and my inhibitions, to be installed in the Bourbon Orleans Hotel in the French Quarter.

The room had all the charm of home—more, since I wouldn't be cleaning it up. I hung the suits in the bathroom, ran the shower, called home, already feeling guilty. Yes, boys, Mommy's at the hotel now and she has a long meeting to go to, let me talk to Daddy. Yes, dear, I'm fine. It was a long ride from the airport, good thing the corporation's paying for this. The hotel is very nice, good thing the corporation's paying for this too. Yes, there's a pool but I doubt I'll have time to use it and anyway, I didn't bring a suit. Not that kind of suit. This isn't a pleasure trip, you know, I'm not on vacation. No. Yes. No. Kiss the boys for me. I love you, too.

If you want to be as conspicuous as possible, be a woman walking almost late into a meeting room full of men who are all gunning to be CEOs. Pick out the two or three other female faces and nod to them even though they're complete strangers, and find a seat near them. Listen to the man at the front of the room say, *Now that we're all here, we can begin*, and know that every man is thinking that means you. Imagine what they are thinking, imagine what they are whispering to each other. Imagine that they know you can't concentrate on the opening presentation because your mind is on your husband and children back home instead of the business at hand when the real reason you can't concentrate is because you're imagining they must all be thinking your mind is on your husband and children back home instead of the business at hand.

Do you know what *they're* thinking about, really? They're thinking about the French Quarter. Those who have been there before are thinking about jazz and booze in go-cups and bars where the women are totally nude, totally, and those who haven't been there before are wondering if everything's as wild as they say.

Finally the presentation ended and the discussion period following the presentation ended (the women had nothing to discuss so as not to be perceived as the ones delaying the after-hours jaunt into the French Quarter). Tomorrow, nine o'clock in the Hyatt, second-floor meeting room. Don't let's be too hung over to make it, boys, ha, ha. Oh, and girls too, of course, ha, ha.

The things you hear when you don't have a crossbow.

Demure, I took a cab back to the Bourbon Orleans, intending to leave a wake-up call for 6:30, ignoring the streets already filling up. In early May, with Mardi Gras already a dim memory? Was there a big convention in town this week, I asked the cabdriver.

No, ma'am, he told me (his accent—Creole or Cajun? I don't know—made it more like *ma'ahm*). De Quarter always be jumpin', and the weather be so lovely.

This was lovely? I was soaked through my drip-dry white blouse and the suitcoat would start to smell if I didn't take it off soon. My crisp, boardroom coiffure had gone limp and trickles of sweat were tracking leisurely along my scalp. Product management was meant to live in air-conditioning (we call it climate control, as though we really could, but there is no controlling this climate).

At the last corner before the hotel, I saw him standing at the curb. Tight jeans, red shirt knotted above the navel to show off the washboard stomach. Definitely not executive material; executives are required to be doughy in that area and the area to the south of that was never delineated quite so definitely as it was in this man's jeans.

Some sixth sense made him bend to see who was watching him from the backseat of the cab.

"Mamma, mamma!" he called and kissed the air between us. "You wanna go to a party?" He came over to the cab and motioned for me to roll the window all the way down. I slammed the lock down on the door and sat back, clutching my sensible black purse.

"C'mon, mamma!" He poked his fingers through the small opening of the window. "I be good to you!" The golden hair was honey from peroxide but the voice was honey from the comb. The light changed and he snatched his fingers away just in time.

"I'll be waiting!" he shouted after me. I didn't look back.

"What was all that about?" I asked the cabdriver.

"Just a wild boy. Lotta wild boys in the Quarter, ma'am." We pulled up next to the hotel and he smiled over his shoulder at me, his teeth just a few shades lighter than his coffee-colored skin. "Anytime you want to find a wild boy for yourself, this is where you look." It came out more like *dis is wheah you look*. "You got a nice company sends you to the Quarter for doin' business."

I smiled back, overtipped him, and escaped into the hotel.

It wasn't even a consideration, that first night. Wake-up call for 6:30, just as I'd intended, to leave time for showering and breakfast, like the good wife and mother and executive I'd always been.

Beignets for breakfast. Carl had told me I must have beignets for breakfast if I were going to be in New Orleans. He'd bought some beignet mix and tried to make some for me the week before I'd left. They'd come out too thick and heavy and only the kids had been able to eat them, liberally dusted with powdered sugar. If I found a good place for beignets, I would try to bring some home, I'd decided, for my lovely, tolerant, patient husband, who was now probably making thick, heavy pancakes for the boys. Nice of him to sacrifice some of his vacation time to be home with the boys while Mommy was out of town. Mommy had never gone out of town on business before. Daddy had, of course; several times. At those times, Mommy had never been able to take any time away from the office though, so she could be with the boys while Daddy was out of town. Too much work to do; if you want to keep those sensible black pumps on the fast track, you can't be putting your family before the work. Lots of women lose out that way, you know, Martha?

I knew.

No familiar faces in the restaurant, but I wasn't looking for any. I moved my tray along the line, took a beignet and poured myself some of the famous Louisiana chicory coffee before I found a small table under a ceiling fan. No air-conditioning and it was already up in the eighties. I made a concession and took off my jacket. After a bite of the beignet, I made another and unbuttoned the top two buttons of my blouse. The pantyhose already felt sticky and uncomfortable. I had a perverse urge to slip off to the ladies' room and take them off. Would anyone notice or care? That would leave me with nothing under the half-slip. Would anyone guess? There goes a lady executive with no pants on. In the heat, it was not unthinkable. No underwear at all was not unthinkable. Everything was binding. A woman in a gauzy caftan breezed past my table, glancing down at me with careless interest. Another out-of-towner, yes. You can tell—we're the only ones not dressed for the weather.

"All right to sit here, ma'am?"

I looked up. He was holding a tray with one hand, already straddling the chair across from me, only waiting my permission to sink down and join me. Dark, curly hair, just a bit too long, darker eyes, smooth skin the color of overcreamed coffee. Tank top over jeans. He eased himself down and smiled. I must have said yes.

"All the other tables're occupied or ain't been bussed, ma'am. Hope you don't mind, you a stranger here and all." The smile was as slow and honeyed as the voice. They all talked in honey tones here. "Eatin' you one of our nice beignets, I see. First breakfast in the Quarter, am I right?"

I used a knife and fork on the beignet. "I'm here on business."

"You have a very striking face."

I risked a glance up at him. "You're very kind." Thirty-five and up is striking, if the world is feeling kind.

"When your business is done, shall I see you in the Quarter?"

"I doubt it. My days are very long." I finished the beignet quickly, gulped the coffee. He caught my arm as I got up. It was a jolt of heat, like being touched with an electric wand.

"I have a husband and three children!" It was the only thing I could think to say.

"You don't want to forget your jacket."

It hung limply on the back of my chair. I wanted to forget it badly, to have an excuse to go through the day of meetings and seminars in shirt sleeves. I put the tray down and slipped the jacket on. "Thank you."

"Name is Andre, ma'am." The dark eyes twinkled. "My heart will surely break if I don't see you tonight in the Quarter."

"Don't be silly."

"It's too hot to be silly, ma'am."

"Yes. It is," I said stiffly. I looked for a place to take the tray.

"They take it away for you. You can just leave it here. Or you can stay and have another cup of coffee and talk to a lonely soul." One finger plucked at the low scoop of the tank top. "I'd like that."

"A cabdriver warned me about wild boys," I said, holding my purse carefully to my side.

"I doubt it. He may have told you but he didn't warn you. And I ain't a boy, ma'am."

Sweat gathered in the hollow between my collarbones and spilled downward. He seemed to be watching the trickle disappear down into my blouse. Under the aroma of baking breads and pastries and coffee, I caught a scent of something else.

"Boys stand around on street corners, they shout rude remarks, they don't know what a woman is."

"That's enough," I snapped. "I don't know why you picked me out for your morning's amusement. Maybe because I'm from out of town. You wild boys get a kick out of annoying the tourists, is that it? If I see you again, I'll call a cop." I stalked out and pushed myself through the humidity to hail a cab. By the time I reached the Hyatt, I might as well not have showered.

"I'm skipping out on this afternoon's session," the woman whispered to me. Her badge said she was Frieda Fellowes, of Boston, Massachusetts. "I heard the speaker last year. He's the biggest bore in the world. I'm going shopping. Care to join me?"

I shrugged. "I don't know. I have to write up a report on this when I get home and I'd better be able to describe everything in detail."

She looked at my badge. "You must work for a bunch of real hard-asses up in Schenectady." She leaned forward to whisper to the other woman sitting in the row ahead of us, who nodded eagerly.

They were both missing from the afternoon session. The speaker was the biggest bore in the world. The men had all conceded to shirt sleeves. Climate control failed halfway through the seminar and it broke up early, releasing us from the stuffiness of the meeting room into the thick air of the city. I stopped in the lobby bathroom and took off my pantyhose, rolled them into an untidy ball and stuffed them in my purse before getting a cab back to my own hotel.

One of the men from my firm phoned my room and invited me to join him and the guys for drinks and dinner. We met in a crowded little place called Messina's, four male executives and me. It wasn't until I excused myself and went to the closet-sized bathroom that I realized I'd put my light summer slacks on over nothing. A careless mistake, akin to starting off to the supermarket on Saturday morning in my bedroom slippers. Mommy's got a lot on her mind. Martha, the No-Pants Executive. Guess what, dear, I went out to dinner in New Orleans with four men and forgot to wear panties. Well, women do reach their sexual peak at thirty-five, don't they, honey?

The heat was making me crazy. No air-conditioning here either, just fans, pushing the damp air around.

I rushed through the dinner of red beans and rice and hot sausage; someone ordered a round of beers and I gulped mine down to cool the sausage. No one spoke much. Martha's here, better keep it low-key, guys. I decided to do them a favor and disappear after the meal. There wouldn't be much chance of running into me at any of the nude bars, nothing to be embarrassed about. Thanks for tolerating my presence, fellas.

But they looked a little puzzled when I begged off anything further. The voice blew over to me as I reached the door, carried on a wave of humidity pushed by one of the fans: "Maybe she's got a headache tonight." General laughter.

Maybe all four of you together would be a disappointment, boys. Maybe you don't know what a woman is, either.

They didn't look especially wild, either.

I had a drink by the pool instead of going right up to the hotel room. Carl would be coping with supper and homework and whatnot. Better to call later, after they were all settled down.

I finished the drink and ordered another. It came in a plastic cup, with apologies from the waiter. "Temporarily short on crystal tonight, ma'am. Caterin' a private dinner here. Hope you don't mind a go-cup this time."

"A what?"

The man's smile was bright. "Go-cup. You take it and walk around with it."

"That's allowed?"

"All over the Quarter, ma'am." He moved on to another table.

So I walked through the lobby with it and out into the street, and no one stopped me.

Just down at the corner, barely half a block away, the streets were filling up again. Many of the streets seemed to be pedestrians only. I waded in, holding the go-cup. Just to look around. I couldn't really come here and not look around.

"It's supposed to be a whorehouse where the girls swung naked on velvet swings."

I turned away from the high window where the mannequin legs had been swinging in and out to look at the man who had spoken to me. He was a head taller than I was, long-haired, attractive in a rough way.

"Swung?" I said. "You mean they don't anymore?"

He smiled and took my elbow, positioning me in front of an open doorway, pointed in. I looked; a woman was lying naked on her stomach under a mirror suspended overhead. Perspiration gleamed on her skin.

"Buffet?" I said. "All you can eat, a hundred dollars?"

The man threw back his head and laughed heartily. "New in the Quarter, ain'tcha?" Same honey in the voice. They caress you with their voices here, I thought, holding the crumpled go-cup tightly. It was a different one; I'd had another drink since I'd come out and it hadn't seemed like a bad idea at all, another drink, the walking around, all of it. Not by myself, anyway.

Something brushed my hip. "You'll let me buy you another, won'tcha?" Dark hair, dark eyes; young. I remembered that for a long time.

Wild creatures in lurid long dresses catcalled screechily from a second-floor balcony as we passed below on the street. My eyes were heavy with heat and alcohol but I kept walking. It was easy with him beside me, his arm around me and his hand resting on my hip.

Somewhere along the way, the streets grew much darker and the crowds disappeared. A few shadows in the larger darkness; I saw them leaning against street signs; we passed one close enough to smell a mixture of perfume and sweat and alcohol and something else.

"Didn't nobody never tell you to come out alone at night in this part of the Quarter?" The question was amused, not reproving. They caress you with their voices down here, with their voices and the darkness and the heat, which gets higher as it gets darker. And when it gets hot enough, they melt and flow together and run all over you, more fluid than water.

What are you doing?

I'm walking into a dark hallway; I don't know my footing, I'm glad there's someone with me.

What are you doing?

I'm walking into a dark room to get out of the heat, but it's no cooler here and I don't really care after all.

What are you doing?

I'm overdressed for the season here; this isn't Schenectady in the spring, it's New Orleans, it's the French Quarter.

What are you doing?

I'm hitting my sexual peak at thirty-five.

"What are you doing?"

Soft laughter. "Oh, honey, don't you know?"

The Quarter was empty at dawn, maybe because it was raining. I found my way back to the Bourbon Orleans in the downpour anyway. It shut off as suddenly as a suburban lawn sprinkler just as I reached the front door of the hotel.

I fell into bed and slept the day away, no wake-up calls, and when I opened my eyes, the sun was going down and I remembered how to find him.

You'd think there would have been a better reason: my husband ignored me or my kids were monsters or my job was a dead end or some variation on the midlife crisis. It wasn't any of those things. Well, the seminars *were* boring, but nobody gets that bored. Or maybe they did and I'd just never heard about it.

It was the heat.

The heat gets inside you. Then you get a fever from the heat, and from fever you progress to delirium and from delirium into another state of being. Nothing is real in delirium. No, scratch that: everything is real in a different way. In delirium, everything floats, including time. Lighter than air, you slip away. Day breaks apart from night, leaves you with scraps of daylight. It's all right—when it gets that hot, it's too hot to see, too hot to bother looking. I remembered dark hair, dark eyes, but it was all dark now, and in the dark it was even hotter than in the daylight.

It was the heat. It never let up. It was the heat and the smell. I'll never be able to describe that smell except to say that if it were a sound, it would have been round and mellow and sweet, just the way it tasted. As if he had no salt in his body at all. As if he had been distilled from the heat itself, and salt had just been left behind in the process.

It was the heat.

And then it started to get cool.

It started to cool down to the eighties during the last two days of the conference and I couldn't find him. I made a halfhearted showing at one of the seminars after a two-day absence. They stared, all the men and the women, especially the one who had asked me to go shopping.

"I thought you'd been kidnapped by white slavers," she said to me during the break. "What happened? You don't look like you feel so hot."

"I feel very hot," I said, helping myself to the watery lemonade punch the hotel had laid out on a table. With beignets. The sight of them turned my stomach and so did the punch. I put it down again. "I've been running a fever."

She touched my face, frowning slightly. "You don't feel feverish. In fact, you feel pretty cool. Clammy, even."

"It's the air-conditioning," I said, drawing back. Her fingers were cold, too cold to tolerate. "The heat and the air-conditioning. It's fucked me up."

Her eyes widened.

"*Messed* me up, excuse me. I've been hanging around my kids too long."

"Perhaps you should see a doctor. Or go home."

"I've just got to get out of this air-conditioning," I said, edging toward the door. She followed me, trying to object. "I'll be fine as soon as I get out of this air-conditioning and back into the heat."

"No, *wait*," she called insistently. "You may be suffering from heatstroke. I think that's it—the clammy skin, the way you look—"

"It's not heatstroke, I'm freezing in this goddam refrigerator. Just leave me the fuck alone and I'll be *fine!*"

I fled, peeling off my jacket, tearing open the top of my blouse. I couldn't go back, not to that awful air-conditioning. I would stay out where it was warm.

I lay in bed with the windows wide open and the covers pulled all the way up. One of the men from my company phoned; his voice sounded too casual when he pretended I had reassured him. Carl's call only twenty minutes later was not a surprise. I'm fine, dear. You don't sound fine. I am, though. Everyone is worried about you. Needlessly. I think I should come down there. No, stay where you are, I'll be fine. No, I think I should come and get you. And I'm telling you to stay where you are. That does it, you sound weird, I'm getting the next flight out and your mother can stay with the boys. You stay where you are, goddammit, or I might not come home, is that clear?

Long silence.

Is someone there with you?

More silence.

I said, is someone there with you?

It's just the heat. I'll be fine, as soon as I warm up.

Sometime after that, I was sitting at a table in a very dark place that was almost warm enough. The old woman sitting across from me occasionally drank delicately from a bottle of beer and fanned herself, even though it was only almost warm.

"It's such pleasure when it cool down like dis," she said in her slow honey-voice. Even the old ladies had honey-voices here. "The heat be a beast."

I smiled, thinking for a moment that she'd said *bitch*, not *beast*. "Yeah. It's a bitch all right but I don't like to be cold."

"No? Where you from?"

"Schenectady. Cold climate."

She grunted. "Well, the heat don't be a bitch, it be a beast. He be a beast."

"Who?"

"Him. The heat beast." She chuckled a little. "My grandma woulda called him a loa. You know what dat is?"

"No."

She eyed me before taking another sip of beer. "No. I don't know whether that good or bad for you, girl. Could be deadly either way, someone who don't like to be cold. What you doin' over here anyway? Tourist Quarter three blocks thataway."

"I'm looking for a friend. Haven't been able to find him since it's cooled down."

"Grandma knew they never named all de loa. She said new ones would come when they found things be willin' for 'em. Or when they named by someone. Got nothin' to do with the old religion anymore. Bigger than the old religion. It's all de world now." The old woman thrust her face forward and squinted at me. "What friend *you* got over here? No outta-town white girl got a friend over here."

"I do. And I'm not from out of town anymore."

"Get out." But it wasn't hostile, just amusement and condescension and a little disgust. "Go buy you some tourist juju and tell everybody you met a mamba in N'awlins. Be some candyass somewhere sell you a nice, fake love charm."

"I'm not here for that," I said, getting up. "I came for the heat."

"Well, girl, it's cooled down." She finished her beer.

Sometime after that, in another place, I watched a man and a woman dancing together. There were only a few other people on the floor in front of the band. I couldn't really make sense of the music, whether it was jazz or rock or whatever. It was just the man and the woman I was paying attention to. Something in their movements was familiar. I was thinking he would be called by the heat in them, but it was so damned cold in there, not even ninety degrees. The street was colder. I pulled the jacket tighter around myself and cupped my hands around the coffee mug. That famous Louisiana chicory coffee. Why couldn't I get warm?

It grew colder later. There wasn't a warm place in the Quarter, but people's skins seemed to be burning. I could see the heat shimmers rising from their bodies. Maybe I was the only one without a fever now.

Carl was lying on the bed in my hotel room. He sat up as soon as I opened the door. The heat poured from him in waves and my first thought was to throw myself on him and take it, take it all, and leave him to freeze to death.

"Wait!" he shouted but I was already pounding down the hall to the stairs.

Early in the morning, it was an easy thing to run through the Quarter. The sun was already beating down but the light was thin, with little warmth. I couldn't hear Carl chasing me, but I kept running, to the other side of the Quarter, where I had first gone into the shadows. Glimpse of an old woman's face at a window; I remembered her, she remembered me. Her head nodded, two fingers beckoned. Behind her, a younger face watched in the shadows. The wrong face.

I came to a stop in the middle of an empty street and waited. I was getting colder; against my face, my fingers were like living icicles. It had to be only eighty-eight or eighty-nine degrees, but even if it got to ninety-five or above today, I wouldn't be able to get warm.

He had it. He had taken it. Maybe I could get it back.

The air above the buildings shimmied, as if to taunt. Warmth, here, and here, and over here, what's the matter with you, frigid or something?

Down at the corner, a police car appeared. Heat waves rippled up from it, and I ran.

"Hey."

The man stood over me where I sat shivering at a corner table in the place that bragged it had traded slaves a hundred years ago. He was the color of rich earth, slightly built with carefully waved black hair. Young face; the wrong face, again.

"You look like you in the market for a sweater."

"Go away." I lifted the coffee cup with shuddering hands. "A thousand sweaters couldn't keep me warm now."

"No, honey." They caressed you with their voices down here. He took the seat across from me. "Not that kind of sweater. Sweater I mean's a person, special kinda person. Who'd you meet in the Quarter? Good-lookin' stud, right? Nice, wild boy, maybe not white but white enough for you?"

"Go away. I'm not like that."

"You know what you like now, though. Cold. Very cold woman. Cold woman's no good. Cold woman'll take all the heat out of a man, leave him frozen dead."

I didn't answer.

"So you need a sweater. Maybe I know where you can find one."

"Maybe you know where I can find *him*."

The man laughed. "That's what I'm sayin', cold woman." He took off his light, white suitcoat and tossed it at me. "Wrap up in that and come on."

The fire in the hearth blazed, flames licking out at the darkness. Someone kept feeding it, keeping it burning for hours. I wasn't sure who, or if it was only one person, or how long I sat in front of the fire, trying to get warm.

Sometime long after the man had brought me there, the old woman said, "Burnin' all day now. Whole Quarter oughta feel the heat by now. Whole *city*."

"*He'll* feel it, sure enough." The man's voice. "He'll feel it, come lookin' for what's burnin'." A soft laugh. "Won't he be surprised to see it's his cold woman."

"Look how the fire wants her."

The flames danced. I could sit in the middle of them and maybe then I'd be warm.

"Where did he go?" The person who asked might have been me.

"Went to take a rest. Man sleeps after a bender, don't you know. He oughta be ready for more by now."

I reached out for the fire. A long tongue of flame licked around my arm; the heat felt so good.

"Look how the fire wants her."

Soft laugh. "If it wants her, then it should have her. Go ahead, honey. Get in the fire."

On hands and knees, I climbed up into the hearth, moving slowly, so as not to scatter the embers. Clothes burned away harmlessly.

To sit in fire is to sit among a glory of warm, silk ribbons touching everywhere at once. I could see the room now, the heavy drapes covering the windows, the dark faces, one old, one young, gleaming with sweat, watching me.

"You feel 'im?" someone asked. "Is he comin'?"

"He's comin', don't worry about that." The man who had brought me smiled at me. I felt a tiny bit of perspiration gather at the back of my neck. Warmer; getting warmer now.

I began to see him; he was forming in the darkness, coming together, pulled in by the heat. Dark-eyed, dark-haired, young, the way he had been. He was there before the hearth and the look on that young face as he peered into the flames was hunger.

The fire leaped for him; I leaped for him and we saw what it was we really had. No young man; no man.

The heat be a beast.

Beast. Not really a loa, something else; I knew that, somehow. Sometimes it looks like a man and sometimes it looks like hot honey in the darkness.

What are you doing?

I'm taking darkness by the eyes, by the mouth, by the throat.

What are you doing?

I'm burning alive.

What are you doing?

I'm burning the heat beast and I have it just where I want it. All the heat anyone ever felt, fire and body heat, fever, delirium. Delirium has eyes; I push them in with my thumbs. Delirium has a mouth; I fill it with my fist. Delirium has a throat; I tear it out. Sparks fly like an explosion of tiny stars and the beast spreads its limbs in surrender, exposing its white-hot core. I bend my head to it and the taste is sweet, no salt in his body at all.

What are you doing?

Oh, honey, don't you know?

I took it back.

In the hotel room, I stripped off the shabby dress the old woman had given me and threw it in the trash can. I was packing when Carl came back.

He wanted to talk; I didn't. Later he called the police and told them everything was all right, he'd found me and I was coming home with him. I was sure they didn't care. Things like that must happen in the Quarter all the time.

In the ladies' room at the airport, the attendant sidled up to me as I was bent over the sink splashing cold water on my face and asked if I were all right.

"It's just the heat," I said.

"Then best you go home to a cold climate," she said. "You do better in a cold climate from now on."

I raised my head to look at her reflection in the spotted mirror. I wanted to ask her if she had a brother who also waved his hair. I wanted to ask her why he would bother with a cold woman, why he would care.

She put both hands high on her chest, protectively. "The beast sleeps in cold. *You* tend him now. Maybe you keep him asleep for good."

"And if I don't?"

She pursed her lips. "Then you gotta problem."

In summer, I keep the air-conditioning turned up high at my office, at home. In the winter, the kids complain the house is too cold and Carl grumbles a little, even though we save so much in heating bills. I tuck the boys in with extra blankets every night and kiss their foreheads, and later in our bed, Carl curls up close, murmuring how my skin is always so warm.

It's just the heat.

KRISTINE KATHRYN RUSCH

Skin Deep

New writer Kristine Kathryn Rusch is one of the fastest-rising and most prolific young authors on the scene today, and she must certainly be one of the busiest. In addition to editing *Pulphouse*, the new quarterly anthology series billed as "the hardback magazine," she is also a frequent contributor to *Amazing, Aboriginal SF, Isaac Asimov's Science Fiction Magazine*, and elsewhere. She lives in Eugene, Oregon.

In the poignant story that follows, she demonstrates that more than beauty can be skin deep. . . .

SKIN DEEP

Kristine Kathryn Rusch

"More pancakes, Colin?"

Cullaene looked down at his empty plate so that he wouldn't have to meet Mrs. Fielding's eyes. The use of his alias bothered him more than usual that morning.

"Thank you, no, ma'am. I already ate so much I could burst. If I take another bite, Jared would have to carry me out to the fields."

Mrs. Fielding shot a glance at her husband. Jared was using the last of his pancake to sop up the syrup on his plate.

"On a morning as cold as this, you should eat more," she said as she scooped up Cullaene's plate and set it in the sterilizer. "You could use a little fat to keep you warm."

Cullaene ran his hand over the stubble covering his scalp. Not taking thirds was a mistake, but to take some now would compound it. He would have to watch himself for the rest of the day.

Jared slipped the dripping bit of pancake into his mouth. He grinned and shrugged as he inclined his head toward his wife's back. Cullaene understood the gesture. Jared had used it several times during the week Cullaene worked for them. The farmer knew that his wife seemed pushy, but he was convinced that she meant well.

"More coffee, then?" Mrs. Fielding asked. She stared at him as if she were waiting for another mistake.

"Please." Cullaene handed her his cup. He hated the foreign liquid that colonists drank in gallons. It burned the back of his throat and churned restlessly in his stomach. But he didn't dare say so.

Mrs. Fielding poured his coffee, and Cullaene took a tentative sip as Lucy entered the kitchen. The girl kept tugging her loose sweater over her skirt. She slipped into her place at the table and rubbed her eyes with the heel of her hand.

"You're running late, little miss," her father said gently.

Lucy nodded. She pushed her plate out of her way and rested both elbows on the table. "I don't think I'm going today, Dad."

"Going?" Mrs. Fielding exclaimed. "Of course, you'll go. You've had a perfect attendance record for three years, Luce. It's no time to break it now—"

"Let her be, Elsie," Jared said. "Can't you see she doesn't feel well?"

The girl's skin was white, and her hands were trembling. Cullaene frowned. She made him nervous this morning. If he hadn't known her parentage, he would have thought she was going to have her first Change. But the colonists had hundreds of diseases with symptoms like hers. And she was old enough to begin puberty. Perhaps she was about to begin her first menstrual period.

Apparently, Mrs. Fielding was having the same thoughts, for she placed her hand on her daughter's forehead. "Well, you don't have a fever," she said. Then her eyes met Cullaene's. "Why don't you men get busy? You have a lot to do today."

Cullaene slid his chair back, happy to leave his full cup of coffee sitting on the table. He pulled on the thick jacket that he had slung over the back of his chair and let himself out the back door.

Jared joined him on the porch. "Think we can finish plowing under?"

Cullaene nodded. The great, hulking machine sat in the half-turned field like a sleeping monster. In a few minutes, Cullaene would climb into the cab and feel the strange gears shiver under his fingers. Jared had said that the machine was old and delicate, but it had to last at least three more years—colonist's years— or they would have to do the seeding by hand. There was no industry on the planet yet. The only way to replace broken equipment was to send to Earth for it, and that took time.

Just as Cullaene turned toward the field, a truck floated onto the landing. He began to walk, as if the arrival of others didn't concern him, but he knew they were coming to see him. The Fieldings seldom had visitors.

"Colin!" Jared was calling him. Cullaene stopped, trying not to panic. He had been incautious this time. Things had happened too fast. He wondered what the colonists would do. Would they imprison him, or would they hurt him? Would they give him a chance to explain the situation and then let him go?

Three colonists, two males and a female, were standing outside the truck. Jared was trying to get them to go toward the house.

"I'll meet you inside," Cullaene shouted back. For a moment he toyed with running. He stared out over the broad expanse of newly cultivated land, toward the forest and rising hills beyond it. Somewhere in there he might find an enclave of his own people, a group of Abandoned Ones who hadn't assimilated, but the chances of that were small. His people had always survived by adaptation. The groups of Abandoned Ones had grown smaller every year.

He rubbed his hands together. His skin was too dry. If only he could pull off this self-imposed restraint for an hour, he would lie down in the field and encase himself in mud. Then his skin would emerge as soft and pure as the fur on Jared's cats. But he needed his restraint now more than ever. He pulled his jacket tighter and let himself into the kitchen once more.

He could hear the voices of Lucy and her mother rise in a heated discussion from upstairs. Jared had pressed the recycle switch on the old coffee maker, and it was screeching in protest. The three visitors were seated around the table, the woman in Cullaene's seat, and all of them turned as he entered the room.

He nodded and sat by the sterilizer. The heat made his back tingle, and the unusual angle made him feel like a stranger in the kitchen where he had supped for over a week. The visitors stared at him with the same cold look he had seen on the faces of the townspeople.

"This is Colin," Jared said. "He works for me."

Cullaene nodded again. Jared didn't introduce the visitors, and Cullaene wondered if it was an intentional oversight.

"We would like to ask you a few questions about yourself," the woman said. She leaned forward as she spoke, and Cullaene noted that her eyes were a vivid blue.

"May I ask why?"

Jared's hand shook as he poured the coffee. "Colin, it's customary around here—"

"No," the woman interrupted. "It is not customary. We're talking with all the strangers. Surely your hired man has heard of the murder."

Cullaene started. He took the coffee cup Jared offered him, relieved that his own hand did not shake. "No, I hadn't heard."

"We don't talk about such things in this house, Marlene," Jared said to the woman.

Coffee cups rattled in the silence as Jared finished serving everyone. The older man, leaning against the wall behind the table, waited until Jared was through before he spoke.

"It's our first killing in *this* colony, and it's a ghastly one. Out near the ridge, we found the skin of a man floating in the river. At first, we thought it was a body because the water filled the skin like it would fill a sack. Most of the hair was in place, hair so black that when it dried its highlights were blue. We couldn't find any clothes—"

"—or bones for that matter," the other man added.

"That's right," the spokesman continued. "He had been gutted. We scoured the area for the rest of him, and up on the ridge we found blood."

"A great deal of it," Marlene said. "As if they had skinned him while he was still alive."

Cullaene had to wrap his fingers around the hot cup to keep them warm. He hadn't been careful enough. Things had happened so swiftly that he hadn't had a chance to go deeper into the woods. He felt the fear that had been quivering in the bottom of his stomach settle around his heart.

"And so you're questioning all of the strangers here to see if they could have done it." He spoke as if he were more curious than frightened.

Marlene nodded. She ran a long hand across her hairline to catch any loose strands.

"I didn't kill anyone," Cullaene said. "I'll answer anything you ask."

They asked him careful, probing questions about his life before he had entered their colony, and he answered with equal care, being as truthful as he possibly could. He told them that the first colony he had been with landed on ground unsuitable for farming. The colonists tried hunting and even applied for a mining permit, but nothing worked. Eventually, most returned to Earth. He remained, traveling from family to family, working odd jobs while he tried to find a place to settle. As he spoke, he mentioned occasional details about himself, hoping that the sparse personal comments would prevent deeper probing. He told them about the Johansens whose daughter he had nearly married, the Cassels who taught him how to cultivate land, and the Slingers who nursed him back to health after a particularly debilitating illness. Cullaene told them every place he had ever been except the one place they were truly interested in—the woods that bordered the Fieldings' farm.

He spoke in a gentle tone that Earthlings respected. And he watched Jared's face because he knew that Jared, of any of them, would be the one to realize that Cullaene was not and never had been a colonist. Jared had lived on the planet for fifteen years. Once he had told Cullaene proudly that Lucy, though an orphan, was the first member of this colony born on the planet.

The trust in Jared's eyes never wavered. Cullaene relaxed slightly. If Jared didn't recognize him, no one would.

"They say that this is the way the natives commit murder," Marlene said when Cullaene finished. "We've heard tales from other colonies of bodies—both human and Riiame—being found like this."

Cullaene realized that she was still questioning him. "I never heard of this kind of murder before."

She nodded. As if by an unseen cue, all three of them stood. Jared stood with them. "Do you think Riiame could be in the area?" he asked.

"It's very likely," Marlene said. "Since you live so close to the woods, you should probably take extra precautions."

"Yes." Jared glanced over at his well-stocked gun cabinet. "I plan to."

The men nodded their approval and started out the door. Marlene turned to Cullaene. "Thank you for your cooperation," she said. "We'll let you know if we have any further questions."

Cullaene stood to accompany them out, but Jared held him back. "Finish your coffee. We have plenty of time to get to the fields later."

After they went out the door, Cullaene took his coffee and moved to his own seat. Lucy and her mother were still arguing upstairs. He took the opportunity to indulge himself in a quick scratch of his hands and arms. The heat had made the dryness worse.

He wondered if he had been convincing. The three looked as if they had already decided what happened. A murder. He shook his head.

A door slammed upstairs, and the argument grew progressively louder. Cullaene glanced out the window over the sterilizer. Jared was still talking with the three visitors. Cullaene hoped they'd leave soon. Then maybe he'd talk to Jared, explain as best he could why he could no longer stay.

"Where are you going?" Mrs. Fielding shouted. Panic touched the edge of her voice.

"Away from you!" Lucy sounded on the verge of tears. Cullaene could hear her stamp her way down the stairs. Suddenly, the footsteps stopped. "No! You stay away from me! I need time to think!"

"You can't have time to think! We've got to find out what's wrong."

"Nothing's wrong!"

"Lucy—"

"You take another step and I swear I'll leave!" Lucy backed her way into the kitchen, slammed the door, and leaned on it. Then she noticed Cullaene, and all the fight left her face.

"How long have you been here?" she whispered.

He poured his now-cold coffee into the recycler that they had set aside for him. "I won't say anything to your father, if that's what you're worried about. I don't even know why you were fighting."

There was no room left in the sterilizer, so he set the cup next to the tiny boiler that purified the ground water. Lucy slid a chair back, and it creaked as she sat in it. Cullaene took another glance out the window. Jared and his visitors seemed to be arguing.

What would he do if they decided he was guilty? He couldn't disappear. They had a description of him that they would send to other colonies. He could search for the Abandoned Ones, but even if he found them, they might not take him in. He had lived with the colonists all his life. He looked human, and sometimes, he even felt human.

Something crashed behind him. Cullaene turned in time to see Lucy stumble over her chair as she backed away from the overturned coffee maker. Coffee ran down the wall, and the sterilizer hissed. He hurried to her side, moved the chair, and got her to a safer corner of the kitchen.

"Are you all right?" he asked.

She nodded. A tear slipped out of the corner of her eye. "I didn't grab it tight, I guess."

"Why don't you sit down. I'll clean it up—" Cullaene stopped as Lucy's tear landed on the back of his hand. The drop was heavy and lined with red. He watched it leave a pink trail as it rolled off his skin onto the floor. Slowly, he looked up into her frightened eyes. More blood-filled tears threatened. He wiped one from her eyelashes and rolled it around between his fingertips.

Suddenly, she tried to pull away from him, and he tightened his grip on her arm. He slid back the sleeve of her sweater. The flesh hung in folds around her elbow and wrist. He touched her wrist lightly and noted that the sweat from her pores was also rimmed in blood.

"How long?" he whispered. "How long has this been happening to you?"

The tears began to flow easily now. It looked as if she were bleeding from her eyes. "Yesterday morning."

He shook his head. "It had to start sooner than that. You would have itched badly. Like a rash."

"A week ago."

He let her go. Poor girl. A week alone without anyone telling her anything. She would hurt by now. The pain and the weakness would be nearly intolerable.

"What is it?" Her voice was filled with fear.

Cullaene stared at her, then, as the full horror finally reached him. He had been prepared from birth for the Change, but Lucy thought she was human. And suddenly he looked out the window again at Jared. Jared, who had found the orphaned girl without even trying to discover anything about the type of life form he raised. Jared, who must have assumed that because the child looked human, she was human.

She was rubbing her wrist. The skin was already so loose that the pressure of his hand hadn't left a mark on it.

"It's normal," he said. "It's the Change. The first time—the first time can be painful, but I can help you through it."

The instant he said the words, he regretted them. If he helped her, he'd have to stay. He was about to contradict himself when the kitchen door clicked shut.

Mrs. Fielding looked at the spilled coffee, then at the humped skin on Lucy's arm. The older woman seemed frightened and vulnerable. She held out her hand to her daughter, but Lucy didn't move. "She's sick," Mrs. Fielding said.

"Sick?" Cullaene permitted himself a small ironic smile. These people didn't realize what they had done to Lucy. "How do you know? You've never experienced anything like this before, have you?"

Mrs. Fielding was flushed. "Have you?"

"Of course, I have. It's perfectly normal development in an adult Riiame."

"And you'd be able to help her?"

The hope in her voice mitigated some of his anger. He could probably trust Mrs. Fielding to keep his secret. She had no one else to turn to right now. ''I was able to help myself.''

''You're Riiame?'' she whispered. Suddenly, the color drained from her face. ''Oh, my God.''

Cullaene could feel a chill run through him. He'd made the wrong choice. Before he was able to stop her, she had pulled the porch door open. ''Jared!'' she called. ''Get in here right away! Colin—Colin says he's a Riiame!''

Cullaene froze. She couldn't be saying that. Not now. Not when her daughter was about to go through one of life's most painful experiences unprepared. Lucy needed him right now. Her mother couldn't help her, and neither could the other colonists. If they tried to stop the bleeding, it would kill her.

He had made his decision. He grabbed Lucy and swung her horizontally across his back, locking her body in position with his arms. She was kicking and pounding on his side. Mrs. Fielding started to scream. Cullaene let go of Lucy's legs for a moment, grabbed the doorknob, and let himself out into the hallway. Lucy had her feet braced against the floor, forcing him to drag her. He continued to move swiftly toward the front door. When he reached it, he yanked it open and ran into the cold morning air.

Lucy had almost worked herself free. He shifted her slightly against his back and managed to capture her knees again. The skin had broken where he touched her. She would leave a trail of blood.

The girl was so frightened that she wasn't even screaming. She hit him in the soft flesh of his side, then leaned over and bit him. The pain almost made him drop her. Suddenly, he spun around and tightened his grip on her.

''I'm trying to help you,'' he said. ''Now stop it.''

She stopped struggling and rested limply in his arms. Cullaene found himself hating the Fieldings. Didn't they know there would be questions? Perhaps they could explain the Change as a disease, but what would happen when her friends began to shrivel with age and she remained as young and lovely as she was now? Who would explain that to her?

He ran on a weaving path through the trees. If Jared was thinking, he would know where Cullaene was taking Lucy. But all Cullaene needed was time. Lucy was so near the Change now that it wouldn't take too long to help her through it. But if the others tried to stop it, no matter how good their intentions, they could kill or disfigure the girl.

Cullaene was sobbing air into his lungs. His chest burned. He hadn't run like this in a long time, and Lucy's extra weight was making the movements more difficult. As if the girl could read his thoughts, she began struggling again. She bent her knees and jammed them as hard as she could into his kidneys. He almost tripped, but managed to right himself just in time. The trees were beginning to thin up ahead, and he smelled the thick spice of the river. It would take the others a while to reach him. They couldn't get the truck in here. They would have to come by foot. Maybe he'd have enough time to help Lucy and to get away.

Cullaene broke into the clearing. Lucy gasped as she saw the ridge. He had to bring her here. She needed the spicy water—and the height. He thought he could hear someone following him now, and he prayed he would have enough time. He had so much to tell her. She had to know about the pigmentation changes, and the possibilities of retaining some skin. But most of all, she had to do what he told her, or she'd be deformed until the next Change, another ten years away.

He bent in half and lugged her up the ridge. The slope of the land was slight enough so that he kept his balance, but great enough to slow him down. He could feel Lucy's heart pounding against his back. The child thought he was going to kill her, and he didn't know how he would overcome that.

When he reached the top of the ridge, he stood, panting, looking over the caramel-colored water. He didn't dare release Lucy right away. They didn't have much time, and he had to explain what was happening to her.

She had stopped struggling. She gripped him as if she were determined to drag him with her when he flung her into the river. In the distance, he could hear faint shouts.

"Lucy, I brought you up here for a reason," he said. Her fingers dug deeper into his flesh. "You're going through what my people call the Change. It's normal. It—"

"I'm not one of your people," she said. "Put me down!"

He stared across the sluggish river into the trees beyond. Even though he had just begun, he felt defeated. The girl had been human for thirteen years. He couldn't alter that in fifteen minutes.

"No, you're not." He set her down, but kept a firm grasp of her wrists. Her sweater and skirt were covered with blood. "But you were born here. Have you ever seen this happen to anyone else?"

He grabbed a loose fold of skin and lifted it. There was a sucking release as the skin separated from the wall of blood. Lucy tried to pull away from him. He drew her closer. "Unfortunately, you believe you are human and so the first one to undergo this. I'm the only one who can help you. I'm a Riiame. This has happened to me."

"You don't look like a Riiame."

He held back a sharp retort. There was so much that she didn't know. Riiame were a shape-shifting people. Parents chose the form of their children at birth. His parents had had enough foresight to give him a human shape. Apparently, so had hers. But she had only seen the Abandoned Ones who retained the shape of the hunters that used to populate the planet's forests.

A cry echoed through the woods. Lucy looked toward it, but Cullaene shook her to get her attention again. "I am Riiame," he said. "Your father's friends claimed to have found a body here. But that body they found wasn't a body at all. It was my skin. I just went through the Change. I shed my skin just as you're going to. And then I came out to find work in your father's farm.''

''I don't believe you,'' she said.

''Lucy, you're bleeding through every pore in your body. Your skin is loose. You feel as if you're floating inside yourself. You panicked when you saw your form outlined in blood on the sheets this morning, didn't you? And your mother, she noticed it, too, didn't she?''

Lucy nodded.

''You have got to trust me because in a few hours the blood will go away, the skin you're wearing now will stick to the new skin beneath it, and you will be ugly and deformed. And in time, the old skin will start to rot. Do you want that to happen to you?''

A bloody tear made its way down Lucy's cheek. ''No,'' she whispered.

''All right then.'' Cullaene wouldn't let himself feel relief. He could hear unnatural rustlings coming from the woods. ''You're going to have to leave your clothes here. Then go to the edge of the ridge, reach your arms over your head to stretch the skin as much as you can, and jump into the river. It's safe, the river is very deep here. As soon as you can feel the cold water on every inch of your body, surface, go to shore, and wrap yourself in mud. That will prevent the itching from starting again.''

The fear on her face alarmed him. ''You mean I have to strip?''

He bit back his frustration. They didn't have time to work through human taboos. ''Yes. Or the old skin won't come off.''

Suddenly, he saw something flash in the woods below. It looked like the muzzle of a heat gun. Panic shot through him. Why was he risking his life to help this child? As soon as he emerged at the edge of the ridge, her father would kill him. Cullaene let go of Lucy's wrists. Let her run if she wanted to. He was not going to let himself get killed. Not yet.

But to his surprise, Lucy didn't run. She turned her back and slowly pulled her sweater over her head. Then she slid off the rest of her clothes and walked to the edge of the ridge. Cullaene knew she couldn't feel the cold right now. Her skin was too far away from the nerve endings.

She reached the edge of the ridge, her toes gripping the rock as tightly as her fingers had gripped his arm, and then she turned to look back at him. ''I can't,'' she whispered.

She was so close. Cullaene saw the blood working under the old skin, trying to separate all of it. ''You have to,'' he replied, keeping himself in shadow. ''Jump.''

Lucy looked down at the river below her, and a shiver ran through her body. She shook her head.

"Do—?" Cullaene stopped himself. If he went into the open, they'd kill him. Then he stared at Lucy for a moment, and felt his resolve waver. "Do you want me to help you?"

He could see the fear and helplessness mix on her face. She wasn't sure what he was going to do, but she wanted to believe him. Suddenly, she set her jaw with determination. "Yes," she said softly.

Cullaene's hands went cold. "All right. I'm going to do this quickly. I'll come up behind you and push you into the river. Point your toes and fall straight. The river is deep and it moves slow. You'll be all right."

Lucy nodded and looked straight ahead. The woods around them were unnaturally quiet. He hurried out of his cover and grabbed her waist, feeling the blood slide away from the pressure of his hands. He paused for a moment, knowing that Jared and his companions would not shoot while he held the girl.

"Point," he said, then pushed.

He could feel the air rush through his fingers as Lucy fell. Suddenly, a white heat blast stabbed his side, and he tumbled after her, whirling and flipping in the icy air. He landed on his stomach in the thick, cold water, knocking the wind out of his body. Cullaene knew that he should stay under and swim away from the banks, but he needed to breathe. He clawed his way to the surface, convinced he would die before he reached it. The fight seemed to take forever, and suddenly he was there, bobbing on top of the river, gasping air into his empty lungs.

Lucy's skin floated next to him, and he felt a moment of triumph before he saw Jared's heat gun leveled at him from the bank.

"Get out," the farmer said tightly. "Get out and tell me what you did with the rest of her before I lose my head altogether."

Cullaene could still go under and swim for it, but what would be the use? He wouldn't be able to change his pigmentation for another ten years or so, and if he managed to swim out of range of their heat guns, he would always be running.

With two long strokes, Cullaene swam to the bank and climbed out of the water. He shivered. It was cold, much too cold to be standing wet near the river. The spice aggravated his new skin's dryness.

Marlene, gun in hand, stood next to Jared, and the two other men were coming out of the woods.

"Where's the rest of her?" Jared asked. His arm was shaking. "On the ridge?"

Cullaene shook his head. He could have hit the gun from Jared's hand and run, but he couldn't stand to see the sadness, the defeat in the man who had befriended him.

"She'll be coming out of the water in a minute."

"You lie!" Jared screamed, and Cullaene saw with shock that the man had nearly snapped.

"No, she will." Cullaene hesitated for a moment. He didn't want to die to keep his people's secret. The Riiame always adapted. They'd adapt this time, too. "She's Riiame. You know that. This is normal for us."

"She's my daughter!"

"No, she's not. She can't be. This doesn't happen to humans."

A splash from the river bank drew his attention. Lucy pulled herself up alongside the water several feet from them. Her skin was fresh, pink and clean, and her bald head reflected patches of sunlight. She gathered herself into a fetal position and began to rock.

Cullaene started to go to her, but Jared grabbed him. Cullaene tried to shake his arm free, but Jared was too strong for him.

"She's not done yet," Cullaene said.

Marlene had come up beside them. "Let him go, Jared."

"He killed my daughter." Jared's grip tightened on Cullaene's arm.

"No, he didn't. She's right over there."

Jared didn't even look. "That's not my Lucy."

Cullaene swallowed hard. His heart was beating in his throat. He should have run when he had the chance. Now Jared was going to kill him.

"That is Lucy," Marlene said firmly. "Let him go, Jared. He has to help her."

Jared looked over at the girl rocking at the edge of the river bank. His hold loosened, and finally he let his hands drop. Cullaene took two steps backward and rubbed his arms. Relief was making him dizzy.

Marlene had put her arm around Jared as if she, too, didn't trust him. She was watching Cullaene to see what he'd do next. If he ran, she'd get the other two to stop him. Slowly, he turned away from them and went to Lucy's side.

"You need mud, Lucy," he said as he dragged her higher onto the bank. She let him roll her into a cocoon. When he was nearly through, he looked at the man behind him.

Jared had dropped his weapon and was staring at Lucy's skin as it made its way down the river. Marlene still clutched her gun, but her eyes were on Jared, not Cullaene.

"Is she Riiame?" Marlene asked Jared.

The farmer shook his head. "I thought she was human!" he said. Then he raised his voice as if he wanted Cullaene to hear. "I thought she was human!"

Cullaene took a handful of mud and started painting the skin on Lucy's face. She had closed her eyes and was lying very still. She would need time to recover from the shock.

"I thought they were going to kill her," Jared said brokenly. "There were two of them and she was so little and I thought they were going to kill her." His voice dropped. "So I killed them first."

Cullaene's fingers froze on Lucy's cheek. Jared had killed Lucy's parents because they didn't look human. Cullaene dipped his hands in more mud and continued working. He hoped they would let him leave when he finished.

He placed the last of the mud on the girl's face. Jared came up beside him. "You're Riiame too, aren't you? And you look human."

Cullaene washed the mud from his shaking hands. He was very frightened. What would he do now? Leave with Lucy, and try to teach the child that she wasn't human at all? He turned to face Jared. "What are you going to do with Lucy?"

"Will she be okay?" the farmer asked.

Cullaene stared at Jared for a moment. All the color had drained from the farmer's face, and he looked close to tears. Jared had finally realized what he had done.

"She should be," Cullaene said. "But someone has to explain this to her. It'll happen again. And there are other things."

He stopped, remembering his aborted love affair with a human woman. Ultimately, their forms had proven incompatible. He wasn't really human, although it was so easy to forget that. He only appeared human.

"Other things?"

"Difficult things." Cullaene shivered again. He would get ill from these wet clothes. "If you want, I'll take her with me. You won't have to deal with her then."

"No." Jared reached out to touch the mud-encased girl, but his hand hovered over her shell, never quite resting on it. "She's my daughter. I raised her. I can't just let her run off and disappear."

Cullaene swallowed heavily. He didn't understand these creatures. They killed Abandoned Ones on a whim, professed fear and hatred of the Riiame, and then would offer to keep one in their home.

"That was your skin that they found, wasn't it?" Jared asked. "This just happened to you."

Cullaene nodded. His muscles were tense. He wasn't sure what Jared was going to do.

"Why didn't you tell us?"

Cullaene looked at Jared for a moment. Because, he wanted to say, the woman I loved screamed and spat at me when she found out. Because one farmer nearly killed me with an axe. Because your people don't know how to cope with anything different, even when *they* are the aliens on a new planet.

"I didn't think you'd understand," he said. Suddenly, he grabbed Jared's hand and set it on the hardening mud covering Lucy's shoulder. Then he stood up. There had to be Abandoned Ones in these woods. He would find them if Jared didn't kill him first. He started to walk.

"Colin," Jared began, but Cullaene didn't stop. Marlene reached his side and grabbed him. Cullaene glared at her, but she didn't let go. He was too frightened to hit her, too frightened to try to break free. If she held him, maybe they weren't going to kill him after all.

She ripped open the side of Cullaene's shirt and examined the damage left by the heat blast. The skin was puckered and withered, and Cullaene suddenly realized how much it ached.

"Can we treat this?" she asked.

"Are you asking for permission?" Cullaene could barely keep the sarcasm from his voice.

"No." The woman looked down and blushed deeply as some humans did when their shame was fullest. "I was asking if we had the skill."

Cullaene relaxed enough to smile. "You have the skill."

"Then," she said. "May we treat you?"

Cullaene nodded. He allowed himself to be led back to Jared's side. Jared was staring at his daughter, letting tears fall onto the cocoon of mud.

"You can take her out of there soon," Cullaene said. "Her clothes are up on the ridge. I'll get them."

And before anyone could stop him, Cullaene went into the woods and started up the ridge. He could escape now. He could simply turn around and run away. But he wasn't sure he wanted to do that.

When he reached the top of the ridge, he peered down at Jared, his frightened daughter, and the woman who protected them. They had a lot of explaining to do to Lucy. But if she was strong enough to survive the Change, she was strong enough to survive anything.

Cullaene draped her bloody clothes over his arm and started back down the ridge. When he reached the others, he handed the clothes to Marlene. Then Cullaene crouched beside Jared. Carefully, Cullaene made a hole in the mud and began to peel it off Lucy. Jared watched him for a moment. Then, he slipped his fingers into a crack, and together the alien and the native freed the girl from her handmade shell.

D. ALEXANDER SMITH

Dying in Hull

D. Alexander Smith lives in Cambridge, Massachusetts, not far from the setting of "Dying in Hull," and is currently working as co-editor on a shared-world anthology of *Future Boston* stories. His novels include *Marathon, Rendezvous,* and, most recently, *Homecoming,* but the eloquent, bittersweet, and moving tale that follows is, annoyingly enough, his first short-story sale.

DYING IN HULL

D. Alexander Smith

In the wee hours of February 12, 2004, Ethel Goodwin Cobb clumped down the oak staircase to check the water level in her dining room. She always checked her floor when the sea was lowest, no matter whether ebb tide came during the day or, as this time, in the dark of night.

Moonlight from the window reflected on the empty hardwood floor, a pale milky rhombus. A thin glistening sheen of still water lay over the wood, bright and smooth like mirror glass.

Blinking sleepily, Ethel sat her chunky body on the next-to-bottom step and leaned forward to press her big square thumb down into the rectangular puddle. She felt the moisture and withdrew her now-wet hand. Water slid in to cover the briefly-bare spot, and in seconds, the surface was motionless and perfect, her mark gone.

She yawned and shook herself like a disgruntled dog.

Gunfire in the harbor had disturbed her rest; she had slept fitfully until the alarm had gone off. Well, she was awake now. Might as well start the day.

The rose-pattern wallpaper was rippled, discolored with many horizontal lines from rising high water marks. It was crusty at eye level but sodden and peeling where it met the floorboards. Above the waterline, Ethel had filled her dining room with photographs of the town of Hull—houses, streets, beaches, the rollercoaster at Paragon Park—and the people who had lived there. Pictures of the past, left behind in empty houses by those who had fled and forgotten.

Ethel carefully touched the floor again, licking her thumb afterwards to taste the brine. "Wet," she muttered. "No doubt about it." For a moment she hung her head, shoulders sagging, then slapped her palms against the tops of her knees. "That's that." She rose slowly and marched back upstairs to dress.

Cold air drafts whiffled through the loose window frames as she quickly donned her checked shirt, denim overalls, and wool socks. The sky outside was dark gray, with just a hint of dawn. Her bedroom walls were adorned with more photographs like those downstairs. As the water rose with the passing months and years, she periodically had to rearrange things, bringing pictures up from below and finding space in the bathroom, on the stairway, or in her makeshift second-floor kitchen.

Crossing to the white wooden mantelpiece, she hefted the letter. Ethel read what she had written, scowling at her spiky penmanship, then folded the paper twice, scoring the creases with her fingernail. She sealed it in an envelope, licked the stamp and affixed it with a thump. Returning to the bed, Ethel stuck the letter in her shirt pocket and pulled on her knee-high wellingtons.

By the time she descended again to the first floor, the tide had risen to cover the bottom step. Ethel waded over to her front door and put on her yellow slicker and her father's oilskin sou'wester, turning up the hat's front brim.

The door stuck, expanded by the moisture. She wrenched it open and stepped out, resolving to plane it again when she returned. Closing the door behind her, she snapped its cheap padlock shut.

Queequeg floated high and dry, tethered to the porch by lines from his bow and stern. Ethel unwrapped the olive-green tarpaulin from his motor and captain's console. When she boarded her boat, the white Boston whaler rocked briefly, settling deeper into the water that filled K Street. After checking the outboard's propeller to verify that no debris had fouled its blades, Ethel pushed *Queequeg*'s motor back to vertical, untied his painters, and poled away from her house.

She turned the ignition and the big ninety-horse Evinrude roared to life, churning water and smoke. Blowing on her hands to warm them, she eased *Queequeg*'s throttle forward and burbled east down K to the ruins of Beach Avenue.

Dawn burnished the horizon, illuminating the pewter-gray scattered clouds. Submerged K Street was a silver arrow that sparkled with a thousand moving diamonds. The air was bright with cold, tangy with the scents of kelp and mussels, the normally rough winter ocean calm now that last night's nor'easter had passed.

She stood at the tiller sniffing the breeze, her stocky feet planted wide against the possibility of *Queequeg* rolling with an ocean swell, her hands relaxed on the wheel. They headed north past a line of houses on their left, Ethel's eyes darting like a general inspecting the wounded after battle.

As the town of Hull sank, its houses had fallen to the Atlantic, singly or in whole streets. These windward oceanfronts, unshielded from the open sea, were the first to go. Black asphalt shingles had been torn from their roofs and walls by many storms. Porches sagged or collapsed entirely. Broken windows and doors were covered with Cambodian territorial chop signs of the Ngor, Pran, and Kim waterkid gangs. Some homes had been burned out, the soot rising from their empty windowframes like the petals of black flowers.

A girl's rusted blue motor scooter leaned against the front stairs of 172 Beach.

Barnacles grew on its handlebars. Mary Donovan and her parents had lived here, Ethel remembered, before she moved to downtown Boston and became an accountant. A good student who had earned one of Ethel's few A-pluses, Mary had ridden that scooter to high school every day, even in the snow, until the water had made riding impossible.

Beach Avenue had been vacant from end to end for years. Still, Ethel always began her day here. It was a reminder and a warning. Her tough brown eyes squinted grimly as the whaler chugged in the quiet, chill day.

"I could have told you folks," Ethel addressed the ghosts of the departed owners. "You don't stop the sea."

Sniffling—cold air made her nose run—she turned down P Street. For three hundred years her ancestors had skippered their small open boats into Hull's rocky coastal inlets, its soft marshy shallows, to harvest the sea. In the skeleton of a town, Ethel Cobb, the last in her family, lived on the ocean's bounty—even if it meant scavenging deserted homes.

Like 16 P just ahead. She throttled back and approached cautiously.

16 P's front door was open, all its lights out. The Cruzes have left, Ethel thought with regret. The last family on P Street. Gone.

Cautiously, she circled the building once to verify that no other combers were inside.

Decades of salt winds had silvered its cedar shingles. Foundation cracks rose like ivy vines up the sides of its cement half-basement. Sprung gutters hung loose like dangled fishing rods. She killed the steel-blue Evinrude and drifted silently toward the two-story frame house.

Luisa Cruz had been born in 16 P, Ethel remembered, in the middle of the Blizzard of '78, when Hull had been cut off from the mainland. A daydreamer, Luisa had sat in the fourth row and drawn deft caricatures of rock stars all over her essay questions.

So the Cruz family had moved, Ethel thought sadly. Another one gone. Were any left?

She looped *Queequeg*'s painter over the porch banister and splashed up 16 P's steps, towing a child's oversize sailboat behind her. The front door had rusted open and Ethel went inside.

Empty soda and beer squeezebottles floated in the foyer, and there was a vaguely disturbing smell. Ethel slogged through soggy newspapers to the kitchen. Maria Cruz had made tea in this kitchen, she recalled, while they had talked about Luisa's chances of getting into Brandeis.

An ancient refrigerator stood in a foot and a half of water. She dragged the door open with a wet creak. Nothing.

The pantry beyond yielded a box of moist taco shells and three cans of tomato paste. Ethel checked the expiration dates, nodded, and tossed them into her makeshift barrow.

What little furniture remained in the living room was rotten and mildewed. The bedroom mattress was green-furred and stank. The bureau's mahogany veneer had curled away from the expanding maple underneath. When Ethel leaned her arm on the dresser, a lion's-claw foot broke. It collapsed slowly into the sawdust-flecked water like an expiring walrus.

Out fell a discolored Polaroid snapshot: Luisa and her brother in graduation cap and gown. I was so proud of her I could have burst, Ethel remembered. Drying the photo carefully, she slipped it into her breast pocket.

On an adjacent high shelf, built into the wall above the attached headboard, were half a dozen paperback books, spines frayed and twisted, their covers scalped. Luisa had been a good reader, a child who wanted to learn so much it had radiated from her like heat.

Pleased, Ethel took them all.

In the bathroom, she found a mirror embossed with the Budweiser logo. With her elbow, Ethel cleaned the glass. The round wrinkled face that grinned back at her had fueled rumors that she had been a marine. The mirror would probably fetch a few dollars at the flea market, maybe more to a memorabilia collector.

Only the front bedroom left to comb, she thought. Good combing. Thank you, Cruz family.

A vulture, Joan Gordon had called her once. "You're just a vulture, eating decay," her friend had said, with the certainty of a mainlander.

"I'm a Cobb," Ethel had answered thickly, gripping the phone. "We live on the sea. My grandfather Daniel Goodwin was lobstering when he was nine."

"What you're doing isn't fishing. It's theft. Just like the waterkids."

"It's *not* like the kids!" Ethel had shouted.

"It's *stealing*," Joan had challenged her.

"No! Just taking what the sea gives. Housecombing is like lobstering." She had clung to her own words for reassurance.

"What you take belongs to other people," her friend had said vehemently.

"Not after they leave," Ethel shot back. "Then it's the ocean's."

Joan switched tacks. "It's dangerous to live in Hull."

"Those folks that left didn't have to go. I'm staying where my roots are."

"Your roots are *underwater*, Ethel!" Joan entreated. "Your town is disappearing."

"It is not," Ethel insisted. "Don't say that."

"Come live in our building. We have a community here."

"Bunch of old folks. Don't want to live with old folks."

"Plenty of people here younger than you."

"Living in a tower's not for me. Closed in, a prisoner. Afraid to go out. Wouldn't like it."

"How do you know? You've never visited me."

"Anyhow, I can't afford it."

She seldom spoke with Joan now. The subject had worn her feelings raw.

"Damn it, Joan," she said in 16 P's hallway, "why did you have to leave?"

The front bedroom door was ajar in a foot and a half of water. She pushed and heard it butt against something. Slowly she craned her neck around.

The two oriental corpses floated on their faces, backs arched, arms and legs hanging down into brown water swirled with red. Ethel gagged at the stench. The youths' long black hair waved like seaweed, their shoulders rocking limply. Catfish and eels nibbled on waving tendrils of human skin and guts.

Retching, Ethel grabbed one of the boys under his armpit and hauled him over onto his back. The bodies had been gutted, bullets gouged out of their chests, leaving no evidence. Periwinkle snails crawled in bloody sockets where the killers had cut out their victims' eyes and sliced off their lips. Each youth's left hand had been amputated. Ethel searched the water until she found one, a bloated white starfish with a Pran gang tattoo on its palm.

She remembered last night's gunshots in Hull Bay. You did not deserve this, she thought to the ruined face, letting it slip back into the water. No one deserved this, not even waterkids.

Of course she knew who did it. Everyone knew who executed waterkids. That was the point. The men on Hog Island *wanted* you to know. They wanted Hull to themselves. The bodies were reminders. And incentive.

In the distance she heard the chatter of several approaching engines. More Cambodian waterkids coming. Hastily she wiped vomit from her mouth and rushed out of the house.

Jumping into the whaler, she untied *Queequeg*'s painter and turned his key, shoving the throttle down hard as his engine caught. But not quickly enough. Before she could get away, four dark gray whalers surrounded her, Pran gang chop signs airbrushed beautifully onto their fiberglass gunwales.

"Hey, grandma." Their leader stood cockily in the stern of his boat while his helmsman grinned. He wore immaculate brown leather pants and a World War II flight jacket, unmarked by spray or moisture. "What's your hurry? Seen a ghost?"

Queequeg rocked slightly as the waves from their sudden arrival washed underneath him. "Yes," Ethel answered.

"Find anything valuable?"

"Nothing you'd want." Unconsciously she touched her breast pocket. "Nothing you can fence."

"Really? Let's see." His boat drifted up against hers and he leaped across into her stern, landing on sure sea legs. "You keep your stuff here?" he scornfully pointed at the plastic sailboat, mugging for his guffawing friends. He kicked it over with his boot and rummaged around among the floorboards. "Hey, Wayne! Huang! We got any use for taco shells?" He held them aloft.

"No, man," they answered gleefully.

"All right, grandma, guess we'll have to look elsewhere." He dropped the box and turned. As she started to relax, he wheeled. "What's in your pocket?"

"I beg your pardon?"

"In your pocket," he snapped.

"A letter and a photograph," she said steadily.

"A naked man, maybe?" the Pran leader chortled. "Let's see it." She opened her sou'wester and handed the picture to him. Waving it like a small fan, he stepped back into his own boat. "Worthless." He pointed it at her like a prod. "Pran gang combs *first*, grandma. Understand? Otherwise the next time I won't just tip over your toy boat. You understand?" He tossed the photo over his shoulder.

Ethel watched it flutter down onto the water, and nodded. "I understand."

He gestured and they started their engines, moving down P Street toward the empty house.

Ethel debated with herself. Keeping silent was too risky—they could always find her later. "Check the front bedroom," she called after them.

He stopped the engine and swung back. "What?" he asked ominously.

"Check the front bedroom. Your two missing friends are there."

The Cambodian teenager's broad face whitened. "Dead?"

She nodded mutely.

"Those bastards," he said softly.

"I'm sorry." She clasped her hands before her.

"*Sorry*?" he shrieked in misery, the hurt child suddenly breaking through his tough façade. "What do you know about sorry?" Their boats leapt away. "What do *you* know about sorry?"

As the sounds of their engines receded, Ethel slowly let out her breath. Hands trembling, she engaged *Queequeg*'s throttle and slowly circled. Sure enough, the snapshot was suspended about three feet below the surface. Ethel lifted her gaffing net and dragged it by the spot, scooping up the picture. The water had curled it and she dried it on her thigh, then returned it to her pocket.

Glancing back at the boats now moored at 16 P, she quickly cut in the whaler's engine with a roar, carving a double white plume behind her.

For the rest of the morning Ethel and *Queequeg* combed the alphabet streets on Hull's submerged flatlands. Nearly all of these houses had long since been abandoned, and she neither stopped nor slowed. Frequently she twisted to check behind her, but there was no sign of the waterkids.

By eleven she had finished W, X, and Y, tiny alleyways that butted against Allerton Hill. Trees at its base were gray and leafless, drowned by the rising seawater. Terry Flaherty had lived on W, she remembered. A short chubby boy with big eyes and a giggle that never stopped, he was someplace in Connecticut now, selling mutual funds. Probably forgotten all the eleventh-grade American history she'd taught him.

As she passed Allerton Point, she looked across the harbor to glass-and-steel Boston. The downtown folks were talking about building walls to hold back the sea that rose as the city sank, but with no money, Hull literally could not afford to save itself. Every storm took more houses, washing out the ground underneath so they fell like sandcastles.

Ethel's house at 22 K was on the far leeward side, as safe as you could be on the flatland, but even it had suffered damage and was endangered.

Town government was disintegrating. People no longer paid property taxes, no longer voted. Nobody ran for selectman, nobody cared. For protection, folks relied on themselves or bought it from Hog Island or the Cambodian waterkids. At night, the long black peterborough boats moved sleekly in the harbor, navigating by infrared. Ethel stayed inside then.

Most of Hull High School was submerged, the brick portico columns standing like piers in the shallow water. The football field was a mudflat.

Forty-one years of history students, all gone, all memories.

When she was young, her students had sniggered that Ethel was a dyke. As she aged, firmly single and unromantic, they had claimed she was a transsexual wrestler. When she reached fifty, they had started saying she was eccentric. At sixty, they had called her crazy.

The jibes always hurt, though she concealed it. After each year was over, fortunately, all she could remember were the names and faces of those whose lives she had affected.

Standing at *Queequeg*'s bow, she left a long scimitar of foam as she circled the buildings. The old school was disappearing, windows shattered, corridors full of stagnant water. She had taken *Queequeg* inside once before to her old classroom, but was eventually driven out by the reek of decomposing flesh from a cat that had been trapped inside and starved.

Ethel closed her eyes, hearing once again the clatter of the period bell, the clamor as kids ran through the corridors, talking at the top of their lungs. Mothers whom she taught had sent their daughters to Hull High School. In her last few years, she had even taught a few granddaughters of former students. Made you proud.

The high school was shut down, dark, and noiseless. Seagulls perched on its roof were her only companions.

To break her mood, she swung onto the open sea and opened the throttle for the five-mile run to South Boston.

The water, hard as a rock this morning, pounded into her calves and knees as the Boston whaler's flat bottom washboarded across the harbor. *Queequeg* kicked up spray over his teak and chrome bow as she slalomed among dayglo styrofoam lobster buoys, tasting the salt spume on her lips.

Behind and above her, a cawing flock of gulls followed, braiding the air. *Queequeg*'s wake pushed small fish close to the surface, under the sharp eyes of the waiting gray and white birds. One after another, the gulls swooped like a line of fighter aircraft. Their flapping wings skimming the waves, they dipped their beaks just enough to catch a fish, then soared back into line.

Hunting and feeding, they escorted her across the harbor until she slowed and docked at the pier.

"Hey, Jerry," Ethel said when she entered the store. "Got a letter for you." She unzipped her slicker and pulled it out. "Mail it for me?"

The storekeeper squinted at the address. "Joan Gordon? Doesn't she live in that senior citizen community in Arlington?"

"Old folks home, you mean."

"Whatever." He suppressed a smile. "You could call her."

"Got no phone."

"No, from here."

"Rather write."

"Okay. What are you writing about?"

Ethel shook her head. "None of your beeswax."

"All right," he laughed, "we've been friends too long for me to complain. How you doing?"

"I get by."

He leaned on the counter. "I worry about you."

"Oh, don't start."

"Sorry." He turned away and began rearranging cans.

"I'm okay," she answered, touched as always.

"Hull gets worse every day." He looked at her over his shoulder. "I see the news."

"Nonsense," Ethel replied with bravado, dismissing his fears with a wave of her hand. "Journalists always exaggerate. Besides, one day *Boston* will be underwater too, same as us."

"I know." Jerry sighed. "I go down to the bathhouse every Sunday for my swim. The sea's always higher. Maybe we should move away, like Joan did. Chicago or Dallas. Somewhere. Anywhere with no ocean."

She laughed. "What would I do in Dallas, Jerry? How would I live?"

"You could teach school. You've taught me more right here in this store than all the history books I ever read."

"Thanks, Jerry. But I'm sixty-eight years old. No one would hire me."

He was quiet. "Then I'd take care of you," he said finally, kneading his hands.

She looked through the window at the pier, where *Queequeg* bobbed on the waves. "Couldn't do it, Jerry," she said. It was hard to find breath. "Too old to move."

"Yeah. Sure." He wiped his forehead and cleared his throat. "Got your usual all set." He put two orange plastic bags on the counter.

"Did my check come through?" Ethel looked suspicious. "Can't take your credit."

"Of course it did. It always comes through. It's electronic."

She peered inside, shifting cans and boxes. "All right, where is it?"

He scowled and rubbed his balding head. "Hell, you shouldn't eat that stuff. Rots your teeth and wrecks your digestion and I don't *know* what."

"I want my two-pound box of Whitman's coconut, dammit."

"Ethel, you're carrying too much weight. It'll strain your heart."

"Been eating candy all my life, and it hasn't hurt me yet. Wish you'd stop trying to dictate my diet."

"Okay, okay." He sighed and threw up his hands, then pulled down the embossed yellow box. "No charge." He held it out.

"Can't accept your charity, Jerry. You know that."

"That's not it." He was hurt and offended. "It's my way of saying I'm sorry I tried to keep it away from you." He gestured with the box. "Please?"

Ethel took the chocolates. "Thank you, Jerry," she replied somberly, laying her right hand flat on the cover. "You've been a good friend."

"Don't talk like that!" the grocer said in exasperation. "Every time you come in here, you sound like you got one foot in the grave. It's not wholesome."

"Was different this morning." Ethel sat down, the candy held tightly in her lap. Her voice was faint, distant. "This morning I *saw* it. Saw my future in the water. Sooner or later, I'm going to pass away. No sense denying that." She kicked her right foot aimlessly. "Maybe I should have accepted when you proposed."

"Still could," he said, wistful. "But you won't."

"No." She shook her head just a bit.

"Stubborn."

"Not stubborn." She was gentle. "Wouldn't be fair. You can't live in Hull. You've said so before."

"Ethel." Jerry wiped his hands on his apron. "I read the paper. Houses are falling into the ocean or burning down. Dangerous evil kids are running loose."

"I can handle the waterkids," she said defiantly.

"No, you *can't*," he insisted. "Drugs and crime and I don't *know* what. Why won't you leave?"

"It's my home," Ethel said in a troubled voice. "My family. Friends." She waved her hands. "My world. What I know."

Jerry rubbed his head again. "That world isn't *there* any more. The people you knew—they're all gone. It's past. Over."

"Got no place to go," she muttered, biting her thumbnail. "Cobbs and Goodwins have lived in Hull since colonial times. That's something to preserve. Elijah Goodwin was a merchant captain. Sailed to China in 1820. Put flowers on his grave every Sunday noon after church. Rain or shine or Cambodian kids. Put flowers on all the Cobbs and Goodwins on Telegraph Hill. Telegraph's an island now, but they will still be in that ground when all the flatland has gone under. Somebody has to remember them."

"Cripes, don't be so morbid." He came around behind her, put his arm around her shoulder and rubbed it.

"I suppose." She leaned her head in the crook of his elbow.

Cars and buses passed in the street outside, sunlight reflecting off their windshields. He patted her shoulder.

She covered his hand with hers. "Thanks, Jerry. You're a good man."

After a moment, she rose and kissed his cheek, then hefted the bags, one to an arm. "Well, that's that," she called with returning jauntiness. "See you next Friday."

Lost in memories, she let *Queequeg* take his return trip more slowly. Islands in the harbor were covered with trees and shrubs, reminding her of great submerged whales. When she neared Hog Island, at the entrance to Hull Bay, she kept a respectful distance. The Meagher boys had lived there—Dennis, Douglas, Dana, Donald, and Dapper. Their mother had always shouted for them in the order of their birth. Five rambunctious Boston-Irish hellions in seven years, usually with a black eye or a skinned knee.

No families lived on Hog now. Castellated gray buildings had grown upward from the old Army fortress underneath. Thieves and smugglers and murderers lived in them, men who drove deep-keeled power yachts without finesse, like machetes through a forest.

Tough sentries carrying binoculars stood lookout as she passed, scanning the horizon like big-eyed insects, their rifles out of sight. Ethel shivered. Delinquent waterkids she could evade, but the organized evil on Hog was shrewd and ruthless.

The fish feeding on that poor child's face, Ethel thought. The people who still lived on Hull. The men on Hog. The Cambodian kids. One way or another, all took their livelihoods from the remains of a town whose time was past. Eventually they would extract Hull's last dollar, and they would all leave. And, in time, the rising sea would engulf everything.

K Street was falling into shadow when she returned. Her house needed a coat of paint, but would last long enough without one, she thought wryly. The dark-green first-floor shutters were closed and nailed shut as a precaution, but her light was still burning in 22 K's bedroom window. Always leave a light on, so everyone knows you're still on guard.

A gang symbol was sprayed on her front door.

Pran chop, she realized with a sick feeling in her gut, remembering the morning's encounter.

Her padlock was untouched, though the waterkids could have easily forced it.

The chop was a message: this is a Pran house.

Perhaps their form of thanks.

safely inside, Ethel took off her sou'wester and slicker, shook the wet salt spray off them, and hung them on the pegs. She unloaded her groceries and stacked her day's combings. Tomorrow she would sell them in the Quincy flea market.

All but the photo. Ethel took it from her pocket and smiled at Luisa's young face. She found a spot on the wall barely large enough and tacked it up, stepping back to admire her work.

As the sun set on the golden bay, she made supper: soup, salad, and cheese sandwiches that she grilled on the woodburning stove she had installed on the second floor. Seagulls wheeled over the marsh flats, snatching clams in their beaks. Rising high over the coastline, the birds dropped their prey to smash open on the wet shoreline rocks. Then the gulls landed and ate the helpless, exposed animal inside the broken shell.

When she was done, Ethel went onto the upper porch and put down her bowl and plate. The birds converged, jostling for the last scraps, hungry and intense, like schoolchildren in gray and white uniforms.

Sitting in her rocking chair, her box of Whitman's coconut firmly on her stomach, Ethel thought about the letter she had mailed that morning.

Today the ocean took my ground floor. One day it will take my house. It's going to reclaim South Boston and Dorchester and Back Bay. Folks will go on denying it like I've tried to, but it won't stop until it's through with all of us.

Enclosed is my will. Had a Cohasset lawyer write it up so it's legal. You get everything. You don't have to comb for it, Joan. It's yours.

Except *Queequeg*. The boat goes to Jerry. He'll never use it, but he'll care for it, and it's no use to you in your tower.

After I'm gone, burn the place down. With me in it. At high tide so the fire won't spread. Nobody will bother you. Nobody else lives around here anyway. No one else has lived here for years.

22 K is a Cobb house. Always been a Cobb house. No squatters here. Give it all to the sea.

But take the pictures first. Put them on your walls. Remember me. Remember me.

Should have left years ago. Can't now.

Wish you'd stayed, Joan. Miss you.

Ethel

The houses around her were black hulks, silent like trees. The crescent moon rose, silvering the ocean. Ethel heard the gulls call to one another, smelled the sea as it licked the beach. In the distance, boats moved on the bay, dots of green and red light, thin black lines of wake.

"God, I love it here," she said suddenly, full of contentment.

KATHE KOJA

Distances

Here's an unsettling study of the kind of sacrifices that must sometimes be made if you're going to bridge the immense distances of time and space . . . and death.

This was Kathe Koja's second sale, and she is already receiving attention as one of the most exciting new writers around. She has subsequently made several more sales to *Isaac Asimov's Science Fiction Magazine*. She lives in Willowbrook, Illinois.

DISTANCES

Kathe Koja

Michael, naked on the table, hospital reek curling down his throat, the base of his skull rich with the ache it has had every day since the first one, will probably never lose. He remembers that day: parts of him stone-numb, other parts prickling and alive; moving to make sure he still could; exhilaration; and the sense of the jacks. They had said he would not, physically could not, feel the implants. Wrong—needle-slim, they seemed like pylons, silver pillars underskin.

He is tall, under the straps; his feet are cold. Three months' postsurgery growth of yellow hair, already curling. Grey eyes' glance roams the ceiling, bare peripherals.

He shifts, a little; the attendant gives him a faraway scowl. The old familiar strap-in: immobilize the head, check CNS response, check for fluid leak, check check check. "I am *fine*," he growls, chin strap digging into his jawline, "just fucking fine," but the attendant, rhino-sized, silent, ignores him entirely.

The ceiling monitor lights, bright and unexpected. Now what?

A woman, dark hair, wide mouth, cheekbones like a cat's, white baggy labcoat shoulders. "Hi," she says. "Doing all right?"

"Just ducky," tightmouthed, tin man with rusted jaw. Don't tell me, he thinks, more tests. "Who're you? A doctor?"

She appears to find this pretty funny. "Not hardly. I'm your handler. My name's Halloran." Something offscreen causes that wide mouth to turn down, impatient curvature. "I'll be in in a couple of minutes, we've got a meeting— Yeah I *heard* you!" and the screen blanks.

Check-up over, Michael rubs the spots where the straps were. "Excuse me," he says to the attendant. "That woman who was just onscreen—you know her?"

"Yeah, I know her." The attendant seems affronted. "She's a real bitch."

That charcoal drawl, bass whisper from babyface: "Oh good. I hate synthetics."

* * *

"So who's he? General Custer?"

Halloran beside him, scent of contraband chocolate mints, slipping him handfuls. They are part of a ten-pair group in an egg-shaped conference room, white jacket and bald head droning away in accentless medspeak at the chopped-down podium. The air is ripe with dedication.

"That's Bruce, Dr. Bruce, the director. You're supposed to be listening to this."

"I am. Just not continuously."

Dreamy genius meets genius-dreamer. Bad kids in the back of the class, jokes and deadpan, catching on faster than anyone anyway. NASA'd done its profile work magnificently this time: the minute of physical meeting told them that, told them also that, if it was engineered (and it was), so what: it's great. Maybe all the other pairs feel the same. That's the goal, anyway. NASA believes there must be something better than a working relationship between handler and glasshead, more than a merely professional bond.

"He always snort like that when he talks?"

"You should hear him when he's not talking."

Dr. Bruce: ". . . bidirectional. The sealed fiber interface, or SFI, affords us—"

"Glass fibers for glass heads."

"Beats an extension cord."

Her hair is a year longer than his, but looking in the mirror would show Michael the back of her skull: it's his. Handlers are first-generation glassheads, just technically imperfect enough to warrant a new improved version—but hey, don't feel bad, you're still useful. We can put you to work training your successors, the ones who'll fly where you can never go; train them to do what you want to; brutally practical demonstration of the Those Who Can't principle. But who better to handle a glasshead but a glasshead?

". . . which by now I'm sure you're all used to." Dr. Bruce again. "But these are extremely important tests. We'll be using the results to determine your final project placement. I know Project Arrowhead is the plum assignment, but the others are valuable, very much so, if not as strictly 'glamorous.' " He says it that way, quotes and all, into a room that suddenly stinks of raw tension. "Handlers, you'll be final-prepping the tandem quarters. Also there's a meeting at 1700. Subjects—"

"That's you," sucking on a mint. Hint of chocolate on those wide lips.

"Actually I'm more of an object."

"—under supervisory care for the balance of the day. Everyone, please remember and observe the security regulations."

"No shootouts in the hallways, huh?"

"No. But don't worry." Halloran gives him a sideways look. "We'll figure out a way to have fun."

*   *   *

Arrowhead: inhouse they call it "Voyager's big brother." Far, far away: Proxima Centauri. The big news came from the van de Kamp lunar telescope, where the results of new proper motion studies confirmed what everyone had, happily, suspected: bedrock evidence of at least three planets. At *least*. The possibility of others, and the complexity of their facefirst exploration, precluded the use of even the most sophisticated AI probe. Build new ones, right? No. Something better.

Thus Arrowhead. And glasshead tech gives it eyes and ears, with almost zero lagtime. This last is accomplished by beaucoup-FTL comlink: two big tin cans on a tachyon string. The tech itself was diplomatically extorted from the Japanese, who nearly twelve years before had helped to construct and launch the machine half of Arrowhead, engineered to interface with a human component that did not yet exist, and proved far more difficult to develop.

At last: the glassheads. Manned exploration without live-body risk and inherent baggage. Data absorbed by the lucky subject through thinnest fibers, jacked from receiving port into said subject's brain. The void as seen by human eyes.

Who wanted a humdrum assignment like sneaking spysat, or making tanks squaredance, when you could ride Arrowhead and be Cortez?

"Hey. State of the art barracks." Michael takes a slow self-conscious seat on the aggressively new, orthopedically sound bed. "Kinda makes you glad this isn't the bad old days, when NASA got the shitty end of every stick."

"Oh yeah, they thought of everything but good taste." Halloran's voice is exquisitely tired. She settles on the other side of the bed, one foot up, one dangling, and talks—inevitably—of Arrowhead. As she speaks her face shifts and changes play across the mobile muscles, taut stalks of bone. She could be a woman talking of her lover, explaining to a stranger. One hand rubs the back of her neck, erratic rhythm.

"It was so *nuts*," that first group. "Everybody just out for blood. Especially me and Ferrante." Paranoia, envy, round-the-clock jockeying, rumors of sabotage and doctored scores. "Everybody in high-gear bastard twenty-four hours a day. It was all I could think of. I'd wake up in the middle of the night, my heart's going a mile a minute, thinking, Did Bruce see my scores today, really *see* them? I mean does he know I'm the only one who can *do* this?" Her hands stray from neck to hair, weave and twist among the dark locks. Her want shines like a lamp.

"You got it, didn't you." It's no question, and she knows it.

"Yeah, I got it. That's how they found out the tech wasn't up to spec." Her voice is absolutely level. "Fucked up, you know, in a simulator. When they told me I'd never be able to go, in any capacity—and I thought of them all, believe me—when they told me, I wanted to just cut out the jacks and die." She says this without self-pity, without the faintest taint of melodrama, as if it is the only natural thing to want under the circumstances. "Then they told me about Plan B. Which is you."

"And so you stayed."

"And so I stayed."

Quiet. The sonorous hum of air, recirculating. Low nimbus of greenish light around Michael's head, his glance down, almost shy, trying to see those days, knowing her pain too well to imagine it. Halloran's hand grabs at her neck; he knows it aches.

"You better not fuck me up, Michael."

"I won't."

"I know."

Silence. Where another would retreat, he pushes forward. "Know what I was doing, when they called me? When they told me I made the cut?"

"What?" Her hands leave her neck, clasp, unclasp, settle like skittish birds. "What were you doing?"

"Singing," promptly, grinning, delighted with the memory. "It was late, they were trying to find me all day and I didn't know it. I was sure I hadn't made it and I was sad, and pissed, so I went down to the bar and started drinking, and by midnight I was up onstage. And at twenty after one—I'll never forget it— this guy comes up to me and says, Hey Michael, some guy from NASA's on the phone, he wants to talk to you. And I knew it! And you know what else?" He leans forward, not noticing then that she loves this story almost as much as he does, not surprised that a comparative stranger can share this glee so fully. "I'd been drinkin' all night, right, and I should've been drunk, but I wasn't. Not till he called." He laughs, still floored, having the joy of it all over again. "I was so drunk when I talked to him, I thought Boy you must sound like a real *ripe* asshole, boy, but I was so happy I didn't give a shit." He laughs again. "I hung up and went back onstage and sang like a son of a bitch till four thirty in the morning, and then I got some eggs and grits and got on the plane for Atlanta."

She puts up an eyebrow. "What's the name of the band?"

"Chronic Six. Chronics one through five busted up." It is the perfect question, and nobody's surprised, or surprised that they're not.

Early days: the pairs, teams as Bruce calls them, solidify. Very little talk between them, and all of it polite. Scrupulous. The glassheads-turned-handlers are avid to better last time's run: they sniff the way old packmates will, hunt weaknesses and soft spots, watch around the clock. The ones they want most are Halloran and her smartass protegé; the Two-Headed Monster; the self-proclaimed Team Chronic.

Too-loud music from their quarters, morning ritual of killer coffee drunk only from twin black handleless mugs, labcoats sleeve-slashed and mutilated, "Team

Chronic'' in black laundry marker across the back, chocolate mints and slogans and mystic aggression, attitude with a capital A. Her snap and his drawl, her detail-stare and his big-picture sprawl, their way of finishing each other's sentences, of knowing as if by eyeless instinct what the other will do. Above all, their way of winning. And winning.

"Everybody hates us," Halloran at meal break, murmuring behind a crust of lunch. "They hated me, too, before."

Michael shrugs with vast satisfaction. "All the world hates a winner."

"*And*," smiling now, coffee steam fragrant around bright eyes, "they can't even scream teacher's pet, because Bruce hates us too."

"Bruce doesn't hate us. He loathes us."

They're laughing this over when: "Halloran." White hand on her shoulder, faint smell of mustard: Ferrante. Old foe, pudgy in immaculate whites, handsome heavy face bare with anger. Behind him, standing like a duelist's second, Ruthann Duvall, his glasshead, her expression aping his. The whole cafeteria is watching.

"I want to talk to you, Halloran."

"Feel free. I've had all my shots."

"Shots is right," Ferrante says. He is obviously on the verge of some kind of fury-fit. "You're *enhanced*," meaning chemically enhanced, meaning illegally doctored; no Inquisitor could have denounced her with more élan. Everyone leans forward, spectators around the cockfight pit. "I'd think that even you would recognize that you're disrupting the integrity of the whole project, but that's never mattered to you, has it? *Or*," sparing, then, a look for Michael, who sits finger-linked and mild, looking up at Ferrante with what appears to be innocent interest, "your foul-mouthed shadow."

Halloran, cocked head, voice sweet with insult: "Oh, I know the species of bug that's up *your* ass—you're stuck in second best and you can't figure out why. Well, let me make it crystal for you, slim: you suck."

"What if I go to Dr. Bruce and ask for a chem scan?"

"What if I jack you into the sanitation system, you big piece of shit?"

His fat white hand clops on her shoulder, shoving her so she slews into Michael and both nearly topple. Immediately she is on her feet, on the attack, pursuing, slapping, driving him towards the cafeteria door. Michael, beside her, grabs the avenging arms: "Let him go, the son of a bitch," and indeed Ferrante takes almost indecent advantage of the moment, leaves, with Ruthann Duvall—contemptuously shaking her still-nearly-bald head—following, muttering, in her mentor's wake.

"Fuck you too, tennis ball head!" Halloran yells, then notices a strange sound coming from Michael: the grunt of suppressed laughter. It's too much, it blows out of him, hands on thighs and bent over with hilarity, and somebody else joins and somebody else too and finally the whole room is laughing. Even Halloran, who is first to stop.

"Let's go," she says.

Michael rubs helplessly at his eyes. "Tennis ball head!" He can't stop laughing.

Third week. Long, long day. In their quarters, blast music on, Michael bare-chested on the floor, Halloran rubbing her neck, the muscles thick and painful. Michael watches her, the sore motions.

"Do your jacks ever hurt?"

"*No!*"

"Mine do. All the time."

"No they *don't!* They're not supposed to!"

He raises his brows at her vehemence, waits.

"All right," she says at last, "you're right. They hurt. But I thought it was because I'm—you know. Defective." Fiercely: "*You're* not defective. It must just be phantom pain."

"A phantom pain in the ass." He sits up, pushes her hands away, begins to massage her hunched shoulders. "Listen, Halloran." His hands are very strong. "There isn't anything wrong with me. Got that? Nothing. So relax." He squeezes, harder and harder, forcing the muscles to give.

"So," squeezing, "when do we jack?"

"We've been jacking all damn day."

"I mean together."

"I don't know." Pleasure in her voice, the pain lessening. "That's up to Bruce, he does all the scheduling."

"The hell with Bruce. Let's do it now."

"*What?*" Even she, rebel, has not considered this. "We can't," already wondering why not, really—if they can jack into the computer—"It's never been done, that I know of, not so early."

"Now we *really* have to." He's already on his feet, making for his labcoat, taking from the inner breast pocket a two-meter length of fiber, cased in protective cord, swings it gently jackend like a pendulum at Halloran, a magic tool, you are getting verrrrry sleeeepy. "Come on," he says. "Just for fun."

There is no resisting. "All right," she says. "Just wait a minute." There's a little timer on her wall desk; she sets it for ten minutes. "When this times out, so do we. Agreed?"

"Sure thing." He's already plugged in, conjurer's hands, quicker than her eye. He reaches up to guide her down. "Ready?"

"Yeah."

They've jacked in simulation, to prepare; it is, now, the difference between seeing the ocean and swimming, seeing food and eating. They are swamped with it, carried, tumbled, at the moment of mutual entry eyes flash wide, twinned, seeing, knowing, hot with it, incredible

Michael it's *strong* stronger than I thought it would
know I know great *look* at this
and faster than belief thoughts and images burst between them, claiming them,
devouring them as they devour, all of each shown to the other without edit or
exception, all of it running the link, the living line, a knowing vaster than any
other, unthinkably complex, here, now, us, look look see *this*, without any words;
they dance the long corridors of memory, and pain, and sorrow, see old fears,
old joys, dead dreams, new happinesses bright as silver streamers, nuance of
being direct and pure, sledgehammer in the blood, going on forever, profound
communion and

finally it is Halloran who pulls back, draws them out, whose caution wakes
enough to warn that time is over. They unplug simultaneously, mutual shudder
of disunity, a chill of spirit strong enough to pain. They sit back, stunned; the
real world is too flat after such a dimensionless feast.

Words are less than useless. In silence is comfort, the knowing—*knowing*—
that one lives who knows you beyond intimacy; two souls, strung hard, adrift on
the peculiar fear of the proud, the fear of being forced to go naked in terrible
weakness and distress, and finding here the fear is toothless, that knowing and
being utterly known could be, is, not exposure but safety, the doctrine of ultimate
trust made perfect by glasshead tech.

They move into each other's arms, still not speaking.

Tears are running down Michael's face; his eyes are closed.

Halloran's hands are ice-cold on his wrists.

"We've been jacked all night," she says, "it's almost morning."

She can feel his body shaking, gently, the slow regular hitching of his chest.
She has never loved anyone so much in all her life.

Is it chance, rogue coincidence, that the next day Bruce schedules a dual jack,
a climatizer as he calls it? Between them, there is much secret hilarity, expressed
in a smile here, a less-than-gesture there, and when they do dual, for real and on
the record, they swoop and march in flawless tandem, working as one; the sim-
ulated tasks are almost ridiculously simple to complete, and perfectly.

Bruce still loathes them, but is undeniably impressed. "There's something
about them," he tells a subordinate, who tells someone else, who mentions it
sotto voce at dinner break, mostly to piss off Ferrante, who is nobody's favorite
either. Michael and Halloran hear, too, but go on eating, serene, prefab biscuits
and freeze-dried stew.

The tests seem, now, redundant, and Michael is impatient, growing more so.
He lusts for the void, can almost taste its unforgiving null. "What is this shit?"
he complains one night, face sideways-pressed into pillow, Halloran's small hands
strong on back and buttocks. "The damn thing'll be there and back before we
ever get a chance to ride it."

More tests. NASA is stultifyingly thorough.

More tests. Intense. Ruthann Duvall vomits her morning sausage in simulation; the sausage, of course, is very real. "Don't you know," Michael tells her, "that's not the way to send back your breakfast?"

More tests.

"Fuck!" Halloran feels like wrecking something. She contents herself with smokebomb curses. "This is getting to me, you know that, this is really fucking *getting* to me."

Maybe even Bruce, the king of caution, has had enough. The waiting is driving everyone mad, madder than before, the daily speculation, the aura of tension thick as gasoline smoke. Surely they must know, those testers, those considerers of results, surely they must know who is meant to fly, who is the best.

They don't need a victory party. They are a victory party.

No one is really, truly, happy for them. Michael is no darling, and this is Halloran's second sweep; besides, Team Chronic has rubbed too many raw spots to be favorites now. All the others can hope for, in their darkest moments, is project failure, but then of course they feel like shits: nobody really wants Arrowhead to fail, no matter who's riding it.

The winners are wild in their joy; the strain has broken, the goal achieved, the certainty blue-ribbon and bright confirmed. They order up beer, the closest they can get to champagne, and one by one, team by team, the others drift by to join in. Ferrante and Duvall do not, of course, attend, instead spending the evening reviewing data, searching for the flaw that cannot be found.

Everyone gets drunk, yells, laughs loud. Even in losing out there is a certain comfort—at least the waiting is over. And their assignments, while (as Bruce noted) not "glamorous," are still interesting, worthy of excitement. Everyone talks about what they're going to do, while silently, unanimously, envying the radiant Michael.

Somebody takes a picture: Michael, beer in hand, mutilated labcoat and denim cap askew, sneakered feet crossed at the ankles, hair a halo and eyes—they are —like stars; one arm around Halloran, dark, intent, a flush on her cheekbones, hair pushed messily back, wearing a button on her lapel—if you look very closely at the picture you can read the words: "Has The World Gone Mad, Or Am I At Work?"

His work area is almost ludicrously bare. The physical jacking in, 2mm cord running to a superconducting supercomputer—that's all. The comlink system is housed elsewhere. In contrast to the manual backup equipment, resembling the cockpit of a suborbital fighter in its daunting complexity, he could be in a broom closet.

He has taken almost obsessive care to furnish his domain. Totems of various meanings and symbolisms are placed with fastidious precision. His bicycle bottle of mineral water, here; the remnants of his original labcoat, draped over his chairback here; his handleless black mug, sticky, most times, with aging grounds, here; pertinent memos and directives that no one must disturb, in this messy heap here; a bumpersticker that reads "Even if I gave a shit, I still wouldn't care," pasted at a strict diagonal across the wall before him; and, in the place of honor, the party-picture.

He loves his work.

It goes without saying, but he does. He cannot imagine, now, another way to live, as if, meeting by chance the lover he has always dreamed of, he thinks of life without her scent and kiss, her morning joke. Riding Arrowhead is all he ever expected, dreamed it to be, only better, better. He does his work—now, guiding Arrowhead through systems check in deceleration mode, realtime course correction to prepare for the big show—and has his play, the sheer flying, ecstasy of blackness, emptiness at his fingertips, in his mouth, flowing over his pores so hungry for mystery that they soak like new sponges. He eats it, all of it, drunk with delight, absorbing every morsel.

In their quarters is a remote terminal. It goes unused.

Other handlers work their subjects still, guiding them through maintenance routines, or geosynchronous dances, or linkups close and far; they are needed, to some degree; their tech has uses. Not that the subjects will not leave them behind, to NASA's prosaic mercies, to other work for handlers whose glassheads have outstripped them. They are on their way out. It was the pre-est of preordained. But not just yet.

Halloran is useless.

Her tech cannot fly Arrowhead—*that* was graphically proved. She cannot interface directly with the audacious bundle streaking across heaven; cannot in fact guide Michael; he is already far beyond her abilities. Despite any projections to the contrary, she has no function. She is required, now, only to keep Michael happy, on an even keel; when he stabilizes, breaks completely to harness, she will no longer be even marginally necessary.

She has busywork, of course. She "charts." She "observes." She "documents." She is strictly prohibited to use the room remote. It will hurt her. She knows this.

She is in the room one twilight, finishing the last of her daily "reports." She is wearing a castoff flightsuit, the irony of which only she can honestly appreciate. Her hair is clubbed back in a greasy bow. She refuses to think about the future. Sometimes, at night, her stomach aches so sourly she wants to scream, knows she will, doesn't.

"Hi." Michael, tray in hand, smile he tries to make natural. Her pain makes him miserable. He goes, every day, where she is technologically forbidden to enter: she stands at the gate while he soars inside. There is never any hint that she begrudges: she would scream like a banshee if ever came the slightest whisper of withdrawal from the project. He is as close as she can get; even the light of the fire is warmth, of a kind.

"Brought you some slop. Here," and sets it before her, gentle, seats himself at her side. "Mind if I graze?"

"Help yourself."

He eats, or tries to. She messes the food, rubs it across the plate, pretends. "Music?" she asks, trying to do her part.

"Sure. How 'bout some Transplant?"

"Okay." She turns it on, the loudest of the blast purveyors, nihilism in 4/4 time. "Good run today?"

"Great. You see the sheets?"

"Yeah. Outstanding."

He cannot answer that. They play at eating for a little while longer, Transplant thrashing in the background; then Michael shoves the tray aside.

"Jack with me," he says, pleads, commands.

This is what she lives for. "Okay," she says.

Inner workings, corridors, a vastness she can know, share. O, she tells him. Without words, trying to hide what cannot be hidden, trying to bear the brunt. He sees, knows, breaks into her courage, as he does each time; his way of sharing it, of taking what he can onto his shoulders. Don't, he says. No, she says.

Wordless, they undress, fit bodies together, make physical love. He is crying. He often cries, now. She is dry-eyed, wet below. The pleasure suffuses, brings its own panacea, is enough for the moment. They ride those waves, peak after peak, trailing down, whispering sighs into each other's open mouths. Her sweat smells sweet to him, like nothing else. He licks her shoulders. He has stopped crying, but only just.

To stay jacked this way too long, after a day of Arrowhead, will exhaust him, perhaps mar his efficiency. She is the one who broaches a stop.

No

Don't be an asshole yes

No

I am

and she does. He grapples, wide-eyed, for a moment, tears free his own jack. "Don't *do* that!" he cries, then sinks back, rubbing rough at his neck.

"I don't want to hurt you," she says, and the cry she has withheld so sternly for so long breaks out; she weeps, explosion, and he holds her, helpless. What to do, what to do; nothing. Nothing to do.

The symptoms are subtle.

Besides the nighttime bellyache, which Halloran has learned to ignore if not subdue, come other things, less palatable. Her jacks pain her, sometimes outrageously. Her joints hurt. She has no appetite. It is so difficult to sleep that she has requested, and received, barbiturates. The fact that they gave her no argument about the drugs makes her wonder. Do they A) just not care if she dopes herself stupid or B) have another reason, i.e., more requests? Is everybody breaking down?

Incredibly, yes. The handlers are beginning—in the startlingly crude NASAspeak—to corrode. The glassheads are still okay, doing swimmingly, making hay with their billion-dollar tech. The handlers are slowly going to shit, each in his or her own destructive orbit but with some symptoms universal. Entropy, Halloran thinks, laughing in a cold hysteric way. Built-in byebye.

But it is not built in. She accesses Bruce's files, breaking their so-called security with contemptuous angry ease, finds that this situation is as shocking to the brass as it is to the handlers. The ex-glassheads. Broken glassheads.

No one is discussing it, not that she knows of. In the cafeteria, at the now-infrequent meetings, she searches them, looks minute and increasingly desperate, hunting their dissolution: does Ryerson look thinner? Wickerman's face seems blotchy. Ferrante has big bags under his eyes. She knows they are watching her, too, seeing her corrosion, drawing conclusions that must inevitably coincide. While in the meantime hell freezes over, waiting for Bruce to bring it up.

She says nothing to Michael about any of it. When they jack, the relief of not having to think about it sweeps her mind clean; she is there, in that moment, in a way she is never anywhere else, at any time, anymore.

Bruce comes to see her one morning. She logs off, faces him, feels the numb patches around lips and wrist begin to throb.

"We don't understand it," he begins.

"Yeah, I know."

"There are various treatments being contemplated." He looks genuinely distressed. For the first time it begins to dawn: this is more than breakdown. This is death. Or maybe. Probably. Otherwise why the careful face, the eyes that won't, will *not*, meet hers. Her voice rises, high vowels, hating the fear of it but unable to quell.

"We're thinking of relocating you," Bruce says. "All the handlers."

"Where?"

"South Carolina," he says. "The treatments—" Pause. "We don't want the subjects . . . we don't want to dismay them."

Dismay? "What am I supposed to tell him?" She is shouting. No, she is screaming. "What am I supposed to *tell* him? That I'm going on VACATION?!" Really sceaming now. Get hold of yourself, girl, part of her says, while the other keeps making noise.

"For God's sake, Halloran!" Bruce is shaking her. That in itself quiets her down; it's so damned theatrical. For God's Sake Halloran! oh ha ha ha, HA HA HA stop it!

"We have no concrete plans, yet," he says, when she is calm enough to listen. "In fact if you have any ideas—about how to inform the subjects—" He looks at her, hopeful.

Get out, Bruce. I can't think about dying with that face of yours in the room. "I'll be sure and send you a memo." It is dismissal; the tone comes easy. In the face of death, getting reprimanded seems, somehow, unimportant. Ha HA: you better stop it or you're going to flip right out.

No more bogus "reports." She sits, stares at her hands, thinking of Michael flying in the dark, thinking of that other dark, the real dark, the biggest dark of all. Oh God, not me. Please not me.

"Something's wrong."
Michael, holding her close, his breath in her damp hair.
"Something's *bad* wrong, Halloran, and you better tell me what it is."
Silence.
"Halloran—"
"I don't . . . I don't want to—" dismay "—worry you. It's a metabolic disturbance," and how easily, how gracefully, the lies roll off her tongue. She could give lessons. Teach a course. A short course. "Don't get your balls in an uproar," and she laughs.

"You," he says, measured, considering, "are a fucking liar." He is plugged in, oh yes, he's going to get to the bottom of this and none of her bullshit about metabolic disturbances, and he pins her down, jacks her in. One way or another he's going to find out what the hell's going on around here.

He finds out.

"South Carolina, what the hell do you mean South Carolina!"
"That's where they want to send us. Some kind of treatment center, a clinic." Voice rough and exhausted from hours of crying, of fighting to comfort. "Bruce seems to think—well, you know, you saw." She is so immensely tired, and somehow, selfishly, relieved: they share this, too. "Don't ask me, I—"
"Why can't they do whatever they have to do right here?" There is that in him that refuses to think of it in any way other than a temporary malfunction. She will be treated, she will be cured. "Why do they have to send you away?"
"You know why."
"How the fuck can I work anyway!" He is the one screaming, now. "How do they expect me to do anything!"
The bond, the tie that binds, cuts deeper than NASA intended, or wants. For all the teams it is the same: the glassheads, even those whose handlers have, like Halloran, become token presences, *want their handlers*. They *need* them. Bruce and his people are in the unhappy position of trying to separate high-strung children from their very favorite stuffed animals now that the stuffing is coming out. *And*

trying to disguise the disintegration at the same time. It is the quintessential no-win situation. Uncountable dollars down the drain with one batch, the other batch sniffing stress and getting antsy and maybe not able to work at all.

And for the closest of them, Team Chronic, it is even worse. How do Siamese twins, *happy* Siamese twins, feel when the scalpel bites?

"Just a little more."

"Stop it." She is surly in her pain. "You're not my mother. Stop trying to make me eat."

"You have to eat, asshole!" He is all at once furious, weeks' worth of worry geysering now. "How do you ever expect to get better if you don't eat?"

"I'm not going to get better!"

"Yes you are. Don't even say that. You are going to get better." He says each word with the unshakable conviction of terror. "And you'd be getting better faster if you'd just cooperate a little."

"Stop it! Stop making it my fault!" She stands up, shaking; an observer, seeing her last a year ago, would be shocked silent at her deterioration. She is translucent with her illness; not ugly or wasted, but simply less and less *there*. "*They* did this to me!" She scratches at her neck, wild, as if trying to dig out the jacks. "*They* made me sick! It's not my fault, Michael, none of it is my fault!"

He starts to cry. "I know I know," hands over his face, "I know I know I know," monotonously, and she sweeps the tray from the table, slapping food on floor, spattering walls, kicking the plastic plate into flight. Then, on her knees beside him, exhausted from the strain of anger, her arms around him, rocking him gently back and forth as he grips her forearms, and sobs as if his heart will break, as if his body will splinter with the force. "I know," she says, softly, into his ear. "I know just how you feel. Don't cry. Please, don't cry."

"There goes the bastard," says a subordinate to Bruce, as Michael slips past them down the corridor. "One minute he's tearing your head off because you touched his coffee cup, the next minute he won't even answer you or acknowledge you're alive."

"He's under enormous stress, Lou."

"Yeah, I know." Lou bites a knuckle, considering. "You don't think he'll—*do* anything, do you? To himself?"

"No." Bruce looks unsure.

"How about Arrowhead?"

"No." Very sure. "He's totally committed to the project, that I know. His performance is still perfect," which is simple truth. Michael's work is excellent, his findings impeccable; essential. It is his refuge; he clings to it as fiercely and stubbornly as he clings to Halloran.

Bruce, and Lou, and all the Lous, are meeting today, to decide the next step in the separation process. The tandem quarters will be vacated; each handler—how empty the title sounds now!—will be put on a ward; the glassheads will be housed in new quarters, with no memories in their walls or under their beds. This move will just be done, no discussion, no chance of input or hysterics or tantrums. Better for everyone, they tell each other solemnly. For them, too, but they don't say it. This daily tragedy is wearing everybody down.

The move is a success, with one exception.

"No," Michael says, with the simplicity of imminent violence. "Nope," hand on the door, very calm. "No, she's not moving anywhere, I don't care who decided, I don't care about anything. She's staying right here and you can go tell Bruce to fuck himself." And the door closes. Bruce is consulted. He says, Let them be for today and we'll think of something else tomorrow.

What they think of is ways to mollify the other teams. Halloran is not moved. Arrowhead is, at bedrock, *the* project, essential. Everything else is a tangent. If consistent, outstanding results are obtained—as they are—then ways can be found, any ways, to keep them coming; the glasshead project in toto is not such a crushing success, what with the first batch proving unsuitable and then unusable, that they can afford to tamper with that which produces its only reason for existing, its reason, to be crude, for any budget at all. Without Arrowhead they can all fold up their tents tomorrow. And the data in itself is so compelling that it is unthinkable that the project not continue.

So Halloran stays.

A conversation tires her; her feet swell and deflate, swell and deflate, with grim comic regularity; her lips bleed, her gums. She plays Transplant, very loud, tells Michael she wishes she could jack right into the music so as to feel it, literally, in her bones. She lets him do almost everything for her, when he is there; it calms and pleases him, as much as he can be pleased, anymore. When they make love he holds her like china, like thinnest crystal that a thought could shatter. They spend a lot of time in tears.

"Oh this is old," she whispers, stroking his back as he lies atop her. "This is just getting so old."

There is no answer to that, so he gives none. He is too tired even to cry, or pound fists, or scream that their treatments are shit, shit! He feels her heart beat. It seems so strong. How can anyone who looks so sick have such a robust heartbeat? Thank God for it. Let it beat forever, till he and all the world is dust.

"Know what?"

"What?"

"Know what I'd like to do, more than anything?"

He raises himself from her, moves to his side, cradles her that way. "What would you like to do?"

"Arrowhead."

The word makes a silence. Vacuum. Each knows what the other is thinking.

Finally, Michael: "It's a neurological strain. A *big* strain. You might—it could hurt you."

She laughs, not sarcastically, with genuine humor. "What a tragedy *that* would be."

More silence.

"There isn't a lot left," she says, very gently, "that I can do. This," running her hand down his body, her touch ethereal. "And that. Just one. Just one ride."

He doesn't answer. He can't answer. Anything he says would be cruel. She puts her hand on his cheek, strokes his skin, the blond stubble. There is a lot she could say, many things: If you love me—one last chance—last favor. She would rather die, and for her it is not an academic pronouncement, than say those things, any of those things.

"All I care about," he says finally, his voice deeper than she has ever heard it, "is that I don't want to be a part of something that hurts you. But I guess it's already too late, isn't it?"

For her, there is no answer to that.

Much later: "You really want to do it?"

He can feel her nod in the dark.

"*Shit.*"

"Okay," Michael says, for the tenth time. "It'll take me a couple minutes to get there, get plugged in. I'll get going, and then this—" indicating a red LED "—will pulse. You jack in then. Okay?"

"Please, Mister," in a little girl's voice, undertone of pure delight, "how do you work this thing?"

"Okay, okay. I'm sorry." He is smiling too, finally. "Fasten your seatbelt, then." She is pale with excitement, back almost painfully rigid, his denim cap jaunty on her head. When he kisses her, he tastes the coppery flavor of blood. He leaves, to march down the hall like Ghenghis Khan.

Halloran's heart is thrashing as she jacks in, to the accompaniment of the LED. She feels Michael at once, a strong presence, then—go.

The slow dazzle of the slipstream night, rushing over her like black water, rich phosphorescence, things, passing, the alien perfection of Arrowhead, the flow and flower of things whose names she knows but now cannot fathom or try, the sense of flying, literal arrowhead splicing near to far, here to there, cutting, riding, past the farthest edge—it is wonder beyond dreams, more than she could have wished, for either of them. Worth everything, every second of every pain, every impatience and disappointment, of the last two years. She does not think these things in words, or terms; the concept of rightness unfolds, origami, as she flies, and if she could spare the second she would nod Yes, that's so.

Michael, beside her, feels this rightness too; on his own or as a gift from her, he cannot tell, would not bother making the distinction. She is in ecstasy, she is inside him, they are both inside Arrowhead. He could ride this way forever, world without end.

They find out, of course, Bruce and the others; almost at once. There is a warning monitor that is made to detect just this thing. They are in the tandem quarters, they forcibly unplug her. Michael feels her leaving, the abrupt disunity, and eyes-open screams, hands splayed across the air, as Arrowhead gives a lurch. As soon as she is out of the system she collapses. Grinning.

Bruce teeters on the edge of speechlessness. One assistant says, voice loud with disbelief, "Do you have any idea what you've just done to yourself? Do you know what's—"

"No," she corrects, from the bottom of the tunnel, faces ringing her like people looking down a manhole. "No, *you* have no idea."

South Carolina is a lot farther away than Proxima Centauri.

KIM NEWMAN

Famous Monsters

Here's a sort of madcap, black-humored, alternate-world *Hollywood Babylon*, complete with Selenites and betentacled B-picture Martians, courtesy of new writer Kim Newman.

Kim Newman is a film critic who lives in London, England. His critical study *Horror: 100 Best Books*, written in collaboration with Stephen Jones, is just out from Xanadu.

FAMOUS MONSTERS

Kim Newman

You know, I wouldn't be doing this picture if it weren't for Chaney Junior's liver. In all the obits, they said it was a heart attack, but anyone who knew Lon knows better. Doing all these interviews with the old-timers, you must have heard the stories. They don't tell the half of it. I didn't get to work with Lon till well past his prime. Past my prime too, come to that. It was some Abbott and Costello piece of shit in the 50s. Already, he looked less human than I do. Wattles, gut, nose, the whole fright mask. And the stink. Hell, but he was a good old bastard. Him and me and Brod Crawford used to hit all the bars on the Strip Friday and Saturday nights. We used to scare up a commotion, I can tell you. I guess we were a disgrace. I quit all that after I got a tentacle shortened in a brawl with some hophead beatniks over on Hollywood Boulevard. I leaked ichor all over Arthur Kennedy's star. That's all gone now, anyway. There aren't any bars left I can use. It's not that they won't serve me—the Second War of the Worlds was, like, twenty-five years ago now, and that's all forgotten—but no one stocks the stuff any more. It's easy enough to get. Abattoirs sell off their leavings for five cents a gallon. But this California heat makes it go rancid and rubbery inside a day.

Anyway, just before Lon conked out—halfway through a bottle of Wild Turkey, natch—he signed up with Al to do this picture. It was called *The Mutilation Machine* back then. It's *Blood of the Cannibal Creature* now. Al will change it. He always does. The footage with Scott Brady and the bike gang is from some dodo Al never got finished in the 60s. *Something a-Go-Go?* Lousy title. *Cycle Sadists a-Go-G0*, that's it. It must be great being a film historian, huh? What with all this confusion and crapola? Do you know how they were paying Lon? Bottles. When Al wanted him to walk across a room in a scene, he'd have the assistant director hold up a bottle of hooch off-camera and shake it. Lon would careen across the set, knocking things and people over, and go for the booze, and Al would get his shot. I don't suppose I'm all that much better off.

One of the backers is a wholesale butcher, and he's kicking in my fee in pig blood. I know you think that sounds disgusting, but don't knock it until you've tried it.

For a while, it looked like Lon would last out the picture. Al got the scene where he's supposed to pull this kootch-kootch dancer's guts out. He was playing Groton the Mad Zombie, by the way. So it's not Chekhov. Al has already cut the scene together. Okay, so there's some scratching on the neg. Al can fix it. He's going to put on some more scratches, and make them look like sparks flying out of Lon. Groton is supposed to be electric. Or atomic. One or the other. The girl keeps laughing while Lon gets his mitts inside her sweater, but they can dub some screams in, and music and growling and it'll be okay. At least, it'll be as okay as anything ever is in Al's movies. Did you catch *Five Bloody Graves*? It was a piece of shit. After this, he wants to do a picture with Georgina Spelvin and the Ritz Brothers called *The Fucking Stewardesses*. You can bet he'll change *that* title.

But one scene is all there is of Lon. So, when he buys the farm Al calls me up. I don't have an agent any more, although I used to be with the William Morris crowd. I do all my deals myself. I couldn't do a worse job than some of the people in this business. I used to be handled by a guy called Dickie Nixon, a real sleazo scumbag. He was the one who landed me in *Orbit Jocks*, and screwed me out of my TV residuals. Anyway, I know Al. I worked for him once before, on *Johnny Blood Rides Roughshod*. That was the horror western that was supposed to put James Dean back on the top. What a joke. The fat freak kept falling off his horse. It turned out to be a piece of shit. Al and me worked something out on this one, and so here I am in Bronson Caverns again, playing Groton the Mad Zombie. They've rewritten the script so I can be Lon in all the early scenes. I know it sounds ridiculous, what with the shape and everything. But, hell, I can cram myself into a pair and a half of jeans and a double-size poncho. In the new script, my character is a Martian—I mean, I can't play an Eskimo, can I?—but when John Carradine zaps me with the Mutilation Machine I turn into a human being. Well, into Groton the Mad Zombie. It's the most challenging part that's come my way in years, even if the film is going to be a total piece of shit. I'm hoping my performance will be a tribute to Lon. I've got the voice down. "George, lookit duh rabbits, George." Now, I working on the walk. That's difficult. You people walk all weird. No matter how long I hang around you, I still can't figure out how you manage with just the two legs.

I'm an American citizen, by the way, I was hatched in Los Angeles. Put it down to the Melting Pot. Mom flopped down in the 20s, when the Old World political situation started going to hell. She'd been through WW I and couldn't face that again. It's in the culture, I guess. When your head of government is called the High War Victor you know you're in trouble. I'm not that way. I'm

mellow. A typical native Californian, like my twenty-eight brood siblings. I'm
the only one of us left now. The rest all died off or went back to the skies. I can't
let go. It's showbiz, you know. It's in the ichor. You must understand that if you
do all these interviews. What do you call it, oral history? It's important, I suppose.
Someone should take all this down before we all die out. Did you get to Rathbone?
There was a guy with some stories. I never got on with him though, despite all
those pictures we did together. He lost some relatives in the First War of the
Worlds, and never got around to accepting that not all non-terrestrials were vicious
thugs.

I suppose you'll want to know how I got into the movies? Well, I'm that one
in a million who started as an extra. It was in the late 30s, when I'd barely brushed
the eggshell out of my slime. Four bucks a day just for hanging around cardboard
nightclubs or walking up and down that street where the buildings are just front-
ages. In *Swing Time*, I'm in the background when Fred and Ginger do their ''Pick
Yourself Up'' routine. They were swell, although Rogers put my name down on
some list of communist sympathizers in the 50s and I nearly had to go before
HUAC. Do I look like a commie? Hell, how many other Americans can blush
red, white and blue? I didn't stay an extra long. I suppose I'm noticeable. There
were very few of us in Hollywood, and so I started getting bit parts. Typically,
I'd be a heavy in a saloon fight, or an underworld hanger-on. If you catch *The
Roaring Twenties* on a re-run, look out for me during the massacre in the Italian
restaurant. Cagney gets me in the back. It's one of my best deaths. I've always
been good at dying.

My big break came when 20th Century-Fox did the Willie K'ssth films.
Remember? Rathbone played Inspector Willie K'ssth of the Selenite Police Force.
*Willie K'ssth Takes Over, Willie K'ssth and The Co-Eds, Willie K'ssth On
Broadway*, and so on. There were more than twenty of them. I was Jimbo,
Willie's big, dumb Martian sidekick. I did all the comedy relief scenes—going
into a tentacle-flapping fright in haunted houses, getting hit on the head and
seeing animated stars in fight sequences. The films don't play much now, because
of the Selenite pressure groups. They hate the idea of a human actor in the
role. And when Earl Derr Biggers was writing the books in the 20s, the Grand
Lunar had them banned on the Moon. I don't see what they were bothered
about. Willie always spots the killer and comes out on top. He usually gets to
make a bunch of human beings look ridiculous as well. In not one of the books
or movies did Jimbo ever guess who the murderer was, even when it was bla-
tantly obvious. And it usually was. For a while, I was typed as the dumb, scared
Martie. Some of my siblings said I was projecting a negative image of the race,
but there was a Depression on and I was the only one of the brood in regular
work. I've got nothing against Selenites, by the way, although the Grand Lunar
has always had a rotten Sapient Rights record. It's no wonder so many of them
headed for the Earth.

After the New York Singe, I was quickly dropped from the series. We were half-way through shooting *Willie K'ssth on Coney Island* when the studio quietly pulled my contract. They rewrote Jimbo as a black chauffeur called Wilbur Wolverhampton and got Stepin Fetchit to do the role. They still put out the film under its original title, even though there wasn't a Coney Island any more. I'd have sued, but there was a wave of virulent Anti-Martian feeling sweeping the country. That was understandable, I guess. I had relatives in New York, too. Suddenly, forty years of cultural exchange was out of the porthole and we were back to interspecial hatred. Nobody cared that Mom was a refugee from High War Victor Uszthay in the first place, and that since his purges most of her brood siblings were clogging up the canals. I was pulled out of my apartment by the Beverly Hills cops and roughed up in a basement. They really did use rubber hoses. I'll never forget that. I ended up in an internment camp, and the studio annexed my earnings. The hate mail was really nasty. We were out in the desert, which wasn't so bad. I guess we're built for deserts. But at night people in hoods would come and have bonfires just outside the perimeter. They burned scarecrows made to look like Martians and chanted lots of blood and guts slogans. That was disturbing. And the guards were a bit free with the cattle prods. It was a shameful chapter in the planet's history, but no one's researched it properly yet. The last interview I did was with some Martian-American professor doing a thesis on Roosevelt's treatment of so-called "enemy aliens." He was practically a hatchling, and didn't really understand what we'd had to go through. I bet his thesis will be a piece of shit. There were rumours about this camp in Nevada where the guards stood back and let a mob raze the place to the ground with the Marties still in it. And who knows what happened in Europe and Asia?

Then the cylinders started falling, and the war effort got going. Uszthay must have been a bigger fool than we took him for. With Mars' limited resources, he couldn't possibly keep the attack going for more than six months. And Earth had cavorite, while he was still using nineteenth-century rocket cannons. Do you know how many cylinders just landed in the sea and sunk? So, Roosevelt got together with the world leaders in Iceland—Hitler, Stalin, Oswald Cabal—and they geared up for Earth's counterinvasion. Finally, I got all the hassles with my citizenship sorted out, and the authorities reluctantly admitted I had as much right to be called an American as any other second generation immigrant. I had to carry a wad of documentation the size of a phone book, but I could walk the streets freely. Of course, if I did I was still likely to get stoned. I did most of my travelling in a curtained car. According to what was left of my contract, I owed 20th a couple of movies. I assumed they'd pay me off and I'd wind up in an armaments factory, but no, as soon as I was on the lot I was handed a stack of scripts. Suddenly, everyone was making war pictures.

The first was *Mars Force*, which I did for Howard Hawks. I was loaned to Warners for that. It was supposed to be a true story. I don't know if you remember, but the week after the Singe a handful of foolhardy volunteers climbed into their Cavor Balls and buzzed the red planet. They didn't do much damage, but it was Earth's first retaliative strike. In the movie, they were after the factories where the elements for the heat rays were being synthesized. In real life, they just flattened a couple of retirement nests and got rayed down. In *Mars Force*, I played the tyrannical Security Victor at the factories. I spent most of the film gloating over a crystal-scope, looking at stock footage of the smoking plains where New York used to be. I also got to drool over a skinny terrestrial missionary, snivel in fear as the brave Earthmen flew over in their Christmas tree ornaments and be machine-gunned to death by John Garfield. It was typical propaganda shit, but it was a pretty good picture. It stands up a lot better than most of the other things I did back then.

I was typecast for the rest of the war. I've raped more nurses than any actor alive—although what I was supposed to see in you sandpaper-skinned bipeds is beyond me. And I did a lot of plotting, scheming, saluting, backstabbing, bombing, blasting, cackling, betraying, sneering and strutting. I saw more action than Patton and Rommel put together, and without ever stepping off the backlots. The furthest I ever went for a battle was Griffith Park. I had a whole set of shiny, slimy uniforms. I played every rank we had going. In *Heat Ray!*, I even got to play Uszthay, although that's like asking Mickey Mouse to play John the Baptist. I soon lost count of the number of times I had to swear to crush the puny planet Earth in my lesser tentacles. I got killed a lot. I was shot by Errol Flynn in *Desperate Journey*, bombed by Spencer Tracy in *Thirty Seconds Over Krba-Gnsk*, and John Wayne got me in *Soaring Tigers*, *The Sands of Grlshnk* and *The Fighting Seabees*. In *Lunaria*, Bogart plugs me as I reach for the crystalphone on the launchfield. Remember that one? Everyone says it's a classic. It got the Academy Award that year. Claude Rains asks Bogart why he came to Lunaria, and Bogart says he came for the atmosphere. "But there's no atmosphere on the Moon," says Rains. "I was misinformed." I wanted the role of the freedom fighter who floats off to Earth with Ingrid Bergman at the end, but Jack Warner chickened out of depicting a sympathetic Martie and they made the character into a Selenite. Paul Henried could never keep his antennae straight. I had to make do with being another Inferior War Victor. No one believed there were any anti-Uszthay Martians. That's typical earthbound thinking.

Then the war ended, and suddenly there were no more Martian roles. In fact, suddenly there were no more Martians period. The allies did a pretty fair job of depopulating the old planet. Since then, we've been a dying race. We're feeble, really. Every time the 'flu goes round, I have to go to funerals. There was a rash of anti-war movies. There always is after the zapping is over. Remember *A Walk in the Dust* or *Terrestrial Invaders*? I didn't get work in those. All you ever saw of the Martian troops were bodies. There were plenty of newsreel scenes of big-eyed orphans waving their tentacles at the camera in front of the sludging ruins of their nests. Those movies didn't do any business. The whole solar system was tired of war. They started making musicals. I can't do what you people call dancing, so those were lean years. I did a bit of investing, and set up my own business. I thought I'd hit on the ideal combination. I opened a Martian bar and a kosher butcher's shop back-to-back. The Jews got the meat, and the Marties got the drainings. It was a good idea, and we did okay until the riots. I lost everything then, and went back to acting.

I did some dinner theatre. Small roles. I thought my best performance was as Dr Chasuble in *The Importance of Being Earnest*, but there weren't many managements willing to cast me in spite, rather than because, of my race. I tried to get the backing to put on *Othello* in modern dress with the Moor as a Martian, but no one was interested. When Stanley Kramer bought up *Worlds Apart*, the hot best-seller about the persecution of Martians on Earth, I put in a bid for the lead, but Stanley had to say no. By then, I was too associated with the stereotype Jimbo Martie. He said audiences wouldn't take me seriously. Maybe he was right, but I'd have liked to take a shot at it. As you must know, Ptyehshdneh got the part and went on to be the first non-terrestrial to walk off with the Best Actor statuette on Oscar night. I'm not bitter, but I can't help thinking that my career in the last twenty years would have been very different if Kramer had taken the chance. Ptyeh' is such a pretty Martie, if you know what I mean. Not much slime on his hide.

Of course, Willie K'ssth came back on television in the early 50s. They made twenty-six half-hour episodes with Tom Conway under the beak and me back as dumb Jimbo. The series is still in syndication on graveyard shift TV. I get fan mail from nostalgia-buff insomniacs and night watchmen all over the country. It's nice to know people notice you. I saw one of those episodes recently. It was a piece of shit. But at the time it was a job, right? It didn't last long, and I was more or less on the skids for a couple of years. I was on relief between guest spots. I'm in a classic *Sergeant Bilko*, where they're trying to make a movie about the canal Bilko is supposed to have taken in the war. Doberman wins a Dream Date With a Movie Star in a contest and all the platoon try to get the ticket off him. Finally, Bilko gets the ticket and turns up at the Hollywood nightspot, and I turn out to be the Dream Date Star. Phil Silvers has a terrific talent, and it was nice just to be funny for a change. We worked out a good little routine with the drinks and the cocktail umbrellas. I'd like to have done more comedy, but when you've got tentacles producers don't think you can milk a laugh. I popped out of a box on *Laugh-In* once.

The 60s were rough, I guess. I had a little bit of a drink problem, but you must have heard about that. You've done your research, right? Well, skipping the messy parts of the story, I ended up in jail. It was only a couple of cows all told, but I exsanguinated them all right. No excuses. Inside, I got involved in the protest movement. I was in with lots of draft evaders. They gave me some LSD, and I wound up signing a lot of petitions and, outside, going on plenty of marches. Hell, everybody now thinks the War on Mercury was a waste of time, but the planet was gung-ho about it back then. Those little jelly-breathers never did anyone any harm, but you'd creamed one planet and got a taste for it. That's what I think. I did a bit of organizational work for the Aliens' League, and spoke on campuses. I was on President Kissinger's enemies list. I'm still proud of that.

I had a few film roles while all this was going in. Nothing spectacular, but I kept my face on the screen. I was the priest in *The Miracle of Mare Nostrum*, Elvis' partner in the spear-fishing business in *She Ain't Human*, and Doris Day's old boyfriend in *With Six You Get Eggroll*. The films were mostly pieces of shit. I'm unbilled in a couple of Sinatra-Martin movies because I knocked around with the Rat Pack for a couple of summers before I got politics. I get a tentacle down Angie Dickinson's decolleté in *Ocean's 11*. I know you're going to ask me about *Orbit Jocks*. I was just naive. Again, no excuses. When I shot my scenes, I thought it was a documentary. They had a whole fake script and everything. I took the job because of the trip to Mars. I'd never been before, and I wanted to discover my roots. I stood in front of landmarks reading out stuff about history. Then the producers sliced in all the hardcore stuff later. I don't know if you've seen the film, but the Martian in all the sex scenes is not me. It's hard to tell with a steel cowl, but he's got all his tentacles.

I'm not retired. I won't retire until they plough me under. But I'm being more selective. I'll take a picture if I can pal around with any of the other old-timers. I was in something called *Vampire Coyotes* last year, with Leslie Howard, Jean Harlow and Sidney Greenstreet. I don't mind working on low-budget horror movies. It's more like the old days. The big studios these days are just cranking out bland television crap. I was asked to be a guest villian on *Columbo*, but I turned it down and they got Robert Culp instead. I went to a science fiction film convention last year. Forrest J. Ackerman interviewed me on stage. He's a great guy. When I finally turn tentacles-up, I'm having it in my will that I be stuffed and put in his basement with the Creature From the Black Lagoon and all that other neat stuff. Lon would have gone for that too, but humans are prejudiced against auto-icons. It's a pity. I hope Forry can make do with just Lon's liver. It was the heart and soul of the man, anyway.

After this, I've got a three-picture deal with Al. That's not as big a thing as it sounds, since he'll shoot them simultaneously. *Blood of the Brain Eaters, Jessie's Girls* and *Martian Exorcist*. Then, I might go to the Philippines and make this movie they want me to do with Nancy Kwan. Okay, so it'll be a piece of shit . . .

If I had it all over again, do you know what? I'd do everything different. For a start, I'd take dancing lessons . . .

LUCIUS SHEPARD

The Scalehunter's Beautiful Daughter

Lucius Shepard is one of the most popular new writers to enter SF in a decade or more. Shepard won the John W. Campbell Award in 1985 as the year's Best New Writer, and no year since has gone by without him adorning the final ballot for one major award or another, and often for several. In 1987, he won the Nebula Award for his landmark novella ''R & R'' and in 1988 he picked up a World Fantasy Award for his monumental short-story collection *The Jaguar Hunter*. His first novel was the acclaimed *Green Eyes*; his second the bestselling *Life During Wartime*; he is at work on two more. Born in Lynchburg, Virginia, he now lives somewhere in the wilds of Nantucket.

Here he takes us to a land dominated by the immobile but still-living body of an immense, mountain-huge dragon, enchanted into stillness in some sorcerous battle in the unimaginably distant past, so long ago that forests and villages have sprung up on the dragon's mountainous flanks . . . and then takes us *inside* the great dragon to explore a whole new world of enchantment and brutality, terror and wonder, strange dangers and stranger beauties.

THE SCALEHUNTER'S BEAUTIFUL DAUGHTER

Lucius Shepard

1

Not long after the Christlight of the world's first morning faded, when birds still flew to heaven and back, and even the wickedest things shone like saints, so pure was their portion of evil, there was a village by the name of Hangtown that clung to the back of the dragon Griaule, a vast mile-long beast who had been struck immobile yet not lifeless by a wizard's spell, and who ruled over the Carbonales Valley, controlling in every detail the lives of the inhabitants, making known his will by the ineffable radiations emanating from the cold tonnage of his brain. From shoulder to tail, the greater part of Griaule was covered with earth and trees and grass, from some perspectives appearing to be an element of the landscape, another hill among those that ringed the valley; except for sections cleared by the scalehunters, only a portion of his right side to the haunch, and his massive neck and head remained visible, and the head had sunk to the ground, its massive jaws halfway open, itself nearly as high as the crests of the surrounding hills. Situated almost eight hundred feet above the valley floor and directly behind the fronto-parietal plate, which overhung the place like a mossy cliff, the village consisted of several dozen shacks with shingled roofs and walls of weathered planking, and bordered a lake fed by a stream that ran down onto Griaule's back from an adjoining hill; it was hemmed in against the shore by thickets of choke-cherry, stands of stunted oak and hawthornes, and but for the haunted feeling that pervaded the air, a vibrant stillness similar to the atmosphere of an old ruin, to someone standing beside the lake it would seem he was looking out upon an ordinary country settlement, one a touch less neatly ordered than most, littered as it was with the bones and entrails of skizzers and flakes and other parasites that infested the dragon, but nonetheless ordinary in the lassitude that governed it, and the shabby dress and hostile attitudes of its citizenry.

Many of the inhabitants of the village were scalehunters, men and women who scavenged under Griaule's earth-encrusted wings and elsewhere on his body, searching for scales that were cracked and broken, chipping off fragments and selling these in Port Chantay, where they were valued for their medicinal virtues. They were well paid for their efforts, but were treated as pariahs by the people of the valley, who rarely ventured onto the dragon, and their lives were short and fraught with unhappy incident, a circumstance they attributed to the effects of Griaule's displeasure at their presence. Indeed, his displeasure was a constant preoccupation, and they spent much of their earnings on charms that they believed would ward off its evil influence. Some wore bits of scale around their necks, hoping that this homage would communicate to Griaule the high regard in which they held him, and perhaps the most extreme incidence of this way of thinking was embodied by the nature given by the widower Riall to his daughter Catherine. On the day of her birth, also the day of his wife's death, he dug down beneath the floor of his shack until he reached Griaule's back, laying bare a patch of golden scale some six feet long and five feet wide, and from that day forth for the next eighteen years he forced her to sleep upon the scale, hoping that the dragon's essence would seep into her and so she would be protected against his wrath. Catherine complained at first about this isolation, but she came to enjoy the dreams that visited her, dreams of flying, of otherworldly climes (according to legend, dragons were native to another universe to which they traveled by flying into the sun); lying there sometimes, looking up through the plank-shored tunnel her father had dug, she would feel that she was not resting on a solid surface but was receding from the earth, falling into a golden distance.

Riall may or may not have achieved his desired end; but it was evident to the people of Hangtown that propinquity to the scale had left its mark on Catherine, for while Riall was short and swarthy (as his wife had also been), physically unprepossessing in every respect, his daughter had grown into a beautiful young woman, long-limbed and slim, with fine golden hair and lovely skin and a face of unsurpassed delicacy, seeming a lapidary creation with its voluptuous mouth and sharp cheekbones and large eloquent eyes, whose irises were so dark that they could be distinguished from the pupils only under the strongest of lights. Not alone in her beauty did she appear cut from different cloth from her parents; neither did she share their gloomy spirit and cautious approach to life. From earliest childhood she went without fear to every quarter of the dragon's surface, even into the darkness under the wing joints where few scalehunters dared go; she believed she had been immunized against ordinary dangers by her father's tactics, and she felt there was a bond between herself and the dragon, that her dreams and good looks were emblems of both a magical relationship and consequential destiny, and this feeling of invulnerability—along with the confidence instilled by her beauty—gave rise to a certain egocentricity and shallowness of character. She was often disdainful, careless in the handling of lovers' hearts, and though she did not stoop to duplicity—she had no need of that—she took pleasure in stealing the men whom other women loved. And yet she considered herself a good woman. Not a saint, mind you. But she honored her father and kept the house clean and did her share of work, and though she had her faults, she had taken steps—half-steps, rather—to correct them. Like most people, she had no clear moral determinant, depending upon taboos and specific circumstances to modify her behavior, and the "good," the principled, was to her a kind of intellectual afterlife to which she planned some day to aspire, but only after she had exhausted the potentials of pleasure and thus gained the experience necessary for the achievement of such an aspiration. She was prone to bouts of moodiness, as were all within the sphere of Griaule's influence, but generally displayed a sunny disposition and optimistic cast of thought. This is not to say, however, that she was a Pollyanna, an innocent. Through her life in Hangtown she was familiar with treachery, grief, and murder, and at eighteen she had already been with a wide variety of lovers. Her easy sexuality was typical of Hangtown's populace, yet because of her beauty and the jealousy it had engendered, she had acquired the reputation of being exceptionally wanton. She was amused, even somewhat pleased, by her reputation, but the rumors surrounding her grew more scurrilous, more deviant from the truth, and eventually there came a day when they were brought home to her with a savagery that she could never have presupposed.

Beyond Griaule's frontal spike, which rose from a point between his eyes, a great whorled horn curving back toward Hangtown, the slope of the skull flattened out into the top of his snout, and it was here that Catherine came one foggy morning, dressed in loose trousers and a tunic, equipped with scaling hooks and ropes and chisels, intending to chip off a sizeable piece of cracked scale she had noticed near the dragon's lip, a spot directly above one of the fangs. She worked at the piece for several hours, suspended by linkages of rope over Griaule's lower jaw. His half-open mouth was filled with a garden of evil-looking plants, the calloused surface of his forked tongue showing here and there between the leaves like nodes of red coral; his fangs were inscribed with intricate patterns of lichen, wreathed by streamers of fog and circled by raptors who now and then would plummet into the bushes to skewer some unfortunate lizard or vole. Epiphytes bloomed from splits in the ivory, depending long strings of interwoven red and purple blossoms. It was a compelling sight, and from time to time Catherine would stop working and lower herself in her harness until she was no more than fifty feet above the tops of the bushes and look off into the caliginous depths of Griaule's throat, wondering at the nature of the shadowy creatures that flitted there.

The sun burned off the fog, and Catherine, sweaty, weary of chipping, hauled herself up to the top of the snout and stretched out on the scales, resting on an elbow, nibbling at a honey pear and gazing out over the valley with its spiny green hills and hammocks of thistle palms and the faraway white buildings of Teocinte, where that very night she planned to dance and make love. The air became so warm that she stripped off her tunic and lay back, bare to the waist, eyes closed, daydreaming in the clean springtime heat. She had been drifting between sleep and waking for the better part of an hour, when a scraping noise brought her alert. She reached for her tunic and started to sit up; but before she could turn to see who or what had made the sound, something fell heavily across her ribs, taking her wind, leaving her gasping and disoriented. A hand groped her breast, and she smelled winey breath.

"Go easy, now," said a man's voice, thickened with urgency. "I don't want nothing half of Hangtown ain't had already."

Catherine twisted her head, and caught a glimpse of Key Willen's lean, sallow face looming above her, his sardonic mouth hitched at one corner in a half-smile.

"I told you we'd have our time," he said, fumbling with the tie of her trousers.

She began to fight desperately, clawing at his eyes, catching a handful of his long black hair and yanking. She threw herself onto her stomach, clutching at the edge of a scale, trying to worm out from beneath him; but he butted her in the temple, sending white lights shooting through her skull. Once her head had cleared, she found that he had flipped her onto her back, had pulled her trousers down past her hips and penetrated her with his fingers; he was working them in and out, his breath coming hoarse and rapid. She felt raw inside, and she let out a sharp, throat-tearing scream. She thrashed about, tearing at his shirt, his hair, screaming again and again, and when he clamped his free hand to her mouth, she bit it.

"You bitch! You . . . goddamn. . . ." He slammed the back of her head against the scale, climbed atop her, straddling her chest and pinning her shoulders with his knees. He slapped her, wrapped his hand in her hair, and leaned close, spittle flying to her face as he spoke. "You listen up, pig! I don't much care if you're awake . . . one way or the other, I'm gonna have my fun." He rammed her head into the scale again. "You hear me? Hear me?" He straightened, slapped her harder. "Hell, I'm having fun right now."

"Please!" she said, dazed.

"Please?" He laughed. "That mean you want some more?" Another slap. "You like it?"

Yet another slap.

"How 'bout that?"

Frantic, she wrenched an arm free, in reflex reaching up behind her head, searching for a weapon, anything, and as he prepared to slap her again, grinning, she caught hold of a stick—or so she thought—and swung it at him in a vicious arc. The point of the scaling hook, for such it was, sank into Key's flesh just back of his left eye, and as he fell, toppling sideways with only the briefest of outcries, the eye filled with blood, becoming a featureless crimson sphere like a rubber ball embedded in the socket. Catherine shrieked, pushed his legs off her waist and scrambled away, encumbered by her trousers, which had slipped down about her knees. Key's body convulsed, his heels drumming the scale. She sat staring at him for a long seamless time, unable to catch her breath, to think. But swarms of black flies, their translucent wings shattering the sunlight into prism, began landing on the puddle of blood that spread wide as a table from beneath Key's face, and she became queasy. She crawled to the edge of the snout and looked away across the checkerboard of fields below toward Port Chantay, toward an alp of bubbling cumulus building from the horizon. Her chest hollowed with cold, and she started to shake. The tremors passing through her echoed the tremor she had felt in Key's body when the hook had bit into his skull. All the sickness inside her, her shock and disgust at the violation, at confronting the substance of death, welled up in her throat and her stomach emptied. When she had finished she cinched her trousers tight, her fingers clumsy with the knot. She thought she should do something. Coil the ropes, maybe. Store the harness in her pack. But these actions, while easy to contemplate, seemed impossibly complex to carry out. She shivered and hugged herself, feeling the altitude, the distances. Her cheeks were feverish and puffy; flickers of sensation—she pictured them to be iridescent worms—tingled nerves in her chest and legs. She had the idea that everything was slowing, that time had flurried and was settling the way river mud settles after the passage of some turbulence. She stared off toward the dragon's horn. Someone was standing there. Coming toward her, now. At first she watched the figure approach with a defiant disinterest, wanting to guard her privacy, feeling that if she had to speak she would lose control of her emotions. But as the figure resolved into one of her neighbors back in Hangtown—Brianne, a tall young woman with brittle good looks, dark brown hair and an olive complexion—she relaxed from this attitude. She and Brianne were not friends; in fact, they had once been rivals for the same man. However, that had been a year and more in the past, and Catherine was relieved to see her. More than relieved. The presence of another woman allowed her to surrender to weakness, believing that in Brianne she would find a fund of natural sympathy because of their common sex.

"My God, what happened?" Brianne kneeled and brushed Catherine's hair back from her eyes. The tenderness of the gesture burst the dam of Catherine's emotions, and punctuating the story with sobs, she told of the rape.

"I didn't mean to kill him," she said. "I . . . I'd forgotten about the hook."

"Key was looking to get killed," Brianne said. "But it's a damn shame you had to be the one to help him along." She sighed, her forehead creased by a worry line. "I suppose I should fetch someone to take care of the body. I know that's not. . . ."

"No, I understand . . . it has to be done." Catherine felt stronger, more capable. She made as if to stand, but Brianne restrained her.

"Maybe you should wait here. You know how people will be. They'll see your face"—she touched Catherine's swollen cheeks "—and they'll be prying, whispering. It might be better to let the mayor come out and make his investigation. That way he can take the edge off the gossip before it gets started."

Catherine didn't want to be alone with the body any longer, but she saw the wisdom in waiting and agreed.

"Will you be all right?" Brianne asked.

"I'll be fine . . . but hurry."

"I will." Brianne stood; the wind feathered her hair, lifted it to veil the lower half of her face. "You're sure you'll be all right?" There was an odd undertone in her voice, as if it were really another question she was asking, or—and this, Catherine thought, was more likely—as if she were thinking ahead to dealing with the mayor.

Catherine nodded, then caught at Brianne as she started to walk away. "Don't tell my father. Let me tell him. If he hears it from you, he might go after the Willens."

"I won't say a thing, I promise."

With a smile, a sympathetic pat on the arm, Brianne headed back toward Hangtown, vanishing into the thickets that sprang up beyond the frontal spike. For a while after she had gone, Catherine felt wrapped in her consolation; but the seething of the wind, the chill that infused the air as clouds moved in to cover the sun, these things caused the solitude of the place and the grimness of the circumstance to close down around her, and she began to wish she had returned to Hangtown. She squeezed her eyes shut, trying to steady herself, but even then she kept seeing Key's face, his bloody eye, and remembering his hands on her. Finally, thinking that Brianne had had more than enough time to accomplish her task, she walked up past the frontal spike and stood looking out along the narrow trail that wound through the thickets on Griaule's back. Several minutes elapsed, and then she spotted three figures—two men and a woman—coming at a brisk pace. She shaded her eyes against a ray of sun that had broken through the overcast, and peered at them. Neither man had the gray hair and portly shape of Hangtown's mayor. They were lanky, pale, with black hair falling to their shoulders, and were carrying unsheathed knives. Catherine couldn't make out their faces, but she realized that Brianne must not have set aside their old rivalry, that in the spirit of vengeance she had informed Key's brothers of his death.

Fear cut through the fog of shock, and she tried to think what to do. There was only one trail and no hope that she could hide in the thickets. She retreated toward the edge of the snout, stepping around the patch of drying blood. Her only chance for escape would be to lower herself on the ropes and take her refuge in Griaule's mouth; however, the thought of entering so ominous a place, a place shunned by all but the mad, gave her pause. She tried to think of alternatives, but there were none. Brianne would no doubt have lied to the Willens, cast her as the guilty party, and the brothers would never listen to her. She hurried to the edge, buckled on the harness and slipped over the side, working with frenzied speed, lowering in ten and fifteen foot drops. Her view of the mouth lurched and veered—a panorama of bristling leaves and head-high ferns, enormous fangs hooking up from the jaw and pitch-dark emptiness at the entrance to the throat. She was fifty feet from the surface when she felt the rope jerking, quivering; glancing up, she saw that one of the Willens was sawing at it with his knife. Her heart felt hot and throbbing in her chest, her palms were slick. She dropped half the distance to the jaw, stopping with a jolt that sent pain shooting through her spine and left her swinging back and forth, muddle-headed. She began another drop, a shorter one, but the rope parted high above and she fell the last twenty feet, landing with such stunning force that she lost consciousness.

She came to in a bed of ferns, staring up through the fronds at the dull brick-colored roof of Griaule's mouth, a surface festooned with spiky dark green epiphytes, like the vault of a cathedral that had been invaded by the jungle. She lay still for a moment, gathering herself, testing the aches that mapped her body to determine if anything was broken. A lump sprouted from the back of the head, but the brunt of the impact had been absorbed by her rear end, and though she felt pain there, she didn't think the damage was severe. Moving cautiously, wincing, she came to her knees and was about to stand when she heard shouts from above.

"See her?"

"Naw . . . you?"

"She musta gone deeper in!"

Catherine peeked between the fronds and saw two dark figures centering networks of ropes, suspended a hundred feet or so overhead like spiders with simple webs. They dropped lower, and panicked, she crawled on her belly away from the mouth, hauling herself along by gripping twists of dead vine that formed a matte underlying the foliage. After she had gone about fifty yards she looked back. The Willens were hanging barely a dozen feet above the tops of the bushes, and as she watched they lowered out of sight. Her instincts told her to move deeper into the mouth, but the air was considerably darker where she now kneeled than where she had landed—a grayish green gloom—and the idea of penetrating the greater darkness of Griaule's throat stalled her heart. She listened for the Willens and heard slitherings, skitterings, and rustles. Eerie whistles that, although soft, were complex and articulated. She imagined that these were not the cries of tiny creatures but the gutterings of breath in a huge throat, and she had a terrifying sense of the size of the place, of her own relative insignificance. She couldn't bring herself to continue in deeper, and she made her way toward the side of the mouth, where thick growths of ferns flourished in the shadow. When she reached a spot at which the mouth sloped upward, she buried herself among the ferns and kept very still.

Next to her head was an irregular patch of pale red flesh, where a clump of soil had been pulled away by an uprooted plant. Curious, she extended a forefinger and found it cool and dry. It was like touching stone or wood, and that disappointed her; she had, she realized, been hoping the touch would affect her in some extreme way. She pressed her palm to the flesh, trying to detect the tic of a pulse, but the flesh was inert, and the rustlings and the occasional beating of wings overhead were the only signs of life. She began to grow drowsy, to nod, and she fought to keep awake. But after a few minutes she let herself relax. The more she examined the situation, the more convinced she became that the Willens would not track her this far; the extent of their nerve would be to wait at the verge of the mouth, to lay siege to her, knowing that eventually she would have to seek food and water. Thinking about water made her thirsty, but she denied the craving. She needed rest far more. And removing one of the scaling hooks from her belt, holding it in her right hand in case some animal less cautious than the Willens happened by, she pillowed her head against the pale red patch of Griaule's flesh and was soon fast asleep.

2

Many of Catherine's dreams over the years had seemed sendings rather than distillations of experience, but never had she had one so clearly of that character as the dream she had that afternoon in Griaule's mouth. It was a simple dream, formless, merely a voice whose words less came to her ear than enveloped her, steeping her in their meanings, and of them she retained only a message of reassurance, of security, one so profound that it instilled in her a confidence that lasted even after she waked into a world gone black, the sole illumination being the gleams of reflected firelight that flowed along the curve of one of the fangs. It was an uncanny sight, that huge tooth glazed with fierce red shine, and under other circumstances she would have been frightened by it; but in this instance she did not react to the barbarity of the image and saw it instead as evidence that her suppositions concerning the Willens had been correct. They had built a fire near the lip and were watching for her, expecting her to bolt into their arms. But she had no intention of fulfilling their expectations. Although her confidence flickered on and off, although to go deeper into the dragon seemed irrational, she knew that any other course offered the certainty of a knife stroke across the neck. And, too, despite the apparent rationality of her decision, she had an unshakeable feeling that Griaule was watching over her, that his will was being effected. She had a flash vision of Key Willen's face, his gaping mouth and blood-red eye, and recalled her terror at his assault. However, these memories no longer harrowed her. They steadied her, resolving certain questions that—while she had never asked them —had always been there to ask. She hadn't been to blame in any way for the rape, she had not tempted Key. But she saw that she had left herself open to tragedy by her aimlessness, by her reliance on a vague sense of destiny to give life meaning. Now it appeared that her destiny was at hand, and she understood that its violent coloration might have been different had *she* been different, had she engaged the world with energy and not with a passive attitude. She hoped that knowing all this would prove important, but she doubted that it would, believing that she had gone too far on the wrong path for any degree of knowledge to matter.

It took all her self-control to begin her journey inward, feeling her way along the side of the throat, pushing through ferns and cobwebs, her hands encountering unfamiliar textures that made her skin crawl, alert to the burbling of insects and other night creatures. On one occasion she was close to turning back, but she heard shouts behind her, and fearful that the Willens were on her trail, she kept going. As she started down an incline, she saw a faint gleam riding the curve of the throat wall. The glow brightened, casting the foliage into silhouette, and eager to reach the source, she picked up her pace, tripping over roots, vines snagging her ankles. At length the incline flattened out, and she emerged into a large chamber, roughly circular in shape, its upper regions lost in darkness; upon the floor lay pools of black liquid; mist trailed across the surface of the pools, and whenever the mist lowered to touch the liquid, a fringe of yellowish red flame would flare up, cutting the shadows on the pebbled skin of the floor and bringing to light a number of warty knee-high protuberances that spouted among the pools—these were deep red in color, perforated around the sides, leaking pale threads of mist. At the rear of the chamber was an opening that Catherine assumed led farther into the dragon. The air was warm, dank, and a sweat broke out all over her body. She balked at entering the chamber; in spite of the illumination, it was less a human place than the mouth. But once again she forced herself onward, stepping carefully between the fires and, after discovering that the mist made her giddy, giving the protuberances a wide berth. Piercing whistles came from above. The notion that this might signal the presence of bats caused her to hurry, and she had covered half the distance across when a man's voice called to her, electrifying her with fear.

"Catherine!" he said. "Not so fast!"

She spun about, her scaling hook at the ready. Hobbling toward her was an elderly white-haired man dressed in the ruin of a silk frock coat embroidered with gold thread, a tattered ruffled shirt, and holed satin leggings. In his left hand he carried a gold-knobbed cane, and at least a dozen glittering rings encircled his bony fingers. He stopped an arms-length away, leaning on his cane, and although Catherine did not lower her hook, her fear diminished. Despite the eccentricity of his appearance, considering the wide spectrum of men and creatures who inhabited Griaule, he seemed comparatively ordinary, a reason for caution but no alarm.

"Ordinary?" The old man cackled. "Oh yes, indeed! Ordinary as angels, as unexceptional as the idea of God!" Before she had a chance to wonder at his knowledge of her thoughts, he let out another cackle. "How could I not know them? We are every one of us creatures of his thought, expressions of his whim. And here what is only marginally evident on the surface becomes vivid reality, inescapable truth. For here—'' he poked the chamber floor with his cane ''— here we live in the medium of his will.'' He hobbled a step closer, fixing her with a rheumy stare. ''I have dreamed this moment a thousand times. I know what you will say, what you will think, what you will do. He has instructed me in all your particulars so that I may become your guide, your confidant.''

''What are you talking about?'' Catherine hefted her hook, her anxiety increasing.

''Not 'what,' '' said the old man. ''Who.'' A grin split the pale wrinkled leather of his face. ''His Scaliness, of course.''

''Griaule?''

''None other.'' The old man held out his hand. ''Come along now, girl. They're waiting for us.''

Catherine drew back.

The old man pursed his lips. ''Well, I suppose you could return the way you came. The Willens will be happy to see you.''

Flustered, Catherine said, ''I don't understand. How can you know. . . .''

''Know your name, your peril? Weren't you listening? You are of Griaule, daughter. And more so than most, for you have slept at the center of his dreams. Your entire life has been prelude to this time, and your destiny will not be known until you come to the place from which his dreams arise . . . the dragon's heart.'' He took her hand. ''My name is Amos Mauldry. Captain Amos Mauldry, at your service. I have waited years for you . . . years! I am to prepare you for the consummate moment of your life. I urge you to follow me, to join the company of the feelies and begin your preparation. But—'' he shrugged ''—the choice is yours. I will not coerce you more than I have done . . . except to say this. Go with me now, and when you return you will discover that you have nothing to fear of the Willen brothers.''

He let loose of her hand and stood gazing at her with calm regard. She would have liked to disregard his words, but they were in such accord with all she had ever felt about her association with the dragon, she found that she could not. ''Who,'' she asked, ''are the feelies?''

He made a disparaging noise. ''Harmless creatures. They pass their time in copulating and arguing among themselves over the most trivial of matters. Were they not of service to Griaule, keeping him free of certain pests, they would have no use whatsoever. Still, there are worse folk in the world, and they do have moments in which they shine.'' He shifted impatiently, tapped his cane on the chamber floor. ''You'll meet them soon enough. Are you with me or not?''

Grudgingly, her hook at the ready, Catherine followed Mauldry toward the opening at the rear of the chamber and into a narrow, twisting channel illuminated by a pulsing golden light that issued from within Griaule's flesh. This radiance,

Mauldry said, derived from the dragon's blood, which, while it did not flow, was subject to fluctuations in brilliance due to changes in its chemistry. Or so he believed. He had regained his light-hearted manner, and as they walked he told Catherine he had captained a cargo ship that plied between Port Chantay and the Pearl Islands.

"We carried livestock, breadfruit, whale oil," he said. "I can't think of much we didn't carry. It was a good life, but hard as hard gets, and after I retired . . . well, I'd never married, and with time on my hands. I figured I owed myself some high times. I decided I'd see the sights, and the sight I most wanted to see was Griaule. I'd heard he was the First Wonder of the World . . . and he was! I was amazed, flabbergasted. I couldn't get enough of seeing him. He was more than a wonder. A miracle, an absolute majesty of a creature. People warned me to keep clear of the mouth, and they were right. But I couldn't stay away. One evening—I was walking along the edge of the mouth—two scalehunters set upon me, beat and robbed me. Left me for dead. And I would have died if it hadn't been for the feelies." He clucked his tongue. "I suppose I might as well give you some of their background. It can't help but prepare you for them . . . and I admit they need preparing for. They're not in the least agreeable to the eye." He cocked an eye toward Catherine, and after a dozen steps more he said, "Aren't you going to ask me to proceed."

"You didn't seem to need encouragement," she said.

He chuckled, nodding his approval. "Quite right, quite right." He walked on in silence, his shoulders hunched and head inclined, like an old turtle who'd leaned to get about on two legs.

"Well?" said Catherine, growing annoyed.

"I knew you'd ask," he said, and winked at her. "I didn't know who they were myself at first. If I had known I'd have been terrified. There are about five or six hundred in the colony. Their numbers are kept down by childbirth mortality and various other forms of attrition. They're most of them the descendants of a retarded man named Feely who wandered into the mouth almost a thousand years ago. Apparently he was walking near the mouth when flights of birds and swarms of insects began issuing from it. Not just a few, mind you. Entire populations. Wellsir, Feely was badly frightened. He was sure that some terrible beast had chased all these lesser creatures out, and he tried to hide from it. But he was so confused that instead of running away from the mouth, he ran into it and hid in the bushes. He waited for almost a day . . . no beast. The only sign of danger was a muffled thud from deep within the dragon. Finally his curiosity overcame his fear, and he went into the throat." Mauldry hawked and spat. "He felt secure there. More secure than on the outside, at any rate. Doubtless Griaule's doing, that feeling. He needed the feelies to be happy so they'd settle down and be his exterminators. Anyway, the first thing Feely did was to bring in a madwoman he'd known in Teocinte, and over the years they recruited other madmen who happened along. I was the first sane person they'd brought into the fold. They're extremely chauvinistic regarding the sane. But of course they were directed by Griaule to take me in. He knew you'd need someone to talk to.'' He prodded the wall with his cane. ''And now this is my home. More than a home. It's my truth, my love. To live here is to be transfigured.''

''That's a bit hard to swallow,'' said Catherine.

''Is it, now? You of all those who dwell on the surface should understand the scope of Griaule's virtues. There's no greater security than that he offers, no greater comprehension than that he bestows.''

''You make him sound like a god.''

Mauldry stopped walking, looking at her askance. The golden light waxed bright, filling in his wrinkles with shadows, making him appear to be centuries old. ''Well, what do you think he is?'' he asked with an air of mild indignation. ''What else could he be?''

Another ten minutes brought them to a chamber even more fabulous than the last. In shape it was oval, like an egg with a flattened bottom stood on end, an egg some one hundred and fifty feet high and a bit more than half that in diameter. It was lit by the same pulsing golden glow that had illuminated the channel, but here the fluctuations were more gradual and more extreme, ranging from a murky dimness to a glare approaching that of full daylight. The upper two thirds of the chamber wall was obscured by stacked ranks of small cubicles, leaning together at rickety angles, a geometry lacking the precision of the cells of a honeycomb, yet reminiscent of such, as if the bees that constructed it had been drunk. The entrances of the cubicles were draped with curtains, and lashed to their sides were ropes, rope ladders, and baskets that functioned as elevators, several of which were in use, lowering and lifting men and women dressed in a style similar to Mauldry: Catherine was reminded of a painting she had seen depicting the roof warrens of Port Chantay; but those habitations, while redolent of poverty and despair, had not as did these evoked an impression of squalid degeneracy, of order lapsed into the perverse. The lower portion of the chamber (and it was in this area that the channel emerged) was covered with a motley carpet composed of bolts of silk and satin and other rich fabrics, and seventy or eighty people were strolling and reclining on the gentle slopes. Only the center had been left clear, and there a gaping hole led away into yet another section of the dragon; a system of pipes ran into the hole, and Mauldry later explained that these carried the wastes of the colony into a pit of acids that had once fueled Griaule's fires. The dome of the chamber was choked with mist, the same pale stuff that had been vented from the protuberances in the previous chamber; birds with black wings and red markings on their heads made wheeling flights in and out of it, and frail scarves of mist drifted throughout. There was a sickly sweet odor to the place, and Catherine heard a murmurous rustling that issued from every quarter.

"Well," said Mauldry, making a sweeping gesture with his cane that included the entire chamber. "What do you think of our little colony?"

Some of the feelies had noticed them and were edging forward in small groups, stopping, whispering agitatedly among themselves, then edging forward again, all with the hesitant curiosity of savages; and although no signal had been given, the curtains over the cubicle entrances were being thrown back, heads were poking forth, and tiny figures were shinnying down the ropes, crowding into baskets, scuttling downward on the rope ladders, hundreds of people beginning to hurry toward her at a pace that brought to mind the panicked swarming of an anthill. And on first glance they seemed as alike as ants. Thin and pale and stooped, with sloping, nearly hairless skulls, and weepy eyes and thick-lipped slack mouths, like ugly children in their rotted silks and satins. Closer and closer they came, those in front pushed by the swelling ranks at their rear, and Catherine, unnerved by their stares, ignoring Mauldry's attempts to soothe her, retreated into the channel. Mauldry turned to the feelies, brandishing his cane as if it were a victor's sword, and cried, "She is here! He has brought her to us at last! She is here!"

His words caused several of those at the front of the press to throw back their heads and loose a whinnying laughter that went higher and higher in pitch as the golden light brightened. Others in the crowd lifted their hands, palms outward, holding them tight to their chests, and made little hops of excitement, and others yet twitched their heads from side to side, cutting their eyes this way and that, their expressions flowing between belligerence and confusion, apparently unsure of what was happening. This exhibition, clearly displaying the feelies' retardation, the tenuousness of their self-control, dismayed Catherine still more. But Mauldry seemed delighted and continued to exhort them, shouting, "She is here," over and over. His outcry came to rule the feelies, to orchestrate their movements. They began to sway, to repeat his words, slurring them so that their response was in effect a single word, "Shees'eer, Shees'eer," that reverberated through the chamber, acquiring a rolling echo, a hissing sonority, like the rapid breathing of a giant. The sound washed over Catherine, enfeebling her with its intensity, and she shrank back against the wall of the channel, expecting the feelies to break ranks and surround her; but they were so absorbed in their chanting, they appeared to have forgotten her. They milled about, bumping into one another, some striking out in anger at those who had impeded their way, others embracing and giggling, engaging in sexual play, but all of them keeping up the chorus of shouts.

Mauldry turned to her, his eyes giving back gleams of the golden light, his face looking in its vacuous glee akin to those of the feelies, and holding out his hands to her, his tone manifesting the bland sincerity of a priest, he said, "Welcome home."

3

Catherine was housed in two rooms halfway up the chamber wall, an apartment that adjoined Mauldry's quarters and was furnished with a rich carpeting of silks and furs and embroidered pillows; on the walls, also draped in these materials, hung a mirror with a gem-studded frame and two oil paintings—this bounty, said Mauldry, all part of Griaule's horde, the bulk of which lay in a cave west of the valley, its location known only to the feelies. One of the rooms contained a large basin for bathing, but since water was at a premium—being collected from points at which it seeped in through the scales—she was permitted one bath a week and no more. Still, the apartment and the general living conditions were on a par with those in Hangtown, and had it not been for the feelies, Catherine might have felt at home. But except in the case of the woman Leitha, who served her meals and cleaned, she could not overcome her revulsion at their inbred appearance and demented manner. They seemed to be responding to stimuli that she could not perceive, stopping now and then to cock an ear to an inaudible call or to stare at some invisible disturbance in the air. They scurried up and down the ropes to no apparent purpose, laughing and chattering, and they engaged in mass copulations at the bottom of the chamber. They spoke a mongrel dialect that she could barely understand, and they would hang on ropes outside her apartment, arguing, offering criticism of one another's dress and behavior, picking at the most insignificant of flaws and judging them according to an intricate code whose niceties Catherine was unable to master. They would follow her wherever she went, never sharing the same basket, but descending or ascending alongside her, staring, shrinking away if she turned her gaze upon them. With their foppish rags, their jewels, their childish pettiness and jealousies, they both irritated and frightened her; there was a tremendous tension in the way they looked at her, and she had the idea that at any moment they might lose their awe of her and attack.

She kept to her rooms those first weeks, brooding, trying to invent some means of escape, her solitude broken only by Leitha's ministrations and Mauldry's visits. He came twice daily and would sit among the pillows, declaiming upon Griaule's majesty, his truth. She did not enjoy the visits. The righteous quaver in his voice aroused her loathing, reminding her of the mendicant priests who passed now and then through Hangtown, leaving bastards and empty purses in their wake. She found his conversation for the most part boring, and when it did not bore, she found it disturbing in its constant references to her time of trial at the dragon's heart. She had no doubt that Griaule was at work in her life. The longer she remained in the colony, the more vivid her dreams became and the more certain she grew that his purpose was somehow aligned with her presence there. But the pathetic condition of the feelies shed a wan light on her old fantasies of a destiny entwined with the dragon's, and she began to see herself in that wan light, to experience a revulsion at her fecklessness equal to that she felt toward those around her.

"You are our salvation," Mauldry told her one day as she sat sewing herself a new pair of trousers—she refused to dress in the gilt and satin rags preferred by the feelies. "Only you can know the mystery of the dragon's heart, only you can inform us of his deepest wish for us. We've known this for years."

Seated amid the barbaric disorder of silks and furs, Catherine looked out through a gap in the curtains, watching the waning of the golden light. "You hold me prisoner," she said. "Why should I help you?"

"Would you leave us, then?" Mauldry asked. "What of the Willens?"

"I doubt they're still waiting for me. Even if they are, it's only a matter of which death I prefer, a lingering one here or a swift one at their hands."

Mauldry fingered the gold knob of his cane. "You're right," he said. "The Willens are no longer a menace."

She glanced up at him.

"They died the moment you went down out of Griaule's mouth," he said. "He sent his creatures to deal with them, knowing you were his at long last."

Catherine remembered the shouts she'd heard while walking down the incline of the throat. "What creatures?"

"That's of no importance," said Mauldry. "What is important is that you apprehend the subtlety of his power, his absolute mastery and control over your thoughts, your being."

"Why?" she asked. "Why is that important?" He seemed to be struggling to explain himself, and she laughed. "Lost touch with your god, Mauldry? Won't he supply the appropriate cant?"

Mauldry composed himself. "It is for you, not I, to understand why you are here. You must explore Griaule, study the miraculous workings of his flesh, involve yourself in the intricate order of his being."

In frustration, Catherine punched at a pillow. "If you don't let me go, I'll die! This place will kill me. I won't be around long enough to do any exploring."

"Oh, but you will." Mauldry favored her with an unctuous smile. "That, too, is known to us."

Ropes creaked, and a moment later the curtains parted, and Leitha, a young woman in a gown of watered blue taffeta, whose bodice pushed up the pale nubs of her breasts, entered bearing Catherine's dinner tray. She set down the tray. "Be mo', ma'am?" she said. "Or mus' I later c'meah." She gazed fixedly at Catherine, her close-set brown eyes blinking, fingers plucking at the folds of her gown.

"Whatever you want." Catherine said.

Leitha continued to stare at her, and only when Mauldry spoke sharply to her did she turn and leave.

Catherine looked down disconsolately at the tray and noticed that in addition to the usual fare of greens and fruit (gathered from the dragon's mouth) there were several slices of underdone meat, whose reddish hue appeared identical to the color of Griaule's flesh. "What's this?" she asked, poking at one of the slices.

"The hunters were successful today," said Mauldry. "Every so often hunting parties are sent into the digestive tract. It's quite dangerous, but there are beasts there that can injure Griaule. It serves him that we hunt them, and their flesh nourishes us." He leaned forward, studying her face. "Another party is going out tomorrow. Perhaps you'd care to join them. I can arrange it if you wish. You'll be well protected."

Catherine's initial impulse was to reject the invitation, but then she thought that this might offer an opportunity for escape; in fact, she realized that to play upon Mauldry's tendencies, to evince interest in a study of the dragon, would be a wise move. The more she learned about Griaule's geography, the greater chance there would be that she would find a way out.

"You said it was dangerous. . . . How dangerous?"

"For you? Not in the least. Griaule would not harm you. But for the hunting party, well . . . lives will be lost."

"And they're going out tomorrow?"

"Perhaps the next day as well. We're not sure how extensive an infestation is involved."

"What kind of beast are you talking about?"

"Serpents of a sort."

Catherine's enthusiasm was dimmed, but she saw no other means of taking action. "Very well. I'll go with them tomorrow."

"Wonderful, wonderful!" It took Mauldry three tries to heave himself up from the cushion, and when at last he managed to stand, he leaned on his cane, breathing heavily. "I'll come for you early in the morning."

"You're going, too? You don't seem up to the exertion."

Mauldry chuckled. "It's true, I'm an old man. But where you're concerned, daughter, my energies are inexhaustible." He performed a gallant bow and hobbled from the room.

Not long after he had left, Leitha returned. She drew a second curtain across the entrance, cutting the light, even at its most brilliant, to a dim effusion. Then she stood by the entrance, eyes fixed on Catherine. "Wan' mo' fum Leitha?" she asked.

The question was not a formality. Leitha had made it plain by touches and other signs that Catherine had but to ask and she would come to her as a lover. Her deformities masked by the shadowy air, she had the look of a pretty young girl dressed for a dance, and for a moment, in the grip of loneliness and despair, watching Leitha alternately brightening and merging with gloom, listening to the unceasing murmur of the feelies from without, aware in full of the tribal strangeness of the colony and her utter lack of connection, Catherine felt a bizarre arousal.

But the moment passed, and she was disgusted with herself, with her weakness, and angry at Leitha and this degenerate place that was eroding her humanity. "Get out," she said coldly, and when Leitha hesitated, she shouted the command, sending the girl stumbling backwards from the room. Then she turned onto her stomach, her face pressed into a pillow, expecting to cry, feeling the pressure of a sob building in her chest; but the sob never manifested, and she lay there, knowing her emptiness, feeling that she was no longer worthy of even her own tears.

Behind one of the cubicles in the lower half of the chamber was hidden the entrance to a wide circular passage ringed by ribs of cartilage, and it was along this passage the next morning that Catherine and Mauldry, accompanied by thirty male feelies, set out upon the hunt. They were armed with swords and bore torches to light the way, for here Griaule's veins were too deeply embedded to provide illumination; they walked in a silence broken only by coughs and the soft scraping of their footsteps. The silence, such a contrast from the feelies' usual chatter, unsettled Catherine, and the flaring and guttering of the torches, the apparition of a backlit pale face turned toward her, the tingling acidic scent that grew stronger and stronger, all this assisted her impression that they were lost souls treading some byway in Hell.

Their angle of descent increased, and shortly thereafter they reached a spot from which Catherine had a view of a black distance shot through with intricate networks of fine golden skeins, like spiderwebs of gold in a night sky. Mauldry told her to wait, and the torches of the hunting party moved off, making it clear that they had come to a large chamber; but she did not understand just how large until a fire suddenly bloomed, bursting into towering flames: and enormous bonfire composed of sapling trunks and entire bushes. The size of the fire was impressive in itself, but the immense cavity of the stomach that it partially revealed was more impressive yet. It could not have been less than two hundred yards long, and was walled with folds of thin whitish skin figured by lacings and branchings of veins, attached to curving ribs covered with even thinner skin that showed their every articulation. A quarter of the way across the cavity, the floor declined into a sink brimming with a dark liquid, and it was along a section of the wall close to the sink that the bonfire had been lit, its smoke billowing up toward a bruised patch of skin some fifty feet in circumference with a tattered rip at the center. As Catherine watched the entire patch began to undulate. The hunting party gathered beneath it, ranged around the bonfire, their swords raised. Then, with ponderous slowness a length of thick white tubing was extruded from the rip, a gigantic worm that lifted its blind head above the hunting party, opened a mouth fringed with palps to expose a dark red maw and emitted a piercing squeal that touched off echoes and made Catherine put her hands to her ears. More and more of the worm's body emerged from the stomach wall, and she marveled at the courage of the hunting party, who maintained their ground. The worm's squealing became unbearably loud as smoke enveloped it; it lashed about, twisting and probing at the air with its head, and then, with an even louder cry, it fell across the bonfire, writhing, sending up showers of sparks. It rolled out of the fire, crushing several of the party; the others set to with their swords, hacking in a frenzy at the head, painting streaks of dark blood over the corpse-pale skin. Catherine realized that she had pressed her fists to her cheeks and was screaming, so involved was she in the battle. The worm's blood spattered the floor of the cavity, its skin was charred and blistered from the flames, and its head was horribly slashed, the flesh hanging in ragged strips. But it continued to squeal, humping up great sections of its body, forming an arch over groups of attackers and dropping down upon them. A third of the hunting party lay motionless, their limbs sprawled in graceless attitudes, the remnants of the bonfire—heaps of burning branches—scattered among them; the rest stabbed and sliced at the increasingly torpid worm, dancing away from its lunges. At last the worm lifted half its body off the floor, its head held high, silent for a moment, swaying with the languor of a mesmerized serpent. It let out a cry like the whistle of a monstrous tea kettle, a cry that seemed to fill the cavity with its fierce vibrations, and fell, twisting once and growing still, its maw half-open, palps twitching in the register of some final internal function.

The hunting party collapsed around it, winded, drained, some leaning on their swords. Shocked by the suddenness of the silence, Catherine went a few steps out into the cavity, Mauldry at her shoulder. She hesitated, then moved forward again, thinking that some of the party might need tending. But those who had fallen were dead, their limbs broken, blood showing on their mouths. She walked alongside the worm. The thickness of its body was three times her height, the skin glistening and warped by countless tiny puckers and tinged with a faint bluish cast that made it all the more ghastly.

"What are you thinking?" Mauldry asked.

Catherine shook her head. No thoughts would come to her. It was as if the process of thought itself had been canceled by the enormity of what she had witnessed. She had always supposed that she had a fair idea of Griaule's scope, his complexity, but now she understood that whatever she had once believed had been inadequate, and she struggled to acclimate to this new perspective. There was a commotion behind her. Members of the hunting party were hacking slabs of meat from the worm. Mauldry draped an arm about her, and by that contact she became aware that she was trembling.

"Come along," he said. "I'll take you home."

"To my room, you mean?" Her bitterness resurfaced, and she threw off his arm.

"Perhaps you'll never think of it as home," he said. "Yet nowhere is there a place more suited to you." He signaled to one of the hunting party, who came toward them, stopped to light a dead torch from a pile of burning branches.

With a dismal laugh, Catherine said, "I'm beginning to find it irksome how you claim to know so much about me."

"It's not you I claim to know," he said, "though it has been given me to understand something of your purpose. But—" he rapped the tip of his cane against the floor of the cavity "—he by whom you are most known, *him I* know well."

4

Catherine made three escape attempts during the next two months, and thereafter gave up on the enterprise; with hundreds of eyes watching her, there was no point in wasting energy. For almost six months following the final attempt she became dispirited and refused to leave her rooms. Her health suffered, her thoughts paled, and she lay abed for hours, relieving her life in Hangtown, which she came to view as a model of joy and contentment. Her inactivity caused loneliness to bear in upon her. Mauldry tried his best to entertain her, but his mystical obsession with Griaule made him incapable of offering the consolation of a true friend. And so, without friends or lovers, without even an enemy, she sank into a welter of self-pity and began to toy with the idea of suicide. The prospect of never seeing the sun again, of attending no more carnivals at Teocinte . . . it seemed too much to endure. But either she was not brave enough or not sufficiently foolish to take her own life, and deciding that no matter how vile or delimiting the circumstance, it promised more than eternal darkness, she gave herself to the one occupation the feelies would permit her: the exploration and study of Griaule.

Like one of those enormous Tibetan sculptures of the Buddha constructed within a tower only a trifle larger than the sculpture itself, Griaule's unbeating heart was a dimpled golden shape as vast as a cathedral and was enclosed within a chamber whose walls left a gap six feet wide around the organ. The chamber could be reached by passing through a vein that had ruptured long ago and was now a wrinkled brown tube just big enough for Catherine to crawl along it; to make this transit and then emerge into that narrow space beside the heart was an intensely claustrophobic experience, and it took her a long, long while to get used to the process. Even after she had grown accustomed to this, it was still difficult for her to adjust to the peculiar climate at the heart. The air was thick with a heated stinging scent that reminded her of the brimstone stink left by a lightning stroke, and there was an atmosphere of imminence, a stillness and tension redolent of some cthonic disturbance that might strike at any moment. The blood at the heart did not merely fluctuate (and here the fluctuations were erratic, varying both in range of brilliance and rapidity of change); it circulated—the movement due to variations in heat and pressure—through a series of convulsed inner chambers, and this eddying in conjunction with the flickering brilliance threw patterns of light and shadow on the heart wall, patterns as complex and fanciful as arabesques that drew her eye in. Staring at them, Catherine began to be able to predict what configurations would next appear and to apprehend a logic to their progression; it was nothing that she could put into words, but watching the play of light and shadow produced in her emotional responses that seemed keyed to the shifting patterns and allowed her to make crude guesses as to the heart's workings. She learned that if she stared too long at the patterns, dreams would take her, dreams notable for their vividness, and one particularly notable in that it recurred again and again.

The dream began with a sunrise, the solar disc edging up from the southern horizon, its rays spearing toward a coast strewn with great black rocks that protruded from the shallows, and perched upon them were sleeping dragons; as the sun warmed them, light flaring on their scales, they grumbled and lifted their heads and with the snapping sound of huge sails filling with wind, they unfolded their leathery wings and went soaring up into an indigo sky flecked with stars arranged into strange constellations, wheeling and roaring their exultation . . . all but one dragon, who flew only a brief arc before coming disjointed in midflight and dropping like a stone into the water, vanishing beneath the waves. It was an awesome thing to see, this tumbling flight, the wings billowing, tearing, the fanged mouth open, claws grasping for purchase in the air. But despite its beauty, the dream seemed to have little relevance to Griaule's situation. He was in no danger of falling, that much was certain. Nevertheless, the frequency of the dream's recurrence persuaded Catherine that something must be amiss, that perhaps Griaule feared an attack of the sort that had stricken the flying dragon. With this in mind she began to inspect the heart, using her hooks to clamber up the steep slopes of the chamber walls, sometimes hanging upside down like a blond spider above the glowing, flickering organ. But she could find nothing out of order, no imperfections—at least as far as she could determine—and the sole result of the inspection was that the dream stopped occurring and was replaced by a simpler dream in which she watched the chest of a sleeping dragon contract and expand. She could make no sense of it, and although the dream continued to recur, she paid less and less attention to it.

Mauldry, who had been expecting miraculous insights from her, was depressed when none were forthcoming. "Perhaps I've been wrong all these years," he said. "Or senile. Perhaps I'm growing senile."

A few months earlier, Catherine, locked into bitterness and resentment, might have seconded his opinion out of spite; but her studies at the heart had soothed her, infused her both with calm resignation and some compassion for her jailers —they could not, after all, be blamed for their pitiful condition—and she said to Mauldry, "I've only begun to learn. It's likely to take a long time before I understand what he wants. And that's in keeping with his nature, isn't it? That nothing happens quickly?"

"I suppose you're right," he said glumly.

"Of course I am," she said. "Sooner or later there'll be a revelation. But a creature like Griaule doesn't yield his secrets to a casual glance. Just give me time."

And oddly enough, though she had spoken these words to cheer Mauldry, they seemed to ring true.

She had started her explorations with minimal enthusiasm, but Griaule's scope was so extensive, his populations of parasites and symbiotes so exotic and intriguing, her passion for knowledge was fired and over the next six years she grew zealous in her studies, using them to compensate for the emptiness of her life. With Mauldry ever at her side, accompanied by small groups of the feelies, she mapped the interior of the dragon, stopping short of penetrating the skull, warned off from that region by a premonition of danger. She sent several of the more intelligent feelies into Teocinte, where they acquired beakers and flasks and books and writing materials that enabled her to build a primitive laboratory for chemical analysis. She discovered that the egg-shaped chamber occupied by the colony would—had the dragon been fully alive—be pumped full of acids and gasses by the contraction of the heart muscle, flooding the channel, mingling in the adjoining chamber with yet another liquid, forming a volatile mixture that Griaule's breath would—if he so desired—kindle into flame; if he did not so desire, the expansion of the heart would empty the chamber. She distilled from these liquids and from that she derived a potent narcotic that she named brianine after her nemesis, and from a lichen growing on the outer surface of the lungs, she derived a powerful stimulant. She catalogued the dragon's myriad flora and fauna, covering the walls of her rooms with lists and charts and notations on their behaviors. Many of the animals were either familiar to her or variants of familiar forms. Spiders, bats, swallows, and the like. But as was the case on the dragon's surface, a few of them testified to his otherworldly origins, and perhaps the most curious of them was Catherine's metahex (her designation for it), a creature with six identical bodies that thrived in the stomach acids. Each body was approximately the size and color of a worn penny, fractionally more dense than a jellyfish, ringed with cilia, and all were in a constant state of agitation. She had at first assumed the metahex to be six creatures, a species that traveled in sixes, but had begun to suspect otherwise when—upon killing one for the purposes of dissection—the other five bodies had also died. She had initiated a series of experiments that involved menacing and killing hundreds of the things, and had ascertained that the bodies were connected by some sort of field—one whose presence she deduced by process of observation—that permitted the essence of the creature to switch back and forth between the bodies, utilizing the ones it did not occupy as a unique form of camouflage. But even the metahex seemed ordinary when compared to the ghostvine, a plant that she discovered grew in one place alone, a small cavity near the base of the skull.

None of the colony would approach that region, warned away by the same sense of danger that had afflicted Catherine, and it was presumed that should one venture too close to the brain, Griaule would mobilize some of his more deadly inhabitants to deal with the interloper. But Catherine felt secure in approaching the cavity, and leaving Mauldry and her escort of feelies behind, she climbed the steep channel that led up to it, lighting her way with a torch, and entered through an aperture not much wider than her hips. Once inside, seeing that the place was lit by veins of golden blood that branched across the ceiling, flickering like the blown flame of a candle, she extinguished the torch; she noticed with surprise that except for the ceiling, the entire cavity—a boxy space some twenty feet long, about eight feet in height—was fettered with vines whose leaves were dark green, glossy, with complex veination and tips that ended in minuscule hollow tubes. She was winded from the climb, more winded—she thought—than she should have been, and she sat down against the wall to catch her breath; then, feeling drowsy, she closed her eyes for a moment's rest. She came alert to the sound of Mauldry's voice shouting her name. Still drowsy, annoyed by his impatience, she called out, "I just want to rest a few minutes!"

"A few minutes?" he cried. "You've been there three days! What's going on? Are you all right?"

"That's ridiculous!" She started to come to her feet, then sat back, stunned by the sight of a naked woman with long blond hair curled up in a corner not ten feet away, nestled so close to the cavity wall that the tips of leaves half-covered her body and obscured her face.

"Catherine!" Mauldry shouted. "Answer me!"

"I . . . I'm all right! Just a minute!"

The woman stirred and made a complaining noise.

"Catherine!"

"I said I'm all right!"

The woman stretched out her legs; on her right hip was a fine pink scar, hook-shaped, identical to the scar on Catherine's hip, evidence of a childhood fall. And on the back of the right knee, a patch of raw, puckered skin, the product of an acid burn she'd suffered the year before. She was astonished by the sight of these markings, but when the woman sat up and Catherine understood that she was staring at her twin—identical not only in feature, but also in expression, wearing a resigned look that she had glimpsed many times in her mirror—her astonishment turned to fright. She could have sworn she felt the muscles of the woman's face shifting as the expression changed into one of pleased recognition, and in spite of her fear, she had a vague sense of the woman's emotions, of her burgeoning hope and elation.

"Sister," said the woman; she glanced down at her body, and Catherine had a momentary flash of doubled vision, watching the woman's head decline and seeing as well naked breasts and belly from the perspective of the woman's eyes.

Her vision returned to normal, and she looked at the woman's face . . . *her* face. Though she had studied herself in the mirror each morning for years, she had never had such a clear perception of the changes that life inside the dragon had wrought upon her. Fine lines bracketed her lips, and the beginnings of crows' feet radiated from the corners of her eyes. Her cheeks had hollowed, and this made her cheekbones appear sharper; the set of her mouth seemed harder, more determined. The high gloss and perfection of her youthful beauty had been marred far more than she had thought, and this dismayed her. However, the most re-markable change—the one that most struck her—was not embodied by any one detail but in the overall character of the face, in that it exhibited character, for— she realized—prior to entering the dragon it had displayed very little, and what little it *had* displayed had been evidence of indulgence. It troubled her to have this knowledge of the fool she had been thrust upon her with such poignancy.

As if the woman had been listening to her thoughts, she held out her hand and said, "Don't punish yourself, sister. We are all victims of our past."

"What are you?" Catherine asked, pulling back. She felt the woman was a danger to her, though she was not sure why.

"I am you." Again the woman reached out to touch her, and again Catherine shifted away. The woman's face was smiling, but Catherine felt the wash of her frustration and noticed that the woman had leaned forward only a few degrees, remaining in contact with the leaves of the vines as if there were some attachment between them that she could not break.

"I doubt that." Catherine was fascinated, but she was beginning to be swayed by the intuition that the woman's touch would harm her.

"But I am!" the woman insisted. "And something more, besides."

"What more?"

"The plant extracts essences," said the woman. "Infinitely small constructs of the flesh from which it creates a likeness free of the imperfections of your body. And since the seeds of your future are embodied by these essences, though they are unknown to you, I know them . . . for now."

"For now?"

The woman's tone had become desperate. "There's a connection between us . . . surely you feel it?"

"Yes."

"To live, to complete that connection, I must touch you. And once I do, this knowledge of the future will be lost to me. I will be as you . . . though separate. But don't worry. I won't interfere with you, I'll live my own life." She leaned forward again, and Catherine saw that some of the leaves were affixed to her back, the hollow tubes at their tips adhering to the skin. Once again she had an awareness of danger, a growing apprehension that the woman's touch would drain her of some vital substance.

"If you know my future," she said, "then tell me . . . will I ever escape Griaule."

Mauldry chose this moment to call out to her, and she soothed him by saying that she was taking some cuttings, that she would be down soon. She repeated her question, and the woman said, "Yes, yes, you will leave the dragon," and tried to grasp her hand. "Don't be afraid. I won't harm you."

The woman's flesh was sagging, and Catherine felt the eddying of her fear.

"Please!" she said, holding out both hands. "Only your touch will sustain me. Without it, I'll die!"

But Catherine refused to trust her.

"You must believe me!" cried the woman. "I am your sister! My blood is yours, my memories!" The flesh upon her arms had sagged into billows like the flesh of an old woman, and her face was becoming jowly, grossly distorted. "Oh, please! Remember the time with Stel below the wing . . . you were a maiden. The wind was blowing thistles down from Griaule's back like a rain of silver. And remember the gala in Teocinte? Your sixteenth birthday. You wore a mask of orange blossoms and gold wire, and three men asked for your hand. For God's sake, Catherine! Listen to me! The major . . . don't you remember him? The young major? You were in love with him, but you didn't follow your heart. You were afraid of love, you didn't trust what you felt because you never trusted yourself in those days."

The connection between them was fading, and Catherine steeled herself against the woman's entreaties, which had begun to move her more than a little bit. The woman slumped down, her features blurring, a horrid sight, like the melting of a wax figure, and then, an even more horrid sight, she smiled, her lips appearing to dissolve away from teeth that were themselves dissolving.

"I understand," said the woman in a frail voice, and gave a husky, glutinous laugh. "Now I see."

"What is it?" Catherine asked. But the woman collapsed, rolling onto her side, and the process of deterioration grew more rapid; within the span of a few minutes she had dissipated into a gelatinous grayish white puddle that retained the rough outline of her form. Catherine was both appalled and relieved; however, she couldn't help feeling some remorse, uncertain whether she had acted in self-defense or through cowardice had damned a creature who was by nature no more reprehensible than herself. While the woman had been alive—if that was the proper word—Catherine had been mostly afraid, but now she marveled at the apparition, at the complexity of a plant that could produce even the semblance of a human. And the woman had been, she thought, something more vital than mere likeness. How else could she have known her memories? Or could memory, she wondered, have a physiological basis? She forced herself to take samples of the woman's remains, of the vines, with an eye toward exploring the mystery. But she doubted that the heart of such an intricate mystery would be accessible to her primitive instruments. This was to prove a self-fulfilling prophecy, because she really did not want to know the secrets of the ghostvine, leery as to what might be brought to light concerning her own nature, and with the passage of time, although she thought of it often and sometimes discussed the phenomenon with Mauldry, she eventually let the matter drop.

5

Though the temperature never changed, though neither rain nor snow fell, though the fluctuations of the golden light remained consistent in their rhythms, the seasons were registered inside the dragon by migrations of birds, the weaving of cocoons, the birth of millions of insects at once; and it was by these signs that Catherine—nine years after entering Griaule's mouth—knew it to be autumn when she fell in love. The three years prior to this had been characterized by a slackening of her zeal, a gradual wearing down of her enthusiasm for scientific knowledge, and this tendency became marked after the death of Captain Mauldry from natural causes; without him to serve as a buffer between her and the feelies, she was overwhelmed by their inanity, their woeful aspect. In truth, there was not much left to learn. Her maps were complete, her specimens and notes filled several rooms, and while she continued her visits to the dragon's heart, she no longer sought to interpret the dreams, using them instead to pass the boring hours. Again she grew restless and began to consider escape. Her life was being wasted, she believed, and she wanted to return to the world, to engage more vital opportunities than those available to her in Griaule's many-chambered prison. It was not that she was ungrateful for the experience. Had she managed to escape shortly after her arrival, she would have returned to a life of meaningless frivolity; but now, armed with knowledge, aware of her strengths and weaknesses, possessed of ambition and a heightened sense of morality, she thought she would be able to accomplish something of importance. But before she could determine whether or not escape was possible, there was a new arrival at the colony, a man whom a group of feelies—while gathering berries near the mouth—had found lying unconscious and had borne to safety. The man's name was John Colmacos, and he was in his early thirties, a botanist from the university at Port Chantay who had been abandoned by his guides when he insisted on entering the mouth and had subsequently been mauled by apes that had taken up residence in the mouth. He was lean, rawboned, with powerful, thick-fingered hands and fine brown hair that would never stay combed. His long-jawed, horsey face struck a bargain between homely and distinctive, and was stamped with a perpetually inquiring expression, as if he were a bit perplexed by everything he saw. His blue eyes were large and intricate, the irises flecked with green and hazel, appearing surprisingly delicate in contrast to the rest of him.

Catherine, happy to have rational company, especially that of a professional in her vocation, took charge of nursing him back to health—he had suffered fractures of the arm and ankle, and was badly cut about the face; and in the course of this she began to have fantasies about him as a lover. She had never met a man with his gentleness of manner, his lack of pretense, and she found it most surprising that he wasn't concerned with trying to impress her. Her conception of men had been limited to the soldiers of Teocinte, the thugs of Hangtown, and everything about John fascinated her. For a while she tried to deny her feelings, telling herself that she would have fallen in love with almost anyone under the circumstances, afraid that by loving she would only increase her dissatisfaction with her prison; and, too, there was the realization that this was doubtless another of Griaule's manipulations, his attempt to make her content with her lot, to replace Mauldry with a lover. But she couldn't deny that under any circumstance she would have been attracted to John Colmacos for many reasons, not the least of which was his respect for her work with Griaule, for how she had handled adversity. Nor could she deny that the attraction was mutual. That was clear. Although there were awkward moments, there was no mooniness between them; they were both watching what was happening.

"This is amazing," he said one day while going through one of her notebooks, lying on a pile of furs in her apartment. "It's hard to believe you haven't had training."

A flush spread over her cheeks. "Anyone in my shoes, with all that time, nothing else to do, they would have done no less."

He set down the notebook and measured her with a stare that caused her to lower her eyes. "You're wrong," he said. "Most people would have fallen apart. I can't think of anybody else who could have managed all this. You're remarkable."

She felt oddly incompetent in the light of this judgment, as if she had accorded him ultimate authority and were receiving the sort of praise that a wise adult might bestow upon an inept child who had done well for once. She wanted to explain to him that everything she had done had been a kind of therapy, a hobby to stave off despair; but she didn't know how to put this into words without sounding awkward and falsely modest, and so she merely said, "Oh," and busied herself with preparing a dose of brianine to take away the pain in his ankle.

"You're embarrassed," he said. "I'm sorry . . . I didn't mean to make you uncomfortable."

"I'm not . . . I mean, I. . . ." She laughed. "I'm still not accustomed to talking."

He said nothing, smiling.

"What is it?" she said, defensive, feeling that he was making fun of her.

"What do you mean?"

"Why are you smiling?"

"I could frown," he said, "if that would make you comfortable."

Irritated, she bent to her task, mixing paste in a brass goblet studded with uncut emeralds, then molding it into a pellet.

"That was a joke," he said.

"I know."

"What's the matter?"

She shook her head. "Nothing."

"Look," he said. "I don't want to make you uncomfortable . . . I really don't. What am I doing wrong?"

She sighed, exasperated with herself. "It's not you," she said. "I just can't get used to you being here, that's all."

From without came the babble of some feelies lowering on ropes toward the chamber floor.

"I can understand that," he said. "I. . . ." He broke off, looked down and fingered the edge of the notebook.

"What were you going to say?"

He threw back his head, laughed. "Do you see how we're acting? Explaining ourselves constantly . . . as if we could hurt each other by saying the wrong word."

She glanced over at him, met his eyes, then looked away.

"What I meant was, we're not that fragile," he said, and then, as if by way of clarification, he hastened to add: "We're not that . . . vulnerable to one another."

He held her stare for a moment, and this time it was he who looked away and Catherine who smiled.

If she hadn't known she was in love, she would have suspected as much from the change in her attitude toward the dragon. She seemed to be seeing everything anew. Her wonder at Griaule's size and strangeness had been restored, and she delighted in displaying his marvelous features to John—the orioles and swallows that never once had flown under the sun, the glowing heart, the cavity where the ghostvine grew (though she would not linger there), and a tiny chamber close to the heart lit not by Griaule's blood but by thousands of luminous white spiders that shifted and crept across the blackness of the ceiling, like a night sky whose constellations had come to life. It was in this chamber that they engaged in their first intimacy, a kiss from which Catherine—after initially letting herself be swept away—pulled back, disoriented by the powerful sensations flooding her body, sensations both familiar and unnatural in that she hadn't experienced them for so long, and startled by the suddenness with which her fantasies had become real.

Flustered, she ran from the chamber, leaving John, who was still hobbled by his injuries, to limp back to the colony alone.

She hid from him most of that day sitting with her knees drawn up on a patch of peach-colored silk near the hole at the center of the colony's floor, immersed in the bustle and gabble of the feelies as they promenaded in their decaying finery. Though for the most part they were absorbed in their own pursuits, some sensed her mood and gathered around her, touching her, making the whimpering noises that among them passed for expressions of tenderness. Their pasty doglike faces ringed her, uniformly sad, and as if sadness were contagious, she started to cry. At first her tears seemed the product of her inability to cope with love, and then it seemed she was crying over the poor thing of her life, the haplessness of her days inside the body of the dragon; but she came to feel that her sadness was one with Griaule's, that this feeling of gloom and entrapment reflected his essential mood, and that thought stopped her tears. She'd never considered the dragon an object deserving of sympathy, and she did not now consider him such; but perceiving him imprisoned in a web of ancient magic, and the Chinese puzzle of lesser magics and imprisonments that derived from that original event, she felt foolish for having cried. Everything, she realized, even the happiest of occurrences, might be a cause for tears if you failed to see it in terms of the world that you inhabited; however, if you managed to achieve a balanced perspective, you saw that although sadness could result from every human action, you had to seize the opportunities for effective action which came your way and not question them, no matter how unrealistic or futile they might appear. Just as Griaule had done by finding a way to utilize his power while immobilized. She laughed to think of herself emulating Griaule even in this abstract fashion, and several of the feelies standing beside her echoed her laughter. One of the males, an old man with tufts of gray hair poking up from his pallid skull, shuffled near, picking at a loose button on his stiff, begrimed coat of silver-embroidered satin.

"Cat'rine mus' be easy sweetly, now?" he said. "No mo' bad t'ing?"

"No," she said. "No more bad thing."

On the other side of the hole a pile of naked feelies were writhing together in the clumsiness of foreplay, men trying to penetrate men, getting angry, slapping one another, then lapsing into giggles when they found a woman and figured out the proper procedure. Once this would have disgusted her, but no more. Judged by the attitudes of a place not their own, perhaps the feelies were disgusting; but this *was* their place, and Catherine's place as well, and accepting that at last, she stood and walked toward the nearest basket. The old man hustled after her, fingering his lapels in a parody of self-importance, and, as if he were the functionary of her mood, he announced to everyone they encountered, "No mo' bad t'ing, no mo' bad t'ing."

*   *   *

Riding up in the basket was like passing in front of a hundred tiny stages upon which scenes from the same play were being performed—pale figures slumped on silks, playing with gold and bejeweled baubles—and gazing around her, ignoring the stink, the dilapidation, she felt she was looking out upon an exotic kingdom. Always before she had been impressed by its size and grotesqueness; but now she was struck by its richness, and she wondered whether the feelies' style of dress was inadvertent or if Griaule's subtlety extended to the point of clothing this human refuse in the rags of dead courtiers and kings. She felt exhilarated, joyful; but as the basket lurched near the level on which her rooms were located, she became nervous. It had been so long since she had been with a man, and she was worried that she might not be suited to him . . . then she recalled that she'd been prone to these worries even in the days when she had been with a new man every week.

She lashed the basket to a peg, stepped out onto the walkway outside her rooms, took a deep breath and pushed through the curtains, pulled them shut behind her. John was asleep, the furs pulled up to his chest. In the fading half-light, his face—dirtied by a few days' growth of beard—looked sweetly mysterious and rapt, like the face of a saint at meditation, and she thought it might be best to let him sleep; but that, she realized, was a signal of her nervousness, not of compassion. The only thing to do was to get it over with, to pass through nervousness as quickly as possible and learn what there was to learn. She stripped off her trousers, her shirt, and stood for a second above him, feeling giddy, frail, as if she'd stripped off much more than a few ounces of fabric. Then she eased in beneath the furs, pressing the length of her body to his. He stirred but didn't wake, and this delighted her; she liked the idea of having him in her clutches, of coming to him in the middle of a dream, and she shivered with the apprehension of gleeful, childish power. He tossed, turned onto his side to face her, still asleep, and she pressed closer, marveling at how ready she was, how open to him. He muttered something, and as she nestled against him, he grew hard, his erection pinned between their bellies. Cautiously, she lifted her right knee atop his hip, guided him between her legs and moved her hips back and forth, rubbing against him, slowly, slowly, teasing herself with little bursts of pleasure. His eyelids twitched, blinked open, and he stared at her, his eyes looking black and wet, his skin stained a murky gold in the dimness. "Catherine," he said, and she gave a soft laugh, because her name seemed a power the way he had spoken it. His fingers hooked into the plump meat of her hips as he pushed and prodded at her, trying to find the right angle. Her head fell back, her eyes closed, concentrating on the feeling that centered her dizziness and heat, and then he was inside her, going deep with a single thrust, beginning to make love to her, and she said, "Wait, wait," holding him immobile, afraid for an instant, feeling too much, a black wave of sensation building, threatening to wash her away.

"What's wrong?" he whispered. "Do you want . . ."

"Just wait . . . just for a bit." She rested her forehead against his, trembling, amazed by the difference that he made in her body; one moment she felt buoyant, as if their connection had freed her from the restraints of gravity, and the next moment—whenever he shifted or eased fractionally deeper—she would feel as if all his weight were pouring inside her and she was sinking into the cool silks.

"Are you all right?"

"Mmm." She opened her eyes, saw his face inches away and was surprised that he didn't appear unfamiliar.

"What is it?" he asked.

"I was just thinking."

"About what?"

"I was wondering who you were, and when I looked at you, it was as if I already knew." She traced the line of his upper lip with her forefinger. "Who are you?"

"I thought you knew already."

"Maybe . . . but I don't know anything specific. Just that you were a professor."

"You want to know specifics?"

"Yes."

"I was an unruly child," he said. "I refused to eat onion soup, I never washed behind my ears."

His grasp tightened on her hips, and he thrust inside her, a few slow, delicious movements, kissing her mouth, her eyes.

"When I was a boy," he said, quickening his rhythm, breathing hard between the words, "I'd go swimming every morning. Off the rocks at Ayler's Point . . . it was beautiful. Cerulean water, palms. Chickens and pigs foraging. On the beach."

"Oh, God!" she said, locking her leg behind his thigh, her eyelids fluttering down.

"My first girlfriend was named Penny . . . she was twelve. Redheaded. I was a year younger. I loved her because she had freckles. I used to believe . . . freckles were . . . a sign of something. I wasn't sure what. But I love you more than her."

"I love you!" She found his rhythm, adapted to it, trying to take him all inside her. She wanted to see where they joined, and she imagined there was no longer any distinction between them, that their bodies had merged and were sealed together.

"I cheated in mathematics class, I could never do trigonometry. God . . . Catherine."

His voice receded, stopped, and the air seemed to grow solid around her, holding her in a rosy suspension. Light was gathering about them, frictive light from a strange heatless burning, and she heard herself crying out, calling his name, saying sweet things, childish things, telling him how wonderful he was, words like the words in a dream, important for their music, their sonority, rather than for any sense they made. She felt again the building of a dark wave in her belly. This time she flowed with it and let it carry her far.

"Love's stupid," John said to her one day months later as they were sitting in the chamber of the heart, watching the complex eddying of golden light and whorls of shadow on the surface of the organ. "I feel like a damn sophomore. I keep finding myself thinking that I should do something noble. Feed the hungry, cure a disease." He made a noise of disgust. "It's as if I just woke up to the fact that the world has problems, and because I'm so happily in love, I want everyone else to be happy. But stuck. . . ."

"Sometimes I feel like that myself," she said, startled by this outburst. "Maybe it's stupid, but it's not wrong. And neither is being happy."

"Stuck in here," he went on, "there's no chance of doing anything for ourselves, let alone saving the world. As for being happy, that's not going to last . . . not in here, anyway."

"It's lasted six months," she said. "And if it won't last here, why should it last anywhere?"

He drew up his knees, rubbed the spot on his ankle where it had been fractured.

"What's the matter with you? When I got here, all you could talk about was how much you wanted to escape. You said you'd do anything to get out. It sounds now that you don't care one way or the other."

She watched him rubbing the ankle, knowing what was coming. "I'd like very much to escape. Now that you're here, it's more acceptable to me. I can't deny that. That doesn't mean I wouldn't leave if I had the chance. But at least I can think about staying here without despairing."

"Well, I can't! I. . . ." He lowered his head, suddenly drained of animation, still rubbing his ankle. "I'm sorry, Catherine. My leg's hurting again, and I'm in a foul mood." He cut his eyes toward her. "Have you got that stuff with you?"

"Yes." She made no move to get it for him.

"I realize I'm taking too much," he said. "It helps pass the time."

She bristled at that and wanted to ask if she was the reason for his boredom; but she repressed her anger, knowing that she was partly to blame for his dependency on the brianine, that during his convalescence she had responded to his demands for the drug as a lover and not as a nurse.

An impatient look crossed his face. "Can I have it?"

Reluctantly she opened her pack, removed a flask of water and some pellets of brianine wrapped in cloth, and handed them over. He fumbled at the cloth, hurrying to unscrew the cap of the flask, and then—as he was about to swallow two of the pellets—he noticed her watching him. His face tightened with anger, and he appeared ready to snap at her. But his expression softened, and he downed the pellets, held out two more. "Take some with me," he said. "I know I have to stop. And I will. But let's just relax today, let's pretend we don't have any troubles . . . all right?"

That was a ploy he had adopted recently, making her his accomplice in addiction and thus avoiding guilt; she knew she should refuse to join him, but at the moment she didn't have the strength for an argument. She took the pellets, washed them down with a swallow of water and lay back against the chamber wall. He settled beside her, leaning on one elbow, smiling, his eyes muddied-looking from the drug.

"You do have to stop, you know," she said.

His smile flickered, then steadied, as if his batteries were running low. "I suppose."

"If we're going to escape," she said, "you'll need a clear head."

He perked up at this. "That's a change."

"I haven't been thinking about escape for a long time. It didn't seem possible . . . it didn't even seem very important, anymore. I guess I'd given up on the idea. I mean just before you arrived, I'd been thinking about it again, but it wasn't serious . . . only frustration."

"And now?"

"It's become important again."

"Because of me, because I keep nagging about it?"

"Because of both of us. I'm not sure escape's possible, but I was wrong to stop trying."

He rolled onto his back, shielding his eyes with his forearm as if the heart's glow were too bright.

"John?" The name sounded thick and sluggish, and she could feel the drug taking her, making her drifty and slow.

"This place," he said. "This goddamn place."

"I thought—" she was beginning to have difficulty in ordering her words "—I thought you were excited by it. You used to talk. . . ."

"Oh, I am excited!" He laughed dully. "It's a storehouse of marvels. Fantastic! Overwhelming! It's too overwhelming. The feeling here. . . ." He turned to her. "Don't you feel it?"

"I'm not sure what you mean."

"How could you stand living here for all these years? Are you that much stronger than me, or are you just insensitive?"

"I'm . . ."

"God!" He turned away, stared at the heart wall, his face tattooed with a convoluted flow of light and shadow, then flaring gold. "You're so at ease here. Look at that." He pointed to the heart. "It's not a heart, it's a bloody act of magic. Every time I come here I get the feeling it's going to display a pattern that'll make me disappear. Or crush me. Or something. And you just sit there looking at it with a thoughtful expression as if you're planning to put in curtains or repaint the damn thing.''

"We don't have to come here anymore.''

"I can't stay away," he said, and held up a pellet of brianine. "It's like this stuff.''

They didn't speak for several minutes . . . perhaps a bit less, perhaps a little more. Time had become meaningless, and Catherine felt that she was floating away, her flesh suffused with a rosy warmth like the warmth of lovemaking. Flashes of dream imagery passed through her mind: a clown's monstrous face; an unfamiliar room with tilted walls and three-legged blue chairs; a painting whose paint was melting, dripping. The flashes lapsed into thoughts of John. He was becoming weaker every day, she realized. Losing his resilience, growing nervous and moody. She had tried to convince herself that sooner or later he would become adjusted to life inside Griaule, but she was beginning to accept the fact that he was not going to be able to survive here. She didn't understand why, whether it was due—as he had said—to the dragon's oppressiveness or to some inherent weakness. Or a combination of both. But she could no longer deny it, and the only option left was for them to effect an escape. It was easy to consider escape with the drug in her veins, feeling aloof and calm, possessed of a dreamlike overview; but she knew that once it wore off she would be at a loss as to how to proceed.

To avoid thinking, she let the heart's patterns dominate her attention. They seemed abnormally complex, and as she watched she began to have the impression of something new at work, some interior mechanism that she had never noticed before, and to become aware that the sense of imminence that pervaded the chamber was stronger than ever before; but she was so muzzy-headed that she could not concentrate upon these things. Her eyelids drooped, and she fell into her recurring dream of the sleeping dragon, focusing on the smooth scaleless skin of its chest, a patch of whiteness that came to surround her, to draw her into a world of whiteness with the serene constancy of its rhythmic rise and fall, as unvarying and predictable as the ticking of a perfect clock.

Over the next six months Catherine devised numerous plans for escape, but discarded them all as unworkable until at last she thought of one that—although far from foolproof—seemed in its simplicity to offer the least risk of failure. Though without brianine the plan would have failed, the process of settling upon this particular plan would have gone faster had drugs not been available; unable to resist the combined pull of the drug and John's need for companionship in his addiction, she herself had become an addict, and much of her time was spent lying at the heart with John, stupefied, too enervated even to make love. Her feelings toward John had changed; it could not have been otherwise, for he was not the man he had been. He had lost weight and muscle tone, grown vague and brooding, and she was concerned for the health of his body and soul. In some ways she felt closer than ever to him, her maternal instincts having been engaged by his dissolution; yet she couldn't help resenting the fact that he had failed her, that instead of offering relief, he had turned out to be a burden and a weakening influence; and as a result whenever some distance arose between them, she exerted herself to close it only if it was practical to do so. This was not often the case, because John had deteriorated to the point that closeness of any sort was a chore. However, Catherine clung to the hope that if they could escape, they would be able to make a new beginning.

The drug owned her. She carried a supply of pellets wherever she went, gradually increasing her dosages, and not only did it affect her health and her energy, it had a profound effect upon her mind. Her powers of concentration were diminished, her sleep became fitful, and she began to experience hallucinations. She heard voices, strange noises, and on one occasion she was certain that she had spotted old Amos Mauldry among a group of feelies milling about at the bottom of the colony chamber. Her mental erosion caused her to mistrust the information of her senses and to dismiss as delusion the intimations of some climactic event that came to her in dreams and from the patterns of light and shadow on the heart; and recognizing that certain of her symptoms—hearkening to inaudible signals and the like—were similar to the behavior of the feelies, she feared that she was becoming one of them. Yet this fear was not so pronounced as once it might have been. She sought now to be tolerant of them, to overlook their role in her imprisonment, perceiving them as unwitting agents of Griaule, and she could not be satisfied in hating either them or the dragon; Griaule and the subtle manifestations of his will were something too vast and incomprehensible to be a target for hatred, and she transferred all her wrath to Brianne, the woman who had betrayed her. The feelies seemed to notice this evolution in her attitude, and they became more familiar, attaching themselves to her wherever she went, asking questions, touching her, and while this made it difficult to achieve privacy, in the end it was their increased affection that inspired her plan.

One day, accompanied by a group of giggling, chattering feelies, she walked up toward the skull, to the channel that led to the cavity containing the ghostvine. She ducked into the channel, half-tempted to explore the cavity again; but she decided against this course and on crawling out of the channel, she discovered that the feelies had vanished. Suddenly weak, as if their presence had been an actual physical support, she sank to her knees and stared along the narrow passage of pale red flesh that wound away into a golden murk like a burrow leading to a shining treasure. She felt a welling up of petulant anger at the feelies for having deserted her. Of course she should have expected it. They shunned this area like. . . . She sat up, struck by a realization attendant to that thought. How far, she wondered, had the feelies retreated? Could they have gone beyond the side passage that opened into the throat? She came to her feet and crept along the passage until she reached the curve. She peeked around it, and seeing no one, continued on, holding her breath until her chest began to ache. She heard voices, peered around the next curve, and caught sight of eight feelies gathered by the entrance to the side passage, their silken rags agleam, their swords reflecting glints of the inconstant light. She went back around the curve, rested against the wall; she had trouble thinking, in shaping thought into a coherent stream, and out of reflex she fumbled in her pack for some brianine. Just touching one of the pellets acted to calm her, and once she had swallowed it she breathed easier. She fixed her eyes on the blurred shape of a vein buried beneath the glistening ceiling of the passage, letting the fluctuations of light mesmerize her. She felt she was blurring, becoming golden and liquid and slow, and in that feeling she found a core of confidence and hope.

There's a way, she told herself; *My God, maybe there really is a way.*

By the time she had fleshed out her plan three days later, her chief fear was that John wouldn't be able to function well enough to take part in it. He looked awful, his cheeks sunken, his color poor, and the first time she tried to tell him about the plan, he fell asleep. To counteract the brianine she began cutting his dosage, mixing it with the stimulant she had derived from the lichen growing on the dragon's lung, and after a few days, though his color and general appearance did not improve, he became more alert and energized. She knew the improvement was purely chemical, that the stimulant was a danger in his weakened state; but there was no alternative, and this at least offered him a chance at life. If he were to remain there, given the physical erosion caused by the drug, she did not believe he would last another six months.

It wasn't much of a plan, nothing subtle, nothing complex, and if she'd had her wits about her, she thought, she would have come up with it long before; but she doubted she would have had the courage to try it alone, and if there was trouble, then two people would stand a much better chance than one. John was elated by the prospect. After she had told him the particulars he paced up and down in their bedroom, his eyes bright, hectic spots of red dappling his cheeks, stopping now and again to question her or to make distracted comments.

"The feelies," he said. "We . . . uh . . . we won't hurt them?"

"I told you . . . not unless it's necessary."

"That's good, that's good." He crossed the room to the curtains drawn across the entrance. "Of course it's not my field, but . . ."

"John?"

He peered out at the colony through the gap in the curtains, the skin on his forehead washing from gold to dark. "Uh-huh."

"What's not your field?"

After a long pause he said, "It's not . . . nothing."

"You were talking about the feelies."

"They're very interesting," he said distractedly. He swayed, then moved sluggishly toward her, collapsed on the pile of furs where she was sitting. He turned his face to her, looked at her with a morose expression. "It'll be better," he said. "Once we're out of here, I'll . . . I know I haven't been . . . strong. I haven't been . . ."

"It's all right," she said, stroking his hair.

"No, it's not, it's not." Agitated, he struggled to sit up, but she restrained him, telling him not to be upset, and soon he lay still. "How can you love me?" he asked after a long silence.

"I don't have any choice in the matter." She bent to him, pushing back her hair so it wouldn't hang in his face, kissed his cheek, his eyes.

He started to say something, then laughed weakly, and she asked him what he found amusing.

"I was thinking about free will," he said. "How improbable a concept that's become. Here. Where it's so obviously not an option."

She settled down beside him, weary of trying to boost his spirits. She remembered how he'd been after his arrival: eager, alive, and full of curiosity despite his injuries. Now his moments of greatest vitality—like this one—were spent in sardonic rejection of happy possibility. She was tired of arguing with him, of making the point that everything in life could be reduced by negative logic to a sort of pitiful reflex if that was the way you wanted to see it. His voice grew stronger, this prompted—she knew—by a rush of the stimulant within his system.

"It's Griaule," he said. "Everything here belongs to him, even the most fleeting of hopes and wishes. What we feel, what we think. When I was a student and first heard about Griaule, about his method of dominion, the omnipotent functioning of his will, I thought it was foolishness pure and simple. But I was an optimist, then. And optimists are only fools without experience. Of course I didn't think of myself as an optimist. I saw myself as a realist. I had a romantic notion that I was alone, responsible for my actions, and I perceived that as being a noble beauty, a refinement of the tragic . . . that state of utter and forlorn independence. I thought how cozy and unrealistic it was for people to depend on gods and demons to define their roles in life. I didn't know how terrible it would be to realize that nothing you thought or did had any individual importance, that everything, love, hate, your petty likes and dislikes, was part of some unfathomable scheme. I couldn't comprehend how worthless that knowledge would make you feel."

He went on in this vein for some time, his words weighing on her, filling her with despair, pushing hope aside. Then, as if this monologue had aroused some bitter sexuality, he began to make love to her. She felt removed from the act, imprisoned within walls erected by his dour sentences; but she responded with desperate enthusiasm, her own arousal funded by a desolate prurience. She watched his spread-fingered hands knead and cup her breasts, actions that seemed to her as devoid of emotional value as those of a starfish gripping a rock; and yet because of this desolation, because she wanted to deny it and also because of the voyeuristic thrill she derived from watching herself being taken, used, her body reacted with unusual fervor. The sweaty film between them was like a silken cloth, and their movements seemed more accomplished and supple than ever before; each jolt of pleasure brought her to new and dizzying heights. But afterward she felt devastated and defeated, not loved, and lying there with him, listening to the muted gabble of the feelies from without, bathed in their rich stench, she knew she had come to the nadir of her life, that she had finally united with the feelies in their enactment of a perturbed and animalistic rhythm.

Over the next ten days she set the plan into motion. She took to dispensing little sweet cakes to the feelies who guarded her on her daily walks with John, ending up each time at the channel that led to the ghostvine. And she also began to spread the rumor that at long last her study of the dragon was about to yield its promised revelation. On the day of the escape, prior to going forth, she stood at the bottom of the chamber, surrounded by hundreds of feelies, more hanging on ropes just above her, and called out in ringing tones, "Today I will have word for you! Griaule's word! Bring together the hunters and those who gather food, and have them wait here for me! I will return soon, very soon, and speak to you of what is to come!"

The feelies jostled and pawed one another, chattering, tittering, hopping up and down, and some of those hanging from the ropes were so overcome with excitement that they lost their grip and fell, landing atop their fellows, creating squirming heaps of feelies who squalled and yelped and then started fumbling with the buttons of each other's clothing. Catherine waved at them, and with John at her side, set out toward the cavity, six feelies with swords at their rear.

John was terribly nervous and all during the walk he kept casting backward glances at the feelies, asking questions that only served to unnerve Catherine. "Are you sure they'll eat them?" he said. "Maybe they won't be hungry."

"They always eat them while we're in the channel," she said. "You know that."

"I know," he said. "But I'm just . . . I don't want anything to go wrong." He walked another half a dozen paces. "Are you sure you put enough in the cakes?"

"I'm sure." She watched him out of the corner of her eye. The muscles in his jaw bunched, nerves twitched in his cheek. A light sweat had broken on his forehead, and his pallor was extreme. She took his arm. "How do you feel?"

"Fine," he said. "I'm fine."

"It's going to work, so don't worry . . . please."

"I'm fine," he repeated, his voice dead, eyes fixed straight ahead.

The feelies came to a halt just around the curve from the channel, and Catherine, smiling at them, handed them each a cake; then she and John went forward and crawled into the channel. There they sat in the darkness without speaking, their hips touching. At last John whispered, "How much longer?"

"Let's give it a few more minutes . . . just to be safe."

He shuddered, and she asked again how he felt.

"A little shaky," he said. "But I'm all right."

She put her hand on his arm; his muscles jumped at the touch. "Calm down," she said, and he nodded. But there was no slackening of his tension.

The seconds passed with the slowness of sap welling from cut bark, and despite her certainty that all would go as planned, Catherine's anxiety increased. Little shiny squiggles, velvety darknesses blacker than the air, wormed in front of her eyes. She imagined that she heard whispers out in the passage. She tried to think of something else, but the concerns she erected to occupy her mind materialized and vanished with a superficial and formal precision that did nothing to ease her, seeming mere transparencies shunted across the vision of a fearful prospect ahead. Finally she gave John a nudge and they crept from the channel, made their way cautiously along the passage. When they reached the curve beyond which the feelies were waiting, she paused, listened. Not a sound. She looked out. Six bodies lay by the entrance to the side passage; even at that distance she could spot the half-eaten cakes that had fallen from their hands. Still wary, they approached the feelies, and as they came near, Catherine thought that there was something unnatural about their stillness. She knelt beside a young male, caught a whiff of loosened bowel, saw the rapt character of death stamped on his features and realized that in measuring out the dosages of brianine in each cake, she had not taken the feelies' slightness of build into account. She had killed them.

"Come on!" said John. He had picked up two swords; they were so short, they looked toylike in his hands. He handed over one of the swords and helped her to stand. "Let's go . . . there might be more of them!"

He wetted his lips, glanced from side to side. With his sunken cheeks and hollowed eyes, his face had the appearance of a skull, and for a moment, dumbstruck by the realization that she had killed, by the understanding that for all her disparagement of them, the feelies were human, Catherine failed to recognize him. She stared at them—like ugly dolls in the ruins of their gaud—and felt again that same chill emptiness that had possessed her when she had killed Key Willen. John caught her arm, pushed her toward the side passage; it was covered by a loose flap, and though she had become used to seeing the dragon's flesh everywhere, she now shrank from touching it. John pulled back the flap, urged her into the passage, and then they were crawling through a golden gloom, following a twisting downward course.

In places the passage was only a few inches wider than her hips, and they were forced to worm their way along. She imagined that she could feel the immense weight of the dragon pressing in upon her, pictured some muscle twitching in reflex, the passage constricting and crushing them. The closed space made her breathing sound loud, and for a while John's breathing sounded even louder, hoarse and labored. But then she could no longer hear it, and she discovered that he had fallen behind. She called out to him, and he said, "Keep going!"

She rolled onto her back in order to see him. He was gasping, his face twisted as if in pain. "What's wrong?" she cried, trying to turn completely, constrained from doing so by the narrowness of the passage.

He gave her a shove. "I'll be all right. Don't stop!"

"John!" She stretched out a hand to him, and he wedged his shoulder against her legs, pushing her along.

"Damn it . . . just keep going!" He continued to push and exhort her, and realizing that she could do nothing, she turned and crawled at an even faster pace, seeing his harrowed face in her mind's eye.

She couldn't tell how many minutes it took to reach the end of the passage; it was a timeless time, one long unfractionated moment of straining, squirming, pulling at the slick walls, her effort fueled by her concern; but when she scrambled out into the dragon's throat, her heart racing, for an instant she forgot about John, about everything except the sight before her. From where she stood the throat sloped upward and widened into the mouth, and through that great opening came a golden light, not the heavy mineral brilliance of Griaule's blood, but a fresh clear light, penetrating the tangled shapes of the thickets in beams made crystalline by dust and moisture—the light of day. She saw the tip of a huge fang hooking upward, stained gold with the morning sun, and the vault of the dragon's mouth above, with its vines and epiphytes. Stunned, gaping, she dropped her sword and went a couple of paces toward the light. It was so clean, so pure, its allure like a call. Remembering John, she turned back to the passage. He was pushing himself erect with his sword, his face flushed, panting.

"Look!" she said, hurrying to him, pointing at the light. "God, just look at that!" She steadied him, began steering him toward the mouth.

"We made it," he said. "I didn't believe we would."

His hand tightened on her arm in what she assumed was a sign of affection; but then his grip tightened cruelly, and he lurched backward.

"John!" She fought to hold onto him, saw that his eyes had rolled up into his head.

He sprawled onto his back, and she went down on her knees beside him, hands fluttering above his chest, saying, "John? John?" What felt like a shiver passed through his body, a faint guttering noise issued from his throat, and she knew, oh, she knew very well the meaning of that tremor, that signal passage of breath. She drew back, confused, staring at his face, certain that she had gotten things wrong, that in a second or two his eyelids would open. But they did not. "John?" she said, astonished by how calm she felt, by the measured tone of her voice, as if she were making a simple inquiry. She wanted to break through the shell of calmness, to let out what she was really feeling, but it was as if some strangely lucid twin had gained control over her muscles and will. Her face was cold, and she got to her feet, thinking that the coldness must be radiating from John's body and that distance would be a cure. The sight of him lying there frightened her, and she turned her back on him, folded her arms across her chest. She blinked against the daylight. It hurt her eyes, and the loops and interlacings of foliage standing out in silhouette also hurt her with their messy complexity, their disorder. She couldn't decide what to do. Get away, she told herself. Get out. She took a hesitant step toward the mouth, but that direction didn't make sense. No direction made sense, anymore.

Something moved in the bushes, but she paid it no mind. Her calm was beginning to crack, and a powerful gravity seemed to be pulling her back toward the body. She tried to resist. More movement. Leaves were rustling, branches being pushed aside. Lots of little movements. She wiped at her eyes. They were no tears in them, but something was hampering her vision, something opaque and thin, a tattered film. The shreds of her calm, she thought, and laughed . . . more a hiccup than a laugh. She managed to focus on the bushes and saw ten, twenty, no, more, maybe two or three dozen diminutive figures, pale mongrel children in glittering rags standing at the verge of the thicket. She hiccuped again, and this time it felt nothing like a laugh. A sob, or maybe nausea. The feelies shifted nearer, edging toward her. The bastards had been waiting for them. She and John had never had a chance of escaping.

Catherine retreated to the body, reached down, groping for John's sword. She picked it up, pointed it at them. "Stay away from me," she said. "Just stay away, and I won't hurt you."

They came closer, shuffling, their shoulders hunched, their attitudes fearful, but advancing steadily all the same.

"Stay away!" she shouted. "I swear I'll kill you!" She swung the sword, making a windy arc through the air. "I swear!"

The feelies gave no sign of having heard, continuing their advance, and Catherine, sobbing now, shrieked for them to keep back, swinging the sword again and again. They encircled her, standing just beyond range. "You don't believe me?" she said. "You don't believe I'll kill you? I don't have any reason not to." All her grief and fury broke through, and with a scream she lunged at the feelies, stabbing one in the stomach, slicing a line of blood across the satin and gilt chest of another. The two she had wounded fell, shrilling their agony, and the rest swarmed toward her. She split the skull of another, split it as easily as she might have a melon, saw gore and splintered bone fly from the terrible wound, the dead male's face nearly halved, more blood leaking from around his eyes as he toppled, and then the rest of them were on her, pulling her down, pummeling her, giving little fey cries. She had no chance against them, but she kept on fighting, knowing that when she stopped, when she surrendered, she would have to start feeling, and that she wanted badly to avoid. Their vapid faces hovered above her, seeming uniformly puzzled, as if unable to understand her behavior, and the mildness of their reactions infuriated her. Death should have brightened them, made them—like her—hot with rage. Screaming again, her thoughts reddening, pumped with adrenaline, she struggled to her knees, trying to shake off the feelies who clung to her arms. Snapping her teeth at fingers, faces, arms. Then something struck the back of her head, and she sagged, her vision whirling, darkness closing in until all she could see was a tunnel of shadow with someone's watery eyes at the far end. The eyes grew wider, merged into a single eye that became a shadow with leathery wings and a forked tongue and a belly full of fire that swooped down, open-mouthed, to swallow her up and fly her home.

7

The drug moderated Catherine's grief . . . or perhaps it was more than the drug. John's decline had begun so soon after they had met, it seemed she had become accustomed to sadness in relation to him, and thus his death had not overwhelmed her, but rather had manifested as an ache in her chest and a heaviness in her limbs, like small stones she was forced to carry about. To rid herself of that ache, that heaviness, she increased her use of the drug, eating the pellets as if they were candy, gradually withdrawing from life. She had no use for life any longer. She knew she was going to die within the dragon, knew it with the same clarity and certainty that accompanied all Griaule's sendings—death was to be her punishment for seeking to avoid his will, for denying his right to define and delimit her.

After the escape attempt, the feelies had treated her with suspicion and hostility; recently they had been absorbed by some internal matter, agitated in the extreme, and they had taken to ignoring her. Without their minimal companionship, without John, the patterns flowing across the surface of the heart were the only thing that took Catherine out of herself, and she spent hours at a time watching them, lying there half-conscious, registering their changes through slitted eyes. As her addiction worsened, as she lost weight and muscle tone, she became even more expert in interpreting the patterns, and staring up at the vast curve of the heart, like the curve of a golden bell, she came to realize that Mauldry had been right, that the dragon was a god, an universe unto itself with its own laws and physical constants. A god that she hated. She would try to beam her hatred at the heart, hoping to cause a rupture, a seizure of some sort; but she knew that Griaule was impervious to this, impervious to all human weapons, and that her hatred would have as little effect upon him as an arrow loosed into an empty sky.

One day almost a year after John's death she waked abruptly from a dreamless sleep beside the heart, sitting bolt upright, feeling that a cold spike had been driven down the hollow of her spine. She rubbed sleep from her eyes, trying to shake off the lethargy of the drug, sensing danger at hand. Then she glanced up at the heart and was struck motionless. The patterns of shadow and golden radiance were changing more rapidly than ever before, and their complexity, too, was far greater than she had ever seen; yet they were as clear to her as her own script: pulsings of darkness and golden eddies flowing, unscrolling across the dimpled surface of the organ. It was a simple message, and for a few seconds she refused to accept the knowledge it conveyed, not wanting to believe that this was the culmination of her destiny, that her youth had been wasted in so trivial a matter; but recalling all the clues, the dreams of the sleeping dragon, the repetitious vision of the rise and fall of its chest. Mauldry's story of the first feelie, the exodus of animals and insects and birds, the muffled thud from deep within the dragon after which everything had remained calm for a thousand years . . . she knew it must be true.

As it had done a thousand years before, and as it would do again a thousand years in the future, the heart was going to beat.

She was infuriated, and she wanted to reject the fact that all her trials and griefs had been sacrifices made for the sole purpose of saving the feelies. Her task, she realized, would be to clear them out of the chamber where they lived before it was flooded with the liquids that fueled the dragon's fires; and after the chamber had been emptied, she was to lead them back so they could go on with the work of keeping Griaule pest-free. The cause of their recent agitation, she thought, must have been due to their apprehension of the event, the result of one of Griaule's sendings; but because of their timidity they would tend to dismiss his warning, being more frightened of the outside world than of any peril within the dragon. They would need guidance to survive, and as once he had chose Mauldry to assist her, now Griaule had chosen her to guide the feelies.

She staggered up, as befuddled as a bird trapped between glass walls, making little rushes this way and that; then anger overcame confusion, and she beat with her fists on the heart wall, bawling her hatred of the dragon, her anguish at the ruin he had made of her life. Finally, breathless, she collapsed, her own heart pounding erratically, trying to think what to do. She wouldn't tell them, she decided; she would just let them die when the chamber flooded, and this way have her revenge. But an instant later she reversed her decision, knowing that the feelies' deaths would merely be an inconvenience to Griaule, that he would simply gather a new group of idiots to serve him. And besides, she thought, she had already killed too many feelies. There was no choice, she realized; over the span of almost eleven years she had been maneuvered by the dragon's will to this place and moment where, by virtue of her shaped history and conscience, she had only one course of action.

Full of muddle-headed good intentions, she made her way back to the colony, her guards trailing behind, and when she had reached the chamber, she stood with her back to the channel that led toward the throat, uncertain of how to proceed.

Several hundred feelies were milling about the bottom of the chamber, and others were clinging to ropes, hanging together in front of one or another of the cubicles, looking in that immense space like clusters of glittering, many-colored fruit; the constant motion and complexity of the colony added to Catherine's hesitancy and bewilderment, and when she tried to call out to the feelies, to gain their attention, she managed only a feeble, scratchy noise. But she gathered her strength and called out again and again, until at last they were all assembled before her, silent and staring, hemming her in against the entrance to the channel, next to some chests that contained the torches and swords and other items used by the hunters. The feelies gawped at her, plucking at their gaudy rags; their silence seemed to have a slow vibration. Catherine started to speak, but faltered; she took a deep breath, let it out explosively and made a second try.

"We have to leave," she said, hearing the shakiness of her voice. "We have to go outside. Not for long. Just for a little while . . . a few hours. The chamber, it's going. . . ." She broke off, realizing that they weren't following her. "The thing Griaule has meant me to learn," she went on in a louder voice, "at last I know it. I know why I was brought to you. I know the purpose for which I have studied all these years. Griaule's heart is going to beat, and when it does the chamber will fill with liquid. If you remain here, you'll all drown."

The front ranks shifted, and some of the feelies exchanged glances, but otherwise they displayed no reaction.

Catherine shook her fists in frustration. "You'll die if you don't listen to me! You have to leave! When the heart contracts, the chamber will be flooded . . . don't you understand?" She pointed up to the mist-hung ceiling of the chamber. "Look! The birds . . . the birds have gone! They know what's coming! And so do you! Don't you feel the danger? I know you do!"

They edged back, some of them turning away, entering into whispered exchanges with their fellows.

Catherine grabbed the nearest of them, a young female dressed in ruby silks. "Listen to me!" she shouted.

"Liar, Cat'rine, liar," said one of the males, jerking the female away from her. "We not goin' be mo' fools."

"I'm not lying! I'm not!" She went from one to another, putting her hands on their shoulders, meeting their eyes in an attempt to impress them with her sincerity. "The heart is going to beat! Once . . . just once. You won't have to stay outside long. Not long at all."

They were all walking away, all beginning to involve themselves in their own affairs, and Catherine, desperate, hurried after them, pulling them back, saying, "Listen to me! Please!" Explaining what was to happen, and receiving cold stares in return. One of the males shoved her aside, baring his teeth in a hiss, his eyes blank and bright, and she retreated to the entrance of the channel, feeling rattled and disoriented, in need of another pellet. She couldn't collect her thoughts, and she looked around in every direction as if hoping to find some sight that would steady her; but nothing she saw was of any help. Then her gaze settled on the chests where the swords and torches were stored. She felt as if her head were being held in a vise and forced toward the chests, and the knowledge of what she must do was a coldness inside her head—the unmistakable touch of Griaule's thought. It was the only way. She saw that clearly. But the idea of doing something so extreme frightened her, and she hesitated, looking behind her to make sure that none of the feelies were keeping track of her movements. She inched toward the chests, keeping her eyes lowered, trying to make it appear that she was moving aimlessly. In one of the chests were a number of tinderboxes resting beside some torches; she stooped, grabbed a torch and one of the tinderboxes, and went walking briskly up the slope. She paused by the lowest rank of cubicles, noticed that some of the feelies had turned to watch her; when she lit the torch, alarm surfaced in their faces and they surged up the slope toward her. She held the torch up to the curtains that covered the entrance to the cubicle, and the feelies fell back, muttering, some letting out piercing wails.

"Please!" Catherine cried, her knees rubbery from the tension, a chill knot in her breast. "I don't want to do this! But you have to leave!"

A few of the feelies edged toward the channel, and encouraged by this, Catherine shouted, "Yes! That's it! If you'll just go outside, just for a little while, I won't have to do it!"

Several feelies entered the channel, and the crowd around Catherine began to erode, whimpering, breaking into tears, trickles of five and six at a time breaking away and moving out of sight within the channel, until there were no more than thirty of them left within the chamber, forming a ragged semi-circle around her. She would have liked to believe that they would do as she had suggested without further coercion on her part, but she knew that they were all packed into the channel or the chamber beyond, waiting for her to put down the torch. She gestured at the feelies surrounding her, and they, too, began easing toward the channel; when only a handful of them remained visible, she touched the torch to the curtains.

She was amazed by how quickly the fire spread, rushing like waves up the silk drapes, following the rickety outlines of the cubicles, appearing to dress them in a fancywork of reddish yellow flame, making crispy, chuckling noises. The fire seemed to have a will of its own, to be playfully seeking out all the intricate shapes of the colony and illuminating them, the separate flames chasing one another with merry abandon, sending little trains of fire along poles and stanchions, geysering up from corners, flinging out fiery fingers to touch tips across a gap.

She was so caught up in this display, her drugged mind finding in it an aesthetic, that she forgot all about the feelies, and when a cold sharp pain penetrated her left side, she associated this not with them but thought it a side-effect of the drug, a sudden attack brought on by her abuse of it. Then, horribly weak, sinking to her knees, she saw one of them standing next to her, a male with a pale thatch of thinning hair wisping across his scalp, holding a sword tipped with red, and she knew that he had stabbed her. She had the giddy urge to speak to him, not out of anger, just to ask a question that she wasn't able to speak, for instead of being afraid of the weakness invading her limbs, she had a terrific curiosity about what would happen next, and she had the irrational thought that her executioner might have the answer, that in his role as the instrument of Griaule's will he might have some knowledge of absolutes. He spat something at her, an accusation or an insult made inaudible by the crackling of the flames, and fled down the slope and out of the chamber, leaving her alone. She rolled onto her back, gazing at the fire, and the pain seemed to roll inside her as if it were a separate thing. Some of the cubicles were collapsing, spraying sparks, twists of black smoke boiling up, smoldering pieces of blackened wood tumbling down to the chamber floor, the entire structure appearing to ripple through the heat haze, looking unreal, an absurd construction of flaming skeletal framework and billowing, burning silks, and growing dizzy, feeling that she was falling upward into that huge fiery space, Catherine passed out.

She must have been unconscious for only a matter of seconds, because nothing had changed when she opened her eyes, except that a section of the fabric covering the chamber floor had caught fire. The flames were roaring, the snap and cracking of timbers as sharp as explosions, and her nostrils were choked with an acrid stink. With a tremendous effort that brought her once again to the edge of unconsciousness, she came to her feet, clutching the wound in her side, and stumbled toward the channel; at the entrance she fell and crawled into it, choking on the smoke that poured along the passageway. Her eyes teared from the smoke, and she wriggled on her stomach, pulling herself along with her hands. She nearly passed out half a dozen times before reaching the adjoining chamber, and then she staggered, crawled, stopping frequently to catch her breath, to let the pain of her wound subside, somehow negotiating a circuitous path among the pools of burning liquid and the pale red warty bumps that sprouted everywhere. Then into the throat. She wanted to surrender to the darkness there, to let go, but she kept going, not motivated by fear, but by some reflex of survival, simply obeying the impulse to continue for as long as it was possible. Her eyes blurred, and darkness frittered at the edges of her vision. But even so, she was able to make out the light of day, the menagerie of shapes erected by the interlocking branches of the thickets, and she thought that now she could stop, that this had been what she wanted—to see the light again, not to die bathed in the uncanny radiance of Griaule's blood.

She lay down, lowering herself cautiously among a bed of ferns, her back against the side of the throat, the same position—she remembered—in which she had fallen asleep that first night inside the dragon so many years before. She started to slip, to dwindle inside herself, but was alerted by a whispery rustling that grew louder and louder, and a moment later swarms of insects began to pour from the dragon's throat, passing overhead with a whirring rush and in such density that they cut off most of the light issuing from the mouth. Far above, like the shadows of spiders, apes were swinging on the vines that depended from the roof of the mouth, heading for the outer world, and Catherine could hear smaller animals scuttling through the brush. The sight of these flights made her feel accomplished, secure in what she had done, and she settled back, resting her head against Griaule's flesh, as peaceful as she could ever recall, almost eager to be done with life, with drugs and solitude and violence. She had a moment's worry about the feelies, wondering where they were; but then she realized that they would probably do no differently than had their remote ancestor, that they would hide in the thickets until all was calm.

She let her eyes close. The pain of the wound had diminished to a distant throb that scarcely troubled her, and the throbbing made a rhythm that seemed to be bearing her up. Somebody was talking to her, saying her name, and she resisted the urge to open her eyes, not wanting to be called back. She must be hearing things, she thought. But the voice persisted, and at last she did open her eyes. She gave a weak laugh on seeing Amos Mauldry kneeling before her, wavering and vague as a ghost, and realized that she was seeing things, too.

"Catherine," he said. "Can you hear me?"

"No," she said, and laughed again, a laugh that sent her into a bout of gasping; she felt her weakness in a new and poignant way, and it frightened her.

"Catherine?"

She blinked, trying to make him disappear; but he appeared to solidify as if she were becoming more part of his world than that of life. "What is it, Mauldry?" she said, and coughed. "Have you come to guide me to heaven . . . is that it?"

His lips moved, and she had the idea that he was trying to reassure her of something; but she couldn't hear his words, no matter how hard she strained her ears. He was beginning to fade, becoming opaque, proving himself to be no more than a phantom; yet as she blacked out, experiencing a final moment of panic, Catherine could have sworn that she felt him take her hand.

She walked in a golden glow that dimmed and brightened, and found herself staring into a face; after a moment, a long moment, because the face was much different than she had imagined it during these past few years, she recognized that it was hers. She lay still, trying to accommodate to this state of affairs, wondering why she wasn't dead, puzzling over the face and uncertain as to why she wasn't afraid; she felt strong and alert and at peace. She sat up and discovered that she was naked, that she was sitting in a small chamber lit by veins of golden blood branching across the ceiling, its walls obscured by vines with glossy dark green leaves. The body—her body—was lying on its back, and one side of the shirt it wore was soaked with blood. Folded beside the body was a fresh shirt, trousers, and resting atop these was a pair of sandals.

She checked her side—there was no sign of a wound. Her emotions were a mix of relief and self-loathing. She understood that somehow she had been conveyed to this cavity, to the ghostvine, and her essences had been transferred to a likeness, and yet she had trouble accepting the fact, because she felt no different than she had before . . . except for the feelings of peace and strength, and the fact that she had no craving for the drug. She tried to deny what had happened, to deny that she was now a thing, the bizarre contrivance of a plant, and it seemed that her thoughts, familiar in their ordinary process, were proofs that she must be wrong in her assumption. However, the body was an even more powerful evidence to the contrary. She would have liked to take refuge in panic, but her overall feeling of well-being prevented this. She began to grow cold, her skin pebbling, and reluctantly she dressed in the clothing folded beside the body. Something hard in the breast pocket of the shirt. She opened the pocket, took out a small leather sack; she loosed the tie of the sack and from it poured a fortune of cut gems into her hand: diamonds, emeralds, and sunstones. She put the sack back into the pocket, not knowing what to make of the stones, and sat looking at the body. It was much changed from its youth, leaner, less voluptuous, and in the repose of death, the face had lost its gloss and perfection, and was merely the face of an attractive woman . . . a disheartened woman. She thought she should feel something, that she should be oppressed by the sight, but she had no reaction to it; it might have been a skin she had shed, something of no more consequence than that.

She had no idea where to go, but realizing that she couldn't stay there forever, she stood and with a last glance at the body, she made her way down the narrow channel leading away from the cavity. When she emerged into the passage, she hesitated, unsure of which direction to choose, unsure, too, of which direction was open to her. At length, deciding not to tempt Griaule's judgment, she headed back toward the colony, thinking that she would take part in helping them rebuild; but before she had gone ten feet she heard Mauldry's voice calling her name.

He was standing by the entrance to the cavity, dressed as he had been that first night—in a satin frock coat, carrying his gold-knobbed cane—and as she approached him, a smile broke across his wrinkled face, and he nodded as if in approval of her resurrection. "Surprised to see me?" he asked.

"I . . . I don't know," she said, a little afraid of him. "Was that you . . . in the mouth?"

He favored her with a polite bow. "None other. After things settled down, I had some of the feelies bear you to the cavity. Or rather I was the instrument that effected Griaule's will in the matter. Did you look in the pocket of your shirt?"

"Yes."

"Then you found the gems. Good, good."

She was at a loss for words at first. "I thought I saw you once before," she said finally. "A few years back."

"I'm sure you did. After my rebirth—" he gestured toward the cavity "—I was no longer of any use to you. You were forging your own path and my presence would have hampered your process. So I hid among the feelies, waiting for the time when you would need me." He squinted at her. "You look troubled."

"I don't understand any of this," she said. "How can I feel like my old self, when I'm obviously so different?"

"Are you?" he asked. "Isn't sameness or difference mostly a matter of feeling?" He took her arm, steered her along the passage away from the colony. "You'll adjust to it, Catherine. I have, and I had the same reaction as you when I first awoke." He spread his arms, inviting her to examine him. "Do I look different to you? Aren't I the same old fool as ever?"

"So it seems," she said drily. She walked a few paces in silence, then something occurred to her. "The feelies . . . do they. . . ."

"Rebirth is only for the chosen, the select. The feelies receive another sort of reward, one not given me to understand."

"You call this a reward? To be subject to more of Griaule's whims? And what's next for me? Am I to discover when his bowels are due to move?"

He stopped walking, frowning at her. "Next? Why, whatever pleases you, Catherine. I've been assuming that you'd want to leave, but you're free to do as you wish. Those gems I gave you will buy you any kind of life you desire."

"I can leave?"

"Most assuredly. You've accomplished your purpose here, and you're your own agent now. *Do* you want to leave?"

Catherine looked at him, unable to speak, and nodded.

"Well, then." He took her arm again. "Let's be off."

As they walked down to the chamber behind the throat and then into the throat itself, Catherine felt as one is supposed to feel at the moment of death, all the memories of her life within the dragon passing before her eyes with their attendant emotions—her flight, her labors and studies, John, the long hours spent beside the heart—and she thought that this was most appropriate, because she was not re-entering life but rather passing through into a kind of afterlife, a place beyond death that would be as unfamiliar and new a place as Griaule himself had once seemed. And she was astounded to realize that she was frightened of these new possibilities, that the thing she had wanted for so long could pose a menace and that it was the dragon who now offered the prospect of security. On several occasions she considered turning back, but each time she did, she rebuked herself for her timidity and continued on. However, on reaching the mouth and wending her way through the thickets, her fear grew more pronounced. The sunlight, that same light that not so many months before had been alluring, now hurt her eyes and made her want to draw back into the dim golden murk of Griaule's blood; and as they neared the lip, as she stepped into the shadow of a fang, she began to tremble with cold and stopped, hugging herself to keep warm.

Mauldry took up a position facing her, jogged her arm. "What is it?" he asked. "You seem frightened."

"I am," she said; she glanced up at him. "Maybe . . ."

"Don't be silly," he said. "You'll be fine once you're away from here. And—" he cocked his eye toward the declining sun "—you should be pushing along. You don't want to be hanging about the mouth when it's dark. I doubt anything would harm you, but since you're no longer part of Griaule's plan . . . well, better safe than sorry." He gave her a push. "Get along with you, now."

"You're not coming with me?"

"Me?" Mauldry chuckled. "What would I do out there? I'm an old man, set in my ways. No, I'm far better off staying with the feelies. I've become half a feely myself after all these years. But you're young, you've got a whole world of life ahead of you." He nudged her forward. "Do what I say, girl. There's no use in your hanging about any longer."

She went a couple of steps toward the lip, paused, feeling sentimental about leaving the old man; though they had never been close, he had been like a father to her . . . and thinking this, remembering her real father, whom she had scarcely thought of these last years, with whom she'd had the same lack of closeness, that made her aware of all the things she had to look forward to, all the lost things she might now regain. She moved into the thickets with a firmer step, and behind her, old Mauldry called to her for a last time.

"That's my girl!" he sang out. "You just keep going, and you'll start to feel at rights soon enough! There's nothing to be afraid of . . . nothing you can avoid, in any case! Goodbye, goodbye!"

She glanced back, waved, saw him shaking his cane in a gesture of farewell, and laughed at his eccentric appearance: a funny little man in satin rags hopping up and down in that great shadow between the fangs. Out from beneath that shadow herself, the rich light warmed her, seeming to penetrate and dissolve all the coldness that had been lodged in her bones and thoughts.

"Goodbye!" cried Mauldry. "Goodbye! Don't be sad! You're not leaving anything important behind, and you're taking the best parts with you. Just walk fast and think about what you're going to tell everyone. They'll be amazed by all you've done! Flabbergasted! Tell them about Griaule! Tell them what he's like, tell them all you've seen and all you've learned. Tell them what a grand adventure you've had!"

8

Returning to Hangtown was in some ways a more unsettling experience than had been Catherine's flight into the dragon. She had expected the place to have changed, and while there *had* been minor changes, she had assumed that it would be as different from its old self as was she. But standing at the edge of the village, looking out at the gray weathered shacks ringing the fouled shallows of the lake, thin smokes issuing from tin chimneys, the cliff of the fronto-parietal plate casting its gloomy shadow, the chokecherry thickets, the hawthornes, the dark brown dirt of the streets, three elderly men sitting on cane chairs in front of one of the shacks, smoking their pipes and staring back at her with unabashed curiosity . . . superficially it was no different than it had been ten years before, and this seemed to imply that her years of imprisonment, her death and rebirth had been of small importance. She did not demand that they be important to anyone else, yet it galled her that the world had passed through those years of ordeal without significant scars, and it also imbued her with the irrational fear that if she were to enter the village, she might suffer some magical slippage back through time and reinhabit her old life. At last, with a hesitant step, she walked over to the men and wished them a good morning.

"Mornin'," said a paunchy fellow with a mottled bald scalp and a fringe of gray beard, whom she recognized as Tim Weedlon. "What can I do for you, ma'am? Got some nice bits of scale inside."

"That place over there—" she pointed to an abandoned shack down the street, its roof holed and missing the door "—where can I find the owner?"

The other man, Mardo Koren, thin as a mantis, his face seamed and blotched, said, "Can't nobody say for sure. Ol' Riall died . . . must be goin' on nine, ten years back."

"He's dead?" She felt weak inside, dazed.

"Yep," said Tim Weedlon, studying her face, his brow furrowed, his expression bewildered. "His daughter run away, killed a village man name of Willen and vanished into nowhere . . . or so ever'body figured. Then when Willen's brothers turned up missin', people thought ol' Riall must done 'em. He didn't deny it. Acted like he didn't care whether he lived or died."

"What happened?"

"They had a trial, found Riall guilty." He leaned forward, squinting at her. "Catherine . . . is that you?"

She nodded, struggling for control. "What did they do with him?"

"How can it be you?" he said. "Where you been?"

"What happened to my father?"

"God, Catherine. You know what happens to them that's found guilty of murder. If it's any comfort, the truth come out finally."

"They took him in under the wing . . . they left him under the wing?" Her fists clenched, nails pricking hard into her palm. "Is that what they did?" He lowered his eyes, picked at a fray on his trouserleg.

Her eyes filled, and she turned away, facing the mossy overhang of the fronto-parietal plate. "You said the truth came out."

"That's right. A girl confessed to having seen the whole thing. Said the Willens chased you into Griaule's mouth. She woulda come forward sooner, but ol' man Willen had her feared for her life. Said he'd kill her if she told. You probably remember her. Friend of yours, if I recall. Brianne.'' She whirled around, repeated the name with venom.

"Wasn't she your friend?" Weedlon asked.

"What happened to her?"

"Why . . . nothing," said Weedlon. "She's married, got hitched to Zev Mallison. Got herself a batch of children. I 'spect she's home now if you wanna see her. You know the Mallison place, don'tcha?"

"Yes."

"You want to know more about it, you oughta drop by there and talk to Brianne."

"I guess . . . I will, I'll do that."

"Now tell us where you been, Catherine. Ten years! Musta been something important to keep you from home for so long."

Coldness was spreading through her, turning her to ice. "I was thinking, Tim . . . I was thinking I might like to do some scaling while I'm here. Just for old time's sake, you know." She could hear the shakiness in her voice and tried to smooth it out; she forced a smile. "I wonder if I could borrow some hooks."

"Hooks?" He scratched his head, still regarding her with confusion. "Sure, I suppose you can. But aren't you going to tell us where you've been? We thought you were dead."

"I will, I promise. Before I leave . . . I'll come back and tell you all about it. All right?"

"Well, all right." He heaved up from his chair. "But it's a cruel thing you're doing, Catherine."

"No crueler than what's been done to me," she said distractedly. "Not half so cruel."

"Pardon," said Tim. "How's that?"

"What?"

He gave her a searching look and said, "I was telling you it was a cruel thing, keeping an old man in suspense about where you've been. Why you're going to make the choicest bit of gossip we've had in years. And you came back with . . ."

"Oh! I'm sorry," she said. "I was thinking about something else."

The Mallison place was among the larger shanties in Hangtown, half a dozen rooms, most of which had been added on over the years since Catherine had left; but its size was no evidence of wealth or status, only of a more expansive poverty. Next to the steps leading to a badly hung door was a litter of bones and mango skins and other garbage. Fruit flies hovered above a watermelon rind; a gray dog with its ribs showing slunk off around the corner, and there was a stink of fried onions and boiled greens. From inside came the squalling of a child. The shanty looked false to Catherine, an unassuming façade behind which lay a monstrous reality—the woman who had betrayed her, killed her father—and yet its drabness was sufficient to disarm her anger somewhat. But as she mounted the steps there was a thud as of something heavy falling, and a woman shouted. The voice was harsh, deeper than Catherine remembered, but she knew it must belong to Brianne, and that restored her vengeful mood. She knocked on the door with one of Tim Weedlon's scaling hooks, and a second later it was flung open and she was confronted by an olive-skinned woman in torn gray skirts—almost the same color as the weathered boards, as if she were the quintessential product of the environment—and gray streaks in her dark brown hair. She looked Catherine up and down, her face hard with displeasure, and said, "What do you want?"

It was Brianne, but Brianne warped, melted, disfigured as a waxwork might be disfigured by heat. Her waist gone, features thickened, cheeks sagging into jowls. Shock washed away Catherine's anger, and shock, too, materialized in Brianne's face. "No," she said, giving the word an abstracted value, as if denying an inconsequential accusation; then she shouted it: "No!" She slammed the door, and Catherine pounded on it, crying, "Damn you! Brianne!"

The child screamed, but Brianne made no reply.

Enraged, Catherine swung the hook at the door; the point sank deep into the wood, and when she tried to pull it out, one of the boards came partially loose; she pried at it, managed to rip it away, the nails coming free with a shriek of tortured metal. Through the gap she saw Brianne cowering against the rear wall of a dilapidated room, her arms around a little boy in shorts. Using the hook as a lever, she pulled loose another board, reached in and undid the latch. Brianne pushed the child behind her and grabbed a broom as Catherine stepped inside.

"Get out of here!" she said, holding the broom like a spear.

The gray poverty of the shanty made Catherine feel huge in her anger, too bright for the place, like a sun shining in a cave, and although her attention was fixed on Brianne, the peripheral details of the room imprinted themselves on her: the wood stove upon which a covered pot was steaming; an overturned wooden chair with a hole in the seat; cobwebs spanning the corners, rat turds along the wall; a rickety table set with cracked dishes and dust thick as fur beneath it. These things didn't arouse her pity or mute her anger; instead, they seemed extensions of Brianne, new targets for hatred. She moved closer, and Brianne jabbed the broom at her. "Go away," she said weakly. "Please . . . leave us alone!"

Catherine swung the hook, snagging the twine that bound the broom straws and knocking it from Brianne's hands. Brianne retreated to the corner where the wood stove stood, hauling the child along. She held up her hand to ward off another blow and said, "Don't hurt us."

"Why not? Because you've got children, because you've had an unhappy life?" Catherine spat at Brianne. "You killed my father!"

"I was afraid! Key's father . . ."

"I don't care," said Catherine coldly. "I don't care why you did it. I don't care how good your reasons were for betraying me in the first place."

"That's right! You never cared about anything!" Brianne clawed at her breast. "You killed my heart! You didn't care about Glynn, you just wanted him because he wasn't yours!"

It took Catherine a few seconds to dredge that name up from memory, to connect it with Brianne's old lover and recall that it was her callousness and self-absorption that had set the events of the past ten years in motion. But although this roused her guilt, it did not abolish her anger. She couldn't equate Brianne's crimes with her excesses. Still, she was confused about what to do, uncomfortable now with the very concept of justice, and she wondered if she should leave, just throw down the hook and leave vengeance to whatever ordering principle governed the fates in Hangtown. Then Brianne shifted her feet, made a noise in her throat and Catherine felt rage boiling up inside her.

"Don't throw that up to me," she said with flat menace. "Nothing I've done to you merited what you did to me. You don't even know what you did!" She raised the hook, and Brianne shrank back into the corner. The child twisted its head to look at Catherine, fixing her with brimming eyes, and she held back.

"Send the child away," she told Brianne.

Brianne leaned down to the child. "Go to your father," she said.

"No, wait," said Catherine, fearing that the child might bring Zev Mallison.

"Must you kill us both?" said Brianne, her voice hoarse with emotion. Hearing this, the child once more began to cry.

"Stop it," Catherine said to him, and when he continued to cry, she shouted it.

Brianne muffled the child's wails in her skirts. "Go ahead!" she said, her face twisted with fear. "Just do it!" She broke down into sobs, ducked her head and waited for the blow. Catherine stepped close to Brianne, yanked her head back by the hair, exposing her throat, and set the point of the hook against the big vein there. Brianne's eyes rolled down, trying to see the hook; her breath came in gaspy shrieks, and the child, caught between the two women, squirmed and wailed. Catherine's hand was trembling, and that slight motion pricked Brianne's skin, drawing a bead of blood. She stiffened, her eyelids fluttered down, her mouth fell open—an expression, at least so it seemed to Catherine, of ecstatic expectation. Catherine studied the face, feeling as if her emotions were being purified, drawn into a fine wire; she had an almost aesthetic appreciation of the stillness gathering around her, the hard poise of Brianne's musculature, the sensitive pulse in the throat that transmitted its frail rhythm along the hook, and she restrained herself from pressing the point deeper, wanting to prolong Brianne's suffering.

But then the hook grew heavy in Catherine's hands, and she understood that the moment had passed, that her need for vengeance had lost the immediacy and thrust of passion. She imagined herself skewering Brianne, and then imagined dragging her out to confront a village tribunal, forcing her to confess her lies, having her sentenced to be tied up and left for whatever creatures foraged beneath Griaule's wing. But while it provided her a measure of satisfaction to picture Brianne dead or dying, she saw now that anticipation was the peak of vengeance, that carrying out the necessary actions would only harm her. It frustrated her that all these years and the deaths would have no resolution, and she thought that she must have changed more than she had assumed to put aside vengeance so easily; this caused her to wonder again about the nature of the change, to question whether she was truly herself or merely an arcane likeness. But then she realized that the change had been her resolution, and that vengeance was an artifact of her old life, nothing more, and that her new life, whatever its secret character, must find other concerns to fuel it apart from old griefs and unworthy passions. This struck her with the force of a revelation, and she let out a long sighing breath that seemed to carry away with it all the sad vibrations of the past, all the residues of hates and loves, and she could finally believe that she was no longer the dragon's prisoner. She felt new in her whole being, subject to new compulsions, as alive as tears, as strong as wheat, far too strong and alive for this pallid environment, and she could hardly recall now why she had come.

She looked at Brianne and her son, feeling only the ghost of hatred, seeing them not as objects of pity or wrath, but as unfamiliar, irrelevant, lives trapped in the prison of their own self-regard, and without a word she turned and walked to the steps, slamming the hook deep into the boards of the wall, a gesture of fierce resignation, the closing of a door opening onto anger and the opening of one that led to uncharted climes, and went down out of the village, leaving old Tim Weedlon's thirst for gossip unquenched, passing along Griaule's back, pushing through thickets and fording streams, and not noticing for quite some time that she had crossed onto another hill and left the dragon far behind. Three weeks later she came to Cabrecavela, a small town at the opposite end of the Carbonales Valley, and there, using the gems provided her by Mauldry, she bought a house and settled in and began to write about Griaule, creating not a personal memoir but a reference work containing an afterword dealing with certain metaphysical speculations, for she did not wish her adventures published, considering them banal by comparison to her primary subjects, the dragon's physiology and ecology. After the publication of her book, which she entitled *The Heart's Millennium*, she experienced a brief celebrity; but she shunned most of the opportunities for travel and lecture and lionization that came her way, and satisfied her desire to impart the knowledge she had gained by teaching in the local school and speaking privately with those scientists from Port Chantay who came to interview her. Some of these visitors had been colleagues of John Colmacos, yet she never mentioned their relationship, believing that her memories of the man needed no modification; but perhaps this was less than an honest self-appraisal, perhaps she had not come to terms with that portion of her past, for in the spring five years after she had returned to the world she married one of these scientists, a man named Brian Ocoi, who in his calm demeanor and modest easiness of speech appeared cast from the same mold as Colmacos. From that point on little is known of her other than the fact that she bore two sons and confined her writing to a journal that has gone unpublished. However, it is said of her—as is said of all those who perform similar acts of faith in the shadows of other dragons yet unearthed from beneath their hills of ordinary-seeming earth and grass, believing that their bond serves through gentle constancy to enhance and not further delimit the boundaries of this prison world—from that day forward she lived happily ever after. Except for the dying at the end. And the heartbreak in-between.

HONORABLE MENTIONS

1988

Brian W. Aldiss, "Traveler, Traveler, Seek Your Wife in the Forests of This Life," *F & SF*, Nov.

Ray Aldridge, "The Touch of the Hook," *F & SF*, Apr.

Poul Anderson, "The Comrade," *Analog*, Jun.

——, "The Deserter," *New Destinies*, Summer.

Kim Antieau, "Listening for the General," *Twilight Zone*, Feb.

Isaac Asimov, "Christmas Without Rodney," *IAsfm*, Mid-Dec.

Scott Baker, "The Sins of the Fathers," *Ripper!*

Clive Barker, "How Spoiler's Bleed," *F & SF*, Oct.

John Barnes, "Delicate Stuff," *Amazing*, Jul.

——, "The Limit of Vision," *IAsfm*, Jul.

——, "Under the Covenant Stars," *IAsfm*, Apr.

Neal Barrett, Jr., "Ginny Sweethips' Flying Circus," *IAsfm*, Feb.

——, "Stairs," *IAsfm*, Sept.

Amy Bechtel, "The Circus Horse," *Analog*, Jun.

M. Shayne Bell, "Nicoji," *IAsfm*, Mar.

Gregory Benford and Paul A. Carter, "Proserpina's Daughter," *Synergy 3*.

Michael Bishop, "The Calling of Paisley Coldpony," *IAsfm*, Jan.

Terry Boren, "Sliding Rock," *A Very Large Array*.

Ben Bova, "Diamond Sam," *F & SF*, Nov.

Steven R. Boyett, "Emerald City Blues," *Midnight Graffiti*, Fall.

Scott Bradfield, "Dazzle," *Other Edens II*.

R. V. Branham, "Lady with Teddy Bear," *IAsfm*, Dec.

John Brunner, "An Entry That Did Not Appear in Domesday Book," *Amazing*, Mar.

Edward Bryant, "Chrysalis," *Tropical Chills*.

——, "While She Was Out," *Pulphouse*, Fall.

Christopher Burns, "Babel," *Interzone 25*.

Pat Cadigan, "Addicted to Love," *Wild Cards V*.

————, "The Edge," *Ripper!*

————, "My Brother's Keeper," *IAsfm*, Jun.

————, "Two," *F & SF*, Jan.

Jack Cady, "By Reason of Darkness," *Prime Evil*.

Orson Scott Card, "Dowser," *IAsfm*, Dec.

Leonard Carpenter, "Recrudescence," *Amazing*, Jan.

Susan Casper, "The Cleaning Lady," *Twilight Zone*, Apr.

Sarah Clemens, "A Good Night's Work," *Ripper!*

B. W. Clough, "Ain't Nothin' but a Hound Dog," *Twilight Zone*, Jun.

David E. Cortesi, "Lost Child," *Amazing*, Jul.

Ronald Anthony Cross, "The Country Store," *F & SF*, Oct.

Jack Dann, "Tea," *IAsfm*, Apr.

———— and Jack C. Haldeman II, "Sentry," *F & SF*, Feb.

Avram Davidson, "El Vilvoy de las Islas," *IAsfm*, Aug.

————, "One Morning With Samuel, Dorothy, and William," *IAsfm*, Mid-Dec.

Bradley Denton, "The Hero of the Night," *F & SF*, Jan.

Thomas M. Disch, "Voices of the Kill," *Full Spectrum*.

George Alec Effinger, "Posterity," *F & SF*, Nov.

————, "Slow, Slow Burn," *Playboy*, May.

Greg Egan, "Scatter My Ashes," *Interzone 23*.

M. J. Engh, "The Lovesick Simurgh," *Arabesques*.

Elizabeth Engstrom, "Fogarty and Fogarty," *F & SF*, Apr.

Harlan Ellison, "The Function of Dream Sleep," *Midnight Graffiti*, #1.

Sharon N. Farber, "The Last Thunder Horse West of the Mississippi," *IAsfm*, Nov.

————, "On the Edge," *Omni*, Dec.

Michael Flynn, "Remember'd Kisses," *Analog*, Dec.

————, "The Steel Driver," *Analog*, Jun.

John M. Ford, "Camelot Station," *Invitation to Camelot*.

————, "Preflash," *Silver Scream*.

Karen Joy Fowler, "Lily Red," *IAsfm*, Jul.

Robert Frazier, "Retrovision," *IAsfm*, Aug.

————, "Tags," *IAsfm*, Apr.

————, "Things He Cannot Name Are Lost," *Twilight Zone*, Apr.

Esther M. Friesner, "Wake-Up Call," *IAsfm*, Dec.

Gregory Frost, "Lizaveta," *IAsfm*, Mid-Dec.

Michael Galloglach, "All in a Day's Work," *Twilight Zone*, Aug.

Peter T. Garratt, "Our Lady of Springtime," *Interzone 25*.

Annie Gerard, "The Boys From Stormville," *Analog*, Feb.

Lisa Goldstein, "After the Master," *IAsfm*, Apr.

————, "Death Is Different," *IAsfm*, Sept.

Felix C. Gotschalk, "Nakajima Cyberspace," *F & SF*, Jun.

Terrence M. Green & Andrew Weiner, "Twenty-Two Steps to the Apocalypse,"
   IAsfm, Jan.
Russell Griffin, "Planesong," *F & SF*, Sept.
Karen Haber, "Madre de Dios," *F & SF*, May.
M. John Harrison, "The Great God Pan," *Prime Evil*.
Howard V. Hendrix, "The Last Impression of Linda Vista," *Aboriginal SF*, May-
   Jun.
Alexander Jablokov, "Deathbinder," *IAsfm*, Feb.
———, "Many Mansions," *IAsfm*, Apr.
Philip C. Jennings, "The Bishop's Decision," *IAsfm*, Mar.
———, "Doctor Quick," *Aboriginal SF*, Sept.
———, "Messiah," *IAsfm*, Jun.
———, "The Spokesthing," *Amazing*, Jul.
James B. Johnson, "The 'Ciders," *F & SF*, Mar.
Gwyneth Jones, "The Eastern Succession," *IAsfm*, Feb.
James Killus, "Heart's Desire," *Twilight Zone*, Oct.
Garry Kilworth, "On The Watchtower at Plataea," *Other Edens II*.
Stephen King, "Dedication," *Night Visions 5*.
Stephen Kraus, "Frame Of Reference," *Analog*, May.
Nancy Kress, "Craps," *IAsfm*, Mar.
———, "Philippa's Hands," *Full Spectrum*.
———, "Spillage," *F & SF*, Apr.
Marc Laidlaw, "Bruno's Shadow," *Omni*, Aug.
———, "Shalamari," *IAsfm*, Dec.
Geoffrey A. Landis, "Ripples in the Dirac Sea," *IAsfm*, Oct.
———, "Vacuum States," *IAsfm*, Jul.
David Langford, "Blit," *Interzone 25*.
Joe R. Lansdale, "Night They Missed the Horror Show," *Silver Scream*.
———, "Not From Detroit," *Midnight Graffiti*, Fall.
Tanith Lee, "Foolish, Wicked, Clever and Kind," *Arabesques*.
———, "The Kingdoms of the Air," *Weird Tales*, Summer.
Stephen Leigh, "Evening Shadow," *IAsfm*, Aug.
Bob Leman, "The Time of the Worm," *F & SF*, Mar.
Bruce McAllister, "Songs From a Far Country," *IAsfm*, Feb.
Paul J. McAuley, "Inheritance," *F & SF*, Nov.
———, "Karl and the Ogre," *Interzone 23*.
Robert R. McCammon, "Night Calls the Green Falcon," *Silver Scream*.
Jack McDevitt, "The Fourth Moxie Branch," *Full Spectrum*.
———, "Last Contact," *IAsfm*, Jun.
———, "Sunrise," *IAsfm*, Mar.
Ian McDonald, "King Of Morning, Queen of Day," *IAsfm*, Apr.
Tom Maddox, "The Robot and the One You Love," *Omni*, Mar.

Elissa Malcohn, "Moments of Clarity," *Full Spectrum*.
Barry N. Malzberg and Jack Dann, "Blues and the Abstract Truth," *F & SF*, Jan.
Phillip Mann, "Lux in Tenebris," *Interzone 24*.
Diane Mapes, "The Huntress," *Argos*, Winter.
George R. R. Martin, "The Skin Trade," *Night Visions 5*.
Lisa Mason, "Deus Ex Machina," *IAsfm*, Dec.
———, "Guardian," *IAsfm*, Oct.
Victor Milan, "Brass," *IAsfm*, Nov.
John J. Miller, "Ouroboros," *A Very Large Array*.
Elizabeth Mitchell, "Animals," *Twilight Zone*, Oct.
Elizabeth Moon, "Too Wet to Plow," *Analog*, Mar.
Richard Mueller, "Meditations on the Death of Cortes," *IAsfm*, Sept.
Pat Murphy, "Good-Bye, Cynthia," *IAsfm*, Apr.
Jamil Nasir, "The Darkness Beyond," *Aboriginal SF*, May–Jun.
O. Niemand, "Put Your Hands Together," *IAsfm*, Feb.
Charles Oberndorf, "Mannequins," *Full Spectrum*.
Rebecca Ore, "Ice-Gouged Lakes, Glacier-Bound Times," *Amazing*, Jul.
Frederik Pohl, "Waiting for the Olympians," *IAsfm*, Aug.
Steven Popkes, "The Color Winter," *IAsfm*, Aug.
W. T. Quick, "Goin' Down Daze," *Analog*, Aug.
———, "The Healing," *Analog*, Nov.
Elaine Radford, "To Be an Auk," *Aboriginal SF*, Mar–Apr.
Hillary Rettig, "Through Alien Eyes," *IAsfm*, Jul.
Kim Stanley Robinson, "The Lunatics," *Terry's Universe*.
Rudy Rucker and Paul D. Filippo, "Instability," *F & SF*, Sept.
Richard Paul Russo, "Listen to My Heartbeat," *IAsfm*, Jan.
Robert Sampson, "A Gift of the People," *Full Spectrum*.
Robert J. Sawyer, "Golden Fleece," *Amazing*, Sept.
Josephine Saxon, "Getting Together," *Other Edens II*.
Stanley Schmidt, "Floodgate," *Twilight Zone*, Oct.
Carter Scholz, "Transients," *Terry's Universe*.
Ronnie Seagren, "Listening," *Full Spectrum*.
Bob Shaw, "Dark Night in Toyland," *Interzone 26*.
Charles Sheffield, "The Courts of Xanadu," *IAsfm*, Apr.
———, "Dead Meat," *Tropical Chills*.
Lucius Shepard, "A Wooden Tiger," *F & SF*, Oct.
———, "Jack's Decline," *Ripper!*
———, "Life of Buddha," *Omni*, May.
———, "Nomans Land," *IAsfm*, Oct.
Robert Silverberg, "At Winter's End," *IAsfm*, Jan.
———, "Hannibal's Elephants," *Omni*, Oct.

————, "We Are for the Dark," *IAsfm*, Oct.

Dan Simmons, "Iverson's Pits," *Night Visions 5*.

————, "Metastasis," *Night Visions 5*.

————, "Two Minutes Forty-Five Seconds," *Omni*, Apr.

Melinda Snodgrass, "Requiem," *A Very Large Array*.

Martha Soukup, "Having Keith," *IAsfm*, Jun.

Norman Spinrad, "Journals Of The Plague Years," *Full Spectrum*.

————, "La Vie Continue," *Other Americas*.

Allen M. Steele, "Live From the Mars Hotel," *IAsfm*, Mid-Dec.

Bruce Sterling, "The Gulf Wars," *Omni*, Feb.

Peter Straub, "The Juniper Tree," *Prime Evil*.

Somtow Sucharitkul, "The Madonna of the Wolves" *IAsfm*, Nov.

————, (as S. P. Somtow) "Anna and the Ripper of Siam," *Ripper!*

Tim Sullivan, "Father to the Man," *IAsfm*, Oct.

Michael Swanwick, "A Midwinter's Tale," *IAsfm*, Dec.

Keith Taylor, "Men From the Plane of Lir," *Weird Tales*, Fall.

————, "The Unlawful Hunter," *Weird Tales*, Spring.

Melanie Tem, "Chameleon," *IAsfm*, Mar.

Steve Rasnic Tem, "Grim Monkeys," *Tropical Chills*.

Jessie Thompson, "Snowfall," *F & SF*, Sept.

James Tiptree, Jr., "The Earth Doth Like a Snake Renew," *IAsfm*, Apr.

Harry Turtledove, "Freedom," *IAsfm*, Jun.

————, "Trapping Run," *IAsfm*, Feb.

————, "Gentlemen of the Shade," *Ripper!*

Vernor Vinge, "The Blabber," *New Destinies VI*.

Eric Vinicoff, "The Great Martian Railroad Race," *IAsfm*, Aug.

Howard Waldrop, "Wild, Wild Horses," *Omni*, Jun.

Ian Watson, "The Flies of Memory," *IAsfm*, Sept.

————, "Joan's World," *IAsfm*, Mid-Dec.

Lawrence Watt-Evans, "An Infinity of Karen," *Amazing*, Sept.

Don Webb, "Common Superstitions," *IAsfm*, Oct.

————, "Second Honeymoon," *New Pathways*, Jul.

————, "Souvenirs From a Damnation," *Pulphouse*, Fall.

Andrew Weiner, "The Egg," *Amazing*, Sept.

————, "The Grandfather Problem," *IAsfm*, Aug.

James White, "Sanctuary," *Analog*, Dec.

Dean Whitlock, "Miriam, Messiah," *F & SF*, Jan.

————, "Winter Solstice," *IAsfm*, Dec.

Rick Wilber, "Suffer the Children," *IAsfm*, Apr.

Cherry Wilder, "The House on Cemetery Street," *IAsfm*, Dec.

Kate Wilhelm, "Isosceles," *Terry's Universe*.

Walter Jon Williams, "Flatline," *IAsfm*, Aug.

————, "Mortality," *Wild Cards V*.

Chet Williamson, "The Music of the Dark Time," *Twilight Zone*, Jun.

Connie Willis, "Ado," *IAsfm*, Jan.

F. Paul Wilson, "Wires," *New Destinies*, Summer.

Gene Wolfe, "Houston, 1943," *Tropical Chills*.

————, "The Tale of the Rose and the Nightingale," *Arabesques*.

Dave Wolverton, "The Sky Is an Open Highway," *IAsfm*, Jul.

William F. Wu, "On a Phantom Tide," *Pulphouse*, Fall.

Thomas Wylde, "The Cage of Pain," *IAsfm*, Mar.

Jane Yolen, "Memories of A Bottle Djinni," *Arabesques*.

————, "The Quiet Monk," *IAsfm*, Mar.

Roger Zelazny, "Deadboy Donner and the Firestone Cup," *Terry's Universe*.